FUNGI OF USSURI RIVER VALLEY

Edited by
Y. Li and Z. M. Azbukina

Supported by

National Natural Science Foundation of China
Fund from Modern Agricultural Systematics of Industry and Technology (MOA)
Major Program of Jilin Province (10ZDGG003)
948 Project of China
Public Welfare Industry Research Foundation of China

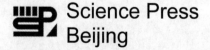
Science Press
Beijing

Responsible Editor: Han Xuezhe

ISBN: 978-7-03-030326-4

Summary

The present work sums up the current knowledge on the occurrence and distribution of fungi in Ussuri River Valley. It is the result of a three year study based on the collections made in 2003, 2004, and 2009. In all 2862 species are recognized. In the enumeration, the fungi are listed alphabetically by genus and species for each major taxonomic groups. Collection data include the hosts, place of collection, collecting date, collector(s) and field or herbarium number. This is the most comprehensive checklist of fungi to date in the Ussuri region and useful reference material to all those who are interested in Mycology.

Contributors

AZBUKINA, Z. M.

Institute of Biology & Soil Science, Far East Branch of the Russian Academy of Sciences, No. 159, Prospekt Stoletiya, Vladivostok, Russia.
(E-mail add.: cryptogamy@ibss.dvo.ru)

BAU, T.

Engineering Research Center of Chinese Ministry of Education for Edible and Medicinal Fungi, Jilin Agricultural University,
No. 2888, Xincheng Street, Changchun City, 130118, Jilin Province, China
(E-mail add.: junwusuo@126.com)

BOGACHEVA, A. V.

Institute of Biology & Soil Science, Far East Branch of the Russian Academy of Sciences, No. 159, Prospekt Stoletiya, Vladivostok, Russia
(E-mail add.: cryptogamy@ibss.dvo.ru)

BULAKH, E. M.

Institute of Biology & Soil Science, Far East Branch of the Russian Academy of Sciences, No. 159, Prospekt Stoletiya, Vladivostok, Russia
(E-mail add.: bulakh@ibss.dvo.ru)

EGOROVA, L. N.

Institute of Biology & Soil Science, Far East Branch of the Russian Academy of Sciences, No. 159, Prospekt Stoletiya, Vladivostok, Russia
(E-mail add.: egorova@ibss.dvo.ru)

GOVOROVA, O. K.

Institute of Biology & Soil Science, Far East Branch of the Russian Academy of Sciences, No. 159, Prospekt Stoletiya, Vladivostok, Russia
(E-mail add.: cryptogamy@ibss.dvo.ru)

LI, Y.

Engineering Research Center of Chinese Ministry of Education for Edible and Medicinal Fungi, Jilin Agricultural University.
No. 2888, Xincheng Street, Changchun City, 130118, Jilin Province, China.

(E-mail add.: yuli966@126.com)

LIU, P.

Engineering Research Center of Chinese Ministry of Education for Edible and Medicinal Fungi, Jilin Agricultural University .

No. 2888, Xincheng Street, Changchun City, 130118, Jilin Province, China.

(E-mail add.: puliu1982@yahoo.com)

VASILYEVA, L. N.

Institute of Biology & Soil Science, Far East Branch of the Russian Academy of Sciences,

No. 159, Prospekt Stoletiya, Vladivostok, Russia

(E-mail add.: vasilyeva@biosoil.ru)

ZHUANG, J.Y.

Engineering Research Center of Chinese Ministry of Education for Edible and Medicinal Fungi, Jilin Agricultural University

No. 2888, Xincheng Street, Changchun City, 130118, Jilin Province, China.

(E-mail add.: zhuangjyun@im.ac.cn)

Introduction

Yu LI, Zinaida M. AZBUKINA

Rising in mountainous region at the extreme south end of Primorsky Territory and flowing north to join the Amur (Heilongjiang River) near Khabarovsk and Fuyuan, Ussuri River forms a boundary between Primorsky Territory of Russian Far East and Northeast China. A west tributary of upper course of the river is outlet for Lake Khanka (Xingkaihu). The climate of the Ussuri valley is continental but influenced by the monsoon to some extent, with annual precipitation of about 500-600 mm and annual temperatures ranging between 3-4°C in the south and about 2°C in the north. The vegetation is mainly coniferous broad-leaved mixed forest. The characteristic tree species include *Pinus koraiensis* Siebold & Zucc., *Quercus mongolica* Fisch. ex Ledeb., *Tilia amurensis* Rupr., *Fraxinus mandshurica* Rupr., *Phellodendron amurense* Rupr., *Juglans mandshurica* Maxim., etc. In the south of Ussuri, the forest vegetation also includes a significant component of endemic trees such as *Abies holophylla* Maxim., *Pinus takahasii* Nakai, *Acer mandshuricum* Maxim., etc.

The Ussuri region in Russia is often considered to be one of the best mycologically documented areas. However, little detailed information has been available for a sizable area in China's side of the river. The rapid economical development in this region is accompanied by a large amount of loss of natural habitat, especially at China's side. Therefore, investigation of fungal biodiversity of this region is extremely urgent. The aim of this study is to acquire further knowledge of fungal biodiversity in the whole Ussuri region extending across the bounds of two countries and to publish a checklist of taxa collected at both sides of the river. We believe that the assessment of fungal biodiversity in the region could lay the foundations for future mycological conservation plans and measures.

Floristic field surveys were carried out by mycologists of Institute of Biology and Soil Science, Far East Branch of the Russian Academy of Sciences, Vladivostok, and Engineering Research Center of Chinese Ministry of Education for Edible and Medicinal Fungi, Jilin Agricultural University, Changchun. Collectors include Y. Li, Z.M. Azbukina, T. Bau, A.V. Bogacheva, E.M. Bulakh, L.N. Vasilyeva, L.N. Egorova, O.K. Govorova, J.Y. Zhuang, and P. Liu. A total of 40 days was spent in fieldwork in September of 2003, August of 2004, and July of 2009. Our efforts were largely focused on areas of Chinese territory including northern side of Lake Khanka (Xingkaihu), Hulin, Raohe and Fuyuan, and areas of Russian territory including the southern side of Lake Khanka, Ussuriysk, Vladivostok, and the surrounding areas of Khabarovsk. The result is a checklist of 2862 species, based on our own studies on the collections mainly made by the investigators mentioned above. Earlier collections made by other investigators are also included. Within the major taxonomic groups, the fungi are listed alphabetically by genus and species. Specimen collection data include the host or substrate, place of collections, collecting date, collector (s), field or herbarium number. In addition, we have also included some literature records without citation of specimens, checked from earlier or more recent publications in order to enrich the checklist to the full extent. The specimens are preserved at the Herbarium of Institute of Mycology, Jilin Agricultural University, Changchun, China (HMJAU) and the Herbarium of Institute of Biology and Soil Science, Far East Branch of the Russian Academy of Sciences, Vladivostok, Russia (VLA). The main identification system used in this book is referring to "The Dictionary of Fungi (9th edition)" except a few changes.

The work was supported by National Natural Science Foundation of China (Project No. 30510154, 30770005), 948 Project of China (Project No. 2006-G11(3)-2), Fund from Ministry of Agriculture of China Project, Public Welfare Industry Research Foundation of China (Project No. nyhyzx07-008), National Science and Technology Supporting Plan of China (Project No. 2008BADA1B03(01-1)), and 863 Project of China (Project No. 2007AA021506). We generally acknowledge the assistance and support provided us throughout the field work by Administration Bureau of Ussuriysk Nature Reserve, Administration Bureau of Khanka Nature Reserve, staffs of Heilongjiang Bayi Agricultural University, and staffs of Northeast Forestry University in Harbin.

Contents

Ascomycetes: Sordariomycetidae, Dothideomycetidae, Erysiphomycetidae, Rhytismomycetidae

Larissa N. VASILYEVA

The checklist that follows is based upon specimens collected by the author in Russia (Primorsky Territory: Ussuriysk Nature Reserve, Khanka Nature Reserve, Big Khekhtsir Nature Reserve, Bastak Nature Reserve) and China (Heilongjiang Province: Xingkaihu Nature Reserve, Weihushan Nature Reserve, in the vicinity of Sanjiang Nature Reserve, as well as in and around Hulin, Raohe, and Fuyuan).

Only 20 species of pyrenomycetes and loculoascomycetes has been reported previously for Heilongjiang Province (Teng, 1964; Kobayashi, Zhao, 1989), and eight of these were collected again in the Ussuri River Valley, namely *Cryptosphaeria populina* (Pers.) Sacc. (now *C. lygniota*), *Diatrype tumida* Ellis & Everh. (now *Eutypella leprosa*), *Diatrypella favacea* (Fr.) Nitschke, *Dothidea collecta* (Schwein.) Ellis & Everh. (now *D. puccinioides*), *Hypospilina oharana* (Y. Nisik. & H. Matsumoto) Katum. & Y. Harada (now *Stegophora oharana*), *Hypoxylon marginatum* (Schwein.) Berk. (now *H. annulatum*), *Polystigma fulvum* DC., and "*Xylaria corniformis*" (Fr.) Fr. However, results obtained in recent studies have indicated that the specimens of the latter species from the north-eastern Asia should be re-identified as *Xylaria primorskensis* Y.-M. Ju, H.-M. Hsieh, Lar.N. Vassiljeva & Akulov (Ju et al., 2009).

While reporting *Hypoxylon rubiginosum* (Pers. : Fr.) Fr., Teng (1964) has followed Miller's (1961) concept of that species, but the latter has been recognized as also including *H. perforatum* (Schwein. : Fr.) Fr. Only *H. perforatum* was found again in Heilongjiang Province, although *H. rubiginosum* could have been expected. As to *Daldinia concentrica* (Bolton : Fr.) Ces. et De Not. (Teng, 1964), this species seems to be excluded from the checklists of fungi collected in East Asia. Drs. Yu-Ming Ju and Marc Stadler (pers. comm.) unanimously think that *D. concentrica* does not occur here and all the collections under this name should be reconsidered.

Sometimes, it was difficult to judge the occurrence of a particular species because of differences in species concepts. Thus, the checklist contains *Biscogniauxia pezizoides*, which is not reported for China. However, the concept of *B. repanda* (Fr. : Fr.) Kuntze that is used (Teng, 1964) (as *Nummularia repanda*) might encompass the former species. Unfortunately, Teng almost never referred to the host plants of stromatic pyrenomycetes, which are not so plurivorous as they were once thought to be. In the case of two last species, *B. repanda* is restricted to *Sorbus* spp., while *B. pezizoides* occurs on *Ulmus* spp. (rarely on *Acer* spp.). Some other examples of "segregates" that were not known in China previously are *Rosellinia corticium* and *Diatrype macounii*, which could be identified as *Rosellinia aquila* (Fr. : Fr.) De Not. and *Diatrype bullata* (Hoffm. : Fr.) Fr., respectively (Teng, 1964; Tai, 1979; Eriksson, Yue, 1988).

A number of species described from the Russian Far East (Vasilyeva, 1998) were also found in China. Examples include *Chromendothia citrina*, *Cryptosphaeria exornata*, *Daldinia gelatinoides*, *Melogramma corylina*. The species newly found in China are marked by a single asterisk. This information was derived as a result of studying numerous published works (Teng, 1964; Tai, 1979; Eriksson, Yue, 1988; Yuan, Zhao, 1993; Liu, Doi, 1995; Liang et al., 1995; Abe, Liu, 1996; Liu et al., 2000; Zhuang, Sun, 2001; Liu et al., 2002; Wang, Liu, 2002; Zhang, Zhuang, 2003; Bau, 2005; Zhuang, 2005; Luo, Zhuang, 2008). The species newly recorded in East Asia (either in Russia or in China) are marked by two asterisks. Several new species were described recently. These are *Rossmania ukurunduensis* (Vasilyeva, 2001), *Daldinia carpinicola* (Vasilyeva, Stadler, 2008), *Diaporthella corylina*, *Leucodiaporthe juglandis*, *Leucostoma pseudoniveum*, *Phragmodiaporthe padi* (Vasilyeva et al., 2007). Types of three latter species were collected in Heilongjiang Province. These species known only from north-eastern Asia are marked by three asterisks.

The division of the class Ascomycetes into subclasses is given in accordance with the electronic resource www.biolib.cz except for the group Rhytismomycetidae created informally for the order Rhytismatales.

ASCOMYCETES

SORDARIOMYCETIDAE

CALOSPHAERIALES

CALOSPHAERIACEAE

Calosphaeria pusilla (Wahlenb.) P. Karst.
 On dead branches of *Betula* sp., Raohe, 7 Aug. 2004, L.N. Vasilyeva, VLA P-1450.

CORONOPHORALES

CORONOPHORACEAE

* Coronophora angustata Fuckel
 On dead branches of *Betula* sp., Fuyuan: Chuangxin, 5 Aug. 2004, L.N. Vasilyeva, VLA

P-1469.

** *Fracchiaea subcongregata* (Berk. & M.A. Curtis) Ellis & Everh.

On dead branch of *Acer* sp., Big Khekhtsir Nature Reserve, 27 Aug. 1983, L.N. Vasilyeva, VLA P-1397. - The name of this species was indicated (Vasilyeva, 1998) as a synonym of *F. broomeana* (Berk.) Petch, but the latter species has larger ascospores.

Loranitschkia viticola Lar.N. Vassiljeva.

On dead *Vitis amurensis* Rupr., Ussuriysk Nature Reserve, 27 Aug. 1989, L.N. Vasilyeva, VLA P-235; Bastak Nature Reserve, 19 Aug. 2004, L.N. Vasilyeva, VLA P-334.

Nitschkia floridana Fitzp.

On decayed wood, Ussuriysk Nature Reserve, 21 Aug. 1989, L.N. Vasilyeva, VLA P-357.

Tympanopsis confertula (Schwein.) Lar.N. Vassiljeva

On dead branches of *Fraxinus* sp., Big Khekhtsir Nature Reserve, 28 Aug. 1983, L.N. Vasilyeva, VLA P-1373. - On wood, Hulin: Dongfanghong, Sept. 3, 2003, L.N. Vasilyeva, VLA P-1731.

DIAPORTHALES

GNOMONIACEAE

Apiothecium vepris (Delacr.) Lar.N. Vassiljeva

On dead stems of *Rubus sachalinensis* Lévl., Big Khekhtsir Nature Reserve, 25 Aug. 1983, L.N. Vasilyeva, VLA P-1865.

* *Gnomonia setacea* (Pers. : Fr.) Ces. & De Not.

On dead leaves of *Quercus mongolica* Fisch. ex Ledeb., Hulin: 854 State Farm, 2 Sept. 2003, L.N. Vasilyeva, VLA P-1903.

Mamiania fimbriata (Pers.: Fr.) Ces. & De Not.

On living leaves of *Carpinus cordata* Blume, Ussuriysk Nature Reserve, 11 Sept. 1962, I.A. Bunkina, VLA P-238.

Mamianiella coryli (Batsch : Fr.) Höhn.

On living leaves of *Corylus mandshurica* Maxim., Ussuriysk Nature Reserve, Sept. 1953, I.A. Bunkina, VLA P-259.

Plagiostoma devexum (Desm.) Fuckel

On dead stems of *Polygonum* sp., Big Khekhtsir Nature Reserve, 22 Aug. 1983, L.N. Vasilyeva, VLA P-1042.

Stegophora oharana (Y. Nisik. & H. Matsumoto) Petr.

On living leaves of *Ulmus japonica* (Rehd.) Sarg., Ussuriysk Nature Reserve, 30 Sept. 1962, L. Gurskaya, VLA P-368; Big Khekhtsir Nature Reserve, 26 Jun. 1981, V.N. Frolova,

VLA P-373.

VALSACEAE

*** Allantoporthe tessella** (Pers. : Fr.) Petr.   Plate 1: 1

On dead branches of *Salix* spp., Ussuriysk Nature Reserve, 27 Aug. 1989, L.N. Vasilyeva, VLA P-1; Raohe, 7 Aug. 2004, L.N. Vasilyeva, VLA P-1904.

Anisogramma anomala (Peck) E. Müll.

On living branches of *Corylus mandshurica* Maxim., Ussuriysk Nature Reserve, 28 Aug. 1989, L.N. Vasilyeva, VLA P-22. - On living branches of *Corylus heterophylla* Fisch. ex Trautv., Khanka Nature Reserve, 18 Jun. 2003, L.N. Vasilyeva, VLA P-20; Bastak Nature Reserve, 19 Aug. 2004, L.N. Vasilyeva, VLA P-25.

**** Diaporthe crataegi** (Curr.) Nitschke

On dead branches of *Crataegus pinnatifida* Bunge, Khanka Nature Reserve, L.N. Vasilyeva, 18 Jun. 2003, VLA P-1846.

Diaporthe decedens (Fr.) Fuckel

On dead branches of *Corylus heterophylla* Fisch. ex Trautv., Bastak Nature Reserve, 19 Aug. 2004, L.N. Vasilyeva, VLA P-56.

Diaporthe fibrosa (Pers. : Fr.) Nitschke

On dead branches of *Rhamnus ussuriensis* Ja. Vassil., Khanka Nature Reserve, 19 Jun. 2003, L.N. Vasilyeva, VLA P-1860.

Diaporthe oncostoma (Duby) Fuckel

On dead branches of *Maackia amurensis* Rupr. et Maxim., Bastak Nature Reserve, 19 Aug. 2004, L.N. Vasilyeva, VLA P-901.

***** Diaporthella corylina** Lar.N. Vassilyeva   Plate 1: 2

On dying stems of *Corylus* sp., Fuyuan, 4 Aug. 2004, L.N. Vasilyeva, VLA P-1866.

Hercoporthe coryli Lar.N. Vassiljeva

On dead branches of *Corylus mandshurica* Maxim., Ussuriysk Nature Reserve, 29 Aug. 1989, L.N. Vasilyeva, VLA P-159 .

***** Leucodiaporthe juglandis** Lar.N. Vassiljeva   Plate 1: 3

On dead branches of *Juglans mandshurica* Maxim., Hulin, 2 Sept. 2003, L.N. Vasilyeva, VLA P-1867.

*** Leucodiaporthe maackii** (Lar.N. Vassiljeva) M.E. Barr & Lar.N. Vassiljeva (= *Cryphonectria maackii* Lar.N. Vassilyeva)   Plate 1: 4

On *Maackia amurensis* Rupr. et Maxim., Big Khekhtsir Nature Reserve, 12 Oct. 1981, L.N. Vasilyeva, VLA P-1362; Ussuriysk Nature Reserve, 29 Aug. 1989, L.N. Vasilyeva, VLA P-332; Hulin: 854 State Farm, 2 Sept. 2003, L.N. Vasilyeva, VLA P-1905; Bastak Nature Reserve, 18 Aug. 2004, L.N. Vasilyeva, VLA P-234.

Leucostoma diatrypa (Fr. : Fr.) Höhn.

On dead branches of *Betula* sp., Ussuriysk Nature Reserve, 23 Aug. 1989, L.N. Vasilyeva, VLA P-212.

** ***Leucostoma excipienda*** (P. Karst.) Lar.N. Vassiljeva

On dead branches of *Padus avium* Mill., Weihushan Nature Reserve: Northern Tiger Forest Garden, 9 Aug. 2004, L.N. Vasilyeva, VLA P-1670.

*** ***Leucostoma pseudoniveum*** Lar.N. Vassiljeva   Plate 1: 5

On the bark of *Populus* sp., Fuyuan, 4 Aug. 2004, L.N. Vasilyeva, VLA P-1906; Bastak Nature Reserve, 19 Aug. 2004, L.N. Vasilyeva, VLA P-1907.

* ***Melanconis carthusiana*** Tul.

On *Juglans mandshurica* Maxim., Ussuriysk Nature Reserve, 14 Aug. 1989, L.N. Vasilyeva, VLA P-271; Hulin: 854 State Farm, 2 Sept. 2003, L.N. Vasilyeva, VLA P-1908.

* ***Melanconis leiphaemia*** (Fr. : Fr.) Lar.N. Vassiljeva

On *Quercus mongolica* Fisch. ex Ledeb., Big Khekhtsir Nature Reserve, 23 Aug. 1983, L.N. Vasilyeva, VLA P-796; Hulin: Hutou, 4 Sept. 2003, L.N. Vasilyeva, VLA P-1683; Fuyuan, 4 Aug. 2004, L.N. Vasilyeva, VLA P-1682.

* ***Melanconis stilbostoma*** (Fr. : Fr.) Tul.

On dead branches of *Betula* sp., Big Khektsir Nature Reserve, 18 Oct. 1981, L.N. Vasilyeva, VLA P-1839; Hulin: 854 State Farm, 2 Sept. 2003, L.N. Vasilyeva, VLA P-1688.

Melanconis thelebola (Fr.) Sacc.

On dead branches of *Alnus hirsuta* (Spach) Fisch. ex Rupr., Ussuriysk Nature Reserve, 12 Aug. 1989, L.N. Vasilyeva, VLA P-338.

* ***Ophiovalsa betulae*** (Tul. & C. Tul.) Petr.

On dead branches of *Betula* sp., Sanjiang Nature Reserve: Dongxing cun, 5 Aug. 2004, L.N. Vasilyeva, VLA P-1702.

** ***Ophiovalsa corylina*** (Tul. & C. Tul.) Petr.

On dead branches of *Corylus heterophylla* Fisch. ex Trautv., Khanka Nature Reserve, 18 Jun. 2003, L.N. Vasilyeva, VLA P-1851.

Ophiovalsa suffusa (Fr. : Fr.) Petr.

On dead branches of *Alnus hirsuta* (Spach) Turcz. ex Rupr., Bastak Nature Reserve, 18 Aug. 2004, L.N. Vasilyeva, VLA P-1849.

Ophiovalsa tiliae (Tul. & C. Tul.) Petr.

On dead branches of *Tilia* sp., Khanka Nature Reserve, 21 Jun. 2004, L.N. Vasilyeva, VLA P-1852.

*** ***Phragmodiaporthe padi*** Lar. N. Vassiljeva

On dead branches of *Padus avium* Mill., Weihushan Nature Reserve, Northern Tiger Forest Garden, 9 Aug. 2004, L.N. Vasilyeva, VLA P-1870.

*** *Rossmania ukurunduensis* Lar.N. Vassiljeva

On dead branches of *Acer ukurunduense* Trautv. et Mey., Big Khekhtsir Nature Reserve, 28 Aug. 1983, L.N. Vasilyeva, VLA P-360.

Valsa ambiens (Pers. : Fr.) Fr.   Plate 1: 6

On dead branches of *Ulmus japonica* (Rehd.) Sarg., Ussuriysk Nature Reserve, 21 Oct. 1956, I.A. Bunkina, VLA P-721. - On dead branches *Tilia amurensis* Rupr., Hulin, 2 Sept. 2003, L.N. Vasilyeva, VLA P-1735.

Valsa ceratosperma (Tode : Fr.) Maire

On dead branches of deciduous trees, Ussuriysk Nature Reserve, 23 Aug. 1989, L.N. Vasilyeva, VLA P-375; Hulin: Dongfanghong, 3 Sept. 2003, L.N. Vasilyeva, VLA P-1736.

* _Valsa germanica_ Nitschke

On dead branches of *Salix* sp., Weihushan Nature Reserve: Northern Tiger Forest Garden, 9 Aug. 2004, L.N. Vasilyeva, VLA P-1737.

** _Valsa leucostomoides_ Peck

On dead branches of *Acer* sp., Big Khekhtsir Nature Reserve, 16 Oct. 1981, L.N. Vasilyeva, VLA P-1853.

Valsa salicina (Pers. : Fr.) Fr.

On dead branches of *Salix* spp., Ussuriysk Nature Reserve, 21 Oct. 1956, A.A. Ablakatova, VLA P-731; Big Khekhtsir Nature Reserve, 16 Aug. 2004, L.N. Vasilyeva, VLA P-1864.

Valsa sordida Nitschke

On dead branches of *Salix* sp., Big Khekhtsir Nature Reserve, 19 Sept. 1982, L.N. Vasilyeva, VLA P-376. - On dead branches of *Populus* sp., Raohe: Shengli State Farm, 6 Sept. 2003, L.N. Vasilyeva, VLA P-1871.

DIATRYPALES

DIATRYPACEAE

Amphisphaerella lonicericola (Z.Q. Yuan & Z.Y. Zhao) Lar.N. Vassiljeva

On dead branches of *Lonicera* sp., Ussuriysk Nature Reserve, 29 Aug. 1989, L.N. Vasilyeva, VLA P-442.

Amphisphaerella xylostei (Pers. : Fr.) Munk

On dead branches of *Lonicera* sp., Ussuriysk Nature Reserve, 27 Aug. 1989, L.N. Vasilyeva, VLA P-445.

Azbukinia ferruginea (Fuckel) Lar.N. Vassiljeva

In wood of dead branches *Fraxinus* spp., Big Khekhtsir Nature Reserve, 25 Sept. 1982, L.N. Vasilyeva, VLA P-29; Ussuriysk Nature Reserve, 18 Aug. 1989, L.N. Vasilyeva,

VLA P-30.

Biscogniauxia cinereolilacina (J.H. Mill.) Pouzar

On *Tilia amurensis* Rupr., Ussuriysk Nature Reserve, 27 Aug. 1989, L.N. Vasilyeva, VLA P-13; Big Khekhtsir Nature Reserve, 15 Aug. 2004, L.N. Vasilyeva, VLA P-16; Bastak Nature Reserve, 19 Aug. 2004, L.N. Vasilyeva, VLA P-19.

* ***Biscogniauxia granmoi*** Lar.N. Vassiljeva

On *Padus avium* Mill., Big Khekhtsir Nature Reserve, 24 Sept. 1982, L.N. Vasilyeva, VLA P-33; Ussuriysk Nature Reserve, 10 Aug. 1989, L.N. Vasilyeva, VLA P-38; Khanka Nature Reserve, 21 Jun. 2003, L.N. Vasilyeva, VLA P-34; Hulin: Wulindong, 4 Sept. 2003, L.N. Vasilyeva, VLA P-1430.

Biscogniauxia mandshurica Lar.N. Vassiljeva   Plate 2: 7

On dead branches *Malus mandshurica* (Maxim.) Kom., Ussuriysk Nature Reserve, 23 Aug. 1989, L.N. Vasilyeva, VLA P-39; Khanka Nature Reserve, 21 Jun. 2003, L.N. Vasilyeva, VLA P-40.

Biscogniauxia marginata (Fr. : Fr.) Pouzar

On dead branches of *Malus baccata* (L.) Borkh., Khanka Nature Reserve, 21 Jun. 2004, L.N. Vasilyeva, VLA P-1850.

Biscogniauxia maritima Lar.N. Vassiljeva

On dead branches of *Quercus mongolica* Fisch. ex Ledeb., Ussuriysk Nature Reserve, 28 Aug. 1989, L.N. Vasilyeva, VLA P-45; Bastak Nature Reserve, 18 Aug. 2004, L.N. Vasilyeva, VLA P-42.

Biscogniauxia mediterranea (De Not.) Kuntze

On dead branches of *Quercus mongolica* Fisch. ex Ledeb., Big Khekhtsir Nature Reserve, 24 Sept. 1982, L.N. Vasilyeva, VLA P-1408; Khanka Nature Reserve, 18 Jun. 2003, L.N. Vasilyeva, VLA P-1862; Hulin: 854 State Farm, 2 Sept. 2003, L.N. Vasilyeva, VLA P-1437; Sanjiang Nature Reserve: Dongxing cun, 5 Aug. 2004, L.N. Vasilyeva, VLA P-1438.

** ***Biscogniauxia mediterranea*** var. ***microspora*** (J.H. Mill.) Y.M. Ju & J.D. Rogers

On dead branches of *Corylus heterophylla* Fisch. ex Trautv., Khanka Nature Reserve, 18 Jun. 2003, L.N. Vasilyeva, VLA P-1861.

* ***Biscogniauxia pezizoides*** (Ellis & Everh.) Kuntze   Plate 2: 8

On dead branches of *Ulmus* spp., Big Khekhtsir Nature Reserve, 22 Aug. 1983, L.N. Vasilyeva, VLA P-278; Ussuriysk Nature Reserve, 27 Aug. 1989, L.N. Vasilyeva, VLA P-273; Khanka Nature Reserve, 21 Jun. 2003, L.N. Vasilyeva, VLA P-272; Xingkaihu Nature Reserve, 1 Sept. 2003, L.N. Vasilyeva, VLA P-1439; Fuyuan, 4 Aug. 2004, L.N. Vasilyeva, VLA P-1441. - On dead branches of *Acer mono* Maxim., Hulin: Wulindong, 4 Sept. 2003, L.N. Vasilyeva, VLA P-1442.

** ***Biscogniauxia simplicior*** Pouzar

On dead branches of *Rhamnus* spp., Big Khekhtsir Nature Reserve, 20 Jun. 2000, L.N.

Vasilyeva, VLA P-1773; Khanka Nature Reserve, 21 Jun. 2003, L.N. Vasilyeva, VLA P-1863.

* Biscogniauxia succenturiata (Tode : Fr.) Kuntze

On *Quercus mongolica* Fisch. ex Ledeb., Xingkaihu Nature Reserve, 1 Sept. 2003, L.N. Vasilyeva, VLA P-1444.

Camarops polysperma (Mont.) J.H. Mill.

On dead branches of *Alnus hirsuta* (Spach) Turcz. ex Rupr., Big Khekhtsir Nature Reserve, 2 Aug. 2000, K.N. Tkachenko, VLA P-1403.

* Cryptosphaeria exornata Lar.N. Vassiljeva   Plate 2: 9

On dead branches and trunks of *Fraxinus* spp., Big Khekhtsir Nature Reserve, 24 Aug. 1983, L.N. Vasilyeva, VLA P-290; Ussuriysk Nature Reserve, 23 Aug. 1989, L.N. Vasilyeva, VLA P-300; Khanka Nature Reserve, 21 Jun. 2003, L.N. Vasilyeva, VLA P-289; Hulin: Dongfanghong, Sept. 3, 2003, L.N. Vasilyeva, VLA P-1477.

Cryptosphaeria lygniota (Fr.) Auersw.

On dead branches of *Populus* spp., Big Khekhtsir Nature Reserve, 19 Aug. 1983, L.N. Vasilyeva, VLA P-1872; Ussuriysk Nature Reserve, 28 Aug. 1989, L.N. Vasilyeva, VLA P-1873; Xingkaihu Nature Reserve, 1 Sept. 2003, L.N. Vasilyeva, VLA P-1478.

Cryptosphaeria subcutanea (Wahlenb. : Fr.) Rappaz

On dead branches of *Salix* sp., Ussutiysk Nature Reserve, 23 Aug. 1989, L.N. Vasilyeva, VLA P-305.

Cryptosphaeria venusta Lar.N. Vassiljeva   Plate 2: 10

On dead branches of *Betula* spp., Big Khekhtsir Nature Reserve, 27 Aug. 1983, L.N. Vasilyeva, VLA P-314; Ussutiysk Nature Reserve, 13 Aug. 1989, L.N. Vasilyeva, VLA P-312.

*** Cryptovalsaria rossica Lar.N. Vassiljeva & S.L. Stephenson

On living trunk of *Alnus hirsuta* (Spach) Turcz. ex Rupr., Big Khekhtsir Nature Reserve, 2 Aug. 2000, K.N. Tkachenko, VLA P-1118.

Diatrype acericola De Not.

On dead branches of *Acer mono* Maxim., Big Khekhtsir Reserve, 28 Aug. 1983, L.N. Vasilyeva, VLA P-67; Ussuriysk Nature Reserve, 23 Aug. 1989, L.N. Vasilyeva, VLA P-78; Khanka Nature Reserve, 21 Jun. 2003, L.N. Vasilyeva, VLA P-69; Bastak Nature Reserve, 19 Aug. 2004, L.N. Vasilyeva, VLA P-68.

Diatrype albopruinosa (Schwein.) Cooke   Plate 2: 11

On dead branches of *Maackia amurensis* Rupr. et Maxim., Sanjiang Nature Reserve: Dongxing cun, 5 Aug. 2004, L.N. Vasilyeva, VLA P-1489. - On dead branches of *Padus avium* Mill., Weihushan Nature Reserve: Northern Tiger Forest Garden, 9 Aug. 2004, L.N. Vasilyeva, VLA P-1488.

Diatrype hypoxyloides De Not.

On dead branches of *Quercus mongolica* Fisch. ex Ledeb., Big Khekhtsir Nature Reserve, 25 Sept. 1982, L.N. Vasilyeva, VLA P-416; Ussuriysk Nature Reserve, 28 Aug. 1989, L.N.

Vasilyeva, VLA P-396; Raohe, 7 Aug. 2004, L.N. Vasilyeva, VLA P-1502.

** *Diatrype macounii* Ellis et Everh.   Plate 2: 12

On dead branches of *Salix* sp., Hulin: Dongfanghong, 3 Sept. 2003, L.N. Vasilyeva, VLA P-1503.

Diatrype platystoma (Schwein. : Fr.) Berk.

On dead branches of deciduous trees, Big Khekhtsir Nature Reserve, 13 Oct. 1983, L.N. Vasilyeva, VLA P-97. - On dead branches *Acer* spp., Big Khekhtsir Nature Reserve, 22 Sept. 1982, L.N. Vasilyeva, VLA P-96; Khanka Nature Reserve, 21 Jun. 2003, L.N. Vasilyeva, VLA P-1855. - On dead branches *Betula* spp., Big Khekhtsir Nature Reserve, 19 Oct. 1981, L.N. Vasilyeva, VLA P-99; Hulin: Dongfanghong, 3 Sept. 2003, L.N. Vasilyeva, VLA P-1504. - On dead branches of *Crataegus* spp., Ussuriysk Nature Reserve, 15 Aug. 1989, L.N. Vasilyeva, VLA P-81; Big Khekhtsir Nature Reserve, 22 Aug. 1983, L.N. Vasilyeva, VLA P-101. - On dead branches of *Corylus mandshurica* Maxim., Big Khekhtsir Nature Reserve, 19 Oct. 1981, L.N. Vasilyeva, VLA P-102. - On dead branches of *Juglans mandshurica* Maxim., Big Khekhtsir Nature Reserve, 22 Sept. 1982, L.N. Vasilyeva, VLA P-100. - On dead branches of *Quercus mongolica* Fisch. ex Ledeb., Ussuriysk Nature Reserve, 23 Aug. 1987, L.N. Vasilyeva, VLA P-82.

** *Diatrype spilomea* Syd.

On dead branches of *Acer* spp., Ussuriysk Nature Reserve, 28 Apr. 1956, I.A. Bunkina, VLA P-402; Big Khekhtsir Nature Reserve, 27 Aug. 1983, L.N. Vasilyeva, VLA P-1370; Bastak Nature Reserve, 18 Aug. 2004, L.N. Vasilyeva, VLA P-91.

Diatrype stigma (Hoffm. : Fr.) Fr.

On dead branches of *Corylus heterophylla* Fisch. ex Trautv. and *Tilia amurensis* Rupr., Bastak Nature Reserve, 19 Aug. 2004, L.N. Vasilyeva, VLA P-404, P-1823. - On *Quercus mongolica* Fisch. ex Ledeb., Big Khekhtsir Nature Reserve, 23 Aug. 1983, L.N. Vasilyeva, VLA P-411.

** *Diatrype subaffixa* (Schwein.) Cooke

On dead branches of *Padus avium* Mill., Ussuriysk Nature Reserve, 27 Aug. 1989, L.N. Vasilyeva, VLA P-417.

* *Diatrype undulata* (Pers. : Fr.) Fr.

On dead branches of *Betula* spp., Big Khekhtsir Nature Reserve, 27 Aug. 1983, L.N. Vasilyeva, VLA P-410; Fuyuan, 4 Aug. 2004, L.N. Vasilyeva, VLA P-1532.

** *Diatrypella circumvallata* (Nees : Fr.) Fuckel

On dead branches of *Corylus* spp., Ussuriysk Nature Reserve, 23 Oct. 1956, I.A. Bunkina, VLA P-128; Big Khekhtsir Nature Reserve, 19 Aug. 1983, L.N. Vasilyeva, VLA P-127.

Diatrypella decorata Nitschke

On dead branches of *Betula* spp., Big Khekhtsir Nature Reserve, 25 Aug. 1983, L.N. Vasilyeva, VLA P-431; Ussuriysk Nature Reserve, 13 Aug. 1989, L.N. Vasilyeva, VLA P-430;

Khanka Nature Reserve, 18 Jun. 2003, L.N. Vasilyeva, VLA P-432; Raohe: Shengli State Farm, 6 Sept. 2003, L.N. Vasilyeva, VLA P-1537.

Diatrypella favacea (Fr.) Ces. & De Not.

On dead branches of *Betula* spp., Big Khekhtsir Nature Reserve, 20 Aug. 1983, L.N. Vasilyeva, VLA P-420; Sanjiang Nature Reserve: Dongxing cun, 5 Aug. 2004, L.N. Vasilyeva, VLA P-1542.

** *Diatrypella informis* Ellis & Everh.

On dead branches of *Carpinus cordata* Blume, Ussuriysk Nature Reserve, 19 Aug. 1989, L.N. Vasilyeva, VLA P-2265.

Diatrypella melaena Nitschke

On dead branches of *Betula* spp., Big Khekhtsir Nature Reserve, 21 Aug. 1983, L.N. Vasilyeva, VLA P-481.

* *Diatrypella placenta* Rehm

On dead branches of *Alnus hirsuta* (Spach) Turcz. ex Rupr., Big Khekhtsir Nature Reserve, 25 Sept. 1982, L.N. Vasilyeva, VLA P-490; Hulin: Dongfanghong, 3 Sept. 2003, L.N. Vasilyeva, VLA P-1547. - On dead branches of *Betula* spp., Big Khekhtsir Nature Reserve, 22 Sept. 1982, L.N. Vasilyeva, VLA P-492; Sanjiang Nature Reserve: Dongxing cun, 5 Aug. 2004, L.N. Vasilyeva, VLA P-1546.

Diatrypella pulvinata Nitschke

On dead branches of *Quercus mongolica* Fisch. ex Ledeb., Big Khekhtsir Nature Reserve, 23 Aug. 1983, L.N. Vasilyeva, VLA P-508; Ussuriysk Nature Reserve, 13 Aug. 1989, L.N. Vasilyeva, VLA P-494.

* *Diatrypella tocciaena* De Not.

On dead branches of *Alnus hirsuta* (Spach) Turcz. ex Rupr., Big Khekhtsir Nature Reserve, 16 Aug. 2004, L.N. Vasilyeva, VLA P-141; Raohe, 7 Aug. 2004, L.N. Vasilyeva, VLA P-1548.

Diatrypella verrucaeformis (Ehrh. : Fr.) Nitschke

On dead branches of *Betula* sp., Hulin: 854 State Farm, 2 Sept. 2003, L.N. Vasilyeva, VLA P-1550.

* *Eutypa crustata* (Fr.) Sacc.

On dead branches of *Ulmus* spp., Big Khekhtsir Nature Reserve, 22 Aug. 1983, L.N. Vasilyeva, VLA P-1874; Ussuriysk Nature Reserve, 23 Aug. 1989, L.N. Vasilyeva, VLA P-1875; Xingkaihu Nature Reserve, 1 Sept. 2003, L.N. Vasilyeva, VLA P-1876.

Eutypa lata (Pers. : Fr.) Tul. & C. Tul.

On wood, Big Khekhtsir Nature Reserve, 14 Oct. 1981, L.N. Vasilyeva, VLA P-1909; Ussuriysk Nature Reserve, 12 Aug. 1989, L.N. Vasilyeva, VLA P-1912.

Eutypa lejoplaca (Fr. : Fr.) Fuckel

On wood, Ussuriysk Nature Reserve, 29 Aug. 1989, L.N. Vasilyeva, VLA P-1910.

Eutypa maura (Fr. : Fr.) Tul.

On wood of *Ulmus japonica* (Rehd.) Sarg., Big Khekhtsir Nature Reserve, 21 Aug. 1983, L.N. Vasilyeva, VLA P-1911.

Eutypa macrospora (Nitschke) Sacc.

On dead branches of a deciduous tree, Big Khekhtsir Nature Reserve, 28 Aug. 1983, L.N. Vasilyeva, VLA P-1878.

Eutypa spinosa (Pers. : Fr.) Tul.

On wood of deciduous trees, Ussuriysk Nature Reserve, 16 Oct. 1953, L.N. Vassiljeva, VLA P-1913.

* *Eutypella alni* (Fr.) Lar.N. Vassiljeva

On dead branches and trunks of *Alnus hirsuta* (Spach) Turcz. ex Rupr., Big Khekhtsir Nature Reserve, 16 Sept. 1982, L.N. Vasilyeva, VLA P-530; Ussuriysk Nature Reserve, 28 Aug. 1989, L.N. Vasilyeva, VLA P-529; Hulin: Wulindong, 4 Sept. 2003, L.N. Vasilyeva, VLA P-1573; Raohe, 7 Aug. 2004, L.N. Vasilyeva, VLA P-1571.

Eutypella cerviculata (Fr. : Fr.) Sacc.

On dead branches of *Betula platyphylla* Sukacz., Big Khekhtsir Nature Reserve, 27 Aug. 1983, L.N. Vasilyeva, VLA P-783; Ussuriysk Nature Reserve, 14 Aug. 1989, L.N. Vasilyeva, VLA P-782.

Eutypella leprosa (Fr.) Berl.

On dead branches of *Crataegus* sp., Khanka Nature Reserve, 21 Jun. 2003, L.N. Vasilyeva, VLA P-1914. - On dead branches of *Lespedeza* spp., Big Khekhtsir Nature Reserve, 25 Sept. 1982, L.N. Vasilyeva, VLA P-1915; Xingkaihu Nature Reserve, 1 Sept. 2003, L.N. Vasilyeva, VLA P-1584. - On dead branches of *Ulmus japonica* (Rehd.) Sarg., Big Khekhtsir Nature Reserve, 19 Aug. 1983, L.N. Vasilyeva, VLA P-1916. - On dead stems of *Vitis amurensis* Rupr., Big Khekhtsir Nature Reserve, 22 Aug. 1983, L.N. Vasilyeva, VLA P-1917.

* *Eutypella prunastri* (Pers. : Fr.) Sacc.

On dead branches of *Padus maackii* (Rupr.) Kom., Big Khekhtsir Nature Reserve, 23 Aug. 1983, L.N. Vasilyeva, VLA P-787; Ussuriysk Nature Reserve, 10 Aug. 1989, L.N. Vasilyeva, VLA P-786; Hulin: Dongfanghong, 3 Sept. 2003, L.N. Vasilyeva, VLA P-1586.

Eutypella scoparia (Schwein. : Fr.) Ellis & Everh.

On dead branches of *Lonicera* sp., Ussuriysk Nature Reserve, 15 Aug. 1989, L.N. Vasilyeva, VLA P-788. - On dead branches of a deciduous tree, Hulin: Dongfanghong, 3 Sept. 2003, L.N. Vasilyeva, VLA P-1589.

Eutypella stellulata (Fr. : Fr.) Sacc.

On dead branches of *Ulmus* spp., Ussuriysk Nature Reserve, 9 Aug. 1989, L.N. Vasilyeva, VLA P-790; Khanka Nature Reserve, 21 Jun. 2003, L.N. Vasilyeva, VLA P-789.

Flageoletia leptasca (Peck & Clint.) Höhn.

On dead branches of *Maackia amurensis* Rupr. et Maxim., Big Khekhtsir Nature Reserve,

24 Sept. 1982, L.N. Vasilyeva, VLA P-791.

Lopadostoma gastrinum (Fr.) Traverso

On dead branches of *Quercus mongolica* Fisch. ex Ledeb., Big Khekhtsir Nature Reserve, 23 Aug. 1983, L.N. Vasilyeva, VLA P-793; Ussuriysk Nature Reserve, 13 Aug. 1989, L.N. Vasilyeva, VLA P-497.

* *Lopadostoma microsporum* (P. Karst.) P.M.D. Martin

On dead trunk of *Alnus hirsuta* (Spach) Fisch. ex Rupr., Fuyuan: Chuangxin, 5 Aug. 2004, L.N. Vasilyeva, VLA P-1674.

* *Melogramma corylina* Lar.N. Vassiljeva

On dead branches of *Corylus* sp., Sanjiang Nature Reserve: Dongxing cun, 5 Aug. 2004, L.N. Vasilyeva, VLA P-1693.

Peridoxylon petersii (Berk. & M.A. Curtis) Shear

On wood of a deciduous tree, Bastak Nature Reserve, 8 Sept. 2001, E.M. Bulakh, VLA P-687.

Phorcys corylina Lar.N. Vassiljeva

On dead branches of *Corylus mandshurica* Maxim., Ussuriysk Nature Reserve, 13 Aug. 1989, L.N. Vasilyeva, VLA P-812.

* *Valsaria foedans* (P. Karst.) Sacc.

On dead branches of *Alnus hirsuta* (Spach) Turcz. ex Rupr. and *Betula* sp., Hulin: Dongfanghong, Sept 3, 2003, L.N. Vasilyeva, VLA P-1739, P-1738.

Valsaria insitiva (Fr.) Ces. & De Not.

On dead branches of *Quercus mongolica* Fisch. ex Ledeb., Big Khekhtsir Nature Reserve, 22 Sept. 1982, L.N. Vasilyeva, VLA P-823.

PHYLLACHORALES

PHYLLACHORACEAE

Phyllachora graminis (Pers. : Fr.) Fuckel

On living leaves of *Calamagrostis* sp., Big Khekhtsir Nature Reserve, 23 Sept. 1982, L.N. Vasilyeva, VLA P-1310.

POLYSTIGMATALES

POLYSTIGMATACEAE

* *Polystigma fulvum* DC.

On living leaves of *Padus avium* Mill., Ussuriysk Nature Reseve, 13 Aug. 1958, VLA P-815, I.A. Bunkina; Big Khekhtsir Nature Reserve, 8 Aug. 1981, L.N. Vasilyeva, VLA P-814;

Weihushan Nature Reserve: Northern Tiger Forest Garden, 9 Aug. 2004, L.N. Vasilyeva, VLA P-1708.

Polystigma ussuriensis (Jacz. & Natalyina) Prots.

On living leaves of *Prunus* spp., Gornotayezhnoye, 28 Sept. 1961, A.A. Ablakatova, VLA P-817.

CRYPHONECTRIACEAE

* ***Chromendothia citrina*** Lar. N. Vassiljeva

On dead branches of *Quercus mongolica* Fisch. ex Ledeb., Hulin: 854 State Farm, 2 Sept. 2003, L.N. Vasilyeva, VLA P-1460.

Cryphonectria japonica (Tak. Kobay. & Kaz. Itô) Gryzenh. & M.J. Wingf.

On dead branches of *Quercus mongolica* Fisch. ex Ledeb., Khanka Nature Reserve, 19 Jun. 2003, L.N. Vasilyeva, VLA P-468.

HYPOCREALES

HYPOCREACEAE

Calonectria cyanogena (Desm.) Lar. N. Vassiljeva

On dead stems of a cereal, Hulin: 854 State Farm, 2 Sept. 2003, L.N. Vasilyeva, VLA P-1449.

Claviceps purpurea Tul.

In ovaries of different grasses, Big Khekhtsir Nature Reserve, Ussuriysk Nature Reserve (Koval, 1991).

Cordyceps coccinea Penz. & Sacc.

On pupas of Lepidoptera, Big Khekhtsir Nature Reserve, Ussuriysk Nature Reserve (Koval, 1991).

Cordyceps corallomyces A. Møller

On larvae of Diptera, Hulin: Dongfanghong, 3 Sept. 2003, A.V. Bogacheva, VLA P-1467; Ussuriysk Nature Reserve (Koval, 1991).

Cordyceps deflectens Penz. & Sacc.

On pupas and lavae of Lepidoptera, Big Khekhtsir Nature Reserve, Ussuriysk Nature Reserve (Koval, 1991).

Cordyceps dipterigena Berk. & Broome

On different flies, Ussuriysk Nature Reserve (Koval, 1991).

Cordyceps entomorrhiza (Diks.) Fr.

On larvae of Coleoptera, Big Khekhtsir Nature Reserve, Ussuriysk Nature Reserve (Koval, 1991).

Cordyceps flavor-brunnescens Henn.

On larvae and pupas of Lepidoptera, Ussuriysk Nature Reserve (Koval, 1991).

Cordyceps kobayasii Koval

On pupas and imago of Cicadidae, Ussuriysk Nature Reserve (Koval, 1991).

Cordyceps laxcroixii Har. & Pat.

On larvae of Lepidoptera, Ussuriysk Nature Reserve (Koval, 1991).

Cordyceps martiales Speg.

On larvae of Coleoptera, Ussuriysk Nature Reserve (Koval, 1991).

Cordyceps militaris (Fr.) Link

On larvae and pupas of Lepidoptera, Big Khekhtsir Nature Reserve, Ussuriysk Nature Reserve (Koval, 1991).

Cordyceps nutans Pat.

On forest bugs (*Fentatoma* sp.), Hulin: Dongfanghong, 3 Sept. 2003, VLA P-1468; Ussuriysk Nature Reserve (Koval, 1991).

Cordyceps owariensis Kobayasi

On larvae of Cicadidae, Ussuriysk Nature Reserve (Koval, 1991).

Cordyceps polyarthra A. Møller

On larvae and pupas of Lepidoptera, Big Khekhtsir Nature Reserve, Ussuriysk Nature Reserve (Koval, 1991).

Cordyceps pseudoinsignis Moureau

On larvae of *Melolontha* sp. (Coleoptera), Ussuriysk Nature Reserve (Koval, 1991).

Cordyceps sphecocephala (Klotzsch) Berk. et M.A. Curtis

On wasps, Ussuriysk Nature Reserve (Koval, 1991).

Cordyceps stylophora Berk. & Broome

On lavae of Elateridae (Coleoptera), Ussuriysk Nature Reserve (Koval, 1991).

Cordyceps superficialis (Peck) Sacc.

On larvae and pupas of Coleoptera, Ussuriysk Nature Reserve (Koval, 1991).

Cordyceps takaomontana Yakush. & Kumaz.

On larvae and pupas of Lepidoptera, Ussuriysk Nature Reserve (Koval, 1991).

Cordyceps tuberculata (Lebert) Maire

On butterflies, Big Khekhtsir Nature Reserve, Ussuriysk Nature Reserve (Koval, 1991).

Cordyceps unilateralis (Tul.) Sacc.

On ants, Big Khekhtsir Nature Reserve, Ussuriysk Nature Reserve (Koval, 1991).

Cordyceps variegata Moureau

On larvae and pupas of Lepidoptera, Big Khekhtsir Nature Reserve (Koval, 1991).

Cosmospora episphaeria (Tode : Fr.) Rossman & Samuels

On old stromata of *Diatrype* sp., Big Khekhtsir Nature Reserve, 20 Aug. 1983, L.N. Vasilyeva, VLA P-462.

Cosmospora purtonii (Grev.) Rossman & Samuels

On old stromata of a diaporthalean fungus, Big Khekhtsir Nature Reserve, 25 Sept. 1982, L.N. Vasilyeva, VLA P-465.

Cosmospora vilior (Starbäck) Rossman & Samuels

On old stromata of *Ustulina deusta* (Hoffm. : Fr.) Lind, Ussuriysk Nature Reserve, 28 Aug. 1989, L.N. Vasilyeva, VLA P-464. - This species was indicated before as *Dialonectria ustulinae* (Teng) Lar.N. Vassiljeva (Vasilyeva, 1998).

Creopus testacea Lar. N. Vassiljeva

On wood, Ussuriysk Nature Reserve, 10 Aug. 1989, L.N. Vasilyeva, VLA P-1877.

Epichloe typhina (Pers. : Fr.) Tul.

On living stems of *Calamagrostis langsdowffii* (Link) Trin., Big Khekhtsir Nature Reserve, 22 Sept. 1982, L.N. Vasilyeva, VLA P-1259.

* *Hypocrea cerebriformis* Berk.

On decayed wood, Ussuriysk Nature Reserve, 2 Sept. 1962, M.M. Nazarova, VLA P-160; Weihushan Nature Reserve: Northern Tiger Forest Garden, 9 Aug. 2004, E.M. Bulakh, VLA P-1603.

Hypocrea fungicola (P. Karst.) Sacc.

On decayed fruit bodies of *Fomitopsis pinicola* (Sw.) P. Karst., Ussuriysk Nature Reserve, 12 Aug. 1989, L.N. Vasilyeva, VLA P-1918.

** *Hypocrea megalosulphurea* Yoshim. Doi

On fruit bodies of *Exidia* sp. from dead branches of *Corylus heterophylla* Fisch. ex Trautv., Bastak Nature Reserve, 19 Aug. 2004, L.N. Vasilyeva, VLA P-92.

Hypomyces subiculosus (Berk. et M. A. Curtis) Höhn.

On fruit bodies of *Coryolus* sp., Ussuriysk Nature Reserve, 18 Aug. 1989, L.N. Vasilyeva, VLA P-795.

Myrmaeciella caraganae Höhn.

On dead branches of *Maackia amurensis* Rupr. et Maxim., Big Khekhtsir Nature Reserve, 24 Sept. 1982, L.N. Vasilyeva, VLA P-801.

Nectria cinnabarina (Tode : Fr.) Fr.

On dead stems of *Aralia elata* (Miq.) Seem., Ussuriysk Nature Reserve, 11 Oct. 1953, L.N. Vassiljeva, VLA P-809; Big Khekhtsir Nature Reserve, 21 Aug. 1983, VLA P-803. - On dead branches of *Ribes* sp., *Schizandra chinensis* (Turcz.) Baill. and *Sorbaria sorbifolia* (L.) A. Br., Ussuriysk Nature Reserve, 28 Aug. 1989, L.N. Vasilyeva, VLA P-805; 28 May 1957, A.A. Ablakatova, VLA P-807; 16 Sept. 1962, L. Gurskaya, VLA P-808. - On dead branches of *Ulmus* spp., Big Khekhtsir Nature Reserve, 28 Aug. 1983, L.N. Vasilyeva, VLA P-802; Ussuriysk Nature Reserve, 21 Aug. 1989, L.N. Vasilyeva, VLA P-806.

Pleonectria balsamea (Cooke & Peck) Lar. N. Vassiljeva

On dead branches of *Abies nephrolepis* (Trautv.) Maxim., Big Khekhtsir Nature Reserve,

19 Oct. 1981, L.N. Vasilyeva, VLA P-1898.

Podostroma alutacea (Pers. : Fr.) G.F. Atk.   Plate 3: 13

On wood, Khanka Nature Reserve, 29 Jul. 2007, E.M. Bulakh, VLA P-1376.

** ***Podostroma leucopus*** P. Karst.

In forest litter, Upper Ussuri Station, 9 Sept. 1975, E.M. Bulakh, VLA P-1374; Bastak Nature Reserve, 17 Aug. 2000, E.M. Bulakh, VLA P-1375.

** ***Podostroma giganteum*** S. Imai   Plate 3: 14

On wood, Bastak Nature Reserve, 8 Sept. 2001, E.M. Bulakh, VLA P-358.

Sarawakus frustulosus (Berk. & M.A. Curtis) Lar.N. Vassiljeva

On wood, Ussuriysk Nature Reserve, 29 Aug. 1989, L.N. Vasilyeva, VLA P-822; Khanka Nature Reserve, 21 Jun. 2003, L.N. Vasilyeva, VLA P-1848; Xingkaihu Nature Reserve, 1 Sept. 2003, L.N. Vasilyeva, VLA P-1726; Fuyuan: Chuangxin, 5 Aug. 2004, L.N. Vasilyeva, VLA P-1725.

Scoleconectria cucurbitula (Tode : Fr.) C. Booth

On dead branches of *Larix gmelinii* (Rupr.) Rupr., Big Khekhtsir Nature Reserve, 24 Sept. 1982, L.N. Vasilyeva, VLA P-761.

Torrubiella leiopus (Mains) Kobayasi et Shimizu

On spiders, Big Khekhtsir Nature Reserve (Koval, 1991).

Torrubiella liberiana Mains

On ants in forest litter, Big Khekhtsir Nature Reserve (Koval, 1991).

XYLARIALES

XYLARIACEAE

*** ***Daldinia carpinicola*** Lar.N. Vassiljeva & M. Stadler   Plate 3: 15

On dead trunks of *Carpinus cordata* Blume, Ussuriysk Nature Reserve, 18 Sept. 1996, L.N. Vasilyeva, VLA P-1776.

*** ***Daldinia childiae*** J. D. Rogers & Y. M. Ju

On logs, Big Khekhtsir Nature Reserve, 17 Oct. 1981, L.N. Vasilyeva, VLA P-1119; Ussuriysk Nature Reserve, 18 Sept. 1996, L.N. Vasilyeva, VLA P-1762. - On bark, Hulin: Dongfanghong, 3 Sept. 2003, L.N. Vasilyeva, VLA P-1751. - On dead trunk of *Fraxinus* sp., Fuyuan, 4 Aug. 2004, L.N. Vasilyeva, VLA P-1747. - On dead trunk of *Quercus mongolica* Fisch. ex Ledeb., near Sanjiang Nature Reserve: Dongxing cun, 5 Aug. 2004, L.N. Vasilyeva, VLA P-1748. - On dead trunk of *Acer* sp., Raohe: Shengli State Farm, 6 Aug. 2004, E.M. Bulakh, VLA P-1746.

* ***Daldinia gelatinoides*** Lar.N. Vassiljeva

On logs, Sanjiang Nature Reserve: Dongxing cun, 5 Aug. 2004, L.N. Vasilyeva, VLA

P-1786.

Entoleuca mammata (Wahlenb.) J.D. Rogers & Y.M. Ju

On dead branches of *Populus* sp., Ussuriysk Nature Reserve, 23 Aug. 1989, L.N. Vasilyeva, VLA P-150.

Entonaema cinnabarina (Cooke & Massee) Lloyd　　　Plate 3: 16

On dead trees of *Padus avium* Mill., Ussuriysk Nature Reserve, 18 Sept. 1996, L.N. Vasilyeva, VLA P-327.

Hypoxylon annulatum (Schwein. : Fr.) Mont.

On dead branches of *Quercus mongolica* Fisch. ex Ledeb., Big Khekhtsir Nature Reserve, 23 Aug. 1983, L.N. Vasilyeva, VLA P-927; Ussuriysk Nature Reserve, 10 Aug. 1989, L.N. Vasilyeva, VLA P-928; Xingkaihu Nature Reserve, 1 Sept. 2003, L.N. Vasilyeva, VLA P-1609; Hulin: Wulindong, 4 Sept. 2003, L.N. Vasilyeva, VLA P-1607; Raohe, 7 Aug. 2004, L.N. Vasilyeva, VLA P-1610; Bastak Nature Reserve, 18 Aug. 2004, L.N. Vasilyeva, VLA P-925.

Hypoxylon crocopeplum Berk. & M.A. Curtis

On wood, Ussuriysk Nature Reserve, 10 Aug. 1989, L.N. Vasilyeva, VLA P-1899.

** *Hypoxylon dearnessii* Y.-M. Ju & J.D. Rogers

On dead branches of *Acer ukurunduense* Trautv. et Mey, Big Khekhtsir Nature Reserve, 20 Jun. 2000, L.N. Vasilyeva, VLA P-1104.

Hypoxylon fuscopurpureum (Schwein. : Fr.) M.A. Curtis (= *Hypoxylon vogesiacum* (Pers.) Sacc. var. *microsporum* J.H. Mill.)

On dead branches of *Corylus* spp., Big Khekhtsir Nature Reserve, 12 Oct. 1981, L.N. Vasilyeva, VLA P-1919.

Hypoxylon fuscum (Pers. : Fr.) Fr.

On dead branches of *Alnus hirsuta* (Spach) Turcz. ex Rupr., Big Khekhtsir Nature Reserve, 16 Sept. 1982, L.N. Vasilyeva, VLA P-173; Ussuriysk Nature Reserve, 27 Aug. 1989, L.N. Vasilyeva, VLA P-166; Hulin: Wulindong, 4 Sept. 2003, L.N. Vasilyeva, VLA P-1628. - On dead branches of *Betula platyphylla* Sukacz., Ussuriysk Nature Reserve, 29 Oct. 1956, I.A. Bunkina, VLA P-167. - On dead branches of *Corylus* spp., Ussuriysk Nature Reserve, 28 Apr. 1956, I.A. Bunkina, VLA P-163; Big Khekhtsir Nature Reserve, 12 Oct. 1981, L.N. Vasilyeva, VLA P-168; Bastak Nature Reserve, 19 Aug. 2004, L.N. Vasilyeva, VLA P-169.

Hypoxylon howeianum Peck

On bark of *Betula* sp., Raohe: Shengli State Farm, 6 Aug. 2004, L.N. Vasilyeva, VLA P-1636. - On dead branches of *Corylus* sp., Raohe, 7 Aug. 2004, E.M. Bulakh, VLA P-1635. - On dead branches of a deciduous tree, Hulin: Wulindong, 4 Sept. 2003, L.N. Vasilyeva, VLA P-1634.

* *Hypoxylon laschii* Nitschke

On dead branches of *Populus* sp., Xingkaihu Nature Reserve, 1 Sept. 2003, L.N. Vasilyeva, VLA P-1639.

* *Hypoxylon moravicum* Pouzar

On dead branches of *Fraxinus* spp., Big Khekhtsir Nature Reserve, 16 Oct. 1982, L.N. Vasilyeva, VLA P-966; Hulin: Dongfanghong, 3 Sept. 2003, L.N. Vasilyeva, VLA P-1641.

Hypoxylon multiforme (Fr. : Fr.) Fr.

On dead trunks of *Betula* spp., Big Khekhtsir Nature Reserve, 20 Aug. 1983, L.N. Vasilyeva, VLA P-967; Ussuriysk Nature Reserve, 11 Aug. 1989, L.N. Vasilyeva, VLA P-969; Hulin: Dongfanghong, 3 Sept. 2003, L.N. Vasilyeva, VLA P-1641; Bastak Nature Reserve, 21 Aug. 2004, E.M. Bulakh, VLA P-968.

* *Hypoxylon perforatum* (Schwein.: Fr.) Fr.

On dead branches of *Acer* spp., Ussuriysk Nature Reserve, 23 Oct. 1956, I.A. Bunkina, VLA P-186; Big Khekhtsir Nature Reserve, 19 Oct. 1981, L.N. Vasilyeva, VLA P-175. - On dead branches of *Betula* sp., Bastak Nature Reserve, 18 Aug. 2004, L.N. Vasilyeva, VLA P-185. - On dead branches of *Carpinus cordata* Blume, *Ligustrina amurensis* Rupr. and *Salix gracilistyla* Miq., Ussuriysk Nature Reserve, 11 Aug. 1960, L.N. Vassiljeva, VLA P-184; 29 May 1958, I.A. Bunkina. VLA P-192; 8 Sept. 1963, L. Smekalina, VLA P-193. - On dead branches of *Fraxinus* spp., Ussuriysk Nature Reserve, 23 Oct. 1956, I.A. Bunkina, VLA P-181; Big Khekhtsir Nature Reserve, 14 Oct. 1981, L.N. Vasilyeva, VLA P-176; Khanka Nature Reserve, 21 Jun. 2003, L.N. Vasilyeva, VLA P-180. - On dead branches of *Corylus* sp., *Juglans mandshurica* Maxim. and *Ulmus japonica* (Rehd.) Sarg., Big Khekhtsir Nature Reserve, 12 Oct. 1981, L.N. Vasilyeva, VLA P-177; 22 Sept. 1982, L.N. Vasilyeva, VLA P-178; 13 Oct. 1981, L.N. Vasilyeva, VLA P-179. - On dead branches of *Malus* sp., Ussuriysk: Gornotayezhnoe, 16 Oct. 1954, A.A. Ablakatova, VLA P-182. - On dead branches of *Padus maackii* (Rupr.) Kom., Hulin: Dongfanghong, 3 Sept. 2003, L.N. Vasilyeva, VLA P-1645.

Hypoxylon pseudoillitum Lar.N. Vassiljeva

On wood, Big Khekhtsir Nature Reserve, 16 Sept. 1981, L.N. Vasilyeva, VLA P-1842; Ussuriysk Nature Reserve, 28 Aug. 1989, L.N. Vasilyeva, VLA P-194. - This species is a member of *Nemania* but the new combination is not made yet.

Hypoxylon rubiginosum (Pers. : Fr.) Fr.

On wood, Ussuriysk Nature Reserve, 18 Aug. 1989, L.N. Vasilyeva, VLA P-978; Big Khekhtsir Nature Reserve, 15 Aug. 2004, L.N. Vasilyeva, VLA P-198.

Hypoxylon sphaeriostomum (Schwein.) Sacc.

On wood, Ussuriysk Nature Reserve, 18 Sept. 1996, L.N. Vasilyeva, VLA P-979.

Hypoxylon ulmophilum Lar.N. Vassiljeva

On dead branches of *Ulmus* spp., Big Khekhtsir Nature Reserve, 14 Oct. 1981, L.N. Vasilyeva, VLA P-573; Ussuriysk Nature Reserve, 18 Sept. 1996, L.N. Vasilyeva, VLA P-566; Khanka Nature Reserve, 21 Jun. 2003, L.N. Vasilyeva, VLA P-882.

Hypoxylon vogesiacum (Pers.) Sacc.

On wood, Big Khekhtsir Nature Reserve, 16 Jun. 2000, L.N. Vasilyeva, VLA P-986.

*** *Pyrenomyxa morganii* M. Stadler, Laessøe & Lar.N. Vassiljeva

On log, Ussuriysk: Gotnotayozhnoye, 18 Sept. 2001, L.N. Vasilyeva, VLA P-942.

Rosellinia conferta Lar.N. Vassiljeva

On dead branches of *Maackia amurensis* Rupr. et Maxim., Big Khekhtsir Nature Reserve, 14 Oct. 1981, L.N. Vasilyeva, VLA P-574.

* *Rosellinia corticium* (Schwein. : Fr.) Sacc.

On dead branches of *Betula* spp., Big Khekhtsir Nature Reserve, 28 Aug. 1983, L.N. Vasilyeva, VLA P-707; Bastak Nature Reserve, 18 Aug. 2004, L.N. Vasilyeva, VLA P-1856. - On bark of deciduous trees, Hulin: Dongfanghong, 3 Sept. 2003, L.N. Vasilyeva, VLA P-1716.

Rosellinia tienpinensis Teng

On the bark of living trunk of *Quercus mongolica* Fisch. ex Ledeb., Ussuriysk: Gotnotayozhnoye, 23 Jul. 2002, E.M. Bulakh, VLA P-946.

* *Thuemenella cubispora* (Ellis et Holw.) Boedijn

On dead branches of *Padus avium* Mill., Weihushan Nature Reserve: Northern Tiger Forest Garden, 9 Aug. 2004, L.N. Vasilyeva, VLA P-1728.

Ustulina deusta (Hoffm. : Fr.) Lind

On logs, Big Khekhtsir Nature Reserve, 19 Aug. 1983, L.N. Vasilyeva, VLA P-767; Ussuriysk Nature Reserve, 23 Aug. 1975, M.M. Nazarova, VLA P-763; Hulin: 854 State Farm, 2 Sept. 2003, L.N. Vasilyeva, VLA P-1733; Weihushan Nature Reserve: Northern Tiger Forest Garden, 9 Aug. 2004, L.N. Vasilyeva, VLA P-1734.

*** *Xylaria primorskensis* Y.M. Ju, H.M. Hsieh, Lar.N. Vassiljeva & Akulov

On wood, Ussuriysk Nature Reserve, 28 Aug. 1989, L.N. Vasilyeva, VLA P-391; Hulin: Dongfanghong, Sept. 3, 2003, L.N. Vasilyeva, VLA P-1742; Raohe: Shengli State Farm, 6 Aug. 2004, L.N. Vasilyeva, VLA P-1743; Big Khekhtsir Nature Reserve, 15 Aug. 2004, L.N. Vasilyeva, VLA P-385; Bastak Nature Reserve, 18 Aug. 2004, L.N. Vasilyeva, VLA P-380.

Xylaria cubensis (Mont.) Fr.

On wood, Ussuriysk Nature Reserve, 21 Aug. 1989, L.N. Vasilyeva, VLA P-1920.

Xylaria hypoxylon (L.) Grev.

On wood, Big Khekhtsir Nature Reserve, 27 Aug. 1983, L.N. Vasilyeva, VLA P-1921.

Xylaria polymorpha (Pers.: Fr.) Grev.

On wood, Ussuriysk Nature Reserve, 26 Aug. 1956, I. A. Bunkina, VLA P-1901.

SORDARIALES

LASIOSPHAERIACEAE

Bombardia lignicola (Fuckel) Kirschst.

On decayed wood, Ussuriysk Nature Reserve, 28 Aug. 1989, L.N. Vasilyeva, VLA P-51.

Coniochaeta sphaeroidea Lar.N. Vassiljeva

On decayed wood, Ussuriysk Nature Reserve, 18 Sept. 1996, L.N. Vasilyeva, VLA P-53.

Lasiosphaeria hirsuta (Fr. : Fr.) Ces. & De Not.

On decayed wood, Big Khekhtsir Nature Reserve, 28 Aug. 1983, L.N. Vasilyeva, VLA P-201; Ussuriysk Nature Reserve, 23 Aug. 1989, L.N. Vasilyeva, VLA P-203; Hulin: Dongfanghong, 3 Sept. 2003, L.N. Vasilyeva, VLA P-1656; Bastak Nature Reserve, 18 Aug. 2004, L.N. Vasilyeva, VLA P-1371.

Lasiosphaeria hispida (Tode : Fr.) Fuckel.

On decayed wood, Big Khekhtsir Nature Reserve, 18 Oct. 1981, L.N. Vasilyeva, VLA P-205; Ussuriysk Nature Reserve, 17 Aug. 1996, L.N. Vasilyeva, VLA P-204.

Lasiosphaeria ovina (Pers. : Fr.) Ces. & De Not.

On decayed wood, Ussuriysk Nature Reserve, 18 Aug. 1996, L.N. Vasilyeva, VLA P-441; Hulin: Wulindong, 4 Sept. 2003, L.N. Vasilyeva, VLA P-1658; Raohe, 7 Aug. 2004, L.N. Vasilyeva, VLA P-1657.

Lasiosphaeria strigosa (Alb. et Schwein.: Fr.) Sacc.

On wood of *Betula* sp., Ussuriysk Nature Reserve, 16 Aug. 1989, L.N. Vasilyeva, VLA P-2144.

DOTHIDEOMYCETIDAE

PSEUDOSPHAERIALES

MASSARIACEAE

Massaria inquinans (Tode : Fr.) De Not.

On dead branches of *Acer* sp., Big Khekhtsir Nature Reserve, 25 Sept. 1982, L.N. Vasilyeva, VLA P-1387.

Massaria mirabilis Lar.N. Vassiljeva

On dead branches of *Morus alba* L., Ussuriysk: Gornotayozhnoye, 24 Sept. 1984, L.N. Vasilyeva, VLA P-1922.

* ***Massaria pyri*** G.H. Otth

On dead branches of *Padus avium* Mill., Ussuriysk Nature Reserve, 27 Aug. 1989, L.N. Vasilyeva, VLA P-1902; Weihushan Nature Reserve: Northern Tiger Forest Garden, 9 Aug. 2004, L.N. Vasilyeva, VLA P-1678.

DOTHIDEALES

DOTHIDEACEAE

Botryosphaeria dothidea (Moug. : Fr.) Ces. & De Not.

On dead branches of *Sorbaria sorbifolia* (L.) A. Br., Big Khekhtsir Nature Reserve, 28

Aug. 1983, L.N. Vasilyeva, VLA P-1404.

Botryosphaeria obtusa (Schwein.) Shoemaker

On dead branches of *Juglans mandshurica* Maxim., Hulin, 2 Sept. 2003, L.N. Vasilyeva, VLA P-1445.

Dothidea puccinioides (DC.) Fr.

On dead branches of *Lespedeza* sp., Big Khekhtsir Nature Reserve, 24 Sept. 1982, L.N. Vasilyeva, VLA P-1881. - On dead branches of *Phellodendron amurense* Rupr., Hulin: 854 State Farm, 2 Sept. 2003, L.N. Vasilyeva, VLA P-1557.

Sydowia polyspora (Bref. & Tavel) E. Müll.

On dead branches of *Abies nephrolepis* (Trautv.) Maxim., Big Khekhtsir Nature Reserve, 19 Oct. 1981, L.N. Vasilyeva, VLA P-1923.

MYCOSPHAERELLACEAE

Mycosphaerella punctiformis (Fr.) J. Schröt.

On dead leaves of *Tilia amurensis* Rupr., Big Khekhtsir Nature Reserve, 10 Apr. 1982, A.A. Lonchakov, VLA P-1880.

PLEOSPORALES

PLEOSPORACEAE

* Leptosphaeria conoidea (De Not.) Sacc.

On dead stems of *Artemisia* sp., Big Khekhtsir Nature Reserve, 27 Aug. 1983, L.N. Vasilyeva, VLA P-576. - On dead stems of *Aconitum* sp., Hulin: Dongfanghong, 3 Sept. 2003, L.N. Vasilyeva, VLA P-1659.

Leptosphaeria gloeospora (Berk. & M.A. Curtis) Sacc.

On dead stems of *Prenanthes tatarinowii* Maxim., Ussuriysk Nature Reserve, 23 Aug. 1989, L.N. Vasilyeva, VLA P-575.

* Leptosphaeria millefolii (Fuckel) Niessl.

On dead herbaceous stems, Ussuriysk Nature Reserve, 12 Aug. 1989, L.N. Vasilyeva, VLA P-579; Hulin: Dongfanghong, 3 Sept. 2003, L.N. Vasilyeva, VLA P-1662; Raohe: Shengli State Farm, 6 Sept. 2003, L.N. Vasilyeva, VLA P-1665; Raohe, 7 Aug. 2004, L.N. Vasilyeva, VLA P-1664.

Leptosphaeria ogilviensis (Berk. & Broome) Ces. & De Not.

On dead stems of *Cirsium* sp., Fuyuan, 4 Aug. 2004, L.N. Vasilyeva, VLA P-1666.

Ophiobolus rubellus (Pers. : Fr.) Sacc.

On dead stems of *Adenocaulon himalaicus* Edgew., Ussuriysk Nature Reserve, 12 Aug.

1989, L.N. Vasilyeva, VLA P-683. - On dead stems of *Veratrum* sp., Big Khekhtsir Nature Reserve, L.N. Vasilyeva, 25 Aug. 1983, VLA P-684.

DIDYMOSPHAERIACEAE

Didymosphaeria eleutherococci Lar. N. Vassiljeva

On dead stems of *Eleutherococcus senticosus* (Rupr. et Maxim.) Maxim., Big Khekhtsir Nature Reserve, 22 Aug. 1983, L.N. Vasilyeva, VLA P-511; Ussuriysk Nature Reserve, 29 Aug. 1989, VLA P-509.

Massarina eburnea (Tul.) Sacc.

On dead branches of *Lonicera edulis* Turcz. ex Freyn, Big Khekhtsir Nature Reserve, 18 Oct. 1981, L.N. Vasilyeva, VLA P-1924.

FENESTELLACEAE

Fenestella fenestrata (Berk. & Broome) J. Schröt.

On dead branches of *Tilia amurensis* Rupr., Bastak Nature Reserve, 19 Aug. 2004, L.N. Vasilyeva, VLA P-1847.

MELANOMMATALES

MELANOMMATACEAE

Byssosphaeria rhodomphala (Berk.) Cooke

On bark and wood of *Phellodendron amurensis* Rupr., Big Khekhtsir Nature Reserve, 23 Aug. 1983, L.N. Vasilyeva, VLA P-448; Ussuriysk Nature Reserve, 23 Aug. 1989, L.N. Vasilyeva, VLA P-452. - On bark of *Maackia amurensis* Rupr. et Maxim., Ussuriysk Nature Reserve, 12 Aug. 1989, L.N. Vasilyeva, VLA P-109; Bastak Nature Reserve, 18 Aug. 2004, L.N. Vasilyeva, VLA P-108.

Cucurbitaria berberidis (Pers. : Fr.) Gray

On dead branches of *Berberis amurensis* Rupr., Big Khekhtsir Nature Reserve, 25 Sept. 1982, L.N. Vasilyeva, VLA P-1241.

Cucurbitaria caraganae P. Karst.

On dead branches of *Maackia amurensis* Rupr. et Maxim., Big Khekhtsir Nature Reserve, 24 Sept. 1982, L.N. Vasilyeva, VLA P-1248; Sanjiang Nature Reserve: Dongxing cun, 5 Aug. 2004, L.N. Vasilyeva, VLA P-1487.

Pseudotrichia mutabilis (Pers. : Fr.) Wehm.

On wood, Ussuriysk Nature Reserve, 15 Aug. 1989, L.N. Vasilyeva, VLA P-1925.

Thaxteriella lignicola Teng

On wood, Big Khekhtsir Nature Reserve, 20 Aug. 1983, L.N. Vasilyeva, VLA P-874.

LOPHIOSTOMATALES

LOPHIOSTOMATACEAE

Lophiostoma appendiculatum Fuckel

On wood, Ussuriysk Nature Reserve, 12 Aug. 1989, L.N. Vasilyeva, VLA P-1900.

Platystomum compressum (Pers. : Fr.) Trevis.

On wood, Big Khekhtsir Nature Reserve, 21 Jul. 1983, L.N. Vasilyeva, VLA P-697; Ussuriysk Nature Reserve, 23 Aug. 1989, L.N. Vasilyeva, VLA P-695.

CHAETOTHYRIALES

STIGMATEACEAE

Stigmatea circinans (Fr.) Fr.

On living leaves of *Geranium* sp., Ussuriysk Nature Reserve, 12 Aug. 1989, L.N. Vasilyeva, VLA P-897.

Stigmatea waldsteiniae (Sawada) Lar.N. Vassiljeva

On living leaves of *Waldsteinia ternata* (Steph.) Fritsch., Ussuriysk Nature Reserve, 28 Apr. 1956, I.A. Bunkina, VLA P-900.

Phaeocryptopus nudus (Peck) Petr.

On wilting needles of *Abies nephrolepis* (Trautv.) Maxim., Ussuriysk Nature Reserve, 21 Aug. 1989, L.N. Vasilyeva, VLA P-1926.

HERPOTRICHIELLACEAE

Acanthostigma scleracanthoides Penz. & Sacc.

On wood, Big Khekhtsir Nature Reserve, 20 Aug. 1983, L.N. Vasilyeva, VLA P-437; Ussuriysk Nature Reserve, 28 Aug. 1989, L.N. Vasilyeva, VLA P-440.

Berlesiella mansonii (Schol-Schwarz) Lar. N. Vassiljeva

On wood of a coniferous tree, Big Khektsir Nature Reserve, 20 Aug. 1983, L.N. Vasilyeva, VLA P-446.

HYSTERIALES

HYSTERIACEAE

Glonium lineare (Fr.) De Not.

On wood, Ussuriysk Nature Reserve, 23 Aug. 1989, L.N. Vasilyeva, VLA P-1927; Hulin:

Wulindong, 4 Sept. 2003, L.N. Vasilyeva, VLA P-1597.

* *Glonium macrosporum* N. Amano

On wood of conifers, Big Khekhtsir Nature Reserve, 19 Aug. 1983, L.N. Vasilyeva, VLA P-550; Ussuriysk Nature Reserve, 21 Aug. 1989, L.N. Vasilyeva, VLA P-548; Hulin: Dongfanghong, 3 Sept. 2003, L.N. Vasilyeva, VLA P-1598.

***Hysterium macrosporum* W.R. Gerard**

On wood of coniferous trees, Big Khekhtsir Nature Reserve, 19 Aug. 1983, L.N. Vasilyeva, VLA P-844; Ussuriysk Nature Reserve, 18 Sept. 1996, L.N. Vasilyeva, VLA P-841.

***Hysterium vermiforme* Massee**

On wood of a coniferous tree, Ussuriysk Nature Reserve, 13 Sept. 1989, L.N. Vasilyeva, VLA P-846.

***Hysterographium curvatum* (Fr.) Rehm**

On wood, Ussuriysk Nature Reserve, 18 Sept. 1996, L.N. Vasilyeva, VLA P-847.

***Hysterographium flexuosum* (Schwein.) Sacc.**

On wood, Ussuriysk Nature Reserve, 11 Aug. 1989, L.N. Vasilyeva, VLA P-848.

** *Hysterographium formosum* (Cooke) Sacc.

On wood of a coniferous tree, Raohe: Shengli State Farm, 6 Aug. 2004, L.N. Vasilyeva, VLA P-1653. - Zogg (1962) placed the name of this fungus under *H. mori* (Schwein.) Rehm but the specimen differs in ascospore size (20-24 × 12-14 μm) and ascospore septation.

***Mytilinidion tortile* (Schwein.) Elllis & Everh.**

On dead branches of *Pinus koraiensis* Siebold et Zucc., Ussuriysk Nature Reserve, 28 Aug. 1989, L.N. Vasilyeva, VLA P-864.

PATELLARIALES

PATELLARIACEAE

***Karschia nigerrima* Sacc.**

On wood, Ussuriysk Nature Reserve, 23 Aug. 1989, L.N. Vasilyeva, VLA P-1928.

***Lecanidion atratum* (Hedw.) Endl.**

On *Phellodendron amurense* Rupr., Big Khekhtsir Nature Reserve, 22 Aug. 1983, L.N. Vasilyeva, VLA P-1879.

***Tryblidaria fenestrata* (Cooke & Peck) M.E. Barr**

On dead branches of *Lonicera* sp., Ussuriysk Nature Reserve, 18 Aug. 1989, L.N. Vasilyeva, VLA P-1113.

ERYSIPHOMYCETIDAE

ERYSIPHALES

ERYSIPHACEAE

Erysiphe aquilegiae DC.

On living leaves of *Aquilegia oxysepala* Trautv. et Mey., Ussuriysk Nature Reserve, 18 Aug. 1961, A.A. Ablakatova, VLA P-1274. - On living leaves of *Caltha* sp., Big Khekhtsir Nature Reserve, 16 Sept. 1982, L.N. Vasilyeva, VLA P-1277.

Erysiphe arabidis R.Y. Zheng & G.Q. Chen

On living leaves of *Arabis pendula* L., Ussuriysk Nature Reserve, 30 Aug. 1953, I.A. Bunkina, VLA P-1181; Big Khekhtsir Nature Reserve, 22 Aug. 1983, L.N. Vasilyeva, VLA P-1180.

Erysiphe artemisiae Grev.

On living leaves of *Artemisia rubripes* Nakai, Big Khekhtsir Nature Reserve, 14 Sept. 1973, I.A. Bunkina, VLA P-1282.

Erysiphe biocellata Ehrenb.

On living leaves of *Scutellaria ussuriensis* (Regel) Kudo, Ussuriysk Nature Reserve, 13 Jul. 1956, I.A. Bunkina, VLA P-1283; Big Khekhtsir Nature Reserve, 24 Aug. 1980, E.M. Bulakh, VLA P-1285.

Erysiphe bunkiniana U. Braun

On living leaves of *Rabdosia excisa* (Maxim.) Hara, Big Khekhtsir Nature Reserve, 14 Sept. 1973, I.A. Bunkina, VLA P-1287.

Erysiphe chloranthi (Golovin & Bunkina) U. Braun

On living leaves of *Chloranthus japonicus* Siebold, Ussuriysk Nature Reserve, 30 Aug. 1953, I.A. Bunkina, VLA P-1883.

Erysiphe cichoracearum DC.

On living leaves of *Inula* sp., Ussuriysk Nature Reserve, 11 Sept. 1961, I.A. Bunkina, VLA P-1291. - On living leaves of *Pterocypsela triangulata* (Maxim.) Shih and *Sonchus* sp., Big Khekhtsir Nature Reserve, 14 Sept. 1973, I.A. Bunkina, VLA P-1290, P-1288.

Erysiphe galeopsidis DC.

On living leaves of *Lamium barbatum* Siebold et Zucc., Ussuriysk Nature Reserve, 30 Aug. 1953, I.A. Bunkina, VLA P-1884.

Erysiphe geraniacearum U. Braun & Simonyan

On living leaves of *Geranium sibiricum* L. Ussuriysk Nature Reserve, 30 Aug. 1953, I.A. Bunkina, VLA P-1885.

Erysiphe graminis DC.

On living leaves of *Neomolinia mandshurica* (Maxim.) Honda, Ussuriysk Nature

Reserve, 30 Aug. 1953, I.A. Bunkina, VLA P-1886.

Erysiphe heraclei DC.

On living leaves of *Sium suave* Walt., Big Khekhtsir Nature Reserve, 2 Sept. 1980, E.M. Bulakh, VLA P-1194.

Erysiphe hommae U. Braun

On living leaves of *Elsholtzia serotina* Kom., Ussuriysk Nature Reserve, 30 Aug. 1953, I.A. Bunkina, VLA P-1296. - On living leaves of *Elsholtzia ciliata* (Thunb.) Hyl., 16 Sept. 1982, L.N. Vasilyeva, VLA P-1294.

Erysipphe krumbholzii U. Braun

On living leaves of *Chrysosplenium pilosum* Maxim., Ussuriysk Nature Reserve, 8 Jul. 1956, I.A. Bunkina, VLA P-1297.

Erysiphe magnicellulata U. Braun

On living leaves of *Polemonium* sp., Ussuriysk Nature Reserve, 30 Aug. 1953, I.A. Bunkina, VLA P-1298.

Erysiphe paeoniae R.Y. Zheng & G.Q. Chen

On living leaves of *Paeonia oreogeton* S. Moore, Ussuriysk Nature Reserve, 13 Jul. 1956, I.A. Bunkina, VLA P-1299.

Erysiphe pisi DC.

On living leaves of *Vicia cracca* L., Big Khekhtsir Nature Reserve, 14 Sept. 1973, I.A. Bunkina, VLA P-1195.

Erysiphe polygoni DC.

On living leaves of *Polygonum aviculare* L., Big Khekhtsir Nature Reserve, 3 Sept. 1980, N. Shaposhnikova, VLA P-1196.

Erysiphe ranunculi Grev.

On living leaves of *Thalictrum filamentosum* L., Big Khekhtsir Nature Reserve, 14 Sept. 1973, I.A. Bunkina, VLA P-1197.

Erysiphe sedi U. Braun

On living leaves of *Sedum auzoon* L., Ussuriysk Nature Reserve, 10 Sept. 1955, I.A. Bunkina, VLA P-1887.

Erysiphe sordida L. Junell

On living leaves of *Plantago asiatica* L., Big Khekhtsir Nature Reserve, 14 Sept. 1973, I.A. Bunkina, VLA P-1198.

Erysiphe thuemenii U. Braun

On living leaves of *Potentilla centigrana* Maxim., Ussuriysk Nature Reserve, 10 Sept. 1955, I.A. Bunkina, VLA P-1888.

Erysiphe trifolii Grev.

On living leaves of *Lathyrus humilis* (Ser.) Spreng., Ussuriysk Nature Reserve, 21 Oct. 1956, I.A. Bunkina, VLA P-1889.

Erysiphe ulmariae Desm.

On living leaves of *Filipendula palmata* (Pall.) Maxim., Big Khekhtsir Nature Reserve, 16 Sept. 1982, L.N. Vasilyeva, VLA P-1199.

Erysiphe urticae (Wallr.) S. Blumer

On living leaves of *Urtica angustifolia* Fisch. ex Hornem., Ussuriysk Nature Reserve, 21 Oct. 1956, I.A. Bunkina, VLA P-1890.

Erysiphe valerianae (Jacz.) S. Blumer

On living leaves of *Valeriana fauriei* Briq., Ussuriysk Nature Reserve, 30 Aug. 1953, I.A. Bunkina, VLA P-1891.

Microsphaera aceris Bunkina

On living leaves of *Acer barbinerve* Maxim., Ussuriysk Nature Reserve, 10 Sept. 1955, I.A. Bunkina, VLA P-342.

Microsphaera alphitoides Griffon & Maubl.

On living leaves of *Quercus mongolica* Fisch. ex Ledeb., Ussuriysk Nature Reserve, 21 Oct. 1956, I.A. Bunkina, VLA P-343.

Microsphaera azaleae U. Braun

On living leaves of *Rhododendron mucronulatum* Turcz., Ussuriysk Nature Reserve, 21 Oct. 1956, I.A. Bunkina, VLA P-1892.

Microsphaera berberidis (DC.) Lév.

On living leaves of *Berberis amurensis* Rupr., Big Khekhtsir Nature Reserve, Jul. 1982, Z.M. Azbukina, VLA P-1206.

Microsphaera deutziae Bunkina

On living leaves of *Deutzia amurensis* (Regel) Airy Shaw, Ussuriysk Nature Reserve, 13 Jul. 1956, I.A. Bunkina, VLA P-1893.

Microsphaera friesii Lév.

On living leaves of *Rhamnus davurica* Pall., Ussuriysk Nature Reserve, 28 Sept. 1961, I.A. Bunkina, VLA P-1894.

Microsphaera hommae U. Braun

On living leaves of *Corylus mandshurica* Maxim., Ussuriysk Nature Reserve, 21 Oct. 1956, I.A. Bunkina, VLA P-1929.

Microsphaera lonicerae (DC.) G. Winter

On living leaves of *Lonicera maackii* (Rupr.) Herd., Ussuriysk Nature Reserve, Aug. 1961, I.A. Bunkina, VLA P-347.

Microsphaera menispermi Howe

On living leaves of *Menispermum dauricum* DC., Ussuriysk Nature Reserve, 30 Aug. 1953, I.A. Bunkina, VLA P-1930.

Microsphaera schizandrae Sawada

On living leaves of *Schisandra chinensis* (Turcz.) Baill., Ussuriysk Nature Reserve, Sept.

1961, I.A. Bunkina, VLA P-1931.

Microsphaera securinegae F.L. Tai et C.T. Wei

On living leaves of *Securinega suffruticosa* (Pall.) Rehd., Ussuriysk Nature Reserve, 21 Oct. 1956, I.A. Bunkina, VLA P-1932.

Microsphaera syringae (Schwein.) Magnus

On living leaves of *Ligustrina amurensis* Rupr., Ussuriysk Nature Reserve, 13 Jul. 1956, I.A. Bunkina, VLA P-1933.

Phyllactinia actinidiae (Jacz.) Bunkina

On living leaves of *Actinidia kolomikta* (Maxim.) Maxim., Ussuriysk Nature Reserve, 1 Sept. 1956, I.A. Bunkina, VLA P-1934.

Phyllactinia fraxini (DC.) Fuss.

On living leaves of *Fraxinus* sp., Ussuriysk Nature Reserve, 21 Oct. 1956, I.A. Bunkina, VLA P-1935.

Phyllactinia mali (Duby) U. Braun

On living leaves of *Malus mandshurica* (Maxim.) Kom., Aug. 1961, I.A. Bunkina, VLA P-1936.

Phyllactinia philadelphi (Jacz.) Bunkina

On living leaves of *Philadelphus tenuifolius* Rupr. et Maxim., Big Khekhtsir Nature Reserve, 13 Oct. 1981, L.N. Vasilyeva, VLA P-1210.

Podosphaera clandestina (Wallr. : Fr.) Lév.

On living leaves of *Crataegus* sp., Big Khekhtsir Nature Reserve, 13 Oct. 1981, L.N. Vasilyeva, VLA P-1211.

Podosphaera minor Howe

On living leaves of *Spiraea salicifolia* L., Ussuriysk Nature Reserve, 30 Aug. 1953, I.A. Bunkina, VLA P-1937.

Sphaerotheca aphanis (Wallr.) U. Braun

On living leaves of *Comarum palustre* L., Big Khekhtsir Nature Reserve, O.K. Govorova, 24 Sept. 1982, VLA P-1217.

Sphaerotheca balsaminae (Wallr.) Kari

On living leaves of *Impatiens noli-tangere* L., Big Khekhtsir Nature Reserve, 16 Sept. 1982, L.N. Vasilyeva, VLA P-1226.

Sphaerotheca erigerontis-canadensis (Lév.) L. Junell

On living leaves of *Prenanthes tatarinowii* Maxim., Ussuriysk Nature Reserve, 30 Aug. 1953, I.A. Bunkina, VLA P-1938.

Sphaerotheca euphorbiae (Castagne) E.S. Salmon

On living leaves of *Euphorbia komaroviana* Prokh., Ussuriysk Nature Reserve, 1 Sept. 1956, I.A. Bunkina, VLA P-1939.

Sphaerotheca fusca (Fr.) S. Blumer

On living leaves of *Sigesbeckia orientalis* L., Big Khekhtsir Nature Reserve, 19 Sept.

1983, L.N. Vasilyeva, VLA P-1342.

Sphaerotheca veronicae (Jacz.) Bunkina

On living leaves of *Veronicastrum sibiricum* (L.) Pennell, Big Khekhtsir Nature Reserve, 23 Aug. 1983, L.N. Vasilyeva, VLA P-1347.

Sphaerotheca xanthii (Castagne) L. Junell

On living leaves of *Adenocaulon adhaerescens* Maxim., Ussuriysk Nature Reserve, 1 Sept. 1956, I.A. Bunkina, VLA P-1940.

Uncinula actinidiae (Hara) Miyabe

On living leaves of *Actinidia kolomikta* (Maxim.) Maxim., Ussuriysk Nature Reserve, Sept. 1959, I.A. Bunkina, VLA P-1895; Big Khekhtsir Nature Reserve, 28 Aug. 1983, L.N. Vasilyeva, VLA P-1350.

Uncinula adunca (Wallr. : Fr.) Lév.

On living leaves of *Salix caprea* L., Big Khekhtsir Nature Reserve, 14 Sept. 1983, L.N. Vasilyeva, VLA P-1352.

Uncinula betulae Homma

On living leaves of *Betula davurica* Pall., Ussuriysk Nature Reserve, 21 Oct. 1956, I.A. Bunkina, VLA P-1941.

Uncinula bicornis (Wallr. : Fr.) Lév.

On living leaves of *Acer mono* Maxim., Ussuriysk Nature Reserve, 1 Sept. 1956, I.A. Bunkina, VLA P-1897.

Uncinula clandenstina (Biv.) J. Schröt.

On living leaves of *Ulmus japonica* (Rehd.) Sarg., Ussuriysk Nature Reserve, Sept. 1961, I.A. Bunkina, VLA P-1942.

Uncinula crataegi Bunkina

On living leaves of *Crataegus maximowiczii* C.K. Schneid., Ussuriysk Nature Reserve, 21 Oct. 1956, I.A. Bunkina, VLA P-1943.

Uncinula fraxini Miyabe

On living leaves of *Fraxinus mandshurica* Rupr., Ussuriysk Nature Reserve, 30 Aug. 1953, I.A. Bunkina, VLA P-1944.

Uncinula ljubarskii Golovin

On living leaves of *Acer pseudosieboldianum* (Pax) Kom., Ussuriysk Nature Reserve, 21 Oct. 1956, I.A. Bunkina, VLA P-1945.

Uncinula miyabei (E.S. Salmon) Sacc. et Syd.

On living leaves of *Alnus hirsuta* (Spach) Fisch. ex Rupr., Ussuriysk Nature Reserve, 28 Sept. 1961, I.A. Bunkina, VLA P-1946.

RHYTISMOMYCETIDAE

RHYTISMATALES

RHYTISMATACEAE

Coccomyces dentatus (Kunze et J.C. Schmidt : Fr.) Sacc.

On dead leaves of *Quercus mongolica* Fisch. ex Ledeb., Hulin: 854 State Farm, 2 Sept. 2003, VLA P-1463.

Coccomyces tumidus (Fr.) De Not.

On dead leaves of *Quercus mongolica* Fisch. ex Ledeb., Fuyuan, 4 Aug. 2004, VLA P-1464.

Colpoma quercinum (Pers.: Fr.) Wallr.

On dead branches of *Quercus mongolica* Fisch. ex Ledeb., Ussuriysk Nature Reserve, 30 May 1958, VLA P-769, I.A. Bunkina; Khanka Nature Reserve, 18 Jun. 2003, VLA P-788; Fuyuan, 4 Aug. 2004, VLA P-1466.

Hypoderma commune (Fr.) Duby

On dead herbaceous stems, Fuyuan, 4 Aug. 2004, VLA P-1606.

*** Hypoderma rubi*** (Pers.: Fr.) De Not.

On dead stems of *Rubus* sp., Hulin: Dongfanghong, 3 Sept. 2003, VLA P-1947.

**** Lophodermium abietis*** Rostr.

On dead needles of *Picea* sp., Big Khekhtsir Nature Reserve, 16 Jun. 2000, VLA P-861.

Lophodermium laricinum Duby

On dead needles of *Larix* sp., Fuyuan, 4 Aug. 2004, VLA P-1948.

**** Lophodermium petiolicolum*** Fuckel

On dead leaves of *Quercus mongolica* Fisch. ex Ledeb., Khanka Nature Reserve, 18 Jun. 2003, VLA P-637; Raohe: Shengli State Farm, 6 Sept. 2003, VLA P-1677.

Rhytisma punctatum (Pers.: Fr.) Fr.

On living leaves of *Acer pseudosieboldianum* (Pers.) Kom. and *A. barbinerve* Maxim., Ussuriysk Nature Reserve, 11 Oct. 1956, I.A. Bunkina, VLA P-866; Upper Ussuri Station, 23 Sept. 1977, Z.M. Azbukina, VLA P-877.

REFERENCES

Abe Y, Liu Z L. An annotated list of xylariaceous and diatrypaceous fungi collected from Mt. Fengyangshan and Mt. Baishanzu, Zhejiang Province in east China. Bull. Nat. Sci. Mus. (Tokyo), 1995, 21: 75-86.

Bau T. Higher taxa of Ascomycota in Jilin Province, China. Journal of Fungal Research, 2005, 3: 1-6. (in

Chinese)

Eriksson O E, Yue J Z. The Pyrenomycetes of China, an annotated chcklist. Univ. of Umea. Umea. 1988, 1-88.

Ju, Y M, Hsieh H M, Vasilyeva L, Akulov A. Three new *Xylaria* species from Russian Far East. Mycologia, 2009, 101: 548-553.

Kobayashi T, Zhao J Z. Notes on diseases of woody plants and their causal fungi in Heilongjiang Province, China (1). Trans. Mycol. Soc. Japan, 1989, 30: 277-293.

Koval E Z. The order Claviciptales Nannf. 1991, 143-243. In Azbukina Z M. (ed.) *Lower* plants, fungi, and mosses of the Russian Far East. Vol. II. Nauka. Leningrad. (in Russian)

Liang Z Q, Liu A Y, Fan M Z, Guo C. Several species of *Cordyceps* in northwest area. Acta Mycologica Sinica, 1995, 14: 237-240.

Liu P G, Doi Y. The Hypocreaceae of China I. *Hypocrea pezizoides* with pale green conidia from southern Yunnan, China. Bull. Nat. Sci. Mus. (Tokyo), 1995, 21: 179-188.

Liu P G, Doi Y, Wang X H, Wang Q B. The Hypocreaceae of China. III. Some fungicolous species of the genus *Hypocrea*. Mycosystema, 2000, 19: 317-327.

Liu P G, Wang X H, Yu F Q, Zheng H D. The Hypocreaceae of China. IV. Some new records of the genus *Hypocrea* for China. Mycotaxon, 2002, 82: 463-474.

Luo J, Zhuang W J. Two new species of *Cosmospora* (Nectriaceae, Hypocreales) from China. Fungal Diversity, 2008, 31: 83-93.

Miller J H. A monograph of the world species of *Hypoxylon*. Athens, 1961, 1-158.

Tai F L. Sylloge Fungorum Sinicorum. Beijing: Science Press, 1979, 1-1527.

Teng S C. Fungi from China. Beijing: Science Press. 1964, 1-808. (in Chinese)

Vasilyeva L N. Pyrenomycetes and Loculoascomycetes. In Azbukina Z M. (ed.) Lower plants, fungi, and mosses of the Russian Far East. Vol. IV. Nauka. Saint-Petersburg, 1998, 1-419. (in Russian)

Vasilyeva L N. Pyrenomycetes of the Ruassian Far East-Additions and corrections. 1. *Rossmania ukurunduensis* gen. et sp. nov. Mycoscience, 2001, 42: 399-401.

Vasilyeva L N, Rossman A Y, Farr D L. New species of the Diaporthales from Eastern Asia and eastern North America. Mycologia, 2007, 99: 852-859.

Vasilyeva L N, Stadler M. Pyrenomycetes of the Russian Far East 3. Three new *Daldinia* species (Xylariaceae). Mycotaxon, 2008, 104: 287-296.

Wang X H, Liu P G. The Hypocreaceae of China V. The genus *Podostroma*. Mycosystema, 2002, 21: 156-161.

Yuan Z Q, Zhao Z Y. Studies on the genera *Amphisphaerella*, *Coniochaeta* and *Rosellinia* of Xinjing, China. Acta Mycologica Sinica, 1993, 12: 180-186.

Zhang X M, Zhuang W Y. Re-examination of Bionectriaceae and Nectriaceae (Hypocreales) from temperate China on deposit in HMAS. Nova Hedwigia, 2003, 76: 191-200.

Zhuang W Y. Ascomycota III. Taphrinomycetidae, Eurotiomycetidae, Dothideomycetidae, and Sordariomycetidae. Fungi of northwestern China. 2005, 113-124. In Zhuang W Y. (ed.) Fungi of northwestern China. Mycotaxon Ltd. Ithaca.

Zhuang W Y, Sun S X. Ascomycetes excluding discomycetes and lichens. 2001: 64-130. In Zhuang W Y.

(ed.) Higher fungi of tropical China. Beijing: Mycotaxon Ltd.

Zogg H. Die Hysteriaceae s.str. und Lophiaceae unter besonderer Berücksichtigung der mitteleuropaeischen Formen. Beitr. Krypt. Fl. Schweiz, 1962, 11(3): 1-190.

Micromycetes: Zygomycetes, Anamorphic Fungi; Ascomycetes

Lina N. EGOROVA

The studies of micromycete biota of Ussuri valley have revealed more than 700 species of fungi belonging to different taxonomic groups. Among them 43 species (50 subspecific taxa) from 13 genera belong to class Zygomycetes. The representatives of class Ascomycetes include 35 species from 18 genera. Moreover, 614 species (621 subspecific taxa) from 155 genera of anamorphic fungi are indicated. The most important groups are soil fungi (more than 400 species) and causal agents of fungal diseases of plant leaves (about 200 species). An annotated check-list is based on the author investigation of soil fungi (Egorova, 1968, 1978, 1984, 1986a, 2003; Egorova, Zhukovskaya, 1974; Egorova, Svishch, 1975; Zhukovskaya, Egorova, 1976; Egorova, Oksenyuk, 1983). In addition, the results of study of causal agents of fungal diseases have been included (Egorova, 1991, 1992, 1999, 2007a; Egorova, Oksenyuk, Blokhina, 1986; Egorova, Oksenyuk, 1987; Egorova, Kalantaevskaya, 2000) and the records of micromycetes in different reserves were supplemented (Egorova, 1986b, 1990, 2006, 2007b, c). The literature data on mycobiota of the Ussuriysk Nature Reserve (Bunkina, Nazarova, 1978; Melnik, 1990; Braun, Melnik, 1998) and Ussuriysk vicinity (Ablakatova, 1965; Gornostay, 1971; Azbukina et al., 1980; Martyniyuk, 2003) have been taken into account. The identification of specimens collected by A.V. Bogacheva at Chinese territory of Ussuri River Valley has provided 44 species from 35 genera of anamorphic fungi.

ZYGOMYCOTA

ZYGOMYCETES

MUCORALES

MUCORACEAE

Absidia coerulea Bainier

In soil of deciduous forest, Ussuriysk Nature Reserve. - In soil of oak forest, Big Khekhtsir Nature Reserve.

Absidia corymbifera (Cohn) Sacc. et Trotter

In soil of coniferous-broad-leaved forest, Ussuriysk Nature Reserve. - In soil of birch forest, Big Khekhtsir Nature Reserve. - In rhizosphere of apple-tree and on roots of fruit seedlings, Dalnerechensk.

Absidia glauca Hagem

In soil of coniferous-broad-leaved forest, Ussuriysk Nature Reserve.

Absidia spinosa Lendn.

In forest and meadow soil, Ussuriysk Nature Reserve. - In soil of coniferous-broad-leaved forest, Big Khekhtsir Nature Reserve.

Actinomucor elegans (Eidam) C.R. Benj. et Hesselt.

In soil of coniferous-broad-leaved forest, Ussuriysk Nature Reserve, Big Khekhtsir Nature Reserve. - In soil of vineyard, Ussuriysk: Gornotayozhnoye.

Circinella muscae (Sorokin) Berl. et De Toni

In soil of vineyard, Ussuriysk: Gornotayozhnoye.

Gongronella butleri (Lendn.) Peyronel et Dal Vesco

In forest and meadow soil, Ussuriysk Nature Reserve. - In rhizosphere of apple-tree, Dalnerechensk. - In soil of coniferous-broad-leaved forest, Big Khekhtsir Nature Reserve.

Mucor abundans Povah

In paddy soil, on roots of *Oryza sativa* L., Khanka Lake region.

Mucor adventitius Oudem.

In soil of vineyard, Ussuriysk: Gornotayozhnoye. - In rhizosphere of apple-tree and pear-tree seedlings, Dalnerechensk.

Mucor circinelloides Tiegh. f. *circinelloides*

In soil of coniferous-broad-leaved forest, Ussuriysk Nature Reserve. - In soil of swampy meadow, Big Khekhtsir Nature Reserve. - In soil of vineyard, Ussuriysk: Gornotayozhnoye. - In paddy soil, on roots of *Oryza sativa* L., Khanka Lake region. - In rhizosphere of apple-tree seedlings, Dalnerechensk.

Mucor circinelloides f. *janssenii* (Lendn.) Schipper

In soil of coniferous-broad-leaved forest, Ussuriysk Nature Reserve, Big Khekhtsir Nature Reserve. - In paddy soil, on roots of *Oryza sativa* L., Khanka Lake region.

Mucor circinelloides f. *griseocyanus* (Hagem) Schipper

On roots of *Oryza sativa* L., Khanka Lake region.

Mucor erectus Bainier

In soil of coniferous-broad-leaved forest, Ussuriysk Nature Reserve.

Mucor genevensis Lendn.

In soil of oak forest, Ussuriysk Nature Reserve. - In soil of birch forest, Upper Ussuri Station.

Mucor guilliermondii Nadson et Philippow

In soil of oak forest, Ussuriysk Nature Reserve. - In soil of coniferous forest, Upper Ussuri Station.

Mucor hiemalis Wehmer f. *hiemalis*

In forest and meadow soil, Ussuriysk Nature Reserve, Upper Ussuri Station, Big Khekhtsir Nature Reserve. - In soil of vineyard, Ussuriysk: Gornotayozhnoye. - In paddy soil, on roots of *Oryza sativa* L., Khanka Lake region. - In rhizosphere and on roots of fruit-tree seedlings, Dalnerechensk.

Mucor hiemalis f. *corticola* (Hagem) Schipper

In forest and meadow soil, Ussuriysk Nature Reserve. - In soil of fir forest, Upper Ussuri Station. - In paddy soil, on roots of *Oryza sativa* L., Khanka Lake Region.

Mucor hiemalis f. *silvaticus* (Hagem) Schipper

In soil of ash forest, Ussuriysk Nature Reserve. - In soil of coniferous-broad-leaved forest, Upper Ussuri Station.

Mucor lausannensis Lendn.

In soil of ash forest, Ussuriysk Nature Reserve. - In soil of coniferous forest, Upper Ussuri Station. - In paddy soil, on roots of *Oryza sativa* L., Khanka Lake region.

Mucor mucedo Fresen.

In soil of birch forest, Big Khekhtsir Nature Reserve. - In paddy soil, Khanka Lake region.

Mucor piriformis A. Fisch.

In soil of vineyard, Ussuriysk: Gornotayozhnoye.

Mucor plumbeus Bonord.

In forest and meadow soil, Ussuriysk Nature Reserve, Upper Ussuri Station, Big Khekhtsir Nature Reserve. - In soil of vineyard, Ussuriysk: Gornotayozhnoye. - On roots of apple-tree, cherry-tree, plum-tree, apricot-tree, Dalnerechensk.

Mucor racemosus Fresen. f. *racemosus*

In soil of coniferous-broad-leaved forest, Ussuriysk Nature Reserve. - In soil of coniferous forest, Upper Ussuri Station. - In paddy soil, Khanka Lake region. - In soil of vineyard: Ussuriysk: Gornotayozhnoye.

Mucor racemosus f. *sphaerosporus* (Hagem) Schipper

In rhizosphere of apple-tree, Dalnerechensk.

Mucor ramosissimus Samouts.

In paddy soil, on roots of *Oryza sativa* L., Khanka Lake region.

Mucor rouxianus (Calmette) Wehmer

In paddy soil, on roots of *Oryza sativa* L., Khanka Lake region.

Mucor saturninus Hagem

In rhizosphere of apple-tree seedlings, Dalnerechensk. - On roots of *Oryza sativa* L.,

Khanka Lake region.

Mucor strictus Hagem

In paddy soil, Khanka Lake region.

Mucor zonatus Milko

In soil of coniferous-broad-leaved forest, Ussuriysk Nature Reserve. - In soil of birch forest, Upper Ussuri Station. - In paddy soil, on roots of *Oryza sativa* L., Khanka Lake region.

Rhizopus arrhizus A. Fisch. var. **arrhizus**

In soil of coniferous-broad-leaved forest, Ussuriysk Nature Reserve. - In paddy soil, on roots and seeds of *Oryza sativa* L., Khanka Lake region.

Rhizopus microsporus Tiegh. var. **chinensis** (Saito) Schipper et Stalpers

In paddy soil, on sprouts of *Oryza sativa* L., Khanka Lake region.

Rhizopus microsporus var. **rhizopodiformis** (Cohn) Schipper et Stalpers

In paddy soil, Khanka Lake region.

Rhizopus stolonifer (Ehrenb.) Vuill.

In forest and meadow soil, Ussuriysk Nature Reserve. - On seeds of *Zea mays* L., Ussuriysk vicinity. - In soil of swampy meadow, Upper Ussuri Station. - In soil of vineyard, Ussuriysk: Gornotayozhnoye. - In paddy soil, on seeds of *Oryza sativa* L., Khanka Lake region. - In rhizosphere and on roots of fruit-tree seedlings, Dalnerechensk.

Zygorhynchus heterogamus (Vuill.) Vuill.

In paddy soil, Khanka Lake region.

Zygorhynchus japonicus Komin.

In soil of coniferous-broad-leaved forest, Ussuriysk Nature Reserve, Big Khekhtsir Nature Reserve. - In soil of vineyard, Ussuriysk: Gornotayozhnoye. - In rhizosphere of apple-tree and pear-tree, Dalnerechensk.

Zygorhynchus moelleri Vuill.

In soil of coniferous-broad-leaved forest, Ussuriysk Nature Reserve, Upper Ussuri Station, Big Khekhtsir Nature Reserve. - In soil of vineyard, Ussuriysk: Gornotayozhnoye. - In rhizosphere of apple-tree and pear-tree seedlings, Dalnerechensk.

CUNNINGHAMELLACEAE

Cunninghamella echinulata (Thaxt.) Thaxt. ex Blakeslee

In rhizosphere of apple-tree and pear-tree, Dalnerechensk. - In soil of vineyard, Ussuriysk: Gornotayozhnoye.

Cunninghamella elegans Lendn.

In rhizosphere of apple-tree and pear-tree, Dalnerechensk.

MYCOTYPHACEAE

Mycotypha microspora Fenner

In soil of vineyard, Ussuriysk: Gornotayozhnoye.

THAMNIDIACEAE

Thamnidium elegans Link

In rhizosphere of apple-tree and pear-tree, Dalnerechensk.

SYNCEPHALASTRACEAE

Syncephalastrum racemosum Cohn ex J. Schröt.

In soil of vineyard, Ussuriysk: Gornotayozhnoye.

MORTIERELLALES

MORTIERELLACEAE

Mortierella gamsii Milko

In forest soil, Ussuriysk: Gornotayozhnoye.

Mortierella jenkinii (A.L. Sm.) Naumov

In paddy soil, Khanka Lake region.

Mortierella polycephala Coem.

In paddy soil, Khanka Lake region.

Mortierella pusilla Oudem.

In soil of vineyard, Ussuriysk: Gornotayozhnoye.

Mortierella stylospora Dixon-Stew.

In soil of coniferous-broad-leaved forest, Ussuriysk Nature Reserve, Upper Ussuri Station, Big Khekhtsir Nature Reserve.

UMBELOPSIDACEAE

Umbelopsis isabellina (Oudem.) W. Gams

In forest and meadow soil, Ussuriysk Nature Reserve, Big Khekhtsir Nature Reserve.

Umbelopsis ramanniana (Möller) W. Gams

In soil of coniferous-broad-leaved forest, Ussuriysk Nature Reserve, Big Khekhtsir Nature Reserve. - In soil of vineyard, Ussuriysk: Gornotayozhnoye. - In paddy soil, Khanka Lake region.

Umbelopsis vinacea (Dixon-Stew.) Arx

In soil of coniferous-broad-leaved forest, Ussuriysk Nature Reserve, Big Khekhtsir Nature Reserve, Upper Ussuri Station.

ANAMORPHIC FUNGI

HYPHOMYCETES

HYPHOMYCETALES

MONILIACEAE

Acremonium alternatum Link

On roots of *Oryza sativa* L., Khanka Lake region.

Acremonium breve (Sukapure et Thirum.) W. Gams

In soil of ash forest, Ussuriysk Nature Reserve. - In soil of coniferous-broad-leaved forest, Big Khekhtsir Nature Reserve.

Acremonium butyri (J.F.H. Beyma) W. Gams

In soil of coniferous-broad-leaved forest, Ussuriysk Nature Reserve.

Acremonium charticola (J. Lindau) W. Gams

In soil of coniferous-broad-leaved forest, Ussuriysk Nature Reserve. - In rhizosphere of apple-tree and pear-tree, Dalnerechensk. - On roots, seeds, stems of *Oryza sativa* L., Khanka Lake region.

Acremonium hyalinulum (Sacc.) W. Gams

On roots of *Oryza sativa* L., Khanka Lake region.

Acremonium minutisporum (Sukapure et Thirum.) W. Gams

On roots of *Oryza sativa* L., Khanka Lake region.

Acremonium persicinum (Nicot) W. Gams

On roots of *Oryza sativa* L., Khanka Lake region.

Acremonium roseogriseum (S.B. Saksena) W. Gams

In soil of coniferous-broad-leaved forest, Ussuriysk Nature Reserve, Big Khekhtsir Nature Reserve.

Acremonium roseum (Oudem.) W. Gams

In soil of oak forest, Ussuriysk Nature Reserve. - In soil of fir forest, Big Khekhtsir Nature Reserve. - In paddy soil, Khanka Lake region. - In rhizosphere of apple-tree and pear-tree, Dalnerechensk.

Acremonium strictum W. Gams

In soil of coniferous-broad-leaved forest, Ussuriysk Nature Reserve, Big Khekhtsir

Nature Reserve.

Acrostalagmus albus Preuss

In soil of vineyard, Ussuriysk: Gornotayozhnoye. - In rhizosphere of apple-tree seedlings, Dalnerechensk. - On roots and seeds of *Panax ginseng* C.A. Mey., Ussuriysk Nature Reserve, Ussuriysk: Gornotayozhnoye.

Aphanocladium album (Preuss) W. Gams

In soil of oak forest, Ussuriysk Nature Reserve.

Arthrobotrys arthrobotryoides (Berl.) Lindau

In soil of coniferous-broad-leaved forest, Ussuriysk Nature Reserve.

Arthrobotrys oligospora Fresen.

In soil of vineyard, Ussuriysk: Gornotayozhnoye.

Aspergillus awamori Nakaz.

In rhizosphere of apple-tree, Dalnerechensk.

Aspergillus candidus Link

In soil of ash forest, in forest litter, Ussuriysk Nature Reserve. - On fallen leaves of *Fraxinus mandshurica* Rupr., Ussuriysk: Gornotayozhnoye. - In rhizosphere of pear-tree seedlings, Dalnerechensk.

Aspergillus clavatus Desm.

In soil of coniferous-broad-leaved forest. - In soil of vineyard, Ussuriysk: Gornotayozhnoye.

Aspergillus flavipes (Bainier et R. Sartory) Thom et Church

In rhizosphere of apple-tree and pear-tree seedlings, Dalnerechensk.

Aspergillus flavus Link var. *flavus*

In soil of ash forest, oak forest, Ussuriysk Nature Reserve. - On seeds of *Zea mays* L., Ussuriysk vicinity. - In forest and meadow soil, Big Khekhtsir Nature Reserve. - In paddy soil, on seeds of *Oryza sativa* L., Khanka Lake region. - In rhizosphere and on roots of apple-tree and pear-tree seedlings, Dalnerechensk.

Aspergillus flavus var. *oryzae* (Ahlb.) M.J. Smiley, Robnet et Wicklow

In soil of ash forest, Ussuriysk Nature Reserve. - On seeds of *Oryza sativa* L., Khanka Lake region.

Aspergillus fumigatus Fresen.

In soil of coniferous-broad-leaved forest, Ussuriysk Nature Reserve, Big Khekhtsir Nature Reserve. - On seeds of *Zea mays* L., Ussuriysk vicinity. - In soil of vineyard, Ussuriysk: Gornotayozhnoye. - In paddy soil, Khanka Lake region. - In rhizosphere of apple-tree and pear-tree seedlings, Dalnerechensk.

Aspergillus janus Raper et Thom

In soil of coniferous-broad-leaved forest, Ussuriysk Nature Reserve, Upper Ussuri Station, Big Khekhtsir Nature Reserve.

Aspergillus japonicus Saito

In soil of coniferous-broad-leaved forest, Ussuriysk Nature Reserve. - On roots of apple-tree, Dalnerechensk.

Aspergillus melleus Yukawa

In rhizosphere of pear-tree, Dalnerechensk.

Aspergillus microviridocitrinus Costantin et Lucet

In rhizosphere of plum-tree seedlings, Dalnerechensk.

Aspergillus niger Tiegh. var. ***niger***

In forest and meadow soil, Ussuriysk Nature Reserve, Big Khekhtsir Nature Reserve. - In soil of vineyard, on fallen rotten berries of *Schisandra chinensis* (Turcz.) Baill., *Rubus crataegifolius* Bunge, *Vitis amurensis* Rupr., Ussuriysk: Gornotayozhnoye. - In paddy soil, on seeds of *Oryza sativa* L., Khanka Lake region. - On seeds of *Zea mays* L., Ussuriysk vicinity. - In rhizosphere of apple-tree and pear-tree seedlings, Dalnerechensk.

Aspergillus niger var. ***nanus*** Al-Musallam

In rhizosphere of pear-tree seedlings, Dalnerechensk.

Aspergillus ochraceus G. Wilh.

In soil of coniferous-broad-leaved forest, Ussuriysk Nature Reserve, Big Khekhtsir Nature Reserve. - In soil of vineyard, Ussuriysk: Gornotayozhnoye. - In rhizosphere of apple-tree and pear-tree seedlings, Dalnerechensk.

Aspergillus parasiticus Speare

In paddy soil, on seeds of *Oryza sativa* L., Khanka Lake region.

Aspergillus penicillioides Speg.

In soil of coniferous-broad-leaved forest, Big Khekhtsir Nature Reserve.

Aspergillus pseudoglaucus Blochwitz

In paddy soil, on seeds of *Oryza sativa* L., Khanka Lake region.

Aspergillus repens (Corda) Sacc.

In rhizosphere of apple-tree and pear-tree seedlings, Dalnerechensk.

Aspergillus restrictus G. Sm.

In rhizosphere of apple-tree and pear-tree seedlings, Dalnerechensk.

Aspergillus sydowii (Bainier et Sartory) Thom et Church

In soil of coniferous-broad-leaved forest, Ussuriysk Nature Reserve, Big Khekhtsir Nature Reserve, Upper Ussuri Station.

Aspergillus terreus Thom

In rhizosphere of apple-tree and pear-tree seedlings, Dalnerechensk.

Aspergillus ustus (Bainier) Thom et Church.

In soil of vineyard, Ussuriysk: Gornotayozhnoye.

Aspergillus versicolor (Vuill.) Tiraboschi

In soil of coniferous-broad-leaved forest, Ussuriysk Nature Reserve, Big Khekhtsir

Nature Reserve, Upper Ussuri Station. - In soil of vineyard, Ussuriysk: Gornotayozhnoye. - In paddy soil, on seeds of *Oryza sativa* L., Khanka Lake region. - In rhizosphere of apple-tree and pear-tree seedlings, Dalnerechensk.

Aspergillus wentii Wehmer

In soil of coniferous-broad-leaved forest, Ussuriysk Nature Reserve.

Beauveria felina (DC.) J.W. Carmich.

In soil of oak forest, Ussuriysk Nature Reserve.

Bostrichonema polygoni (Unger) J. Schröt.

On leaves of *Polygonum aviculare* L., Big Khekhtsir Nature Reserve.

Botrytis argillaceae Cooke

On fallen leaves of *Quercus mongolica* Fisch. ex Ledeb., Ussuriysk Nature Reserve.

Botrytis carnea Schumach.

In soil of coniferous-broad-leaved forest, Ussuriysk Nature Reserve.

Botrytis cinerea Pers.

In soil of coniferous-broad-leaved forest, on leaves of *Panax ginseng* C.A. Mey., *Veratrum dahuricum* (Turch.) Loes., *Maackia amurensis* Maxim. et Rupr., Ussuriysk Nature Reserve. - In soil of vineyard, on flowers and fruits of *Malus mandshurica* (Maxim.) Kom., *Pyrus ussuriensis* Maxim., on berries of *Vitis amurensis* Rupr., *Fragaria orientalis* Losinsk., *Rubus crataegifolius* Bunge, *Cerasus maximowiczii* (Rupr.) Kom., *Actinidia kolomicta* (Maxim.) Maxim., *Schisandra chinensis* (Turcz.) Baill., Ussuriysk: Gornotayozhnoye. - In rhizosphere of apple-tree and pear-tree seedlings, Dalnerechensk. - In paddy soil, on seeds of *Oryza sativa* L., Khanka Lake region. - On leaves of *Gypsophila serotina* Hayne ex Wild., *Lysimachia davurica* Ledeb., *Viola acuminata* Ledeb., Big Khekhtsir Nature Reserve. - On leaves of *Ledum palustre* L., *Philadelphus tenuifolius* Rupr. et Maxim., *Thalictrum filamentosum* Maxim., Bastak Nature Reserve. - On grass stems and leaves, Hulin: 854 State Farm, Fuyuan.

Botrytis elliptica (Berk.) Cooke

On leaves and stems of *Hemerocallis middendorfii* Trautv. et Mey., Big Khekhtsir Nature Reserve.

Botrytis epigaea Link

In soil of ash forest, Ussuriysk Nature Reserve. - In soil of swampy meadow, Big Khekhtsir Nature Reserve. - In forest and meadow soil, Upper Ussuri Station.

Botrytis pyramidalis (Bonord.) Sacc.

In soil of ash forest, Ussuriysk Nature Reserve. - In soil of coniferous forest, Upper Ussuri Station. - In paddy soil, Khanka Lake region.

Cercosporella chaerophylli Aderh.

On leaves of *Anthriscus sylvestris* (L.) Hoffm., Ussuriysk Nature Reserve.

Cercosporella echinulata Garbowsky

On leaves of *Stellaria bungeana* Fenzl., Ussuriysk Nature Reserve.

Cercosporella euonymi Erikss.

On leaves of *Euonymus sacrosancta* Koidz., Ussuriysk Nature Reserve.

C*ercosporella exilis* Davis

On leaves of *Phryma asiatica* (Hara) O. et I. Degener, Ussuriysk Nature Reserve.

Cercosporella leptospermum (Peck) Davis

On leaves of *Eleutherococcus sessiliflorus* (Rupr. et Maxim.) S.Y. Hu, *Aralia elata* (Miq.) Seem., Ussuriysk Nature Reserve. - On leaves of *Aralia* sp., Fuyuan.

Cercosporella veratri Peck

On leaves of *Veratrum lobelianum* Bernh., Bastak Nature Reserve.

Cercosporella virgaureae (Thüm.) Allesch.

On leaves of *Solidago pacifica* Juz., Ussuriysk Nature Reserve.

Chrysonilia sitophila (Mont.) Arx

In soil of ash forest, Ussuriysk Nature Reserve.

Chrysosporium inops J.W. Carmich.

In paddy soil, Khanka Lake region.

Chrysosporium merdarium (Ehrenb.) J.W. Carmich.

In paddy soil, Khanka Lake region.

Chrysosporium parvum J.W. Carmich.

In paddy soil, Khanka Lake region.

Clonostachys rosea (Preuss) Mussat f. *rosea*

In soil of coniferous-broad-leaved forest, Ussuriysk Nature Reserve. - In soil of vineyard, Ussuriysk: Gornotayozhnoye. - In paddy soil, on roots and seeds of *Oryza sativa* L., Khanka Lake region. - In rhizosphere of apple-tree, Dalnerechensk.

Clonostachys rosea f. *catenulata* (J.C. Gilman et E.V. Abbott) Schroers

In paddy soil, Khanka Lake region. - In rhizosphere of apple-tree, Dalnerechensk.

Cylindrocladium scoparium J.V. Morgan

On needles and roots of seedlings of *Pinus koraiensis* Siebold et Zucc., Big Khekhtsir Nature Reserve.

Cylindrophora hoffmannii Dasz.

In soil of ash forest, Ussuriysk Nature Reserve.

Eriomycopsis lasiosphaeriicola U. Braun et Melnik

On ascocarps of *Lasiosphaeria hirsuta* (Fr.: Fr.) Ces. et De Not. from bark of *Populus* sp., Ussuriysk Nature Reserve.

Geotrichum candidum Link

In soil of coniferous-broad-leaved forest, Ussuriysk Nature Reserve. - In soil of vineyard, Ussuriysk: Gornotayozhnoye. - In paddy soil, Khanka Lake region.

Gliocephalotrichum simplex (J.A. Mey.) B.J. Wiley et E.G. Simmons

In soil of coniferous forest, Upper Ussuri Station.

Gliocladiopsis tenuis (Bugnic.) Crous et M.J. Wingf.

In paddy soil, Khanka Lake region.

Gliocladium penicillioides J.C. Gilman et E.V.Abbott

In soil of coniferous-broad-leaved forest, Ussuriysk Nature Reserve. - In soil of vineyard, Ussuriysk: Gornotayozhnoye. - In rhizosphere of apple-tree, Dalnerechensk.

Lecanicillium lecanii (Zimm.) Zare et W. Gams

In forest and meadow soil, Ussuriysk Nature Reserve.

Mariannaea elegans (Corda) Samson

In soil of ash forest, Ussuriysk Nature Reserve.

Mariannaea camptospora Samson

In paddy soil, Khanka Lake region.

Metarhizium anisopliae (Metschn.) Sorok.

In paddy soil, Khanka Lake region.

Monilia brunnea J.C. Gilman et E.V.Abbott

In soil of vineyard, Ussuriysk: Gornotayozhnoye. - In paddy soil, Khanka Lake region.

Monilia crataegi Died.

On flowers and leaves of *Crataegus pinnatifida* Bunge, Ussuriysk: Gornotayozhnoye.

Monilia fructigena Pers.

On fruits of *Schisandra chinensis* (Turcz.) Baill., *Prinsepia sinensis* (Oliv.) Bean., Ussuriysk Nature Reserve. - On fruits of *Malus mandshurica* (Maxim.) Kom., *Pyrus ussuriensis* Maxim., *Prunus domestica* L., *Prunus ussuriensis* Koval. et Kostina, on berries of *Vitis amurensis* Rupr., *Actinidia arguta* (Siebold. et Zucc.) Planch. ex Miq., Ussuriysk: Gornotayozhnoye.

Monilia kusanoi Henn.

On flowers, leaves and fruits of *Cerasus sachalinensis* (Fr. Schmidt) Kom., *Padus maackii* (Rupr.) Kom., Ussuriysk: Gornotayozhnoye.

Monilia laxa (Ehrenb.) Sacc. et Voglino

On flowers, leaves and fruits of *Cerasus tomentosa* (Thunb.) Wall., on fruits of *Prunus ussuriensis* Koval. et Kostina, *Actinidia arguta* (Siebold. et Zucc.) Planch. ex Miq., *Actinidia kolomikta* (Maxim.) Maxim., *Vitis amurensis* Rupr., *Armeniaca mandshurica* (Maxim.) Skvorts., *Armeniaca sibirica* (L.) Lam., *Armeniaca vulgaris* Lam., *Padus maackii* (Rupr.) Kom., Ussuriysk: Gornotayozhnoye.

Monilia linhartiana Sacc.

On leaves of *Padus asiatica* Kom., Ussuriysk: Gornotayozhnoye.

Monilia pruinosa Cooke et Massee

In soil of vineyard, Ussuriysk: Gornotayozhnoye.

Monocillium indicum S.B. Saksena

In soil of fir forest, Upper Ussuri Station.

Monocillium constrictum W. Gams

In paddy soil, Khanka Lake region.

Monocillium exsolum Bat. et J.W. Heine

In paddy soil, Khanka Lake region.

Paecilomyces carneus (Dusche et R. Heim) A.H.S. Br. et G. Sm.

In soil of coniferous-broad-leaved forest, Ussuriysk Nature Reserve, Big Khekhtsir Nature Reserve. - In soil of vineyard, Ussuriysk: Gornotayozhnoye. - In paddy soil, Khanka Lake region. - In rhizosphere of apple-tree, Dalnerechensk.

Paecilomyces inflatus (Burnside) J.W. Carmich.

In paddy soil, Khanka Lake region.

Paecilomyces farinosus (Holmsk.) A.H.S. Br. et G. Sm.

In paddy soil, Khanka Lake region.

Paecilomyces lilacinus (Thom) Samson

In soil of coniferous-broad-leaved forest, Ussuriysk Nature Reserve. - In paddy soil, Khanka Lake region. - In rhizosphere of apple-tree and pear-tree seedlings, Dalnerechensk.

Paecilomyces marquandii (Massee) S. Hughes

In soil of coniferous-broad-leaved forest, Ussuriysk Nature Reserve. - In rhizosphere of apple-tree and pear-tree seedlings, Dalnerechensk.

Paecilomyces puntonii (Vuill.) Nann.

On roots of *Oryza sativa* L., Khanka Lake region.

Paecilomyces variotii Bainier

In soil of coniferous-broad-leaved forest, Ussuriysk Nature Reserve, Big Khekhtsir Nature Reserve. - In paddy soil, Khanka Lake region. - In rhizosphere of apple-tree and pear-tree seedlings, Dalnerechensk.

Paecilomyces viridis Segretain, Fromentin, Destombes, Brygoo et Dodin ex Samson

In paddy soil, Khanka Lake region.

Paecilomyces xylariiformis (Lloyd) Samson

In paddy soil, Khanka Lake region.

Penicillium aculeatum Raper et Fennell

In soil of coniferous-broad-leaved forest, Ussuriysk Nature Reserve, Upper Ussuri Station. - In paddy soil, Khanka Lake region.

Penicillium adametzi K.M. Zalessky

In soil of coniferous-broad-leaved forest, Ussuriysk Nature Reserve. - In soil of vineyard, Ussuriysk: Gornotayozhnoye. - In rhizosphere of apple-tree and pear-tree seedlings, Dalnerechensk.

Penicillium albidum Sopp

In soil of ash forest, Ussuriysk Nature Reserve. - In paddy soil, Khanka Lake region.

Penicillium atramentosum Thom

In soil of coniferous forest, Big Khekhtsir Nature Reserve.

Penicillium aurantiogriseum Dierckx var. ***aurantiogriseum***

In soil of coniferous-broad-leaved forest, Ussuriysk Nature Reserve, Big Khekhtsir Nature Reserve. - In soil of vineyard, Ussuriysk: Gornotayozhnoye. - On seeds of *Triticum aestivum* L., Ussuriysk vicinity. - In paddy soil, on seeds of *Oryza sativa* L., Khanka Lake region. - In rhizosphere of apple-tree and pear-tree seedlings, Dalnerechensk.

Penicillium aurantiogriseum var. ***viridicatum*** (Westling) Frisvad et Filt.

In soil of coniferous-broad-leaved forest, Ussuriysk Nature Reserve, Big Khekhtsir Nature Reserve. - In soil of vineyard, Ussuriysk: Gornotayozhnoye. - In rhizosphere of apple-tree and pear-tree seedlings, Dalnerechensk.

Penicillium brevicompactum Dierckx

In soil of coniferous-broad-leaved forest, Ussuriysk Nature Reserve, Big Khekhtsir Nature Reserve. - In soil of vineyard, Ussuriysk: Gornotayozhnoye. - On seeds of *Triticum aestivum* L., Ussuriysk vicinity. - In paddy soil, on seeds of *Oryza sativa* L., Khanka Lake region. - In rhizosphere of apple-tree and pear-tree seedlings, Dalnerechensk.

Penicillium camemberti Thom

In soil of coniferous-broad-leaved forest, Ussuriysk Nature Reserve, Upper Ussuri Station. - In soil of vineyard, Ussuriysk: Gornotayozhnoye. - In paddy soil, Khanka Lake region. - In rhizosphere of apple-tree and pear-tree seedlings, Dalnerechensk.

Penicillium canescens Sopp

In soil of coniferous-broad-leaved forest, Ussuriysk Nature Reserve, Upper Ussuri Station. - In soil of vineyard, Ussuriysk: Gornotayozhnoye. - On seeds of *Triticum aestivum* L., Ussuriysk vicinity. - In paddy soil, on seeds of *Oryza sativa* L., Khanka Lake region. - In rhizosphere of apple-tree and pear-tree seedlings, Dalnerechensk.

Penicillium chermesinum Biourge

In soil of ash forest, Ussuriysk Nature Reserve. - In soil of birch forest, Big Khekhtsir Nature Reserve. - In soil of vineyard, Ussuriysk: Gornotayozhnoye. - In paddy soil, Khanka Lake region. - In rhizosphere of apple-tree and pear-tree seedlings, Dalnerechensk.

Penicillium chrysogenum Thom

In forest and meadow soil, Ussuriysk Nature Reserve. - In soil of birch forest, Big Khekhtsir Nature Reserve. - In soil of vineyard, Ussuriysk: Gornotayozhnoye. - On seeds of *Triticum aestivum* L., Ussuriysk vicinity. - In paddy soil, on seeds of *Oryza sativa* L., Khanka Lake region. - In rhizosphere of apple-tree, Dalnerechensk.

Penicillium citreonigrum Dierckx

In soil of coniferous-broad-leaved forest, Ussuriysk Nature Reserve. - In soil of vineyard, Ussuriysk: Gornotayozhnoye. - In paddy soil, Khanka Lake region. - In rhizosphere of apple-tree and pear-tree seedlings, Dalnerechensk.

Penicillium citrinum Thom

In forest and meadow soil, Ussuriysk Nature Reserve. - In soil of swampy meadow, Big Khekhtsir Nature Reserve. - In soil of vineyard, Ussuriysk: Gornotayozhnoye. - On seeds of *Triticum aestivum* L., Ussuriysk vicinity. - In paddy soil, on seeds of *Oryza sativa* L., Khanka Lake region. - In rhizosphere of apple-tree, Dalnerechensk.

Penicillium commune Thom

In soil of coniferous-broad-leaved forest, Ussuriysk Nature Reserve, Big Khekhtsir Nature Reserve. - In soil of vineyard, Ussuriysk: Gornotayozhnoye. - In paddy soil, Khanka Lake region. - In rhizosphere of apple-tree and pear-tree seedlings, Dalnerechensk.

Penicillium corylophilum Dierckx

In soil of coniferous-broad-leaved forest, Ussuriysk Nature Reserve, Big Khekhtsir Nature Reserve. - In soil of vineyard, Ussuriysk: Gornotayozhnoye. - In paddy soil, Khanka Lake region.

Penicillium cyaneum (Bainier et Sartory) Biourge

In soil of vineyard, Ussuriysk: Gornotayozhnoye.

Penicillium dangeardii Pitt

In soil of vineyard, Ussuriysk: Gornotayozhnoye. - On seeds of *Triticum aestivum* L., Ussuriysk vicinity. - In paddy soil, on seeds of *Oryza sativa* L., Khanka Lake region.

Penicillium decumbens Thom

In forest and meadow soil, Ussuriysk Nature Reserve, Big Khekhtsir Nature Reserve. - In soil of vineyard, Ussuriysk: Gornotayozhnoye. - In paddy soil, Khanka Lake region. - In rhizosphere of apple-tree and pear-tree, Dalnerechensk.

Penicillium dierckxii Biourge

In soil of coniferous-broad-leaved forest, Ussuriysk Nature Reserve, Upper Ussuri Station. - In soil of vineyard, Ussuriysk: Gornotayozhnoye. - In rhizosphere of apple-tree and pear-tree, Dalnerechensk.

Penicillium diversum Raper et Fennell

In soil of ash forest, Ussuriysk Nature Reserve. - In soil of vineyard, Ussuriysk: Gornotayozhnoye.

Penicillium dodgei Pitt

On roots of *Oryza sativa* L., Khanka Lake region.

Penicillium duclauxii Delacr.

In soil of vineyard, Ussuriysk: Gornotayozhnoye. - In rhizosphere of apple-tree and pear-tree seedlings, Dalnerechensk.

Penicillium emmonsii Pitt

In soil of vineyard, Ussuriysk: Gornotayozhnoye. - In paddy soil, Khanka Lake region. - In rhizosphere of apple-tree and pear-tree seedlings, Dalnerechensk.

Penicillium expansum Link

In soil of coniferous-broad-leaved forest, Ussuriysk Nature Reserve, Big Khekhtsir

Nature Reserve, Upper Ussuri Station. - In soil of vineyard, on fallen fruits of *Prunus ussuriensis* Koval. et Kostina, *Actinidia arguta* (Siebold. et Zucc.) Planch. ex Miq., *Malus mandshurica* (Maxim.) Kom., *Pyrus ussuriensis* Maxim., on berries of *Vitis amurensis* Rupr., *Fragaria orientalis* Losinsk., Ussuriysk: Gornotayozhnoye. - On seeds of *Triticum aestivum* L., Ussuriysk vicinity. - In paddy soil, on seeds of *Oryza sativa* L., Khanka Lake region. - In rhizosphere of apple-tree and pear-tree, Dalnerechensk.

Penicillium funiculosum Thom

In forest and meadow soil, Ussuriysk Nature Reserve. - On seeds of *Triticum aestivum* L., Ussuriysk vicinity. - In paddy soil, on seeds of *Oryza sativa* L., Khanka Lake region.

Penicillium fuscum (Sopp) Raper et Thom

In soil of oak forest, Ussuriysk Nature Reserve. - In soil of vineyard, Ussuriysk: Gornotayozhnoye. - In paddy soil, Khanka Lake region, in rhizosphere of apple-tree and pear-tree, Dalnerechensk.

Penicillium glabrum (Wehmer) Westling

In forest and meadow soil, Ussuriysk Nature Reserve, Big Khekhtsir Nature Reserve. - In soil of vineyard, Ussuriysk: Gornotayozhnoye. - In rhizosphere of apple-tree and pear-tree, Dalnerechensk.

Penicillium gladioli Machacek

In paddy soil, Khanka Lake region, in rhizosphere of apple-tree and pear-tree seedlings, Dalnerechensk.

Penicillium granulatum Bainier

In rhizosphere of apple-tree and pear-tree, Dalnerechensk.

Penicillium griseofulvum Dierckx

In soil of coniferous-broad-leaved forest, Ussuriysk Nature Reserve, Big Khekhtsir Nature Reserve, Upper Ussuri Station. - In paddy soil, Khanka Lake region. - In rhizosphere of apple-tree and pear-tree seedlings, Dalnerechensk.

Penicillium herquei Bainier et Sartory

In soil of ash forest, Ussuriysk Nature Reserve, Big Khekhtsir Nature Reserve.

Penicillium hirsutum Dierckx var. **hirsutum**

In soil of broad-leaved forest, Ussuriysk Nature Reserve, Big Khekhtsir Nature Reserve, Upper Ussuri Station. - In soil of vineyard, Ussuriysk: Gornotayozhnoye. - In rhizosphere of apple-tree and pear-tree, Dalnerechensk.

Penicillium humuli J.F.H. Beyma

In paddy soil, Khanka Lake region. - In rhizosphere of apple-tree and pear-tree seedlings, Dalnerechensk.

Penicillium implicatum Biourge

In soil of coniferous-broad-leaved forest, Ussuriysk Nature Reserve, Big Khekhtsir Nature Reserve. - In soil of vineyard, Ussuriysk: Gornotayozhnoye.

Penicillium islandicum Sopp

In soil of oak forest, Big Khekhtsir Nature Reserve. - In paddy soil, Khanka Lake region.

Penicillium italicum Wehmer

In soil of oak forest, Ussuriysk Nature Reserve. - In soil of coniferous-broad-leaved forest, Big Khekhtsir Nature Reserve. - In soil of vineyard, Ussuriysk: Gornotayozhnoye. - In paddy soil, Khanka Lake region. - In rhizosphere of apple-tree and pear-tree, Dalnerechensk.

Penicillium janczewskii K.M. Zalessky

In soil of coniferous-broad-leaved forest, Ussuriysk Nature Reserve, Big Khekhtsir Nature Reserve. - In soil of vineyard, Ussuriysk: Gornotayozhnoye. - In paddy soil, Khanka Lake region. - In rhizosphere of apple-tree, pear-tree, cherry-tree, plum-tree seedlings, Dalnerechensk.

Penicillium jensenii K.M. Zalessky

In soil of coniferous-broad-leaved forest, Ussuriysk Nature Reserve, Big Khekhtsir Nature Reserve, Upper Ussuri Station. - In soil of vineyard, Ussuriysk: Gornotayozhnoye. - In paddy soil, Khanka Lake region. - In rhizosphere of apple-tree and pear-tree, Dalnerechensk.

Penicillium kloeckeri Pitt

In paddy soil, Khanka Lake region.

Penicillium lapidosum Raper et Fennell

In soil of coniferous-broad-leaved forest, Ussuriysk Nature Reserve, Big Khekhtsir Nature Reserve. - In soil of vineyard, Ussuriysk: Gornotayozhnoye. - In paddy soil, Khanka Lake region. - In rhizosphere of apple-tree and pear-tree, Dalnerechensk.

Penicillium lanosum Westling

In soil of coniferous-broad-leaved forest, Ussuriysk Nature Reserve, Big Khekhtsir Nature Reserve. - In soil of vineyard, Ussuriysk: Gornotayozhnoye. - In paddy soil, Khanka Lake region. - In rhizosphere of apple-tree and pear-tree, Dalnerechensk.

Penicillium lehmanii Pitt

On roots and seeds of *Oryza sativa* L., Khanka Lake region.

Penicillium lividum Westling

In soil of vineyard, Ussuriysk: Gornotayozhnoye.

Penicillium miczynskii K.M. Zalessky

In soil of birch forest, Big Khekhtsir Nature Reserve. - In soil of vineyard, Ussuriysk: Gornotayozhnoye. - In paddy soil, on roots and seeds of *Oryza sativa* L., Khanka Lake region.

Penicillium multicolor Grig.-Man. et Porad.

In rhizosphere of apple-tree, Dalnerechensk.

Penicillium nalgiovense Laxa

In paddy soil, Khanka Lake region.

Penicillium ochrochloron Biourge

In soil of coniferous-broad-leaved forest, Ussuriysk Nature Reserve. - In soil of vineyard,

Ussuriysk: Gornotayozhnoye.

Penicillium olsonii Bainier et Sartory

In soil of ash forest, Ussuriysk Nature Reserve.

Penicillium oxalicum Currie et Thom

In soil of oak forest, Ussuriysk Nature Reserve. - In soil of coniferous forest, Upper Ussuri Station. - In soil of vineyard, Ussuriysk: Gornotayozhnoye. - In paddy soil, on roots and seeds of *Oryza sativa* L., Khanka Lake region. - In rhizosphere of apple-tree and pear-tree seedlings, Dalnerechensk.

Penicillium palitans Westling

In soil of coniferous-broad-leaved forest, Ussuriysk Nature Reserve, Big Khekhtsir Nature Reserve, Upper Ussuri Station.

Penicillium paxilli Bainier

In soil of broad-leaved forest, Ussuriysk Nature Reserve. - In soil of coniferous forest, Big Khekhtsir Nature Reserve. - In soil of vineyard, Ussuriysk: Gornotayozhnoye. - In paddy soil, Khanka Lake region. - In rhizosphere of apple-tree, Dalnerechensk.

Penicillium phoeniceum J.F.H. Beyma

In soil of coniferous-broad-leaved forest, Ussuriysk Nature Reserve. - In soil of vineyard, Ussuriysk: Gornotayozhnoye. - In paddy soil, Khanka Lake region.

Penicillium pulvillorum Turfitt

In soil of coniferous-broad-leaved forest, Ussuriysk Nature Reserve.

Penicillium purpurogenum Stoll

In soil of coniferous-broad-leaved forest, Ussuriysk Nature Reserve, Big Khekhtsir Nature Reserve. - In soil of vineyard, Ussuriysk: Gornotayozhnoye. - In paddy soil, Khanka Lake region. - In rhizosphere of pear-tree seedlings, Dalnerechensk.

Penicillium purpurescens (Sopp) Biourge

In soil of coniferous-broad-leaved forest, Ussuriysk Nature Reserve.

Penicillium quercetorum Baghdadi

In soil of oak forest, Ussuriysk Nature Reserve.

Penicillium raistrickii G. Sm.

In soil of coniferous-broad-leaved forest, Ussuriysk Nature Reserve. - In soil of vineyard, Ussuriysk: Gornotayozhnoye. - In paddy soil, Khanka Lake region. - In rhizosphere of apple-tree, Dalnerechensk.

Penicillium rasile Pitt

In paddy soil, on roots and seeds of *Oryza sativa* L., Khanka Lake region.

Penicillium resticulosum Birkinshaw, Raistrick et G. Sm.

In soil of coniferous-broad-leaved forest, Ussuriysk Nature Reserve, Upper Ussuri Station.

Penicillium restrictum J.C. Gilman et E.V. Abbott

In soil of elm forest, Ussuriysk Nature Reserve. - In soil of vineyard, Ussuriysk: Gornotayozhnoye.

Penicillium rolfsii Thom

In paddy soil, on roots of *Oryza sativa* L., Khanka Lake region.

Penicillium roqueforti Thom

In soil of oak forest, Ussuriysk Nature Reserve. - In soil of coniferous forest, Upper Ussuri Station. - In soil of vineyard, Ussuriysk: Gornotayozhnoye.

Penicillium roseopurpureum Dierckx

In soil of coniferous-broad-leaved forest, Ussuriysk Nature Reserve. - In soil of vineyard, Ussuriysk: Gornotayozhnoye. - In paddy soil, on roots of *Oryza sativa* L., Khanka Lake region. - In rhizosphere of apple-tree and pear-tree, Dalnerechensk.

Penicillium rubrum Sopp

In soil of coniferous-broad-leaved forest, Ussuriysk Nature Reserve, Big Khekhtsir Nature Reserve, Upper Ussuri Station. - In soil of vineyard, Ussuriysk: Gornotayozhnoye. - In paddy soil, on roots of *Oryza sativa* L., Khanka Lake region.

Penicillium rugulosum Thom

In soil of coniferous-broad-leaved forest, Ussuriysk Nature Reserve, Big Khekhtsir Nature Reserve. - In paddy soil, Khanka Lake region.

Penicillium sclerotiorum J.F.H. Beyma

In soil of vineyard, Ussuriysk: Gornotayozhnoye. - In rhizosphere of plum-tree seedlings, Dalnerechensk.

Penicillium spiculisporum Lehman

In soil of vineyard, Ussuriysk: Gornotayozhnoye. - In paddy soil, on seeds of *Oryza sativa* L., Khanka Lake region.

Penicillium simplicissimum (Oudem.) Thom

In soil of coniferous-broad-leaved forest, Ussuriysk Nature Reserve, Big Khekhtsir Nature Reserve, Upper Ussuri Station. - In soil of vineyard, Ussuriysk: Gornotayozhnoye. - In paddy soil, on roots of *Oryza sativa* L., Khanka Lake region. - In rhizosphere of apple-tree and pear-tree seedlings, Dalnerechensk.

Penicillium solitum Westling var. ***solitum***

In soil of vineyard, Ussuriysk: Gornotayozhnoye. - In rhizosphere of apple-tree and pear-tree, Dalnerechensk.

Penicillium solitum var. ***crustosum*** (Thom) Bridge, D. Hawksw., Kozak, Onions, R.R.M. Paterson et Sackin

In soil of coniferous-broad-leaved forest, Ussuriysk Nature Reserve, Big Khekhtsir Nature Reserve. - In paddy soil, Khanka Lake region. - In rhizosphere of apple-tree and pear-tree, Dalnerechensk.

Penicillium spinulosum Thom

In forest and meadow soil, Ussuriysk Nature Reserve, Big Khekhtsir Nature Reserve, Upper Ussuri Station. - In soil of vineyard, Ussuriysk: Gornotayozhnoye. - In paddy soil, Khanka Lake region.

Penicillium thomii Maire var. *thomii*

In forest and meadow soil, Ussuriysk Nature Reserve, Big Khekhtsir Nature Reserve, Upper Ussuri Station. - In soil of vineyard, Ussuriysk: Gornotayozhnoye. - In paddy soil, Khanka Lake region. - In rhizosphere of apple-tree and pear-tree, Dalnerechensk.

Penicillium thomii var. *flavescens* Abe

In soil of oak forest, Ussuriysk Nature Reserve.

Penicillium turbatum Westling

In forest and meadow soil, Ussuriysk Nature Reserve. - In soil of vineyard, Ussuriysk: Gornotayozhnoye. - In paddy soil, Khanka Lake region. - In rhizosphere of apple-tree and pear-tree seedlings, Dalnerechensk.

Penicillium variabile Sopp

In soil of coniferous-broad-leaved forest, Ussuriysk Nature Reserve, Upper Ussuri Station.

Penicillium velutinum J.F.H. Beyma

In soil of vineyard, Ussuriysk: Gornotayozhnoye. - In rhizosphere of pear-tree, Dalnerechensk.

Penicillium verrucosum Dierckx

In forest and meadow soil, Ussuriysk Nature Reserve.

Penicillium verruculosum Peyronel

In soil of coniferous-broad-leaved forest, Ussuriysk Nature Reserve. - In paddy soil, Khanka Lake region.

Penicillium vinaceum J.C. Gilman et E.V. Abbott

In soil of ash forest, Ussuriysk Nature Reserve. - In soil of vineyard, Ussuriysk: Gornotayozhnoye. - In rhizosphere of apple-tree and pear-tree, Dalnerechensk.

Penicillium vulpinum (Cooke et Massee) Seifert et Samson

In soil of coniferous-broad-leaved forest, Ussuriysk Nature Reserve, Big Khekhtsir Nature Reserve. - In soil of vineyard, Ussuriysk: Gornotayozhnoye. - In rhizosphere of apple-tree, Dalnerechensk.

Penicillium waksmanii K.M. Zalessky

In soil of coniferous-broad-leaved forest, Ussuriysk Nature Reserve, Big Khekhtsir Nature Reserve, Upper Ussuri Station. - In soil of vineyard, Ussuriysk: Gornotayozhnoye. - In rhizosphere of apple-tree and pear-tree seedlings, Dalnerechensk.

Phacellium alborosellum (Desm.) U. Braun

On dry leaves of *Cerastium holosteoides* Fries, Big Khekhtsir Nature Reserve.

Pseudocercosporella capsellae (Ellis et Everh.) Deighton

On leaves of *Capsella bursa-pastoris* (L.) Medik., Big Khekhtsir Nature Reserve, Bastak Nature Reserve.

Pseudocercosporella magnusiana (Allesh.) U. Braun

On leaves of *Geranium* sp., Ussuriysk Nature Reserve.

Ramularia acris Lindr.

On leaves of *Ranunculus repens* L., Ussuriysk Nature Reserve.

Ramularia actinidiae Ablak.

On leaves of *Actinidia kolomikta* (Maxim.) Maxim., Ussuriysk: Gornotayozhnoye.

Ramularia adoxae (Rabenh.) P. Karst.

On leaves of *Adoxa moschatellina* L., Ussuriysk Nature Reserve.

Ramularia agrimoniae Sacc.

On leaves of *Agrimonia pilosa* Ledeb., Ussuriysk Nature Reserve, Big Khekhtsir Nature Reserve.

Ramularia arvensis Sacc.

On leaves of *Potentilla fragarioides* L., Ussuriysk Nature Reserve, Big Khekhtsir Nature Reserve.

Ramularia balcanica Bubák. et Ranoj.

On leaves of *Cirsium setosum* (Willd.) Bess., Ussuriysk Nature Reserve.

Ramularia cardamines Syd. et P. Syd.

On leaves of *Cardamine leucantha* (Tausch) Schulz., Ussuriysk Nature Reserve.

Ramularia cirsii Allesch.

On leaves of *Cirsium pendulum* Fisch., Ussuriysk Nature Reserve, Hulin: 856 State Farm.

Ramularia chelidonii (Jacz.) Karak.

On leaves of *Hylomecon vernalis* Maxim., Ussuriysk Nature Reserve.

Ramularia coleosporii Sacc.

On rust fungus from leaves of *Phellodendron amurense* Rupr., Ussuriysk Nature Reserve.

Ramularia deusta (Fuckel) K.F. Baker, W.C. Snyder et L.H. Davis

On leaves of *Lathyrus komarovii* Ohwi, Ussuriysk Nature Reserve.

Ramularia didyma Unger

On leaves of *Aconitum* sp., Ussuriysk Nature Reserve. - On leaves of *Ranunculus repens* L., Big Khekhtsir Nature Reserve.

Ramularia filaris Fresen.

On leaves of *Petasites tatewakianus* Kitam., Ussuriysk Nature Reserve.

Ramularia gei (A.G. Eliasson) Lindr.

On leaves of *Geum aleppicum* Jacq., Ussuriysk Nature Reserve, Big Khekhtsir Nature

Reserve.

Ramularia geranii (West.) Fuckel

On leaves of *Geranium oriostemon* Fisch., Big Khekhtsir Nature Reserve.

Ramularia hieracii (Bauml.) Jaap

On leaves of *Hieracium umbellatum* L., Bastak Nature Reserve.

Ramularia lactea (Desm.) Sacc.

On leaves of *Viola acuminata* Ledeb., Ussuriysk Nature Reserve, Big Khekhtsir Nature Reserve.

Ramularia lonicerae Vogl.

On leaves of *Lonicera chrysantha* Turz. ex Ledeb., Big Khekhtsir Nature Reserve. - On leaves of *Lonicera maximowiczii* (Rupr.) Regel, Bastak Nature Reserve. - On leaves of *Lonicera* sp., Raohe.

Ramularia oenotherae-biennis A.I. Ivanov

On leaves of *Oenothera biennis* L., Ussuriysk Nature Reserve.

Ramularia philadelphi Sacc.

On leaves of *Philadelphus tenuifolius* Rupr. et Maxim., Bastak Nature Reserve.

Ramularia picridis Fautrey et Roum.

On leaves of *Picris koreana* (Kitam.) Worosch., Ussuriysk Nature Reserve.

Ramularia plantaginis Ellis et Everh.

On leaves of *Plantago major* L., Big Khekhtsir Nature Reserve.

Ramularia pratensis Sacc.

On leaves of *Rumex crispus* L., Ussuriysk Nature Reserve.

Ramularia rubella (Bonord.) Nannf.

On leaves of *Rumex acetosella* L., Big Khekhtsir Nature Reserve.

Ramularia sambucina Sacc.

On leaves of *Sambucus sibirica* Nakai, Big Khekhtsir Nature Reserve.

Ramularia saussureae Thuem.

On leaves of *Saussurea amurensis* Turcz., Bastak Nature Reserve.

Ramularia schisandrae Ablak. et Koval

On leaves of *Schisandra chinensis* (Turcz.) Baill., Ussuriysk Nature Reserve.

Ramularia silenicola Mass.

On leaves of *Silene macrostyla* Maxim., Bastak Nature Reserve.

Ramularia sorbi Karak.

On leaves of *Sorbus amurensis* Koehn., Ussuriysk Nature Reserve.

Ramularia taraxaci P. Karst.

On leaves of *Taraxacum mongolicum* Hand.-Mazz., *T. officinale* Wigg., Ussuriysk Nature Reserve, Big Khekhtsir Nature Reserve.

Ramularia thalictri Bondartsev

On leaves of *Thalictrum filamentosum* Maxim., Ussuriysk Nature Reserve; Bastak

Nature Reserve.

Ramularia ulmariae Cooke

, On leaves of *Filipendula palmata* Maxim., Ussuriysk Nature Reserve, Bastak Nature Reserve.

Ramularia urticae Ces.

On leaves of *Urtica angustifolia* Fisch. ex Hornem., Big Khekhtsir Nature Reserve.

Rhynchosporium secalis (Oudem.) Davis

On leaves of *Hordeum vulgare* L., Ussuriysk vicinity.

Sarocladium oryzae (Sawada) W. Gams et D. Hawksw.

On leaves of *Oryza sativa* L., Khanka Lake region.

Scopulariopsis brevicaulis (Sacc.) Bainier

In soil of oak forest, Ussuriysk Nature Reserve.

Scopulariopsis brumptii Salv.-Duval

In soil of leaved forest, Ussuriysk Nature Reserve. - In paddy soil, Khanka Lake region.

Scopulariopsis candida (Gueg.) Vuill.

In paddy soil, Khanka Lake region.

Scopulariopsis koningii (Oudem.) Vuill.

In paddy soil, Khanka Lake region.

Sesquicillium candelabrum (Bonord.) W. Gams

On fallen twigs of *Eleutherococcus senticosus* (Rupr. et Maxim.) Maxim., Ussuriysk Nature Reserve, Ussuriysk: Gornotayozhnoye.

Trichoderma aureoviride Rifai

In soil of ash forest, Ussuriysk Nature Reserve. - In paddy soil, Khanka Lake region. - In rhizosphere of apple-tree and pear-tree seedlings, Dalnerechensk.

Trichoderma glaucum E.V. Abbott

In rhizosphere of apple-tree and pear-tree seedlings, Dalnerechensk.

Trichoderma hamatum (Bonord.) Bainier

In soil of coniferous-broad-leaved forest, Ussuriysk Nature Reserve. - In paddy soil, Khanka Lake region.

Trichoderma harzianum Rifai

In paddy soil, Khanka Lake region.

Trichoderma koningii Oudem.

In forest and meadow soil, Ussuriysk Nature Reserve, Big Khekhtsir Nature Reserve, Upper Ussuri Station. - In soil of vineyard, Ussuriysk: Gornotayozhnoye. - In rhizosphere of apple-tree and pear-tree seedlings, Dalnerechensk.

Trichoderma longibrachiatum Rifai

In paddy soil, Khanka Lake region.

Trichoderma piluliferum J. Webster et Rifai

In forest and meadow soil, Big Khekhtsir Nature Reserve.

Trichoderma polysporum (Link) Rifai

In soil of coniferous-broad-leaved forest, Ussuriysk Nature Reserve, Big Khekhtsir Nature Reserve, Upper Ussuri Station. - In paddy soil, Khanka Lake region. - In soil of vineyard, Ussuriysk: Gornotayozhnoye.

Trichoderma viride Pers.

In forest and meadow soil, Ussuriysk Nature Reserve, Big Khekhtsir Nature Reserve. - In paddy soil, on roots and seeds of *Oryza sativa* L., Khanka Lake region. - On seeds of *Zea mays* L., Ussuriysk vicinity. - In rhizosphere of apple-tree, Dalnerechensk.

Trichothecium candidum Wallr.

On stems of *Panax ginseng* C.A. Mey., *Eleutherococcus senticosus* (Rupr. et Maxim.) Maxim., Ussuriysk Nature Reserve.

Trichothecium roseum (Pers.) Link

On dry leaves of *Rosa davurica* Pall., Big Khekhtsir Nature Reserve. - On fallen twigs of *Padus avium* Mill., Ussuriysk Nature Reserve. - On stems and seeds of *Zea mays* L., Ussuriysk vicinity. - In soil of vineyard, Ussuriysk: Gornotayozhnoye. - In paddy soil, on leaves, stems and seeds of *Oryza sativa* L., Khanka Lake region. - In rhizosphere of apple-tree seedlings, Dalnerechensk.

Verticillium nigrescens Pethybr.

In soil of coniferous-broad-leaved forest, Ussuriysk Nature Reserve. - In rhizosphere of cherry-tree, plum-tree, apricot-tree seedlings, Dalnerechensk.

Verticillium tenerum Nees

In soil of coniferous-broad-leaved forest, on fallen twigs of *Carpinus cordata* Blume, Ussuriysk Nature Reserve. - In soil of vineyard, Ussuriysk: Gornotayozhnoye.

Verticillium terrestre (Pers.) Sacc.

In paddy soil, Khanka Lake region.

DEMATIACEAE

Alternaria alternata Keissl.

In forest and meadow soil, on fallen twigs and dry leaves of different plants, Ussuriysk Nature Reserve, Big Khekhtsir Nature Reserve. - In soil of vineyard, Ussuriysk: Gornotayozhnoye. - On seeds of *Zea mays* L., *Triticum aestivum* L., Ussuriysk vicinity. - In paddy soil, on seeds of *Oryza sativa* L., Khanka Lake region. - In rhizosphere of apple-tree seedlings, Dalnerechensk. - On stems and leaves of grasses, Fuyuan, Mishan, Raohe: Shengli State Farm.

Alternaria amaranthi (Peck) J.M. Hook

On leaves of *Amaranthus retroflexus* L., Big Khekhtsir Nature Reserve.

Alternaria brassicicola (Schwein.) Wiltshire

In rhizosphere of apple-tree seedlings, Dalnerechensk.

Alternaria cinerariae Hori et Enjoji

On leaves of *Senecio nemorensis* L., Bastak Nature Reserve.

Alternaria geophila Dasz.

In rhizosphere of apple-tree seedlings, Dalnerechensk.

Alternaria grisea Szilv.

In rhizosphere of pear-tree seedlings, Dalnerechensk.

Alternaria mali Roberts

On leaves of *Malus domestica* Borkh., Ussuriysk: Gornotayozhnoye.

Alternaria oryzae Hara

On seeds of *Oryza sativa* L., Khanka Lake region.

Alternaria tenuissima (Kunze) Wiltshire

In forest and meadow soil, Ussuriysk Nature Reserve. - On seeds and stems of *Oryza sativa* L., Khanka Lake region. - On dry leaves of *Potentilla fragarioides* L., Big Khekhtsir Nature Reserve.

Alternaria vitis Cavara

On leaves of *Vitis amurensis* Rupr., Ussuriysk Nature Reserve.

Arthrinium arundinis (Corda) Dyko et B. Sutton

On dry gramineous stems, Big Khekhtsir Nature Reserve, Hulin: 856 State Farm.

Arthrinium phaeospermum (Corda) M.B. Ellis

In soil of ash forest, on fallen twigs of trees, on dry stems of grasses, Ussuriysk Nature Reserve. - On wood of *Pinus koraiensis* Siebold et Zucc., Big Khekhtsir Nature Reserve. - In soil of vineyard, Ussuriysk: Gornotayozhnoye. - In paddy soil, Khanka Lake region. - In rhizosphere of apple-tree seedlings, Dalnerechensk. - On wood of a deciduous tree, Xingkaihu Nature Reserve, Hulin: 854 State Farm.

Aureobasidium pullulans (de Bary) G. Arnaud

In forest and meadow soil, Ussuriysk Nature Reserve, Upper Ussuri Station, Big Khekhtsir Nature Reserve. - In soil of vineyard, Ussuriysk: Gornotayozhnoye. - In paddy soil, Khanka Lake region. - In rhizosphere of apple-tree and pear-tree seedlings, Dalnerechensk.

Bactrodesmium betulicola M.B. Ellis

On bark of *Betula schmidtii* Regel, Ussuriysk Nature Reserve.

Bipolaris cynodontis (Marignoni) Shoemaker

On leaves of *Muhlenbergia japonica* Steud., Ussuriysk Nature Reserve.

Bipolaris hawaiiensis (M.B. Ellis) J.Y. Uchida et Aragaki

On roots and seeds of *Oryza sativa* L., Khanka Lake region.

Bipolaris leersiae (G.F. Atk.) Shoemaker

On leaves of *Microstegium vimineum* (Trin.) A. Camus, Ussuriysk Nature Reserve.

Bipolaris maydis (Y. Nisik. et C. Miyake) Shoemaker

On leaves, stems and corncobs of *Zea mays* L., Ussuriysk vicinity.

Bipolaris miyakei (Y. Nisiök.) Shoemaker

On leaves of *Eragrostis pilosa* (L.) Beauv., Ussuriysk vicinity.

Bipolaris nodulosa (Berk. et M.A. Curtis) Shoemaker

In soil of vineyard, Ussuriysk: Gornotayozhnoye. - In rhizosphere of pear-tree, Dalnerechensk.

Bipolaris oryzae (Breda de Haan) Shoemaker

On leaves, roots and seeds of *Oryza sativa* L., Khanka Lake region.

Bipolaris ravenelii (M.A. Curtis) Shoemaker

On leaves of *Agrostis gigantea* Roth, Ussuriysk Nature Reserve.

Bipolaris sacchari (E.I. Butler) Shoemaker

On leaves of *Zea mays* L., Ussuriysk vicinity.

Bipolaris setariae (Sawada) Shoemaker

On leaves of *Setaria viridis* (L.) Beauv., *Digitaria ischaemum* (Schreb.) Muehl, Ussuriysk Nature Reserve.

Bipolaris sorokiniana (Sacc.) Shoemaker

On leaves of *Neomolinia mandchurica* (Maxim.) Honda, *Elymus excelsus* Turcz. ex Griseb., *Setaria glauca* (L.) Beauv., Ussuriysk Nature Reserve. - On leaves and seeds of *Zea mays* L., *Triticum aestivum* L., *Hordeum vulgare* L., on sprouts of cereals, Ussuriysk vicinity. - In paddy soil, on seeds of *Oryza sativa* L., Khanka Lake region. - In rhizosphere of apple-tree and pear-tree seedlings, Dalnerechensk.

Bipolaris victoriae (F. Meehan et H.C. Murphy) Shoemaker

On leaves of *Elytrigia repens* (L.) Nevski, *Setaria glauca* (L.) Beauv., *Bromopsis inermis* (Leys.) Holub, *Phleum pratense* L., Ussuriysk Nature Reserve.

Bipolaris zeicola (G.L. Stout) Shoemaker

On leaves and seeds of *Zea mays* L., Ussuriysk vicinity.

Bispora betulina (Corda) S. Hughes

On dead wood of *Betula* sp., Big Khekhtsir Nature Reserve. - On bark of *Betula* sp., Hulin: Dongfanghong.

Botryotrichum piluliferum Sacc. et Marchal

In soil of vineyard, Ussuriysk: Gornotayozhnoye.

Brachysporium obovatum (Berk.) Sacc.

On leaves of *Thalictrum filamentosum* Maxim., Ussuriysk Nature Reserve.

Ceratosporium fuscescens Schwein.

On dry twigs of *Viburnum sargentii* Koehne, Big Khekhtsir Nature Reserve.

Cercospora althaeina Sacc.

On leaves of *Abutilon theophrasti* Medik., Ussuriysk vicinity.

Cercospora angulata G. Winter

On leaves of *Philadelphus tenuifolius* Rupr. et Maxim., Ussuriysk Nature Reserve, Bastak Nature Reserve.

Cercospora duddiae Welles

On leaves of *Allium cepa* L., Ussuriysk vicinity.

Cercospora maianthemi Fuckel

On leaves of *Maianthemum bifolium* (L.) F.W. Schmidt, Bastak Nature Reserve.

Cercospora moricola Cooke

On leaves of *Morus alba* L., Ussuriysk vicinity.

Cercospora negundinis Ellis et Everh.

On leaves of *Acer ginnala* Maxim., Ussuriysk Nature Reserve.

Cercospora paridis Erikss.

On leaves of *Paris manshurica* Kom., Ussuriysk vicinity.

Cercospora physalidis Ellis

On leaves of *Physalis franchetii* Mast., Ussuriysk: Gornotayozhnoye.

Cheiromycella microscopica (P. Karst.) S. Hughes

On fallen twigs of *Salix* sp., Big Khekhtsir Nature Reserve, Raohe: Shengli State Farm.

Chloridium chlamydosporis (J.F.H. Beyma) S. Hughes

In soil of oak forest, Ussuriysk Nature Reserve.

Chloridium virescens var. *caudigerum* (Höhn.) W. Gams et Hol.-Jech.

In rhizosphere of apple-tree and pear-tree seedlings, Dalnerechensk.

Cladorrhinum foecundissimum Sacc. et Marchal

In paddy soil, Khanka Lake region.

Cladosporium atroseptum Pidopl. et Deniak

In soil of swampy meadow, Big Khekhtsir Nature Reserve. - In rhizosphere of apple-tree and pear-tree seedlings, Dalnerechensk.

Cladosporium chlorocephalum (Fresen.) E.W. Mason et M.B. Ellis

In paddy soil, Khanka Lake region.

Cladosporium cladosporioides (Fresen.) G.A. de Vries

In forest and meadow soil, Ussuriysk Nature Reserve, Upper Ussuri Station, Big Khekhtsir Nature Reserve. - In soil of vineyard, Ussuriysk: Gornotayozhnoye. - In paddy soil, on seeds of *Oryza sativa* L., Khanka Lake region. - In rhizosphere of apple-tree and pear-tree seedlings, Dalnerechensk. - On dried leaves of *Rosa davurica* Pall., Big Khekhtsir Nature Reserve. - On fallen leaves of *Lonicera* sp., Xingkaihu Nature Reserve.

Cladosporium elatum (Harz) Nannf.

In paddy soil, Khanka Lake region.

Cladosporium herbarum (Pers.) Link

In forest and meadow soil, on dry leaves and stems of grasses, on fallen twigs of different trees, Ussuriysk Nature Reserve, Upper Ussuri Station, Big Khekhtsir Nature Reserve. - In soil of vineyard, Ussuriysk: Gornotayozhnoye. - In paddy soil, Khanka Lake region. - In rhizosphere of apple-tree and pear-tree seedlings, Dalnerechensk. - On leaves of *Calamagrostis langsdorffii* (Link) Trin., Bastak Nature Reserve. - On gramineous stems and leaves, Mishan, Hulin: Dongfanghong, Raohe: Shengli State Farm.

Cladosporium macrocarpum Preuss

In soil of coniferous-broad-leaved forest, Ussuriysk Nature Reserve.

Cladosporium oxysporum Berk. et M.A. Curtis

In paddy soil, Khanka Lake region.

Cladosporium sphaerospermum Penz.

In soil of ash forest, Ussuriysk Nature Reserve.

Cladosporium tenuissimum Cooke

In soil of oak forest, Ussuriysk Nature Reserve.

Cladosporium variabile (Cooke) G.A. de Vries

In paddy soil, Khanka Lake region.

Coniothecium complanatum (Nees) Sacc.

On leaves of *Acer mono* Maxim., Ussuriysk Nature Reserve.

Conoplea fusca Pers.

On rotten wood, Big Khekhtsir Nature Reserve, Hulin: Dongfanghong.

Conoplea sphaerica Pers.

On fallen twigs of *Abies* sp., *Acer* sp., Big Khekhtsir Nature Reserve. - On rotten wood, Ussuriysk Nature Reserve. - On fallen twigs of *Betula* sp., Raohe.

Cordana pauciseptata Preuss

In soil of ash forest, Ussuriysk Nature Reserve.

Costantinella terrestris (Link) S. Hughes

On rotten wood, Big Khekhtsir Nature Reserve, Xingkaihu Nature Reserve.

Cryptocoryneum condensatum (Wallr.) E.W. Mason et S. Hughes

On fallen twigs of *Philadelphus tenuifolius* Rupr. et Maxim., Big Khekhtsir Nature Reserve.

Curvularia clavata B.L. Jain

On leaves of *Zea mays* L., Ussuriysk vicinity.

Curvularia cymbopogonis (C.W. Dodge) J.W. Groves et Skolko

On leaves of *Digitaria asiatica* Tzvel., Ussuriysk Nature Reserve.

Curvularia lunata (Wakker) Boedijn

In paddy soil, on seeds of *Oryza sativa* L., Khanka Lake region. - On leaves and seeds of *Zea mays* L., Ussuriysk vicinity.

Curvularia pallescens Boedijn

In paddy soil, on seeds of *Oryza sativa* L., Khanka Lake region.

Curvularia ovoidea (Hiroe et N. Watan.) Muntanola

On leaves of *Zea mays* L., Ussuriysk vicinity.

Dactylaria obtriangularia Matsush.

On fruit bodies of *Polystigmina rubrum* (Desm.) Sacc. from leaves of *Padus avium* Mill., Ussuriysk Nature Reserve.

Dendrodochium rubellum Sacc.

On fallen twigs of *Betula* sp., Big Khekhtsir Nature Reserve.

Dictyosporium oblongum (Fuckel) S. Hughes

On rotten wood, Big Khekhtsir Nature Reserve.

Dictyosporium toruloides (Corda) Gueg.

On wood of *Pinus koraiensis* Siebold et Zucc., Ussuriysk Nature Reserve.

Diplococcium spicatum Grove

On fallen twigs of *Pinus koraiensis* Siebold et Zucc., Big Khekhtsir Nature Reserve.

Drechslera avenacea (M.A. Curtis ex Cooke) Shoemaker

On leaves and sprouts of *Avena sativa* L., Ussuriysk vicinity.

Drechslera graminea (Rabenh. ex Schltdl.) Shoemaker

On leaves and seeds of *Hordeum vulgare* L., Ussuriysk vicinity.

Drechslera teres (Sacc.) Shoemaker

On leaves of *Hordeum vulgare* L., Ussuriysk vicinity.

Drechslera zizaniae (Y. Nisik.) Subram. et B.L. Jain

On seeds of *Oryza sativa* L., Khanka Lake region.

Endophragmiella cesatii (Mont.) S. Hughes

On dried twigs of *Rubus matsumuranus* Levl. et Vaniot, Big Khekhtsir Nature Reserve.

Excipularia fusispora (Berk. et Broome) Sacc.

On dry twig of *Lonicera* sp., Big Khekhtsir Nature Reserve.

Exosporium tiliae Link

On bark of *Tilia amurensis* Rupr., Ussuriysk Nature Reserve, Big Khekhtsir Nature Reserve. - On twigs of *Tilia* sp., Hulin: Wulindong.

Exserohilum pedicellatum (A.W. Henry) K.J. Leonard et Suggs

In paddy soil, on roots of *Oryza sativa* L., Khanka Lake region.

Exserohilum rostratum (Drechsler) K.J. Leonard et Suggs

On leaves and seeds of *Zea mays* L., Ussuriysk vicinity.

Exserohilum turcicum (Pass.) K.J. Leonard et Suggs

On leaves of *Zea mays* L., Ussuriysk vicinity.

Gliomastix cerealis (P. Karst.) C.H. Dickinson

In soil of coniferous-broad-leaved forest, Ussuriysk Nature Reserve; Upper Ussuri Station. - In soil of vineyard, Ussuriysk: Gornotayozhnoye. - In rhizosphere of pear-tree, Dalnerechensk.

Gliomastix guttuliformis J.C. Br. et W.B. Kendr.

In soil of coniferous-broad-leaved forest, Ussuriysk Nature Reserve; Upper Ussuri Station. - In soil of vineyard, Ussuriysk: Gornotayozhnoye. - In rhizosphere of apple-tree seedlings, Dalnerechensk.

Gliomastix murorum (Corda) S. Hughes

In soil of coniferous-broad-leaved forest, Ussuriysk Nature Reserve.

Gonytrichum macrocladum (Sacc.) S. Hughes

In soil of elm forest, Ussuriysk Nature Reserve. - In soil of vineyard, Ussuriysk: Gornotayozhnoye. - In rhizosphere of pear-tree, Dalnerechensk.

Helminthosporium macrocarpum Grev.

On twigs of different plants, Ussuriysk Nature Reserve.

Helminthosporium microsorum D. Sacc.

On dried twigs of *Carpinus cordata* Blume, Ussuriysk Nature Reserve.

Helminthosporium velutinum Link

On dried twigs of *Corylus mandshurica* Maxim., *Ulmus laciniata* (Trautv.) Mayr., *Lonicera* sp., Ussuriysk Nature Reserve. - On dry twigs of *Betula mandshurica* (Regel) Nakai, Big Khekhtsir Nature Reserve. - In soil of vineyard, Ussuriysk: Gornotayozhnoye. - In rhizosphere of apple-tree and pear-tree, Dalnerechensk. - On dry twigs of *Lonicera* sp., Raohe.

Heterosporium maydis Lobik

On leaves of *Zea mays* L., Ussuriysk vicinity.

Humicola grisea Traaen

In forest and meadow soil, Ussuriysk Nature Reserve, Upper Ussuri Station, Big Khekhtsir Nature Reserve. - In soil of vineyard, Ussuriysk: Gornotayozhnoye. - In paddy soil, Khanka Lake region. - In rhizosphere of apple-tree and pear-tree seedlings, Dalnerechensk. - On wood of a deciduous tree, Big Khekhtsir Nature Reserve.

Humicola nigrescens Omvik

In soil of broad-leaved forest, Ussuriysk Nature Reserve. - In rhizosphere of apple-tree and pear-tree seedlings, Dalnerechensk.

Monodictys castanea (Wallr.) S. Hughes

On rotten wood, Big Khekhtsir Nature Reserve.

Monodictys levis (Wiltshire) S. Hughes

On wood of *Quercus mongolica* Fisch. ex Ledeb., Big Khekhtsir Nature Reserve. - On wood of a deciduous tree, Hulin: Dongfanghong, Sanjiang Nature Reserve.

Mycocentrospora acerina (R. Hartig) Deighton

On leaves of *Acer pseudosieboldianum* (Pax) Kom., Ussuriysk Nature Reserve, Ussuriysk: Gornotayozhnoye.

Mycovellosiella dioscoreae (Vassiljevsky) N. Pons. et B. Sutton

On leaves of *Dioscorea nipponica* Makino, Ussuriysk Nature Reserve.

Nigrospora oryzae (Berk. et Broome) Petch

On leaves and grains of *Oryza sativa* L., Khanka Lake region.

Oidiodendron echinulatum G.L. Barron

In soil of coniferous-broad-leaved forest, Ussuriysk Nature Reserve.

Oidiodendron flavum Szilv.

In soil of broad-leaved forest, Ussuriysk Nature Reserve.

Oidiodendron tenuissimum (Peck) S. Hughes

In soil of coniferous-broad-leaved forest, Ussuriysk Nature Reserve, Big Khekhtsir Nature Reserve.

Passalora amurensis (Ziling) U. Braun et H.D. Shin

On leaves of *Ligustrina amurensis* Rupr., Ussuriysk Nature Reserve.

Passalora bellynskii (Westend.) U. Braun

On leaves of *Artemisia rubripes* Nakai, *A. sylvatica* Maxim., Ussuriysk Nature Reserve. - On leaves of *Artemisia* sp., Xingkaihu Nature Reserve.

Passalora bupleuri (Pass.) U. Braun

On leaves of *Bupleurum longiradiatum* Turcz., *Anthriscus sylvestris* (L.) Hoffm., Ussuriysk Nature Reserve.

Passalora calystegiae (Speg.) U. Braun

On leaves of *Calystegia sepium* (L.) R. Br., Ussuriysk Nature Reserve.

Passalora circumscissa (Sacc.) U. Braun

On leaves of *Padus avium* Mill., Ussuriysk Nature Reserve. - On leaves of *Padus asiatica* Kom., Ussuriysk: Gornotayozhnoye.

Passalora depressa (Berk. et Broome) Sacc.

On leaves of *Angelica genuflexa* Nutt. ex Torr. et Gray, Ussuriysk: Gornotayozhnoye.

Passalora dubia (Riess) U. Braun

On leaves of *Chenopodium album* L., Ussuriysk vicinity.

Passalora ferruginea (Fuckel) U. Braun et Crous

On leaves of *Artemisia rubripes* Nakai, *A. sylvatica* Maxim., Ussuriysk Nature Reserve. - On leaves of *Artemisia* sp., Xingkaihu Nature Reserve.

Passalora fraxini (DC.) Arx

On leaves of *Fraxinus mandshurica* Rupr., Big Khekhtsir Nature Reserve, Bastak Nature Reserve, Ussuriysk vicinity.

Passalora gotoana (Togashi) U. Braun

On leaves of *Sorbaria sorbifolia* (L.) A. Br., Ussuriysk Nature Reserve, Bastak Nature Reserve, Raohe.

Passalora janseana (Racib.) U. Braun

On leaves and seeds of *Oryza sativa* L., Khanka Lake region.

Passalora microsora (Sacc.) U. Braun

On leaves of *Tilia amurensis* Rupr., Ussuriysk Nature Reserve, Bastak Nature Reserve.

Passalora miurae (Syd. et P. Syd.) U. Braun et H.D. Shin

On leaves of *Metaplexis japonica* (Thunb.) Makino, Ussuriysk Nature Reserve.

Passalora rosicola (Pass.) U. Braun

On leaves of *Rosa davurica* Pall., Ussuriysk vicinity.

Passalora sojina (Hara) H.D. Shin et U. Braun

On leaves, stems, seeds of *Glycine max* (L.) Merr., Ussuriysk vicinity.

Passalora thalictrina (Karak.) U. Braun et Melnik

On leaves of *Thalictrum filamentosum* Maxim., Bastak Nature Reserve.

Periconia byssoides Pers.

On leaves of *Phellodendron amurense* Rupr., *Ulmus japonica* (Rehd.) Sarg., *Vicia* sp., *Juglans mandshurica* Maxim., Ussuriysk Nature Reserve. - On dried stems of grasses, Big Khekhtsir Nature Reserve. - On panicles of *Oryza sativa* L., Khanka Lake region. - On stems of grasses, Raohe: Shengli State Farm, Hulin: 856 State Farm.

Periconia cookei E.W. Mason et M.B. Ellis.

On dry leaves of *Prinsepia sinensis* (Oliv.) Bean., Ussuriysk Nature Reserve.

Periconia digitata (Cooke) Sacc.

On panicles of *Oryza sativa* L., Khanka Lake region.

Periconia macrospinosa Lefebvre et Aar J. Johnson

In soil of oak forest, Ussuriysk Nature Reserve.

Phaeoramularia actaeae (Ellis et Everh.) U. Braun

On leaves of *Cimicifuga dahurica* (Turcz.) Maxim., Bastak Nature Reserve.

Phragmocephala glanduliformis (Höhn.) S. Hughes

On bark of *Quercus mongolica* Fisch. ex Ledeb., Ussuriysk Nature Reserve.

Pleurophragmium parvisporum (Preuss.) Hol.-Jech.

On wood of *Betula* sp., Big Khekhtsir Nature Reserve.

Pithomyces chartarum (Berk. et M.A. Curtis) M.B. Ellis.

On dead wood of *Ligustrina amurensis* Rupr., Ussuriysk Nature Reserve. - On dried stems of cereals, Big Khekhtsir Nature Reserve. - On leaves, stems and seeds of *Oryza sativa* L., Khanka Lake region.

Pithomyces maydicus (Sacc.) M.B. Ellis

On leaves of *Oryza sativa* L., Khanka Lake region.

Pollaccia radiosa (Lib.) E. Bald. et Ciff.

On leaves of *Populus davidiana* Dode, Ussuriysk Nature Reserve. - On leaves of *Populus* sp., Hulin: Dongfanghong.

Pollaccia saliciperda (Allesch. et Tubeuff) Arx

On leaves of *Salix rorida* Laksch., Ussuriysk Nature Reserve. - On leaves of *Salix* sp.,

Raohe: Shengli State Farm.

Polythrincium trifolii Kunze

On leaves of *Trifolium repens* L., Ussuriysk Nature Reserve.

Pseudocercospora araliae (Henn.) Deighton

On leaves of *Aralia elata* (Miq.) Seem., Ussuriysk Nature Reserve. - On leaves of *Aralia* sp., Fuyuan.

Pseudocercospora cladrastidis (Jacz.) J.K. Bai et M.Y. Cheng

On leaves of *Maackia amurensis* Maxim. et Rupr., Ussuriysk Nature Reserve, Ussuriysk: Gornotayozhnoye, Big Khekhtsir Nature Reserve, Bastak Nature Reserve.

Pseudocercospora dictamni (Fuckel) U. Braun et Crous

On leaves of *Dictamnus dasycarpus* Turcz., Bastak Nature Reserve.

Pseudocercospora juglandis (Kellerm. et Swingle) U. Braun et Crous

On leaves, twigs, fruits of *Juglans mandshurica* Maxim., Ussuriysk: Gornotayozhnoye.

Pseudocercospora latens (Ellis et Everh.) Y.L. Guo et X.J. Liu

On leaves of *Lespedeza bicolor* Turcz., Ussuriysk: Gornotayozhnoye.

Pseudocercospora mali (Ellis et Everh.) Deighton

On leaves of *Malus domestica* Borkh., Ussuriysk: Gornotayozhnoye.

Pseudocercospora opuli (Höhn.) U. Braun et Crous

On leaves of *Viburnum sargentii* Koehne, Ussuriysk Nature Reserve, Ussuriysk: Gornotayozhnoye.

Pseudocercospora vitis (Lév.) Speg.

On leaves of *Vitis amurensis* Rupr., Ussuriysk Nature Reserve, Ussuriysk: Gornotayozhnoye.

Pseudospiropes leptotrichus (Cooke et Ellis) M.B. Ellis

On wood, Ussuriysk Nature Reserve.

Pyricularia oryzae Cavara

On leaves, stems and panicle of *Oryza sativa* L., Khanka Lake region.

Pyricularia grisea Sacc.

In paddy soil, Khanka Lake region.

Spadicoides bina (Corda) S. Hughes

On bark of *Maackia amurensis* Rupr. et Maxim., Big Khekhtsir Nature Reserve.

Sporidesmium leptosporum (Sacc. et Roum.) S. Hughes.

On dry twigs of *Acer* sp., *Eleutherococcus senticosus* (Rupr. et Maxim.) Maxim., Big Khekhtsir Nature Reserve.

Stachybotrys alternans Bonord.

In soil of vineyard, Ussuriysk: Gornotayozhnoye.

Stachybotrys chartarum (Ehrenb.) S. Hughes

In soil of broad-leaved forest, Ussuriysk Nature Reserve. - In soil of vineyard, Ussuriysk:

Gornotayozhnoye. - On dry stems of grasses, Big Khekhtsir Nature Reserve. - On fallen twigs of *Lonicera* sp., Raohe.

Stachybotrys cylindrospora C.N. Jensen

In soil of ash forest, Ussuriysk Nature Reserve.

Stachybotrys dichroa Grove

In soil of coniferous-broad-leaved forest, Ussuriysk Nature Reserve.

Stemphylium botryosum Sacc.

On leaves of *Allium ochotense* Prokh., Big Khekhtsir Nature Reserve. - In rhizosphere of apple-tree and pear-tree seedlings, Dalnerechensk.

Stemphylium cirsii (Lindau) E.G. Simmons

On leaves of *Cirsium pendulum* Fisch. ex DC., Big Khekhtsir Nature Reserve, Bastak Nature Reserve, Hulin: 856 State Farm.

Stemphylium lycopersici (Enjoji) W. Yamam.

In paddy soil, Khanka Lake region.

Stemphylium sarciniforme (Cavara) Wiltshire

On leaves of *Trifolium repens* L., Big Khekhtsir Nature Reserve.

Stemphylium verruculosum (Zimm.) Sacc.

In soil of oak forest, Ussuriysk Nature Reserve. - In paddy soil, Khanka Lake region. - In rhizosphere of apple-tree and pear-tree seedlings, Dalnerechensk.

Stenella subsanguinea (Ellis et Everh.) U. Braun

On leaves of *Maianthemum dilatatum* (Wood) Nels. et Macbr., Bastak Nature Reserve.

Stigmina carpophila (Lév.) M.B. Ellis

On fruits of *Prunus ussuriensis* Koval. et Kostina, Ussuriysk Nature Reserve.

Stigmina negundinis (Berk. et M.A. Curtis) M.B. Ellis

On leaves of *Acer mono* Maxim., Ussuriysk Nature Reserve.

Taeniolella stilbospora (Corda) S. Hughes

In soil of ash forest, Ussuriysk Nature Reserve. - In soil of oak forest, on fallen twigs of a deciduous tree, Big Khekhtsir Nature Reserve. - In soil of vineyard, Ussuriysk: Gornotayozhnoye. - In rhizosphere of apple-tree and pear-tree seedlings, Dalnerechensk. - On fallen twigs of a deciduous tree, Hulin: Dongfanghong.

Taeniolella stricta (Corda) S. Hughes

On wood of *Betula* sp., Big Khekhtsir Nature Reserve, Raohe.

Taeniolina scripta (P. Karst.) P.M. Kirk

On wood of a deciduous tree, Big Khekhtsir Nature Reserve.

Thermomyces lanuginosus Tsikl.

In paddy soil, on seeds of *Oryza sativa* L., Khanka Lake region.

Torula expansa Pers.

In rhizosphere and on roots of pear-tree seedlings, Dalnerechensk.

Torula herbarum (Pers.) Link

In forest and meadow soil, on fallen twigs of trees and shrubs, Ussuriysk Nature Reserve. - In rhizosphere and on roots of pear-tree, Dalnerechensk. - On dry stems of grasses, Big Khekhtsir Nature Reserve, Fuyuan.

Torula terrestris Misra

On roots of *Oryza sativa* L., Khanka Lake region.

Trichocladium asperum Harz

In forest and meadow soil, Ussuriysk Nature Reserve. - In soil of vineyard, Ussuriysk: Gornotayozhnoye. - In rhizosphere and on roots of fruit-tree seedlings, Dalnerechensk. - On wood of a deciduous tree, Big Khekhtsir Nature Reserve, Hulin: Dongfanghong.

Trichocladium opacum (Corda) S. Hughes

In forest soil, Ussuriysk Nature Reserve. - In paddy soil, on roots of *Oryza sativa* L., Khanka Lake region.

Trimmatostroma betulinum (Corda) S. Hughes

On dry twigs of *Betula* sp., Big Khekhtsir Nature Reserve, Raohe.

Trimmatostroma salicis Corda

On twigs of *Salix* sp., Big Khekhtsir Nature Reserve, Raohe: Shengli State Farm.

Ulocladium chartarum (Preuss) E.G. Simmons

On bark of coniferous tree, Big Khekhtsir Nature Reserve, Fuyuan.

Ulocladium consortiale (Thüm.) E.G. Simmons

In paddy soil, on root of *Oryza sativa* L., Khanka Lake region.

Virgariella atra S. Hughes.

On fallen twigs of *Fraxinus mandshurica* Rupr., Ussuriysk Nature Reserve, Big Khekhtsir Nature Reserve.

Xylohypha nigrescens (Pers.) E.W. Mason

On twigs of *Lonicera praeflorans* Batal., Ussuriysk Nature Reserve. - On fallen twigs of *Tilia amurensis* Rupr., Big Khekhtsir Nature Reserve. - On twigs of *Lonicera* sp., Xingkaihu Nature Reserve.

TUBERCULARIALES

TUBERCULARIACEAE

Cylindrocarpon candidum (Link) Wollenw.

In forest soil, Ussuriysk Nature Reserve.

Cylindrocarpon destructans (Zinssm.) Sholten

In forest soil, Ussuriysk Nature Reserve, Big Khekhtsir Nature Reserve. - In rhizosphere and on roots of fruit-tree seedlings, Dalnerechensk.

Cylindrocarpon didymum (Harting) Wollenw.

In forest soil, Ussuriysk Nature Reserve, Big Khekhtsir Nature Reserve. - In rhizosphere and on roots of fruit-tree seedlings, Dalnerechensk.

Epicoccum nigrum Link

In forest soil, on dead wood, Ussuriysk Nature Reserve. - On leaves and seeds of *Zea mays* L., *Triticum aestivum* L., Ussuriysk vicinity. - On dried stems of cereals, Big Khekhtsir Nature Reserve. - On leaves, stems and seeds of *Oryza sativa* L., Khanka Lake region. - On wood, Hulin: Wulindong.

Fusarium aquaeductuum (Rabenh. et Radlk.) Sacc.

On fallen leaves and dried stems of grasses, Ussuriysk Nature Reserve. - In paddy soil, on roots of *Oryza sativa* L., Khanka Lake region. - In rhizosphere and on roots of fruit-tree seedlings, Dalnerechensk.

Fusarium avenaceum (Fr.) Sacc.

In paddy soil, on seeds of *Oryza sativa* L., Khanka Lake region. - In rhizosphere and on roots of fruit-tree seedlings, Dalnerechensk. - On seeds of *Zea mays* L., on roots, stems and seeds of *Triticum aestivum* L., Ussuriysk vicinity.

Fusarium coeruleum Libb. ex Sacc.

In paddy soil, Khanka Lake region.

Fusarium culmorum (W.G. Sm.) Sacc.

In swampy meadow soil, Big Khekhtsir Nature Reserve. - In soil of vineyard, Ussuriysk: Gornotayozhnoye. - On roots and seeds of *Oryza sativa* L., Khanka Lake region. - On leaves, stems, roots and seeds of *Triticum aestivum* L., on seeds and stems of *Zea mays* L., Ussuriysk vicinity.

Fusarium gibbosum Appel et Wollenw.

In forest soil, Big Khekhtsir Nature Reserve. - In paddy soil, on seeds of *Oryza sativa* L., Khanka Lake region. - In rhizosphere of fruit-tree seedlings, Dalnerechensk.

Fusarium graminearum Schwabe

In meadow soil, on dry stems of grasses, Ussuriysk Nature Reserve. - On roots, stems and seeds of *Oryza sativa* L., Khanka Lake region. - On leaves, stems, roots and seeds of *Triticum aestivum* L., on stems and seeds of *Zea mays* L., Ussuriysk vicinity.

Fusarium heterosporum Nees et T. Nees

In paddy soil, on seeds of *Oryza sativa* L., Khanka Lake region. - On seeds of *Triticum aestivum* L., Ussuriysk vicinity. - In rhizosphere and on roots of fruit-tree seedlings, Dalnerechensk.

Fusarium incarnatum (Desm.) Sacc.

In soil of vineyard, Ussuriysk: Gornotayozhnoye. - In paddy soil, Khanka Lake region. - In rhizosphere and on roots of fruit-tree seedlings, Dalnerechensk.

Fusarium javanicum Koord.

In rhizosphere and on roots of fruit-tree seedlings, Dalnerechensk.

Fusarium lateritium Nees

On fruits of *Prinsepia sinensis* (Oliv.) Bean, on twigs of *Eleutherococcus senticosus* (Rupr. et Maxim.) Maxim. and *Aralia elata* (Miq.) Seem., Ussuriysk Nature Reserve.

Fusarium merismoides Corda

In paddy soil, Khanka Lake region.

Fusarium moniliforme J. Sheld.

In soil of oak forest, Big Khekhtsir Nature Reserve. - On stems and seeds of *Zea mays* L., on seeds of *Triticum aestivum* L., Ussuriysk vicinity. - In paddy soil, on seeds of *Oryza sativa* L., Khanka Lake region. - In rhizosphere and on roots of fruit-tree seedlings, Dalnerechensk.

Fusarium oxysporum Schltdl.

In forest and meadow soil, Ussuriysk Nature Reserve. - In soil of vineyard, Ussuriysk: Gornotayozhnoye. - On leaves, roots and seeds of *Triticum aestivum* L., Ussuriysk vicinity. - In paddy soil, on seeds of *Oryza sativa* L., Khanka Lake region. - In rhizosphere and on roots of fruit-tree seedlings, Dalnerechensk.

Fusarium oxysporum f. sp. *conglutinans* (Wollenw.) W.C. Snyder et H.N. Hansen

In paddy soil, on seeds of *Oryza sativa* L., Khanka Lake region. - In rhizosphere and on roots of fruit-tree seedlings, Dalnerechensk.

Fusarium poae (Peck) Wollenw.

On seeds of *Triticum aestivum* L., Ussuriysk vicinity.

Fusarium sambucinum Fuckel var. *sambucinum*

In soil of vineyard, Ussuriysk: Gornotayozhnoye. - In paddy soil, Khanka Lake region. - In rhizosphere and on roots of fruit-tree seedlings, Dalnerechensk. - On roots of *Panax ginseng* C.A. Mey., Ussuriysk Nature Reserve.

Fusarium sarcochroum (Desm.) Sacc.

In paddy soil, Khanka Lake region.

Fusarium solani (Mart.) Sacc.

In soil of meadow and oak forest, Ussuriysk Nature Reserve. - On stems and seeds of *Zea mays* L., Ussuriysk vicinity. - In soil of birch forest, Big Khekhtsir Nature Reserve. - In soil of vineyard, Ussuriysk: Gornotayozhnoye. - In paddy soil, Khanka Lake region. - In rhizosphere and on roots of fruit-tree seedlings, Dalnerechensk.

Fusarium sporotrichioides Sherb.

On seeds of *Panax ginseng* C.A. Mey., Ussuriysk Nature Reserve. - On sprouts of *Schisandra chinensis* (Turcz.) Baill., Ussuriysk: Gornotayozhnoye. - On roots and seeds of *Triticum aestivum* L., Ussuriysk vicinity. - On seeds of *Oryza sativa* L., Khanka Lake region.

Myrothecium cinctum (Corda) Sacc.

In rhizosphere of apple-tree, Dalnerechensk.

Myrothecium indicum P. Rama Rao

In rhizosphere of pear-tree, Dalnerechensk.

Myrothecium inundatum Tode

In forest soil, Ussuriysk Nature Reserve.

Myrothecium roridum Tode

In forest soil, Ussuriysk Nature Reserve; Big Khekhtsir Nature Reserve. - In soil of vineyard, Ussuriysk: Gornotayozhnoye. - In rhizosphere of fruit-tree seedlings, Dalnerechensk.

Myrothecium verrucaria (Alb. et Shwein.) Ditmar

In soil of coniferous-broad-leaved forest, Ussuriysk Nature Reserve; Big Khekhtsir Nature Reserve. - In soil of vineyard, Ussuriysk: Gornotayozhnoye. - In paddy soil, on leaves and roots of *Oryza sativa* L., Khanka Lake region. - In rhizosphere of fruit-tree seedlings, Dalnerechensk.

Tubercularia vulgaris Tode

On twigs of different trees and shrubs, Ussuriysk Nature Reserve. - On twigs of *Betula* sp., Big Khekhtsir Nature Reserve. - On twigs of *Sorbaria* sp., Raohe.

STILBELLALES

STILBELLACEAE

Doratomyces stemonitis (Pers.) F.J. Morton et G. Sm.

In soil of coniferous-broad-leaved forest, Ussuriysk Nature Reserve; Big Khekhtsir Nature Reserve. - In soil of vineyard, Ussuriysk: Gornotayozhnoye. - In rhizosphere of fruit-tree seedlings, Dalnerechensk. - On dried grasses, Big Khekhtsir Nature Reserve, Fuyuan, Mishan.

Graphium bulbicola Henn.

In soil of coniferous-broad-leaved forest, Ussuriysk Nature Reserve. - In soil of vineyard, Ussuriysk: Gornotayozhnoye. - In rhizosphere of fruit-tree seedlings, Dalnerechensk.

Graphium penicillioides Corda

On twigs of *Alnus hirsuta* (Spach) Turcz. ex Rupr., Big Khekhtsir Nature Reserve. - On twigs of *Alnus* sp., Hulin: Walindong.

Graphium putredinis (Corda) S. Hughes

On leaves of *Oryza sativa* L., Khanka Lake region.

Nematographium stilboideum (Corda) Goid.

On twigs of *Philadelphus tenuifolius* Rupr. et Maxim., Ussuriysk Nature Reserve.

Stilbella aciculosa (Ellis et Everh.) Seifert

On wood of a coniferous tree and fallen twigs of *Pinus koraiensis* Siebold. et Zucc., Big Khekhtsir Nature Reserve.

Stilbella bulbicola Henn.

In soil of coniferous-broad-leaved forest, Ussuriysk Nature Reserve. - On roots of apricot-tree seedlings, Dalnerechensk.

Stilbella fusca (Sacc.) Seifert

On fruits of *Juglans mandshurica* Maxim., Ussuriysk Nature Reserve.

COELOMYCETES

SPHAEROPSIDALES

SPHAERIOIDACEAE

Aplosporella clintonii (Peck) Petr. et Syd.

On twigs of *Acer pseudosieboldianum* (Pax) Kom., Ussuriysk Nature Reserve.

Aposphaeria difformis Sacc.

On wood of *Salix gracilistyla* Miq., Ussuriysk Nature Reserve.

Ascochyta doronici Allesch.

On leaves of *Hieracium umbellatum* L., Bastak Nature Reserve.

Ascochyta ischaemi Sacc.

On leaves of *Zea mays* L., Ussuriysk vicinity.

Ascochyta juglandis Boltsh.

On leaves of *Juglans mandshurica* Maxim., Ussuriysk Nature Reserve.

Ascochyta procenkoi Melnik

On leaves of *Schisandra chinensis* (Turz.) Baill., Ussuriysk Nature Reserve.

Ascochyta sonchi (Sacc.) Grove

On leaves of *Sonchus arvensis* L., Ussuriysk Nature Reserve.

Ascochyta tenerrima Sacc. et Roum.

On leaves of *Lonicera* sp., Ussuriysk Nature Reserve, Sanjiang Nature Reserve.

Ascochyta veratri Cav.

On leaves of *Veratrum lobelianum* Bernh., Bastak Nature Reserve.

Camarosporium cladrastidis Henn.

On twigs of *Maackia amurensis* Rupr. et Maxim., Ussuriysk Nature Reserve.

Camarosporium macrosporum (Berk. et Broome) Sacc.

On fallen twigs of a deciduous tree, Ussuriysk Nature Reserve.

Camarosporium xylostei Sacc.

On dry twigs of *Lonicera praeflorens* Batal., Ussuriysk Nature Reserve.

Cicinobolus cesatii de Bary

On fungus of Erysiphales, Ussuriysk Nature Reserve.

Coniothyrium fuckelii Sacc.

On twigs of *Maackia amurensis* Rupr. et Maxim., in forest and meadow soil, Ussuriysk

Nature Reserve. - In soil of vineyard, Ussuriysk: Gornotayozhnoye. - In rhizosphere of fruit-tree seedlings, Dalnerechensk.

Coniothyrium japonicum I. Miyake

On leaves and panicle of *Oryza sativa* L., Khanka Lake region.

Coniothyrium oryzae Cav.

On leaves, stems, panicles of *Oryza sativa* L., Khanka Lake region.

Corniculariella spina (Berk. et Ravenel) DiCosmo

On twigs of *Fraxinus rhynchophylla* Hance, Ussuriysk Nature Reserve.

Cytonaema spinella (Kalchbr.) Höhn.

On twigs of *Acer ukurunduense* Trautv. et C.A. Mey., Big Khekhtsir Nature Reserve.

Cytospora caprea Fuckel

On twigs of *Salix* spp., Ussuriysk Nature Reserve, Raohe: Shengli State Farm.

Cytospora chrysosperma (Pers.) Fr.

On twigs of *Populus* spp., *Salix* spp., Ussuriysk Nature Reserve, Hulin: Dongfanghong.

Cytospora leucosperma (Pers.) Fr.

On twigs of *Ulmus japonica* (Rehd.) Sarg. and *Acer mono* Maxim., Ussuriysk Nature Reserve.

Cytospora leucostoma (Pers.) Sacc.

On twigs of *Populus* spp. and *Schisandra chinensis* (Turz.) Baill., Ussuriysk Nature Reserve.

Cytospora personata Fr.

On twigs of *Betula mandshurica* (Regel) Nakai, Ussuriysk Nature Reserve.

Cytospora pruinosa Defago

On twigs of *Fraxinus mandshurica* Rupr., Ussuriysk Nature Reserve.

Cytospora rubescens Fr.

On twigs of *Padus avium* Mill., Ussuriysk Nature Reserve.

Cytospora sacculus (Schwein.) Gvrit.

On twigs of *Pinus koraiensis* Siebold et Zucc., Ussuriysk Nature Reserve.

Cytospora vitis Mont.

On twigs of *Vitis amurensis* Rupr., Ussuriysk Nature Reserve.

Cytosporina ludibunda Sacc.

On twigs of *Populus maximowiczii* A. Henry and *Salix caprea* L., Ussuriysk Nature Reserve.

Diplodia atrata (Desm.) Sacc.

On twigs of *Acer barbinerve* Maxim., Ussuriysk Nature Reserve.

Diplodia clandestina Durieu et Mont.

On twigs of *Rhamnus davurica* Pall., Ussuriysk Nature Reserve.

Diplodia opuli Pass.

On twigs of *Viburnum burejaeticum* Regel et Herd., Ussuriysk Nature Reserve.

Diplodia salicina Lév.

On twigs of   *Salix gracilistyla* Miq., Ussuriysk Nature Reserve.

Diplodia spiraeina Sacc.

On twigs of *Spiraea salicifolia* L., Ussuriysk Nature Reserve.

Diplodiella oryzae I. Miyake

On leaves and panicles of *Oryza sativa* L., Khanka Lake region.

Fusicoccum quercus Oudem.

In soil of oak forest, Ussuriysk Nature Reserve.

Hendersonia acicola Munch. et Tubeuff

On needles of *Pinus koraiensis* Siebold et Zucc., Ussuriysk Nature Reserve.

Hendersonia oryzae I. Miyake.

In paddy soil, Khanka Lake region.

Hendersonia sarmentorum Westend.

On twigs of *Padus avium* Mill., Ussuriysk Nature Reserve.

Hendersonia ulmea (P. Karst.) Berl. et Voglino

On twigs of *Ulmus japonica* (Rehd.) Sarg., Ussuriysk Nature Reserve.

Macrophoma excelsa P. Karst.

On twigs of *Pinus koraiensis* Siebold et Zucc., Ussuriysk Nature Reserve.

Micropera padina (Pers.) Sacc.

On twigs of *Corylus* sp. and *Padus* sp., Ussuriysk Nature Reserve.

Micropera sorbi Thüm.

On twigs of *Sorbaria sorbifolia* (L.) A. Br., Ussuriysk Nature Reserve.

Microsphaeropsis olivacea (Bonord.) Höhn.

On twigs of *Betula* sp. and *Acer mono* Maxim., Ussuriysk Nature Reserve.

Phoma abietis Briard

On needles of *Abies holophylla* Maxim., Ussuriysk Nature Reserve.

Phoma aceris-negundinis Arcang.

On twigs of *Acer pseudosieboldianum* (Pax) Kom. and *A. barbinerve* Maxim., Ussuriysk Nature Reserve.

Phoma actinidiae Ablak. et Koval

On twigs of *Actinidia kolomikta* (Maxim.) Maxim., Ussuriysk Nature Reserve.

Phoma araliae Cooke et Massee

On twigs of *Eleutherococcus senticosus* (Rupr. et Maxim.) Maxim., Ussuriysk Nature Reserve.

Phoma crataegi Sacc.

On twigs of *Crataegus pinnatifida* Bunge, Ussuriysk Nature Reserve.

Phoma equiseti Desm.

On stems of *Equisetum* sp., Ussuriysk Nature Reserve.

Phoma glumicola Speg.

On stems, leaves and seeds of *Oryza sativa* L., Khanka Lake region.

Phoma herbarum Westend.

In soil of coniferous-broad-leaved forest, Ussuriysk Nature Reserve; Big Khekhtsir Nature Reserve. - In soil of vineyard, Ussuriysk: Gornotayozhnoye. - In rhizosphere of fruit-tree seedlings, Dalnerechensk. - On dried stem of a grass, Big Khekhtsir Nature Reserve.

Phoma humicola J.C. Gilman et E.V. Abbott.

In soil of coniferous-broad-leaved forest, Ussuriysk Nature Reserve. - In rhizosphere of fruit-tree seedlings, Dalnerechensk.

Phoma necatrix Thüm.

On stems, leaves and seeds of *Oryza sativa* L., Khanka Lake region.

Phoma minutispora P.N. Mathur

In paddy soil, on stems, leaves and seeds of *Oryza sativa* L., Khanka Lake region.

Phoma oblongata Briard et Har.

On twigs of *Ulmus japonica* (Rehd.) Sarg., Ussuriysk Nature Reserve.

Phoma phellodendri Bres.

On twigs of *Phellodendron amurense* Rupr., Ussuriysk Nature Reserve.

Phoma philadelphi Cooke

On twigs of *Philadelphus tenuifolius* Rupr. et Maxim., Ussuriysk Nature Reserve.

Phoma pomorum Thüm.

On leaves of *Padus maackii* (Rupr.) Kom., Ussuriysk Nature Reserve.

Phoma schisandrae Ablak. et Koval

On twigs of *Schisandra chinensis* (Turcz.) Baill., Ussuriysk Nature Reserve.

Phoma securinegae Syd.

On twigs of *Securinega suffruticosa* (Pall.) Rehder, Ussuriysk Nature Reserve.

Phoma trachelii Allesch.

On twigs of *Campanula punctata* Lam., Ussuriysk Nature Reserve.

Phoma vitis Bonord.

On stems of *Vitis amurensis* Rupr., Ussuriysk Nature Reserve.

Phoma zeae-maydis Punith.

On leaves of *Zea mays* L., Ussuriysk vicinity.

Phomopsis cladrastidis Petr.

On twigs of *Maackia amurensis* Rupr. et Maxim., Ussuriysk Nature Reserve.

Phomopsis juglandina (Sacc.) Höhn.

On twigs of *Juglans mandshurica* Maxim., Ussuriysk Nature Reserve.

Phomopsis lebiseyi (Sacc.) Died.

On twigs of *Acer mono* Maxim., Ussuriysk Nature Reserve.

Phomopsis oryzae-sativae Punith.

On leaves and seeds of *Oryza sativa* L., Khanka Lake region.

Phomopsis quercella Sacc.et Roum.

On twigs of *Querqus mongolica* Fisch. ex Ledeb., Ussuriysk Nature Reserve.

Phomopsis quercina (Sacc.) Höhn.

On fallen trunk of *Querqus mongolica* Fisch. ex Ledeb., Ussuriysk Nature Reserve.

Phomopsis rosae (Schulzer et Sacc.) Died.

On twigs of *Rosa rugosa* Thunb., Ussuriysk Nature Reserve.

Phyllosticta acanthopanacis Syd.

On leaves of *Eleutherococcus sessiliflorus* (Rupr. et Maxim.) S.Y. Hu, Ussuriysk Nature Reserve.

Phyllosticta acerina Allesch.

On leaves of *Acer mandschuricum* Maxim., Ussuriysk Nature Reserve.

Phyllosticta aconitina Petr.

On leaves of *Aconitum albo-violaceum* Kom., Ussuriysk Nature Reserve.

Phyllosticta actinidiae Ablak. et Koval

On leaves of *Actinidia arguta* (Sieb. et Zucc.) Planch., Ussuriysk Nature Reserve.

Phyllosticta angelicae Sacc.

On leaves of *Angelica dahurica* (Fisch.) Benth. et Hook, Ussuriysk Nature Reserve.

Phyllosticta arisaematis Bunkina et Koval

On leaves of *Arisaema amurense* Maxim., Ussuriysk Nature Reserve.

Phyllosticta asperulae Grove

On leaves of *Rubia sylvatica* (Maxim.) Nakai, Ussuriysk Nature Reserve.

Phyllosticta betulina Sacc.

On leaves of *Betula* sp., Ussuriysk Nature Reserve.

Phyllosticta bupleuri (Fuckel) Sacc.

On leaves of *Bupleurum longiradiatum* Turcz., Ussuriysk Nature Reserve.

Phyllosticta caprifolii (Opiz.) Sacc.

On leaves of *Lonicera maximowiczii* (Rupr.) Regel and *L. gibbiflora* (Rupr.) Dippel, Ussuriysk Nature Reserve. - On leaves of *Lonicera* sp., Sanjiang Nature Reserve.

Phyllosticta cardamines amorae Petr.

On leaves of *Cardamine leucantha* (Tausch) O.E. Schulz., Ussuriysk Nature Reserve.

Phyllosticta chloranthi Bunkina et Koval

On leaves of *Chloranthus japonicus* Sieb., Ussuriysk Nature Reserve.

Phyllosticta coronaria Pass.

On leaves of *Philadelphus tenuifolius* Rupr. et Maxim., Ussuriysk Nature Reserve.

Phyllosticta convallariae Pers.

On leaves of *Polygonatum* sp., Ussuriysk Nature Reserve.

Phyllosticta deutziae Ellis et Everh.

On leaves of *Deutzia amurensis* (Regel) Airy-Schow., Ussuriysk Nature Reserve.

Phyllosticta everhartii Sacc. et P. Syd.

On leaves of *Aralia elata* (Miq.) Seem., Ussuriysk Nature Reserve.

Phyllosticta fraxini Ellis et G. Martin

On leaves of *Fraxinus mandshurica* Rupr., Ussuriysk Nature Reserve.

Phyllosticta gei Bres.

On leaves of *Geum aleppicum* Jacq., Ussuriysk Nature Reserve.

Phyllosticta grossulariae Sacc.

On leaves of *Ribes* sp., Ussuriysk Nature Reserve.

Phyllosticta japonica I. Miyake

On leaves of *Oryza sativa* L., Khanka Lake region.

Phyllosticta lantanae Pass.

On leaves of *Viburnum sargentii* Koehne, Ussuriysk Nature Reserve.

Phyllosticta menispermi Pass.

On leaves of *Menispermum dauricum* DC., Ussuriysk Nature Reserve.

Phyllosticta miurai I. Miyake

On leaves of *Oryza sativa* L., Khanka Lake region.

Phyllosticta negundinis Sacc. et Speg.

On leaves of *Acer barbinerve* Maxim., Ussuriysk Nature Reserve.

Phyllosticta oryzicola Hara

On leaves of *Oryza sativa* L., Khanka Lake region.

Phyllosticta panacis Nakata et Takim.

On leaves of *Panax ginseng* C.A. Mey., Ussuriysk Nature Reserve.

Phyllosticta phellodendri Bunkina et Koval.

On leaves of *Phellodendron amurense* Rupr., Ussuriysk Nature Reserve.

Phyllosticta phlomidis Bondartsev et Lebedeva

On leaves of *Leonurus heterophyllus* Sweet, Ussuriysk Nature Reserve.

Phyllosticta phrymae Bunkina

On leaves of *Phryma leptostachya* L., Ussuriysk Nature Reserve.

Phyllosticta platanoides Sacc.

On leaves of *Acer mandschuricum* Maxim., Ussuriysk Nature Reserve.

Phyllosticta prenanthis Bunkina

On leaves of *Prenanthes tatarinowii* Maxim., Ussuriysk Nature Reserve.

Phyllosticta thalictri Westend.

On leaves of *Thalictrum filamentosum* Maxim., Ussuriysk Nature Reserve.

Phyllosticta tiliae Sacc. et Speg.

On leaves of *Tilia amurensis* Rupr., Ussuriysk Nature Reserve.

Phyllosticta viticola Sacc. et Speg.

On leaves of *Vitis amurensis* Rupr., Ussuriysk Nature Reserve.

Phyllosticta vulgaris Desm.

On leaves of *Lonicera praeflorens* Batal., Ussuriysk Nature Reserve.

Pyrenochaeta berberidis (Sacc.) Brunaud

On twigs of *Padus avium* Mill., Ussuriysk Nature Reserve.

Rhabdospora nebulosa (Desm.) Sacc.

On stems of *Angelica* sp., Ussuriysk Nature Reserve.

Septoria adoxae Fuckel

On leaves of *Adoxa moschatellina* L., Ussuriysk Nature Reserve.

Septoria ascochytoides Sacc.

On leaves of *Filipendula palmata* (Pall.) Maxim., Bastak Nature Reserve.

Septoria astericola Ellis et Everh.

On leaves of *Aster incisus* Fisch., Ussuriysk Nature Reserve.

Septoria brunneola (Fr.) Niessl.

On leaves of *Convallaria keiskii* Miq., Bastak Nature Reserve.

Septoria bunkinae Teterevn.

On leaves of *Cimicifuga simplex* Wormsk., Ussuriysk Nature Reserve.

Septoria caricis Pass.

On leaves of *Carex* sp., Ussuriysk Nature Reserve.

Septoria chelidonii Desm.

On leaves of *Chelidonium majus* L., Ussuriysk Nature Reserve.

Septoria convolvuli Desm.

On leaves of *Calystegia sepium* (L.) R. Br., Ussuriysk Nature Reserve.

Septoria crataegi J. Kickx.

On leaves of *Crataegus pinnatifida* Bunge, Ussuriysk Nature Reserve.

Septoria dimera Sacc.

On leaves of *Silene macrostyla* Maxim., Bastak Nature Reserve.

Septoria euonymi Rabenh.

On leaves of *Euonymus sacrosancta* Koidz., Ussuriysk Nature Reserve.

Septoria falcispora Z.A. Demidova

On panicles of *Oryza sativa* L., Khanka Lake region.

Septoria geranii Roberge ex Desm.

On leaves of *Geranium sibiricum* L., Ussuriysk Nature Reserve.

Septoria letendreana Sacc.

On leaves of *Juglans mandshurica* Maxim., Ussuriysk Nature Reserve.

Septoria maydis Schulzer et Sacc.

On leaves of *Zea mays* L., Ussuriysk vicinity.

Septoria menispermi Thüm.

On leaves of *Menispermum dauricum* DC., Ussuriysk Nature Reserve.

Septoria mitellae Ellis et Everh.

On leaves of *Mitella nuda* L., Ussuriysk Nature Reserve.

Septoria miyakei Sacc. et Traverso

On panicles of *Oryza sativa* L., Khanka Lake region.

Septoria mougeoti Sacc. et Roum.

On leaves of *Hieracium umbellatum* L., Bastak Nature Reserve.

Septoria oryzae Catt.

On leaves of *Oryza sativa* L., Khanka Lake region.

Septoria oxalidis Lind

On leaves of *Oxalis acetosella* L., Ussuriysk Nature Reserve.

Septoria plectranthi Ziling

On leaves of *Rabdosia excisa* (Maxim.) Hara, Ussuriysk Nature Reserve.

Septoria pisi Westend.

On stems of *Vicia venosa* (Willd. et Link) Maxim., Ussuriysk Nature Reserve.

Septoria podagrariae Lasch.

On leaves of *Aegopodium alpestre* Ledeb., Ussuriysk Nature Reserve.

Septoria rubi Westend.

On leaves of *Rubus crataegifolius* Bunge, Ussuriysk Nature Reserve.

Septoria sambucina Peck

On leaves of *Sambucus koreana* Nakai, Ussuriysk Nature Reserve.

Septoria saussureae Thüm.

On leaves of *Saussurea amurensis* Turcz., Bastak Nature Reserve.

Septoria sublineolata Thüm.

On leaves of *Veratrum lobelianum* Bernh., Bastak Nature Reserve.

Septoria tritici Desm.

On leaves of *Triticum aestivum* L., Ussuriysk vicinity.

Septoria viburni Westend.

On leaves of *Viburnum sargentii* Koehne, Ussuriysk Nature Reserve.

Septoria vincetoxici (C. Schub.) Auersw.

On leaves of *Cynanchum acuminatifolium* Hemsley, Ussuriysk Nature Reserve.

Septoria xylostei Sacc. et G. Winter

On leaves of *Lonicera gibbiflora* (Rupr.) Dippel, Ussuriysk Nature Reserve. - On leaves of *Lonicera* sp., Sanjiang Nature Reserve.

Septoria zeae G.L. Stout

On leaves of *Zea mays* L., Ussuriysk vicinity.

Septoria zeina G.L. Stout

On leaves of *Zea mays* L., Ussuriysk vicinity.

Sphaerellopsis filum (Biv.) B. Sutton

On rust fungus from leaves of *Rubus crataegifolius* Bunge, Ussuriysk Nature Reserve.

Sphaeronema acerinum Peck

On twigs of *Acer pseudosieboldianum* (Pax) Kom., Ussuriysk Nature Reserve.

Sphaeronema cylindricum Fr.

On twigs of *Salix* sp., *Maackia amurensis* Rupr. et Maxim. and *Philadelphus tenuifolius* Rupr. et Maxim., Ussuriysk Nature Reserve.

Sphaeropsis demersa (Bonord.) Sacc.

On twigs of *Padus avium* Mill. and *Spiraea* sp., Ussuriysk Nature Reserve.

Sphaeropsis malorum Berk.

On twigs of *Malus mandshurica* (Maxim.) Kom., Ussuriysk Nature Reserve.

Sphaeropsis populi Ellis et Barthol.

On twigs of *Populus koreana* Rehder, Ussuriysk Nature Reserve.

Sphaeropsis salicis Ellis et Barthol.

On twigs of *Salix* sp., Ussuriysk Nature Reserve.

Sphaeropsis syringae (Fr.) Peck et Cooke

On twigs of *Syringa amurensis* Rupr., Ussuriysk Nature Reserve.

Sphaeropsis viburni Ellis et Dearn.

On twigs of *Viburnum sargentii* Koehne and *V. burejaeticum* Regel et Herd., Ussuriysk Nature Reserve.

ZYTHIACEAE

Rhodosticta caraganae Woron.

On leaves of *Caragana ussuriensis* Pojark., Ussuriysk Nature Reserve.

LEPTOSTROMATACEAE

Discosia artocreas (Tode) Fr.

On leaves of *Euonymus sacrosancta* Koidz., *Geum aleppicum* Jacq., *Panax ginseng* C.A. Mey. and *Betula* sp., Ussuriysk Nature Reserve.

Discosia clypeata De Not.

On fallen leaves of *Maackia amurensis* Rupr. et Maxim., Ussuriysk Nature Reserve.

Leptostroma abietum Ziling

On needles of *Abies holophylla* Maxim., Ussuriysk Nature Reserve.

Leptostroma caricinum Fr.

On leaves of *Carex* sp., Ussuriysk Nature Reserve.

Leptostromella hysterioides (Fr.) Sacc.

On stems of *Dictamnus dasycarpus* Turcz., Ussuriysk Nature Reserve.

Leptothyrium protuberans (Lév.) Sacc.

On leaves of *Fragaria orientalis* Losinsk., Ussuriysk Nature Reserve.

Melasmia acerina Lév.

On leaves of *Acer mono* Maxim. and *A. pseudosieboldianum* (Pax) Kom., Ussuriysk Nature Reserve.

Melasmia lonicerae Jacz.

On leaves of *Lonicera* spp., Ussuriysk Nature Reserve, Sanjiang Nature Reserve.

Melasmia punctata Sacc.et Roum.

On leaves of *Acer pseudosieboldianum* (Pax) Kom. and *A. barbinerve* Maxim., Ussuriysk Nature Reserve.

Piggotia ulmi (Grev.) Keissl.

On leaves of *Ulmus japonica* (Rehd.) Sarg., Ussuriysk Nature Reserve.

EXCIPULACEAE

Dinemasporium cytosporoides (Sacc.) Sutton

On twigs of *Quercus mongolica* Fisch. ex Ledeb., Big Khekhtsir Nature Reserve.

Dinemasporium strigosum (Pers.) Sacc.

On stems and leaves of *Miscanthus sacchariflorus* (Maxim.) Benth., Big Khekhtsir Nature Reserve.

MELANCONIALES

MELANCONIACEAE

Asteroma frondicola (Fr. ex Ficinus et Schubert) M. Morelet

On leaves of *Populus* spp., Ussuriysk Nature Reserve.

Colletotrichum circinans (Berk.) Voglino

On leaves of *Hemerocallis middendorfii* Trautv. et C.A. Mey., Big Khekhtsir Nature Reserve.

Colletotrichum coccodes (Wallr.) S. Hughes

On leaves of *Ligustrina amurensis* Rupr., Ussuriysk Nature Reserve.

Colletotrichum dematium (Pers.) Grove

On stems of *Panax ginseng* C.A. Mey., *Angelica* sp., *Anthriscus almula* (Woron.) B.

Schischk., on leaves of *Aralia elata* (Miq.) Seem., *Convallaria keiskei* Miq., *Galium* sp., *Jeffersonia dubia* Benth. et Hook, in forest soil, Ussuriysk Nature Reserve. - On leaves of *Lilium pensylvanicum* Ker.-Gavl., Big Khekhtsir Nature Reserve. - On leaves of *Maianthemum dilatatum* (Wood) Nels. et Macbr., *Convallaria keiskii* Miq., *Thalictrum filamentosum* Maxim., *Veratrum lobelianum* Bernh., Bastak Nature Reserve. - On leaves of *Aralia* sp., Fuyuan.

Colletotrichum dictamni Hollos

On leaves of *Dictamnus dasycarpus* Turcz., Ussuriysk Nature Reserve, Bastak Nature Reserve.

Colletotrichum gloeosporioides (Penz.) Penz. et Sacc.

On leaves of *Viola acuminata* Ledeb., Big Khekhtsir Nature Reserve.

Colletotrichum graminicola (Ces.) G.W. Wilson

On leaves of *Zea mays* L., Ussuriysk vicinity.

Colletotrichum panacicola Nakata et Takim.

On leaves and seeds of *Panax ginseng* C.A. Mey., Ussuriysk: Gornotayozhnoye.

Cryptocline conigena (Sacc. et Roum.) Arx

On needles of *Abies* sp., Ussuriysk Nature Reserve.

Cylindrosporium aceris Jacz.

On leaves of *Acer mandshuricum* Maxim., Ussuriysk Nature Reserve.

Cylindrosporium quercus Sorokin

On leaves of *Quercus mongolica* Fisch. ex Ledeb., Ussuriysk Nature Reserve.

Didymosporium profusum (Grev.) Fr.

On fallen twigs of *Quercus mongolica* Fisch. ex Ledeb., Ussuriysk Nature Reserve.

Dinemasporium cytosporoides (Sacc.) B. Sutton

On twigs of *Quercus mongolica* Fisch. ex Ledeb., Big Khekhtsir Nature Reserve.

Dinemasporium strigosum (Pers.) Sacc.

On leaves and stems of *Miscanthus sacchariflorus* (Maxim.) Benth., Big Khekhtsir Nature Reserve.

Diploceras kriegerianum (Bres.) Nag Raj

On leaves of *Chamaenerion angustifolium* (L.) Scop., Big Khekhtsir Nature Reserve.

Discula umbrinella (Berk. et Broome) M. Morelet

On leaves of *Quercus mongolica* Fisch. ex Ledeb., Ussuriysk Nature Reserve, Bastak Nature Reserve.

Kabatia periclymeni (Desm.) M. Morelet

On leaves of *Lonicera praeflorens* Batal., Ussuriysk Nature Reserve.

Kabatia lonicerae (Harkn.) Höhn.

On leaves of *Lonicera praeflorens* Batal., Ussuriysk Nature Reserve.

Marssonina manschurica (Naumov) Karak.

On leaves of *Juglans mandshurica* Maxim., Ussuriysk Nature Reserve.

Marssonina populi (Lib.) Magnus

On leaves of *Populus davidiana* Dode, Ussuriysk Nature Reserve.

Marssonina potentillae (Desm.) Magnus

On leaves of *Fragaria orientalis* Losinsk., Ussuriysk Nature Reserve.

Marssonina viticola (I. Miyake) F.L. Tai

On leaves of *Vitis amurensis* Rupr., Ussuriysk Nature Reserve.

Pestalotiopsis breviseta (Sacc.) Steyaert

On leaves of *Betula* sp., Ussuriysk Nature Reserve.

Pestalotiopsis funerea (Desm.) Steyaert

On flower stalk of *Panax ginseng* C.A. Mey., Ussuriysk Nature Reserve.

Pestalotiopsis uvicola (Speg.) Bissett

On leaves of *Vitis amurensis* Rupr., Ussuriysk Nature Reserve.

Pestalotiopsis virgatula (Kleb.) Steyaert

In soil of vineyard, Ussuriysk: Gornotayozhnoye.

Seimatosporium lichenicola (Corda) Shoemaker et E. Müll.

On leaves of *Lonicera praeflorens* Batal., Ussuriysk Nature Reserve.

Stegonsporium betulae Bres.

On fallen twigs of *Betula* sp., Ussuriysk Nature Reserve.

Truncatella hartigii (Tubeuff) Steyaert

In soil of ash forest, Ussuriysk Nature Reserve.

ASCOMYCOTA

ASCOMYCETES

EUROTIALES

TRICHOCOMACEAE

Byssochlamys fulva Olliver et G. Sm.

In paddy soil, Khanka Lake region.

Emericella nidulans (Eidam) Vuill.

In soil of coniferous-broad-leaved forest, Ussuriysk Nature Reserve, Big Khekhtsir Nature Reserve.

Emericellopsis minima Stolk

In soil of vineyard, Ussuriysk: Gornotayozhnoye.

Emericellopsis terricola J.F.H. Beyma

In soil of vineyard, Ussuriysk: Gornotayozhnoye.

Eupenicillium javanicum (J.F.H. Beyma) Stolk et D.B. Scott

In soil of coniferous-broad-leaved forest, Ussuriysk Nature Reserve, Big Khekhtsir Nature Reserve.

Eupenicillium levitum (Raper et Fennell) Stolk et D.B. Scott

In paddy soil, on roots and seeds of *Oryza sativa* L., Khanka Lake region.

Eurotium amstelodami L. Mangin

In soil of coniferous-broad-leaved forest, Ussuriysk Nature Reserve, Big Khekhtsir Nature Reserve.

Eurotium herbariorum (F.H. Wigg.) Link

In soil of ash forest, Ussuriysk Nature Reserve.

Talaromyces avellaneus Stolk et Samson

In soil of coniferous-broad-leaved forest, Ussuriysk Nature Reserve.

PSEUDEUROTIACEAE

Pseudeurotium ovale Stolk

In paddy soil, Khanka Lake region.

Pseudeurotium zonatum J.F.H. Beyma

In paddy soil, Khanka Lake region.

ONYGENALES

GYMNOASCACEAE

Arachniotus aurantiacus (Kamyschko) Arx.

In paddy soil, Khanka Lake region.

Arachniotus ruber (Tiegh.) J. Schröt.

In garden soil, Dalnerechensk.

Arachniotus terrestris Raillo

In garden soil, Dalnerechensk.

Gymnoascus reessii Baran.

In soil of coniferous-broad-leaved forest, Ussuriysk Nature Reserve, Big Khekhtsir Nature Reserve, Upper Ussuri Station. - In paddy soil, Khanka Lake region. - In rhizosphere of apple-tree and pear-tree seedlings, Dalnerechensk.

Pseudogymnoascus roseus Raillo

In soil of oak forest, Ussuriysk Nature Reserve, Big Khekhtsir Nature Reserve. - In rhizosphere of apple-tree and pear-tree seedlings, Dalnerechensk. - In paddy soil, on roots of *Oryza sativa* L., Khanka Lake region.

SORDARIALES

SORDARIACEAE

Gelasinospora calospora (Mouton) C. Moreau

In paddy soil, on roots of *Oryza sativa* L., Khanka Lake region.

Gelasinospora tetrasperma Dowding

In paddy soil, on roots of *Oryza sativa* L., Khanka Lake region.

Sordaria fimicola (Roberge ex Desm.) Ces. et De Not.

In soil of coniferous-broad-leaved forest, Ussuriysk Nature Reserve, Big Khekhtsir Nature Reserve. - In rhizosphere of apple-tree and pear-tree seedlings, Dalnerechensk.

CHAETOMIACEAE

Chaetomidium fimeti (Fuckel) Zopf

In garden soil, Dalnerechensk.

Chaetomium circinatum Chivers

In soil of coniferous-broad-leaved forest, Ussuriysk Nature Reserve, Big Khekhtsir Nature Reserve.

Chaetomium cochlioides Palliser

In soil of oak forest, Ussuriysk Nature Reserve. - In paddy soil, on roots and seeds of *Oryza sativa* L., Khanka Lake region. - In rhizosphere of apple-tree and pear-tree seedlings, Dalnerechensk.

Chaetomium elatum Kunze

In soil of elm forest, Ussuriysk Nature Reserve. - In soil of vineyard, Ussuriysk: Gornotayozhnoye. - In rhizosphere of apple-tree seedlings, Dalnerechensk.

Chaetomium fibripilium L.M. Ames

On seeds of *Oryza sativa* L., Khanka Lake region.

Chaetomium funicola Cooke

On roots of *Oryza sativa* L., Khanka Lake region.

Chaetomium globosum Kunze

In forest soil, Ussuriysk Nature Reserve, Ussuriysk: Gornotayozhnoye, Big Khekhtsir Nature Reserve. - In rhizosphere of apple-tree and pear-tree seedlings, Dalnerechensk.

Chaetomium homopilatum Omvik

In paddy soil, Khanka Lake region.

Chaetomium indicum Corda

On seeds of *Oryza sativa* L., Khanka Lake region.

Chaetomium olivaceum Cooke et Ellis

In soil of broad-leaved forest, Ussuriysk Nature Reserve.

Chaetomium spirale Zopf

In forest soil, Ussuriysk Nature Reserve. - In paddy soil, Khanka Lake region. - In rhizosphere of apple-tree and pear-tree seedlings, Dalnerechensk.

Farrowia seminuda (L.M. Ames) D. Hawksw.

In paddy soil, on seeds of *Oryza sativa* L., Khanka Lake region.

Thielavia microspora Mouch.

In paddy soil, on roots of *Oryza sativa* L., Khanka Lake region.

Thielavia tetraspora (Lodhi et J.H. Mirza) Arx

In paddy soil, Khanka Lake region.

DOTHIDEALES

SPORORMIACEAE

Preussia fleischhakii (Auersw.) Cain

In rhizosphere of apple-tree, Dalnerechensk.

Westerdykella multispora (Saito et Minoura ex Cain) Ceip et Milko

In paddy soil, on roots of *Oryza sativa* L., Khanka Lake region.

REFERENCES

Ablakatova A A. Mycoflora and main fungal diseases of fruit trees and berry plants in the southern Far East. Nauka. Moscow-Leningrad, 1965, 1-145. (in Russian)

Azbukina Z M, Barbayanova T A, Lukiyanchikov V P, Zaitseva A V. Causal agents of cereals fungal diseases. 1980, 84-225. In Azbukina Z M. (ed.) Causal agents of agricultural plants diseases in the Far East. Nauka. Moscow. (in Russian)

Braun U, Melnik V A. *Eriomycopsis lasiosphaeriicola* sp. nov. - hyperparasitic hyphomycete from the Far East of Russia. Mikologiya i Fitopatologiya, 1998, 32: 3-6.

Bunkina I A, Nazarova M M. Fungi. 1978, 36-114. In Kharkevich S S. (ed.) Flora and vegetation of Ussuriysk Nature Reserve. Nauka. Moscow. (in Russian)

Egorova L N. Investigation of soil mycoflora of vineyard in Primorje. Mikologiya i Fitopatologiya, 1968, 2: 449-452. (in Russian)

Egorova L N. Soil mycoflora. 1978, 105-110. In Kharkevich S S. (ed.) Flora and vegetation of Ussuriysk Nature Reserve. Nauka. Moscow. (in Russian)

Egorova L N. Zygomycetes, Hyphomycetes, Coelomycetes. 1984, 24: 61-64. In Azbukina Z M & Kharkevich S S. (eds.) Flora and vegetation of Upper Ussuri Station. Vladivostok. (in Russian)

Egorova L N. Soil fungi of the Far East. Hyphomycetes. Nauka. Leningrad, 1986a, 1-191. (in Russian)

Egorova L N. Zygomycetes, Plectomycetes, Hyphomycetes, Coelomycetes. 1986b, 32: 68-70. In Azbukina Z M & Kharkevich S S. (eds.) Flora and vegetation of Big Khekhtsir Nature Reserve (Khabarovsk region). Vladivostok: Far East. Sci. Center. (in Russian)

Egorova L N. Saprotrophic Hyphomycetes newly found in the Far East. 1990, 113-116. In Vasilyeva L N. Cryptogamic studies in the Far East. Vladivostok: Far East Branch Russ. Acad. Sci. (in Russian)

Egorova L N. *Cercospora* and related hyphomycete genera in the Soviet Far East. Mykologiya i Fitopatologiya,1991, 25: 288-294. (in Russian)

Egorova L N. The genus *Ramularia* Unger and its allies from the Far East. Mykologiya i Fitopatologiya, 1992, 26: 177-182. (in Russian)

Egorova L N. The genus *Alternaria* and allied hyphomycetes from the Russan Far East. Mykologiya i Fitopatologiya, 1999, 33: 13-18. (in Russian)

Egorova L N. Soil ascomycetes from the Russian Far East. Mykologiya i Fitopatologiya, 2003, 37: 13-21. (in Russian)

Egorova L N. Zygomycetes, Hyphomycetes, Coelomycetes, soil ascomycetes. 2006, 139-141, 216-234. In Vasilyeva L N & Besdeleva T A. (eds.) Flora, vegetation and mycobiota of the reserve "Ussuriysky". Dalnauka. Vladivostok. (in Russian)

Egorova L N. Micromycetes-contaminants of cereals grains in the Primorsky Region. Advances in Medical Mycology, 2007a, 9: 83-85. (in Russian)

Egorova L N. Anamorphic fungi from the Big Khekhtsir Nature Reserve (Khabarovsk Region). Mykologiya i Fitopatologiya, 2007b, 41: 120-125. (in Russian)

Egorova L N. Micromycetes as causal agents of plants leaf spot diseases in Bastak Nature Reserve. 2007c, 44-46. In Kalinin A Ju. (ed.) Materials of the Scientific-practical Conference, devoted to the 10-th anniversary of Bastak Nature Reserve. Reserve "Bastak". Birobidzan. (in Russian)

Egorova L N, Kalantaevskaya O G. Species composition and distribution of fusaria causing the wheat-ear disease in Primorsky Region. 2000, 224-229. In Chayka A K. (ed.) Selection and seed-growing of agricultural plants as the basis of agriculture development in Far-Eastern Region. Novosibirsk. (in Russian)

Egorova L N, Oksenyuk G I. Species composition of fungi in rice field soils of the Maritime Area. Mykologiya i Fitopatologiya, 1983, 17: 97-102. (in Russian)

Egorova L N, Oksenyuk G I. Causal agents of rice fungal diseases in Primorsky Region. Vladivostok: Far East Branch Russ. Acad. Sci., 1987, 1-38. (in Russian)

Egorova L N, Oksenyuk G I, Blokhina M V. Mycoflora of the rice seeds in Primorsky Region, 1986, 106-125. In Vasilyeva L N. (ed.) Flora and systematics of the cryptogamic plants in the Far East. Far East. Sci. Center. Vladivostok. (in Russian)

Egorova L N, Svishch L G. Mycoflora of rhizosphere and roots of pome fruits in Maritime Area. Mykologiya i Fitopatologiya, 1975, 9: 283-288. (in Russian)

Egorova L N, Zhukovskaya S A. Study on garden soil mycoflora in gardens of the Primorsky Region, 1974: 101-112. In Vassiljeva L N. (ed.) Cryptogamic plants of the Soviet Far East. Far East. Sci. Center. Vladivostok. (in Russian)

Gornostay V I. Far Eastern species of *Helminthosporium* on cereals. Mykologiya i Fitopatologiya, 1971, 5: 76-79. (in Russian)

Martyniyuk T D. Causal agents of corn (Zea mays) fungal leaves diseases in Primorsky Region. Mykologiya i Fitopatologiya, 2003, 37: 80-85. (in Russian)

Melnik V A. Deuteromycetes of the Soviet Far East. I. Fungi of Primorsky Region, 1990, 117-127. In Vasilyeva L N. (ed.) Cryptogamic studies in the Far East. Vladivostok: Far East Branch Russ. Acad. Sci. (in Russian)

Zhukovskaya S A, Egorova L N. Mycoflora of the fruit-tree nursery gardens in Primorsky Region. In Vassiljeva L N & Nazarova M M. (eds.) Lower plants of the Far East. Vladivostok: Far East. Sci. Center, 1976. (in Russian)

Non-lichenized Discomycetes: Leotiomycetidae and Pezizomycetidae

Anna V. BOGACHEVA

Discomycetes in the Ussuri River Valley are characterized by exceptional taxonomic diversity and include 277 species from 99 genera, 20 families and 3 orders (Kullman, 1982; Raitviir, 1991; Bogacheva, 1998). Most of them occur in mixed coniferous-broad-leaved forests and are widely distributed in temperate zone.

The earliest information on discomycetes of the Ussuriysk Nature Reserve could be found in L.N. Vassiljeva's (1960) paper. She has reported 5 species of operculate discomycetes. As a result of M.M. Nazarova's collections of 1961-1963 which were identified by A.G. Raitviir, 31 species were added to the biota of discomycetes in this reserve (Vasilyeva, Nazarova, 1967). Later, V.P. Prokhorov (1993) has found two coprotrophic discomycetes in the same collections, namely *Fimaria coprina* Eckbl. and *F. porcina* Svrček et Kubička. By the end of the 1980s, the 43 species from the order *Pezizales* and 42 species from the order *Leotiales* were known in the reserve (Bunkina, Nazarova, 1978; Kullman, 1982; Raitviir, 1991). The investigations of discomycetes at this territory in the 1990s have provided 58 additional species, namely 27 species from the order *Pezizales* and 31 species from the order *Leotiales* (Bogacheva, 1998).

The Upper Ussuri Station, along with the Ussuriysk Nature Reserve, settles down on the western slopes of the Sikhote-Alin Mountains. At this place, 41 species of discomycetes from 24 genera belonging in 9 families and 2 orders were found (Kullman, 1982; Azbukina et al., 1984; Raitviir, 1991). Fungi are considerably less studied in the Khabarovsk Territory, Jewish Autonomous Region and Amur Region. For example, only sixteen species of discomycetes were revealed in the Big Khekhtsir Nature Reserve.

In this paper there are data on distribution and species composition of discomycetes in the Amur River basin that have not been published earlier. The material was supplemented with collections from the Khabarovsky and Primorsky Territories conducted during the field seasons in July-September in 2003 and 2004. To identify the specimens we used monographic papers on discomycete taxonomy (Rehm, 1896; Teng, 1939; Seaver, 1942, 1951; Dennis, 1960; Moser, 1963; Naumov, 1964; Smitskaya, 1980; Kullman, 1982; Spooner, 1987; Hühtinen, 1989; Raitviir, 1991). Taxonomy construction is provided according to "Ainsworth and Bisby's Dictionary of the fungi" (Kirk et al., 2001).

LEOMYCETIDAE

HELOTIALES

BULGARIACEAE

Bulgaria inquinans (Pers.: Fr.) Fr.

On bark of *Quercus mongolica* Fisch. ex Ledeb., Ussuriysk Nature Reserve, 29 Sept. 1961, Vassiljeva L. N., VLA D-81; Tikhorechnoye, 13 Jul. 2004, Bulakh E. M., VLA D-2505; Ussuriysk: Gornotayozhnoye, 23 Jul. 2002, Bulakh E. M., VLA D-1774; Upper-Ussuri Station, 27 Aug. 1973, Bulakh E. M., VLA D-79.

CUDONIACEAE

Cudonia circinans (Pers.: Fr.) Fr.

On soil in conifer-broad-leaved forest, Ussuriysk Nature Reserve, 4 Sept. 1963, Nazarova M. M., VLA D-180; Upper-Ussuri Station, 29 Aug. 1973, Bulakh E. M., VLA D-192, 27 Jun. 1974, Bulakh E. M., VLA D-177, 12 Aug. 1974, Bulakh E. M., VLA D-176, 7 Sept. 1975, Bulakh E. M., VLA D-199; Hulin: Dongfanghong, 3 Sept. 2003, Bogacheva A. V., VLA D-2640.

Cudonia monticola Mains

On litter in conifer-broad-leaved forest, Ussuriysk: Gornotayozhnoye, 19 Sept. 2001, Vassiljeva L. N., VLA D-1729.

Spathularia flavida Pers.: Fr.

On soil and litter in conifer forest, Big Khekhtsir Nature Reserve, 25 Aug. 1983, Bulakh E. M., VLA D-1388, 7 Sept. 1983, Bulakh E. M., VLA D-1392; Upper-Ussuri Station, 15 Aug. 1974, Bulakh E. M., VLA D-1357; Mishan, 9 Aug. 2004, Bogacheva A. V., VLA D-2631.

Spathularia rufa Swartz.

On soil in conifer-broad-leaved forest, Hulin: 856 State Farm, 2 Sept. 2003, Bogacheva A. V., VLA D-2488; Hulin: Dongfanghong, 3 Sept. 2003, Bogacheva A. V., VLA D-2660.

DERMATEACEAE

Calloria kansensis Ellis et Everh.

On woody debris in conifer-broad-leaved forest, Ussuriysk Nature Reserve, 15 Jul. 1961, Nazarova M. M., VLA D-86.

Calloria neglecta (Lib.) B. Hein

On dying twigs of *Vaccinium uliginosum* L., Ussuriysk Nature Reserve, VLA D-85.

Dermatella pumilionis (Rehm) Sacc.

On conifer woody debris, Big Khekhtsir Nature Reserve, 20 Jul. 2004, Bogacheva A. V., VLA D-2860, 15 Aug. 2004, Bogacheva A. V., VLA D-2859.

Dermea ariaea (Pers.: Fr.) Tul.

On dying twigs of *Sorbaria sorbifolia* (L.) A. Br., Ussuriysk Nature Reserve, VLA D-268.

Dermea cerasi (Pers.: Fr.) Fr.

On dying twigs of *Cerasus maximowiczii* (Rupr.) Kom., Ussuriysk Nature Reserve, VLA D-251.

Dermea crypta Cooke

On twigs of *Rhododendron* sp., Ussuriysk Nature Reserve, VLA D-2274.

Dermea padi (Alb. et Schwein.) Fr.

On woody debris in conifer-broad-leaved forest, Ussuriysk Nature Reserve, VLA D-267.

Dermea prunastri (Pers.) Fr.

On dying twigs of *Prunus ussuriensis* Koval. et Kostina and *Armeniaca mandshurica* (Maxim.) B. Skvortz., Ussuriysk Nature Reserve, 16 Jul. 1956, 10 Jun. 1957, Ablakatova A. A., VLA D-260, VLA D-257; Ussuriysk: Gornotayozhnoye, 21 Jul. 1955, Ablakatova A. A., VLA D-261, 24 Jul. 1957, Ablakatova A. A., VLA D-258.

Leptotrochila cerastiorum (Wallr.) Schüepp.

On fallen leaves of *Cerastium holosteoides* Fries, Ussuriysk Nature Reserve, VLA D-1719.

Leptotrochila ranunculi (Fr.) Schüepp.

On fallen leaves of *Ranunculus* sp., Ussuriysk Nature Reserve, VLA D-278.

Mollisia amenticola (Sacc.) Rehm

On catkins of *Alnus hirsuta* (Spach) Turcz. ex Rupr., Ussuriysk Nature Reserve, VLA D-2589.

Mollisia atrata (Pers.) P. Karst.

On dying twigs of *Rubus* sp., Big Khekhtsir Nature Reserve, 24 Jul. 2004, Bogacheva A. V., VLA D-2863, VLA D-2864.

Mollisia caesia (Fuckel) Sacc.

On woody debris in broad-leaved forest, Big Khekhtsir Nature Reserve, 15 Aug. 2004, Bogacheva A. V., VLA D-2857.

Mollisia caespitica P. Karst.

On woody debris in conifer-broad-leaved forest, Big Khekhtsir Nature Reserve, 29 Jul. 2004, Bogacheva A. V., VLA D-2899.

Mollisia cinerea (Batsch) P. Karst.

On fallen twigs of *Abies* sp., *Acer* sp., *Quercus mongolica* Fisch. ex Ledeb., *Populus* sp., Hulin: Dongfanghong, 3 Sept. 2003, Bogacheva A. V., VLA D-2656; Big Khekhtsir Nature Reserve, 23 Jul. 2004, Bogacheva A. V., VLA D-2800.

Mollisia discolor (Mont.) W. Phillips var. *longispora* Le Gal

On bark of *Alnus hirsuta* (Spach) Turcz. ex Rupr., Big Khekhtsir Nature Reserve, 27 Jul. 2004, Bogacheva A. V., VLA D-2861.

Mollisia encoelioides Rehm

On woody debris in broad-leaved forest, Hulin: Dongfanghong, 3 Sept. 2003, Bogacheva A. V., VLA D-2625.

Mollisia hydrophila P. Karst.

On grass stems, Big Khekhtsir Nature Reserve, 24 Jul. 2004, Bogacheva A. V., VLA D-2795.

Mollisia lilacina Clem.

On woody debris in broad-leaved forest, Raohe, 7 Aug. 2004, Bogacheva A. V., VLA D-2674.

Mollisia minutella (Sacc.) Rehm

On stems of umbelliferous plant, Mishan, 8 Aug. 2004, Bogacheva A. V., VLA D-2700.

Mollisia polygoni (Lasch) Gillet

On stems of umbelliferous plant, Fuyuan, 4 Aug. 2004, Bogacheva A. V., VLA D-2714.

Mollisia pumilionis Rehm

On conifer woody debris in conifer-broad-leaved forest, Big Khekhtsir Nature Reserve, 29 Jul. 2004, Bogacheva A. V., VLA D-1017.

Mollisia trabincola Rehm

On woody debris in broad-leaved forest, Hulin: Wulindong, 4 Sept. 2003, Bogacheva A. V., VLA D-2604.

Niptera hypogaea (Bresad.) Rehm

On stems of umbelliferous plant, Hulin: Dongfanghong, 3 Sept. 2003, Bogacheva A. V., VLA D-2633.

Niptera melanophaea Rehm

On *Carex* sp., Ussuriysk Nature Reserve, VLA D-939.

Niptera melatephra (Lasch) Rehm

On grass stems, Fuyuan, 4 Aug. 2004, Bogacheva A. V., VLA D-2717; Sanjiang Nature Reserve: Dongxing cun, 5 Aug. 2004, Bogacheva A. V., VLA D-2710; Raohe: Shengli State Farm, 6 Aug. 2004, Bogacheva A. V., VLA D-2716; Raohe, 7 Aug. 2004, Bogacheva A. V., VLA D-2715.

Niptera pulla (W. Phillips et Keith) Boud.

On twigs of *Betula mandshurica* (Regel) Nakai, Big Khekhtsir Nature Reserve, 29 Jul.

2004, Bogacheva A. V., VLA D-2822.

Niptera ramincola Rehm

On bark of *Alnus hirsuta* (Spach) Turcz. ex Rupr.; Hulin: Wulindong, 4 Sept. 2003, Bogacheva A. V., VLA D-2638.

Pezicula acericola (Peck) Sacc.

On bark of *Acer ginnala* Maxim., Big Khekhtsir Nature Reserve, 24 Jul. 2004, Bogacheva A. V., VLA D-2794.

Pseudopeziza trifolii (Biv.-Bern.: Fr.) Fuckel

On *Trifolium* sp., Ussuriysk: Gornotayozhnoye, 20 Jul. 1957, Ablakatova A. A., VLA D-1171.

Pyrenopeziza arundinacea (DC.) Boud.

On stems of grasses, Big Khekhtsir Nature Reserve, 24 Jul. 2004, Bogacheva A. V., VLA D-2789, 26 Jul. 2004, Bogacheva A. V., VLA D-2813.

Pyrenopeziza atrata (Pers.) Fuckel

On stems of *Artemisia* sp., Big Khekhtsir Nature Reserve, 24 Jul. 2004, Bogacheva A. V., VLA D-1189.

Pyrenopeziza benesuada (Tul.) Gremmen

On dying twigs of *Betula mandshurica* (Regel) Nakai, Big Khekhtsir Nature Reserve, 20 Jul. 2004, Bogacheva A. V., VLA D-2917, 16 Aug. 2004, Bogacheva A. V., VLA D-2862.

Tapesia culcitella (Cooke et Ellis) Sacc.

On woody debris in broad-leaved forest, Raohe, 7 Aug. 2004, Bogacheva A. V., VLA D-2675.

Tapesia fusca (Pers.) Fuckel

On grass stems, Big Khekhtsir Nature Reserve, 26 Jul. 2004, Bogacheva A. V., VLA D-2782. - On twigs of *Alnus hirsuta* (Spach) Turcz. ex Rupr., Big Khekhtsir Nature Reserve, 27 Jul. 2004, Bogacheva A. V., VLA D-2821. - On twigs of *Acer* sp., Big Khekhtsir Nature Reserve, 23 Jul. 2004, Bogacheva A. V., VLA D-2791.

Tapesia knieffii (Wallr.) J. Kuntze

On grass stems, Big Khekhtsir Nature Reserve, 26 Jul. 2004, Bogacheva A. V., VLA D-1419; Hulin: Dongfanghong, 3 Sept. 2003, Bogacheva A. V., VLA D-2502.

Tapesia lividofusca (Fr.) Rehm

On twigs of *Betula* sp., Raohe, 7 Aug. 2004, Bogacheva A. V., VLA D-2713. - On twigs of *Salix* sp., Big Khekhtsir Nature Reserve, 27 Jul. 2004, Bogacheva A. V., VLA D-2819.

Tapesia mollisioides (Schwein.) Sacc.

On grass stems, Fuyuan, 4 Aug. 2004, Bogacheva A. V., VLA D-2692. - The substrate is unusual for this species.

GEOGLOSSACEAE

Geoglossum alveolatum (E.J. Durand ex Rehm) E.J. Durand

On woody debris in conifer-broad-leaved forest, Ussuriysk Nature Reserve, 20 Sept. 1975, Nazarova M. M., VLA D-1975.

Geoglossum atropurpureum Batsch: Fr.

On sand, Big Khekhtsir Nature Reserve, 27 Jul. 2004, Bogacheva A. V., VLA D-281.

Geoglossum fallax E.J. Durand

On soil and woody debris, Ussuriysk Nature Reserve (Raitviir, 1991).

*Geoglossum glabru*m Pers.

On conifer woody debris, Big Khekhtsir Nature Reserve (Raitviir, 1991).

Geoglossum glutinosum Pers.: Fr.

On soil, Big Khekhtsir Nature Reserve (Raitviir, 1991).

Geoglossum umbratile Sacc.

On litter in broad-leaved forest, Hulin: Dongfanghong, 3 Sept. 2003, Bogacheva A. V., VLA D-2661.

Trichoglossum hirsutum (Pers.: Fr.) Boud.

On woody debris in conifer-broad-leaved forest, Ussuriysk Nature Reserve, 24 Aug. 1975, Nazarova M. M., VLA D-1438.

HELOTIACEAE

Ascocoryne cylichnium (Tul.) Korf

On wood of deciduous trees in conifer-broad-leaved forest, Ussuriysk Nature Reserve, 18 Sept. 1961, Vassiljeva L. N., VLA D-1517; Upper-Ussuri Station, 12 Sept. 1974, Bulakh E. M., VLA D-1571.

Ascocoryne sarcoides (Jacq.) J.W. Groves et D.E. Wilson

On wood of *Tilia amurensis* Rupr., Ussuriysk Nature Reserve, 14 Aug. 1961, Vassiljeva L. N., VLA D-1519; Big Khekhtsir Nature Reserve, 15 Aug. 2004, Bogacheva A. V., VLA D-2834, 17 Aug. 2004, Bogacheva A. V., VLA D- 2544; Hulin: 854 State Farm, 2 Sept. 2003, Bogacheva A. V., VLA D-2498, Dongfanghong, 3 Sept. 2003, Bogacheva A. V., VLA D-2497; Raohe, 7 Aug. 2004, Bogacheva A. V., VLA D-2677.

Ascotremella faginea (Peck) Seaver

On fallen twigs in broad-leaved forest, Hulin: Dongfanghong, 3 Sept. 2003, Bogacheva A. V., VLA D-2600.

Ascotremella turbinata Seaver

On wood of *Fraxinus mandshurica* Rupr., Ussuriysk: Gornotayozhnoye, 13 Aug. 2002, Bogacheva A. V., VLA D-1875.

Belonioscypha miniata Kanouse

On dying herbaceous stems, Ussuriysk: Gornotayozhnoye, 13 Aug. 2002, Bogacheva A. V., VLA D-1819.

Bisporella citrina (Batsch: Fr.) Korf et S.E. Carp.

On wood of deciduous trees in conifer-broad-leaved forest, Ussuriysk Nature Reserve, 25 Aug. 1961, Vassiljeva L. N., VLA D-97; Big Khekhtsir Nature Reserve, 17 Aug. 2004, Bogacheva A. V., VLA D-2520; Hulin: Dongfanghong, 3 Sept. 2003, Bogacheva A. V., VLA D-2663; Hulin: Wulindong, 4 Sept. 2003, Bogacheva A. V., VLA D-2637; Mishan, 9 Aug. 2004, Bogacheva A. V., VLA D-2676.

Bisporella subpallida (Rehm) Dennis

On woody debris in broad-leaved forest, Hulin: Dongfanghong, 3 Sept. 2003, Bogacheva A. V., VLA D-2659.

Bulgariella pulla (Fr.) P. Karst.

On wood in broad-leaved forest, Hulin: Dongfanghong, 3 Sept. 2003, Bogacheva A. V., VLA D-2503; Raohe: Shengli State Farm, 7 Aug. 2004, Bogacheva A. V., VLA D-2694.

Chlorencoelia torta (Schwein.) J.R. Dixon

On wood of deciduous trees in broad-leaved forest, Hulin: Dongfanghong, 3 Sept. 2003, Bogacheva A. V., VLA D- 2504; Hulin: Wulindong, 4 Sept. 2003, Bogacheva A. V., VLA D-2649; Sanjiang Nature Reserve: Dongxing cun, 05 Aug. 2004, Bogacheva A. V., VLA D-2650.

Chlorencoelia versiformis (Pers.) J.R. Dixon

On wood of deciduous trees in conifer-broad-leaved forest, Ussuriysk Nature Reserve, 6 Sept. 1961, Vassiljeva L. N., VLA D-156, 16 Aug. 1968, Nazarova M. M., VLA D-147, 02 Nov. 1975, Nazarova M. M., VLA D-151; Ussuriysk: Gornotayozhnoye, 4 Aug. 2002, Bulakh E. M., VLA D-1830, 13 Aug. 2002, Bogacheva A. V., VLA D-1841; Hulin: 854 State Farm, 2 Sept. 2003, Bogacheva A. V., VLA D-2599; Hulin: Dongfanghong, 3 Sept. 2003, Bogacheva A. V., VLA D-2605.

Chlorociboria aeruginascens (Nyl.) Kanouse ex C.S. Ramamurthi, Korf et L.R. Batra

On bark and twigs of *Betula* sp., Ussuriysk Nature Reserve, 7 Sept. 1962, Nazarova M. M., VLA D-115, 18 Aug. 1963, Nazarova M. M., VLA D-119, 26 Aug. 1975, Nazarova M. M., VLA D-118, 20 Aug. 1994, Bogacheva A. V., VLA D-1730; Hulin: Dongfanghong, 3 Sept. 2003, Bogacheva A. V., VLA D-2658; Hulin: Wulindong, 4 Sept. 2003, Bogacheva A. V., VLA D-2601; Big Khekhtsir Nature Reserve, 23 Jul. 2004, Bogacheva A. V., VLA D-2793, 27 Jul. 2004, Bogacheva A. V., VLA D-2799, 28 Jul. 2004, Bogacheva A. V., VLA D-2824; Raohe, 7 Aug. 2004, Bogacheva A. V., VLA D-2651.

Chlorociboria aeruginosa (Oeder) Seaver ex C.S. Ramamurthi, Korf et L.R. Batra

On bark and twigs of *Chosenia arbutifolia* (Pall.) A. Skvorts., Ussuriysk Nature Reserve, 28 Aug. 1958, Bunkina I. A., VLA D-127, 20 Sept. 1962, Koval E. Z., VLA D- 124; Ussuriysk:

Gornotayozhnoye, 13 Aug. 2002, Bogacheva A. V., VLA D-1881; Upper-Ussuri Station, 16 Aug. 1974, Bulakh E. M., VLA D-1580; Big Khekhtsir Nature Reserve, 17 Aug. 2004, Bogacheva A. V., VLA D-2537; Hulin: Dongfanghong, 3 Sept. 2003, Bogacheva A. V., VLA D-2496; Hulin: Wulindong, 4 Sept. 2003, Bogacheva A. V., VLA D-2646; Raohe: Shengli State Farm, 6 Sept. 2003, Bogacheva A. V., VLA D-2647; Raohe, 07 Aug. 2004, Bogacheva A. V., VLA D-2645.

Cordierites boedijnii W.Y. Zhuang

On wood of *Betula mandshurica* (Regel) Nakai, Ussuriysk: Gornotayozhnoye, 13 Aug. 2002, Bogacheva A. V., VLA D-1849.

Crocicreas coronatum (Bull.) S.E. Carp.

On dying herbaceous stems, Raohe: Shengli State Farm, 6 Aug. 2004, Bogacheva A. V., VLA D-2707. - On stems of *Urtica* sp., Hulin: Dongfanghong, 3 Sept. 2003, Bogacheva A. V., VLA D-2665.

Crocicreas cyathoideum (Bull.) S.E. Carp.

On dying herbaceous stem, Ussuriysk Nature Reserve, 2 Sept. 1975, Nazarova M. M., VLA D-1161.

Crocicreas subhyalinum (Rehm) S.E. Carp.

On fallen leaves of *Ulmus* sp., Raohe, 7 Aug. 2004, Bogacheva A. V., VLA D-2705.

Godronia spiraea (Rehm) Seaver

On dying twigs of *Sorbaria sorbifolia* (L.) A. Br., Ussuriysk Nature Reserve, 11 Jun. 1959, Bunkina I. A., VLA D-303.

Godronia uberiformis Groves

On woody debris in broad-leaved forest, Raohe, 7 Aug. 2004, Bogacheva A. V., VLA D-2719.

Godronia urceolus (Alb. et Schwein.) P. Karst.

On twigs of *Spiraea media* Franz Schmidt and *Sorbaria sorbifolia* (L.) A. Br., Ussuriysk Nature Reserve, 18 Jun. 1958, Bunkina I. A., VLA D-302, 10 Jun. 1959, Bunkina I. A., VLA D-301.

Gorgoniceps aridula (P. Karst.) P. Karst.

On conifer woody debris, Raohe, 7 Aug. 2004, Bogacheva A. V., VLA D-2648.

Hymenoscyphus albidus (Roberge ex Desm.) W. Phillips

On petioles in litter, Hulin: 854 State Farm, 2 Sept. 2003, Bogacheva A. V., VLA D-2613; Big Khekhtsir Nature Reserve, 22 Jul. 2004, Bogacheva A. V., VLA D-2798; Raohe: Shengli State Farm, 6 Aug. 2004, Bogacheva A. V., VLA D-2695; VLA D-2697.

Hymenoscyphus calyculus (Sowerby) W. Phillips

On wood of deciduous trees, dying herbaceous stems, fallen acorns of *Quercus mongolica* Fisch. ex Ledeb., Hulin: 854 State Farm, 2 Sept. 2003, Bogacheva A. V., VLA D-2618; Big Khekhtsir Nature Reserve, 27 Jul. 2004, Bogacheva A. V., VLA D-2855, 16 Aug.

2004, Bogacheva A. V., VLA D-2839.

Hymenoscyphus caudatus (P. Karst.) Dennis

On leaves of deciduous trees in conifer-broad-leaved forest, Ussuriysk Nature Reserve, 6 Aug. 1962, Nazarova M. M., VLA D-546; Hulin: 854 State Farm, 2 Sept. 2003, Bogacheva A. V., VLA D-2611; Hulin: Dongfanghong, 3 Sept. 2003, Bogacheva A. V., VLA D-2508; Hulin: Wulindong, 4 Sept. 2003, Bogacheva A. V., VLA D-2593, VLA D-2612; Big Khekhtsir Nature Reserve, 26 Jul. 2004, Bogacheva A. V., VLA D-2787, 27 Jul. 2004, Bogacheva A. V., VLA D-2814, 16 Aug. 2004, Bogacheva A. V., VLA D-2853. - On leaves of *Lonicera* sp., Mishan, 8 Aug. 2004, Bogacheva A. V., VLA D-2698.

Hymenoscyphus epiphyllus (Pers.) Rehm ex Kauffman.

On dying herbaceous stems, Ussuriysk: Gornotayozhnoye, 13 Aug. 2002, Bogacheva A. V., VLA D-1818. - On leaves of *Salix* sp., Raohe: Shengli State Farm, 6 Aug. 2004, Bogacheva A. V., VLA D-2726. - On fallen leaves of *Corylus* sp., Big Khekhtsir Nature Reserve, 23 Jul. 2004, Bogacheva A. V., VLA D-2803, 16 Aug. 2004, Bogacheva A. V., VLA D-2837, VLA D-2847.

Hymenoscyphus fructigenus (Bull.) Fr.

On fallen acorns of *Quercus mongolica* Fisch. ex Ledeb., Ussuriysk Nature Reserve, 4 Sept. 1968, Nazarova M. M., VLA D-566, 10 Sept. 1968, Nazarova M. M., VLA D-565. - On petioles of *Fraxinus* sp., Hulin: 854 State Farm, 2 Sept. 2003, Bogacheva A. V., VLA D-2620; Big Khekhtsir Nature Reserve, 27 Jul. 2004, Bogacheva A. V., VLA D-2818.

Hymenoscyphus herbarum (Pers.) Dennis

On dying herbaceous stems, Ussuriysk: Gornotayozhnoye, 13 Aug. 2002, Bogacheva A. V., VLA D-1820; Xingkaihu Nature Reserve, 1 Sept. 2003, Bogacheva A. V., VLA D-2615; Hulin: 854 State Farm, 2 Sept. 2003, Bogacheva A. V., VLA D-2608, VLA D-2639; Hulin: Wulindong, 4 Sept. 2003, Bogacheva A. V., VLA D-2481, VLA D-2627, VLA D-2632; Big Khekhtsir Nature Reserve, 26 Jul. 2004, Bogacheva A. V., VLA D-2786; 27 Jul. 2004, Bogacheva A. V., VLA D- 2792, VLA D-2844, 28 Jul. 2004, Bogacheva A. V., VLA D-2852; Raohe: Shengli State Farm, 6 Aug. 2004, Bogacheva A. V., VLA D-2722; Raohe, 7 Aug. 2004, Bogacheva A. V., VLA D-2703; Mishan, 08 Aug. 2004, Bogacheva A. V., VLA D-2709.

Hymenoscyphus imberbis (Bull.) Dennis

On wood and bark of *Betula mandshurica* (Regel) Nakai, Upper-Ussuri Station, 16 Aug. 1975, Bulakh E. M., VLA D-1585.

Hymenoscyphus immutabilis (Fuckel) Dennis

On leaves of *Betula* sp., Raohe, 7 Aug. 2004, Bogacheva A. V., VLA D-2711.

Hymenoscyphus phyllogenon (Rehm) Kuntze

On fallen leaves in conifer-broad-leaved forest, Big Khekhtsir Nature Reserve, 10 Jul. 2004, Bogacheva A. V., VLA D-2769.

Hymenoscyphus pileatus (P. Karst.) Kuntze

On fallen leaves, Big Khekhtsir Nature Reserve, 26 Jul. 2004, Bogacheva A. V., VLA D-2846, 17 Aug. 2004, Bogacheva A. V., VLA D-2559; Hulin: 856 State Farm, 2 Sept. 2003, Bogacheva A. V., VLA D-2487, VLA D-2610; Hulin: Wulindong, 4 Sept. 2003, Bogacheva A. V., VLA D-2595. - On stems in litter, Big Khekhtsir Nature Reserve, 26 Jul. 2004, Bogacheva A. V., VLA D-2816.

Hymenoscyphus repandus (W. Phillips) Dennis

On stems in conifer-broad-leaved forest, Big Khekhtsir Nature Reserve, 23 Jul. 2004, Bogacheva A. V., VLA D-2815.

Hymenoscyphus robustior (P. Karst.) Dennis

On grass stems, Hulin: 854 State Farm, 2 Sept. 2003, Bogacheva A. V., VLA D-2622.

Hymenoscyphus salicellus (Fr.) Dennis

On twigs of *Populus* sp., Mishan, 8 Aug. 2004, Bogacheva A. V., VLA D-2725; Big Khekhtsir Nature Reserve, 24 Jul. 2004, Bogacheva A. V., VLA D-2845, 16 Aug. 2004, Bogacheva A. V., VLA D-2848, VLA D-2841.

Hymenoscyphus scutula (Pers.: Fr.) W. Phillips

On plant debris in conifer-broad-leaved forest, Upper-Ussuri Station, 16 Aug. 1974, Bulakh E. M., VLA D-1586; Xingkaihu Nature Reserve, 1 Sept. 2003, Bogacheva A. V., VLA D-2507, VLA D-2616; Hulin: Dongfanghong, 3 Sept. 2003, Bogacheva A. V., VLA D-2506, VLA D-2617; Hulin: Wulindong, 4 Sept. 2003, Bogacheva A. V., VLA D-2594; Raohe: Shengli State Farm, 6 Sept. 2003, Bogacheva A. V., VLA D-2628; Big Khekhtsir Nature Reserve, 16 Jul. 2004, Bogacheva A. V., VLA D-2840, 26 Jul. 2004, Bogacheva A. V., VLA D-2850, 27 Jul. 2004, Bogacheva A. V., VLA D-2817, 16 Aug. 2004, Bogacheva A. V., VLA D-2851; Fujuan, 4 Aug. 2004, Bogacheva A. V., VLA D-2727; Raohe: Shengli State Farm, 6 Aug. 2004, Bogacheva A. V., VLA D-2696, VLA D-2724; Raohe, 7 Aug. 2004, Bogacheva A. V., VLA D-2702, VLA D-2723, VLA D-2740; Mishan, 8 Aug. 2004, Bogacheva A. V., VLA D-2699.

Hymenoscyphus subferrugineus (Nyl.) Dennis

On twigs of *Sorbaria* sp., Raohe, 7 Aug. 2004, Bogacheva A. V., VLA D-2721.

Ionomidotis fulvotingens (Berk. et M.A. Curtis) E.K. Cash

On wood of *Quercus mongolica* Fisch. ex Ledeb., Ussuriysk: Gornotayozhnoye, 13 Aug. 2002, Bogacheva A. V., VLA D-1884.

Midotis irregularis (Cooke) Sacc.

On wood of deciduous trees in conifer-broad-leaved forest, Ussuriysk Nature Reserve, 10 Sept. 1962, Nazarova M. M., VLA D-810.

Ombrophila violacea (Hedw.) Fr.

On wood of deciduous trees in conifer-broad-leaved forest, Ussuriysk Nature Reserve, 18 Sept. 1961, Vassiljeva L. N., VLA D-950.

Pezizella discreta (P. Karst.) Dennis

On dying herbaceous stems in conifer-broad-leaved forest, Big Khekhtsir Nature Reserve, 27 Jul. 2004, Bogacheva A. V., VLA D-2790.

Tatraea macrospora (Peck) Baral

On woody debris in conifer-broad-leaved forest, Ussuriysk Nature Reserve, 11 Sept. 1961, Vassiljeva L. N., VLA D-1204, 18 Aug. 1963, Nazarova M. M., VLA D-1206.

Tympanis pinastri (Pers.) Tul. et C. Tul.

On twigs of *Abies* sp., Ussuriysk Nature Reserve, 17 Jul. 1957, Koval E. Z, VLA D-1481, 14 Aug. 1958, Bunkina I. A., VLA D-1487; Upper-Ussuri Station, 17 Aug. 1974, Bulakh E. M., VLA D-1589.

HYALOSCYPHACEAE

Albotricha albotestacea (Desm.) Raitv.

On grass stems, Ussuriysk Nature Reserve, Upper-Ussuri Station (Raitviir, 1991).

Albotricha kamtschatica (Raitv.) Raitv.

On stems of *Filipendula* sp., Upper-Ussuri Station (Raitviir, 1991).

Arachnopeziza cornuta (Ellis) Korf

On woody debris, Hulin: Dongfanghong, 3 Sept. 2003, Bogacheva A. V., VLA D-2623. - On fallen stems of *Equisetum* sp., Mishan, 8 Aug. 2004, Bogacheva A. V., VLA D-2680.

Brunnipila cannabina (Rehm) Raitv. et Järv

On fern, Shengli State Farm, 6 Aug. 2004, Bogacheva A. V., VLA D-2670.

(The substrate is unusual for this species). - On stems of *Filipendula* sp., Raohe: Shengli State Farm, 6 Aug. 2004, Bogacheva A. V., VLA D-2681.

Brunnipila clandestina (Bull.) Baral

On twigs of *Spiraea salicifolia* L. and *Rubus* sp., Big Khekhtsir Nature Reserve, 27 Jul. 2004, Bogacheva A. V., VLA D-2856.

Calycellina phalaridis (Lib. ex P. Karst.) Höhn.

On grass stems, Hulin: Dongfanghong, 3 Sept. 2003, Bogacheva A. V., VLA D-2602.

Calycellina punctata (Fr.) Lowen et E.J. Dumont

On fallen leaves of *Betula* sp., Hulin: Dongfanghong, 03 Sept. 2003, Bogacheva A. V., VLA D-2666; Raohe, 7 Aug. 2004, Bogacheva A. V., VLA D-2720. - On fallen leaves of *Quercus mongolica* Fisch. ex Ledeb., Hulin: Dongfanghong, 3 Sept. 2003, Bogacheva A. V., VLA D-2636 - On dying stems, Hulin: Wulindong, 4 Sept. 2003, Bogacheva A. V., VLA D-2672. (The substrate is unusual for this species).

Calycellina viridiflavescens (Rehm) Raitv.

On fallen twigs of *Salix* sp., Big Khekhtsir Nature Reserve, 22 Jul. 2004, Bogacheva A. V., VLA D-2788.

Ciliolarina neglecta Huhtinen

On cones of *Pinus korajensis* Ziebold et Zucc., Big Khekhtsir Nature Reserve (Raitviir, 1991).

Cistella orientalis Raitv.

On stem debris, Hulin: Dongfanghong, 3 Sept. 2003, Bogacheva A. V., VLA D-2480.

Clavidisculum caricis Raitv.

On dying stems of *Equisetum* sp., Big Khekhtsir Nature Reserve, 26 Jul. 2004, Bogacheva A. V., VLA D-2898. - The substrate is unusual for this species.

Dasyscyphus pudibundus (Quél.) Sacc.

On woody debris (*Quercus mongolica* Fisch. ex Ledeb., *Betula mandshurica* (Regel) Nakai, *Picea* sp.) , Big Khekhtsir Nature Reserve, 23 Jul. 2004, Bogacheva A. V., VLA D-2904.

Hamatocanthoscypha uncipila (Le Gal) Huhtinen

On twigs of *Betula* sp., Raohe, 7 Aug. 2004, Bogacheva A. V., VLA D-2712.

Hyalopeziza ciliata Fuckel

On fallen leaves of *Tilia amurensis* Rupr. and *Acer* sp., Big Khekhtsir Nature Reserve (Raitviir, 1991).

Hyaloscypha albohyalina (P. Karst.) Boud. var. *albohyalina*

On woody debris, Big Khekhtsir Nature Reserve (Raitviir, 1991).

Incrucipulum ciliare (Schrad.: Fr.) Baral

On fallen leaves of *Quercus mongolica* Fisch. ex Ledeb., Big Khekhtsir Nature Reserve, 27 Jul. 2004, Bogacheva A. V., VLA D-2913, 29 Jul. 2004, Bogacheva A. V., VLA D-2895; Fuyuan, 4 Aug. 2004, Bogacheva A. V., VLA D-2684; Raohe: Shengli State Farm, 6 Aug. 2004, Bogacheva A. V., VLA D-2701. - On grass stems, Sanjiang Nature Reserve: Dongxing cun, 5 Aug. 2004, Bogacheva A. V. VLA D-2669. (The substrate is unusual for this species).

Incrucipulum sinegoricum (Raitv.) Raitv.

On dying stems, Big Khekhtsir Nature Reserve, 27 Jul. 2004, Bogacheva A. V., VLA D-2858; Fuyuan, 4 Aug. 2004, Bogacheva A. V., VLA D-2690.

Lachnellula calyciformis (Willd.: Fr.) Dharne

On wood of *Abies* sp., Ussuriysk Nature Reserve, 23 Jul. 1959, Koval E. Z., VLA D-597; Big Khekhtsir Nature Reserve, 24 Jul. 2004, Bogacheva A. V., VLA D-2896. - On twigs of *Larix* sp., Fuyuan, 4 Aug. 2004, Bogacheva A. V., VLA D-2693.

Lachnellula ciliata (Hahn) Dennis

On fallen leaves of *Quercus mongolica* Fisch. ex Ledeb., Ussuriysk Nature Reserve, 8 Aug. 1961, Nazarova M. M., VLA D-215.

Lachnellula fuckelii (Bres. ex Rehm) Dharne

On wood of *Larix gmelinii* (Rupr.) Rupr., Ussuriysk Nature Reserve (Raitviir, 1991).

Lachnellula minuscula Raitv.

On wood of *Abies* sp., Upper-Ussuri Station, 31 Jul. 1974, Bulakh E. M., VLA D-1572; Ussuriysk Nature Reserve (Raitviir, 1991).

Lachnum abnorme (Mont.) J.H. Haines et Dumont

On bark and wood of deciduous trees, Hulin: Dongfanghong, 3 Sept. 2003, Bogacheva A. V., VLA D-2596; Fuyuan, 4 Aug. 2004, Bogacheva A. V., VLA D-2682. - On bark of *Betula mandshurica* (Regel) Nakai, Big Khekhtsir Nature Reserve, 24 Jul. 2004, Bogacheva A. V., VLA D-2900, VLA D-2903. - On bark of *Acer* sp., Big Khekhtsir Nature Reserve, 23 Jul. 2004, Bogacheva A. V., VLA D-2902. - On bark of *Pinus koraiensis* Siebold et Zucc., Big Khekhtsir Nature Reserve, 23 Jul. 2004, Bogacheva A. V., VLA D-2910.

Lachnum alnifolium (Raitv.) Raitv.

On fallen leaves of *Carpinus cordata* Blume, Ussuriysk Nature Reserve, 26 Jun. 2005, Bogacheva A. V., VLA D-2865.

Lachnum barbatum (Kunze) J. Schröt.

On twigs of *Lonicera* sp., Raohe: Shengli State Farm, 6 Sept. 2003, Bogacheva A. V., VLA D-2603.

Lachnum bicolor (Bull.: Fr.) P. Karst.

On wood in conifer-broad-leaved forest, Big Khekhtsir Nature Reserve, 23 Jul. 2004, Bogacheva A. V., VLA D-2921, 26 Jul. 2004, Bogacheva A. V., VLA D-2802, 27 Jul. 2004, Bogacheva A. V., VLA D-2870.

Lachnum bicolor var. *rubi* Bres.

On leaves of *Carex* sp., Raohe: Shengli State Farm, 6 Aug. 2004, Bogacheva A. V., VLA D-2671. (The substrate is unusual for this species.) - On stems of *Rubus* sp., Big Khekhtsir Nature Reserve, 24 Jul. 2004, Bogacheva A. V., VLA D-2911.

Lachnum carneolum (Sacc.) Rehm

On grass stems, Big Khekhtsir Nature Reserve, 24 Jul. 2004, Bogacheva A. V., VLA D-2783; Fuyuan, 4 Aug. 2004, Bogacheva A. V., VLA D-2683.

Lachnum cerinum (Pers.) Nannf.

On twigs of *Rubus sachalinensis* Lévl., and *Pinus sylvestris* L., Ussuriysk Nature Reserve (Raitviir, 1991).

Lachnum clandestinum (Bull.: Fr.) P. Karst.

On twigs of *Lonicera* sp., Big Khekhtsir Nature Reserve, 22 Jul. 2004, Bogacheva A. V., VLA D-2856.

Lachnum clavigerum (Svrček) Raitv.

On stems of *Polygonum* sp., *Chamerion* sp., *Ledum palustre* L., *Vaccinium uliginosum* L., *Aruncus* sp., *Rubus* sp., *Senecio* sp., Ussuriysk Nature Reserve, VLA D-2319; Big Khekhtsir Nature Reserve, 24 Jul. 2004, Bogacheva A. V., VLA D-2291; Upper-Ussuri Station, VLA D-2295.

Lachnum eleuterococcii Raitv.

On *Eleutherococcus senticosus* (Rupr. et Maxim.) Maxim., Upper-Ussuri Station, VLA D-2373. - On twigs of *Lespedeza* sp., Raohe: Shengli State Farm, 6 Sept. 2003, Bogacheva A. V., VLA D-2662.

Lachnum fuscescens (Fr.) P. Karst.

On fallen leaves of *Carpinus cordata* Blume, Ussuriysk Nature Reserve, 10 Jun. 1969, Nazarova M. M., VLA D-211.

Lachnum imbecille P. Karst.

On *Carex* sp., Big Khekhtsir Nature Reserve, 26 Jul. 2004, Bogacheva A. V., VLA D-2854; Raohe, 7 Aug. 2004, Bogacheva A. V., VLA D-2708.

Lachnum macroparaphysatum Raitv.

On fallen leaves of *Acer pseudosieboldianum* (Pax) Kom., *Carpinus cordata* Blume and dying stems of unknown plant, Upper-Ussuri Station, VLA D-744; Big Khekhtsir Nature Reserve, 26 Jul. 2004, Bogacheva A. V. VLA D-2258.

Lachnum marginatum (Cooke) Raitv.

On fallen leaves of *Quercus mongolica* Fisch. ex Ledeb., Ussuriysk Nature Reserve, 20 Jun. 2005, Bogacheva A. V., VLA D-2866.

Lachnum mollissimum P. Karst.

On dying stem of *Urtica* sp., Ussuriysk Nature Reserve, 20 Jun. 2005, Bogacheva A. V., VLA D-743.

Lachnum palearum (Desm.) Raitv.

On grass stems, Big Khekhtsir Nature Reserve, 24 Jul. 2004, Bogacheva A. V., VLA D-2795, VLA D-2796, VLA D-2806, 27 Jul. 2004, Bogacheva A. V., VLA D-2907.

Lachnum papyraceum (P. Karst.) P. Karst.

On twigs of *Betula mandshurica* (Regel) Nakai, Big Khekhtsir Nature Reserve, 29 Jul. 2004, Bogacheva A. V., VLA D-2914.

Lachnum perplexum (Boud.) Korf

On plant debris in broad-leaved forest, Fuyuan, 4 Aug. 2004, Bogacheva A. V. VLA D-2685.

Lachnum pseudocannabinum (Raitv.) Raitv.

On stems of *Filipendula* sp., Raohe: Shengli State Farm, 6 Aug. 2004, Bogacheva A. V., VLA D-2704.

Lachnum pudicelloides (Raitv.) Raitv.

On leaves of a grass, Big Khekhtsir Nature Reserve, 24 Jul. 2004, Bogacheva A. V., VLA D-2897.

Lachnum pygmaeum (Fr.) Bres.

On stems of *Rubus* sp., Big Khekhtsir Nature Reserve, 24 Jul. 2004, Bogacheva A. V., VLA D-2915.

Lachnum rhytismatis (W. Phillips) Nannf.

On fallen leaves of *Quercus mongolica* Fisch. ex Ledeb., Xingkaihu Nature Reserve, 1 Sept., Bogacheva A. V., VLA D-2621.

Lachnum rhodoleucum (Sacc.) Rehm

On stems and leaves of grasses, Big Khekhtsir Nature Reserve, 24 Jul. 2004, Bogacheva A. V., VLA D-2909, VLA D-2918, 26 Jul. 2004, Bogacheva A. V., VLA D-2813; Fuyuan, 4 Aug. 2004, Bogacheva A. V., VLA D-2692.

Lachnum salicariae (Rehm) Raitv.

On dying stems, Ussuriysk: Gornotayozhnoye, 13 Aug. 2002, Bogacheva A. V., VLA D-1817; Ussuriysk Nature Reserve, 20 Jun. 2005, Bogacheva A. V., VLA D-2867; Raohe, 7 Aug. 2004, Bogacheva A. V., VLA D-2706.

Lachnum soppitii (Massee) Raitv.

On fallen leaves of *Quercus mongolica* Fisch. ex Ledeb., Hulin: Dongfanghong, 3 Sept. 2003, Bogacheva A. V., VLA D-2629.

Lachnum tenuissimum (Quél.) Raitv.

On grass stems, Hulin: 854 State Farm, 2 Sept. 2003, Bogacheva A. V., VLA D-2614, VLA D-2668; Sanjiang Nature Reserve: Dongxing cun, 5 Aug. 2004, Bogacheva A. V., VLA D-2686; Big Khekhtsir Nature Reserve, 27 Jul. 2004, Bogacheva A. V., VLA D-2907, VLA D-2912.

Lachnum virgineum (Batsch.: Fr.) P. Karst.

On stems of *Artemisia* sp., Fuyuan, 4 Aug. 2004, Bogacheva A. V., VLA D-2687 - On twigs *Lonicera* sp., Raohe, 7 Aug. 2004, Bogacheva A. V., VLA D-2688. - On twigs of *Sorbaria* sp., Raohe, 7 Aug. 2004, Bogacheva A. V., VLA D-2689. - On twigs of *Rubus* sp., Big Khekhtsir Nature Reserve, 24 Jul. 2004, Bogacheva A. V., VLA D-2864, VLA D-2919. - On wood of *Betula mandshurica* (Regel) Nakai, Big Khekhtsir Nature Reserve, 30 Jul. 2004, Bogacheva A. V., VLA D-2901. - On twigs of *Salix* sp., Big Khekhtsir Nature Reserve, 26 Jul. 2004, Bogacheva A. V., VLA D-2906, 27 Jul. 2004, Bogacheva A. V., VLA D-2905, VLA D-2916.

Lasiobelonium belanense (Svrček) Raitv.

On bark of *Salix* sp., Big Khekhtsir Nature Reserve, 26 Jul. 2004, Bogacheva A. V., VLA D-1550.

Lasiobelonium boreale (Ellis et Holw.) Raitv.

On bark and wood of *Salix* sp., Big Khekhtsir Nature Reserve, 26 Jul. 2004, Bogacheva A. V., VLA D-2389.

Lasiobelonium diervillae Raitv.

On twigs of *Lonicera* sp., Sanjiang Nature Reserve: Dongxing cun, 5 Aug. 2004, Bogacheva A. V., VLA D-2678. - On twigs of *Aralia elata* (Miq.) Seem., Fuyuan, 04 Aug. 2004, Bogacheva A. V., VLA D-2679.

Mollisina uncinata Arendh. et R. Sharma

On fallen leaves of *Quercus mongolica* Fisch. ex Ledeb., Big Khekhtsir Nature Reserve, 26 Jul. 2004, Bogacheva A. V., VLA D-914; Sanjiang Nature Reserve: Dongxing cun, 5 Aug. 2004, Bogacheva A. V., VLA D-2691; Ussuriysk Nature Reserve, 20 Jun. 2005, Bogacheva A. V. VLA D-915.

Perrotia flammea (Alb. et Schwein.: Fr.) Boud.

On twigs of *Lonicera* sp., Xingkaihu Nature Reserve, 1 Sept. 2003, Bogacheva A. V., VLA D-2489.

Phialina lachnobrachya (Desm.) Raitv.

On fallen leaves of *Quercus mongolica* Fisch. ex Ledeb., *Acer* sp., *Tilia amurensis* Rupr., *Betula mandshurica* (Regel) Nakai, *Salix* sp., Big Khekhtsir Nature Reserve (Raitviir, 1991).

Psilachnum inquilinum (P. Karst.) Dennis

On dying roots of *Equisetum* sp., Ussuriysk Nature Reserve, 26 Sept. 1961, Vassiljeva L. N., VLA D-1184.

Rodwayella citrinula (P. Karst.) Spooner et Dennis

On wood of *Alnus hirsuta* (Spach) Turcz. ex Rupr., Ussuriysk Nature Reserve, 7 Sept. 1958, Bunkina I. A., VLA D-505, 16 Aug. 1962, Nazarova M. M., VLA D-510, 30 Aug. 1962, Nazarova M. M., VLA D-512, 20 Sept. 1962, Nazarova M. M., VLA D-502.

Setoscypha lachnobrachyoidea (Raitv.) Raitv.

On fallen leaves of *Quercus mongolica* Fisch. ex Ledeb., *Acer* sp., *Tilia amurensis* Rupr., Ussuriysk Nature Reserve (Raitviir, 1991).

Setoscypha spiraeaicola (Raitv.) Raitv.

On fallen leaves of *Spiraea salicifolia* L., Big Khekhtsir Nature Reserve (Raitviir, 1991).

Solenopezia solenia (Peck) Sacc.

On dying stems, Upper-Ussuri Station (Raitviir, 1991).

Trichopeziza vermispora (Raitv.) Raitv.

On dying stems of *Pteridium* sp., Upper-Ussuri Station, VLA D-2391.

LEOTIACEAE

Leotia lubrica (Scop.) Pers.: Fr.

On soil in conifer forest, Ussuriysk Nature Reserve, 12 Aug. 1962, Nazarova M. M., VLA D-783, 4 Sept. 1963, Nazarova M. M., VLA D-785, 24 Aug. 1975, Nazarova M. M., VLA D-781; Ussuriysk: Gornotayozhnoye, 13 Aug. 2002, Bogacheva A. V., VLA D-1811; Upper-Ussuri Station, 17 Sept. 1974, Bulakh E. M., VLA D-787, VLA D-1677, 20 Aug. 1975, Bulakh E. M., VLA D-1676; Big Khekhtsir Nature Reserve, 3 Aug. 1981, Bulakh E. M., VLA D-784, 17 Aug. 2004, Bogacheva A. V., VLA D-2516; Hulin: Dongfanghong, 3 Sept. 2003, Bogacheva A. V., VLA D-2598; Hulin: Wulindong, 4 Sept. 2003, Bogacheva A. V., VLA

D-2635; Raohe: Shengli State Farm, 6 Sept. 2003, Bogacheva A. V., VLA D-2630.

Leotia marcida Pers.

On litter in conifer-broad-leaved forest, Upper-Ussuri Station, VLA D-1919; Big Khekhtsir Nature Reserve, 3 Aug. 2004, Bogacheva A. V., VLA D-1938.

ORBILIACEAE

Orbilia auricolor (A. Bloxam ex Berk.) Sacc.

On woody debris, Ussuriysk Nature Reserve; Hulin: 856 State Farm, 2 Sept. 2003, Bogacheva A. V., VLA D-2499, Dongfanghong, 3 Sept. 2003, Bogacheva A. V., VLA D-2500; Big Khekhtsir Nature Reserve, 15 Aug. 2004, Bogacheva A. V., VLA D-2830.

Orbilia cardui Velen.

On dying stems in conifer-broad-leaved forest, Upper-Ussuri Station, VLA D-973.

Orbilia delicatula (P. Karst.) P. Karst.

On woody debris in broad-leaved forest, Hulin: Dongfanghong, 3 Sept. 2003, Bogacheva A. V., VLA D-2655; Big Khekhtsir Nature Reserve, 22 Jul. 2004, Bogacheva A. V., VLA D-2809, 24 Jul. 2004, Bogacheva A. V., VLA D-2833, 15 Aug. 2004, Bogacheva A. V., VLA D-2831, 17 Aug. 2004, Bogacheva A. V., VLA D-2554.

Orbilia epipora (Nyl.) P. Karst.

On wood of *Quercus mongolica* Fisch. ex Ledeb. and *Betula* sp., Ussuriysk: Gornotayozhnoye, 13 Aug. 2002, Bogacheva A. V., VLA D-1890; Hulin: Dongfanghong, 3 Sept. 2003, Bogacheva A. V., VLA D-2667; Fuyuan, 4 Aug. 2004, Bogacheva A. V., VLA D-2673.

Orbilia microclava Velen.

On woody debris in conifer-broad-leaved forest, Big Khekhtsir Nature Reserve, 24 Jul. 2004, Bogacheva A. V., VLA D-2808.

Orbilia sarraziniana Boud.

On woody debris in broad-leaved forest, Big Khekhtsir Nature Reserve, 24 Jul. 2004, Bogacheva A. V., VLA D-2832, 17 Aug. 2004, Bogacheva A. V., VLA D-2491; Hulin: Dongfanghong, 3 Sept. 2003, Bogacheva A. V., VLA D-2597; Hulin: Wulindong, 4 Sept. 2003, Bogacheva A. V., VLA D-2644; Sanjiang Nature Reserve: Dongxing cun, 5 Aug. 2004, Bogacheva A. V., VLA D-2643.

RUTSTROEMIACEAE

Rutstroemia bolaris (Batsch: Fr.) Rehm

On woody debris in conifer-broad-leaved forest, Hulin: Dongfanghong, 3 Sept. 2003, Bogacheva A. V., VLA D-2642; Hulin: Wulindong, 4 Sept. 2003, Bogacheva A. V., VLA

D-2653; Sanjiang Nature Reserve: Dongxing cun, 5 Aug. 2004, Bogacheva A. V., VLA D-2652.

Rutstroemia conformata (P. Karst.) Nannf

On wood and leaves of *Betula mandshurica* (Regel) Nakai, Ussuriysk: Gornotayozhnoye, 30 Jul. 2001, Sazanova N. N., VLA D-1949; Big Khekhtsir Nature Reserve, 26 Jul. 2004, Bogacheva A. V., VLA D-2842, 15 Aug. 2004, Bogacheva A. V., VLA D-2843.

Rutstroemia juglandis Raitv.

On petioles of *Juglans mandshurica* Maxim., Ussuriysk Nature Reserve, 25 Aug. 1961, Nazarova M. M., VLA D-1218, 30 Aug. 1962, Nazarova M. M., VLA D-1216, 08 Sept. 1975, Nazarova M. M., VLA D-1220.

Rutstroemia petiolorum (Roberge ex Desm.) W.L. White

On petioles of *Fraxinus mandshurica* Rupr., Ussuriysk Nature Reserve, 24 Aug. 1961, Nazarova M. M., VLA D-1203. - On petioles of *Juglans mandshurica* Maxim., Ussuriysk Nature Reserve, 18 Aug. 1961, Vassiljeva L. N., VLA D-1198.

SCLEROTINIACEAE

Ciborinia foliicola (Cash et Davidson) Whetzel

On fallen leaves of *Salix* sp., Raohe, 7 Aug. 2004, Bogacheva A. V., VLA D-2654.

Sclerotinia sclerotiorum (Lib.) de Bary

On acorns of *Quercus mongolica* Fisch. ex Ledeb., Big Khekhtsir Nature Reserve, 17 Aug. 2004, Bogacheva A. V., VLA D-2571.

Incertae sedis

Microglossum olivaceum (Pers.: Fr.) Gillet

On woody debris in conifer-broad-leaved forest, Big Khekhtsir Nature Reserve, 27 Jul. 2004, Bogacheva A. V., VLA D-2036; Ussuriysk Nature Reserve, VLA D-1583.

Microglossum rufum (Schwein.) Underw.

On woody debris and soil in conifer-broad-leaved forest, Ussuriysk Nature Reserve, 24 Aug. 1975, Nazarova M. M., VLA D-803; Big Khekhtsir Nature Reserve, 25 Aug. 1975, Bulakh E. M. VLA D-801, 15 Sept. 1981, Bulakh E. M., VLA D-804, 10 Jul. 2004, Bogacheva A. V., VLA D-2772.

Microglossum viride (Fr.) Gillet

On soil in conifer-broad-leaved forest, Ussuriysk Nature Reserve, VLA D-799.

PEZIZOMYCETIDAE

PEZIZALES

ASCOBOLACEAE

Ascobolus stercorarius (Bull.) J. Schröt.

On dung of a wild goat, Upper-Ussuri Station, VLA D-18.

DISCINACEAE

Discina ancilis (Pers.) Sacc.

On woody debris and soil in conifer-broad-leaved forest, Ussuriysk Nature Reserve, 26 Apr. 1946, Vassiljeva L. N., VLA D-270, 24 May 1962, Vassiljeva L. N., VLA D-271.

Discina caroliniana (Bosc) Eckblad

On soil in conifer-broad-leaved forest, Ussuriysk Nature Reserve, 18 May 2004, Barkalov V. Yu., VLA D-2483.

Discina venosa (Pers.) Fr.

On soil in conifer-broad-leaved forest, Ussuriysk Nature Reserve, VLA D-269.

Gyromitra ambigua (P. Karst.) Harmaja

On soil and woody debris in conifer forest, Upper-Ussuri Station, 2 Jul. 1974, Bulakh E. M., VLA D-331.

Gyromitra esculenta (Pers.: Fr.) Fr.

On litter in broad-leaved forest, Ussuriysk Nature Reserve, 13 May 2004, Barkalov V. Yu., VLA D-2533.

Gyromitra gigas (Krombh.) Cooke

On conifer woody debris, Upper-Ussuri Station, 20 Jun. 1974, Bulakh E. M., VLA D-327.

Gyromitra infula (Schaeff.) Quél.

On conifer woody debris, Ussuriysk Nature Reserve, Aug. 1968, Nazarova M. M., VLA D- 319; Upper-Ussuri Station, 11 Jun. 1975, Bulakh E. M., VLA D-322.

Neogyromitra ussuriensis (Lj.N. Vassiljeva) Raitv.

On conifer woody debris, Ussuriysk Nature Reserve, 2 Jun. 1961, Nazarova M. M., VLA D-932, May 1974, Nazarova M. M., VLA D-931.

Pseudorhizina sphaerospora (Peck) Pouzar

On woody debris in conifer-broad-leaved forest, Ussuriysk Nature Reserve, 1 Jun. 1961, Nazarova M. M., VLA D-1180, 24 May 1962, Vassiljeva L. N., VLA D-1183.

HELVELLACEAE

Helvella acetabulum (L.) Quél.

On soil in broad-leaved forest, Ussuriysk Nature Reserve, VLA D-2049.

Helvella atra J. König

On soil in broad-leaved forest, Big Khekhtsir Nature Reserve, 29 Jun. 1981, Bulakh E. M., VLA D-440; Ussuriysk: Gornotayozhnoye, 4 Aug. 2002, Bulakh E. M., VLA D-1797; Tikhorechnoye, 30 Jun. 1983, Bulakh E. M., VLA D-443; Big Khekhtsir Nature Reserve, 19 Jul. 2004, Bogacheva A. V., VLA D-2869; Raohe: Shengli State Farm, 6 Sept. 2003, Bogacheva A. V., VLA D-2731.

Helvella chinensis (Velen.) Nannf. et L. Holm

On soil in conifer-broad-leaved forest, Hulin: Dongfanghong, 3 Sept. 2003, Bogacheva A. V., VLA D-2781; Big Khekhtsir Nature Reserve, 24 Jul. 2004, Bogacheva A. V., VLA D-2780.

Helvella corium (O. Weberb.) Massee

On soil in conifer-broad-leaved forest, Ussuriysk Nature Reserve, VLA D-2546.

Helvella crispa (Scop.) Fr.

On soil in conifer-broad-leaved forest, Ussuriysk Nature Reserve, 25 Aug. 1962, Nazarova M. M., VLA D-341, 29 Aug. 2002, Barkalov V. Yu., VLA D-1782; Khanka Nature Reserve, 26 Jul. 2002, Barkalov V. Yu., VLA D-1843, 30 Aug. 2002, Bulakh E. M., VLA D-2047; Ussuriysk: Gornotayozhnoye, 3 Aug. 2002, Bulakh E. M., VLA D-1796, 13 Aug. 2002, Bogacheva A. V., VLA D-1893; Upper-Ussuri Station, 10 Sept. 1975, Bulakh E. M., VLA D-344; Big Khekhtsir Nature Reserve, 13 Aug. 1981, Bulakh E. M., VLA D-356.

Helvella elastica Bull.

On soil and woody debris in conifer-broad-leaved forest, Ussuriysk Nature Reserve, 8 Sept. 1957, Vassiljeva L. N., VLA D-380, 8 Aug. 1959, Bunkina I. A., VLA D-393, 25 Aug. 1962, Nazarova M. M., VLA D-373; Upper-Ussuri Station, 18 Sept. 1974, Bulakh E. M., VLA D-375; Khanka Nature Reserve, 28 Aug. 2002, Bulakh E. M., VLA D-1840; Ussuriysk: Gornotayozhnoye, 13 Aug. 2002, Bogacheva A. V., VLA D-1806; Hulin, 3 Aug. 2003, Bogacheva A. V., VLA D-2753; Raohe: Shengli State Farm, 6 Sept. 2003, Bogacheva A. V., VLA D-2735; Raohe, 7 Aug. 2004, Bogacheva A. V., VLA D-2757; Big Khekhtsir Nature Reserve, 17 Aug. 2004, Bogacheva A. V., VLA D-2566, 15 Aug. 2004, Bogacheva A. V., VLA D-2871.

Helvella ephippium Lév.

On soil in conifer-broad-leaved forest, Ussuriysk Nature Reserve, 24 Aug. 1963, Nazarova M. M., VLA D-433, 12 Sept. 1963, Nazarova M. M., VLA D-435.

Helvella exarata Gillet

On soil in conifer-broad-leaved forest, Ussuriysk Nature Reserve, 21 Aug. 1961,

Vassiljeva L. N., VLA D-431.

Helvella lacunosa Afzel.

On soil in conifer-broad-leaved forest, Ussuriysk Nature Reserve, 12 Sept. 1963, Nazarova M. M., VLA D-426, 18 Aug. 1975, Nazarova M. M., VLA D-427; Tikhorechnoye, 21 Jul. 1998, Bulakh E. M., VLA D-2042; Big Khekhtsir Nature Reserve, 23 Jul. 2004, Bogacheva A. V., VLA D-2872. - On wood of *Quercus mongolica* Fisch. ex Ledeb., Ussuriysk: Gornotayozhnoye, 13 Aug. 2002, Bogacheva A. V., VLA D-1888.

Helvella macropus (Pers.) P. Karst.

On soil in broad-leaved forest, Ussuriysk: Gornotayozhnoye, 13 Aug. 2002, Bogacheva A. V., VLA D-1810; Upper-Ussuri Station, 19 Aug. 1974, Bulakh E. M., VLA D-1614, 22 Aug. 1975, Bulakh E. M., VLA D-404.

Helvella villosa Schaeff.

On soil in conifer-broad-leaved forest, Ussuriysk Nature Reserve, 2 Sept. 1975, Nazarova M. M., VLA D-422.

Midotis irregularis (Cooke) Sacc.

On wood of deciduous trees in conifer-broad-leaved forest, Ussuriysk Nature Reserve, VLA D-810-812.

KARSTENELLACEAE

Karstenella vernalis Harmaja

On fallen twigs of *Sambucus* sp., Big Khekhtsir Nature Reserve, 27 Jul. 2004, Bogacheva A. V., VLA D-2766

MORCHELLACEAE

Morchella elata Fr.

On litter in broad-leaved forest, Ussuriysk Nature Reserve, VLA D-2076.

Morchella esculenta (L.) Pers.

On soil of meadow, Ussuriysk Nature Reserve, 13 May, Barkalov V. Yu., VLA D-2539; Upper-Ussuri Station, 25 May 2004, Bulakh E. M., VLA D-2509.

Morchella vulgaris (Pers.) Boud.

On soil of conifer-broad-leaved forest, Ussuriysk Nature Reserve, 13 May, 1969, Nazarova M. M., VLA D-921.

Ptychoverpa bohemica (Krombrh.) Boud.

On soil in conifer-broad-leaved forest, Ussuriysk Nature Reserve, 14 May 2004, Barkalov V. Yu., VLA D-2518.

Verpa conica (O. F. Müll.) Sw.

On soil in conifer-broad-leaved forest, Upper-Ussuri Station, 22 Jun. 1974, Bulakh E. M.,

VLA D-1513, 11 Jun. 1975, Bulakh E. M., VLA D-1514; Khanka Nature Reserve, 19 May 2004, Bulakh E. M., VLA D-2581.

PEZIZACEAE

Iodophanus difformis (P. Karst.) Kimbr.

On mosses in conifer-broad-leaved forest, Upper-Ussuri Station, VLA D-2228.

Pachyella babingtonii (Berk. et Broome) Boud.

On wood of *Betula mandshurica* (Regel) Nakai, Ussuriysk Nature Reserve, VLA D-1017.

Peziza ampelina Quél.

On bark of *Tilia* sp., Raohe, 7 Aug. 2004, Bogacheva A. V., VLA D-2758.

Peziza arvernensis Boud.

On burned soil, Upper-Ussuri Station, 23 Jul. 1974, Bulakh E. M., VLA D-1607, 11 Jul. 1975, Bulakh E. M., VLA D-1635; Big Khekhtsir Nature Reserve, 24 Jul. 2004, Bogacheva A. V., VLA D-2763.

Peziza badia Pers.

On soil in conifer-broad-leaved forest, Ussuriysk Nature Reserve, Aug. 1962, Nazarova M. M., VLA D-1038; 29 Aug. 1963, Nazarova M. M., VLA D-1056; Ussuriysk: Gornotayozhnoye, 23 Jul. 2002, Govorova O. K., VLA D-1777; Upper-Ussuri Station, 31 Jul. 1974, Bulakh E. M., VLA D-1039, 17 Sept. 1974, Bulakh E. M., VLA D-1041; Khanka Nature Reserve, 26 Jul. 2002, Barkalov V. Yu., VLA D-1827; Big Khekhtsir Nature Reserve, 22 Jul. 2004, Bogacheva A. V., VLA D-2891, 27 Jul. 2004, Bogacheva A. V., VLA D-2759; Sanjiang Nature Reserve: Dongxing cun Nature Reserve, 5 Aug. 2004, Bogacheva A. V., VLA D-2741; Raohe: Shengli State Farm, 6 Aug. 2004, Bogacheva A. V., VLA D-2756, VLA D-2742.

Peziza badiofusca (Boud.) Dennis

On woody debris in litter of conifer-broad-leaved forest, Ussuriysk: Gornotayozhnoye, 13 Aug. 2002, Bogacheva A. V., VLA D-1874; Hulin: Dongfanghong, 3 Sept. 2003, Bogacheva A. V., VLA D-2607.

Peziza cerea Sowerby

On wood in broad-leaved forest, Ussuriysk Nature Reserve, 20 Jun. 2005, Bogacheva A. V., VLA D-2828.

Peziza depressa Pers.

On sandy soil, Hulin: Dongfanghong, 3 Sept. 2003, Bogacheva A. V., VLA D-2774; Mishan, 9 Aug. 2004, Bogacheva A. V., VLA D-2835.

Peziza domiciliana Cooke

On sandy soil, Big Khekhtsir Nature Reserve, 23 Jul. 2004, Bogacheva A. V., VLA

D-2778; Raohe, 7 Aug. 2004, Bogacheva A. V., VLA D-2749.

Peziza fimeti Seaver

On dung, Big Khekhtsir Nature Reserve, 22 Jul. 2004, Bogacheva A. V., VLA D-2873.

Peziza furfuracea (Rehm) Smitska

On wood of *Betula mandshurica* (Regel) Nakai, Ussuriysk Nature Reserve, VLA D-2463.

Peziza gerardii Cooke

On soil in conifer-broad-leaved forest, Upper-Ussuri Station, 12 Aug. 1974, Bulakh E. M., VLA D-1619.

Peziza granulosa Schumach.

On litter and soil in broad-leaved forest, Raohe: Shengli State Farm, 6 Aug. 2004, Bogacheva A. V., VLA D-2738.

Peziza howsei (Boud.) Donadini

On woody debris in conifer-broad-leaved forest, Ussuriysk Nature Reserve, 21 Aug. 2002, Bulakh E. M., VLA D-1842. - On wood of *Betula davurica* Pall., Big Khekhtsir Nature Reserve, 29 Jul. 2004, Bogacheva A. V., VLA D-2894.

Peziza limnaea Maas Geest.

On sandy soil, Hulin: Dongfanghong, 3 Sept. 2003, Bogacheva A. V., VLA D-2775.

Peziza micropus Pers.

On wood of *Populus* sp., Upper-Ussuri Station, 18 Sept. 1974, Bulakh E. M., VLA D-1616; Tykhorechnoye, 27 Oct. 2004, Barkalov V. Yu., VLA D-2619.

Peziza natrophila A.Z.M. Khan

On burned soil, Big Khekhtsir Nature Reserve, 29 Jul. 2004, Bogacheva A. V., VLA D-2779; Mishan, 8 Aug. 2004, Bogacheva A. V., VLA D-2739.

Peziza nivea R. Hedw.: Fr.

On stems of *Calamagrostis langsdorffii* (Link) Trin. and wood of *Fraxinus mandshurica* Rupr., Ussuriysk Nature Reserve (Raitviir, 1991).

Peziza phyllogena Cooke

On soil in conifer-broad-leaved forest, Upper-Ussuri Station, 12 Aug. 1974, Bulakh E. M., VLA D-1615.

Peziza psammobia Rifai

On soil in broad-leaved forest, Big Khekhtsir Nature Reserve, 22 Jul. 2004, Bogacheva A. V., VLA D-2868.

Peziza repanda P. Karst.

On woody debris and soil in conifer-broad-leaved forest, Ussuriysk Nature Reserve, 16 Aug. 1959, Bunkina I. A., VLA D-1075, 31 May 1961, Nazarova M. M., VLA D-1086; Upper-Ussuri Station, 22 Jun. 1974, Bulakh E. M., VLA D-1081, 6 Aug. 1974, Bulakh E. M., VLA D-1078, 2 Jun. 2003, Bulakh E. M., VLA D-2056; Big Khekhtsir Nature Reserve, 27 Jul.

2004, Bogacheva A. V., VLA D-2890.

Peziza rufescens Saut.

On sandy soil in broad-leaved forest, Ussuriysk Nature Reserve, VLA D-333.

Peziza succosa Berk.

On soil in conifer-broad-leaved forest, Ussuriysk Nature Reserve, 4 Aug. 1962, Nazarova M. M., VLA D-1134, 6 Sept. 1963, Nazarova M. M., VLA D-1135; Ussuriysk: Gornotayozhnoye, 13 Aug. 2002, Bogacheva A. V., VLA D-1887.

Peziza succosella (Le Gal & Romagn.) M.M. Moser ex Aviz.-Hersh. & Nemlich

On soil in broad-leaved forest, Ussuriysk: Gornotayozhnoye, 13 Aug. 2002, Bogacheva A. V., VLA D-1876.

Peziza thozetii Berk.

On wood of *Quercus mongolica* Fisch. ex Ledeb., Ussuriysk: Gornotayozhnoye, 13 Aug. 2002, Bogacheva A. V., VLA D-2034.

Peziza verrucosa (Velen.) Smitska

On burned soil, Ussuriysk Nature Reserve, VLA D-577.

Peziza violacea Pers.

On burned soil and woody debris in conifer-broad-leaved forest, Ussuriysk Nature Reserve, 14 Jul. 1945, Vassiljeva L. N., VLA D-1126.

PYRONEMATACEAE

Aleuria aurantia (Pers.) Fuckel

On soil of conifer-broad-leaved forest, Upper-Ussuri Station, 18 Sept. 1974, Bulakh E. M., VLA D-3.

Aleuria bicucullata Boud.

On sandy soil, Big Khekhtsir Nature Reserve, 15 Aug. 2004, Bogacheva A. V., VLA D-2823.

Aleuria rhenana Fuckel

On soil and litter in conifer-broad-leaved forest, Ussuriysk: Gornotayozhnoye, 4 Sept. 2002, Govorova O. K., VLA D-1781.

Anthracobia macrocystis (Cooke) Boud.

On burned soil, Hulin: Sengly Farm, 6 Aug. 2004, Bogacheva A. V., VLA D- 2732.

Caloscypha fulgens (Pers.) Boud.

On soil in conifer-broad-leaved forest, Ussuriysk Nature Reserve, 2 Jun. 1961, Nazarova M. M., VLA D-90.

Cheilymenia fimicola (De Not. et Bagl.) Dennis

On dung of a cow, Big Khekhtsir Nature Reserve, 15 Aug. 2004, Bogacheva A. V., VLA D-586.

Coprobia granulata (Bull.) Boud.

On rabbit dung, Ussuriysk Nature Reserve, 10 Aug. 1961, Vassiljeva L. N., VLA D-472, 24 Aug. 1975, Nazarova M. M., VLA D-170; Big Khekhtsir Nature Reserve, 24 Jul. 2004, Bogacheva A. V., VLA D-2838, 27 Jul. 2004, Bogacheva A. V., VLA D-2920.

Fimaria cervaria (W. Phillips) Brumm.

On burned soil, Big Khekhtsir Nature Reserve, 24 Jul. 2004, Bogacheva A. V., VLA D-2784.

Fimaria coprina Eckblad

On dung, Ussuriysk Nature Reserve, VLA D-299.

Fimaria porcina Svrček et Kubička

On dung, Ussuriysk Nature Reserve, VLA D-297; Upper-Ussuri Station, VLA D-295.

Flavoscypha cantharella (Fr.) Harmaja

On clay, Hulin: Wulindong, 4 Sept. 2003, Bogacheva A. V., VLA D-2748; Raohe: Shengli State Farm, 6 Sept. 2003, Bogacheva A. V., VLA D-2754; Big Khekhtsir Nature Reserve, 16 Aug. 2004, Bogacheva A. V., VLA D-2893.

Flavoscypha phlebophora (Berk. et Broome) Harmaja

On soil in conifer-broad-leaved forest, Ussuriysk Nature Reserve, VLA D-288; Upper-Ussuri Station, VLA D-334.

Geopora arenosa (Fuckel) S. Ahmad

On sandy soil, Ussuriysk Nature Reserve, VLA D-2022; Upper-Ussuri Station, VLA D-581.

Geopora tenuis (Fuckel) T. Schumach.

On soil in broad-leaved forest, Big Khekhtsir Nature Reserve, 16 Aug. 2004, Bogacheva A. V. VLA D-582.

Geopyxis carbonaria (Alb. et Schwein.) Sacc.

On burned soil, Ussuriysk Nature Reserve, 14 May 1945, Vassiljeva L. N., VLA D-287; 23 Jun. 1974, Bulakh E. M., VLA D-1606.

Humaria hemisphaerica (F.N. Wigg.) Fuckel

On woody debris in conifer-broad-leaved forest, Ussuriysk Nature Reserve, 18 Aug. 1962, Nazarova M. M., VLA D-464, 7 Aug. 1975, Nazarova M. M., VLA D-455; Upper-Ussuri Station, 2 Aug. 1972, Bulakh E. M., VLA D-1636, 12 Sept. 1975, Bulakh E. M., VLA D-453; Ussuriysk: Gornotayozhnoye, 3 Aug. 2002, Bulakh E. M., VLA D-1805, 13 Aug. 2002, Bogacheva A. V., VLA D-1869; Khanka Nature Reserve, 26 Jul. 2002, Barkalov V. Yu., VLA D-1765; Big Khekhtsir Nature Reserve, 3 Aug. 1981, Bulakh E. M., VLA D-454; 22 Jul. 2004, Bogacheva A. V., VLA D-2761; 24 Jul. 2004, Bogacheva A. V., VLA D-2760, 28 Jul. 2004, Bogacheva A. V., VLA D-2825; Hulin: Dongfanghong, 3 Sept. 2003, Bogacheva A. V., VLA D-2776; Hutou, 4 Sept. 2003, Bogacheva A. V., VLA D-2755; Raohe, 7 Aug. 2004, Bogacheva, A. V. VLA D-2743.

Humaria velenovsky (Vasek ex Svrček) Korf et Sagara

On soil in conifer-broad-leaved forest, Big Khekhtsir Nature Reserve, 23 Jul. 2004, Bogacheva A. V., VLA D-2805; Raohe: Shengli State Farm, 6 Aug. 2004, Bogacheva A. V., VLA D-2744.

Jafnea fusicarpa (W.R. Gerard) Korf

On soil in conifer-broad-leaved forest, Big Khekhtsir Nature Reserve, 26 Jul. 2004, Bogacheva A. V., VLA D-2887.

Lamprospora polytrichi (Schumach.) Le Gal

On soil in conifer-broad-leaved forest, Ussuriysk Nature Reserve, VLA D-586.

Lamprospora schroeteri Benkert

On burned soil, Ussuriysk: Gornotayozhnoye, VLA D-583.

Leucoscypha leucotricha (Alb. et Schwein.) Boud.

On soil in conifer-broad-leaved forest, Ussuriysk: Gornotayozhnoye, VLA D-588; Upper-Ussuri Station, VLA D-291.

Melastiza cornubiensis (Berk. et Broome) J. Moravec

On soil in conifer-broad-leaved forest, Ussuriysk: Gornotayozhnoye, VLA D-2038; Upper-Ussuri Station, VLA D-589.

Miladina lecithina (Cooke) Svrček

On woody debris in conifer-broad-leaved forest, Big Khekhtsir Nature Reserve, 23 Jul. 2004, Bogacheva A. V., VLA D-2804.

Neottiella hetieri Boud.

On stems of mosses, Ussuriysk Nature Reserve, 6 Sept. 1975, Nazarova M. M., VLA D-1631.

Otidea alutacea (Pers.) Massee

On soil in conifer-broad-leaved forest, Ussuriysk Nature Reserve, 10 Aug. 2002, Tiunova T. M., VLA D-1809; Ussuriysk: Gornotayozhnoye, 13 Aug. 2002, Bogacheva A. V., VLA D-1780; Khanka Nature Reserve, 26 Jul. 2002, Barkalov V. Yu., VLA D-1837; Raohe: Shengli State Farm, 6 Sept. 2003, Bogacheva A. V., VLA D-2624; Mishan, 9 Aug. 2004, Bogacheva A. V., VLA D-2836.

Otidea ampelina Quél.

On soil in conifer-broad-leaved forest, Khanka Nature Reserve, 26 Jul. 2002, Barkalov V. Yu., VLA D-1838.

Otidea cochleata (Huds.) Fuckel

On soil in broad-leaved forest, Ussuriysk: Gornotayozhnoye, 13 Aug. 2002, Bogacheva A. V., VLA D-1808. - On litter in broad-leaved forest, Hulin: Dongfanghong, 3 Sept. 2003, Bogacheva A. V., VLA D-2486; Raohe: Shengli State Farm, 6 Sept. 2003, Bogacheva A. V., VLA D-2479; Sanjiang Nature Reserve: Dongxing cun, 5 Aug. 2004, Bogacheva A. V., VLA D-2730.

Otidea grandis (Pers.) Rehm

On soil in broad-leaved forest, Khanka Nature Reserve, 26 Jul. 2002, Barkalov V. Yu. VLA D-1828; Raohe, 7 Aug. 2004, Bogacheva A. V., VLA D-2729.

Otidea leporina (Batsch) Fuckel

On litter and soil in broad-leaved forest, Raohe: Shengli State Farm, 6 Sept. 2003, Bogacheva A. V., VLA D-2777; Big Khekhtsir Nature Reserve, 23 Jul. 2004, Bogacheva A. V., VLA D-2892; Sanjiang Nature Reserve: Dongxing cun, 5 Aug. 2004, Bogacheva A. V., VLA D-2728.

Otidea onotica (Pers.) Fuckel

On fallen needles in litter, Ussuriysk: Gornotayozhnoye, 23 Jul. 2002, Govorova O. K., VLA D-1835, 13 Aug. 2002, Bogacheva A. V., VLA D-1807.

Psilopezia nummularia Berk.

On woody debris in conifer-broad-leaved forest, Ussuriysk Nature Reserve, 11 Sept. 1961, Vassiljeva L. N., VLA D-1185.

Pulvinula cinnabarina (Fuckel) Boud.

On sand, Ussuriysk Nature Reserve, VLA D-1395.

Scutellinia badio-berbis (Berk. ex Cooke) Kuntze

On woody debris in conifer-broad-leaved forest, Big Khekhtsir Nature Reserve, 22 Jul. 2004, Bogacheva A. V., VLA D-2771.

Scutellinia colensoi Massee ex Le Gal

On wood of *Quercus mongolica* Fisch. ex Ledeb., Ussuriysk: Gornotayozhnoye, 13 Aug. 2002, Bogacheva A. V., VLA D-1889; Hulin: Dongfanghong, 3 Sept. 2003, Bogacheva A. V., VLA D-2606.

Scutellinia crinita (Bull.) Lambotte

On soil or woody debris in conifer-broad-leaved forest, Ussuriysk: Gornotayozhnoye, Ussuriysk Nature Reserve (Kullman, 1982).

Scutellinia minor (Velen.) Svrček

On soil in broad-leaved forest, Big Khekhtsir Nature Reserve, 27 Jul. 2004, Bogacheva A. V., VLA D-2878, 15 Aug. 2004, Bogacheva A. V., VLA D-2884.

Scutellinia olivascens (Cooke) Kuntze

On soil or woody debris, Ussuriysk Nature Reserve, Upper-Ussuri Station (Kullman, 1982).

Scutellinia parvispora J. Moravec

On soil in broad-leaved forest, Big Khekhtsir Nature Reserve, 26 Jul. 2004, Bogacheva A. V., VLA D-2773.

Scutellinia patagonica (Rehm) Gamundí

On wood in broad-leaved forest, Big Khekhtsir Nature Reserve, 20 Jul. 2004, Bogacheva A. V., VLA D-2881.

Scutellinia pennsylvanica (Seaver) Denison

On woody debris in conifer-broad-leaved forest, Ussuriysk: Gornotayozhnoye, 13 Aug. 2002, Bogacheva A. V., VLA D-1872.

Scutellinia scutellata (L.) Lambotte

On woody debris in conifer-broad-leaved forest, Ussuriysk Nature Reserve, 27 Sept. 1961, Nazarova M. M., VLA D-1276, 4 Aug. 1962, Nazarova M. M., VLA D-1272; Ussuriysk: Gornotayozhnoye, 13 Aug. 2002, Bogacheva A. V., VLA D-1813; Raohe: Shengli State Farm, 6 Sept. 2003, Bogacheva A. V., VLA D-2751; Raohe, 7 Aug. 2004, Bogacheva A. V., VLA D-2733; Big Khekhtsir Nature Reserve, 23 Jul. Bogacheva A. V., VLA D-2877, 17 Aug. 2004, Bogacheva A. V., VLA D-2574.

Scutellinia scutellata var. *discreta* Kullman et Raitv.

On woody debris in broad-leaved forest, Hulin: Wulindong, 4 Sept. 2003, Bogacheva A. V., VLA D-2750; Big Khekhtsir Nature Reserve, 27 Jul. 2004, Bogacheva A. V., VLA D-2768.

Scutellinia setosa (Nees) Kuntze

On woody debris in conifer-broad-leaved forest, Ussuriysk Nature Reserve, 28 Aug. 1961, Vassiljeva L. N., VLA D-1300, 15 Aug. 1989, Vassiljeva L. N., VLA D-1327, 5 Sept. 1994, Bogacheva A. V., VLA D-1673; Hulin: Wulindong, 4 Sept. 2003, Bogacheva A. V., VLA D-2752.

Scutellinia subhirtella Svrček

On wood of *Betula* sp., Big Khekhtsir Nature Reserve, 16 Aug. 2004, Bogacheva A. V., VLA D-2883; Sanjiang Nature Reserve: Dongxing cun, 5 Aug. 2004, Bogacheva A. V., VLA D-2734.

Scutellinia trechispora (Berk. et Broome) Lambotte

On soil in broad-leaved forest, Big Khekhtsir Nature Reserve, 22 Jul. 2004, Bogacheva A. V., VLA D-2767, 24 Jul. Bogacheva A. V., VLA D-2876.

Scutellinia umbrarum (Fr.) Lambotte

On wood in conifer-broad-leaved forest, Big Khekhtsir Nature Reserve, 20 Jul. 2004, Bogacheva A. V., VLA D-2885, 22 Jul. 2004, Bogacheva A. V., VLA D-2879.

Sowerbyella imperialis (Peck) Korf

On soil and litter, Tikhorechnoye, 13 Jul. 2004, Bulakh E. M., VLA D-2482; Big Khekhtsir Nature Reserve, 15 Aug. 2004, Bogacheva A. V., VLA D-2888.

Tarzetta catinus (Holmsk.) Korf & J.K. Rogers

On litter in conifer-broad-leaved forest, Big Khekhtsir Nature Reserve, 26 Jul. 2004, Bogacheva A. V., VLA D-2762, 15 Aug. 2004, Bogacheva A. V., VLA D-2889, 17 Aug. 2004, Bogacheva A. V., VLA D-2555; Hulin: Wulindong, 4 Sept. 2003, Bogacheva A. V., VLA D-2485; Raohe: Shengli State Farm, 6 Aug. 2004, Bogacheva A. V., VLA D-2737; Mishan, 8 Aug. 2004, Bogacheva A. V., VLA D-2736. - On woody debris, Upper-Ussuri Station, 27 Jun.

1974, Bulakh E. M., VLA D-1640.

Trichophaea abundans (P. Karst.) Boud.

On sandy soil, Hulin: Dongfanghong, 3 Sept. 2003, Bogacheva A. V., VLA D-2484.

Trichophaea gregaria (Rehm) Boud.

On litter and soil in broad-leaved forest, Fujuan, 4 Aug. 2004, Bogacheva A. V., VLA D-2746; Raohe: Shengli State Farm, 6 Aug. 2004, Bogacheva A. V., VLA D-2747; Raohe, 7 Aug. 2004, Bogacheva A. V., VLA D-2745.

Trichophaea hemisphaerioides (Mouton) Graddon

On soil in conifer-broad-leaved forest, Upper-Ussuri Station, 18 Aug. 1974, Bulakh E. M., VLA D-1595.

Trichophaea hydrida (Sowerby) T. Schumach.

On soil in broad-leaved forest, Big Khekhtsir Nature Reserve, 26 Jul. 2004, Bogacheva A. V., VLA D-2826.

SARCOSCYPHACEAE

Microstoma floccosum (Schwein.) Raitv.

On woody debris in litter, Ussuriysk Nature Reserve, 9 Sept. 1961, Nazarova M. M., VLA D-806, 14 May 1969, Nazarova M. M., VLA D-8; Big Khekhtsir Nature Reserve, 26 Jul. 2004, Bogacheva A. V., VLA D-2764, 9 Aug. 2004, Kurenshykov D. K., VLA D-2874.

Phillipsia domingensis (Berk.) Berk.

On litter in conifer-broad-leaved forest, Ussuriysk: Gornotayozhnoye, 4 Sept. 2002, Govorova O. K., VLA D-1783.

Sarcoscypha coccinea (Jacq.) Sacc.

On fallen twigs of *Picea* sp., Ussuriysk Nature Reserve, 14 Sept. 1975, Nazarova M. M., VLA D-1232, Jun. 1996, Bogacheva A. V., VLA D-1236, 7 May 2004, Bulakh E. M., VLA D-2431; Ussuriysk: Gornotayozhnoye, 13 Aug. 2002, Bogacheva A. V., VLA D-1882; Big Khekhtsir Nature Reserve, 22 Jul. 2004, Bogacheva A. V., VLA D-2770, 9 Aug. 2004, Kurenshykov D. K., VLA D-2875.

Sarcoscypha vassiljevae Raitv.

On fallen twigs in litter, Ussuriysk Nature Reserve, 17 Aug. 1963, Nazarova M. M., VLA D-1238, 28 Aug. 1968, Nazarova M. M., VLA D-1241, 2 Sept. 1975, Nazarova M. M., VLA D-1237; Tikhorechnoye, 10 Aug. 1977, Bulakh E. M., VLA D-1618.

SARCOSOMATACEAE

Sarcosoma amurense Lj.N. Vassiljeva

On fallen twigs of *Picea ajanensis* (Lindl. et Gord.) Fisch. ex Carr., Ussuriysk Nature

Reserve; Upper-Ussuri Station, 6 Aug. 1973, Bulakh E. M., VLA D-1256, 27 Jun. 1974, Bulakh E. M., VLA D-1255; Big Khekhtsir Nature Reserve, 24 Jul. 2004, Bogacheva A. V., VLA D-2765, VLA D-2886.

Urnula craterium (Schwein.) Fr.

On woody debris in broad-leaved forest, Ussuriysk Nature Reserve, 14 May 1969, Nazarova M. M., VLA D-1511, Aug. 1989, Vassiljeva L. N., VLA D-1504, 7 May 2004, Bulakh E. M. . VLA D-2403.

ASCOMYCETES

Insertae sedis

OSTROPALES

STICTIDACEAE

Stictis radiata (L.) Pers.

On stems of *Artemisia* spp., Xingkaihu Nature Reserve, 1 Sept., Bogacheva A. V., VLA D-2641; Hulin: 856 State Farm, 2 Sept. 2003, Bogacheva A. V., VLA D-2501.

REFERENCES

Azbukina Z M, Kharkevich S S. (eds.) The flora of the Upper Ussuri Station (the south of Sikhote-Alin). Vladivostok: Far East Sci. Center, 1984, 1-130. (in Russian)

Bogacheva A V. Discomycetes from Ussuriysky Nature Reserve. Mikologiya i Fitopatologiya, 1998, 32: 1-6. (in Russian)

Bunkina I A, Nazarova M M. Fungi. 1978, 36-104. In Kharkevich S S. (ed.) Flora and vegetation of Ussuriysk Nature Reserve. Nauka. Moscow. (in Russian)

Dennis R W G. British cup fungi. London, 1960, 1-280.

Hühtinen S. A monograph of *Hyaloscypha* and allied genera. Karstenia, 1989 [1990], 29: 45-252.

Kirk P M, Cannon P F, David J C, Stalpers J A. Ainsworth and Bisby's Dictionary of the fungi. CABI Bioscience. Wallingford, 2001, 1-655.

Kullman B B. A revision of the genus *Scutellinia* (Pezizales) in Soviet Union. Tallin, 1982, 1-158. (in Russian)

Moser M. Kleine Kryptogamenflora. Bd IIa. Ascomyceten (Schlauchpilze). Jena. 1963, 1-147.

Naumov N A. The fungal flora of Leningrad region. Vol. 2. Discomycetes. Nauka. Moscow-Leningrad. 1964, 1-256. (in Russian)

Prokhorov V P. Discomycetes coprotrophici in URSS. Novitates systematicae plantarum non vascularium. 1993, 29: 51-58. (in Russian)

Raitviir A G. Helotiales Nannf. 1991, 254-363. In Azbukina Z M. (ed.) Lower plants, fungi, and mosses of the Russian Far East. Vol. II. Nauka. Leningrad. (in Russian)

Rehm H. Die Pilze Deutschlands, Osterreichs und der Schweiz. III. Abteilung. Ascomyceten: Hysteriaceen und Discomyceten. Leipzig. 1896: 1-1334.

Seaver F J. The North American Cup-fungi (Operculates). New York. 1942, 1-377.

Seaver F J. The North American Cup-fungi (Inoperculates). New York. 1951, 1-428.

Smitskaya M F. Flora fungorum RSS Ucrainicae. Discomycetes (Operculatae). Kiev, 1980, 1-224. (in Russian)

Spooner B M. Helotiales of Australasia: Geoglossaceae, Orbiliaceae, Sclerotiniaceae, Hyaloscyphaceae. J. Cramer. Berlin-Stuttgart, 1987, 1-711.

Teng S C. A contribution to our knowledge of the higher fungi of China. Academia Sinica, 1939, 1-614.

Vassiljeva L N. An addition to discomycetes of Primorsky Territory. Reports of the Far East Branch of the Academy of Sciences of the USSR, 1960, 12: 155-156. (in Russian)

Vassiljeva L N, Nazarova M M. Fungi as components of forest phytocoenoses in the south of Primorsky Territory. 1967, 122-164. In Vassiljeva L N, Ivanov G I, Rosenberg V A, Tarankov V I (eds.) Complex stationary investigations in the forests of Primorsky Territory. Leningrad. (in Russian)

Basidiomycetes

Tolgor BAU, Eugenia M. BULAKH, Olga K. GOVOROVA

The studies of macromycetes in the Ussuri River Valley were started by L.V. Lyubarsky in 1929 (wood-destroying fungi) and followed by L.N. Vassiljeva in 1944 (agaricoid and gasteroid fungi). The following check-list includes 1430 species and is based on the extensive authors' collections as well as literature data (Teng, 1939; Parmasto, 1965, 1968, 1982, 1983; Vassiljeva, 1973; Wells, Raitviir, 1977; Tai, 1979; Bondartseva, Parmasto, 1986; Nezdoyminogo, 1990; Wasser, 1990; Kovalenko, 1995; Kõljalg, 1996; Mao, 1998, 2000; Parmasto, Kollom, 2000). Such species as *Resinomycena japonica*, *Xerula globospora*, *X. vinocontusa* are collected in Russia for the first time, whereas *X. hongoi* found in China before (Zhu-Liang Yang, 2000) is the first record in Russia (Petersen, Nagasawa, 2005).

AGARICALES

AGARICACEAE

Agaricus abruptibulbus Peck

On the ground in coniferous forest, Upper Ussuri Station, 26 Aug. 1973, E.M. Bulakh, VLA M-4856; Big Khekhtsir Nature Reserve, 27 Aug. 1983, E.M. Bulakh, VLA M-4378; Birobidzhan: Bastak Nature Reserve, 12 Sept. 2001, VLA M-16368; Ussuriysk Nature Reserve (Vasilyeva & Bezdeleva, 2006).

Agaricus arvensis Schaeff.

On the ground, Raohe, 7 Aug. 2004, Tolgor Bau, HMJAU 3343; Hailin, 9 Aug. 2004, Tolgor Bau, HMJAU 3285; Big Khekhtsir Nature Reserve, 16 Aug. 2004, Tolgor Bau, HMJAU 3300; Ussuriysk Nature Reserve (Vasilyeva & Bezdeleva, 2006).

Agaricus augustus Fr.

On the ground in a park, Ussuriysk, 23 Sept. 1945, L.N. Vassiljeva, VLA M-4393; in oak forest, Nikolaevka, 21 Aug. 2002, E.M. Bulakh, VLA M-19272; Ussuriysk Nature Reserve (Vasilyeva & Bezdeleva, 2006); Big Khekhtsir Nature Reserve (Wasser, 1990).

Agaricus bisporus (J.E. Lange) Pilát

On the ground of meadow, Ussuriysk: Baranovsky, 17 Aug. 1994, E.M. Bulakh, VLA M-4804.

Agaricus bitorquis (Quél.) Sacc.

On the ground of meadow, Novotroitskoye, 14 Jul. 2004, E.M. Bulakh, VLA M-19502.

Agaricus campetris L.   Plate 3: 17

On the ground near the road, Ussuriysk Nature Reserve (Vasilyeva & Bezdeleva, 2006); in a park, Ussuriysk, 23 Sept. 1945, L.N. Vassiljeva, VLA M-4400; in meadow, Khanka Nature Reserve, 28 Aug. 2002, E.M. Bulakh, VLA M-19287; in oak forest, Big Khekhtsir Nature Reserve, 25 Jun. 1981, E.M. Bulakh, VLA M-4403.

Agaricus comptulus Fr.

On the ground in oak forest, Big Khekhtsir Nature Reserve, 12 Aug. 1981, E.M. Bulakh, VLA M-4401; Hulin, Tolgor Bau, HMJAU 3366.

Agaricus cupreobrunneus (Jul. Schäff. et Steer) Pilát

On the ground near the road, Ussuriysk Nature Reserve (Vasilyeva & Bezdeleva, 2006).

Agaricus dulcidulus Schulzer

On the ground in coniferous forest, Upper Ussuri Station, 29 Aug. 1973, E.M. Bulakh, VLA M-4313.

Agaricus impudicus (Rea) Pilát

[= *Agaricus variegatus* (F.H. Møller) Pilát]

On the ground in korean pine-broad-leaved forest, Ussuriysk Nature Reserve, 25 Jul. 2005, E.M. Bulakh, VLA M-20282; in the thicket of *Crataegus*, Khanka Nature Reserve, 22 Jul. 2002, V.Yu. Barkalov, VLA M-19288; in coniferous-broad-leaved forest, Big Khekhtsir Nature Reserve (Wasser, 1990); in broad-leaved forest, Birobidzhan: Bastak Nature Reserve, 19 Aug. 2004, E.M. Bulakh, VLA M-19612.

Agaricus litoralis (Wakef. et A. Pearson) Pilát

(= *Agaricus spissicaulis* (F.H. Møller) F.H. Møller

On the ground in poplar forest, Ussuriysk Nature Reserve (Wasser, 1990).

Agaricus meleagris (J. Schäff.) Pilát

On the ground in korean pine-broad-leaved forest, Ussuriysk (Wasser, 1990).

Agaricus minimus (Ricken) Pilát

On the ground, Ussuriysk Nature Reserve, 15 Oct. 1955, L.N. Vassiljeva , VLA M-4415.

Agaricus moelleri Wasser

(= *Agaricus praeclaresquamosus* A.E. Freeman)

On the ground in forest, Birobidzhan: Bastak Nature Reserve, 18 Aug. 2004, Tolgor Bau, HMJAU 2954.

Agaricus placomyces Peck   Plate 3: 18

On the ground, Ussuriysk Nature Reserve, 16 Aug. 1961, L.N. Vassiljeva, VLA M-4431; in broad-leaved forest, Tikhorechnoye, 13 Jul. 2004, E.M. Bulakh, VLA M-19499; Upper Ussuri Station, 28 Aug. 1973, E.M. Bulakh, VLA M-4416; in coniferous forest, Big Khekhtsir Nature Reserve, 19 Aug. 1983, E.M. Bulakh, VLA M-4424.

Agaricus porphyrizon P.D. Orton

On the ground near the road, Ussuriysk Nature Reserve (Wasser, 1990).

Agaricus purpurellus (F.H. Møller) F.H. Møller

On the ground in willow forest, Khanka Nature Reserve, 25 Jul. 2002, V.Yu. Barkalov, VLA M-19300; in coniferous forest, Upper Ussuri Station, 9 Sept. 1973, E.M. Bulakh, VLA M-4441; in broad-leaved forest, Big Khekhtsir Nature Reserve, 1 Sept. 1983, E.M. Bulakh, VLA M-4435.

Agaricus rusiophyllus Lasch

On the ground in broad-leaved forest, Big Khekhtsir Nature Reserve (Wasser, 1990).

Agaricus semotus Fr.

On the forest litter, Ussuriysk Nature Reserve (Vasilyeva & Bezdeleva, 2006). - On the ground in coniferous forest, Upper Ussuri Station, 9 Sept. 1973, E.M. Bulakh, VLA M-4441; in the korean pine forest, Big Khekhtsir Nature Reserve, 16 Sept. 1975, E.M. Bulakh, VLA M-4455.

Agaricus silvaticus Schaeff.   Plate 4: 19

On the ground in the korean pine-broad-leaved forest, Ussuriysk Nature Reserve, 15 Aug. 1945, L.N. Vassiljeva, VLA M-4465; Big Khekhtsir Nature Reserve, 14 Aug. 1981, E.M. Bulakh, VLA M-4464; Bastak Nature Reserve, 17 Aug. 2002, E.M. Bulakh, VLA M-19311; in broad-leaved forest, Ussuriysk: Gornotayozhnoye, 30 Aug. 1963, M.M. Nazarova, VLA M-4468; Tikhorechnoye, 21 Jul. 1998, E.M. Bulakh, VLA M-10478; Hutou, Tolgor Bau, HMJAU 3301.

Agaricus silvicola (Vittad.) Peck

On the forest litter in broad-leaved forest, Ussuriysk Nature Reserve, 21 Aug. 1975, M.M. Nazarova, VLA M-4479; Birobidzhan: Bastak Nature Reserve, 21 Aug. 2003, E.M. Bulakh, VLA M-192306. - On the ground in pine-oak forest, Nikolaevka, 21 Aug. 2002, E.M. Bulakh, VLA M-19322; in korean pine forest, Upper Ussuri Station, 2 Aug. 1974, E.M. Bulakh, VLA M-4484; in birch forest, Big Khekhtsir Nature Reserve, 2 Sept. 1983, E.M. Bulakh, VLA M-4477, Tolgor Bau, HMJAU 3411; Raohe, 7 Aug. 2004, E.M. Bulakh, VLA M-19598.

Agaricus subrufescens Peck   Plate 4: 20

On the ground in broad-leaved forest, Ussuriysk Nature Reserve, 1 Sept. 1946, L.N. Vassiljeva, VLA M-4509; Big Khekhtsir Nature Reserve, 12 Sept. 1946, L.N. Vassiljeva, VLA M-4510.

Chlorophyllum agaricoides (Czern.) Vellinga

(= *Endoptychum agaricoides* Czern.)

On the ground in broad-leaved forest, Spassk-Dalny, 24 Aug. 1955, L.N. Vassiljeva, VLA M-17923.

Chlorophyllum rhacodes (Vittad.) Vellinga   Plate 4: 21

[= *Macrolepiota rhacodes* (Vittad.) Singer]

On the ground in poplar forest near the road, Upper Ussuri Station, 8 Sept. 2005, E.M. Bulakh, VLA M-20224.

Cystoderma amianthinum (Scop.) Fayod

On the forest litter in fir-broad-leaved forest, Ussuriysk Nature Reserve, 28 Aug. 1965, M.M. Nazarova, VLA M-4945; in dark coniferous forest, Upper Ussuri Station, 17 Sept. 1974, E.M. Bulakh, VLA M-4955; Big Khekhtsir Nature Reserve, 7 Sept. 1983, E.M. Bulakh, VLA M-4962; Birobidzhan: Bastak Nature Reserve, 18 Aug. 2004, Tolgor Bau, HMJAU 3192.

Cystoderma carcharias (Pers.) Fayod

On the forest litter in korean pine forest, Ussuriysk Nature Reserve (Wasser, 1990); Upper Ussuri Station, 23 Jun. 1974, E.M. Bulakh, VLA M-4978; Birobidzhan: Bastak Nature Reserve, 12 Sept. 2001, E.M. Bulakh, VLA M-16379.

Cystoderma cinnabarinum (Alb. et Schwein.) Fayod

On the forest litter in korean pine-broad-leaved forest, Ussuriysk Nature Reserve, 8 Sept. 1975, M.M. Nazarova, VLA M-4989; in broad-leaved forest, Birobidzhan: Bastak Nature Reserve, 16 Aug. 2000, E.M. Bulakh, VLA M-15362.

Cystoderma granulosum (Batsch) Fayod

On the forest litter in korean pine-broad-leaved forest, Ussuriysk Nature Reserve, 1 Sept. 1962, M.M. Nazarova, VLA M-5002; in dark coniferous forest, Upper Ussuri Station, 6 Aug. 1973, E.M. Bulakh, VLA M-5007; Big Khekhtsir Nature Reserve, 14 Aug. 1981, E.M. Bulakh, VLA M-4999; Birobidzhan: Bastak Nature Reserve, 12 Sept. 2001, E.M. Bulakh, VLA M-16866; in deciduous forest, Hulin, 19 Sept. 2004, Tolgor Bau, HMJAU 2612. - On the wood of *Quercus* in the forest litter, Ussuriysk: Gornotayozhnoye, 23 Jul. 2002, E.M. Bulakh, VLA M-19321.

Cystoderma rugosoreticulata (F. Lorinser) Wasser

On the forest litter in dark coniferous forest, Big Khekhtsir Nature Reserve, 20 Aug. 1983, E.M. Bulakh, VLA M-5025.

Cystolepiota hetieri (Boud.) Singer

(= *Lepiota langei* Locq.)

On the forest litter and decayed wood in korean pine-broad-leaved forest, Ussuriysk Nature Reserve, 12 Aug. 1961, L.N. Vassiljeva, VLA M-4696; in broad-leaved forest, Raohe: Shengli State Farm, 6 Aug. 2004, E.M. Bulakh, VLA M-19608.

Cystolepiota lignicola (P. Karst.) Nezdojm.

(= *Lepiota lignicola* P. Karst.)

On the log of *Betula* in korean pine-broad-leaved forest, Ussuriysk Nature Reserve, 20 Sept.1961, L.N. Vassiljeva, VLA M-4740. - On the log of a deciduous tree, Upper Ussuri Station, 20 Aug. 1973, E.M. Bulakh, VLA M-4734; Birobidzhan: Bastak Nature Reserve, 13 Aug. 2000, E.M. Bulakh, VLA M-15191.

Cystolepiota moelleri Knudsen

(= *Lepiota rosea* Rea)

On the forest litter in ash forest, Ussuriysk Nature Reserve, 11 Sept. 1963, M.M. Nazarova, VLA M-4769.

Cystolepiota pseudogranulosa (Berk. et Broome) Sacc.

On the ground in forest, Big Khekhtsir Nature Reserve, 16 Aug. 2004, Tolgor Bau, HMJAU 2776, 2785; Hulin, 9 Aug. 2004, Tolgor Bau, HMJAU 2597; Raohe, 6 Aug. 2004, Tolgor Bau, HMJAU 2630.

Cystolepiota seminuda (Lasch) Gillet

On the forest litter in korean pine-broad-leaved forest, Ussuriysk Nature Reserve, 14 Sept. 1962, M.M. Nazarova, VLA M-4784; in dark coniferous forest, Upper Ussuri Station, 29 Aug. 1973, E.M. Bulakh, VLA M-4771; in oak forest, Big Khekhtsir Nature Reserve, 13 Aug. 1981, E.M. Bulakh, VLA M-4791; Birobidzhan: Bastak Nature Reserve, 21 Aug. 2003, E.M. Bulakh, VLA M-19248.

Lepiota aspera (Pers.) Quél.

[= *Lepiota acutesquamosa* (Weinm.) P. Kumm.]

On the needles and decayed wood in korean pine-broad-leaved forest, Ussuriysk Nature Reserve, 14 Sept. 1975, M.M. Nazarova, VLA M-4530. - On the ground in broad-leaved forest, Tikhorechnoye, 3 Jul. 1979, E.M. Bulakh, VLA M-4537. - On the forest litter in oak-korean pine forest, Upper Ussuri Station, 12 Sept. 1975, E.M. Bulakh, VLA M-4538; in dark coniferous forest, Big Khekhtsir Nature Reserve, 18 Sept. 1946, L.N. Vassiljeva, VLA M-4535, 16 Aug. 2004, Tolgor Bau, HMJAU 2970; Birobidzhan: Bastak Nature Reserve, 14 Aug. 2000, E.M. Bulakh, VLA M-15361.

Lepiota brunneoincarnata Chodat et Martin

On the ground in broad-leaved forest, Birobidzhan: Bastak Nature Reserve, 8 Sept. 2001, E.M. Bulakh, VLA M-16373.

Lepiota castanea Quél.

(= *Lepiota ignicolor* Bres. = *Lepiota ignipes* Locq.)

On the forest litter in korean pine-broad-leaved forest, Ussuriysk Nature Reserve, 20 Aug. 1961, M.M. Nazarova, VLA M-4546; Upper Ussuri Station, 25 Aug. 1973, E.M. Bulakh, VLA M-4551; in broad-leaved forest, Birobidzhan: Bastak Nature Reserve, 21 Aug. 2003, E.M. Bulakh, VLA M-19068; Raohe, 8 Sept. 2003, Tolgor Bau, HMJAU 3046.

Lepiota citrophylla (Berk. et Broome.) Sacc.

On the forest litter in korean pine-broad-leaved forest, Ussuriysk Nature Reserve, 18 Aug. 1961, L.N. Vassiljeva, VLA M-4849; in oak forest, Big Khekhtsir Nature Reserve (Azbukina & Kharkevich, 1986).

Lepiota clypeolaria (Bull.) P. Kumm.

On the forest litter in coniferous-broad-leaved forest, Ussuriysk Nature Reserve, 21 Aug.

1961, L.N. Vassiljeva, VLA M-4599; Big Khekhtsir Nature Reserve, 28 Aug. 1983, E.M. Bulakh, VLA M-4598; in the thicket of *Crataegus* and *Salix*, Khanka Nature Reserve, 25 Jul. 2002, V.Yu. Barkalov, VLA M-19282; in dark coniferous forest, Upper Ussuri Station, 9 Sept. 1973, E.M. Bulakh, VLA M-4564; in broad-leaved forest, Birobidzhan: Bastak Nature Reserve, 6 Sept. 2001, E.M. Bulakh, VLA M-16377; Hulin, 9 Aug. 2004, Tolgor Bau, HMJAU 2570

Lepiota cristata (Bolton) P. Kumm.

On the forest litter in korean pine-broad-leaved forest, Ussuriysk Nature Reserve, 20 Aug. 1961, L.N. Vassiljeva, VLA M-4614; Ussuriysk, 3 Aug. 2003, Tolgor Bau, HMJAU 2806; in korean pine forest, Upper Ussuri Station, 10 Aug. 1974, E.M. Bulakh, VLA M-4621; in oak forest, Khanka Nature Reserve, 28 Aug. 2002, E.M. Bulakh, VLA M-19281; Big Khekhtsir Nature Reserve, 23 Aug. 1983, E.M. Bulakh, VLA M-4630, 16 Aug. 2004, Tolgor Bau, HMJAU 2900; Longwangmiao Mishan, 1 Sept. 2003, Tolgor Bau, HMJAU 3036; Hulin, 9 Aug. 2004, Tolgor Bau, HMJAU 3370; in birch forest, Raohe, 7 Aug. 2004, E.M. Bulakh, VLA M-20404; Birobidzhan: Bastak Nature Reserve, 17 Aug. 2002, E.M. Bulakh, VLA M-17301.

Lepiota echinacea J.E. Lange

On the ground and forest litter in coniferous-broad-leaved forest, Ussuriysk Nature Reserve, 21 Aug. 1961, L.N. Vassiljeva, VLA M-4649; in korean pine-broad-leaved forest, Upper Ussuri Station, 17 Aug. 1974, E.M. Bulakh, VLA M-4652.

Lepiota echinella Quél. et G.E. Bernard

On the ground in broad-leaved forest, Birobidzhan: Bastak Nature Reserve, 17 Aug. 2002, E.M. Bulakh, VLA M-17255.

Lepiota erminea (Fr.) Gillet

[= *Lepiota alba* (Bres.) Sacc.]

On the forest litter in forest, Ussuriysk, 3 Aug. 2003, Tolgor Bau, HMJAU 2840.

Lepiota eriophora Peck

On the forest litter in korean pine-broad-leaved forest, Ussuriysk Nature Reserve, 23 Aug. 1975, M.M. Nazarova, VLA M-4660; in birch forest, Raohe, 7 Aug. 2004, E.M. Bulakh, VLA M-20405.

Lepiota felina (Pers.) P. Karst.

On the forest litter in coniferous-broad-leaved forest, Ussuriysk Nature Reserve, 28 Aug. 1961, L.N. Vassiljeva, VLA M-4677; in korean pine-broad-leaved forest, Upper Ussuri Station, 15 Sept. 1974, E.M. Bulakh, VLA M-4678; in dark coniferous forest, Big Khekhtsir Nature Reserve, 7 Sept. 1983, E.M. Bulakh, VLA M-4675.

Lepiota grangei (Eyre) J.E. Lange

On the ground in broad-leaved forest, Ussuriysk Nature Reserve, 6 Sept. 1963, M.M. Nazarova, VLA M-4685.

Lepiota hetieriana Locq.

On forest litter in coniferous-broad-leaved forest, Ussuriysk Nature Reserve (Wasser, 1990).

Lepiota hystrix F.H. Möller et J.E. Lange

On the forest litter in korean pine-broad-leaved forest, Ussuriysk Nature Reserve, 12 Sept. 1955, L.N. Vassiljeva, VLA M-4704; Upper Ussuri Station, 6 Sept. 1974, E.M. Bulakh, VLA M-4698; in dark coniferous forest, Big Khekhtsir Nature Reserve, 15 Aug. 1981, E.M. Bulakh, VLA M-4706; in broad-leaved forest, Birobidzhan: Bastak Nature Reserve, 18 Aug. 2003, E.M. Bulakh, VLA M-19197.

Lepiota lateritiopurpurea Lj.N. Vassiljeva

On the forest litter in fir-broad-leaved forest, Ussuriysk Nature Reserve, 28 Aug. 1965, M.M. Nazarova, VLA M-4730; in korean pine-broad-leaved forest, Upper Ussuri Station, 9 Sept. 1973, E.M. Bulakh, VLA M-4731.

Lepiota magnispora Murrill

[= *Lepiota ventriospora* Reid = *Lepiota metulaespora* (Berk. et Broome) Sacc.]

On the forest litter in korean pine-broad-leaved forest, Ussuriysk Nature Reserve, 12 Sept. 1955, L.N. Vassiljeva, VLA M-4746; in dark coniferous forest, Upper Ussuri Station, 22 Aug. 1974, E.M. Bulakh, VLA M-4747; Big Khekhtsir Nature Reserve, 20 Aug. 1983, E.M. Bulakh, VLA M-4742; in willow forest, Khanka Nature Reserve, 27 Jul. 2002, V.Yu. Barkalov, VLA M-19100; in broad-leaved forest, Birobidzhan: Bastak Nature Reserve, 19 Aug. 2003, E.M. Bulakh, VLA M-19212.

Lepiota neophana Morgan

On the forest litter in broad-leaved forest, Ussuriysk Nature Reserve, 12 Aug. 1961, L.N. Vassiljeva, VLA M-4753.

Lepiota pseudofelina J.E. Lange

On the forest litter in coniferous-broad-leaved forest, Ussuriysk Nature Reserve, 28 Aug. 1961, L.N. Vassiljeva, VLA M-4757.

Lepiota pseudolilacea Huijsman

(= *Lepiota pseudohelveola* Kühner ex Hora)

On the forest litter and ground in broad-leaved forest, Ussuriysk Nature Reserve, 13 Aug. 1961, M.M. Nazarova, VLA M-4759; Big Khekhtsir Nature Reserve, 3 Sept. 1983, E.M. Bulakh, VLA M-4764; in broad-leaved forest, Khanka Nature Reserve, 8 Aug. 2003, E.M. Bulakh, VLA M-19188; Birobidzhan: Bastak Nature Reserve, 21 Aug. 2003, E.M. Bulakh, VLA M-19293.

Lepiota rhodorrhisa Romagn. et Locq. ex P.D. Orton

On the forest litter in oak forest, Big Khekhtsir Nature Reserve, 13 Aug. 1981, E.M. Bulakh, VLA M-4766.

Lepiota rufipes Morgan

On the log in coniferous-broad-leaved forest, Ussuriysk Nature Reserve, 25 Aug. 1962, M.M. Nazarova, VLA M-4770.

Lepiota subalba Kühner ex P.D. Orton.

On the forest litter in ash forest, Ussuriysk Nature Reserve, 2 Sept. 1962, M.M. Nazarova, VLA M-4832. - On decayed wood, in korean pine forest, Upper Ussuri Station, 10 Aug. 1974, E.M. Bulakh, VLA M-4834.

Lepiota subincarnata J.E. Lange

On the forest litter in korean pine-broad-leaved forest, Ussuriysk Nature Reserve, 24 Aug. 1963, E.M. Bulakh, VLA M-4836; in oak forest, Khanka Nature Reserve, 29 Jul. 2002, E.M. Bulakh, VLA M-19310.

Lepiota tomentella J.E. Lange

On the forest litter in coniferous-broad-leaved forest, Ussuriysk Nature Reserve, 29 Aug. 1963, M.M. Nazarova, VLA M-4838; in oak forest, Big Khekhtsir Nature Reserve, 11 Aug. 1981, E.M. Bulakh, VLA M-4842; Raohe: Shengli State Farm, 6 Aug. 2004, E.M. Bulakh, VLA M-20191.

Lepiota virescens (Speg.) Morgan

On the forest litter in korean pine-broad-leaved forest, Ussuriysk Nature Reserve, 29 Aug. 1946, L.N. Vassiljeva, VLA M-4845.

Lepiota xanthophylla P.D. Orton

On the forest litter in oak forest, Big Khekhtsir Nature Reserve, 12 Aug. 1981, E.M. Bulakh, VLA M-4847.

Leucoagaricus georginae (W.G. Sm.) Candusso

On the forest litter in korean pine-broad-leaved forest, Ussuriysk Nature Reserve, 12 Aug. 1961, L.N. Vassiljeva, VLA M-4907.

Leucoagaricus naucinus (Fr.) Singer   Plate 4: 22

On the ground in a garden, Ussuriysk, 12 Oct. 1945, L.N. Vassiljeva, VLA M-4911; Tikhorechnoye, 4 Aug. 2005, E.M. Bulakh, VLA M-20225.

Leucoagaricus nympharum (Kalchbr.) Bon

[= *Macrolepiota puellaris* (Fr.) M.M. Moser]

On the forest litter in korean pine-broad-leaved forest, Ussuriysk Nature Reserve, 11 Sept. 1955, M.M. Nazarova, VLA M-4890; in dark coniferous forest, Big Khekhtsir Nature Reserve, 14 Aug. 1981, E.M. Bulakh, VLA M-4901. - On the ground in poplar forest, Upper Ussuri Station, 9 Sept. 1976, E.M. Bulakh, VLA M-4889.

Leucoagaricus rubrotinctus (Peck) Singer

On the ground in broad-leaved forest, Tikhorechnoye, 5 Aug. 2005, E.M. Bulakh, VLA M-20287.

Leucoagaricus serenus (Fr.) Bon et Boiffard

[= *Lepiota serena* (Fr.) Sacc.]

On the forest litter in fir-broad-leaved forest, Ussuriysk Nature Reserve, 28 Aug. 1965, M.M. Nazarova, VLA M-4810.

Leucocoprinus americanus (Peck) Redhead

[= *Leucocoprinus bresadolae* (Schulzer) M.M. Moser]

On sawdust in broad-leaved forest, Ussuriysk Nature Reserve (Wasser, 1990).

Leucocoprinus badhamii (Berk et Broome) M.M. Moser

On the forest litter in korean pine-broad-leaved forest, Ussuriysk Nature Reserve, 16 Sept. 1963, M.M. Nazarova, VLA M-4864.

Leucocoprinus cygneus (J.E. Lange) Bon

(= *Lepiota cygnea* J. E. Lange)

On the forest litter in korean pine-broad-leaved forest, Ussuriysk Nature Reserve, 7 Aug. 2003, E.M. Bulakh, VLA M-19193; in the stand of *Abies*, Ussuriysk: Gornotayozhnoye, 23 Jul. 2002, E.M. Bulakh, VLA M-19312; in broad-leaved forest, Upper Ussuri Station, 26 Aug. 1974, E.M. Bulakh, VLA M-4642; in oak forest, Big Khekhtsir Nature Reserve, 13 Aug. 1981, E.M. Bulakh, VLA M-4640; Raohe: Shengli State Farm, 6 Aug. 2004, E.M. Bulakh, VLA M-19637.

Leucocoprinus straminellus (Bagl.) Narducci et Caroti

[= *Leucocoprinus denudatus* (Rabenh.) Singer]

On the ground near the road, Ussuriysk Nature Reserve (Wasser, 1990).

Macrolepiota excoriata (Schaeff.) M.M. Moser

On the ground in broad-leaved forest, Ussuriysk Nature Reserve (Vasilyeva & Bezdeleva, 2006).

Macrolepiota gracilenta (Krombh.) Wasser.

On the ground in coniferous-broad-leaved forest, Ussuriysk Nature Reserve (Vasilyeva & Bezdeleva, 2006); Upper Ussuri Sation, 26 Aug. 1973, E.M. Bulakh, VLA M-4856. - On the forest litter in broad-leaved forest, Big Khekhtsir Nature Reserve, 31 Aug. 1983, E.M. Bulakh, VLA M-4857.

Macrolepiota konradii (Hujsman ex P.D. Orton) M.M. Moser

On the ground in korean pine-broad-leaved forest, Ussuriysk Nature Reserve, 27 Aug. 1963, M.M. Nazarova, VLA M-4860.

Macrolepiota mastoidea (Fr.) Singer

On the ground in a park, Ussuriysk, 23 Sept. 1945, L.N. Vassiljeva, VLA M-4862.

Macrolepiota procera (Scop.) Singer   Plate 4: 23

On the forest litter in korean pine-broad-leaved forest, Ussuriysk Nature Reserve, 23 Aug. 1961, L.N. Vassiljeva, VLA M-4876; in broad-leaved forest, Big Khekhtsir Nature Reserve, 21 Aug. 2004, E.M. Bulakh, VLA M-19568, 18 Aug. 2004, Tolgor Bau, HMJAU 2965; Hulin,

19 Sept. 2003, 19 Sept. 2004, Tolgor Bau, HMJAU 2702, 3051; Birobidzhan: Bastak Nature Reserve, 16 Aug. 2004, Tolgor Bau, HMJAU 2962. - On the ground in the thicket of *Salix* and *Betula*, Khanka Nature Reserve, 29 Jul. 2002, V.Yu. Barkalov, VLA M-19269.

Macrolepiota prominens (Fr.) M.M. Moser

On the ground in deciduous forest, Ussuriysk Nature Reserve, 11 Aug. 1961, L.N. Vassiljeva, VLA M-4881.

Melanophyllum echinatum (Roth) Singer

[= *Melanophyllum haematospermum* (Bull.) Kreisel]

On the forest litter in coniferous-broad-leaved forest, Ussuriysk Nature Reserve, 20 Aug. 1970, M.M. Nazarova, VLA M-4515; Upper Ussuri Station, 11 Sept. 1975, E.M. Bulakh, VLA M-4518.

Melanophyllum eyrei (Massee) Singer

On the forest litter in korean pine-broad-leaved forest, Ussuriysk Nature Reserve, 27 Aug. 1963, M.M. Nazarova, VLA M-4521; in broad-leaved forest, Ussuriysk: Gornotayozhnoye, 4 Jul. 2002, E.M. Bulakh, VLA M-19284.

AMANITACEAE

Amanita baccata (Fr.) Gillet

[= *Amanita agglutinata* (Berk.et M.A. Curtis) Lloyd]

On the ground in korean pine-broad-leaved forest, Ussuriysk Nature Reserve (Vasilyeva & Bezdeleva, 2006); in oak forest, Ussuriysk: Gornotayozhnoye, 30 Aug. 1963, M.M. Nazarova, VLA M-3882; Upper Ussuri Station, 23 Sept. 1995, E.M. Bulakh, VLA M-3888; in birch forest, Raohe, 7 Aug. 2004, E.M. Bulakh, VLA M-19614.

Amanita bivolvata Peck

On the ground in dark coniferous forest, Big Khekhtsir Nature Reserve, 15 Sept. 1981, E.M. Bulakh, VLA M-3893; Birobidzhan: Bastak Nature Reserve, 7 Sept. 2001, E.M. Bulakh, VLA M-16795.

Amanita caesarea (Scop.) Pers.

[= *Amanita hemibapha* (Berk. et Broome) Sacc.]

On the ground in oak forest, Ussuriysk Nature Reserve, 23 Aug. 1975, M.M. Nazarova, VLA M-3902; Novotroitskoye, 21 Aug. 1998, E.M. Bulakh, VLA M-10563; Big Khekhtsir Nature Reserve, 14 Aug. 1980, E.M. Bulakh, VLA M-3914; Birobidzhan: Bastak Nature Reserve, 19 Aug. 2000, E.M. Bulakh, VLA M-15248; Fuyuan, 5 Aug. 2004, Tolgor Bau, HMJAU, 2623, 2563.

Amanita ceciliae (Berk. et Broome) Bas

(= *Amanita inaurata* Secr.)

On the ground in broad-leaved forest, Ussuriysk Nature Reserve, 6 Sept. 1951, L.N.

Vassiljeva, VLA M-4272; Khanka Nature Reserve, 29 Jul. 2007, E.M. Bulakh, VLA M-21511; Big Khekhtsir Nature Reserve, 21 Aug. 1981, E.M.Bulakh, VLA M-4033; in coniferous-broad-leaved forest, Upper Ussuri Station, 22 Aug. 1975, E.M. Bulakh, VLA M-3997; in birch forest, Birobidzhan: Bastak Nature Reserve, 11 Aug. 2006, E.M. Bulakh, VLA M-20951; Raohe, 7 Aug. 2004, E.M. Bulakh, VLA M-19641, Fuyuan, 4 Aug. 2004, E.M. Bulakh, VLA M-19640.

Amanita cothurnata G.F. Atk.

On the ground in coniferous-broad-leaved forest, Ussuriysk Nature Reserve, 26 Aug. 1961, L.N. Vassiljeva, VLA M-3926.

Amanita crocea (Quél.) Singer

On the ground in birch forest, Ussuriysk Nature Reserve, 28 Aug. 1946, L.N. Vassiljeva, VLA M-4012; in oak forest, Ussuriysk: Gornotayozhnoye, 24 Aug. 1945, L.N. Vassiljeva, VLA M-4013; in the thicket of *Salix* and *Betula*, Khanka Nature Reserve, 29 Jul. 2002, E.M. Bulakh. VLA M-19270; in dark coniferous forest, Upper Ussuri Station, 6 Aug. 1973, E.M. Bulakh, VLA M-4017; in oak forest, Big Khekhtsir Nature Reserve, 21 Aug. 1981, E.M. Bulakh, VLA M-4001; Birobidzhan: Bastak Nature Reserve, 13 Aug. 2000, E.M. Bulakh, VLA M-15264.

Amanita flavipes S. Imai   Plate 4: 24

On the ground in oak forest, Ussuriysk: Gornotayozhnoye, 23 Jul. 2002, E.M. Bulakh, VLA M-19299; Big Khekhtsir Nature Reserve, 8 Aug. 1981, E.M. Bulakh, VLA M-3932; Birobidzhan: Bastak Nature Reserve, 8 Sept. 2001, E.M. Bulakh, VLA M-16793.

Amanita fulva (Schaeff.) Fr.

On the ground in dark coniferous forest, Upper Ussuri Station, 29 Aug. 973, E.M. Bulakh, VLA M-3993; Raohe, in forest, 7 Aug. 2004, 8 Aug. 2004, Tolgor Bau, HMJAU 2579, 2640, 2610.

Amanita muscaria (L.) Lam.   Plate 5: 25

On the ground in birch forest, Ussuriysk Nature Reserve, 9 Sept. 2005, E.M. Bulakh, VLA M-20220; Upper Ussuri Station, 13 Sept. 1975, E.M. Bulakh, VLA M-3958; Big Khekhtsir Nature Reserve, 5 Sept. 1983, E.M. Bulakh, VLA M-3961; Birobidzhan: Bastak Nature Reserve, 2 Sept. 2001, E.M. Bulakh, VLA M-20658; Hulin, 3 Aug. 2004, Tolgor Bau, HMJAU, 3050.

Amanita nivalis Grev.

On the ground in dark coniferous forest, Birobidzhan: Bastak Nature Reserve, 13 Aug. 2000, E.M. Bulakh, VLA M-15297.

Amanita pantherina (DC.) Krombh.

On the ground under the tree of *Betula* in korean pine-broad-leaved forest, Ussuriysk Nature Reserve, 11 Sept. 2005, E.M. Bulakh, VLA M-20232; in the thicket of *Salix* and *Betula*, Khanka Nature Reserve, 29 Jul. 2003, E.M. Bulakh, VLA M-19182; in oak forest,

Tikhorechnoye, 28 Jul. 1984, E.M. Bulakh, VLA M-4180; in dark coniferous forest, Upper Ussuri Station, 6 Aug.1973, E.M. Bulakh, VLA M-4194; in broad-leaved forest, Big Khekhtsir Nature Reserve, 11 Aug. 1981, E.M. Bulakh, VLA M-4202; Raohe, 8 Aug. 2004, Tolgor Bau, HMJAU 2755; Fuyuan, 5 Aug. 2004, Tolgor Bau, HMJAU 2530.

Amanita phalloides (Vaill. ex Fr.) Link   Plate 5: 26

On the ground in korean pine-broad-leaved forest, Ussuriyk Nature Reserve, 18 Aug. 1975, M.M. Nazarova, VLA M-4208; in broad-leaved forest, Big Khekhtsir Nature Reserve, 9 Aug. 1981, E.M. Bulakh, VLA M-4214; Birobidzhan: Bastak Nature Reserve, 11 Aug. 2006, E.M. Bulakh, VLA M-20949.

Amanita porphiria Alb. et Schwein.

On the ground in coniferous-broad-leaved forest, Ussuriysk Nature Reserve, 28 Sept. 1946, L.N. Vassiljeva, VLA M-4228; Big Khekhtsir Nature Reserve, 3 Sept. 1983, E.M. Bulakh, VLA M-4227; in dark coniferous forest, Upper Ussuri Station, 2 Aug. 1975, E.M. Bulakh, VLA M-4223; Birobidzhan: Bastak Nature Reserve, 17 Aug. 2000, E.M. Bulakh, VLA M-15262.

Amanita rubescens Pers.   Plate 5: 27

On the ground under the tree of *Betula* in korean pine-broad-leaved forest, Ussuriysk Nature Reserve, VLA M-4244; Tikhorechnoye, 5 Aug. 2005, E.M. Bulakh, VLA M-20185; in dark coniferous forest, Upper Ussuri Station, 19 Aug. 1973, E.M. Bulakh, VLA M-4236; Big Khekhtsir Nature Reserve, 15 Sept.1981, E.M. Bulakh,VLA M-4245.

Amanita spissa (Fr.) P. Kumm.

[= *Amanita excelsa* (Fr.) P. Kumm.]

On the ground in dark coniferous forest, Birobidzhan: Bastak Nature Reserve, 17 Aug. 2000, E.M. Bulakh, VLA M-15480.

Amanita spreta (Peck) Sacc.

On the ground in coniferous-broad-leaved forest, Ussuriysk Nature Reserve, 21 Aug. 1961, L.N. Vassiljeva, VLA M-4262; Tikhorechnoye, 21 Jul. 1998, E.M. Bulakh, VLA M-12061; Big Khekhtsir Nature Reserve, 14 Aug. 1981, E.M. Bulakh, VLA M-4261; in oak forest, Birobidzhan: Bastak Nature Reserve, 10 Sept. 2001, E.M. Bulakh, VLA M-16796; in birch forest, Fuyuan, 4 Aug. 2004, E.M. Bulakh, VLA M-19617; Raohe. 7 Aug. 2004, E.M. Bulakh, VLA M-20279.

Amanita strobiliformis (Paulet et Vittad.) Bertill.

On the ground in dark coniferous forest, Ussuriysk Nature Reserve, 5 Sept. 1996, E.M. Bulakh, VLA M-4252.

Amanita sychnopyramis Corner et Bas f. *subannulata* Hongo

Raohe, Tolgor Bau, HMJAU 3239.

Amanita vaginata (Bull.) Lam.   Plate 5: 28

On the ground under the tree of *Betula* in coniferous-broad-leaved forest, Ussuriysk

Nature Reserve, 22 Aug. 1962, M.M. Nazarova, VLA M-4288; in broad-leaved forest, Khanka Nature Reserve, 28 Jul. 2002, E.M. Bulakh, VLA M-4279; Tikhorechnoye, 21 Jul. 1998, E.M. Bulakh, VLA M-10579; Hulin, 4 Sept. 2003, Tolgor Bau, HMJAU 3024; Fuyuan, 5 Aug. 2004, Tolgor Bau, HMJAU 2549, 2561, 2592, 2688, 2560; in dark coniferous forest, Upper Ussuri Station, 25 Aug. 1975, E.M. Bulakh, VLA M-4294; Big Khekhtsir Nature Reserve, 14 Aug. 1981, E.M. Bulakh, VLA M-4303; 17 Aug. 2004, Tolgor Bau, HMJAU 2782; Birobidzhan: Bastak Nature Reserve, 10 Sept. 2001, E.M. Bulakh, VLA M-16794; Raohe, 7 Aug. 2004, Tolgor Bau, HMJAU 3304.

Amanita verna (Fr.) Lam.

On the ground in korean pine forest, Upper Ussuri Starton, 22 Aug. 1975, E.M. Bulakh , VLA M-4341; in oak forest, Khanka Nature Reserve, 29 Jul. 2007, E.M. Bulakh, VLA M-21512; Big Khekhtsir Nature Reserve, 28 Aug. 1983.

Amanita virosa (Fr.) Bertill.

On the ground in korean pine forest, Upper Ussuri Station, 13 Sept. 1975, E.M. Bulakh, VLA M-4337; in dark coniferous forest, Big Khekhtsir Nature Reserve, 15 Sept. 1981, E.M. Bulakh,VLA M-4333.

Limacella delicata (Fr.) Earle var. *glioderma* (Fr.) Gminder

On decayed wood in coniferous-broad-leaved forest, Ussuriysk Nature Reserve, 2 Sept. 1951, L.N. Vassiljeva, VLA M-4349; in oak forest, Tikhorechnoye, 4 Aug. 2005, E.M. Bulakh, VLA M-20231; Big Khekhtsir Nature Reserve, 18 Aug. 2004, E.M. Bulakh,VLA M-20650; Birobidzhan: Bastak Nature Reserve, 13 Aug. 2000, E.M. Bulakh, VLA M-153698; in korean pine forest, Upper Ussuri Station, 21 Aug. 1974, E.M. Bulakh, VLA M-4352.

Limacella illinita (Fr.) Maire

On the ground in korean pine forest, Upper Ussuri Station, 18 Aug. 1974, E.M. Bulakh, VLA M-4356; in oak forest, Ussuriysk: Gornotayozhnoye, 23 Jul. 2002, E.M. Bulakh, VLA M-17201.

BOLBITIACEAE

Agrocybe cylindracea (DC.) Gillet

On the log of *Ulmus* in broad-leaved forest, Ussuriysk Nature Reserve, 25 Jun. 1970, M.M. Nazarova, VLA M-19471; Birobidzhan: Bastak Nature Reserve, 19 Aug. 2000, E.M. Bulakh, VLA M-15384.

Agrocybe dura (Bolton) Singer

On the ground in broad-leaved forest, Khanka Nature Reserve, 21 Jun. 2003 E.M. Bulakh, VLA M-18349; in dark coniferous forest, Upper Ussuri Station, 3 Sept. 1973, E.M. Bulakh, VLA M-5331; Big Khekhtsir Nature Reserve (Azbukina & Kharkevich, 1986). - On the ground in a garden, Tikhorechnoye, 23 Jun. 2006, E.M. Bulakh, VLA M-20687.

Agrocybe erebia (Fr.) Kühner. ex Singer

On decayed wood in coniferous-broad-leaved forest, Ussuriysk Nature Reserve, 29 Aug. 1963, M.M. Nazarova, VLA M-5487. - On the ground in broad-leaved forest, Hulin, 9 Aug. 2004, E.M. Bulakh, VLA M-19591.

Agrocybe firma (Peck) Singer

On the log in coniferous-broad-leaved forest, Ussuriysk Nature Reserve, 27 Aug. 1983, M.M. Nazarova, VLA M-5448; Upper Ussuri Station, 21 Jun. 1974, E.M. Bulakh, VLA M-5447.

Agrocybe paludosa (J.E. Lange) Kühner et Romagn.

On the ground among grasses and mosses on the edge of a marsh, Khanka Nature Reserve, 21 Jun. 2004, E.M. Bulakh, VLA M-19348.

Agrocybe pediades (Fr.) Fayod

On the ground in the stand of *Pinus koraiensis*, Arkhipovka, 19 Jul. 2002, E.M. Bulakh, VLA M-17463.

Agrocybe praecox (Pers.) Fayod

[= *Agrocybe semiorbicularis* (Bull. ex St. Amans.) Fayod]

On the forest litter in coniferous-broad-leaved forest, Ussuriyk Nature Reserve, 11 Jun. 2002, E.M. Bulakh, VLA M-17211; in broad-leaved forest, Upper Ussuri Station, 18 Jun. 1973, E.M. Bulakh, VLA M-5522; Big Khekhtsir Nature Reserve, 26 Jun. 1981, E.M. Bulakh, VLA M-5547. - On the ground at the edge of a road, Tikhorechnoye, 14 Jul. 2004, E.M. Bulakh, VLA M-19505; Fuyuan, Tolgor Bau, HMJAU 3397.

Bolbitius reticulatus (Pers.) Ricken

On decayed wood, Ussuriysk Nature Reserve, 20 Jun. 2005, E.M. Bulakh, VLA M-20421; Birobidzhan: Bastak Nature Reserve, 21 Aug. 2004, E.M. Bulakh, VLA M-20796. - On the ground, Arkhipovka, 15 Jun. 2003, E.M. Bulakh, VLA M-19167.

Bolbitius vitellinus (Pers.) Fr.

On the forest litter in coniferous-broad-leaved forest, Ussuriysk Nature Reserve, 9 Jul. 1963, M.M. Nazarova, VLA M-5508. - On the ground, Upper Ussuri Station, 25 Jun. 1974, E.M. Bulakh VLA M-5503; Ussuriysk: Gornotayozhnoye, 23 Jul. 2002, E.M. Bulakh, VLA M-17204; Big Khekhtsir Nature Reserve, 22 Jun. 1981, E.M. Bulakh, VLA M-5505.

Conocybe aberrans (Kühner) Kühner

On the forest litter in korean pine forest, Ussuriysk Nature Reserve, 6 Sept. 1982, M.M. Nazarova, VLA M-5427.

Conocybe albipes Hauskn.

[= *Conocybe lactea* (J.E.Lange) Métrod]

On the ground among grasses in meadow, Khanka Nature Reserve , 25 Jul. 2003, E.M. Bulakh, VLA M-19095; Tikhorechnoye, 23 Jun. 2006, E.M. Bulakh, VLA M-20689; Chuguevka, 18 Jul. 2002, E.M. Bulakh, VLA M-17468; Birobidzhan: Bastak Nature Reserve,

14 Aug. 2006, E.M. Bulakh, VLA M-21217; Hulin, 9 Aug. 2004, Tolgor Bau, HMJAU 2595.

Conocybe blattaria (Fr.) Kühner

On the ground in korean pine forest, Ussuriysk Nature Reserve, 12 Jun. 1982, M.M. Nazarova, VLA M-5449; in poplar forest, Upper Ussuri Station, 1 Sept. 1973, E.M. Bulakh. VLA M-5490.

Conocybe brunnea J.E. Lange et Kühner ex Watling

On the log in dark coniferous forest, Ussuriysk Nature Reserve, 21 Aug. 2002, E.M. Bulakh, VLA M-17457; in broad-leaved forest, Ussuriysk: Gornotayozhnoye, 6 Aug. 2003, E.M. Bulakh, VLA M-19229; Big Khekhtsir Nature Reserve, 26 Aug. 1983, E.M. Bulakh, VLA M-5472; in korean pine forest, Upper Ussuri Station, 18 Aug. 1974, E.M. Bulakh, VLA M-5473;

Conocybe cyanopus (G.F. Atk.) Kühner

On the ground in poplar forest, Upper Ussuri Station, 7 Sept. 1973, E.M. Bulakh, VLA M-5444; at the edge of a road, Raohe: Shengli State Farm, 6 Aug. 2004, E.M. Bulakh, VLA M-19654.

Conocybe fibrillosipes Watling

On the forest litter, Birobidzhan: Bastak Nature Reserve, 19 Aug. 2004, E.M. Bulakh, VLA M-20793.

Conocybe filaris (Fr.) Kühner

On the wood in fir-broad-leaved forest, Ussurysk Nature Reserve, 21 Aug. 1981, M.M. Nazarova, VLA M-5435; in poplar forest, Upper Ussuri Station, 11 Sept. 1975, E.M. Bulakh, VLA M-12339; Birobidzhan: Bastak Nature Reserve, 21 Aug. 2003, E.M. Bulakh, VLA M-19208.

Conocybe incarnata (Jul. Schaeff.) Hauskn. et Arnolds

[= *Conocybe fragilis* (Peck) Singer]

On the ground in broad-leaved forest, Big Khekhtsir Nature Reserve, 26 Jun. 1981, E.M. Bulakh, VLA M-5394.

Conocybe mesospora Kühner. ex Watling

On the ground and forest litter in coniferous-broad-leaved forest, Ussuriysk Nature Reserve, 5 Sept. 1962, M.M. Nazarova, VLA M-5380; Upper Ussuri Station, 18 Aug. 1974, E.M. Bulakh, VLA M-15510; in dark coniferous forest, Big Khekhtsir Nature Reserve, 21 Sept. 1983, E.M. Bulakh, VLA M-5398.

Conocybe mutabilis Watling

On the ground among grasses in meadow, Khanka Nature Reserve, 9 Aug. 2003, E.M. Bulakh, VLA M-19244.

Conocybe pilosella (Fr.) Kühner

On the ground in poplar forest, Upper Ussuri Station, 28 Aug. 1973, E.M. Bulakh, VLA M-5389.

Conocybe plicatella (Peck) Kühner

On the ground in coniferous-broad-leaved forest, Big Khekhtsir Nature Reserve, 31 Aug. 1983, E.M. Bulakh, VLA M-5391.

Conocybe pubescens (Gillet) Kühner

On the ground in dark coniferous forest, Big Khekhtsir Nature Reserve, 7 Sept. 1983, E.M. Bulakh, VLA M-5410.

Conocybe rickeniana P.D. Orton

On the ground of meadow, Ussuriysk Nature Reserve, 19 Jun. 2002, E.M. Bulakh, VLA M-17218; in poplar forest, Upper Ussuri Station, 18 Sept. 1974, E.M. Bulakh, VLA M-18403; in dark coniferous forest, Big Khekhtsir Nature Reserve, 15 Aug. 1981, E.M. Bulakh,VLA M-5388; in broad-leaved forest, Raohe, 6 Aug. 2004, E.M. Bulakh, VLA M-20401.

Conocybe rugosa (Peck) Watling

On wood in broad-leaved forest, Birobidzhan: Bastak Nature Reserve, 11 Sept. 2001, E.M. Bulakh, VLA M-16480.

Conocybe semiglobata Kühner. et Watling

On the ground in poplar forest, Upper Ussuri Station, 25 Aug. 1974, E.M. Bulakh, VLA M-5395; in broad-leaved forest, Big Khekhtsir Nature Reserve, 1 Sept. 1983, E.M. Bulakh, VLA M-5420.

Conocybe sienophylla (Berk. et Broome) Singer

On the ground in broad-leaved forest, Upper Ussuri Station, 7 Sept. 1975, E.M. Bulakh, VLA M-18405; Big Khekhtsir Nature Reserve, 3 Aug. 1981, E.M. Bulakh, VLA M-5421.

Conocybe siliginea (Fr.) Kühner

On the forest litter in korean pine-broad-leaved forest, Ussuriysk Nature Reserve, 15 Aug. 1962, M.M. Nazarova, VLA M-5400.

Conocybe subovalis Kühner et Watling

On the ground in korean pine forest, Upper Ussuri Station, 19 Aug. 1974, E.M. Bulakh, VLA M-5373.

Conocybe utriformis P.D. Orton

On the ground in coniferous-broad-leaved forest, Upper Ussuri Station, 18 Aug. 1974, E.M. Bulakh, VLA M-5475.

Descolea flavoannulata (Lj.N. Vasiljeva) E. Horak.

On the ground in coniferous-broad-leaved forest, Ussuriysk Nature Reserve, 20 Aug. 2004, E.M. Bulakh, VLA M-20106; Big Khekhtsir Nature Reserve, 21 Sept. 1983, E.M. Bulakh, M-7358, 16 Aug. 2004, Tolgor Bau HMJAU 3259; in oak forest, Spassk-Dalny: Slavinka, 18 Jul. 1981, E.M. Bulakh, VLA M-7357; Tikhorechnoye, 10 Aug. 2005, E.M. Bulakh, VLA M-20413; Birobidzhan: Bastak Nature Reserve, 13 Aug. 2006, E.M. Bulakh, VLA M-21001; in birch forest, Raohe, 7 Aug. 2004, E.M. Bulakh, VLA M-19541.

COPRINACEAE

Coprinus atramentarius (Bull.) Fr.   Plate 5: 29

On the wood in broad-leaved forest, Ussuriysk Nature Reserve, 19 Sept. 1975, M.M. Nazarova, VLA M-13637; Ussuriysk: Gornotayozhnoye, 12 Aug. 1963, M.M. Nazarova VLA M-5031; Khanka Nature Reserve, 28 Aug. 2002, E.M. Bulakh, VLA M-17740; Upper Ussuri Station, 23 Jun. 1974, E.M. Bulakh, VLA M-5028; in birch forest, Big Khekhtsir Nature Reserve, 30 Jun. 1981, E.M. Bulakh, VLA M-5032; Birobidzhan: Bastak Nature Reserve, 8 Sept. 2001, E.M. Bulakh, VLA M-16869.

Coprinus cinereus (Schaeff.) Gray

On the dung of herbivorous animals in broad-leaved forest, Ussuriysk Nature Reserve, 7 Aug. 2003, E.M. Bulakh, VLA M-18998.

Coprinus comatus (O.F.Müll.) Pers.   Plate 5: 30

On the ground of meadow, Ussuriysk, 10 Sept. 1945, L.N. Vassiljeva, VLA M-5047.

Coprinus cordisporus T. Gibbs

On the dung of herbivorous animals in coniferous-broad-leaved forest, Ussuriysk Nature Reserve, 2 Sept. 1975, M.M. Nazarova, VLA M-5055.

Coprinus disseminatus (Pers.) Gray

On the log in broad-leaved forest, Ussuriysk Nature Reserve, 20 Aug. 2003, E.M. Bulakh, VLA M-20105; in dark coniferous forest, Upper Ussuri Station, 18 Aug. 1974, E.M. Bulakh, VLA M-5061; Big Khekhtsir Nature Reserve, 20 Jun. 1981, E.M. Bulakh, VLA M-5057; Birobidzhan: Bastak Nature Reserve, 21 Aug. 2006, E.M. Bulakh, VLA M-20656.

Coprinus domesticus (Bolton) Gray

On the log in broad-leaved forest, Ussuriysk Nature Reserve, 13 Aug. 1962, M.M. Nazarova, VLA M-5085; in korean pine forest, Upper Ussuri Station, 3 Aug. 1974, E.M. Bulakh, VLA M-5074; Big Khekhtsir Nature Reserve, 26 Jun. 1981, E.M. Bulakh, VLA M-5090. - On the ground in broad-leaved forest, Khanka Nature Reserve, 21 Jul. 2002, V.Yu. Barkalov, VLA M-17216; Birobidzhan: Bastak Nature Reserve, 19 Aug. 2003, E.M. Bulakh, VLA M-18993.

Coprinus flocculosus (DC.) Fr.   Plate 6: 31

On the straw, Tikhorechnoye, 23 Jun. 2006, E.M. Bulakh, VLA M-20688.

Coprinus friesii Quél.

On the stem of *Artemisia* in deciduous forest, Ussuriysk Nature Reserve, 9 Aug. 1961, L.N. Vassiljeva, VLA M-5108; in dark coniferous forest, Upper Ussuri Station, Aug. 1973, E.M. Bulakh, VLA M-5109; Raohe: Shengli State Farm, 6 Aug. 2004, E.M. Bulakh, VLA M-20498. - On the stem of *Carex* in willow forest, Big Khekhtsir Nature Reserve, 24 Jun. 1981, E.M. Bulakh, VLA M-5105; Birobidzhan: Bastak Nature Reserve, 18 Aug. 2002, E.M. Bulakh, VLA M-17297.

Coprinus heptemerus M. Lange et A.H. Sm.

On the dung of cow in the meadow, Khanka Nature Reserve, 9 Aug. 2003, E.M. Bulakh, VLA M-18996. - On the dung of herbivorous animals in broad-leaved forest, Tikhorechnoye, 6 May 1998, E.M. Bulakh, VLA M-5898.

Coprinus hexagonosporus Joss.

On the dung of herbivorous animal, Upper Ussuri Station, Aug. 1973, E.M. Bulakh, VLA M-5115. - On the dung of cow, Tikhorechnoye, 23 Jun. 2006, E.M. Bulakh, VLA M-20649.

Coprinus lagopus (Fr.) Fr.

On the ground in korean pine forest, Ussuriysk Nature Reserve, 19 Jun. 2002, E.M. Bulakh, VLA M-17209; in meadow, Arkhipovka, 2 Jun. 2003, E.M. Bulakh, VLA M-18997. - On the log in willow forest, Khanka Nature Reserve, 21 Jun. 2002, V.Yu. Barkalov, VLA M-17208. - On the forest litter in broad-leaved forest, Big Khekhtsir Nature Reserve, 5 Sept. 1983, E.M. Bulakh, VLA M-5117; Birobidzhan: Bastak Nature Reserve, 8 Sept. 2001, E.M. Bulakh, VLA M-16870.

Coprinus micaceus (Bull.) Fr.   Plate 6: 32

On the log in coniferous-broad-leaved forest, Ussuriysk Nature Reserve, 25 Jun. 1970, M.M. Nazarova, VLA M-5132; in broad-leaved forest, Khanka Nature Reserve, 21 Jun. 2003, E.M. Bulakh, VLA M-18355; Tikhorechnoye, 10 Jul. 1986 E.M. Bulakh, VLA M-5137; in dark coniferous forest, Upper Ussuri Station, 29 Aug. 1973, E.M. Bulakh, VLA M-5131; Big Khekhtsir Nature Reserve (Vasilyeva & Bezdeleva, 2006); Hailin, Tolgor Bau, HMJAU 3223.

Coprinus narcoticus (Betsch) Fr.

On the ground in broad-leaved forest, Upper Ussuri Station, 29 Aug. 1975, E.M. Bulakh, VLA M-13669.

Coprinus niveus (Pers.) Fr.

On the dung of horse in meadow, Khanka Nature Reserve, 22 Jun. 2002, E.M. Bulakh, VLA M-17186.

Coprinus patouillardii Quél.

On the dung of horse, Tikhorechnoye, 6 May 1998, E.M. Bulakh, VLA M-5897. Big Khekhtsir Nature Reserve (Azbukina & Kharkevich, 1986).

Coprinus phlyctidosporus Romagn.

On wood in broad-leaved forest, Khanka Nature Reserve, 29 Jul. 2007, E.M. Bulakh, VLA M-21384.

Coprinus plicatilis (Curtis) Fr.

On shrubs in broad-leaved forest, Ussuriysk Nature Reserve, 9 Aug. 1997, E.M. Bulakh, VLA M-13672; Khanka Nature Reserve, 28 Aug. 2002, E.M. Bulakh, VLA M-17741; in dark coniferous forest, Upper Ussuri Station, 25 Sept.1974, E.M. Bulakh, VLA M-5165. - On the wood in broad-leaved forest, Ussuriysk: Gornotayozhnoye, 5 Aug. 2003, E.M. Bulakh, VLA M-18995; Big Khekhtsir Nature Reserve, 26 Aug. 1983, E.M. Bulakh, VLA M-5164. - On the stem of *Artemisia* in broad-leaved forest, Raohe: Shengli State Farm, 6 Aug. 2004, E.M. Bulakh, VLA M-20407.

Coprinus radiatus (Bolton) Gray

On the dung in broad-leaved forest, Upper Ussuri Station, 12 Sept. 1975, E.M. Bulakh, VLA M-5168.

Coprinus squamosus Morgan

(= *Coprinus romagnesianus* Singer)

On the ground in broad-leaved forest, Tikhorechnoye, 23 Jul. 1998, E.M. Bulakh, VLA M-10504.

Coprinus silvaticus Peck

On the ground in coniferous-broad-leaved forest, Ussuriysk Nature Reserve, 25 Aug. 2002, E.M. Bulakh, VLA M-19061; Tikhorechnoye, 26 Jul. 2006, E.M. Bulakh, VLA M-20679; Upper Ussuri Station, 20 Aug. 1974, E.M. Bulakh, VLA M-13597; Birobidzhan: Bastak Nature Reserve, 18 Aug. 2000, E.M. Bulakh, VLA M-15265.

Coprinus stercoreus Fr.

On the dung in korean pine forest, Upper Ussuri Station, 19 Aug. 1974, E.M. Bulakh, VLA M-5176.

Coprinus truncorum (Scop.) Fr.

On the wood in coniferous-broad-leaved forest, 13 Aug. 2000, E.M. Bulakh, VLA M-15358.

Coprinus xanthotryx Romagn

On the wood in ash forest, Ussuriysk Nature Reserve, 12 Aug. 1961 L.N. Vassiljeva, VLA M-5178.

Lacrymaria lacrymabunda (Bull.) Pat.

[= *Psathyrella velutina* (Pers.) Singer]

On the ground under *Populus* in poplar forest, Ussuriysk Nature Reserve, 22 Sept. 1961, L.N. Vassiljeva, VLA M-5371; Upper Ussuri Station, 9 Sept. 1973, E.M. Bulakh, VLA M-5363; in willow forest, Big Khekhtsir Reserve, 30 Jun. 1981, E.M. Bulakh, VLA M-5361.

Psathyrella appendiculata Fr.

On the decayed wood in korean pine-broad-leaved forest, Ussuriysk Nature Reserve, 16 Sept. 1955, L.N. Vassiljeva, VLA M-5209.

Psathyrella bepellis (Quél.) A.H. Sm.

On the wood in coniferous-broad-leaved forest, Upper Ussuri Station, 25 Jun. 1974, E.M. Bulakh, VLA M-5210.

Psathyrella candolleana (Fr.) Maire

On the wood in korean pine-broad-leaved forest, Ussuriysk Nature Reserve, 18 Aug. 1975, E.M. Bulakh, VLA M-19491; in deciduous forest, Big Khekhtsir Nature Reserve, 21 Jun. 1981, E.M. Bulakh, VLA M-5239. - On the ground in the thicket of *Salix* and *Rhamnus*,

Khanka Nature Reserve, 21 Jun. 2002, V.Yu. Barkalov, VLA M-17188; in dark coniferous forest, Upper Ussuri Station, 24 Jun. 1974, E.M. Bulakh, VLA M-5211; Birobidzhan: Bastak Nature Reserve, 14 Aug. 2000, E.M. Bulakh, VLA M-15376.

Psathyrella cernua (Vahl.) M.M. Moser

On the ground in broad-leaved forest, Ussuriysk Nature Reserve, 7 Sept. 1963, M.M. Nazarova, VLA M-5292; Birobidzhan: Bastak Nature Reserve, 13 Aug. 2000, E.M. Bulakh, VLA M-15247.

Psathyrella chondroderma (Berk. et Broome) A.H. Sm.

On the forest litter in korean pine-broad-leaved forest, Ussuriysk Nature Reserve, 7 Aug. 2003, E.M. Bulakh, VLA M-18412.

Psathyrella conopilus (Fr.) A. Pearson et Dennis

On the log among mosses in korean pine-broad-leaved forest, Ussuriysk Nature Reserve, 28 Aug. 1961, L.N. Vassiljeva, VLA M-5250; Upper Ussuri Station, 19 Jun. 1974, E.M. Bulakh, VLA M-5251.

Psathyrella fusca (Schumach.) M.M.Moser

On the forest litter in korean pine-broad-leaved forest, Ussuriysk Nature Reserve, 23 Oct. 1962, M.M. Nazarova, VLA M-5266; Birobidzhan: Bastak Nature Reserve, 9 Sept. 2001, E.M. Bulakh, VLA M-16865. - On the log of *Acer* in dark coniferous forest, Big Khekhtsir Nature Reserve, 7 Sept. 1983, E.M. Bulakh, VLA M-5268.

Psathyrella gordonii (Berk. et Broome) A. Pearson et Dennis

On the forest litter in broad-leaved forest, Ussuriysk Nature Reserve, 9 Sept. 1955, L.N. Vassiljeva, VLA M-5273.

Psathyrella gracilis (Fr.) Quél.

On the forest litter in korean pine-broad-leaved forest, Ussuriysk Nature Reserve, 19 Sept. 1961, E.M. Bulakh, VLA M-5276. - On the wood in oak forest, Khanka Nature Reserve, 28 Aug. 2002, E.M. Bulakh, VLA M-17482; in coniferous-broad-leaved forest, Upper Ussuri Station, 26 Aug. 1973, E.M. Bulakh, VLA M-5275.

Psathyrella lutensis (Romagn.) M.M. Moser

On the wood in korean pine-broad-leaved forest, Ussuriysk Nature Reserve, 1 Jun. 1961, L.N. Vassiljeva, VLA M-5283; in oak forest, Ussuriysk: Gornotayozhnoye, 5 Aug. 2003, E.M. Bulakh, VLA M-18418; Birobidzhan: Bastak Nature Reserve, 21 Aug. 2003, E.M. Bulakh, VLA M-18417. - On the forest litter in oak forest, Nikolaevka, 19 Sept. 2000, E.M. Bulakh, VLA M-15176.

Psathyrella melanthina (Fr.) Kits van Wav.

On the wood in korean pine-broad-leaved forest, Ussuriysk Nature Reserve, 7 Aug. 2003, E.M. Bulakh, VLA M-18407; in the stand of trees, Ussuriysk: Gornotayozhnoye, 23 Jul. 2001, E.M. Bulakh, VLA M-17469; in broad-leaved forest, Khanka Nature Reserve, 21 Jun. 2003, E.M. Bulakh, VLA M-18343.

Psathyrella multipedata (Peck) A.H. Sm.

On the forest litter in broad-leaved forest, Ussuriysk Nature Reserve, 11 Aug. 1961, L.N. Vassiljeva, VLA M-5285.

Psathyrella obtusata (Pers.) A.H. Sm.

On the forest litter in korean pine-broad-leaved forest, Ussuriysk Nature Reserve, 9 Sept. 1961, L.N. Vassiljeva, VLA M-5289; Birobidzhan: Bastak Nature Reserve, 14 Aug. 2000, E.M. Bulakh, VLA M-15258.

Psathyrella piluliformis (Bull.) P.D. Orton

On the wood in korean pine-broad-leaved forest, Ussuriysk Nature Reserve, 6 Sept. 1975, M.M. Nazarova, VLA M-5279; in broad-leaved forest, Usuriysk: Gornotayozhnoye, 5 Aug. 2003, E.M. Bulakh, VLA M-19003.

Psathyrella pseudocasca (Romagn.) Kits van Wav.

On the forest litter in korean pine-broad-leaved forest, Ussuriysk Nature Reserve, 16 Sept. 1962, M.M. Nazarova, VLA M-5296; in poplar forest, Upper Ussuri Station, 10 Jun. 1975, E.M. Bulakh, VLA M-5294.

Psathyrella pygmaea (Bull.) Singer

On the wood in broad-leaved forest, Ussuriysk Nature Reserve, 13 Jul. 1961, L.N. Vassiljeva, VLA M-5301; Upper Ussuri Station, 18 Sept. 1974, E.M. Bulakh, VLA M-5318; Birobidzhan: Bastak Nature Reserve, 11 Sept. 2001, E.M. Bulakh, VLA M-16873.

Psathyrella sarcocephala (Fr.) Singer

On the ground in korean pine forest, Upper Ussuri Station, 14 Jun. 1975, E.M. Bulakh, VLA M-5325; in aspen forest, Big Khekhtsir Nature Reserve, 29 Jun. 1981, E.M. Bulakh, VLA M-5715.

Psathyrella scobinacea (Fr.) Konrad et Maubl.

On the wood of *Carpinus* in coniferous-broad-leaved forest, Ussuriysk Nature Reserve, 15 Sept. 1961, L.N. Vassiljeva, VLA M-5329.

Psathyrella spadicea (Schaeff.) Singer.

On the wood of *Ulmus* in broad-leaved forest, Ussuriysk Nature Reserve, 8 Sept. 1975, M.M. Nazarova, VLA M-5347. - On the log of *Quercus* in broad-leaved forest, Fuyuan, 4 Aug. 2004, E.M. Bulakh, VLA M-20292; Birobidzhan: Bastak Nature Reserve, 15 Aug. 2002, E.M. Bulakh, VLA M-17290.

Psathyrella sphaerocystis P.D. Orton

On the wood in broad-leaved forest, Birobidzhan: Bastak Nature Reserve, 21 Aug. 2003, E.M. Bulakh, VLA M-18420.

Psathyrella spintrigera (Fr.) Konrad et Maubl.

On the wood in broad-leaved forest, Evseevka, 25 Aug. 1955, L.N. Vassiljeva, VLA M-5358.

ENTOLOMATACEAE

Clitopilus prunulus (Scop.) P. Kumm.

On the ground in oak forest, Novotroitskoye, 14 Jul. 2004, E.M. Bulakh, VLA M-19496; Fuyuan, 5 Aug. 2004, E.M. Bulakh, VLA M- 20390; in birch forest, Big Khekhtsir Nature Reserve, 5 Sept. 1983, E.M. Bulakh, VLA M-3469; Hulin, 9 Aug. 2004, Tolgor Bau, HMJAU 2641; Fuyuan, 5 Aug. 2004, E.M. Bulakh, VLA M-20390.

Entoloma abortivum (Berk. et M.A. Curtis) Donk   Plate 6: 33

On the basis of trunk in korean pine-broad-leaved forest, Ussuriysk Nature Reserve, 17 Sept. 1863, M.M. Nazarova, VLA M-18397; Big Khekhtsir Nature Reserve, 14 Sept. 1981, E.M. Bulakh, VLA M-3506; Birobidzhan: Bastak Nature Reserve, 10 Sept. 2001, E.M. Bulakh, VLA M-16830. - On the ground in coniferous-broad-leved forest, Upper Ussuri Station, 3 Sept.1973, E.M. Bulakh, VLA M-3488.

Entoloma apiculatum (Fr.) Noordel.

On the decayed wood in coniferous-broad-leaved forest, Ussuriysk Nature Reserve (Vasilyeva & Bezdeleva, 2006).

Entoloma araneosum (Quél.) M.M. Moser

[= *Entoloma fulvostrigosum* (Berk et Broome) M.M. Moser]

On the ground in ash forest, Big Khekhtsir Nature Reserve, 11 Aug. 1981, E.M. Bulakh, VLA M-3471.

Entoloma ater (Hongo) Hongo et Izawa

On the ground in forest, Big Khekhtsir Nature Reserve, 15 Aug. 2004, Tolgor Bau, 2949.

Entoloma byssisedum (Pers.) Donk

On the basis of trunk of *Acer* in coniferous-broad-leaved forest, Ussuriysk Nature Reserve, 14 Aug. 1961, L.N. Vassiljeva, VLA M-18401. - On the trunk of *Ulmus* in broad-leaved forest, Big Khekhtsir Nature Reserve, 11 Aug. 1981, E.M. Bulakh, VLA M-18402. - On the wood in oak forest, Raohe: Shangli State Farm, 6 Aug. 2004, E.M. Bulakh, VLA M-19577; Raohe, 7 Aug. 2004, E.M. Bulakh, VLA M-19573.

Entoloma chalybaeum (Pers.) Noordel var. *lazulinum* (Fr.) Noordel.

On the decayed wood in korean pine-broad-leaved forest, Ussuriysk Nature Reserve, 12 Sept. 1955, L.N. Vassiljeva, VLA M-3548. - On the forest litter in oak forest, Big Khekhtsir Nature Reserve, 3 Aug. 1981, E.M. Bulakh, VLA M-3546. - On the ground in broad-leaved forest, Shirokaya Canyon, 31 Aug. 2002, E.M. Bulakh, VLA M-20533.

Entoloma clypeatum (L.) P. Kumm.   Plate 6: 34

On the ground under the tree of *Prunulus* in a garden, Tikhorechnoye, 12 Jun. 1989, E.M. Bulakh, VLA M-3489.

Entoloma crassipes Imazeki et Toki

On the ground in forest, Big Khekhtsir Nature Reserve, 16 Aug. 2004, Tolgor Bau,

HMJAU 2759; Fuyuan, 5 Aug. 2004, Tolgor Bau, HMJAU 2565.

Entoloma dystales (Peck) Sacc.

On the ground in broad-leaved forest, Big Khekhtsir Nature Reserve, 26 Jun. 1981, E.M. Bulakh, VLA M-3517; in birch forest, Raohe, 7 Aug. 2004, E.M. Bulakh, VLA M-20289.

Entoloma griseocyaneum (Fr.) P. Kumm.

On the ground in ash forest, Ussuriysk Nature Reserve, 12 Aug. 1961, L.N. Vassiljeva, VLA M-20506; in oak forest, Usuriysk: Gornotayozhnoye, 9 Sept. 1963, M.M. Nazarova, VLA M-20502.

Entoloma griseorubellum (Lasch) Kalamees et Urbonas

On the ground in broad-leaved forest, Ussuriysk Nature Reserve, 11 Aug. 1961, L.N. Vassiljeva, VLA M-3530; Big Khekhtsir Nature Reserve, 30 Jun. 1981, E.M. Bulakh, VLA M-3529.

Entoloma hirtipes (Schumach.) M.M. Moser

On the log among mosses in coniferous-broad-leaved forest, Ussuriysk Nature Reserve, 25 Aug. 1961, M.M. Nazarova, VLA M-3532.

Entoloma jubatum (Fr.) P. Karst.

On the rotten wood in broad-leaved forest, Birobidzhan: Bastak Nature Reserve, 18 Aug. 2003, E.M. Bulakh, VLA M-19337.

Entoloma juncinum (Kuhn. et Romagn.) Noordel [Vassiljeva, 1973 as *Rhodophyllus junceus* (Fr.) Quél.].

On the ground in broad-leaved forest, Big Khekhtsir Nature Reserve, 28 Aug. 1983, E.M. Bulakh, VLA M-3536. - On the wood in forest litter in dark coniferous forest, Upper Ussuri Station, 12 Aug. 1974, E.M. Bulakh, VLA M-20525; Birobidzhan: Bastak Nature Reserve, 16 Aug. 2002, E.M. Bulakh, VLA M-19354.

Entoloma lampropum (Fr.) Hesler

On the ground in coniferous-broad-leaved forest, Ussuriysk Nature Reserve, 17 Sept. 1963, M.M. Nazarova, VLA M-20528; in korean pine forest, Upper Ussuri Station, 16 Sept. 1975, E.M. Bulakh, VLA M-3545. - On the wood in broad-leaved forest, Ussuriysk: Gornotayozhnoye, 6 Aug. 2003, E.M. Bulakh, VLA M-19332; in dark coniferous forest, Big Khekhtsir Nature Reserve, 7 Sept. 1983, E.M. Bulakh, VLA M-3544; Birobidzhan: Bastak Nature Reserve, 16 Aug. 2002, E.M. Bulakh, VLA M-19346.

Entoloma mammosum (L.) Hesler

On the ground in ash forest, Ussuriysk Nature Reserve (Vasilyeva & Bezdeleva, 2006).

Entoloma neglectum (Lasch) Arnolds

On the forest litter in birch forest, Big Khekhtsir Nature Reserve, 31 Aug. 1983, E.M. Bulakh, VLA M-20488.

Entoloma papillatum (Bres.) Dennis

On the forest litter in korean pine-broad-leaved forest, Ussuriysk Nature Reserve, 26

Sept. 1961, M.M. Nazarova, VLA M-20556; in dark coniferous forest, Upper Ussuri Station, 29 Aug. 1973, E.M. Bulakh, VLA M-20557. - On the wood in coniferous-broad-leaved forest, Big Khekhtsir Nature Reserve, 28 Aug. 1983, E.M. Bulakh, VLA M-3559.

Entoloma parasiticum (Quél.) Kreisel

On the decayed wood in korean pine-broad-leaved forest, Ussuriysk Nature Reserve, 4 Aug. 1962, M.M. Nazarova, VLA M-20560. - On the wood among mosses in broad-leaved forest, Raohe: Shengli State Farm, 6 Aug. 2004, E.M. Bulakh, VLA M-20275.

Entoloma parkensis (Fr.) Noordel.

On the wood in broad-leaved forest, Birobidzhan: Bastak Nature Reserve, 7 Sept. 2001, E.M. Bulakh, VLA M-16876.

Entoloma placidum (Fr.) Noordel.

On the ground in coniferous-broad-leaved forest, 23 Aug. 1973, E.M. Bulakh, VLA M-20569; in broad-leaved forest, Big Khekhtsir Nature Reserve, 10 Sept. 1946, L.N. Vassiljeva, VLA M-20565.

Entoloma plebejum (Kalchbr.) Noordel.

On the ground in broad-leaved forest, Birobidzhan: Bastak Nature Reserve, 11 Sept. 2001, E.M. Bulakh, VLA M-19323.

Entoloma pleopodium (Bull.) Noordel.

(= *Entoloma icterinum* M.M. Moser)

On the ground in birch forest, Big Khekhtsir Nature Reserve, 2 Sept. 1983, E.M. Bulakh, VLA M-3534; Raohe, 7 Aug. 2004, E.M. Bulakh, VLA M-19624.

Entoloma porphyrophaeum (Fr.) P. Karst.

On the ground in deciduous forest, Upper Ussuri Station, 11 Sept. 2002, E.M. Bulakh, VLA M-19327.

Entoloma quadratum (Berk. et M.A. Curtis) Horak

[= *Entoloma salmoneum* (Peck) Sacc.]

On the ground in korean pine-broad-leaved forest, Ussuriysk Nature Reserve, 20 Aug. 2005, E.M. Bulakh, VLA M-20194.

Entoloma rhodopolium (Fr.) P. Kumm.

On the ground in korean pine-broad-leaved forest, Ussuriysk Nature Reserve, 31 Aug. 1962, M.M. Nazarova, VLA M-3572; in oak forest, Khanka Nature Reserve, 30 Aug. 2002, E.M. Bulakh, VLA M-19292; in broad-leaved forest, Tikhorechnoye, 21 Jul. 1998, E.M. Bulakh, VLA M-10568; in dark coniferous forest, Upper Ussuri Station, 17 Sept. 1974, E.M. Bulakh, VLA M-3574; in aspen forest, Big Khekhtsir Nature Reserve, 5 Aug. 1981, E.M. Bulakh, VLA M-3568; Birobidzhan: Bastak Nature Reserve, 19 Aug. 2004, E.M. Bulakh, VLA M-19613; Raohe, 7 Aug. 2004, Tolgor Bau, HMJAU 3233.

Entoloma rusticoides (Gillet) Noordel.

On the ground in broad-leaved forest, Birobidzhan: Bastak Nature Reserve, 11 Sept.

2001, E.M. Bulakh, VLA M-16864.

Entoloma sericeum (Bull.) Quél.

On the forest litter in korean pine-broad-leaved forest, Ussuriysk Nature Reserve, 24 Aug. 1963, M.M. Nazarova, VLA M-3589; in dark coniferous forest, Upper Ussuri Station, 15 Sept. 1974, E.M. Bulakh, VLA M-20631; Big Khekhtsir Nature Reserve, 7 Sept. 1983, E.M. Bulakh, VLA M-3592. - On the ground in oak forest, Khanka Nature Reserve, 30 Aug. 2002, E.M. Bulakh, VLA M-19356; Birobidzhan: Bastak Nature Reserve, 14 Aug. 2000, E.M. Bulakh, VLA M-15355.

Entoloma serrulatum (Peck) Hesler

On the ground in broad-leaved forest, Tikhorechnoye, 6 Aug. 2005, E.M. Bulakh, VLA M-20193; Birobidzhan: Bastak Nature Reserve, 12 Aug. 2000, E.M. Bulakh, VLA M-15356; Raohe: Shengli State Farm, 6 Aug. 2004, E.M. Bulakh, VLA M-20398.

Entoloma speculum (Fr.) Quél.

On the ground in korean pine-broad-leaved forest, Ussuriysk Nature Reserve, 28 Sept. 1946, L.N. Vassiljeva, VLA M-20614. - On the forest litter, Upper Ussuri Station, 15 Aug. 1974, E.M. Bulakh, VLA M-3596; Birobidzhan: Bastak Nature Reserve, 8 Sept. 2001, E.M. Bulakh, VLA M-19341.

Entoloma strigossimum (Rea) Noordel.

On the forest litter in broad-leaved forest, Raohe: Shengli State Farm, 6 Aug. 2004, E.M. Bulakh, VLA M-19631.

Entoloma undatum (Fr.) M.M. Moser

On the ground in coniferous-broad-leaved forest, Ussuriysk Nature Reserve, 7 Sept. 1963, M.M. Nazarova, VLA M-20618; in birch forest, Big Khekhtsir Nature Reserve, 30 Jun. 1981, E.M. Bulakh, VLA M-3598.

Rhodocybe caelata (Fr.) Maire

On the wood in korean pine-broad-leaved forest, Birobidzhan: Bastak Nature Reserve, 17 Aug. 2002, E.M. Bulakh, VLA M-17514.

Rhodocybe falax (Quél.) Singer

On the forest litter in fir-broad-leaved forest, Ussuriysk Nature Reserve, 4 Sept. 1968, M.M. Nazarova, VLA M-3462; in broad-leaved forest, Big Khekhtsir Nature Reserve, 20 Aug. 1983, E.M. Bulakh, VLA M-3463; Birobidzhan: Bastak Nature Reserve, 20 Aug. 2003, E.M. Bulakh, VLA M-19169.

Rhodocybe nitellina (Fr.) Singer

On the forest litter in fir-broad-leaved forest, Ussuriysk Nature Reserve, 21 Aug. 1961, L.N. Vassiljeva, VLA M-18369; in coniferous-broad-leaved forest, Upper Ussuri Station, 29 Aug. 1973, E.M. Bulakh, VLA M-18374; in dark coniferous forest, Big Khekhtsir Nature Reserve, 14 Aug. 1981, E.M. Bulakh, VLA M-18375.

Rhodocybe popinalis (Fr.) Singer

[= *Rhodocybe mundula* (Lasch) Singer]

On the forest litter in fir-broad-leaved forest, Ussuriysk Nature Reserve, 21 Aug. 1961, L.N. Vassiljeva, VLA M-18369; in coniferous-broad-leaved forest, Big Khekhtsir Nature Reserve, 31 Aug. 1983, E.M. Bulakh, VLA M-18367.

HYGROPHORACEAE

Hygrocybe cantharellus (Schwein.) Murrill

On the ground in broad-leaved forest, Ussuriysk Nature Reserve (Vasilyeva & Bezdeleva, 2006); in the thicket of *Spiraea*, Khanka Nature Reserve, 21 Jun. 2004, V.Yu. Barkalov, VLA M-19342; Big Khekhtsir Nature Reserve, 16 Aug. 2004, Tolgor Bau, HMJAU 2779; Birobidzhan: Bastak Nature Reserve, 18 Aug. 2004, Tolgor Bau, HMJAU 2790, 2801, 3188.

Hygrocybe ceracea (Wulfen) P. Kumm.

On the ground in broad-leaved forest, Raohe: Shengli State Farm, 6 Aug. 2004, E.M. Bulakh, VLA M-20214; Birobidzhan: Bastak Nature Reserve, 12 Aug. 2002, E.M. Bulakh, VLA M-17534.

Hygrocybe chlorophana (Fr.) Wünsche

On the ground in broad-leaved forest, Big Khekhtsir Nature Reserve (Azbukina & Kharkevich, 1986).

Hygrocybe coccinea (Schaeff.) P. Kumm.

On the wood and ground in broad-leaved and dark coniferous forests, Big Khekhtsir Nature Reserve (Azbukina & Kharkevich, 1986).

Hygrocybe conica (Scop.) P. Kumm.

On the ground in coniferous-broad-leaved forest, Ussuriysk Nature Reserve (Vasilyeva & Bezdeleva, 2006); Big Khekhtsir Nature Reserve, 15, 16 Aug. 2004, Tolgor Bau, HMJAU 2795, 2892; in broad-leaved forest, Hulin, 9 Aug. 2004, Tolgor Bau, HMJAU 3361, 3362; Raohe: Shengli State Farm, 6 Aug. 2004, E.M. Bulakh, VLA M-20400, 7 Aug. 2004, Tolgor Bau, HMJAU 3210; Birobidzhan: Bastak Nature Reserve,18 Aug. 2004, Tolgor Bau, HMJAU 3242.

Hygrocybe cystidiata Arnolds

On the wood in fir forest, Ussuriysk Nature Reserve, 26 Aug. 1961, L.N. Vassiljeva, VLA M-520.

Hygrocybe flavescens (Kauffm.) Singer

On the ground in broad-leaved forest, Raohe, 7 Aug. 2004, Tolgor Bau, HMJAU 3244; Big Khekhtsir Nature Reserve, 16 Aug. 2004, Tolgor Bau, HMJAU 3196.

Hygrocybe insipida (J.E. Lange ex S. Lundell) M.M. Moser

On the ground in broad-leaved forest, Raohe: Shengli State Farm, 6 Aug. 2004, E.M.

Bulakh, VLA M-19653; Birobidzhan: Bastak Nature Reserve, 22 Aug. 2003, E.M. Bulakh, VLA M-19200.

Hygrocybe laeta (Pers.) P. Kumm.

On the ground and forest litter in coniferous-broad-leaved forest, Ussuriysk Nature Reserve (Vasilyeva & Bezdeleva, 2006); in the thiket of *Crataegus*, Khanka Nature Reserve, 28 Aug. 2003, E.M. Bulakh, VLA M-19257; Birobidzhan: Bastak Nature Reserve, 13 Aug. 2000, E.M. Bulakh, VLA M-15465.

Hygrocybe mucronella (Fr.) P. Karst.

[= *Gliophorus reae* (Maire) Kovalenko]

On the ground in korean pine-broad-leaved forest, Ussuriysk Nature Reserve, 21 Aug. 1975, E.M. Bulakh, VLA M-530; Upper Ussuri Station, 29 Aug. 1973, E.M. Bulakh, VLA M-18374.

Hygrocybe parvula (Peck) Pegler

[= *Pseudohygrocybe parvula* (Peck) Kovalenko]

On the ground in korean pine-broad-leaved forest, Ussuriysk Nature Reserve, 23 Aug. 1961, M.M. Nazarova, VLA M-527; Big Khekhtsir Nature Reserve (Azbukina & Kharkevich, 1986).

Hygrocybe persistens (Britzelm.) Singer

On the ground in broad-leaved forest, Ussuriysk Nature Reserve (Vasilyeva & Bezdeleva, 2006); Raohe: Shengli State Farm, 6 Aug. 2004, E.M. Bulakh, VLA M-19651; Fuyuan, 4 Aug. 2004, E.M. Bulakh, VLA M-16990; Big Khekhtsir Nature Reserve (Azbukina & Kharkevich, 1986); Birobidzhan: Bastak Nature Reserve, 19 Aug. 2000, E.M. Bulakh, VLA M-15399.

Hygrocybe pratensis Murrill

[= *Camarophyllus pratensis* (Pers.) P. Kumm.]

On the ground in korean pine-broad-leaved forest, Ussuriysk Nature Reserve (Vasilyeva & Bezdeleva, 2006); Big Khekhtsir Nature Reserve, Tolgor Bau, HMJAU 3183, 3225; Raohe, Tolgor Bau, HMJAU 3353; Birobidzhan: Bastak Nature Reserve, 13 Aug. 2002, E.M. Bulakh, VLA M-17518.

Hygrocybe psittacina (Schaeff.) P. Kumm.

On the ground in coniferous-broad-leaved forest, Ussuriysk Nature Reserve (Vasilyeva & Bezdeleva, 2006); in birch forest, Raohe, 7 Aug. 2004, E.M. Bulakh, VLA M-20291; in broad-leaved forest, Big Khekhtsir Nature Reserve (Azbukina & Kharkevich, 1986).

Hygrocybe quieta (Kühner) Singer

[= *Pseudohygrocybe obrussea* (Fr.) Kovalenko]

On the ground and decaying wood in broad-leaved forest, Big Khekhtsir Nature Reserve (Azbukina & Kharkevich, 1986).

Hygrocybe swanetica Singer

(= *Pseudohygrocybe swanetica* (Singer) Kovalenko)

On the decayed wood in korean pine-broad-leaved forest, Ussuriysk Nature Reserve (Vasilyeva & Bezdeleva, 2006); Birobidzhan: Bastak Nature Reserve, 16 Aug. 2000, E.M. Bulakh, VLA M-15393.

Hygrocybe virginea (Wulfen) P.D. Orton et Watling

[= *Hygrocybe nivea* (Scop.) P.D. Orton et Watling]

On the ground in korean pine-broad-leaved forest, Ussuriysk Nature Reserve (Vasilyeva & Bezdeleva, 2006); Upper Ussuri Station (Azbukina & Kharkevich, 1984); Raohe: Shengli State Farm, 6 Aug. 2004, E.M. Bulakh, VLA M-20268, Tolgor Bau, HMJAU, 3238, 3248; Hulin, 8 Sept. 2003, Tolgor Bau, HMJAU 3005; Big Khekhtsir Nature Reserve, Tolgor Bau, HMJAU 3249; Birobidzhan: Bastak Nature Reserve, 17 Aug. 2002, E.M. Bulakh, VLA M-17532.

Hygrocybe vitellina (Fr.) P. Karst.

On the ground in korean pine-broad-leaved forest, Birobidzhan: Bastak Nature Reserve, 17 Aug. 2002, E.M. Bulakh, VLA M-17510.

Hygrophorus arbustivus Fr.

On the ground under the trees of *Quercus* in korean pine-broad-leaved forest, Ussuriysk Nature Reserve (Vasilyeva & Bezdeleva, 2006); in oak forest, Novotroitskoye, 14 Jul. 2004, E.M. Bulakh, VLA M-19495.

Hygrophorus camarophyllus (Alb. et Schwein) Dumée, Grandjean et Maire

On the ground in coniferous-broad leaved forest, Ussuriysk Nature Reserve (Vasilyeva & Bezdeleva, 2006).

Hygrophorus chrysodon (Batsch) Fr.

On the ground under the trees of *Quercus* in korean pine-broad-leaved forest, Ussuriysk Nature Reserve, 11 Sept. 2005, E.M. Bulakh, VLA M-20228; Big Khekhtsir Nature Reserve (Azbukina & Kharkevich, 1986); Birobidzhan: Bastak Nature Reserve, 21 Aug. 2003, E.M. Bulakh, VLA M-19067.

Hygrophorus discoideus (Pers.) Fr.

On the ground in dark coniferous forest, Ussuriysk Nature Reserve, 26 Aug. 1966, M.M. Nazarova, VLA M-467.

Hygrophorus eburneus (Bull.) Fr.

On the ground under the trees of *Quercus* in broad-leaved forest, Ussuriysk Nature Reserve (Vasilyeva & Bezdeleva, 2006); Big Khekhtsir Nature Reserve (Azbukina & Kharkevich, 1986).

Hygrophorus erubescens (Fr.) Fr.

On the ground under the trees of *Abies* and *Picea* in dark coniferous forest, Ussuriysk Nature Reserve (Vasilyeva & Bezdeleva, 2006); Big Khekhtsir Nature Reserve (Azbukina & Kharkevich, 1986).

Hygrophorus hedrychii (Velen.) K. Kult.

Under the trees of *Betula* in birch forest, Ussuriysk, 3 Aug. 2003, Tolgor Bau, 2901; Upper Ussuri Station, 8 Sept. 2005, E.M. Bulakh, VLA M-20278.

Hygrophorus lindtneri M. M. Moser

On the ground under the bush of *Corylus* and the tree of *Carpinus* in broad-leaved forest, Ussuriysk Nature Reserve (Vasilyeva & Bezdeleva, 2006); Ussuriysk, 3 Aug. 2003, Tolgor Bau, HMJAU 2901.

Hygrophorus nemoreus (Pers.) Fr.

On the ground in broad-leaved forest, Ussuriysk Nature Reserve, Big Khekhtsir Nature Reserve (Kovalenko, 1995).

Hygrophorus persoonii Arnolds

On the ground under the tree of *Quercus* in broad-leaved forest, Ussuriysk Nature Reserve [(Vasilyeva & Bezdeleva, 2006), as *Hygrophorus limacinus* (Scop.) Fr.].

Hygrophorus pudorinus (Fr.) Fr.

On the ground under the trees of *Abies*, Ussuriysk Nature Reserve (Vasilyeva & Bezdeleva, 2006); Big Khekhtsir Nature Reserve (Kovalenko, 1995); Birobidzhan: Bastak Nature Reserve, 21 Aug. 2003, E.M. Bulakh, VLA M-19227.

Hygrophorus queletii Bres.

Under the tree of *Larix*, Birobidzhan: Bastak Nature Reserve, 12 Sept. 2002, E.M. Bulakh, VLA M-17538.

Hygrophorus russula (Schaeff.) Kauffman

On the ground under the trees of *Quercus*, Ussuriysk Nature Reserve (Vasilyeva & Bezdeleva, 2006); Big Khekhtsir Nature Reserve, 18 Aug. 2004, Tolgor Bau, HMJAU 2890; Birobidzhan: Bastak Nature Reserve, 17 Aug. 2002, E.M. Bulakh, VLA M-17543.

PLUTEACEAE

Pluteus atromarginatus (Konrad) Kühner

On the log of *Pinus koraiensis* in korean pine-broad-leaved forest, Ussuriysk Nature Reserve, 29 Aug. 1963, M.M. Nazarova, VLA M-3599.

Pluteus aurantiorugosus (Trog.) Sacc.

[= *Pluteus coccineus* (Massee) J. E. Lange]

On the log in korean pine-broad-leaved forest, Ussuriysk Nature Reserve, 10 Aug. 1970, M.M. Nazarova, VLA M-3659; Upper Ussuri Station, 7 Sept. 1975, E.M. Bulakh, VLA M-3660; Tikhorechnoye, 21 Jul. 1998, E.M. Bulakh, VLA M-12875; Big Khekhtsir Nature Reserve, 7 Sept. 1989, E.M. Bulakh, VLA M-3662; Hulin, 20 Sept. 2004, Tolgor Bau, HMJAU 2703; Birobidzhan: Bastak Nature Reserve, 19 Aug. 2004, Tolgor Bau, HMJAU 2773.

Pluteus cervinus (Schaeff.) P. Kumm.

[= *Pluteus atricapillus* (Batsch) Fayod]

On the logs of *Betula* in deciduous forest, Ussuriysk Nature Reserve, 3 Sept. 1961, L.N. Vassiljeva, VLA M-3634; Ussuriysk, 3 Aug. 2003, Tolgor Bau, HMJAU 3229; in broad-leaved forest, Birobidzhan: Bastak Nature Reserve, 9 Sept. 2001, E.M. Bulakh, VLA M-20698. - On the wood in korean pine-broad-leaved forest , Upper Ussuri Station, 15 Aug. 1974, E.M. Bulakh, VLA M-3620; Big Khekhtsir Nature Reserve, 22 Jun. 1981 E.M. Bulakh, VLA M-3630; Fujuan, 4 Aug. 2004, E.M. Bulakh, VLA M-19636, Tolgor Bau, HMJAU 3404; Raohe, 7 Aug. 2004, Tolgor Bau, HMJAU 2527; Hulin, 19 Sept. 2004, Tolgor Bau, HMJAU 2704; Hailin Mudanjiang, Aug. 2004, Tolgor Bau, HMJAU 2584.

Pluteus chrysophaeus (Schaeff.) Quél.

On the log of a coniferous tree in korean pine-broad-leaved forest, Ussuriysk Nature Reserve, 14 Sept. 1961, L.N. Vassiljeva, VLA M-3671. - On the log of a deciduous tree in broad-leaved forest, Big Khekhetsir Nature Reserve, 28 Aug. 1946, L.N. Vassiljeva, VLA M-3674.

Pluteus cinereofuscus J.E. Lange

On the basis of trunk of *Ulmus* in ash forest, Ussuriysk Nature Reserve, 16 Aug. 1962, M.M. Nazarova, VLA M-3675.

Pluteus diettrichii Bres.

(= *Pluteus rimulosus* Kühner et Romagn.)

Near the trunk of a deciduous tree in broad-leaved forest, Ussuriysk Nature Reserve, 17 Aug. 1961, L.N. Vassiljeva, VLA M-3814.

Pluteus hiatulus Romagn.

On the log of *Quercus* in korean pine-broad-leaved forest, Ussuriysk Nature Reserve (Vasilyeva & Bezdeleva, 2006).

Pluteus hispidulus (Fr.) Gillet

On the logs of deciduous tree in coniferous-broad-leaved forest, Ussuriysk Nature Reserve, 21 Aug. 1961, L.N.Vassileva, VLA M-3704; in oak forest, Ussuriysk: Gornotayozhnoye, 4 Aug. 2002, E.M. Bulakh, VLA M -19303; Upper Ussuri Station, 11 Sept. 1975, E.M. Bulakh, VLA M-3705; Big Khekhtsir Nature Reserve, 11 Aug. 1981, E.M. Bulakh, VLA M-3702; in birch forest, Raoche, 7 Aug. 2004, E.M. Bulakh, VLA M-19596. - On the log of *Quercus* in broad-leaved forest, Khanka Nature Reserve, 28 Aug. 2002, E.M. Bulakh, VLA M-19315

Pluteus leoninus (Schaeff.) P. Kumm.

On the logs of *Ulmus* in broad-leaved forest, Ussuriysk Nature Reserve, 20 Aug. 1970, M.M. Nazarova, VLA M-3734; Ussuriysk, 4 Aug. 2004, Tolgor Bau, HMJAU 2894; Upper Ussuri Station, 16 Sept. 1974, E.M. Bulakh, VLA M-3726. - On the log in broad-leaved forest, Ussuriysk, 4 Aug. 2003, Tolgor Bau, HMJAU 2894; Khanka Nature Reserve, 21 Aug. 2003,

E.M. Bulakh, VLA M-19186; in dark coniferous forest, Big Khekhtsir Nature Reserve, 19Aug. 1983, E.M. Bulakh, VLA M-3738; Birobidzhan: Bastak Nature Reserve, 13 Aug. 2000, E.M. Bulakh, VLA M-15275.

Pluteus luctuosus Boud.

[= *Pluteus marginatus* (Quél.) Bres.]

On the wood buried in soil in coniferous-broad-leaved forest, Ussuriysk Nature Reserve (Vasilyeva & Bezdeleva, 2006).

Pluteus luteus (Redhead et B. Liu) Redhead

On rotten wood, Ussuriysk, 4 Aug. 2003, Tolgor Bau, HMJAU 2916.

Pluteus nanus (Pers.) P. Kumm.

On the logs in coniferous-broad-leaved forest, Ussuriysk Nature Reserve, 12 Aug. 1961, M.M. Nazarova, VLA M-3775; Ussuriysk, 4 Aug. 2003, Tolgor Bau, HMJAU 3421; Upper Ussuri Station, 8 Aug. 1973, E.M. Bulakh, VLA M-3784; Tikhorechnoye, 2 Jul. 1988, E.M. Bulakh, VLA M-12181; Big Khekhtsir Nature Reserve, 29 Jun. 1981, E.M. Bulakh, VLA M-3793.

Pluteus pellitus (Pers.) P. Kumm.

On the logs in coniferous-broad-leaved forest, Ussuriysk Nature Reserve (Vasilyeva & Bezdeleva, 2006); Raohe, 7 Aug. 2004, Tolgor Bau, HMJAU 3224. - On the log of *Betula* in broad-leaved forest, Tikhorechnoye, 4 Aug. 2004, E.M. Bulakh, VLA M-20290.

Pluteus petasatus (Fr.) Gillet

On the logs in coniferous-broad-leaved forest, Ussuriysk Nature Reserve, 15 Sept. 1961, M.M. Nazarova, VLA M-3798; Big Khekhtsir Nature Reserve, 29 Jun. 1981, E.M. Bulakh, VLA M-3683; in broad-leaved forest, Birobidzhan: Bastak Nature Reserve, 13 Aug. 2006, E.M. Bulakh, VLA M-20988. - On the log of *Betula*, Upper Usuri Station, 26 Aug. 1973, E.M. Bulakh, VLA M-3687.

Pluteus plautus (Weinm.) Gillet

On the wood of a deciduous tree in coniferous-broad-leaved forest, Ussuriysk Nature Reserve, 9 Sept. 1961, M.M. Nazarova, VLA M-3808; Birobidzhan: Bastak Nature Reserve, 19 Aug. 2003, E.M. Bulakh, VLA M-19185.

Pluteus podospileus Sacc. et Cub.

(= *Pluteus minutissimus* Maire)

On the wood of deciduous trees in coniferous-broad-leaved forest, Ussuriysk Nature Reserve, 14 Sept. 1961, M.M. Nazarova, VLA M-3761; Big Khekhtsir Nature Reserve, 20 Jun. 1981, E.M. Bulakh, VLA M-3770; in fir-broad-leaved forest, Birobidzhan: Bastak Nature Reserve, 13 Aug. 2000, E.M. Bulakh, VLA M-15391. - On the log of *Betula*, Upper Ussuri Station, 18 Aug. 1974, E.M. Bulakh, VLA M-3767.

Pluteus romelii (Britzelm.) Lapl.

[= *Pluteus lutescens* (Fr.) Bres.]

On the logs in coniferous-broad-leaved forest, Ussuriysk Nature Reserve, 10 Aug. 1961, M.M. Nazarova, VLA M-3747; in korean pine forest, Upper Ussuri Station, 26 Aug. 1973, E.M. Bulakh, VLA M-3753; in oak forest, Big Khekhtsir Nature Reserve, 12 Aug. 1981, E.M. Bulakh, VLA M-3757; Birobidzhan: Bastak Nature Reserve, 21 Aug. 2003, E.M. Bulakh, VLA M-19239.

Pluteus salicinus (Pers.) P. Kumm.

On the logs of deciduous tree in coniferous-broad-leaved forest, Ussuriysk Nature Reserve, 20 Aug. 1961, L.N. Vassiljeva, VLA M-3820; Ussuriysk, 3 Aug. 2003, Tolgor Bau, HMJAU 2910; Upper Ussuri Station, 10 Aug. 1973, E.M. Bulakh, VLA M-3816; Birobidzhan: Bastak Nature Reserve, 21 Aug. 2003, E.M. Bulakh, VLA M-19240.

Pluteus semibulbosus (Lasch) Gillet

On the logs of deciduous trees in coniferous-broad-leaved forest, Ussuriysk Nature Reserve, 17 Aug. 1962, M.M. Nazarova, VLA M-3824; in broad-leaved forest, Ussuriysk: Gornotayozhnoye, 6 Aug. 2003, E.M. Bulakh, VLA M-19226; in korean pine forest, Upper Ussuri Station, 22 Aug. 1975, E.M. Bulakh, VLA M-3832.

Pluteus thomsonii (Berk. et Broome) Dennis

On the log of *Betula* in broad-leaved forest, Raohe, 7 Aug. 2004, E.M. Bulakh, VLA M-20648.

Pluteus tomentosus Peck

On the wood buried in soil in coniferous-broad-leaved forest, Ussuriysk Nature Reserve, 20 Aug. 1962, M.M. Nazarova, VLA M-3837.

Pluteus umbrosus (Pers.) P. Kumm.

On the logs of deciduous trees in coniferous-broad-leaved forest, Ussuriysk Nature Reserve, 12 Sept. 1961, L.N. Vassiljeva, VLA M-3838; in broad-leaved forest, Ussuriysk: Gornotayozhnoye, 6 Aug. 2003, E.M. Bulakh, VLA M-19216; Tikhorechnoye, 26 Jul. 2006, E.M. Bulakh, VLA M-20681; Upper Ussuri Station, 7 Aug. 1973 E.M. Bulakh, VLA M-3845; Big Khekhtsir Nature Reserve, 1 Sept. 1983, E.M. Bulakh, VLA M-3843; Birobidzhan: Bastak Nature Reserve, 12 Aug. 2000, E.M. Bulakh, VLA M-15390.

Volvariella bombycina (Schaeff.) Singer   Plate 6: 35

On the ground near the road in broad-leaved forest, Ussuriysk Nature Reserve, 6 Sept. 1951, L.N. Vassiljeva, VLA M-3849; Birobidzhan: Bastak Nature Reserve, 16 Aug. 2000, E.M. Bulakh, VLA M-15255. - On the log of *Populus* in coniferous-broad-leaved forest, Upper Ussuri Station, 3 Aug. 1974, E.M. Bulakh, VLA M-3851. - On the wood of *Tilia* in dark coniferous forest, Big Khekhtsir Reserve, 15 Aug. 1981 E.M. Bulakh, VLA M-3857.

Volvariella gloiocephala (DC.) Boekhout et Enderle

[= *Volvariella speciosa* (Fr.) Singer]

On the forest litter in ash forest, Ussuriysk Nature Reserve, 12 Aug. 1961, L.N. Vassiljeva, VLA M-3872; Ussuriysk, 3 Aug. 2003, Tolgor Bau, HMJAU 2960. - On the ground in coniferous-broad-leaved forest, Upper Ussuri Station, 7 Aug. 1973, E.M. Bulakh, VLA M-3858.

Volvariella murinella (Quél.) M.M. Moser

On the wood in coniferous-broad-leaved forest, Ussuriysk Nature Reserve, 28 Aug. 1961, L.N. Vassiljeva, VLA M-3866.

Volvariella pusilla (Pers.) Singer

On the forest litter in coniferous-broad-leaved forest, Ussuriysk Nature Reserve, 10 Aug. 1962, M.M. Nazarova, VLA M-3870; in korean pine forest, Upper Ussuri Station, 15 Aug. 1974, E.M. Bulakh, VLA M-3869.

Volvariella volvacea (Bull.) Singer   Plate 6: 36

On the decayed wood in broad-leaved forest, Ussuriysk Nature Reserve, 6 Aug. 1962, M.M. Nazarova, VLA M-3880; Khanka Nature Reserve, 28 Jul. 2007, E.M. Bulakh, VLA M-21482; Big Khekhtsir Nature Reserve, 23 Sept. 1983, E.M. Bulakh, VLA M-3879; Birobidzhan: Bastak Nature Reserve, 21 Aug. 2004, E.M. Bulakh, VLA M-19595. - On the log of *Ulmus* in korean pine-broad-leaved forest, Upper Ussuri Station, 26 Aug. 1973, E.M. Bulakh, VLA M-3876.

STROPHARIACEAE

Hypholoma capnoides (Fr.) P. Kumm.

On the wood in broad-leaved forest, Ussuriysk Nature Reserve, 25 Sept. 1946, L.N. Vassiljeva, VLA M-5648. - On the wood of *Picea* in dark coniferous forest, Upper Ussuri Station, 15 Sept. 1974, E.M. Bulakh, VLA M-5644; Big Khekhtsir Nature Reserve, 19 Jun. 1974, E.M. Bulakh, VLA M-5667; Birobidzhan: Bastak Nature Reserve, 12 Sept. 2001, E.M. Bulakh, VLA M-16389.

Hypholoma elongatipes (Peck) A.H. Sm.

On the ground of marsh, Birobidzhan: Bastak Nature Reserve, 21 Aug. 2003, E.M. Bulakh, VLA M-19235.

Hypholoma fasciculare (Fr.) P. Kumm.

On the log of a deciduous tree in coniferous-broad-leaved forest, Ussuriysk Nature Reserve, 12 Aug. 1962, M.M. Nazarova, VLA M-5677. - On the wood of *Picea* in dark coniferous forest, Upper Ussuri Station, 15 Sept. 1974, E.M. Bulakh, VLA M-5644. - On the wood in dark coniferous forest, Big Khekhtsir Nature Reserve, 2 Sept. 1983, E.M. Bulakh, VLA M-5671; Birobidzhan: Bastak Nature Reserve, 16 Aug. 2000, E.M. Bulakh, VLA M-15377. - On the rotten wood, Ussuriysk, 3 Aug. 2003, Tolgor Bau, HMJAU 2836, 2846; Hulin, 4 Sept. 2003, 20 Sept. 2004, Tolgor Bau, HMJAU 3007, 3031, 2710; Hutou, 8 Sept. 2003, Tolgor Bau, HMJAU 3024; Raohe, 7 Aug. 2004, Tolgor Bau, HMJAU 2520, 2621; Fuyuan, 5 Aug. 2004, Tolgor Bau, HMJAU 2575.

Hypholoma sublateritium (Schaeff.) Quél.

On the rotten wood, Hulin, 4 Sept. 2003, Tolgor Bau, HMJAU 3058, 3060, 3025.

Kuehneromyces mutabilis (Schäff.) Singer et A. H. Sm. Plate 7: 37

On the wood in korean pine-broad-leaved forest, Ussuriysk Nature Reserve, 21 Sept. 1962, M.M. Nazarova, VLA M-19951; Birobidzhan: Bastak Nature Reserve, 9 Sept. 2001, E.M. Bulakh, VLA M-16381. - On the logs in broad-leaved forest, Ussuriysk: Gornotayozhnoye, 21 Oct. 1944, L.N. Vassiljeva, VLA M-19944; Big Khekhtsir Nature Reserve, 1 Sept. 1983, E.M. Bulakh, VLA M-5846, 15 Aug. 2004, Tolgor Bau, HMJAU 2963. - On wood of *Ulmus* in coniferous-broad-leaved forest, Upper Ussuri Station, 11 Jun. 1975, E.M. Bulakh, VLA M-5903.

Kuehneromyces vernalis (Peck) Singer et A.H. Sm.

On the log in korean pine-broad-leaved forest, Ussuriysk Nature Reserve (Vasilyeva & Bezdeleva, 2006). - On the ground in coniferous-broad-leaved forest, Upper Ussuri Station, 28 Aug. 1973, E.M. Bulakh, VLA M-5919.

Melanotus phillipsii (Berk. & Broome) Singer

On leaves of *Carex* in broad-leaved forest, Birobidzhan: Bastak Nature Reserve, 6 Sept. 2001, E.M. Bulakh, VLA M-16458.

Panaeolina foenisecii (Pers.) Maire Plate 7: 38

On the dung of a cow in meadow, Khanka Nature Reserve, 9 Aug. 2003, E.M. Bulakh , VLA M-18994. - On the ground of meadow, Tikhorechnoye, 14 Jul. 2004, E.M. Bulakh, VLA M-19503, Novotroitskoye, 14 Jul. 2004, E.M. Bulakh, VLA M-19503.

Panaeolus fimicola (Pers.) Gillet

On the dung of a cow in meadow, Khanka Nature Reserve, 9 Aug. 2003, E.M. Bulakh, VLA M-19010; Sokolovka, 18 Jul. 2002, E.M. Bulakh, VLA M-17180. - On the ground of meadow, Chuguevka, 18 Jul. 2002, E.M. Bulakh, VLA M-17180.- Vudalanichi, 15 Jun. 2005, E.M. Bulakh, VLA M-20330.

Panaeolus papilionaceus (Bull.) Quél.

On the dung in broad-leaved forest, Ussuriysk Nature Reserve, 27 Aug. 1963, M.M. Nazarova, VLA M-5181. - On the dung of horse in meadow, Khanka Nature Reserve, 25 Jul. 2003, E.M. Bulakh, VLA M-19111.

Panaeolus semiovatus (Sowerby) S. Lundell et Nannf. var. *semiovatus*

On the dung of a cow in meadow, Khanka Nature Reserve, 9 Aug. 2003, E.M. Bulakh, VLA M-19205. - On the dung in meadow, Arkhipovka, 2 Jun. 2003, E.M. Bulakh, VLA M-19237.

Panaeolus semiovatus var. *phalaenarum* (Fr.) Ew. Gerhardt

On the straw, Galenki, 29 Apr. 2000, E.M. Bulakh, VLA M-13643.

Panaeolus sphinctrinus (Fr.) Quél.

On the dung in poplar forest, Upper Ussuri Station, 6 Aug. 1974, E.M. Bulakh, VLA

M-5199; in dark coniferous forest, Big Khekhtsir Nature Reserve, 14 Aug. 1981, E.M. Bulakh VLA M-5191.

Pholiota adiposa (Batsch) P. Kumm.   Plate 7: 39

On the wood in broad-leaved forest, Yakovlevka: Yelovy pereval, 23 Aug. 1955, L.N. Vassiljeva, VLA M-20002. - On the trunk of *Betula* in coniferous-broad-leaved forest, Upper Ussuri Station, 6 Sept. 2005, E.M. Bulakh, VLA M-20273.

Pholiota albocrenulata (Peck) Sacc.

Near the basis of living trunk of *Populus*, Ussuriysk Nature Reserve, 25 Aug. 1961, L.N. Vassiljeva, VLA M-5724. - On the log of *Betula* in coniferous-broad-leaved forest, Upper Ussuri Station, 12 Sept. 1974, E.M. Bulakh, VLA M-5727; Big Khekhtsir Nature Reserve, 21 Aug. 1983, E.M. Bulakh, VLA M-5719; Hulin, 19 Sep. 2004, Tolgor Bau, HMJAU 2667.

Pholiota alnicola (Fr.) Singer

On the wood in coniferous-broad-leaved forest, Ussuriysk Nature Reserve (Vasilyeva & Bezdeleva, 2006); Upper Ussuri Station, 9 Sept. 1973, E.M. Bulakh, VLA M-5737. - On the ground in birch forest, Big Khekhtsir Nature Reserve, 30 Jun. 1981, E.M. Bulakh, VLA M-5733.

Pholiota astragalina (Fr.) Singer

On the coniferous wood in dark coniferous forest, Ussuriysk Nature Reserve, 24 Aug. 1975, M.M. Nazarova, VLA M-20484; Upper Ussuri Station, 29 Aug. 1973, E.M. Bulakh, VLA M-5741; Big Khekhtsir Nature Reserve, 21 Aug. 1983, E.M. Bulakh, VLA M-5743; Birobidzhan: Bastak Nature Reserve, 13 Aug. 2006, E.M. Bulakh, VLA M-20994.

Pholiota aurivella (Batsch) Fr.   Plate 7: 40

On the trunk of *Salix,* Ussuriysk Nature Reserve, 3 Sept. 1995, E.M. Bulakh, VLA M-5752; Ussuriysk: Gornotayozhnoye, 21 Oct. 1944, L.N. Vassiljeva, VLA M-19960; Upper Ussuri Station, 16 Sept. 2005, E.M. Bulakh, VLA M-19705; Big Khekhtsir Nature Reserve, 23 Aug. 1983, E.M. Bulakh, VLA M-5755; Birobidzhan: Bastak Nature Reserve, 13 Aug. 2002, E.M. Bulakh, VLA M-17494.

Pholiota conissans (Fr.) M.M.Moser

On the trunk of *Salix*, Ussuriysk Nature Reserve, 14 Sept. 1963 M.M. Nazarova, VLA M-20030.

Pholiota flammans (Batsch) P. Kumm.   Plate 7: 41

On the trunk of *Pinus koraiensis* in korean pine-broad-leaved forest, Ussuriysk Nature Reserve, 18 Aug. 1961, L.N. Vassiljeva, VLA M-20055. - On the trunk of *Picea* in coniferous-broad-leaved forest, Upper Ussuri Station, 20 Aug. 1974, E.M. Bulakh, VLA M-5790. - On the trunk of *Betula* in dark coniferous forest, Big Khekhtsir Nature Reserve, 2 Sept. 1983, E.M. Bulakh, VLA M-5791. - On the wood, Hulin, 9 Aug. 2004, Tolgor Bau, HMJAU 2594.

Pholiota gummosa (Lasch) Singer

On the fallen twigs of *Quercus* in korean pine-broad-leaved forest, Ussuriysk Nature Reserve (Vasilyeva & Bezdeleva, 2006).

Pholiota heteroclita (Fr.) Quél.

On the wood in korean pine-broad-leaved forest, Ussuriysk Nature Reserve, 10 Sept. 1968, M.M. Nazarova, VLA M-20481.

Pholiota highlandensis (Peck) A.H. Sm. et Hesler

[= *Pholiota carbonaria* (Fr.) Singer]

On the burnt ground, Upper Ussuri Station, 25 Aug. 1974, E.M. Bulakh, VLA M-5776; Birobidzhan: Bastak Nature Reserve, 13 Aug. 2000, E.M. Bulakh, VLA M-15372.

Pholiota lenta (Pers.) Singer

On the log in coniferous-broad-leaved forest, Ussuriysk Nature Reserve, 14 Sept. 1963, M.M. Nazarova, VLA M-19964; Upper Ussuri Station, 26 Jul. 1974, E.M. Bulakh , VLA M-5807. - On the ground under the tree of *Betula*, in birch forest, Big Khekhtsir Nature Reserve, 15 Sept. 1981, E.M. Bulakh, VLA M-5816.

Pholiota limonella (*Peck*) *Sacc*.

(= *Pholiota squarrosoadiposa* J.E. Lange)

On the log in coniferous-broad-leaved forest, Ussuriysk Nature Reserve, 7 Aug. 2003, E.M. Bulakh, VLA M-19250. - On the wood of *Acer* in dark coniferous forest, Big Khekhtsir Nature Reserve, 15 Sept. 1981, E.M. Bulakh, VLA M-5877.

Pholiota lubrica (Pers.) Singer

On the ground in korean pine-broad-leaved forest, Ussuriysk Nature Reserve, 24 Sept. 1963, M.M. Nazarova, VLA M-19936; in dark coniferous forest, Upper Ussuri Station, 22 Aug. 1975, E.M. Bulakh, VLA M-5826; in birch forest, Big Khekhtsir Nature Reserve, 29 Jun.1981, E.M. Bulakh, VLA M-5827.

Pholiota lucifera (Lasch) Quél.

On the fallen twigs in coniferous-broad-leaved forest, Ussuriysk Nature Reserve, 20 Jun. 1961, L.N. Vassiljeva, M-20017. - On the log in oak forest, Big Khekhtsir Nature Reserve, 26 Jun. 1981, E.M. Bulakh, VLA M-5836; Birobidzhan: Bastak Nature Reserve, 21 Aug. 2003, E.M. Bulakh, VLA M-19183.

Pholiota polychroa (Berk.) A.H. Sm. et H.J. Brodie (as *Pholiota luteofolia* (Peck) Sacc. - Vassiljeva, 1973).

On the trunk of *Salix*, Tikhorechnoye, 21 Jul. 1998, E.M.Bulakh, VLA M-12097. - On the fallen twigs of *Quercus* in korean pine-broad-leaved forest, Upper Ussuri Station, 7 Sept. 1975, E.M. Bulakh, VLA M-5838. - On the fallen twigs of *Corylus* in oak forest, Big Khekhtsir Nature Reserve, 12 Aug. 1981, E.M. Bulakh, VLA M-5839; Birobidzhan: Bastak Nature Reserve, 13 Aug. 2000, E.M. Bulakh, VLA M-17526.

Pholiota populnea (Pers. Kuyper et Tjall.-Beuk.)   Plate 7: 42

[= *Pholiota destruens* (Brond.) Gillet]

On the log of *Populus*, Ussuriysk Nature Reserve (Vasilyeva & Bezdeleva, 2006). - On the wood of *Ulmus* in broad-leaved forest, Upper Ussuri Station, 19 Aug. 1973, E.M. Bulakh, VLA M-5786; Birobidzhan: Bastak Nature Reserve, 14 Aug. 2000, E.M. Bulakh, VLA M-15373.

Pholiota scamba (Fr.) M.M. Moser

On the decayed wood in coniferous-broad-leaved forest, Ussuriysk Nature Reserve (Vassiljeva, 1973).

Pholiota spumosa (Fr.) Singer

On the logs in korean pine-broad-leaved forest, Ussuriysk Nature Reserve, 14 Sept. 1963, L.N. Vassiljeva, VLA M-19957; in oak forest, Khanka Nature Reserve, 19 Jun. 2002, E.M. Bulakh, VLA M-17221; in deciduous forest, Upper Ussuri Station, 9 Sept. 1973, E.M. Bulakh, VLA M-5857; in coniferous-broad-leaved forest, Big Khekhtsir Nature Reserve, 2 Sept. 1983, E.M. Bulakh, VLA M-5852; in forest, Fuyuan, 5 Aug. 2004, Tolgor Bau, HMJAU 2537; Raohe, 7 Aug. 2004, Tolgor Bau, HMJAU 2526; Birobidzhan: Bastak Nature Reserve, 16 Aug. 2001, E.M. Bulakh, VLA M-17809. - On the log of *Quercus* in oak forest, Ussuriysk: Gornotayozhnoye, 9 Sept. 1963, M.M. Nazarova, VLA M-19992.

Pholiota squarrosa (Batsch) P. Kumm.

On the wood in coniferous-broad-leaved forest, Ussuriysk Nature Reserve, 23 Sept. 1995, E.M. Bulakh, VLA M-5873. - On the ground under the tree of *Betula* in broad-leaved forest, Ussuriysk: Gornotayozhnoye, 4 Aug. 2002, E.M. Bulakh, VLA M-19306. - On the ground under the tree of *Quercus* in broad-leaved forest, Birobidzhan: Bastak Nature Reserve, 9 Sept. 2001, E.M. Bulakh, VLA M-16394. - On the log of *Quercus* in korean pine-broad-leaved forest, Upper Ussuri Station, 19 Sept. 1974, E.M. Bulakh, VLA M-5871. - On the wood of *Fraxinus* in coniferous-broad-leaved forest, Big Khekhtsir Nature Reserve, 15 Sept.1981, E.M. Bulakh, VLA M-5874.

Pholiota squarrosoides (Peck) Sacc.

On the log in korean pine-broad-leaved forest, Ussuriysk Nature Reserve, 25 Aug. 2003, E.M. Bulakh, VLA M-19286. - On the logs of *Betula* in dark coniferous forest, Upper Ussuri Station, 29 Aug. 1973, E.M. Bulakh, VLA M-5864; Big Khekhtsir Nature Reserve, 7 Sept. 1983, E.M. Bulakh, VLA M-5867. - On the log of *Alnus*, Birobidzhan: Bastak Nature Reserve, 21 Aug. 2004, E.M. Bulakh, VLA M-20304.

Pholiota subsulphurea A.H. Sm. et Hesler.

On the log of *Betula* in coniferous-broad-leaved forest, Upper Ussuri Station, 22 Jun. 1974, E.M. Bulakh, VLA M-5894.

Pholiota tuberculosa (Schaeff.) P. Kumm.

[= *Pholiota curvipes* (Fr.) Quél.]

On the stumps in coniferous-broad-leaved forest, Ussuriysk Nature Reserve, 16 Sept. 1962, M.M. Nazarova, M-20047; Gaivoron, 28 Jul. 2007, E.M. Bulakh, VLA M-21499.

Pleuroflammula chocoruensis Singer

On the fallen twigs in broad-leaved forest, Ussuriysk Nature Reserve, 3 Sept. 1963, M.M. Nazarova, VLA M-6025. - On the twigs of *Quercus* in oak forest, Khanka Nature Reserve, 19 Jun. 2002, E.M. Bulakh, VLA M-17220; Tikhorechnoye, 13 Jul. 2004, E.M. Bulakh, VLA M-19498. - On the log of *Betula* in dark coniferous forest, Upper Ussuri Station, 6 Aug. 1973, E.M. Bulakh, VLA M-5997; Big Khekhtsir Nature Reserve, 2 Sept. 1983, E.M. Bulakh, VLA M-6012. - On the log of *Phellodendron amurense*, Birobidzhan: Bastak Nature Reserve, 20 Aug. 2003, E.M. Bulakh, VLA M-19029.

Psilocybe coprophila (Bull.) P. Kumm.   Plate 8: 43

On the dung of a horse in meadow, Khanka Nature Reserve, 21 Jun. 2002, E.M. Bulakh, VLA M-17210; in broad-leaved forest, Big Khekhtsir Nature Reserve, 1 Sept.1983, E.M. Bulakh, VLA M-5568.

Psilocybe crobula (Fr.) Singer

On the log in korean pine forest, Upper Ussuri Station, 24 Aug. 1973, E.M. Bulakh, VLA M-5570. - On the forest litter in broad-leaved forest, Birobidzhan: Bastak Nature Reserve, 23 Aug. 2003, E.M. Bulakh, VLA M-19124.

Psilocybe inquilina (Fr.) Bres.

On the dead grass in deciduous forest, Anuchino, 21 Aug. 1955, L.N. Vassiljeva, VLA M-19920. - On the fallen twigs in deciduous forest, Upper Ussuri Station, 8 Aug. 1973, E.M. Bulakh, VLA M-5573; in birch forest, Big Khekhtsir Nature Reserve, 30 Jun. 1981 E.M. Bulakh, VLA M-5985. - On the ground, Barabash-Levada, 12 May 1999, E.M. Bulakh, VLA M-12966.

Psilocybe montana (Pers.) P. Kumm.

On the forest litter and mosses in birch forest, Big Khekhtsir Nature Reserve, 30 Jun. 1981, E.M. Bulakh, VLA M-5567.

Psilocybe paupera Singer.

On the ground in willow forest, Khanka Nature Reserve, 21 Jun. 2002 E.M. Bulakh, VLA M-17232; in deciduous forest, Big Khekhtsir Nature Reserve, 22 Jun. 1981, E.M. Bulakh, VLA M-5524.

Psilocybe phyllogena (Peck) Peck

[= *Psilocybe rhombispora* (Britzelm) Sacc.]

On the forest litter in korean pine-broad-leaved forest, Ussuriysk Nature Reserve, 24 Jun. 1962, M.M. Nazarova, VLA M-19542. - On the wood in coniferous-broad-leaved forest, Upper Ussuri Station, 10 Aug. 1973, E.M. Bulakh, VLA M-5950.

Stropharia aeruginosa (Curtis) Quél.

On the forest litter in korean pine-broad-leaved forest, Ussuriysk Nature Reserve, 20 Aug.

1962, M.M. Nazarova, VLA M-20029; in deciduous forest, Ussuriysk, 2 Aug. 2003, Tolgor Bau, HMJAU 2856; Upper Ussuri Station, 15 Sept. 1973, E.M. Bulakh, VLA M-5590.

Stropharia coronilla (Bull.) Quél.

On the ground in broad-leaved forest, Birobidzhan: Bastak Nature Reserve, 21 Aug. 2003, E.M. Bulakh, VLA M-19224.

Stropharia hornemanii (Fr.) S. Lundell et Nannf.

On the log in coniferous-broad-leaved forest, Upper Ussuri Station, 15 Sept. 1974, E.M. Bulakh, VLA M-5607.

Stropharia inuncta (Fr.) Quél.

On the forest litter in korean pine-broad-leaved forest, Ussuriysk Nature Reserve, 21 Aug. 1962, M.M. Nazarova, VLA M-5614.

Stropharia pseudocyanea (Desm.) Morgan

[= *Stropharia albocyanea* (Desm.) Quél.]

On the forest litter in korean pine-broad-leaved forest, Ussuriysk Nature Reserve, 14 Sept. 19075, M.M. Nazarova, VLA M-5600.

Stropharia rugosoannulata Farl. ex Murrill   Plate 8: 44

On the ground of meadow, Khanka Nature Reserve, 26 Jul. 2002, E.M. Bulakh, VLA M-19317; in coniferous-broad-leaved forest, Upper Ussuri Station, 17 Aug. 1974, E.M. Bulakh, VLA M-5619; Big Khekhtsir Nature Reserve, 1 Jul. 1981, E.M. Bulakh, VLA M-5615.

Stropharia semiglobata (Batsch) Quél.

On the dung of herbivorous animals in korean pine-broad-leaved forest, Ussuriysk Nature Reserve, 10 Sept. 1955, L.N. Vassiljeva, VLA M-5636. - On the dung of a horse in meadow, Khanka Nature Reserve, 9 Aug. 2003, E.M. Bulakh, VLA M-19011; in dark coniferous forest, Big Khekhtsir Nature Reserve, 14 Aug. 1981, E.M. Bulakh, VLA M-5630.

Tubaria furfuracea (Pers.) Gillet

On the culm of a grass in coniferous-broad-leaved forest, Upper Ussuri Station, 22 Jun. 1974, E.M. Bulakh, VLA M-5978. - On the ground in broad-leaved forest, Big Khekhtsir Nature Reserve, 20 Jun.1981, E.M. Bulakh, VLA M-5982.

Tubaria pellucida (Bull.) Fr.

On the log among mosses in broad-leaved forest, Ussuriysk Nature Reserve, 14 Aug. 1961, L.N. Vassiljeva, VLA M-5995.

TRICHOLOMATACEAE

Armillaria mellea (Vahl.) P. Kumm.   Plate 8: 45

On the ground and wood in coniferous-broad-leaved forest, Ussuriysk Nature Reserve (Vasilyeva & Bezdeleva, 2006); Ussuriysk, 3 Aug. 2003, Tolgor Bau, HMJAU 2915; on the basis of trunk, Ussuriysk, 3 Aug. 2003, Tolgor Bau, HMJAU 2913; Khanka Nature Reserve, 27 Jul. 2007, E.M. Bulakh, VLA M-21463; Big Khekhtsir Nature Reserve, 25 Sept. 1983, E.M. Bulakh, VLA M-1282; Birobidzhan: Bastak Nature Reserve, 13 Aug. 2000, E.M. Bulakh, VLA M-15415; Hulin, 4 Sept. 2003, Tolgor Bau, HMJAU 3004; Hulin, 20 Sep. 2003, Tolgor Bau, HMJAU 2699; Raohe, 8 Sep. 2003, Tolgor Bau, HMJAU 3044. - On the ground in deciduous forest, Upper Ussuri Station, 6 Sept. 1974, E.M. Bulakh, VLA M-1268.

Armillaria tabescens (Scop.) Emel

On the wood, Hulin, Tolgor Bau, HMJAU 3298.

Asterophora lycoperdoides (Bull.) Ditmar

On the decayed caps of *Russula nigricans* in korean pine forest, Upper Ussuri Station, 19 Aug. 1974, E.M. Bulakh, VLA M-1402; Birobidzhan: Bastak Nature Reserve, 18 Aug. 2000, E.M. Bulakh, VLA M-15427.

Baeospora myriadophylla (Peck) Singer

On the log in coniferous-broad-leaved forest, Ussuriysk Nature Reserve, 10 Jun., 1969, M.M. Nazarova, VLA M-12155; Big Khekhtsir Nature Reserve, 24 Aug. 1980, E.M. Bulakh, VLA M-3426. - On the log of *Populus* in poplar forest, Upper Ussuri Station, 26 Aug. 1973, E.M. Bulakh, VLA M-3430.

Calocybe carnea (Bull.) Donk.

On the ground in korean pine-broad-leaved forest, Ussuriysk Nature Reserve, 23 Aug. 1961, L.N. Vassiljeva, VLA M-1374.

Calocybe chrysenteron (Bull.) Singer

On the ground in korean pine-broad-leaved forest, Ussuriysk Nature Reserve [(Vasilyeva & Bezdeleva, 2006), as *C. cerina* (Pers.) Singer); in broad-leaved forest, Big Khekhtsir Nature Reserve, 3 Aug. 1981, E.M. Bulakh, VLA M-1382

Calocybe constricta (Fr.) Kühner

[= *Calocybe leucocephala* (Fr.) Singer]

On the forest litter in korean pine-broad-leaved forest, Ussuriysk Nature Reserve, 27 Sept. 1963, M.M. Nazarova, VLA M-1395; in broad-leaved forest, Big Khekhtsir Nature Reserve, 3 Sept. 1983, E.M. Bulakh, VLA M-1396.

Calocybe fallax (Sacc.) Redhead et Singer

[= *Calocybe cerina* (Pers.) Singer sensu Vassiljeva (1973)].

On the ground in korean pine-broad-leaved forest, Ussuriysk Nature Reserve, 23 Aug. 1961, L.N. Vassiljeva, VLA M-1374; Nikolaevka, 21 Sept. 1954, L.N.Vassilleva, VLA M-1373.

Calocybe gambosa (Fr.) Donk

On the ground in a garden, Ussuriysk Nature Reserve, 20 Aug. 1966, E.M. Bulakh, VLA M-206; Birobidzhan: Bastak Nature Reserve, 8 Sept. 2001, E.M. Bulakh, VLA M-16363.

Calocybe ionides (Bull.) Donk

On the forest litter in oak forest, Ussuriysk: Gornotayozhnoye, 23 Jul. 2002, E.M. Bulakh, VLA M-18348; Khanka Nature Reserve, 21 Jun. 2002, V.Yu. Barkalov, VLA M-17193; in aspen forest, Tikhorechnoye, 4 Jul. 1979, E.M. Bulakh, VLA M-1392; in broad-leaved forest, Big Khekhtsir Nature Reserve, 25 Aug. 1981, E.M. Bulakh, VLA M-1389.

Calocybe persicolor (Fr.) Singer

On the forest litter in coniferous-broad-leaved forest, Ussuriysk Nature Reserve, 1 Sept. 1993, E.M. Bulakh, VLA M-1364; in the stand of coniferous trees, Ussuriysk: Gornotayozhnoye, 12 Jul. 2002, E.M. Bulakh, VLA M-442; in korean pine-broad-leaved forest, Upper Ussuri Station, 9 Sept. 1973, E.M. Bulakh, VLA M-5981; Tikhorechnoye, 4 Jul. 1979, E.M. Bulakh, VLA M-1363; in broad-leaved forest, Big Khekhtsir Nature Reserve, 15 Sept. 1981, E.M. Bulakh, VLA M-1368; Raohe, 6 Aug. 2004, E.M. Bulakh, VLA M-20281; Birobidzhan: Bastak Nature Reserve, 16 Aug. 2000, E.M. Bulakh, VLA M-15446.

Campanella boninensis (S. Ito et Imai) Parmasto

On the log of *Tilia* in korean pine-broad-leaved forest, Upper Ussuri Station (Azbukina & Kharkevich, 1984).

Campanella tristis (G. Stev.) Segedin   Plate 8: 46

On the bark of *Tilia* in broad-leaved forest, Ussuriysk Nature Reserve, Jun. 1969, M.M. Nazarova, VLA M-3305; on the twigs of *Actinidia*, Birobidzhan: Bastak Nature Reserve, 10 Aug. 2006, E.M. Bulakh, VLA M-20954.

Cantharellula umbonata (J.F. Gmel.) Singer

On the forest litter in dark coniferous forest, Birobidzhan: Bastak Nature Reserve, 16 Aug. 2000, E.M. Bulakh, VLA M-15497.

Catathelasma ventricosum (Peck) Singer

On the ground under the tree of *Picea* in dark coniferous forest, Ussuriysk Nature Reserve, 5 Sept. 1996, E.M. Bulakh, VLA M-4162; Upper Ussuri Station, 6 Sept. 2005, E.M. Bulakh, VLA M-20223; Birobidzhan: Bastak Nature Reserve, 18 Aug. 2000, E.M. Bulakh, VLA M-15449.

Cellypha goldbachii (Weinm.) Donk

On culms of grasses in meadow, Khanka Nature Reserve, 8 Aug. 2003, E.M. Bulakh, VLA M-17813; in oak forest, Ussuriysk: Gornotayozhnoye, 23 Jul. 2002, E.M. Bulakh, VLA M-17461.

Cheimonophyllum candidissimum (Berk. et M.A. Curtis) Singer

On the logs in korean pine-coniferous-broad-leaved forest, Ussuriysk Nature Reserve, 17 Aug. 2005, E.M. Bulakh, VLA M-20269; Birobidzhan: Bastak Nature Reserve, 9 Aug. 2006, E.M. Bulakh, VLA M-20959. - On the log of *Ulmus* in coniferous-broad-leaved forest, Upper Ussuri Station, 11 Aug. 1990, E.M. Bulakh, VLA M-18410.

Chromosera cyanophylla (Fr.) Redhead, Ammirati et Norvell

[=*Omphalina cyanophylla* (Fr.) Singer]

On the logs in coniferous-broad-leaved forest, Ussuriysk Nature Reserve, 21 Aug. 1961, L.N. Vassiljeva, VLA M-939; in dark coniferous forest, Upper Ussuri Station, 29 Aug. 1973, E.M. Bulakh, VLA M-938.

Chrysomphalina chrysophylla (Fr.) Clémençon

On the log in korean pine-broad-leaved forest, Upper Ussuri Station, 3 Aug. 1974, E.M. Bulakh, VLA M-916; in dark coniferous forest, Big Khekhtsir Nature Reserve, 20 Aug. 1983, E.M. Bulakh, VLA M-924.

Chrysomphalina grossula (Pers.) S Noordel., Redhead et Ammirati

[=*Omphalina grossula* (Pers.) Singer]

On the log of *Pinus koraiensis* in korean pine-broad-leaved forest, Upper Ussuri Station, 10 Aug. 1974, E.M. Bulakh, VLA M-992.

Clitocybe angustissima (Lasch) P. Kumm.

On the forest litter in broad-leaved forest, Ussuriysk Nature Reserve, 3 Sept. 1963, M.M. Nazarova, VLA M-629; in coniferous-broad-leaved forest, Upper Ussuri Station, 20 Aug. 1975, E.M. Bulakh, VLA M-630; Birobidzhan: Bastak Nature Reserve, 16 Aug. 2002, E.M. Bulakh, VLA M-17480.

Clitocybe brumalis (Fr.) Quél.

On the forest litter in korean pine-broad-leaved forest, Upper Ussuri Station, 17 Sept. 1974, E.M. Bulakh, VLA M-632.

Clitocybe candicans (Pers.) P. Kumm.

[= *Clitocybe tuba* (Fr.) Gillet]

On the forest litter in korean pine-broad-leaved forest, Ussuriysk Nature Reserve, 24 Aug. 1963, M.M. Nazarova, VLA M-643; in dark coniferous forest, Upper Ussuri Station, 12 Aug. 1974, E.M. Bulakh, VLA M-636; Birobidzhan: Bastak Nature Reserve, 23 Aug. 2003, E.M. Bulakh, VLA M-19203.

Clitocybe candida Bres.

On the forest litter in korean pine-broad-leaved forest, Ussuriysk Nature Reserve, 7 Aug. 1975, M.M. Nazarova, VLA M-19765.

Clitocybe clavipes (Pers.) P. Kumm.   Plate 8: 47

On the forest litter in coniferous-broad-leaved forest, Ussuriysk Nature Reserve, 8 Aug. 1961, L.N. Vassiljeva, VLA M-675; in dark coniferous forest, Upper Ussuri Station, 10 Sept. 1974, E.M. Bulakh, VLA M-677; Big Khekhtsir Nature Reserve, Tolgor Bau, HMJAU 3412; Birobidzhan: Bastak Nature Reserve, 16 Aug. 2000, E.M. Bulakh, VLA M-15446.

Clitocybe diatreta (Fr.) P. Kumm.

On the forest litter in broad-leaved forest, Ussuriysk Nature Reserve, 6 Sept. 1961, L.N. Vassiljeva, VLA M-684.

Clitocybe ditopa (Fr.) Gillet

On the forest litter in oak forest, Ussuriysk: Gornotayozhnoye, 6 Aug. 2002, E.M. Bulakh, VLA M-17233; Tikhorechnoye, 4 Aug. 2005, E.M. Bulakh, VLA M-20284.

Clitocybe fragrans (With.) P. Kumm.

[*Clitocybe obsoleta* (Batsch) Quél. ss. auct.]

On the forest litter in korean pine-broad-leaved forest, Ussuriysk Nature Reserve, 23 Aug. 1961, L.N. Vassiljeva, VLA M-840; Birobidzhan: Bastak Nature Reserve, 21 Aug. 2004, E.M. Bulakh, VLA M-20899. - On the ground in the stand of *Abies*, Ussuriysk: Gornotayozhnoye, 23 Jul. 2002, E.M. Bulakh, VLA M-19314; - On the forest litter in the thicket in *Craetegus* and *Salix*, Khanka Nature Reserve, 9 Aug. 2003, E.M. Bulakh, VLA M-19177; in coniferous-broad-leaved forest, Upper Ussuri Station, 1 Sept. 1973, E.M. Bulakh, VLA M-692; in birch forest, Raohe, 7 Aug. 2004, E.M. Bulakh, VLA M-20283.

Clitocybe fuscosquamula J.E. Lange

On the forest litter in broad-leaved forest, Hulin, 9 Aug. 2004, E.M. Bulakh, VLA M-20286.

Clitocybe geotropa (Bull.) Quél.

On the forest litter in korean pine-broad-leaved forest, Ussuriysk Nature Reserve, 24 Sept. 1946, L.N. Vassiljeva, VLA M-697; Ussuriysk, Tolgor Bau, HMJAU 2587, 2761; in dark coniferous forest, Big Khekhtsir Nature Reserve, 14 Sept. 1946, L.N. Vassiljeva, VLA M-698.

Clitocybe gibba (Pers.) P. Kumm.   Plate 8: 48

On the forest litter in korean pine-broad-leaved forest, Ussuriysk Nature Reserve, 7 Aug. 1975, M.M. Nazarova, VLA M-714; Ussuriysk, 3 Aug. 2003, Tolgor Bau, HMJAU 2581, 2761; in deciduous forest, Khanka Nature Reserve, 26 Jul. 2002, E.M. Bulakh, VLA M-17453; in dark coniferous forest, Upper Ussuri Station, 10 Sept. 1974, E.M. Bulakh, VLA M-702; in broad-leaved forest, Big Khehtsir Nature Reserve, 8 Aug.1981, E.M. Bulakh, VLA M-706, 15 Aug. 2004, Tolgor Bau, HMJAU 2765, 2947, 2957; Birobidzhan: Bastak Nature Reserve, 12 Aug. 2000, E.M. Bulakh, VLA M-15419; Hutou, 8 Sept. 2003, Tolgor Bau, HMJAU 3020; Hulin, 9 Aug. 2004, 4 Sept. 2003, 8 Sept. 2004, Tolgor Bau, HMJAU 2690, 3043, 2587; Fuyuan, 5 Aug. 2004, Tolgor Bau, HMJAU 2531, 2626.

Clitocybe hydrogramma (Bull. et A. Venturi) P. Kumm.

On the forest litter, in korean pine-broad-leaved forest, Birobidzhan: Bastak Nature Reserve, 16 Aug. 2000, E.M. Bulakh, VLA M-15410.

Clitocybe inornata (Sowerby) Gillet

On the forest litter in korean pine-broad-leaved forest, Ussuriysk Nature Reserve, 19 Aug. 1975, M.M. Nazarova,VLA M-713; in korean pine forest, Upper Ussuri Station, 16 Sept. 1975, E.M. Bulakh, VLA M-744.

Clitocybe nebularis (Batsch) Quél.   Plate 9: 49

On the forest litter in korean pine-broad-leaved forest, Ussuriysk Nature Reserve, 21 Sept. 1975, M.M. Nazarova, VLA M-827; Upper Ussuri Station, 21 Aug. 1975 E.M. Bulakh, VLA M-819; in dark coniferous forest, Big Khekhtsir Nature Reserve, 14 Sept. 1981 E.M. Bulakh, VLA M-817; Birobidzhan: Bastak Nature Reserve, 21 Aug. 2003, E.M. Bulakh, VLA M-19219.

Clitocybe odora (Bull.) P. Kumm.

On the forest litter in oak forest, Ussuriysk Nature Reserve, 8 Sept. 1975, M.M. Nazarova, VLA M-846; in dark coniferous forest, Upper Ussuri Station, 10 Sept. 1974, E.M. Bulakh, VLA M-748; in broad-leaved forest, Big Khekhtsir Nature Reserve, 31 Aug. 1983, E.M. Bulakh, VLA M-854; Birobidzhan: Bastak Nature Reserve, 13 Aug. 2000, E.M. Bulakh, VLA M-15450.

Clitocybe phyllophila (Pers.) P. Kumm.

[= *Clitocybe cerussata* (Fr.) P. Kumm.]

On the forest litter in korean pine-broad-leaved forest, Ussuriysk Nature Reserve, 19 Sept. 1963, L.N. Vassiljeva, VLA M-658; in deciduous forest, Khanka Nature Reserve, 28 Aug. 2002, E.M. Bulakh, VLA M-19247; in dark coniferous forest, Upper Ussuri Station, 29 Aug. 1973, E.M. Bulakh, VLA M-664; in broad-leaved forest, Big Khekhtsir Nature Reserve, 5 Aug. 1981, E.M. Bulakh, VLA M-668.

Clitocybe squamulosa (Pers.) Fr.

On the forest litter in dark coniferous forest, Upper Ussuri Station, 10 Sept. 1974, E.M. Bulakh, VLA M-748; Big Khekhtsir Nature Reserve, 2 Aug.1974, E.M. Bulakh, VLA M-866.

Clitocybe strigosa Harmaja

On the forest litter in korean pine-broad-leaved forest, Ussuriysk Nature Reserve, 21 Aug. 1970, M.M. Nazarova, VLA M-885.

Clitocybe suaveolens (Fr.) P. Kumm.

On the forest litter in broad-leaved forest, Khanka Nature Reserve, 28 Aug. 2002, E.M. Bulakh, VLA M-19246; in dark coniferous forest, Upper Ussuri Station, 15 Sept. 1974, E.M. Bulakh, VLA M-892; Big Khekhtsir Nature Reserve, 21 Aug. 1983, E.M. Bulakh, VLA M-896.

Clitocybe subalutacea (Batsch) P. Kumm.

On the forest litter in coniferous-broad-leaved forest, Ussuriysk Nature Reserve, 6 Jul. 1962, M.M. Nazarova, VLA M-901; Birobidzhan: Bastak Nature Reserve, 14 Aug. 2000, E.M. Bulakh, VLA M-19138.

Clitocybe trullaeformis (Fr.) P. Karst.

On the forest litter in dark coniferous forest, Upper Ussuri Station, 15 Aug. 1974, E.M. Bulakh, VLA M-908; in broad-leaved forest, Big Khekhtsir Nature Reserve, 8 Aug.1981, E.M. Bulakh, VLA M-903; Birobidzhan: Bastak Nature Reserve, 16 Aug. 2000, E.M. Bulakh, VLA

M-15413.

Clitocybe vibecina (Fr.) Quél.

(= *Clitocybe langei* Singer ex Hora)

On the forest litter in dark coniferous forest, Upper Ussuri Station, 21 Aug. 1975, E.M. Bulakh, VLA M-761.

Clitocybula lacerata (Lasch) Singer

On the log among mosses in korean pine-broad-leaved forest, Ussuriysk Nature Reserve, 23 Aug. 1975, M.M. Nazarova, VLA M-1421. - On the forest litter in korean pine forest, Upper Ussuri Station, 16 Sept. 1975, E.M. Bulakh, VLA M-1411; in dark coniferous forest, Big Khekhtsir Nature Reserve, 15 Sept.1981, E.M. Bulakh, VLA M-1424.

Collybia cirrhata (Schumach.) P. Kumm.

On the decayed caps of mushrooms in forest litter in korean pine-broad-leaved forest, Ussuriysk Nature Reserve, 5 Sept. 1962, M.M. Nazarova, VLA M-1556; Upper Ussuri Station, 26 Aug. 1973, E.M. Bulakh, VLA M-1575; Birobidzhan: Bastak Nature Reserve, 17 Aug. 2000, E.M. Bulakh, VLA M-15406.

Collybia cookei (Bres.) J.D. Arnold

On the log in oak forest, Ussuriysk Nature Reserve, 4 Sept. 1975, M-1639, M.M. Nazarova. - On the stump of coniferous tree in korean pine-broad-leaved forest, Upper Ussuri Station, 14 Sept. 1974, E.M. Bulakh, VLA M-1641.

Collybia porrea (L.) Singer

On the forest litter in coniferous-broad-leaved forest, Ussuriysk Nature Reserve (Vasilyeva & Bezdeleva, 2006).

Collybia tuberosa (Bull.) P. Kumm.

On the forest litter in coniferous-broad-leaved forest, Ussuriysk Nature Reserve, 18 Aug. 19063, M.M. Nazarova, VLA M-1900; in dark coniferous forest, Upper Ussuri Station, 10 Sept. 1974, E.M. Bulakh, VLA M-1896; Big Khekhtsir Nature Reserve, 7 Sept. 1983, E.M. Bulakh, VLA M-1893.

Collybia velutinopunctata Lj.N. Vassiljeva

On the log of *Populus*, Ussuriysk Nature Reserve, 11 Sept. 1955, L.N. Vassiljeva, VLA M-1904.

Crinipellis piceae Singer

On the needles of *Abies* in forest litter in korean pine-broad-leaved forest, Ussuriysk Nature Reserve, 14 Jul. 1961, M.M. Nazarova, VLA M-2490; Upper Ussuri Station, 6 Aug. 1973, E.M. Bulakh, VLA M-2487; in dark coniferous forest, Big Khekhtsir Nature Reserve, 24 Jun. 1981, E.M. Bulakh, VLA M-2489; Birobidzhan: Bastak Nature Reserve, 15 Aug. 2000, E.M. Bulakh, VLA M-15420.

Crinipellis setipes (Peck) Singer

On the forest litter in the thicket of *Salix* and *Rhamnus*, Khanka Nature Reserve, 21 Jun.

2002, E.M. Bulakh, VLA M-17206.

Crinipellis scabella (Alb. et Schwein.) Murrill

[= *Crinipellis stipitaria* (Fr.) Pat.]

On the forest litter in deciduous forest, Khanka Nature Reserve, 4 Aug. 2003, Tolgor Bau, HMJAU 2893.

Crinipellis zonata (Peck) Sacc.   Plate 9: 50

On the fallen twigs in coniferous-broad-leaved forest, Ussuriysk Nature Reserve, 10 Jun. 1969, M.M. Nazarova, VLA M-2506; Big Khekhtsir Nature Reserve, 25 Jun. 1981, E.M. Bulakh, VLA M-2510; Birobidzhan: Bastak Nature Reserve, 17 Aug. 2000, E.M. Bulakh, VLA M-15482; in the thicket of *Crataegus*, Khanka Nature Reserve, 8 Aug. 2003, E.M. Bulakh, VLA M-19153. - On the drying twigs of *Abies* in korean pine forest, Upper Ussuri Station, 23 Jun. 1974, E.M. Bulakh, VLA M-2520.

Delicatula integrella (Pers.) Fayod

On the log of *Abies* in dark coniferous forest, Ussuriysk Nature Reserve, 10 Aug. 1961, L.N. Vassiljeva, VLA M-2537. - On the ground in broad-leaved forest, Ussuriysk: Gornotayozhnoye, 16 Aug. 2005, E.M. Bulakh, VLA M-20288. - On the basis of trunk of *Betula* in korean pine-broad-leaved forest, Upper Ussuri Station, 3 Aug. 1974, E.M. Bulakh, VLA M-2536; in dark coniferous forest, Big Khekhtsir Nature Reserve, 20 Aug. 1983, E.M. Bulakh, VLA M-2551; Birobidzhan: Bastak Nature Reserve, 10 Aug. 2006, E.M. Bulakh, VLA M-20672.

Flammulina velutipes (Curtis) Singer   Plate 9: 51

On the wood in broad-leaved forest, Vladivostok, 2 Aug. 2003, Tolgor Bau, HMJAU 2820; Ussuriysk Nature Reserve, 2 Oct. 2000, E.M. Bulakh, VLA M-13570; Ussuriysk, 3 Aug. 2003, Tolgor Bau, HMJAU 2814; Birobidzhan: Bastak Nature Reserve, 12 Sept. 2001, E.M. Bulakh, VLA M-16491; Hulin, 4 Sept. 2003, 20 Sept. 2004, Tolgor Bau, HMJAU 3053, 2693; Raohe: Shengli State Farm, 6 Aug. 2004, Tolgor Bau, HMJAU 2627. - On the trunk of *Salix* in willow forest, Khanka Nature Reserve, 28 Aug. 2002; Upper Ussuri Station, 9 Aug. 2005, E.M. Bulakh, VLA M- 20692; Big Khekhtsir Nature Reserve, 22 Jun. 1981, E.M. Bulakh, VLA M-3435.

Floccularia luteovirens (Alb. et Schwein.) Pouzar

On the ground in korean pine-broad-leaved forest, Ussuriysk Nature Reserve, 22 Aug. 1995, E.M. Bulakh, VLA M-202; Upper Ussuri Station, 16 Aug. 1974, E.M. Bulakh, VLA M-20147.

Gerronema albidum (Fr.) Singer

On the wood in broad-leaved forest, Arkhipovka, 3 Aug. 2003, E.M. Bulakh,VLA M-18275.

Gloiocephala menieri (Boud.) Singer

On the dead culm and root of *Carex* in marsh, Big Khekhtsir Nature Reserve, 30 Jun.

1981, E.M. Bulakh, VLA M-3373.

Gymnopus confluens (Pers.) Antonin, Halling et Noordel.

[= *Collybia confluens* (Pers.) P. Kumm.]

On the forest litter in korean pine-broad-leaved forest, Ussuriysk Nature Reserve, 4 Aug. 1962, M.M. Nazarova, VLA M-1583; Ussuriysk, 3 Aug. 2003, Tolgor Bau, HMJAU 2988; Upper Ussuri Station, 23 Jun. 1974, E.M. Bulakh, VLA M-1589; in willow forest, Khanka Nature Reserve, 25 Jul. 2002, E.M. Bulakh, VLA M-19278; in dark coniferous forest, Big Khekhtsir Nature Reserve, 7 Sept. 1983, E.M. Bulakh, VLA M-1584, 16 Aug. 2004, Tolgor Bau, HMJAU 2778; Birobidzhan: Bastak Nature Reserve, 16 Aug. 2000, E.M. Bulakh, VLA M-15421; Raohe, 5 Sept. 2003, 7 Aug. 2004, Tolgor Bau, HMJAU 3017, 2538; Fuyuan, 5 Aug. 2004, Tolgor Bau, HMJAU 2515, 2624; Longwangmiao Mishan, 1 Sept. 2003, Tolgor Bau HMJAU 3346.

Gymnopus dryophilus (Bull.) Murrill

On the forest litter in korean pine-broad-leaved forest, Ussuriysk Nature Reserve, 22 Aug. 1968, M.M. Nazarova, VLA M-12174; Ussuriysk, 3 Aug. 2003, Tolgor Bau, HMJAU 2859; Upper Ussuri Station, 8 Aug. 1973, E.M. Bulakh, VLA M-1685, E.M. Bulakh; in deciduous forest, Khanka Nature Reserve, 21 Jun. 2002, E.M. Bulakh, M-17192, 4 Aug. 2003, Tolgor Bau, HMJAU 2838; in dark coniferous forest, Big Khekhtsir Nature Reserve, 24 Jun. 1981, E.M. Bulakh, VLA M-1708; Hulin, 9 Aug. 2004, 5 Sept. 2003, 20 Sept. 2004, Tolgor Bau, HMJAU 2569, 2672, 3014, 3040; Fuyuan, 4 Aug. 2004, Tolgor Bau, HMJAU 2533, 4 Aug. 2004, E.M. Bulakh, VLA M-20298; Birobidzhan: Bastak Nature Reserve, 18 Aug. 2004, Tolgor Bau HMJAU 2945.

Gymnopus fuscopurpureus (Pers.) Antonin, Halling et Noordel.

On the forest litter in korean pine-broad-leaved forest, Ussuriysk Nature Reserve, 20 Sept. 1975, M.M. Nazarova, VLA M-1734; Upper Ussuri Station, 18 Sept. 1974, E.M. Bulakh, VLA M-1733; in oak forest, Tikhorechnoye, 4 Aug. 1979, E.M. Bulakh, VLA M-1755; in dark coniferous forest, Big Khekhtsir Nature Reserve, 27 Aug. 1983, E.M. Bulakh, VLA M-1739; Birobidzhan: Bastak Nature Reserve, 8 Sept. 2001, E.M. Bulakh, VLA M-16496.

Gymnopus hariolorum (Bull.) Antonin, Halling et Noordel.

On the forest litter in oak forest, Ussuriysk Nature Reserve, 6 Sept. 1975, M.M. Nazarova, VLA M-1770; in korean pine-broad-leaved forest, Upper Ussuri Station, 16 Aug. 1974, E.M. Bulakh, VLA M-1768; Birobidzhan: Bastak Nature Reserve, 17 Aug. 2002, E.M. Bulakh, VLA M-17269; in dark coniferous forest, Big Khekhtsir Nature Reserve, 19 Aug. 1983, E.M. Bulakh, VLA M-1764; in birch forest, Raohe, 7 Aug. 2004, E.M. Bulakh, VLA M-20299.

Gymnopus impudicus (Fr.) Antonin, Halling et Noordel.

On the fallen needles in korean pine-broad-leaved forest, Ussuriysk Nature Reserve, 24 Jun. 1964, M.M. Nazarova, VLA M-1811; in dark coniferous forest, Upper Ussuri Station, 20

Jun. 1974, E.M. Bulakh, VLA M-1783; Big Khekhtsir Nature Reserve, 24 Jun. 1981, E.M. Bulakh, VLA M-1785.

Gymnopus ocior (Pers.) Antonin, Halling et Noordel.

[= *Collybia exculpta* (Fr.) Gillet = *Collybia succinea* (Fr.) Quél.]

On the ground of meadow, Khanka Nature Reserve, 22 Jun. 2002, E.M. Bulakh, VLA M-17190; in broad-leaved forest, Tikhorechnoye, 24 Jul. 1998, E.M. Bulakh, VLA M-10507. - On the forest litter in korean pine-broad-leaved forest, Upper Ussuri Station, 9 Aug. 1975, E.M. Bulakh, VLA M-1728.

Gymnopus peronatus (Bolton) Antonin, Halling et Noordel.

On the forest litter in korean pine-broad-leaved forest, Ussuriysk Nature Reserve, 8 Sept. 1975, M.M. Nazarova, VLA M-1867; in the thicket of *Salix* and *Betula*, Khanka Nature Reserve, 25 Jul. 2002, E.M. Bulakh, VLA M-17452; in dark coniferous forest, Big Khekhtsir Nature Reserve, 14 Aug.1981, E.M. Bulakh, VLA M-1856, 15 Aug. 2004, Tolgor Bau, HMJAU 2786; Birobidzhan: Bastak Nature Reserve, 15 Aug. 2000, E.M. Bulakh, VLA M-15424.

Hemimycena cuculata (Pers.) Singer

On the logs in korean pine-broad-leaved forest, Ussuriysk Nature Reserve, 6 Sept. 1962, M.M. Nazarova, VLA M-3374; Upper Ussuri Station, 18 Aug. 1974 E.M. Bulakh, VLA M-4327; in oak forest, Ussuriysk: Gornotayozhnoye, 23 Jul. 2002, E.M. Bulakh, VLA M-17747; Tikhorechnoye, 3 Aug. 2005, E.M. Bulakh, VLA M-20198; in the thicket of *Salix*, Khanka Nature Reserve, 28 Aug. 2002, E.M. Bulakh, VLA M-17771; in broad-leaved forest, Big Khekhtsir Nature Reserve, 15 Sept. 1981, E.M. Bulakh, VLA M-3385; Birobidzhan: Bastak Nature Reserve, 21 Aug. 2003, E.M. Bulakh, VLA M-19159.

Hemimycena gracilis (Quél.) Singer

On the leaf of *Populus* in forest litter, Big Khekhtsir Nature Reserve, 26 Jun. 1981, E.M. Bulakh, VLA M-2529.

Hemimycena hirsuta (Tode) Singer

[= *Hemimycena crispula* (Quél.) Singer]

On the wood in dark coniferous forest, Birobidzhan: Bastak Nature Reserve, 18 Aug. 2000, E.M. Bulakh, VLA M-15290.

Hemimycena lactea (Pers.) Singer

On the decayed wood and forest litter in coniferous-broad-leaved forest, Ussuriysk Nature Reserve (Vasilyeva & Bezdeleva, 2006).

Hemimycena pseudolactea (Kühner) Singer

On the fallen needles in larch forest, Birobidzhan: Bastak Nature Reserve, 18 Aug. 2002, E.M. Bulakh, VLA M-17274.

Hemimycena rickenii (A.H. Sm.) Singer

On the bark of *Quercus* in oak forest, Ussuriysk: Gornotayozhnoye, 23 Jul. 2002, E.M.

Bulakh, VLA M-17767.

Hohenbuehelia angustata (Berk.) Singer

On the log of *Ulmus* in broad-leaved forest, Ussuriysk Nature Reserve, 15 Aug.1970, М.М.Назарова, VLA M-237. - On the log of a coniferous tree in dark coniferous forest, Upper Ussuri Station, 31 Jul. 1974, E.M. Bulakh, VLA M-232.

Hohenbuehelia atrocoerulea (Fr.) Singer

On the trunk of *Acer* in korean pine-broad-leaved forest, Ussuriysk Nature Reserve, 7 Aug. 1975, М.М.Назарова, VLA M-238; Bastak Nature Reserve, 18 Aug. 2002, E.M. Bulakh, VLA M-17298. - On the log of *Abies* in dark coniferous forest, Upper Ussuri Station, 3 Jun. 1974, E.M. Bulakh, VLA M-239. - On the log of *Quercus* in broad-leaved forest, Big Khektsir Nature Reserve, 21 Jun. 1981, E.M. Bulakh, VLA M-248.

Hohenbuehelia cyphelliformis (Berk.) O.K. Mill.

On the stump of *Populus davidiana*, Big Khektsir Nature Reserve, 1 Jun. 1981, E.M. Bulakh, VLA M-257.

Hohenbuehelia mastrucata (Fr.) Singer

On the trunk of *Maackia amurensis* in korean pine-broad-leaved forest, Ussuriysk Nature Reserve (Vasilyeva & Bezdeleva, 2006). - On the log of *Pinus koraiensis* in korean pine-broad-leaved forest, Upper Ussuri Station, 10 Aug. 1974, E.M. Bulakh, VLA M-260.

Hohenbuehelia myxotricha (Lév.) Singer

On the log of *Ulmus* in coniferous-broad-leaved forest, Ussuriysk Nature Reserve (Vasilyeva & Bezdeleva, 2006). - On the fallen twigs of *Corylus* in broad-leaved forest, Ussuriysk: Gornotayozhnoye, 23 Jul. 2003, E.M. Bulakh, VLA M-19042. - On the wood of *Salix* in willow forest, Khanka Nature Reserve, 28 Aug. 2002, E.M. Bulakh, VLA M-17774.

Hohenbuehelia petaloides (Bull.) Schulzer

On the ground in coniferous-broad-leaved forest, Ussuriysk Nature Reserve (Vasilyeva, 1973); Big Khekhtsir Nature Reserve, 29 Jun. 1981, E.M. Bulakh, VLA M-264.

Hohenbuehelia reniformis (G. Mey.) Singer

On the dead branch of a deciduous trees in coniferous-broad-leaved forest, Ussuriysk Nature Reserve (Vasilyeva & Bezdeleva, 2006). - On the wood in forest, Big Khekhtsir Nature Reserve, 17 Aug. 2004, Tolgor Bau, HMJAU 2997.

Hydropus floccipes (Fr.) Singer

On the bark of *Abies* in korean pine-broad-leaved forest, Ussuriysk Nature Reserve, 26 Aug. 1961, M.M. Nazarova, VLA M-2744. - On the twig of *Tilia*, Birobidzhan: Bastak Nature Reserve, 18 Aug. 2000, E.M. Bulakh, VLA M-15285.

Hydropus fuliginarius (Batsch) Singer

On the log of a coniferous tree in korean pine-broad-leaved forest, Ussuriysk Nature Reserve, 23 Jul. 1961, M.M. Nazarova, VLA M-3327. - On the logs of *Pinus koraiensis* in coniferous-broad-leaved forest, Upper Ussuri Station, 21 Aug. 1973, E.M. Bulakh, VLA

M-3323; in deciduous forest, Big Khekhtsir Nature Reserve, 28 Aug. 1983, E.M. Bulakh, VLA M-3331.

Hydropus marginellus (Pers.) Singer

On the log in korean pine-broad-leaved forest, Ussuriysk Nature Reserve, 7 Aug. 1975, M.M. Nazarova, VLA M-3314; Upper Ussuri Station, 10 Aug. 1973, E.M. Bulakh, VLA M-3310; Birobidzhan: Bastak Nature Reserve, 13 Aug. 2000, E.M. Bulakh, VLA M-15287.

Hypsizygus tessulatus (Bull.) Singer   Plate 9: 52

On the trunk of *Tilia* in broad-leaved forest, Ussuriysk Nature Reserve, 20 Sept. 2002, E.M. Bulakh, VLA M-17484. - On the wood in oak forest, Birobidzhan: Bastak Nature Reserve, 15 Aug. 2002, E.M. Bulakh, VLA M-17811. - On the trunk of *Betula* in coniferous-broad-leaved forest, Upper Ussuri Station, 11 Sept. 2002, E.M. Bulakh, VLA M-17226.

Hypsizygus ulmarius (Bull.) Redhead

On the logs of *Ulmus* in korean pine-broad-leaved forest, Ussuriysk Nature Reserve, 1 Sept. 1961, M.M. Nazarova, VLA M-1343; Upper Ussuri Station, 15 Sept. 1974, E.M. Bulakh, VLA M-1349. - On the trunk of *Betula* in dark coniferous forest, Big Khekhtsir Nature Reserve, 15 Sept. 1981, E.M. Bulakh, VLA M-1335.

Laccaria amethystina Cooke   Plate 9: 53

On the ground in oak forest, Ussuriysk Nature Reserve, 15 Aug. 1974, M.M. Nazarova, VLA M-19763; Ussuriysk: Gornotayozhnoye, 9 Sept. 1963, M.M. Nazarova, VLA M-19798; Khanka Nature Reserve, 18 Aug. 2002, E.M. Bulakh, VLA M-19024; Big Khekhtsir Nature Reserve, 30 Jun. 1981, E.M. Bulakh, VLA M-19876; Birobidzhan: Bastak Nature Reserve, 12 Aug. 2002, E.M. Bulakh, VLA M-17262; in birch forest, Tikhorechnoye, 5 Aug. 2005, VLA M-20680; Raohe, 7 Aug. 2004, Tolgor Bau, HMJAU 3363.

Laccaria laccata (Scop.) Fr.

On the ground in korean pine-broad-leaved forest, Ussuriysk Nature Reserve, 20 Sept. 1975, M.M. Nazarova, VLA M-1058; Ussuriysk, 3 Aug. 2003, Tolgor Bau, HMJAU 2932; in the thicket of *Salix*, Khanka Nature Reserve, 26 Jul. 2003, E.M. Bulakh, VLA M-19044, 4 Aug. 2003, Tolgor Bau, HMJAU 2944; in poplar forest, Upper Ussuri Station, 24 Jun. 1974, E.M. Bulakh, VLA M-19748; in birch forest, Big Khekhtsir Nature Reserve, 11 Aug. 1981, E.M. Bulakh, VLA M-19812, 16 Aug. 2004, Tolgor Bau, HMJAU 3187; Birobidzhan: Bastak Nature Reserve, 7 Sept. 2001, E.M. Bulakh, VLA M-16477; Hulin, 4 Sept. 2003, Tolgor Bau, HMJAU 3018, 3028; Hulin, 4 Sept. 2003, 20 Sept. 2004, Tolgor Bau, HMJAU 3045, 2715; Raohe, 6, 7 Aug. 2004, Tolgor Bau, HMJAU 2645, 2536.

Laccaria proxima (Boud.) Pat.   Plate 9: 54

On the ground in larch forest, Birobidzhan: Bastak Nature Reserve, 18 Aug. 2002, E.M. Bulakh, VLA M-17236.

Laccaria tortilis (Bolton) Cooke

On the ground in ash forest, Ussuriysk Nature Reserve, 18 Jul. 1962, М.М.Назарова, VLA M-19729; in the thicket of *Salix*, Khanka Nature Reserve, 21 Jun. 2003, E.M. Bulakh,VLA M-19069; in poplar forest, Upper Ussuri Station, 9 Sept. 1973, E.M. Bulakh, VLA M-19783.

Lampteromyces japonicus (Kawam.) Singer   Plate 10: 55

On the trunk of *Acer*, Ussuriysk Nature Reserve, 3 Sept. 1961, L.N. Vassiljeva, VLA M-134.

Lentinula edodes (Berk) Pegler   Plate 10: 56

On the logs of *Quercus* in korean pine-broad-leaved forest, Ussuriysk Nature Reserve, 6 May 2003, E.M. Bulakh, VLA M-19519; Tikhorechnoye, 26 Jul. 2006, E.M. Bulakh, VLA M-20678.

Lepista caespitosa (Bres.) Singer

On the forest litter in broad-leaved forest, Ussuriysk Nature Reserve, 1 Sept. 1993, E.M. Bulakh, VLA M-1069; in oak forest, Khanka Nature Reserve, 28 Aug. 2002, E.M. Bulakh, VLA M-19134; in dark coniferous forest, Upper Ussuri Station, 10 Sept. 1974, E.M. Bulakh, VLA M-1067; Big Khekhtsir Nature Reserve, 16-17 Sept. 2004, Tolgor Bau, HMJAU 3263, 3309; Birobidzhan: Bastak Nature Reserve, 13 Aug. 2006, E.M. Bulakh, VLA M-20975.

Lepista flaccida (Sowerby) Pat.

[= *Lepista gilva* (Pers.) P. Kumm.]

On the forest litter in korean pine-broad-leaved forest, Ussuriysk Nature Reserve, 14 Sept. 1963, E.M. Bulakh, VLA M-725; Birobidzhan: Bastak Nature Reserve, 17 Aug. 2000, E.M. Bulakh, VLA M-15481.

Lepista glaucocana (Bres.) Singer

On the forest litter in korean pine-broad-leaved forest, Ussuriysk Nature Reserve, 18 Sept. 1961, L.N. Vassiljeva, VLA M-1163; in oak forest, Khanka Nature Reserve, 28 Aug. 2002, E.M. Bulakh, VLA M-17753; Upper Ussuri Station, 12 Sept. 1975 E.M. Bulakh, VLA M-1166; Big Khekhtsir Nature Reserve, 3 Sept. 1983, E.M. Bulakh, VLA M-1080; Birobidzhan: Bastak Nature Reserve, 19 Aug. 2003, E.M. Bulakh, VLA M-19307.

Lepista inversa (Scop.) Pat.

On the forest litter in korean pine-broad-leaved forest, Ussuriysk Nature Reserve, 22 Aug. 1962, M.M. Nazarova, VLA M-753; Upper Ussuri Station, 15 Sept. 1974, E.M. Bulakh, VLA M-752; Birobidzhan: Bastak Nature Reserve, 12 Aug. 2002, E.M. Bulakh, VLA M-17283.

Lepista irina (Fr.) H.E. Bigelow

On the ground in deciduous forest, Hulin, 9 Aug. 2004, Tolgor Bau, HMJAU 3316.

Lepista nuda (Bull.) Cooke   Plate 10: 57

On the forest litter in korean pine-broad-leaved forest, Ussuriysk Nature Reserve, 24 Sept. 1961, L.N. Vassiljeva, VLA M-1095; Ussuriysk, 3 Aug. 2003, Tolgor Bau, HMJAU

2873;

Lepista piperata Ricek

(= *Lepista ricekii* Bon)

On the forest litter in deciduous forest, Hulin, 9 Aug. 2004, Tolgor Bau, HMJAU 3318.

Lepista sordida (Fr.) Singer   Plate 10: 58

On the forest litter in broad-leaved forest, Ussuriysk Nature Reserve, 21 Aug. 1975, M.M. Nazarova, VLA M-1091; in the thicket of *Crataegus*, Khanka Nature Reserve, 25 Jul. 2002, V.Yu. Barkalov, VLA M-19101; in a garden, Osinovka, 11 Sept. 1951, L.N. Vassiljeva, VLA M-1520.

Leucopaxillus alboalutaceus (F.H. Møller et Jul. Schäff.) F.H. Møller

On the forest litter in korean pine-broad-leaved forest, Ussuriysk Nature Reserve, 1 Sept. 1993, E M. Bulakh, VLA M-19198; in dark coniferous forest, Upper Ussuri Station, 8 Sept. 1974, E.M. Bulakh, VLA M-19752; Big Khekhtsir Nature Reserve, 15 Sept. 1981, E.M. Bulakh, VLA M-19809.

Leucopaxillus cerealis (Lasch) Singer

On the forest litter in korean pine-broad-leaved forest, Ussuriysk Nature Reserve, 7 Aug. 1975, M.M. Nazarova, VLA M-19765; in dark coniferous forest, Big Khekhtsir Nature Reserve, 15 Aug. 1981, E.M. Bulakh, VLA M-19721.

Leucopaxillus gentianeus (Quél.) Kotl.

On the forest litter in korean pine-broad-leaved forest, Ussuriysk Nature Reserve, 7 Aug. 1975, M.M. Nazarova, VLA M-19720; in dark coniferous forest, Big Khekhtsir Nature Reserve, 14 Aug. 1981, E.M. Bulakh, VLA M-1493; in broad-leaved forest, Birobidzhan: Bastak Nature Reserve, 21 Aug. 2003, E.M. Bulakh, VLA M-19259.

Leucopaxillus nauseosodulcis (P. Karst.) Singer et A.H. Sm.

On the litter forest and wood in korean pine-broad-leaved forest, Ussuriysk Nature Reserve (Vasilyeva & Bezdeleva, 2006); in korean pine forest, Upper Ussuri Station, 7 Sept. 1975, E.M. Bulakh, VLA M-1975; in broad-leaved forest, Big Khekhtsir Nature Reserve, 3 Sept. 1983, E.M. Bulakh, VLA M-19726.

Leucopaxillus paradoxus (Costantin et L.M. Duffour) Boursier

On the ground in korean pine-broad-leaved forest, Ussuriysk Nature Reserve, 12 Aug. 1945, L.N. Vassiljeva, VLA M- 19757.

Leucopaxillus   tricolor (Peck) Kühner

On the ground in pine forest, Nikolaevka, 19 Sept. 2000, E.M. Bulakh, VLA M-15137.

Lichenomphalina velutina (Quél.) Redhead, Lutzoni, Moncalvo et Vilgalys

[= *Omphalina grisella* (Weinm.) M.M.Moser]

On the ground among mosses in coniferous-broad-leaved forest, Upper Ussuri Station, 24 Jun. 1974, E.M. Bulakh, VLA M-985; Big Khekhtsir Nature Reserve, 24 Jun. 1981, E.M. Bulakh, VLA M-989.

Lyophyllum connatum (Schumach.) Singer

On the ground in korean pine-broad-leaved forest, Ussuriysk Nature Reserve, 11 Sept. 1975, M.M. Nazarova, VLA M-1290; Upper Ussuri Station, 24 Aug. 1973, E.M. Bulakh, VLA M-19837; in dark coniferous forest, Big Khekhtsir Nature Reserve, 2 Sept. 1983, E.M. Bulakh, VLA M-19791; in poplar forest, Birobidzhan: Bastak Nature Reserve, 8 Sept. 2001, E.M. Bulakh, VLA M-13670.

Lyophyllum decastes (Fr.) Singer   Plate 10: 59

On the wood in deciduous forest, Khanka Nature Reserve, 28 Aug. 2002, E.M. Bulakh, VLA M-17800; Upper Ussuri Station, 9 Sept. 1974, E.M. Bulakh, VLA M-1305.

Lyophyllum infumatum (Bres.) Kühner

On the forest litter in oak forest, Ussuriysk: Gornotayozhnoye, 4 Aug. 2002, E.M. Bulakh, VLA M-18329; in deciduous forest, Khanka Nature Reserve, 28 Aug. 2002, E.M. Bulakh, VLA M-17800; in dark coniferous forest, Upper Ussuri Station, 10 Aug. 1973, E.M. Bulakh, VLA M-1313; in dark coniferous forest, Big Khekhtsir Nature Reserve, 25 Jun. 1981, E.M. Bulakh, VLA M-1316.

Lyophyllum leucophaeatum (P. Karst.) P. Karst.

[= *Lyophyllum fumatofoetens* (Secr.) J. Schaeff.]

On the forest litter in korean pine-broad-leaved forest, Ussuriysk Nature Reserve, 10 Sept. 1955, L.N. Vassiljeva, VLA M-1317; in oak forest, Novotroitskoye, 14 Jul. 2004, E.M. Bulakh, VLA M-19500; in dark coniferous forest, Big Khekhtsir Nature Reserve, 14 Sept. 1981, E.M. Bulakh, VLA M-1322; Birobidzhan: Bastak Nature Reserve, 17 Aug. 2002, E.M. Bulakh, VLA M-17545.

Lyophyllum macrosporum Singer

On the decayed wood of coniferous tree in korean pine-broad-leaved forest, Ussuriysk Nature Reserve, 20 Sept. 1975, E.M. Bulakh, VLA M-1513; in broad-leaved forest, Upper Ussuri Station, 6 Sept. 1975, E.M. Bulakh, VLA M-1330; in dark coniferous forest, Big Khekhtsir Nature Reserve, 15 Sept. 1981, E.M. Bulakh, VLA M-1323.

Lyophyllum mephiticum (Fr.) Singer

On the ground in dark coniferous forest, Birobidzhan: Bastak Nature Reserve, 17 Aug. 2001, E.M. Bulakh, VLA M-16875.

Lyophyllum semitale (Fr.) Kühner et Kalamees

On the forest litter in coniferous forest, Upper Ussuri Station, 21 Aug. 1975, E.M. Bulakh, VLA M- 1314; Big Khekhtsir Nature Reserve, 15 Aug. 1981, E.M. Bulakh, VLA M-1315.

Macrocystidia cucumis (Pers.) Joss.   Plate 10: 60

On the ground in korean pine-broad-leaved forest, Ussuriysk Nature Reserve, 17 Aug. 1962, M.M. Nazarova, VLA M-2471; in the stand of coniferous trees, Ussuriysk: Gornotayozhnoye, 23 Jul. 2002, E.M. Bulakh, VLA M-19118; in broad-leaved forest, Upper

Ussuri Station, 21 Aug. 1975, E.M. Bulakh, VLA M-2450; in oak forest, Big Khekhtsir Nature Reserve, 1 Aug. 1981, E.M. Bulakh, VLA M-2467; Birobidzhan: Bastak Nature Reserve, 12 Aug. 2000, E.M. Bulakh, VLA M-15479; Raohe, 7 Aug. 2004, Tolgor Bau, HMJAU 3372; Hulin, 9 Aug. 2004, Tolgor Bau, HMJAU 3173.

Marasmiellus candidus (Bolton) Singer

(= *Gerronema corticiphila* L.N. Vassiljeva)

On the bark of *Tilia* trunk in korean pine-broad-leaved forest, Ussuriysk Nature Reserve, 7 Aug. 1975, M.M. Nazarova, VLA M-556; in the stand of coniferous trees, Ussuriysk: Gornotayozhnoye, 23 Jul. 2002, E.M. Bulakh, VLA M-17187. - On the wood in korean pine-broad-leaved forest, Upper Ussuri Station, 5 Jul. 1973, E.M. Bulakh, VLA M-540; Big Khekhtsir Nature Reserve, 16 Aug. 2004, Tolgor Bau, HMJAU 2930; Birobidzhan: Bastak Nature Reserve, 19 Aug. 2000, E.M. Bulakh, VLA M-15293; Fuyuan, 4 Aug. 2004, Tolgor Bau, HMJAU 2521; Hulin, 9 Aug. 2004, Tolgor Bau, HMJAU 2714, E.M. Bulakh, VLA M-20218.

Marasmiellus ramealis (Bull.) Singer

On the fallen twigs in coniferous-broad-leaved forest, Ussuriysk Nature Reserve, 6 Aug. 1969, M.M. Nazarova, VLA M-2328; Ussuriysk, 3 Aug. 2003, Tolgor Bau, HMJAU 2818; Big Khekhtsir Nature Reserve, 24 Jun. 1981, E.M. Bulakh, VLA M-2324; Birobidzhan: Bastak Nature Reserve, 17 Aug. 2000, E.M. Bulakh, VLA M-15276. - On the fallen twigs of *Salix* in willow forest, Ussuriysk: Gornotayozhnoye, 4 Aug. 2002, E.M. Bulakh, VLA M-19273. - On the trunk of *Corylus* in deciduous forest, Khanka Nature Reserve, 28 Aug. 2002, E.M. Bulakh, VLA M-17776; Fuyuan,4 Aug. 2004, E.M. Bulakh, VLA M-20186. - On the fallen twigs of *Abies* in korean pine-broad-leaved forest, Upper Ussuri Station, 15 Aug. 1974, E.M. Bulakh, VLA M-1920.

Marasmiellus tricolor (Alb. et Schwein.) Singer

On dead culmes of grasses in broad-leaved forest, Ussuriysk: Gornotayozhnoye, 23 Jul. 2002, E.M. Bulakh, VLA M-17471; Ivanovka, 16 Aug. 1964, L.N. Vassiljeva, VLA M-2431. - On dead stems of *Artemisia* in meadow, Khanka Nature Reserve, 18 Jun. 2003, E.M. Bulakh, VLA M-18347. - On the root of *Carex* in marsh, Tikhorechnoye, 23 Jul. 1998, E.M. Bulakh, VLA M-12091.

Marasmiellus vaillantii (Pers.) Singer

(= *Marasmius dryophilus* Lj.N.Vassiljeva)

On the fallen twigs and leaves of *Quercus* in korean pine-broad-leaved forest, Ussuriysk Nature Reserve, 12 Jul. 1962, M.M. Nazarova, VLA M-2009. - On dead leaves of grasses in oak forest, Ussuriysk: Gornotayozhnoye, 4 Aug. 2002, E.M. Bulakh, VLA M-17470. - On the fallen twigs in the thicket of *Crataegus*, Khanka Nature Reserve, 8 Aug. 2003, E.M. Bulakh, VLA M-19146.

Marasmius androsaceus (L.) Fr.   Plate 11: 61

On the fallen needles of *Abies* in korean pine-broad-leaved forest, Ussuriysk Nature Reserve, 3 Sept. 1963, M.M. Nazarova, VLA M-2070; Ussuriysk, 3 Aug. 2003, Tolgor Bau, HMJAU 2866. - On the leaves of forest litter in oak forest, Ussuriysk: Gornotayozhnoye, 23 Jul. 2002, E.M. Bulakh, VLA M-17751. - On the fallen needles of *Pinus koraiensis* in korean pine forest, Upper Ussuri Station, 23 Jun. 1974, E.M. Bulakh, VLA M-2022. - On the fallen needles on *Picea* in dark coniferous forest, Big Khekhtsir Nature Reserve, 21 Jun. 1981, E.M. Bulakh, VLA M-2034.

Marasmius anomalus Peck

(= *Marasmius littoralis* Quél. et Le Bre)

On the leaves of forest litter in korean pine-broad-leaved forest, Ussuriysk Nature Reserve, 4 Sept. 1963, M.M. Nazarova, VLA M-2054; in dark coniferous forest, Upper Ussuri Station, 23 Aug. 1975, E.M. Bulakh, VLA M-2053; Big Khekhtsir Nature Reserve, 15 Sept. 1981, E.M. Bulakh, VLA M-2057; Birobidzhan: Bastak Nature Reserve, 16 Aug. 2000, E.M. Bulakh, VLA M-15243.

Marasmius berteroi (Lév.) Murrill

On the forest litter in korean pine-broad-leaved forest, Ussuriysk Nature Reserve, 6 Aug. 1962, M.M. Nazarova, VLA M-2075; Tikhorechnoye, 4 Aug. 2005, E.M. Bulakh, VLA M-20235; in oak forest, Big Khekhtsir Nature Reserve, 15 Sept. 1981, E.M. Bulakh, VLA M-2345; Birobidzhan: Bastak Nature Reserve, 15 Aug. 2000, E.M. Bulakh, VLA M-15246.

Marasmius bulliardii Quél.

On the fallen leaves in oak forest, Ussuriysk Nature Reserve, 4 Sept. 1975, M.M. Nazarova, VLA M-2135; Ussuriysk: Gornotayozhnoye, 24 Jun. 1963, M.M. Nazarova, VLA M-2131. - On the fallen twigs in the thicket of *Salix* and *Crataegus*, Khanka Nature Reserve, 21 Jun. 2002, E.M. Bulakh, VLA M-17184. - On the fallen needles in dark coniferous forest, Upper Ussuri Station, 26 Aug. 1973, E.M. Bulakh, VLA M-2092; Big Khekhtsir Nature Reserve, 24 Jun. 1981, E.M. Bulakh, VLA M-2090.

Marasmius cohaerens (Alb. et Schwein.) Cooke et Quél.

On the forest litter in korean pine-broad-leaved forest, Ussuriysk Nature Reserve, 24 Aug. 1975, M.M. Nazarova, VLA M-2159; in korean pine forest, Upper Ussuri Station, 18 Sept. 1974, E.M. Bulakh, VLA M-2122; in dark coniferous forest, Big Khekhtsir Nature Reserve, 4 Sept. 1981, E.M. Bulakh, VLA M-2165; Birobidzhan: Bastak Nature Reserve, 19 Aug. 2000, E.M. Bulakh, VLA M-15270; Hulin, 5 Sept. 2003, Tolgor Bau, HMJAU 3037; Hailin Mudanjiang, 9 Aug. 2004, Tolgor Bau HMJAU 3416.

Marasmius collinus (Scop.) Singer

On the forest litter in korean pine-broad-leaved forest, Ussuriysk Nature Reserve, 13 Aug. 1963, M.M. Nazarova, VLA M-2194; in dark coniferous forest, Big Khekhtsir Nature Reserve, 1 Sept. 1983, E.M. Bulakh, VLA M-2196.

Marasmius epiphyllus (Pers.) Fr.

On the fallen leaves in oak forest, Ussuriysk Nature Reserve, 8 Sept. 1975, M.M. Nazarova, VLA M-2205. - On the fallen leaves of *Populus* in poplar forest, Upper Ussuri Station, 1 Sept. 1974, E.M. Bulakh, VLA M-2204. - On the fallen leaves of *Fraxinus* in broad-leaved forest, Big Khekhtsir Nature Reserve, 14 Sept. 1981, E.M. Bulakh, VLA M-2213; on the fallen leaves of *Betula*, Birobidzhan: Bastak Nature Reserve, 16 Aug. 2000, E.M. Bulakh, VLA M-15272.

Marasmius fasciatus Penn.

On the forest litter in korean pine-broad-leaved forest, Ussuriysk Nature Reserve, 17 Aug. 1963, M.M. Nazarova, VLA M-2242; Upper Ussuri Station, 22 Aug. 1974 E.M. Bulakh, VLA M-2257; in oak forest, Ussuriysk, 3 Aug. 2003, Tolgor Bau, HMJAU 2907; Ussuriysk: Gornotayozhnoye, 30 Aug. 1963, M.M. Nazarova, VLA M-2241; Big Khekhtsir Nature Reserve, 8 Aug. 1981, E.M. Bulakh, VLA M-2266; Birobidzhan: Bastak Nature Reserve, 14 Aug. 2000, E.M. Bulakh, VLA M-15447.

Marasmius graminum (Lib.) Berk.

On the forest litter, Ussuriysk, 3 Aug. 2003, Tolgor Bau, HMJAU 2907; Fuyuan, 5 Aug. 2004, Tolgor Bau, HMJAU 2523. - On the dead stems of *Carex*, Big Khekhtsir Nature Reserve, 3 Aug. 1981, E.M. Bulakh, VLA M-2272.

Marasmius limosus Boud. et Quél.

On the dead stems and leaves of *Carex* in broad-leaved forest, Ussuriysk Nature Reserve, 18 Jul. 1962, M.M. Nazarova, VLA M-2280; Upper Ussuri Station, 13 Sept. 1974, E.M. Bulakh, VLA M-2282.

Marasmius lupuletorum (Weinm.) Bres.

On the forest litter in dark coniferous forest, Ussuriysk Nature Reserve, 25 Aug. 1970, M.M. Nazarova, VLA M-2291; Upper Ussuri Station, 16 Aug. 1974, E.M. Bulakh, VLA M-2290.

Marasmius minutus Peck

(= *Marasmius capillipes* Sacc.)

On the fallen leaves in elm-ash forest, Ussuriysk Nature Reserve, 6 Aug. 1961, M.M. Nazarova, VLA M-2102; in oak forest, Ussuriysk: Gornotayozhnoye, 24 Jul. 1963, M.M. Nazarova, VLA M-2149. - On the fallen leaves of *Fraxinus* in broad-leaved forest, Upper Ussuri Station, 7 Aug. 1973, E.M. Bulakh, VLA M-2116; Big Khekhtsir Nature Reserve, 20 Jun. 1981, E.M. Bulakh, VLA M-2114; Birobidzhan: Bastak Nature Reserve, 15 Aug. 2002, E.M. Bulakh, VLA M-17253.

Marasmius oreades (Bolton) Fr.

On the ground among grasses in meadow, Ussuriysk Nature Reserve, 3 Jul. 1990, E.M. Bulakh, VLA M-2322; Ussuriysk: Gornotayozhnoye, 23 Jul. 2002 E.M. Bulakh, VLA M-17191; Khanka Nature Reserve, 8 Aug. 2003, E.M. Bulakh, VLA M-19151; Sokolovka, 18

Jul. 2002, E.M. Bulakh, VLA M-17207; Birobidzhan: Bastak Nature Reserve, 18 Aug. 2004, Tolgor Bau, HMJAU 2996.

Marasmius personatus Berk. et M.A. Curtis

On the forest litter, Hulin, 9 Aug. 2004, Tolgor Bau, HMJAU 2573; Raohe, 7 Aug. 2004, Tolgor Bau, HMJAU 2543.

Marasmius plicatulus Peck

On the forest litter in korean pine-broad-leaved forest, Ussuriysk Nature Reserve, 25 Aug. 1962, M.M. Nazarova, VLA M-2297; Upper Ussuri Station, 18 Aug. 1974, E.M. Bulakh, VLA M-2301; Birobidzhan: Bastak Nature Reserve, 14 Aug. 2000, E.M. Bulakh, VLA M-15245; in oak forest, Khanka Nature Reserve, 25 Jul. 2002, V.Yu. Barkalov, VLA M-17766.

Marasmius scorodonius (Fr.) Fr.

On the basis of trunks of *Picea* and *Pinus koraiensis* in korean pine-broad-leaved forest, Ussuriysk Nature Reserve, 12 Sept. 1999, E.M. Bulakh, VLA M-20108. - On the stump in oak forest, Ussuriysk: Gornotayozhnoye, 24 Jun. 1963, M.M. Nazarova, VLA M-2365. - On the wood in broad-leaved forest, Khanka Nature Reserve, 21 Jun. 2003, E.M. Bulakh, VLA M-18351; Big Khekhtsir Nature Reserve, 21 Jul. 1981, E.M. Bulakh, VLA M-2384; Birobidzhan: Bastak Nature Reserve, 16 Aug. 2000, E.M. Bulakh, VLA M-15267. - On the forest litter in dark coniferous forest, Upper Ussuri Station, 15 Aug. 1974, E.M. Bulakh, VLA M-2373.

Marasmius siccus (Schwein.) Fr.

On the fallen leaves of *Quercus* in korean pine-broad-leaved forest, Ussuriysk Nature Reserve, 9 Aug. 1961, M.M. Nazarova, VLA M-2393. - On the forest litter in oak forest, Ussuriysk, 3 Aug. 2003, Tolgor Bau, HMJAU 2917; Ussuriysk: Gornotayozhnoye, 23 Jul. 2002, E.M. Bulakh, VLA M-17215; in forest, Ussiryisk, 3 Aug. 2003, Tolgor Bau, HMJAU 2917; Khanka Nature Reserve, 28 Aug. 2002, E.M. Bulakh, VLA M-17812, 4 Aug. 2003, Tolgor Bau, HMJAU 2883; in dark coniferous forest, Upper Ussuri Station, 6 Aug. 1973, E.M. Bulakh, VLA M-2405; in broad-leaved forest, Big Khekhtsir Nature Reserve, 3 Aug. 1981, E.M. Bulakh, VLA M-2396, 16 Aug. 2004, Tolgor Bau, HMJAU 2902; Birobidzhan: Bastak Nature Reserve, 6 Sept. 2001, E.M. Bulakh, VLA M-16440; Hulin, 4, 5 Sept. 2003, 9 Aug. 2004, Tolgor Bau, HMJAU 3009, 3022, 2588; Fuyuan, 4 Aug. 2004, Tolgor Bau, HMJAU 2509; Raohe, 7, 8 Aug. 2004, HMJAU 2535, 2650.

Marasmius splachnoides (Hornem.) Fr.

On the fallen leaves of *Quercus* in korean pine-broad-leaved forest, Ussuriysk Nature Reserve, 18 Aug. 1968, M.M. Nazarova, VLA M-2429.

Marasmius wynnei Berk. et Broome

On the forest litter in coniferous-broad-leaved forest, Ussuriysk Nature Reserve, 24 Aug. 1975, M.M. Nazarova, VLA M-2432; in the stand of *Abies*, Ussuriysk: Gornotayozhnoye, 23 Jul. 2002, E.M. Bulakh, VLA M-19085; in oak forest, Big Khekhtsir Nature Reserve, 11 Aug.

1981, E.M. Bulakh, VLA M-2434.

Megacollybia platyphylla (Pers.) Kotl. et Pouzar

On the logs of deciduous trees in korean pine-broad-leaved forest, Ussuriysk Nature Reserve, 7 Aug. 1975, M.M. Nazarova, VLA M-1957; Upper Ussuri Station, 11 Aug.1990, E.M. Bulakh, VLA M-1978. - On the logs of *Betula* in broad-leaved forest, Tikhorechnoye, 28 Aug. 1984, E.M. Bulakh, VLA M-1986; Big Khekhtsir Nature Reserve, 25 Aug. 1983, E.M. Bulakh, VLA M-1970. - On the rotten wood, Hulin, 4 Sep. 2003, Tolgor Bau, HMJAU 3052; Fuyuan, 4 Aug. 2004, Tolgor Bau, HMJAU 2544.

Melanoleuca brevipes (Bull.) Pat.

On the ground in deciduous forest, Ussuriysk Nature Reserve, 10 Sept. 1955, L.N. Vassiljeva, VLA M-19810; in korean pine-broad-leaved forest, Upper Ussuri Station, 12 Sept. 1975, E.M. Bulakh, VLA M-19840.

Melanoleuca cognata (Fr.) Konrad et Maubl.

On the ground in deciduous forest, Hailin Mudanjiang, 9 Aug. 2004, Tolgor Bau, HMJAU 2590.

Melanoleuca grammopodia (Bull.) Murrill

On the forest litter in oak forest, Ussuriysk Nature Reserve, 14 Sept. 1975, M.M. Nazarova, VLA M-20173; Birobidzhan: Bastak Nature Reserve, 27 Aug. 2003, E.M. Bulakh, VLA M-19175; in korean pine-broad-leaved forest, Upper Ussuri Station, 3 Sept. 1975, E.M. Bulakh, VLA M-19736; in the thicket of *Salix*, Khanka Nature Reserve, 25 Jul. 2002, E.M. Bulakh, VLA M-19150; in dark coniferous forest, Big Khekhtsir Nature Reserve, 14 Sept. 1981, E.M. Bulakh, VLA M-19870.

Melanoleuca humilis (Pers.) Pat.

On the decayed wood in broad-leaved forest, Ussuriysk Nature Reserve, 18 Aug. 1961, L.N. Vassiljeva, VLA M-19857; in korean pine-broad-leaved forest, Upper Ussuri Station, 309 1975, E.M. Bulakh, VLA M-19736.

Melanoleuca melaleuca (Pers.) Murrill

On the forest litter in korean pine-broad-leaved forest, Ussuriysk Nature Reserve, 6 Sept. 1962, M.M. Nazarova, VLA M-19806; Upper Ussuri Station, 24 Aug. 1973, E.M. Bulakh, VLA M-19740; in alder forest, Big Khekhtsir Nature Reserve, 25 Aug. 1983, E.M. Bulakh, VLA M-19865; Birobidzhan: Bastak Nature Reserve, Tolgor Bau, HMJAU 3402.

Melanoleuca strictipes (P. Karst.) Jul. Shäff.

On the forest litter in korean pine-broad-leaved forest, Ussuriysk Nature Reserve, 1 Sept. 1946, L.N. Vassiljeva, VLA M-19732.

Melanoleuca verrucipes (Fr.) Singer

On the ground of meadow, Khanka Nature Reserve, 13 Aug. 1975, E.M. Bulakh, VLA M-19874.

Mniopetalum globisporum Donk

On the moss covering the log of *Betula* in dark coniferous forest, Upper Ussuri Station, 15 Aug. 1974, E.M. Bulakh, VLA M-1924.

Mycena acicula (Schaeff.) P. Kumm.

On the wood buried in forest litter in coniferous-broad-leaved forest, Ussuriysk Nature Reserve, 20 Aug. 2004, E.M. Bulakh, VLA M-20104; Ussuriysk, 3 Aug. 2003, Tolgor Bau, HMJAU 2860, 2912; in poplar forest, Upper Ussuri Station, 30 Jun. 1974, E.M. Bulakh, VLA M-2567; in broad-leaved forest, Big Khekhtsir Nature Reserve, 29 Jun. 1981, E.M. Bulakh, VLA M-2565.

Mycena adonis (Bull.) Gray

On the fallen needles in korean pine-broad-leaved forest, Ussuriysk Nature Reserve, 24 Jun. 1962, M.M. Nazarova, VLA M-2596; in birch forest, Ussuriysk: Gornotayozhnoye, 23 Jul. 2002, E.M. Bulakh, VLA M-3149; in korean pine forest, Upper Ussuri Station, 17 Aug. 1974, E.M. Bulakh, VLA M-2601; in dark coniferous forest, Big Khekhtsir Nature Reserve, 1 Sept. 1983, E.M. Bulakh, VLA M-2612, 16 Aug. 2004, Tolgor Bau, HMJAU 3195; Birobidzhan: Bastak Nature Reserve, 17 Aug. 2000, E.M. Bulakh, VLA M-15292.

Mycena alba (Bres.) Kühner

On the log of *Populus davidiana* in aspen forest, Big Khekhtsir Nature Reserve, 29 Jun. 1981, E.M. Bulakh, VLA M-3205.

Mycena alphitophora (Berk.) Sacc.

(= *Mycena osmundicola* J.E. Lange)

On the forest litter in korean pine-broad-leaved forest, Ussuriysk Nature Reserve, 1 Sept. 1962, M.M. Nazarova, VLA M-3043; Upper Ussuri Station, 17 Aug. 1974, E.M. Bulakh, VLA M-2601; Birobidzhan: Bastak Nature Reserve, 17 Aug. 2002, E.M. Bulakh, VLA M-17265.

Mycena amicta (Fr.) Quél.

On the basis of trunk of *Quercus* in coniferous-broad-leaved forest, Ussuriysk Nature Reserve, 5 Aug. 1963, M.M. Nazarova, VLA M-2625. - On the wood in birch forest, Raohe, 7 Aug. 2004, E.M. Bulakh, VLA M-19648.

Mycena californensis Berk. et M.A. Curtis

(= *Mycena elegantula* Peck)

On the cone of *Picea* in forest litter in dark coniferous forest, Upper Ussuri Station, 11 Jun. 1974, E.M. Bulakh, VLA M-2683.

Mycena capillaripes Peck

On the forest litter in korean pine-broad-leaved forest, Ussuriysk Nature Reserve, 13 Aug. 1961, M.M. Nazarova, VLA M-2654; in dark coniferous forest, Upper Ussuri Station, 15 Aug. 1974, E.M. Bulakh, VLA M-2648; Big Khekhtsir Nature Reserve, 2 Sept. 1983, E.M. Bulakh, VLA M-2662; Birobidzhan: Bastak Nature Reserve, 21 Aug. 2003, E.M. Bulakh, VLA M-19271.

Mycena citrinomarginata Gillet

On the forest litter in korean pine forest, Upper Ussuri Station, 26 Jun. 1974, E.M. Bulakh, VLA M-2641; in oak forest, Big Khekhtsir Nature Reserve, 26 Jun. 1981, E.M. Bulakh, VLA M-2631.

Mycena clavicularis (Batsch) Sacc.

On the fallen needles in coniferous-broad-leaved forest, Ussuriysk Nature Reserve, 5 Aug. 1970, M.M. Nazarova, VLA M-2666; in dark coniferous forest, Big Khekhtsir Nature Reserve, 24 Jun. 1981, E.M. Bulakh, VLA M-2664.

Mycena coracina Maas Geest.

On the wood in coniferous-broad-leaved forest, Ussuriysk Nature Reserve, 3 Sept. 1961, L.N. Vassiljeva, VLA M-2630; Birobidzhan: Bastak Nature Reserve, 18 Aug. 2000, E.M. Bulakh, VLA M-15294. - On the forest litter in the thicket of *Salix* and *Rhamnus*, Khanka Nature Reserve, 21 Jun. 2002, E.M. Bulakh, VLA M-17735.

Mycena dryopteriphila Lj. N. Vassiljeva et M. M. Nazarova

On the scales of leaves of *Dryopteris* in korean pine-broad-leaved forest, Ussuriysk Nature Reserve, 6 Sept. 1976, E.M. Bulakh, VLA M-2679; Upper Ussuri Station, 19 Sept. 1974, E.M. Bulakh, VLA M-2721.

Mycena egregia Maas Geest.

On the forest litter in dark coniferous forest, Upper Ussuri Station, 7 Aug. 1973, E.M. Bulakh, VLA M-2955.

Mycena epipterygia (Scop.) Gray

On the forest litter in dark coniferous forest, Ussuriysk Nature Reserve, 19 Sept. 1975, M.M. Nazarova, VLA M-2890; Big Khekhtsir Nature Reserve, 14 Sept. 1981, E.M. Bulakh, VLA M-2706, E.M. Bulakh; in korean pine forest, Upper Ussuri Station, 6 Sept. 1975, E.M. Bulakh, VLA M-2689; in larch forest, Birobidzhan: Bastak Nature Reserve, 18 Aug. 2002, E.M. Bulakh, VLA M-17267.

Mycena erubescens Höhn.

On the forest litter in coniferous-broad-leaved forest, Ussuriysk Nature Reserve, 14 Aug. 1961, M.M. Nazarova, VLA M-2725.

Mycena filopes (Bull.) P. Kumm.

[= *Mycena amygdalina* (Pers.) Singer]

On the forest litter in coniferous-broad-leaved forest, Ussuriysk Nature Reserve, 11 Jun. 1962, M.M. Nazarova, VLA M-2989; Hulin, 9 Aug. 2004, Tolgor Bau, HMJAU 3350, 3371.

Mycena floridula Secr.

On the forest litter in korean pine-broad-leaved forest, Ussuriysk Nature Reserve (Vasilyeva & Bezdeleva, 2006).

Mycena galericulata (Scop.) Gray

On the logs of *Quercus* in coniferous-broad-leaved forest, Ussuriysk Nature Reserve, 9

Aug. 1997, E.M. Bulakh, VLA M-4055; Big Khekhtsir Nature Reserve, 15 Sept. 1981, E.M. Bulakh, VLA M-2806; in dark coniferous forest, Upper Ussuri Station, 10 Sept. 1974, E.M. Bulakh, VLA M-2786. - On the rotten wood, Ussuriysk, 3 Aug. 2003, Tolgor Bau, HMJAU 2868, 2874; Birobidzhan: Bastak Nature Reserve, 21 Aug. 2004, E.M. Bulakh, VLA M-20820.

Mycena galopus (Pers.) P. Kumm.

On the logs of coniferous trees in korean pine-broad-leaved forest, Ussuriysk Nature Reserve, 6 Aug. 1961, L.N. Vassiljeva, VLA M-2807; Anuchino, 21 Aug. 1955, L.N. Vassiljeva, VLA M-2815.

Mycena haematopus (Pers.) P. Kumm.

On the logs of deciduous trees in broad-leaved forest, Ussuriysk Nature Reserve, 20 Aug. 1961, L.N. Vassiljeva, VLA M-2820; Anuchino, 21 Aug. 1955, L.N. Vassiljeva, VLA M-2823; Big Khekhtsir Nature Reserve, 21 Jun. 1981, E.M. Bulakh, VLA M-2832, 15 Aug. 2004, Tolgor Bau, HMJAU 2946; in korean pine-broad-leaved forest, Upper Ussuri Station, 8 Aug. 1973, E.M. Bulakh, VLA M-2825; Hulin, 9 Aug. 2004, Tolgor Bau, HMJAU 3383.

Mycena inclinata (Fr.) Quél.

On the wood in broad-leaved forest, Birobidzhan: Bastak Nature Reserve, 17 Aug. 2002, E.M. Bulakh, VLA M-17254.

Mycena laevigata (Lasch) Gillet

On the logs in korean pine-broad-leaved forest, Ussuriysk Nature Reserve, 2 Jun. 1962, M.M. Nazarova, VLA M-2879; Anuchino, 21 Aug. 1955, L.N. Vassiljeva, VLA M-2893; Upper Ussuri Station, 8 Aug. 1973, E.M. Bulakh, VLA M-2825; in broad-leaved forest, Big Khekhtsir Nature Reserve, 6 Aug. 1973, E.M. Bulakh, VLA M-2885; Birobidzhan: Bastak Nature Reserve, 18 Aug. 2002, E.M. Bulakh, VLA M-17276.

Mycena lamprospora (Corner) E. Horak   Plate 11: 62

On the logs of *Tilia* and *Quercus* in broad-leaved forest, Spassk-Dalny: Slavinka, 18 Jul. 1981, E.M. Bulakh, VLA M-2916; Tikhorechnoye, 20 Jul. 1984, E.M. Bulakh, VLA M-2911; 26 Jul. 2006, VLA M-20677.

Mycena leaiana (Berk.) Sacc.

On the fallen twigs in korean pine-broad-leaved forest, Ussuriysk Nature Reserve, 15 Jul. 1961, M.M. Nazarova, VLA M-2921.

Mycena leptocephala (Pers.) Gillet

On the wood in dark coniferous forest, Ussuriysk Nature Reserve, 3 Sept. 1961, L.N. Vassiljeva, VLA M-2922. - On the forest litter in oak forest, Ussuriysk: Gornotayozhnoye, 4 Aug. 2002, E.M. Bulakh, VLA M-17727; Anuchino, 21 Aug. 1955, L.N. Vassiljeva, VLA M-2928; in broad-leaved forest, Big Khekhtsir Nature Reserve, 6 Jun. 1981, E.M. Bulakh, VLA M-2926; Birobidzhan: Bastak Nature Reserve, 17 Aug. 2000, E.M. Bulakh, VLA M-15295.

Mycena leptophylla Peck

On the wood in forest litter in korean pine-broad-leaved forest, Ussuriysk Nature Reserve, 1 Aug. 1961, L.N. Vassiljeva, VLA M-2923; Tikhorechnoye, 4 Aug. 2005, E.M. Bulakh, VLA M-20297; in broad-leaved forest, Raohe: Shegli State Farm, 6 Aug. 2004, E.M. Bulakh, VLA M-20294.

Mycena lohwagii Singer

On the rhizomes of *Athyrium* in coniferous-broad-leaved forest, Ussuriysk Nature Reserve, 24 Sept. 1975, M.M. Nazarova, VLA M-2943; Upper Ussuri Station, 18 Sept. 1974, E.M. Bulakh, VLA M-2944; Birobidzhan: Bastak Nature Reserve, 21 Aug. 2003, E.M. Bulakh, VLA M-19157.

Mycena maculata P. Karst.

On the logs in broad-leaved forest, Ussuriysk Nature Reserve, 24 Sept. 1961, L.N. Vassiljeva, VLA M-2968; Birobidzhan: Bastak Nature Reserve, 18 Aug. 2003, E.M. Bulakh, VLA M-13082.

Mycena mellea Lj. N. Vassiljeva

On the bark of trunks of *Quercus* in oak forest, Ussuriysk Nature Reserve, 20 Aug. 2003, E.M. Bulakh, VLA M-12259; Khanka Nature Reserve, 9 Aug. 2003, E.M. Bulakh, VLA M-19179. - On the trunk of *Abies* in the stand of coniferous trees, Ussuriysk: Gornotayozhnoye, 23 Jul. 2002, E.M. Bulakh, VLA M-17222. - On the bark of trunk of *Tilia*, Upper Ussuri Station, 27 Jun. 1974, E.M. Bulakh, VLA M-2969. - On the bark of trunk of *Padus*, in coniferous-broad-leaved forest, Big Khekhtsir Nature Reserve, 25 Jun. 1981, E.M. Bulakh, VLA M-2972.

Mycena niveipes (Murrill) Murrill

On the wood in broad-leaved forest, Ussuriysk Nature Reserve, 9 Jul. 1997, E.M. Bulakh VLA M-4064; Khanka Nature Reserve, 28 Aug. 2002, E.M. Bulakh, VLA M-17725; Birobidzhan: Bastak Nature Reserve, 18 Aug. 2003, E.M. Bulakh, VLA M-19309; Raohe: Shengli State Farm, 6 Aug. 2004, E.M. Bulakh, VLA M-20295; in dark coniferous forest, Upper Ussuri Station, 21 Aug. 1974, E.M. Bulakh, VLA M-3020; in coniferous-broad-leaved forest, Big Khekhtsir Nature Reserve, 20 Jun. 1981, E.M. Bulakh, VLA M-3012.

Mycena pelianthina (Fr.) Quél.

On the forest litter in korean pine-broad-leaved forest, Ussuriysk Nature Reserve, 9 Sept. 1997, E.M. Bulakh, VLA M-4068; Tikhorechnoye, 28 Jul. 1984, E.M. Bulakh, VLA M-3076; Upper Ussuri Station, 8 Aug. 1973, E.M. Bulakh, VLA M-3057; in oak forest, Big Khekhtsir Nature Reserve, 11 Aug. 1981, E.M. Bulakh, VLA M-3073; Birobidzhan: Bastak Nature Reserve, 8 Sept. 2001, E.M. Bulakh, VLA M-16500.

Mycena phaeophyla Kühner

On the forest litter in oak forest, Ussuriysk: Gornotayozhnoye, 23 Jul. 2002, E.M. Bulakh, VLA M-17724.

Mycena polygramma (Bull.) Gray

On the wood in korean pine-broad-leaved forest, Ussuriysk Nature Reserve, 9 Sept. 1955, L.N. Vassiljeva, VLA M-3089.

Mycena pterigena (Fr.) P. Kumm.

On the scales of leaves of *Athyrium* in coniferous-broad-leaved forest, Upper Ussuri Station, 15 Sept. 1974, E.M. Bulakh, VLA M-3092; Big Khekhtsir Nature Reserve, 14 Sept. 1981, E.M. Bulakh, VLA M-3094.

Mycena pura (Pers.) P. Kumm.   Plate 11: 63

On the forest litter in coniferous-broad-leaved forest, Ussuriysk Nature Reserve, 14 Sept. 1961, M.M. Nazarova, VLA M-3104; in deciduous forest, Ussuriysk, 3 Aug. 2003, Tolgor Bau, HMJAU 2863, 3265; Khanka Nature Reserve, 26 Jul. 2002, V.Yu. Barkalov, VLA M-17733; in korean pine forest, Upper Ussuri Station, 23 Jun. 1974, E.M. Bulakh, VLA M-3098; in aspen forest, Big Khekhtsir Nature Reserve, 25 Aug. 1983, E.M. Bulakh, VLA M-3113, 15 Aug. 2004, Tolgor Bau, HMJAU 2777, 2882; Birobidzhan: Bastak Nature Reserve, 15 Aug. 2000, E.M. Bulakh, VLA M-15274; Raohe, 7 Aug. 2004, Tolgor Bau, HMJAU 3206. - On the rotten wood, Ussuriysk, 3 Aug. 2003, Tolgor Bau, HMJAU 2863; Hulin, 5 Sept. 2003, 20 Sept. 2004, Tolgor Bau, HMJAU 3016, 2607.

Mycena rorida (Scop.) Quél.

On the fallen needles in coniferous-broad-leaved forest, Ussuriysk Nature Reserve, 26 Aug. 1961, L.N. Vassiljeva, VLA M-3136; in the stand of coniferous trees, Ussuriysk: Gornotayozhnoye, 23 Jul. 2002, E.M. Bulakh, VLA M-17235.

Mycena rubromarginata (Fr.) P. Kumm.

On the forest litter in broad-leaved forest, Ussuriysk Nature Reserve, 15 Aug. 1978, M.M. Nazarova, VLA M-2728.

Mycena septentrionalis Maas Geest.

On the forest litter in korean pine-broad-leaved forest, Ussuriysk Nature Reserve, 10 Sept. 1961, M.M. Nazarova, VLA M-3179; Upper Ussuri Station, 13 Jun. 1975, E.M. Bulakh, VLA M-2980.

Mycena speirea (Fr.) Gillet

On the fallen twigs in korean pine-broad-leaved forest, Upper Ussuri Station, 19 Jun.1974, E.M. Bulakh, VLA M-3142. - On the wood in willow forest, Big Khekhtsir Nature Reserve, 30 Jun. 1981, E.M. Bulakh, VLA M-3143.

Mycena stipata Maas Geest. et Schwöbel

On the logs in korean pine-broad-leaved forest , Ussuriysk Nature Reserve, 3 Sept. 1961, M.M. Nazarova, VLA M-3175; Upper Ussuri Station, 22 Jun. 1974, E.M. Bulakh, VLA M-3160. - On the wood in forest litter, Hulin, 20 Sept. 2004, Tolgor Bau, HMJAU 2616; Hulin, 4 Sep. 2003, Tolgor Bau 3035; Fuyuan, 5 Aug. 2004, Tolgor Bau, HMJAU 2554; Raohe, 7 Aug. 2004, Tolgor Bau, HMJAU 2649.

Mycena strobilicola J. Favre et Kühner

On the fallen needles in the stand of *Pinus*, Ussuriysk: Gornotayozhnoye, 23 Jul. 2002, E.M. Bulakh, VLA M-3091; in korean pine forest, Upper Ussuri Station, 13 Jun. 1975, E.M. Bulakh, VLA M-2640.

Mycena stylobates (Pers.) P. Kumm.

On the forest litter in korean pine-broad-leaved forest, Ussuriysk Nature Reserve, 10 Aug. 1962, M.M. Nazarova, VLA M-3195; in dark coniferous forest, Upper Ussuri Station, 15 Aug. 1974, E.M. Bulakh, VLA M-3189.

Mycena tintinabulum (Batsch) Quél.

On the logs in coniferous-broad-leaved forest, Ussuriysk Nature Reserve, 5 Sept. 1962, M.M. Nazarova, VLA M-3220; Birobidzhan: Bastak Nature Reserve, 16 Aug. 2000, E.M. Bulakh, VLA M-15416.

Mycena ulmicola A.H. Sm.

On the wood in coniferous-broad-leaved forest, Big Khekhtsir Nature Reserve, 7 Sept. 1983, E.M. Bulakh, VLA M-3239; Birobidzhan: Bastak Nature Reserve, 17 Aug. 2000, E.M. Bulakh, VLA M-15292.

Mycena vexans Peck

On the log in korean pine-broad-leaved forest, Ussuriysk Nature Reserve, 27 Aug. 1963, M.M. Nazarova, VLA M-3181. - On the wood of *Pinus koraiensis* in dark coniferous forest, Upper Ussuri Station, 12 Aug. 1974, E.M. Bulakh, VLA M-3163. - On the log of *Quercus* in oak forest, Big Khekhtsir Nature Reserve, 29 Jun. 1981, E.M. Bulakh, VLA M-2931.

Mycena viridomarginata P. Karst.

On the wood in korean pine-broad-leaved forest, Ussuriysk Nature Reserve (Vasilyeva & Bezdeleva, 2006); Anuchino, 3 Aug. 1976, M.M. Nazarova, VLA M-3156; Upper Ussuri Station, 23 Jun. 1974, E.M. Bulakh, VLA M-3161; in broad-leaved forest, Big Khekhtsir Nature Reserve, 20 Jun. 1981, E.M. Bulakh, VLA M-3030; Birobidzhan: Bastak Nature Reserve, 18 Aug. 2000, E.M. Bulakh, VLA M-15286.

Mycena viscosa Secr. ex Maire

On the log of a coniferous tree in korean pine-broad-leaved forest, Ussuriysk Nature Reserve, 23 Aug. 1961, M.M. Nazarova, VLA M-3257. - On the forest litter in korean pine forest, Upper Ussuri Station, 13 Jun. 1974, E.M. Bulakh, VLA M-3243. - On the wood of *Picea* in dark coniferous forest, Big Khekhtsir Nature Reserve, 4 Sept. 1981, E.M. Bulakh, VLA M-3248.

Mycena vitilis (Fr.) Quél.

On the fallen twigs of *Quercus* in forest litter in oak forest, Ussuriysk Nature Reserve, 14 Sept. 1961, L.N. Vassiljeva, VLA M-3293; Big Khekhtsir Nature Reserve, 22 Jun. 1981, E.M. Bulakh, VLA M-3286. - On the forest litter in deciduous forest, Khanka Nature Reserve, 21 Jun. 2002, V.Yu. Barkalov, VLA M-17726; in korean pine-broad-leaved forest, Upper Ussuri

Station 23 Jun. 1973, E.M. Bulakh, VLA M-3277.

Mycenella bryophila (Voglino) Singer

On the forest litter in korean pine-broad-leaved forest, Ussuriysk Nature Reserve, 12 Sept. 1963, M.M. Nazarova, VLA M-2643.

Myxomphalia maura (Fr.) Hora

On the coals at a burnt place, Upper Ussuri Station, 21 Aug. 1974, E.M. Bulakh, VLA M-3338; in pine forest, Nikolaevka, 21 Sept. 1954, L.N. Vassiljeva, VLA M-3339; in oak forest, Raohe: Shengli State Farm, 6 Aug. 2004, E.M. Bulakh, VLA M-20694.

Omphalina discorosea (Pilát) Herink et Kotl.

On the logs of *Ulmus* in broad-leaved forest, Ussuriysk Nature Reserve, 26 Jul. 1970, M.M. Nazarova, VLA M-12228; in oak forest, Tikhorechnoye, 13 Jul 1998, E.M. Bulakh, VLA M-10580; in coniferous-broad-leaved forest, Upper Ussuri Station, 11 Sept. 1975, E.M. Bulakh, VLA M-948; Birobidzhan: Bastak Nature Reserve, 18 Aug. 2000, E.M. Bulakh, VLA M-15428.

Omphalina epichysium (Pers.) Quél.

On the logs of *Ulmus* in korean pine-broad-leaved forest, Ussuriysk Nature Reserve, 12 Sept. 1963, M.M. Nazarova, VLA M-977; in broad-leaved forest, Tikhorechnoye, 13 Jul. 2004, E.M. Bulakh, VLA M-19510; Birobidzhan: Bastak Nature Reserve, 12 Aug. 2002, E.M. Bulakh, VLA M-17280. - On the wood in coniferous-broad-leaved forest, Upper Ussuri Station, 11 Aug. 1990, E.M. Bulakh, VLA M-969; in dark coniferous forest, Big Khekhtsir Nature Reserve, 19 Aug. 1983, E.M. Bulakh, VLA M-967.

Omphalina ericetorum (Bull.) M. Lange

On the logs in korean pine-broad-leaved forest, Ussuriysk Nature Reserve, 2 Jun. 1961, L.N. Vassiljeva, VLA M-1035; in coniferous-broad-leaved forest, Upper Ussuri Station, 9 Jun. 1974, E.M. Bulakh, VLA M-1039; in broad-leaved forest, Big Khekhtsir Nature Reserve, 25 Oct. 1981, E.M. Bulakh, VLA M-1024.

Omphalina luteovitellina (Pilát et Nannf.) M. Lange

On the stump, covered by mosses in korean pine-broad-leaved forest, Ussuriysk Nature Reserve, 25 Aug. 1975, M.M. Nazarova, VLA M-20107.

Omphalina reclinis (Fr.) Quél.

On the forest litter in coniferous-broad-leaved forest, Ussuriysk Nature Reserve, 6 Sept. 1962, M.M. Nazarova, VLA M-1004. - On the log in broad-leaved forest, Big Khekhtsir Nature Reserve, 24 Jun. 1981, E.M. Bulakh, VLA M-1010.

Omphalina striapilea (Fr.) P.D. Orton

On the forest litter in dark coniferous forest, Big Khekhtsir Nature Reserve, 14 Sept. 1981, E.M. Bulakh, VLA M-1022.

Ossicaulis lignatilis (Pers.) Redhead et Ginns

On the logs of deciduous trees in korean pine-broad-leaved forest, Ussuriysk Nature

Reserve, 2 Sept. 1975, M.M. Nazarova, VLA M-776; in broad-leaved forest, Khanka Nature Reserve, 28 Aug. 2002, E.M. Bulakh, VLA M-17803; Big Khekhtsir Nature Reserve, 12 Aug. 1981, E.M. Bulakh, VLA M-800, Tolgor Bau, HMJAU 3422; Birobidzhan: Bastak Nature Reserve, 12 Aug. 2000, E.M. Bulakh, VLA M-15469. - On the log of *Tilia* in korean pine-broad-leaved forest, Upper Ussuri Station, 10 Aug. 1974, E.M. Bulakh, VLA M-766.

Oudemansiella brunneomarginata Lj. N. Vassiljeva

On the log of *Acer* in korean pine-broad-leaved forest , Ussuriysk Nature Reserve, 2 Sept. 1975, M.M. Nazarova, VLA M-1937. - On the log of *Tilia* in korean pine-broad-leaved forest, Upper Ussuri Station, 21 Aug. 1974, E.M. Bulakh, VLA M-1930.

Oudemansiella mucida (Schrad.) Höhn.

On the logs of *Acer* in coniferous-broad-leaved forest, Ussuriysk Nature Reserve, 11 Sept. 1975, M.M. Nazarova, VLA M-1949; Ussuriysk, 3 Aug. 2003, Tolgor Bau, HMJAU 2867; in korean pine-broad-leaved forest, Upper Ussuri Station, 21 Jul. 1974, E.M. Bulakh, VLA M-1950. - On the logs of *Tilia* in broad-leaved forest, Khanka Nature Reserve, 21 Jun. 2003, E.M. Bulakh, VLA M-18340; Big Khekhtsir Nature Reserve, 12 Aug. 1981, E.M. Bulakh, VLA M-11946, 15 Aug. 2004, Tolgor Bau, HMJAU 2906; Raohe: Shengli State Farm, 6 Aug. 2004, Tolgor Bau, HMJAU 2540.

Panellus patellaris (Fr.) Konrad et Maubl.

[= *Tectella patellaris* (Fr.) Murrill]

On the twigs of *Corylus* in coniferous-broad-leaved forest, Upper Ussuri Station, 16 Sept. 1990, E.M. Bulakh, VLA M-303; Birobidzhan: Bastak Nature Reserve, 18 Aug. 2003, E.M. Bulakh, VLA M-19037. - On the fallen twigs in broad-leaved forest, Big Khektsir Nature Reserve, 14 Sept. 1946, L.N. Vassiljeva, VLA M-301.

Panellus ringens (Fr.) Romagn.

On the fallen twigs of *Salix*, Ussuriysk Nature Reserve, 22 Sept. 1963, M.M. Nazarova, VLA M-308. - On the fallen twigs of deciduous trees, Upper Ussuri Station (Azbukina & Kharkevich, 1984).

Panellus rupicola (Massee) Singer

On the stump of *Abies*, Ussuriysk Nature Reserve (Vasilyeva & Bezdeleva, 2006); Ussuriysk, Gornotajoznoe, 21 Oct. 1944, L.N. Vassiljeva, VLA M-312.

Panellus serotinus (Schrad.) Kühner

On the logs of *Tilia*, Ussuriysk Nature Reserve, 10 Oct. 1963, M.M. Nazarova, VLA M-272; Big Khekhtsir Nature Reserve, 14 Sept. 1981, E.M. Bulakh , VLA M-271. - On the logs of *Alnus*, Upper Ussuri Station, 12 Sept. 2002, E.M. Bulakh,VLA M-16954; Bastak Nature Reserve, 21 Aug. 2003, E.M. Bulakh, VLA M-19130. - On the rotten wood in forest, Hulin, 6 Sept. 2003, 19 Sept. 2004, Tolgor Bau, HMJAU 3038, 2705.

Panellus stipticus (Bull.) P. Karst.

On the logs of *Quercus,* Ussuriysk Nature Reserve, 31 Aug. 1962, M.M. Nazarova, VLA

M-334; Ussuriysk: Gornotayozhnoye, 24 Jun. 1963, M.M. Nazarova, VLA M-333. - On the log of *Betula*, Upper Ussuri Station, 22 Jun. 1974, E.M. Bulakh, VLA M-323. -   On the log of *Tilia,* Big Khekhtsir Nature Reserve, 16 Aug. 1980, E.M. Bulakh,VLA M-321. - On the rotten wood, Ussuriysk, 3 Aug. 2003, Tolgor Bau, HMJAU 2807; Birobidzhan: Bastak Nature Reserve, 18 Aug. 2004, Tolgor Bau, HMJAU 2780.

Panellus violaceofulvus (Batsch) Singer

On the logs of deciduous trees, Ussuriysk Nature Reserve, 17 Aug. 1962, M.M. Nazarova,VLA M-349; Khanka Nature Reserve, 27 Jul. 2007, E.M. Bulakh, VLA M-21533; Big Khekhtsir Nature Reserve, 25 Jun. 1981, E.M. Bulakh, M-367; in broad-leaved forest, 8 Aug. 2004, E.M. Bulakh, VLA M-20280; Raohe: Shengli State Farm, 6 Aug. 2004, E.M. Bulakh, VLA M-20280.

Pseudoclitocybe cyathiformis (Bull.) Singer

On the forest litter in deciduous forest, Ussuriysk, 4 Aug. 2003, Tolgor Bau, HMJAU 3264; Khanka Nature Reserve, 25 Jul. 2002, E.M. Bulakh, VLA M-17773. - On the wood in korean pine-broad-leaved forest, Upper Ussuri Station, 8 Aug.1973, E.M. Bulakh, VLA M-1466; in broad-leaved forest, Big Khekhtsir Nature Reserve, 1 Sept. 1983, E.M. Bulakh, VLA M-1484; Birobidzhan: Bastak Nature Reserve, 12 Aug. 2000, E.M. Bulakh, VLA M-15190.

Pseudoomphalina compressipes (Peck) Singer

On the wood and cone of *Pinis koraiensis* in korean pine-broad-leaved forest, Ussuriysk Nature Reserve, 12 Aug. 1962, M.M. Nazarova, VLA M-1445; Upper Ussuri Station, 10 Sept. 1975, E.M. Bulakh, VLA M-1452; Birobidzhan: Bastak Nature Reserve, 17 Aug. 2000, E.M. Bulakh, VLA M-15452.

Pseudoomphalina lignicola Lj. N.Vassiljeva

On the logs of coniferous trees in korean pine-broad-leaved forest, Ussuriysk Nature Reserve, 25 Aug. 1970, M.M. Nazarova, VLA M-1458; in broad-leaved forest, Arkhipovka, 6 Jun. 2004, E.M. Bulakh, VLA M-19329; Birobidzhan: Bastak Nature Reserve, 18 Aug. 2003, E.M. Bulakh, VLA M-19178.

Resinomycena japonica Redhead et Nagas.

On the wood of *Quercus*. Birobidzhan: Bastak Nature Reserve, 18 Aug. 2004, Tolgor Bau, HMJAU 3179.

Resupinatus applicatus (Batsch) Gray

On the wood of a coniferous tree in korean pine-broad-leaved forest, Ussuriysk Nature Reserve, 6 Aug. 1962, M.M. Nazarova, VLA M-282. - On the log of *Quercus* in korean pine-broad-leaved forest, Upper Ussuri Station, 23 Aug. 1974, E.M. Bulakh, VLA M-20102. - On the logs of deciduous trees in broad-leaved forest, Big Khekhtsir Nature Reserve, 21 Aug. 1983, E.M. Bulakh, VLA M-283; Bastak Nature Reserve, 21 Aug. 2005, E.M. Bulakh, VLA M-19160; in birch forest, Fujuan, 4 Aug. 2004, E.M. Bulakh, VLA M-19563.

Resupinatus striatulus (Pers.) Murrill

On the log of a coniferous tree in korean pine-broad-leaved forest, Ussuriysk Nature Reserve, 14 Aug. 1961, L.N. Vassiljeva, VLA M-298. - On the fallen twigs of *Betula* in birch forest, Ussuriysk: Gornotayozhnoye, 23 Jul. 2003, E.M. Bulakh, M-19072.

Resupinatus trichotis (Pers.) Singer

On the wood, Ussuriysk, 3 Aug. 2003, Tolgor Bau, HMJAU 2887. - On the logs of *Quercus* in broad-leaved forest, Tikhorechnoye, 11 Aug. 1977, E.M. Bulakh, VLA M-299; in korean pine-broad-leaved forest, Upper Ussuri Station, 7 Sept. 1975, E.M. Bulakh, M-300, E.M. Bulakh; Big Khekhtsir Nature Reserve, 18 Aug. 2004, Tolgor Bau, HMJAU 3227.

Resupinatus unguicularis (Fr.) Singer

On the log of *Betula* in coniferous-broad-leaved forest, Big Khekhtsir Nature Reserve, 28 Aug. 1983, E.M. Bulakh, VLA M-279.

Rhodocollybia butyracea (Bull.) Lennox   Plate 11: 64

[= *Collybia butyracea* (Bull.) Fr.]

On the forest litter in korean pine-broad-leaved forest, Ussuriysk Nature Reserve, 23 Aug. 1975, M.M. Nazarova, VLA M-1544; Birobidzhan: Bastak Nature Reserve, 10 Aug. 2006, E.M. Bulakh, VLA M-21360; in dark coniferous forest, Upper Ussuri Station, 23 Aug. 1975, E.M. Bulakh, VLA M-1549; in larch forest, Big Khekhtsir Nature Reserve, 30 Jul. 1981, E.M. Bulakh, VLA M-1541.

Rhodocollybia maculata (Alb. et Schwein.) Singer

On the decayed wood in forest litter in korean pine-broad-leaved forest, Ussuriysk Nature Reserve, 18 Sept. 1975, M.M. Nazarova, VLA M-1830; Anuchino, 21 Aug. 1955, L.N. Vassiljeva, M-1840; Birobidzhan: Bastak Nature Reserve, 10 Aug. 2006, E.M. Bulakh, VLA M-21357. - On the stump in korean pine-broad-leaved forest, Upper Ussuri Station, 21 Aug. 1975, E.M. Bulakh, VLA M-1827.

Rhodocollybia prolixa (Hornem.) Antonin et Noordel. var. ***distorta*** (Fr.) Antonin, Halling et Noordel.

On the forest litter in korean pine-broad-leaved forest, Ussuriysk Nature Reserve, 23 Aug. 1961, L.N. Vassiljeva, VLA M-1655; Upper Ussuri Station, 23 Aug. 1975, E.M. Bulakh, VLA M-1657.

Rhodotus palmatus (Bull.) Maire

On the logs of *Ulmus* in korean pine-broad-leaved forest, Ussuriysk Nature Reserve, 4 Sept. 1963, M.M. Nazarova, VLA M-3482; Upper Ussuri Station, 25 Jun. 1974, E.M. Bulakh, VLA M-3476. - On the logs of *Acer* in broad-leaved forest, Big Khekhtsir Nature Reserve, 25 Jun. 1981, E.M. Bulakh, VLA M-3479; Birobidzhan: Bastak Nature Reserve, 16 Aug. 2002, E.M. Bulakh, VLA M-15429.

Rickenella fibula (Bull.) Raithelh

On the wood among mosses in coniferous-broad-leaved forest, Ussuriysk, 3 Aug. 2003,

Tolgor Bau, HMJAU 3273; Ussuriysk Nature Reserve, 7 Aug. 1975, M.M. Nazarova, VLA M-618; Upper Ussuri Station, 25 Aug. 1973, E.M. Bulakh, VLA M-560; Big Khekhtsir Nature Reserve, 25 Jun. 1981, E.M. Bulakh, VLA M-600. - On the ground among mosses in meadow, Khanka Nature Reserve, 21 Jun. 2002, E.M. Bulakh, VLA M-17759; Birobidzhan: Bastak Nature Reserve, 17 Aug. 2000, E.M. Bulakh, VLA M-15279.

Rickenella swartzii (Fr.) Kuyper

On the log among mosses in dark coniferous forest, Upper Ussuri Station, 6 Aug. 1973, E.M. Bulakh, VLA M-3203. - On the ground in broad-leaved forest, Birobidzhan: Bastak Nature Reserve, 16 Aug. 2000, E.M. Bulakh, VLA M-15404.

Ripartites tricholoma (Alb. et Schwein.) P. Karst.

On the ground in korean pine-broad-leaved forest, Ussuriysk Nature Reserve, 2 Sept. 1968, M.M. Nazarova, VLA M-1101; in korean pine forest, Upper Ussuri Station, 16 Sept. 1975, E.M. Bulakh, VLA M-1102.

Tephrocybe putida (Fr.) M.M. Moser

On the forest litter in broad-leaved forest, Ussuriysk Nature Reserve, 15 Aug. 1970, M.M. Nazarova, VLA M-19741.

Tephrocybe rancida (Fr.) Donk

On the forest litter in korean pine-broad-leaved forest, Ussuriysk Nature Reserve, 1 Sept. 1993, E.M. Bulakh, VLA M-1882. - On the ground in oak forest, Ussuriysk: Gornotayozhnoye, 23 Jul. 2003, E.M. Bulakh, VLA M-19276; in dark coniferous forest, Upper Ussuri Station, 6 Sept. 1975, E.M. Bulakh, VLA M-1885; Big Khekhtsir Natuire Reserve, 15 Sept. 1981, E.M. Bulakh, VLA M-1881.

Tetrapyrgos nigripes (Schwein.) E. Horak

On the fallen twigs, Khanka Nature Reserve, 29 Jul. 2007, E.M. Bulakh, VLA M-21534.

Tricholoma acerbum (Bull.) Vent.

On the ground in pine forest, Khorol, 18 Sept. 1954, L.N. Vassiljeva, VLA M-1109; Nikolaevka, 20 Sept. 1954, L.N. Vassiljeva, VLA M-1112.

Tricholoma album (Schaeff.) P. Kumm.

On the ground in oak forest, Ussuriysk Nature Reserve, 23 Aug. 1975, M.M. Nazarova, VLA M-20171; in dark coniferous forest, Upper Ussuri Station, 29 Aug. 1973, E.M. Bulakh, VLA M-20156; Big Khekhtsir Nature Reserve, 15 Sept. 1981, E.M. Bulakh, VLA M-20135; Birobidzhan: Bastak Nature Reserve, 18 Aug. 2003, E.M. Bulakh, VLA M-19196.

Tricholoma atrosquamosum (Cheval.) Sacc.

On the ground in coniferous-broad-leaved forest, Ussuriysk Nature Reserve, 7 Sept. 1968 M.M. Nazarova, VLA M-20075; in dark coniferous forest, Birobidzhan: Bastak Nature Reserve, 17 Aug. 2000, E.M. Bulakh, VLA M-15464.

Tricholoma caligatum (Viv.) Ricken   Plate 11: 65

[= *Tricholoma matsutake* (S. Ito et S. Imai) Singer]

On the ground under the trees of *Quercus* in oak forest, Ussuriysk Nature Reserve (Vasilyeva & Bezdeleva, 2006); Ussuriysk: Gornotayozhnoye, 6 Aug. 2002, E.M. Bulakh, VLA M-17736. - On the ground under the tree of *Pinus densiflora*, Barabash-Levada, 2 Sept. 1997, E.M. Bulakh, VLA M-15097.

Tricholoma cossonianum Maire.

On the ground in broad-leaved forest, Ussuriysk Nature Reserve (Vasilyeva & Bezdeleva, 2006).

Tricholoma flavobrunneum (Fr.) P. Kumm.

On the ground in korean pine-broad-leaved forest, Ussuriysk Nature Reserve, 4 Sept. 1975, E.M. Bulakh, VLA M-1144; in birch forest, Big Khekhtsir Nature Reserve, 2 Sept. 1983, E.M. Bulakh, VLA M-1135.

Tricholoma goniospermum Bres.

On the ground under the tree of *Ulmus* in broad-leaved forest, Ussuriysk Nature Reserve, 24 Aug. 1961, L.N. Vassiljeva, VLA M-1166.

Tricholoma myomyces (Pers.) J.E.Lange

[= *Tricholoma terreum* (Schaeff.) P. Kumm.]

On the ground in coniferous-broad-leaved forest, Ussuriysk Nature Reserve, 7 Sept. 1963, M.M. Nazarova, VLA M-20094; Birobidzhan: Bastak Nature Reserve, 22 Aug. 2003, E.M. Bulakh, VLA M-19253; in korean pine forest, Upper Ussuri Station, 12 Sept. 1974, E.M. Bulakh, M-20125.

Tricholoma orirubens Quél.

On the ground in oak forest, Ussuriysk: Gornotayozhnoye, 4 Jul. 2002, E.M. Bulakh, VLA M-17801; Nikolaevka, 19 Sept. 2000, E.M. Bulakh, VLA M-15146; in korean pine forest, Upper Ussuri Station, 9 Sept. 1975, E.M. Bulakh, VLA M-1176; in dark coniferous forest, Big Khekhtsir Nature Reserve, 15 Sept. 1981, E.M. Bulakh, VLA M-1177.

Tricholoma portentosum (Fr.) Quél.

On the ground in coniferous-broad-leaved forest, Ussuriysk Nature Reserve, 26 Sept. 1946, L.N. Vassiljeva, VLA M-20182; in dark coniferous forest, Upper Ussuri Station, 25 Aug. 1975, E.M. Bulakh, VLA M-20159.

Tricholoma saponaceum (Fr.) P. Kumm.

On the ground in broad-leaved forest, Ussuriysk Nature Reserve, 10 Aug. 1991, E.M. Bulakh, VLA M-2548; in dark coniferous forest, Upper Ussuri Station, 29 Aug. 1973, E.M. Bulakh, VLA M-1224; Big Khekhtsir Nature Reserve, 15 Sept. 1981, E.M. Bulakh, VLA M-1214.

Tricholoma scalpturatum (Fr.) Quél.

On the ground in coniferous-broad-leaved forest, Ussuriysk Nature Reserve (Vasilyeva & Bezdeleva, 2006).

Tricholoma sejunctum (Sowerby) Quél.

On the ground in fir-broad-leaved forest, Ussuriysk Nature Reserve, 14 Sept. 1963, M.M. Nazarova, VLA M-20084; in dark coniferous forest, Big Khekhtsir Nature Reserve, 7 Sept. 1983, E.M. Bulakh, VLA M-20089.

Tricholoma spermaticum (Fr.) Gillet

On the ground in broad-leaved forest, Big Khekhtsir Nature Reserve, 19 Sept. 1946, L.N. Vassiljeva, VLA M-20059.

Tricholoma squarrulosum Bres.

Under the trees of *Abies* in fir-broad-leaved forest, Ussuriysk Nature Reserve, 20 Aug. 2003, E.M. Bulakh, VLA M-19704; Upper Ussuri Station, 9 Sept. 2005, E.M. Bulakh, VLA M-20234.

Tricholoma sulphureum (Bull.) Fr.

On the ground in oak forest, Ussuriysk Nature Reserve, 22 Sept. 1975, VLA M-1232, M.M. Nazarova; in dark coniferous forest, Upper Ussuri Station, 6 Sept. 1975, E.M. Bulakh, VLA M-1229, E.M. Bulakh.

Tricholoma ustale (Fr.) P. Kumm.

On the ground in aspen forest, Khanka Nature Reserve, 28 Aug. 2002, E.M. Bulakh, VLA M-18311; in pine forest, Nikolaevka, 20 Sept. 1954, L.N. Vassiljeva, VLA M-1248; in oak forest, Fuyuan, 5 Aug. 2004, E.M. Bulakh, VLA M-20270 .

Tricholoma vaccinum (Schaeff.) P. Kumm.

On the ground in fir-broad-leaved forest, Ussuriysk Nature Reserve, 19 Sept. 1975, M.M. Nazarova, VLA M-1254; Birobidzhan: Bastak Nature Reserve, 18 Aug. 2003, E.M. Bulakh, VLA M-19255; in dark coniferous forest, Upper Ussuri Station, 6 Sept. 1975, E.M. Bulakh, M-1257; Big Khekhtsir Nature Reserve, 15 Sept. 1981, E.M. Bulakh, VLA M-1252; in larch forest, Birobidzhan: Bastak Nature Reserve, 6 Sept. 2001, E.M. Bulakh, VLA M-16437.

Tricholoma virgatum (Fr.) P. Kumm.

On the ground in fir-broad-leaved forest, Ussuriysk Nature Reserve, 20 Sept. 1975, M.M. Nazarova, VLA M-20098; in korean pine forest, Upper Uussuri Station, 18 Sept. 1974, E.M. Bulakh, VLA M-20061; in dark coniferous forest, Big Khekhtsir Nature Reserve, 7 Sept. 1983, E.M. Bulakh, VLA M-20091.

Tricholomopsis decora (Fr.) Singer

On the logs of coniferous trees in korean pine-broad-leaved forest, Ussuriysk Nature Reserve, 29 Aug. 1963, M.M. Nazarova, VLA M-19885; in dark coniferous forest, Big Khekhtsir Nature Reserve, 14 Aug. 1981, E.M. Bulakh, VLA M-20065. - On the coniferous trunk in korean pine forest, Upper Ussuri Station, 22 Aug. 1974, E.M. Bulakh, VLA M-19844.

Tricholomopsis rutilans (Schaeff.) Singer

On the wood of a coniferous tree in korean pine-broad-leaved forest, Ussuriysk Nature Reserve, 6 Aug. 1962, M.M. Nazarova, VLA M-19859; Ussuriysk, 3 Aug. 2003, Tolgor Bau,

HMJAU 2852; Upper Ussuri Station, 19 Aug. 1973, E.M. Bulakh, VLA M-19826; in dark coniferous forest, Big Khekhtsir Nature Reserve, 14 Aug. 1981, E.M. Bulakh, VLA M-1202; Birobidzhan: Bastak Nature Reserve, 13 Aug. 2006, E.M. Bulakh, VLA M-20980; Hulin, 5 Sept. 2003, Tolgor Bau, HMJAU 3042.

Xeromphalina campanella (Batsch) Maire   Plate 11: 66

On the wood of coniferous trees in korean pine-broad-leaved forest, Ussuriysk Nature Reserve, 23 Aug. 1975, M.M. Nazarova, VLA M-3363; Upper Ussuri Station, 6 Aug. 1973, E.M. Bulakh, VLA M-3340; Big Khekhtsir Nature Reserve, 25 Jun. 1981, E.M. Bulakh, VLA M-3344, 16 Aug. 2004, Tolgor Bau, HMJAU 2787; Birobidzhan: Bastak Nature Reserve, 8 Sept. 2001, E.M. Bulakh, VLA M-16506; Hulin, 5 Sept. 2003, Tolgor Bau, HMJAU 2622.

Xeromphalina cauticinalis (With.) Kühner et Maire

On the fallen needles in korean pine-broad-leaved forest, Ussuriysk Nature Reserve, 4 Sept. 1963, M.M. Nazarova, VLA M-3401; Upper Ussuri Station, 18 Sept. 1974, E.M. Bulakh, VLA M-3399; Big Khekhtsir Nature Reserve, 7 Sept. 1983, E.M. Bulakh, VLA M-3419, 16 Aug. 2004, Tolgor Bau, 2787; Birobidzhan: Bastak Nature Reserve, 17 Aug. 2002, E.M. Bulakh, VLA M-17278.

Xerula globospora R.H. Petersen et Nagas.

On the ground in korean pine-broad-leaved forest, Ussuriysk Nature Reserve, 2 Sept. 1993, E.M. Bulakh, VLA M-1994; in oak forest, Ussuriysk: Gornotayozhnoye, 13 Jul. 2004, E.M. Bulakh, VLA M-19507, as *X. radicata* (Relhan) Dörfelt.

Xerula hongoi (Dörfelt) Z.L. Yang

On the wood in broad-leaved forest, Arkhipovka, 10 Sept. 2002, E.M. Bulakh, VLA M-17224, as *X. longipes* (P. Kumm.) Maire.

Xerula vinocontusa R.H. Petersen et Nagas.

On the ground in korean pine-broad-leaved forest, Ussuriysk Nature Reserve, 15 Sept. 1961, VLA M-1998, L.N. Vassiljeva, 23. Aug. 1975, M.M. Nazarova, VLA M-2003 [(Vasilyeva & Bezdeleva, 2006), as *X. radicata*], 14 Sept. 2005, E.M. Bulakh, VLA M-20438 [(Vasilyeva & Bezdeleva, 2006), as *X. rugosoceps* (G.F. Atk.) Redhead, Ginns et Shoemaker].

ATRACTIELLALES

PHLEOGENACEAE

Phleogena faginea (Fr.) Link

On the rotten wood, Hulin, 5 Sept. 2003, Tolgor Bau, HMJAU 3013.

AURICULARIALES

AURICULARIACEAE

Auricularia auricula-judae (Bull.) Quél.   Plate 12: 67

On the wood of a deciduous tree, Ussuriysk Nature Reserve, 19 Oct. 1990, O.K. Govorova, VLA M-11250. - On the wood of *Tilia,* Ussuriysk: Gornotayozhnoye, 6 Aug. 2003, E.M. Bulakh, VLA M-18534. - On the wood of *Salix*, Khanka Nature Reserve, 21 Jun. 2002, V.Yu. Barkalov, VLA M-18518. - On the wood of *Acer*, Upper Ussuri Station, 31 Aug. 1973, E.M. Bulakh, VLA M-11269. - On the wood, 4 Aug. 2003, Tolgor Bau, HMJAU 2931; Big Khekhtsir Nature Reserve, 24 Sept. 1981, E.M. Bulakh, VLA M-11210; Hulin, 9 Aug. 2004, Tolgor Bau, HMJAU 2675.

Auricularia cornea Ehrenb.

On the wood, Ussuriysk Nature Reserve, 30 Jul. 1992, O.K. Govorova, VLA M-11291. - On the wood of *Abies*, Ussuriysk: Gornotayozhnoye, 21 Oct. 1944, L.N. Vassiljeva, VLA M-11285. - On the wood of *Ulmus*, Upper Ussuri Station, 22 Jun. 1974, E.M. Bulakh, VLA M-11286.

Auricularia fuscosuccinea (Mont.) Henn.

On the log of a deciduous tree, Ussuriysk Nature Reserve (Vasilyeva & Bezdeleva, 2006).

Auricularia mesenterica (Discs.) Pers.

On the wood of *Ulmus,* Ussuriysk Nature Reserve, 2 Aug. 1990, O.K. Govorova, VLA M-11311; Tikhorechnoye, 6 Aug. 1984, E.M. Bulakh, VLA M-11292; Upper Ussuri Station, 20 Aug. 1975, E.M. Bulakh, VLA M-11305.

Auricularia papyraceae Yasuda

On the log of *Sambucus,* Upper Ussuri Station, 10 Aug. 1990, E.M. Bulakh, VLA M-11322.

Auricularia polytricha (Mont.) Sacc.   Plate 12: 68

On the wood, Ussuriysk Nature Reserve, 7 Aug. 2003, E.M. Bulakh, VLA M-18524. - On the wood of *Ulmus*, Upper Ussuri Station, 7 Aug. 1973, E.M. Bulakh, VLA M-11336; Big Khekhtsir Nature Reserve, 19 Aug. 1983, E.M. Bulakh , VLA M-11327. - On the rotten wood, Ussuriysk, 3 Aug. 2003, Tolgor Bau, HMJAU 2828; Vladivostok, 2 Aug. 2003, Tolgor Bau, HMJAU 2845.

Auricularia tenuis (Lév.) Farl.

On the wood, Ussuriysk Nature Reserve, 3 Jul. 1990, O.K. Govorova, VLA M-11348.

BOLETALES

BOLETACEAE

Boletus calopus Pers.

Under the trees of *Qurcus* in korean pine-broad-leaved forest, Ussuriysk Nature Reserve, 2 Sept. 1993, E.M. Bulakh, VLA M-7940; Birobidzhan: Bastak Nature Reserve, 8 Sept. 2001, E.M. Bulakh, VLA M-16420.

Boletus chrysenteron Bull.

Under the trees of *Quercus* in coniferous-broad-leaved forest, Ussuriysk Nature Reserve, 7 Jul. 1963, M.M. Nazarova, VLA M-20219; in oak forest, Ussuriysk: Gornotayozhnoye, 3 Aug. 2002, E.M. Bulakh, VLA M-19051; Khanka Nature Reserve, 29 Jul. 2002, E.M. Bulakh, VLA M-19070; in birch forest, Fuyuan, 8 Aug. 2004, E.M. Bulakh, VLA M-19594; Birobidzhan: Bastak Nature Reserve, 13 Aug. 2006, E.M. Bulakh, VLA M-20996.

Boletus edulis Bull.   Plate 12: 69

Under the trees of *Quercus* in coniferous-broad-leaved forest, Ussuriysk Nature Reserve, 21 Aug. 1961, L.N. Vassiljeva, VLA M-7967; Big Khekhtsir Nature Reserve, 7 Sept. 1983, E.M. Bulakh, VLA M-3419; Birobidzhan: Bastak Nature Reserve, 13 Aug. 2006, E.M. Bulakh, VLA M-20953; in birch forest, Upper Ussuri Station, 20 Aug. 1974, E.M. Bulakh, VLA M-7958; in oak forest, Hulin, 8 Sept. 2003, Tolgor Bau, HMJAU 3039.

Boletus erythropus Fr.   Plate 12: 70

Under the tree of *Quercus* in oak forest, Khanka Nature Reserve, 26 Jul. 2007, E.M. Bulakh, VLA M-21464.

Boletus griseus Frost

[= *Retiboletus griseus* (Frost) Manfr. et Bresinsky]

Under the tree of *Quercus* in oak forest, Ussuriysk: Gorntayozhnoye, 8 Aug. 2002, E.M. Bulakh, VLA M-19031.

Boletus junquilleus (Quél.) Boud.

On the ground in korean pine-broad-leaved forest, Ussuriysk Nature Reserve, 28 Aug. 1961, L.N. Vassiljeva, VLA M-7981.

Boletus luridus Schaeff.

On the ground in oak forest, Novotroitskoye, 19 Jul. 1998, E.M. Bulakh, VLA M-10466; in broad-leaved forest, Upper Ussuri Station, 27 Aug. 1996, E.M. Bulakh, VLA M-7971.

Boletus pulverulentus Opat.

On the ground in broad-leaved forest, Ussuriysk Nature Reserve, 20 Aug. 1961, L.N. Vassiljeva, VLA M-7888.

Boletus queletii Sculzer

On the ground in oak forest, Osinovka, 14 Aug. 1954, L.N. Vassiljeva, VLA M-7982.

Boletus reticulatus Schaeff.

Fuyuan, Tolgor Bau, HMJAU 3288; Hailin. Tolgor Bau, HMJAU 3290, 3299.

Boletus rhodoxanthus (Krombh.) Kallenb.

On the ground under the tree of *Quercus* in korean pine-broad-leaved forest, Ussuriysk Nature Reserve, 31 Aug. 1993, E.M. Bulakh, VLA M-7994.

Boletus rubellus Krombh.

Under the trees of *Quercus* in oak forest, Khanka Nature Reserve, 28 Jul. 2002, E.M. Bulakh, VLA M-19052; Big Khekhtsir Nature Reserve, 28 Aug. 1983, E.M. Bulakh, VLA M-7894.

Boletus speciosus Frost   Plate 12: 71

On the ground in oak forest, Novotroitskoye, 14 Jul. 2004, E.M. Bulakh, VLA M-19501.

Boletus subtomentosus L.

On the ground in korean pine-broad-leaved forest, Ussuriysk Nature Reserve, 23 Aug. 1961, L.N. Vassiljeva, VLA M-7917; in oak forest, Ussuriysk: Gorntayozhnoye, 5 Aug. 2003, E.M. Bulakh, VLA M-19009. - Under the trees of *Qurcus* in oak forest, Khanka Nature Reserve, 28 Aug. 2002, E.M. Bulakh, VLA M-19040; Tikhorechnoye, 5 Aug. 2005, E.M. Bulakh, VLA M-20317; Big Khekhtsir Nature Reserve, 26 Jun. 1981, E.M. Bulakh, VLA M-7900. - Under the trees of *Populus* in poplar forest, Upper Ussuri Station, 20 Aug. 1975, E.M. Bulakh, VLA M-7898; Birobidzhan: Bastak Nature Reserve, 23 Aug. 2003, E.M. Bulakh, VLA M-19007.

Boletus tomentososquamulosus Lj. N. Vassiljeva

On the ground under the tree of *Abies* in coniferous-broad-leaved forest, Ussuriysk Nature Reserve, 26 Aug. 1961, L.N. Vassiljeva, VLA M-8000.

Boletus violaceofuscus Chiu

Under the tree of *Quercus* in oak forest, Biribidzhan: Kazanka, 20 Aug. 2000, E.M. Bulakh, VLA M-15346.

Buchwaldoboletus lignicola (Kallenb.) Pilát

Near the basis of trunk of *Pinus koraiensis* in korean pine-broad-leaved forest, Ussuriysk Nature Reserve (Vasilyeva & Bezdeleva, 2006). - On the coniferous wood in dark coniferous forest, Big Khekhtsir Nature Reserve, 27 Aug. 1983, E.M. Bulakh, VLA M-7928.

Buchwaldoboletus sphaerocephalus (Barla) Watling et T.H. Li

(= *Buchwaldoboletus sulphureus* Watling et N.M. Greg.)

Near the basis of trunk of *Pinus koraiensis* in coniferous-broad-leaved forest, Ussuriysk Nature Reserve, 26 Aug. 1961, L.N. Vassiljeva, VLA M-7930.

Leccinum aurantiacum (Bull.) Gray   Plate 12: 72

On the ground under the trees of *Populus davidiana* in aspen forest, Khanka Nature Reserve, 4 Aug. 2003, Tolgor Bau, HMJAU 2939; Big Khekhtsir Nature Reserve, 28 Jun. 1981, E.M. Bulakh, VLA M-8015, 17 Aug. 2004, Tolgor Bau, HMJAU 3000; Raohe, 7 Aug.

2004, Tolgor Bau, HMJAU 2512, 3390.

Leccinum chromapes (Frost.) Singer

Under the trees of *Betula* in birch forest and korean pine-broad-leaved forest, Ussuriysk Nature Reserve, 16 Sept. 1997, E.M. Bulakh, VLA M-8031; in oak forest, Khanka Nature Reserve, 15 Jul. 2004, E.M. Bulakh, VLA M- 20425; Nikolaevka, 21 Aug. 2002, E.M. Bulakh, VLA M-17475; Fuyuan, 5 Aug. 2004, Tolgor Bau, HMJAU 2552, E.M. Bulakh, VLA M-19585; Birobidzhan: Bastak Nature Reserve, 21 Aug. 2003, E.M. Bulakh, VLA M-19121.

Leccinum extremiorientale Lj. N. Vassiljeva   Plate 13: 73

On the ground under the tree of *Quercus* in korean pine-broad-leaved forest, Ussuriysk Nature Reserve, 10 Aug. 2004, E.M. Bulakh, VLA M-20426.

Leccinum holopus (Rostk.) Watling

On the ground under the tree of *Betula* in birch forest, Ussuriysk: Gornotayozhnoye, 23 Jul. 2002, E.M. Bulakh, VLA M-19060.

Leccinum oxydabile (Singer) Singer

On the ground under the tree of *Betula* in birch forest, Ussuriysk Nature Reserve (Vasilyeva & Bezdeleva, 2006).

Leccinum scabrum (Bull.) Gray

On the ground under the trees of *Betula* in birch forest, Ussuriysk Nature Reserve, 25 Aug. 2005, E.M. Bulakh, VLA M-20427; Khanka Nature Reserve, 26 Jul. 2002, E.M. Bulakh, VLA M-17462; Ussuriysk, 3 Aug. 2003, Tolgor Bau, HMJAU 2934, 2853; Upper Ussuri Station, 20 Aug. 1974, E.M. Bulakh, VLA M-8076; Big Khekhtsir Nature Reserve, 11 Aug. 1981, E.M. Bulakh, VLA M-8081; Hutou, 8 Sept. 2003, Tolgor Bau, HMJAU 3220; Hulin, 9 Sept. 2003, Tolgor Bau, 3057; Fuyuan, 4 Aug. 2004, Tolgor Bau, HMJAU 2568, 2550, 2635, 2559, 2566; Birobidzhan: Bastak Nature Reserve, 10 Aug. 2001, E.M. Bulakh, VLA M-16423.

Leccinum variicolor Watling   Plate 13: 74

On the ground under the trees of *Betula* in moist birch forest, Ussuriysk Nature Reserve, 9 Sept. 1962, M.M. Nazarova, VLA M-20226; in coniferous-broad-leaved forest, Upper Ussuri Station, 6 Sept. 2005, E.M. Bulakh, VLA M-20227; Birobidzhan: Bastak Nature Reserve, 7 Sept. 2001, E.M. Bulakh, VLA M-16505.

Leccinum versipelle (Fr. et Hök.) Snell.

On the ground under the trees of *Betula* in birch forest, Ussuriysk Nature Reserve, 20 Aug. 2005, E.M. Bulakh, VLA M-20428; Khanka Nature Reserve, 19 Jun. 2002, E.M. Bulakh, VLA M-17181; Upper Ussuri Station, 2 Aug. 1974, E.M. Bulakh, VLA M-8090; Big Khekhtsir Nature Reserve, 11 Aug. 1981, E.M. Bulakh, VLA M-20684; Birobidzhan: Bastak Nature Reserve, 20 Aug. 2006, E.M. Bulakh, VLA M-20655.

Suillus americanus (Peck) Snell

Under the trees of *Pinus koraiensis* in coniferous-broad-leaved forest, Ussuriysk Nature

Reserve, 23 Aug. 1962, M.M. Nazarova, VLA M-7731; in korean pine forest, Upper Ussuri Station, 25 Aug. 1974, E.M. Bulakh, VLA M-7743; in dark coniferous forest, Big Khekhtsir Nature Reserve, 14 Sept. 1981, E.M. Bulakh, VLA M-7736; Birobidzhan: Bastak Nature Reserve, 7 Sept. 2001, E.M. Bulakh, VLA M-16456.

Suillus asiaticus (Singer) Kretzer et T.D. Bruns

Under the tree of *Larix*, Birobidzhan: Bastak Nature Reserve, 14 Aug. 2006, E.M. Bulakh, VLA M-20952.

Suillus cavipes (Opat.) A.H. Sm. et Thiers

Under the tree of *Larix*, Birobidzhan: Bastak Nature Reserve, 21 Aug. 2003, E.M. Bulakh, VLA M-19165.

Suillus granulatus (L.) Roussel   Plate 13: 75

Under the trees of *Pinus densiflora* in pine forest, Ussuriysk Nature Reserve, 5 Sept. 1951, L.N. Vassiljeva, VLA M-7758; Khanka Nature Reserve, 27 Jul. 2002, E.M. Bulakh, VLA M-19065. - Under the bush of *Pinus pumila*, Chuguevka: Snezhnaya Mountain, 31 Aug. 1977, M.M. Nazarova, VLA M-15170.

Suillus grevillei (Klotzsch) Singer

Under the trees of *Larix* in larch forest, Ussuriysk Nature Reserve, 9 Sept. 1975, M.M. Nazarova, VLA M-7772; Big Khekhtsir Nature Reserve, 25 Aug. 1983, E.M. Bulakh, VLA M-7765; Birobidzhan: Bastak Nature Reserve, 6 Sept. 2001, E.M. Bulakh, VLA M-16483. Hulin, 8 Sept. 2003, Tolgor Bau, HMJAU 3012.

Suillus luteus (L.) Roussel   Plate 13: 76

Under the trees of *Pinus* in the stand of *Pinus densiflora*, Ussuriysk Nature Reserve, 6 Sept. 1996, E.M. Bulakh, VLA M-7793; in the stand of *Pinus sylvestris*, Khorol, 18 Sept. 1954, L.N. Vassiljeva, VLA M-7799; Hulin, 9 Aug. 2004, Tolgor Bau, HMJAU 2571.

Suillus pictus (Peck) A.H. Sm. et Thiers

Under the trees of *Pinus koraiensis* in korean pine-broad-leaved forest, Ussuriysk Nature Reserve, 18 Aug. 1962, M.M. Nazarova, VLA M-7640; Upper Ussuri Station, 19 Aug. 1974, E.M. Bulakh, VLA M-7650; in dark coniferous forest, Big Khekhtsir Nature Reserve, 14 Sept. 1981, E.M. Bulakh, VLA M-7651; Birobidzhan: Bastak Nature Reserve, 13 Aug. 2000, E.M. Bulakh, VLA M-15305.

Suillus placidus (Bonord.) Singer

Under the trees of *Pinus koraiensis* in korean pine-broad-leaved forest, Ussuriysk Nature Reserve, 5 Aug. 1962, M.M. Nazarova, VLA M-7803; Upper Ussuri Station, 18 Sept. 1974, E.M. Bulakh, VLA M-15175; Big Khekhtsir Nature Reserve, 7 Sept. 1983, E.M. Bulakh, VLA M-7810; Birobidzhan: Bastak Nature Reserve, 17 Aug. 2002, E.M. Bulakh, VLA M-17509.

Suillus plorans (Rolland) Kuntze   Plate 13: 77

Under the trees of *Pinus koraiensis* in korean pine-broad-leaved forest, Ussuriysk Nature Reserve, 20 Aug. 1976, M.M. Nazarova, VLA M-20220; Upper Ussuri Station, 9 Sept. 1973,

E.M. Bulakh, VLA M-7846; Birobidzhan: Bastak Nature Reserve, 12 Sept. 2001, E.M. Bulakh, VLA M-16476; in dark coniferous forest, Big Khekhtsir Nature Reserve, 15 Sept. 1981, E.M. Bulakh, VLA M-7853.

Suillus viscidus (L.) Fr.

[= *Suillus aeruginascens* Secr. ex Snell]

On the ground under the trees of *Larix* in larch forest, Big Khekhtsir Nature Reserve, 28 Aug. 1983, E.M. Bulakh, VLA M-7700; Birobidzhan: Bastak Nature Reserve, 6 Sept. 2001, E.M. Bulakh, VLA M-16048.

CONIOPHORACEAE

Coniophora fusispora (Cooke et Ellis) Cooke

On the wood in dark coniferous forest, Ussuriysk Nature Reserve, 18 Sept. 1961, L.N. Vassiljeva, VLA M-14907.

Coniophora olivacea (Pers.) P. Karst.

On the trunk of a coniferous tree, Ussuriysk Nature Reserve, 18 Aug. 1961, L.N. Vassiljeva, VLA M-14908.

Coniophora puteana (Schumach.) P. Karst.

On the log of *Alnus hirsuta*, Big Khekhtsir Nature Reserve (Azbukina & Kharkevich, 1986). - On the log of *Picea ajanensis*, Upper Ussuri Station (Azbukina & Kharkevich, 1984).

Hydnomerulius pinastri (Fr.) Jarosch et Besl.

On the wood of coniferous trees in a mine, Dalnegorsk, 14 Jul. 1980, Dvuzilnyi, VLA M-15002; Birobidzhan: Bastak Nature Reserve, 13 Aug. 2006, E.M. Bulakh, VLA M-20982.

Jaapia ochroleuca (Bres.) Nanf. et J. Erikss.

[= *Peniophora ochroleuca* (Bres.) Höhn. et Litsch.]

On the wood of *Picea ajanensis*, Chuguevka (Bondartseva & Parmasto, 1986).

Leucogyrophana mollusca (Fr.) Pouzar

On the log of *Picea ajanensis*, Upper Ussuri Station (Azbukina & Kharkevich, 1984);

Pseudomerulius aureus (Fr.) Jülich

On the fallen twigs of *Pinus koraiensis* and *Picea ajanensis*, Upper Ussuri Station (Azbukina & Kharkevich, 1984).

Pseudomerulius curtisii (Berk.) Redhead et Ginns

(= *Paxillus curtisii* Berk.)

On the logs of coniferous trees in birch forest, Ussuriysk Nature Reserve, 23 Aug. 1975, M.M. Nazarova, VLA M-8097; in coniferous-broad-leaved forest, Upper Ussuri Station, 3 Sept. 1975, E.M. Bulakh, VLA M-8097; Birobidzhan: Bastak Nature Reserve, 12 Aug. 2000, E.M. Bulakh, VLA M-15347.

Serpula himantioides (Fr.) P. Karst.

On the logs of *Picea ajanensis*, *Abies nephrolepis*, *Betula lanata* and *Padus maackii*, Upper Ussuri Station (Azbukina & Kharkevich, 1984). - On the log of *Pinus koraiensis* in korean pine-broad-leaved forest, Big Khekhtsir Nature Reserve (Azbukina & Kharkevich, 1986).

Serpula lacrymans (Wulfen) J. Schröt.

On the wood of a building in korean pine-broad-leaved forest, Ussuriysk Nature Reserve, 18 Aug. 2005, E.M. Bulakh, VLA M-20222.

GOMPHIDIACEAE

Chroogomphus purpurascens (Lj.N. Vassiljeva) M.M. Nazarova

Under the trees of *Pinus koraiensis* in korean pine-broad-leaved forest, Ussuriysk Nature Reserve, 1 Sept. 1993, E.M. Bulakh, VLA M-8212; Upper Ussuri Station, 9 Sept. 1975, E.M. Bulakh, VLA M-8211. - Under the tree of *Pinus densiflora* in pine forest, Nikolaevka, 20 Sept. 1954, L.N. Vassiljeva, VLA M-8208. - Under the tree of *Pinus sylvestris* in the stand of *Pinus sylvestris*, Vyazemsky, 2 Oct. 1990, E.M. Bulakh, VLA M-8220.

Chroogomphus rutilus (Schaeff.) O.K. Mill.   Plate 13: 78

Under the trees of *Pinus densiflora* in pine forest, Barabash-Levada: Shirokaya Canyon, 30 Aug. 2002, E.M. Bulakh, VLA M-17464; Nikolaevka, 25 Sept. 1999, E.M. Bulakh, VLA M-12281; in the stand of *Pinus sylvestris*, Big Khekhtsir Nature Reserve, 17 Sept. 2004, E.M. Bulakh, VLA M-19585. - Under the tree of *Pinus koraiensis* in korean pine forest, Upper Ussuri Station, 18 Sept. 1974, E.M. Bulakh, VLA M-15175.

Chroogomphus sibiricus (Singer) O.K. Mill.

Under the tree of *Pinus koraiensis* in korean pine-broad-leaved forest, Ussuriysk Nature Reserve, 31 Aug. 1962, M.M. Nazarova, VLA M-8231.

Gomphidius maculatus (Scop.) Fr.

Under the trees of *Larix* in larch forest, Big Khekhtsir Nature Reserve, 17 Sept. 1946, L.N. Vassiljeva, VLA M-8179; Birobidzhan: Bastak Nature Reserve, 6 Sept. 2001, E.M. Bulakh, VLA M-16427.

GYRODONTACEAE

Gyrodon lividus (Bull.) Fr.

On the ground in broad-leaved forest, Hailin Mudanjiang, 9 Aug. 2004, Tolgor Bau, HMJAU 2577.

Gyroporus castaneus (Bull.) Quél.

On the ground in broad-leaved forest, Ussuriysk Nature Reserve, 17 Aug. 2005, E.M.

Bulakh, VLA M-20258. - Under the the tree of *Quercus*, Birobidzhan: Bastak Nature Reserve, 13 Aug. 2006, E.M. Bulakh, VLA M-20962.

Psiloboletinus lariceti (Singer) Singer

Under the tree of *Larix*, Birobidzhan: Bastak Nature Reserve, 12 Sept. 2001, E.M. Bulakh, VLA M-16448.

HYGROPHOROPSIDACEAE

Hygrophoropsis aurantiaca (Wulfen) Maire   Plate 14: 79

On the forest litter in coniferous broad-leaved forest, Ussuriysk Nature Reserve, 10 Aug. 1961, L.N. Vassiljeva, VLA M-8142. - On the decayed wood in dark coniferous forest, Upper Ussuri Station, 6 Aug. 1973, E.M. Bulakh, VLA M-8149; Big Khekhtsir Nature Reserve, 7 Sept. 1983, E.M. Bulakh, VLA M-8150.

PAXILLACEAE

Omphalotus illudens (Schwein.) Bresinsky et Besl.

[= *Omphalotus olearius* (DC.) Singer]

On the forest litter in korean pine-broad-leaved forest, Ussuriysk Nature Reserve, 2 Sept. 1993, E.M. Bulakh, VLA M-8157.

Paxillus involutus (Batsch) Fr.   Plate 14: 80

On the basis of trunk in oak forest, Ussuriysk Nature Reserve, 4 Sept. 1975, M.M. Nazarova, VLA M-8123. - On the ground in deciduous forest, Ussuriysk, 3 Aug. 2003, Tolgor Bau, HMJAU 2875; Khanka Nature Reserve, 26 Jul. 2002, E.M. Bulakh, VLA M-17754; Big Khekhtsir Nature Reserve, 12 Aug. 1981, E.M. Bulakh, VLA M-8109, 17 Aug. 2004, Tolgor Bau, HMJAU 2792; Hulin, 8 Sept. 2003, Tolgor Bau, HMJAU 2593, 3062; Fuyuan, 5 Aug. 2004, Tolgor Bau, HMJAU 2517, 2634; Raohe, 7 Aug. 2004, Tolgor Bau, HMJAU 2574, 3252, 3355; Birobidzhan: Bastak Nature Reserve, 12 Aug. 2000, E.M. Bulakh, VLA M-15308.

Tapinella panuoides (Batsch) E.-J. Gilbert   Plate 14: 81

[= *Paxillus panuoides* (Fr.) Fr.]

On the wood of a building in korean pine-broad-leaved forest, Ussuriysk Nature Reserve, 7 Aug. 1975, M.M. Nazarova, VLA M-8130. - On the wood of *Picea* in coniferous-broad-leaved forest, Upper Ussuri Station, 23 Aug. 1973, E.M. Bulakh, VLA M-8127; Big Khekhtsir Nature Reserve, 27 Aug. 1983, E.M. Bulakh, VLA M-8133; Birobidzhan: Bastak Nature Reserve, 10 Aug. 2006, E.M. Bulakh, VLA M-20991.

STROBILOMYCETACEAE

Chalciporus piperatus (Bull.) Bataille   Plate 14: 82

On the ground in korean pine-broad-leaved forest, Ussuriysk Nature Reserve, 13 Aug. 1961, L.N. Vassiljeva, VLA M-7844; Birobidzhan: Bastak Nature Reserve, 18 Aug. 2002, E.M. Bulakh, VLA M-17522; Ussuriysk, Tolgor Bau, HMJAU 3409; in dark coniferous forest, Upper Ussuri Station, 29 Aug. 1973, E.M. Bulakh, VLA M-7832; in broad-leaved forest, Big Khekhtsir Reserve, 5 Sept. 1983, E.M. Bulakh, VLA M-7834.

Porphyrellus atrobrunneus Lj.N. Vassiljeva

On the ground under the tree of *Quercus* in oak forest, Big Khekhtsir Nature Reserve, 15 Aug. 2004, E.M. Bulakh, VLA M-20264.

Porphyrellus gracilis (Peck) Singer

On the ground in coniferous-broad-leaved forest, Ussuriysk Nature Reserve, 21 Aug. 1961, L.N. Vassiljeva, VLA M-7538.

Porphyrellus porphyrosporus (Fr.et Hök) E.-J. Gilbert

(= *Porphyrellus pseudoscaber* Secr. ex Singer)

On the ground in coniferous-broad-leaved forest, Ussuriysk Nature Reserve, 26 Aug. 1961, L.N. Vassiljeva, VLA M-7542; in dark coniferous forest, Big Khekhtsir Nature Reserve, 15 Sept. 1981, E.M. Bulakh, VLA M-7550.

Strobilomyces strobilaceus (Scop.) Berk.

Under the trees of *Quercus* in korean pine-broad-leaved forest, Ussuriysk Nature Reserve, 18 Aug. 1963, M.M. Nazarova, VLA M-20221; in oak forest, Ussuriysk: Gornotayozhnoye, 4 Jul. 1945, L.N. Vassiljeva, VLA M-7516; Novotroitskoye, 19 Jul. 1998, E.M. Bulakh, VLA M-10561; Big Khektsir Nature Reserve, 15 Aug. 2004, E.M. Bulakh, VLA M-20265; Birobidzhan: Bastak Nature Reserve, 17 Aug. 2002, E.M. Bulakh, VLA M-17512.

Tylopilus felleus (Bull.) P. Karst.

On the trunk of *Pinus koraiensis* in dark coniferous forest, Big Khekhtsir Nature Reserve, 2 Sept. 1983, E.M. Bulakh, VLA M-8004; Birobidzhan: Bastak Nature Reserve, 18 Aug. 2000, E.M. Bulakh, VLA M-15251.

CANTHARELLALES

APHELLARIACEAE

Aphelaria tuberosa (Grev.) Corner

[= *Tremellodendropsis tuberosa* (Grev.) D.A.Crawford]

On the ground, Ussuriysk Nature Reserve, 18 Aug. 2001, O.K. Govorova , VLA M-15654; Ussuriysk: Gornotayozhnoye, 4 Sept. 2002, O.K. Govorova, VLA M-18717;

Birobidzhan: Bastak Nature Reserve, 19 Aug. 2000, E.M. Bulakh, VLA M-15076.

CANTHARELLACEAE

Cantharellus cibarius Fr.   Plate 14: 83

On the ground under the trees of *Quercus* and *Betula*, Ussuriysk Nature Reserve, 20 Aug. 2005, E.M. Bulakh, VLA M-9408; Ussuriysk: Gornotayozhnoye, 6 Aug. 2002, O.K. Govorova, VLA M-17634; Khanka Nature Reserve, 25 Jul. 2002, V.Yu. Barkalov, VLA M-17633; Upper Ussuri Station, 6 Aug. 1973, E.M. Bulakh, VLA M-15815; Big Khekhtsir Nature Reserve, 11 Aug. 1981, E.M. Bulakh, VLA M-15820; Birobidzhan: Bastak Nature Reserve, 22 Aug. 2003, E.M. Bulakh, VLA M-18991.

Cantharellus infundibuliformis (Scop.) Fr.

[= *Cantharellus tubaeformis* (Bull.) Fr.]

On the ground, Ussuriysk Nature Reserve, 20 Aug. 1961, L.N. Vassiljeva, VLA M-16463. - On the ground among mosses, Big Khekhtsir Nature Reserve, 15 Sept. 1981, E.M. Bulakh, VLA M-16461; Ussuriysk: Gornotayozhnoye, 6 Aug. 2002, O.K. Govorova, VLA M-17668.

Cantharellus lateritius (Berk.) Singer

On the ground, Fuyuan, Tolgor Bau, HMJAU 3219.

CLAVARIACEAE

Clavaria acuta Sowerby

On the ground under deciduous trees, Terekhovka, 27 Aug. 1998, O.K. Govorova, VLA M-12600.

Clavaria argillacea Fr.

On the ground under *Taxus*, Upper Ussuri Station, 22 Aug. 1974, E.M. Bulakh, VLA M-12558.

Clavaria fragilis Holnsk

(= *Clavaria vermicularis* Scop.)

On the ground under deciduous trees, Ussuriysk Nature Reserve, 18 Aug. 2004, O.K. Govorova, VLA M-15652; Terekhovka, 27 Aug. 1998, O.K. Govorova, VLA M-12550; Upper Ussuri Station, 17 Aug. 1974, E.M. Bulakh, VLA M-12530; Big Khehktsir Nature Reserve, 3 Aug. 1981, E.M. Bulakh, VLA M-12544; Raohe, 8 Aug. 2004, Tolgor Bau, HMJAU 2619; Hulin, 5 Sept. 2003, Tolgor Bau, HMJAU 3033; Birobidzhan: Bastak Nature Reserve, 20 Aug. 2003, E.M. Bulakh, VLA M-18678.

Clavaria fumosa Pers.

On the ground under deciduous trees, Ussuriysk Nature Reserve, 8 Sept. 1975, O.K. Govorova, VLA M-12575; Big Khekhtsir Nature Reserve, 1 Sept. 1983, E.M. Bulakh, VLA

M-12579; Birobidzhan: Bastak Nature Reserve, 12 Aug. 2002, E.M. Bulakh, VLA M-15070.

Clavaria purpurea Fr.

On the ground in forest, Raohe, 8 Aug. 2004, Tolgor Bau, HMJAU 2602.

Clavaria zollingeri Lév.

On the ground in korean pine-broad-leaved forest, Upper Ussuri Station (Azbukina & Kharkevich, 1984); Birobidzhan: Bastak Nature Reserve, Tolgor Bau, HMJAU 3276.

Clavulinopsis aurantio-cinnabarina (Schwein.) Corner

On the ground in dark coniferous forest, Big Khehktsir Nature Reserve (Azbukina & Kharkevich, 1986).

Clavulinopsis corniculata (Schaeff.) Corner

[= *Ramariopsis corniculata* (Schaeff.) R.H. Petersen]

On the ground under the trees of *Quercus*, Ussuriysk Nature Reserve, 5 Sept. 2000, O.K. Govorova, VLA M-15045; Upper Ussuri Station, 17 Aug. 1974, E.M. Bulakh VLA M-12144; Big Khekhtsir Nature Reserve, 1 Sept. 1983, E.M. Bulakh, VLA M-12147; Birobidzhan: Bastak Nature Reserve, 21 Aug. 2003, E.M. Bulakh, VLA M-18706.

Clavulinopsis fusiformis (Sowerby) Corner

On the ground under the trees of *Betula* in birch-aspen forest, Big Khehktsir Nature Reserve, 29 Jun. 1981, E.M. Bulakh, VLA M-12617; 15 Aug. 2004, Tolgor Bau HMJAU 2919; Birobidzhan: Bastak Nature Reserve, 18 Aug. 2004, Tolgor Bau, HMJAU 3401.

Clavulinopsis laeticolor (Berk. et M.A. Curtis) R.H. Petrsen

[= *Ramariopsis laeticolor* (Berk. et M.A. Curtis) R.H. Petersen]

On the forest litter, Ussuriysk Nature Reserve, 5 Sept. 2000, O.K. Govorova , VLA M-15026. - On the ground under the trees of *Quercus*, Terekhovka, 27 Aug. 1998, O.K. Govorova, VLA M-12251; Birobidzhan: Bastak Nature Reserve, 16 Aug. 2002, E.M. Bulakh, VLA M-18689. - On the coniferous wood in litter forest of coniferous-broad-leaved forest, Big Khekhtsir Nature Reserve, 14 Aug. 1981, E.M. Bulakh, VLA M-12259.

Clavulinopsis umbrinella (Sacc.) Corner

On the forest litter, Birobidzhan: Bastak Nature Reserve, 8 Sept. 2001, E.M. Bulakh, VLA M-15778.

Macrotyphula fistulosa (Holmsk.) R.H. Petersen

On the ground of the plantation of *Panax ginseng*, Ussuriysk Nature Reserve, 5 Sept. 1958, I.A. Bunkina, VLA M-12483. - On the log of *Picea*, Upper Ussuri Station, 11 Jun. 1975, E.M. Bulakh, VLA M-12486. - On the fallen twigs, Big Khekhtsir Nature Reserve, 15 Sept. 1981, E.M. Bulakh, VLA M-12484.

Multiclavula mucida (Pers.) R.H. Petersen

On the wood covered by mosses, Ussuriysk Nature Reserve, 6 Sept. 1996, O.K. Govorova, VLA M-12312; Upper Ussuri Station (Azbukina & Kharkevich, 1984); Birobidzhan: Bastak Nature Reserve, 18 Aug. 2004, Tolgor Bau, HMJAU 2797.

Ramariopsis asperulispora (G.F. Atk.) Corner

On the ground under deciduous trees, Terekhovka, 27 Aug. 1998, O.K. Govorova , VLA M-12592.

Ramariopsis biformis (G.F. Atk.) R.H. Petersen

On the ground under the trees of *Quercus*, Ussuriysk Nature Reserve (Vasilyeva & Bezdeleva, 2006); Terekhovka, 27 Aug. 1998, O.K. Govorova, VLA M-1264; Birobidzhan: Bastak Nature Reserve, 16 Aug. 2000, E.M. Bulakh, VLA M-15092.

Ramariopsis crocea (Pers.) Corner

On the forest litter, Ussuriysk Nature Reserve (Vasilyeva & Bezdeleva, 2006); Yakovlevka: Yelovy pereval, 23 Aug. 1953, L.N. Vassiljeva, VLA M-12674; Birobidzhan: Bastak Nature Reserve, 17 Aug. 2002, E.M. Bulakh, VLA M-18652.

Ramariopsis kunzei (Fr.) Corner

On the ground under deciduous trees, Ussuriysk Nature Reserve, 18 Aug. 2001, O.K. Govorova, VLA M-15626; Terekhovka, 27 Aug. 1998, O.K. Govorova , VLA M-12191; Upper Ussuri Station, 18 Sept. 1974, E.M. Bulakh , VLA M-12200; Big Khekhtsir Nature Reserve, 9 Aug. 1981, E.M. Bulakh, VLA M-12201; Birobidzhan: Bastak Nature Reserve, 19 Aug. 2003, E.M. Bulakh, VLA M-18675.

Ramariopsis pulchella (Boud.) Corner

On the ground under the trees of *Quercus*, Barabash-Levada: Shirokaya Canyon, 30 Aug. 2002, E.M. Bulakh, VLA M-18705; Birobidzhan: Bastak Nature Reserve, 21 Aug. 2003, E.M. Bulakh, VLA M-18704.

Ramariopsis tenuicola (Bourdot et Galzin) R.H. Petersen

On the ground, Ussuriysk Nature Reserve, 5 Sept. 2000, O.K. Govorova, VLA M-15096.

Ramariopsis tenuiramosa Corner

On the wood of deciduous trees, Khanka Nature Reserve, 26 Jul. 2002, E.M. Bulakh, VLA M-18707.

CLAVARIADELPHACEAE

Clavariadelphus americanus (Corner) Methven

On the ground under the trees of *Quercus*, Ussuriysk Nature Reserve, 4 Sept. 1975, M.M. Nazarova, VLA M-12070; Terekhovka, 27 Aug. 1998, O.K. Govorova,VLA M-12069.

Clavariadelphus ligula (Shaeff.) Donk

On the ground in forest, Big Khekhtsir Nature Reserve, 17 Aug. 2004, Tolgor Bau, HMJAU 2754, 2783.

Clavariadelphus pistillaris (L.) Donk

On the ground under coniferous and deciduous trees, Ussuriysk Nature Reserve, 11 Sept. 1997, O.K. Govorova, VLA M-12100; Barabash-Levada: Shirokaya Canyon, 30 Aug. 2002,

E.M. Bulakh, VLA M-18722; Upper Ussuri Station, 6 Aug. 1975, E.M. Bulakh, VLA M-12095; Kabarga, 10 Aug. 2002, M.P. Tiunov, VLA M-18721; Birobidzhan: Bastak Nature Reserve, 18 Aug. 2002, E.M. Bulakh, VLA M-15075.

Clavariadelphus truncatus (Quél.) Donk

On the ground under coniferous and deciduous trees, Ussuriysk Nature Reserve, 20 Aug. 1962, M.M. Nazarova, VLA M-12063; Upper Ussuri Station, 19 Aug. 1974, E.M. Bulakh, VLA M-12065.

CLAVULINACEAE

Clavulina amethystina (Bull.) Donk

On the ground in broad-leaved forest, Big Khekhtsir Nature Reserve, 18 Aug. 2004, Tolgor Bau, HMJAU 3213.

Clavulina castaneipes (G.F. Atk.) Corner

On the ground in broad-leaved forest, Ussuriysk Nature Reserve (Vasilyeva & Bezdeleva, 2006); Upper Ussuri Station, 23 Aug. 1975, E.M. Bulakh, VLA M-12430; in dark coniferous forest, Big Khekhtsir Nature Reserve, 20 Aug. 1983, E.M. Bulakh, VLA M-12433.

Clavulina cinerea (Bull.) J. Schröt.

On the ground, Ussuriysk Nature Reserve, 18 Aug. 2001, O.K. Govorova , VLA M-15649; Upper Ussuri Station, 23 Aug. 1975, E.M. Bulakh, VLA M-12421; Khabarovsk, 10 Aug. 2002, M.P. Tiunov, VLA M-18739; in deciduous forest, Big Khekhtsir Nature Reserve, 3 Aug. 1981, E.M. Bulakh, VLA M-12400. - On the wood, Ussuriysk: Gornotayozhnoye, 4 Aug. 2002, E.M. Bulakh, VLA M-18337; Birobidzhan: Bastak Nature Reserve, 8 Aug. 2001, E.M. Bulakh, VLA M-15679.

Clavulina coralloides (L.) J. Schröt.   Plate 14: 84

[= *Clavulina cristata* (Holmsk.) J. Schröt.]

On the ground, Ussuriysk Nature Reserve, 18 Aug. 2001, O.K. Govorova, VLA M-15649; Khanka Nature Reserve, 9 Aug. 2003, E.M. Bulakh, VLA M-18674; Osinovka, 14 Aug. 1954, L.N. Vassiljeva,VLA M-12477; Upper Ussuri Station, 25 Aug. 1973, E.M. Bulakh, VLA M-12469; Fuyuan, 5 Aug. 2004, Tolgor Bau, HMJAU 2606; Raohe, 8 Aug. 2004, Tolgor Bau, HMJAU 2655.

Clavulina rugosa (Bull.) J. Schröt.

On the ground under the trees of *Betula* and *Quercus*, Ussuriysk Nature Reserve, 21 Aug. 2001, O.K. Govorova, VLA M-15647; Khanka Nature Reserve, 26 Jul. 2002, E.M. Bulakh, VLA M-18736; Barabash-Levada: Shirokaya Canyon, 30 Aug. 2002, E.M. Bulakh, VLA M-18729; Big Khekhtsir Nature Reserve, 26 Jun. 1981, E.M. Bulakh, VLA M-12453.

CRATERELLACEAE

Craterellus cornucopioides (L.) Pers.   Plate 15: 85

On the ground under the trees of *Quercus*, Ussuriysk Nature Reserve, 21 Aug. 2001, O.K. Govorova, VLA M-15796; Ussuriysk: Gornotayozhnoye, 6 Aug. 2002, O.K. Govorova, VLA M-17570; Nikolaevka, 21 Aug. 2002, O.K. Govorova, VLA M-17556; Barabash-Levada: Shirokaia canyon, 30 Aug. 2002, E.M. Bulakh, VLA M-17559; Big Khekhtsir Nature Reserve, 3 Aug. 1981, E.M. Bulakh, VLA M-15805.

Pseudocraterellus sinuosus (Fr.) Corner

On the ground under the trees of *Quercus*, Big Khekhtsir Nature Reserve, 5 Aug. 1981, E.M. Bulakh, VLA M-15790; Birobidzhan: Bastak Nature Reserve, 20 Aug. 2003, E.M. Bulakh, VLA M-18893.

HYDNACEAE

Climacodon pulcherrimus (Berk. et M.A. Curtis) M.I. Nikol.

On the log of a deciduous tree in coniferous-broad-leaved forest, Upper Ussuri Station (Azbukina & Kharkevich, 1984). - On the log of *Populus davidiana* and other deciduous trees, Big Khekhtsir Nature Reserve (Azbukina & Kharkevich, 1986).

Climacodon septentrionalis (Fr.) P. Karst.

On the trunks of deciduous trees, Ussuriysk Nature Reserve, 14 Aug. 1961, L.N. Vassiljeva, VLA M-16516; Big Khekhtsir Nature Reserve, 18 Aug. 2004, Tolgor Bau, HMJAU 2998. - On the stump of *Betula* in coniferous-broad-leaved forest, Upper Ussuri Station (Azbukina & Kharkevich, 1984).

Hydnum repandum L.

On the ground under the trees of *Quercus*, Ussuriysk Nature Reserve, 5 Sept. 1991, O.K. Govorova, VLA M-15881; Ussuriysk: Gornotayozhnoye, 13 Aug. 2002, O.K. Govorova, VLA M-17578; Terekhovka, 27 Aug. 1998, O.K. Govorova, VLA M-15882; Khanka Nature Reserve, 25 Jul. 2002, V.Yu. Barkalov, VLA M-17591; Upper Ussuri Station, 18 Sept. 1974, E.M. Bulakh, VLA M-15854; Big Khekhtsir Nature Reserve, 3 Aug. 1981, E.M. Bulakh, VLA M-15865, 16 Aug. 2004, Tolgor Bau, HMJAU 3184; Birobidzhan: Bastak Nature Reserve, 23 Aug. 2003, E.M. Bulakh, VLA M-18553; Fuyuan, 5 Aug. 2004, Tolgor Bau, HMJAU 2546, 3405; Raohe, 9 Sept. 2003, Tolgor Bau, HMJAU 3015, 3243.

Hydnum rufescens Pers.

On the ground in korean pine-broad-leaved forest, Upper Ussuri Station (Azbukina & Kharkevich, 1984).

PTERULACEAE

Deflexula ulmi (Peck) Corner

On the wood of *Ulmus* in forest stand, Khorol, 15 Sept. 1951, A. Shiriaev, VLA M-19360.

Pterula subulata Fr.

[= *Pterula multifida* (Chevall.) Fr.]

On the ground in forest, Ussuriysk, 20 Aug. 2002, V.Yu. Barkalov, VLA M-18695; Big Khekhtsir Nature Reserve, 25 Aug. 1983, E.M. Bulakh, VLA M-12707. - On the forest litter, Upper Ussuri Station, 20 Aug. 1975, E.M. Bulakh, VLA M-12703; Big Khekhtsir Nature Reserve, 16 Aug. 2004, Tolgor Bau, HMJAU 2898; Hulin, 9 Aug. 2004, Tolgor Bau, HMJAU 2677; Birobidzhan: Bastak Nature Reserve, 6 Aug. 2001, E.M. Bulakh, VLA M-15696.

SCUTIGERACEAE

Albatrellus ovinus (Schaeff.) Kotl. et Pouzar

On the wood, Ussuriysk Nature Reserve, 6 Sept. 1975, VLA M-15839. - On the ground, Ussuriysk: Gornotayozhnoye, 4 Aug. 2002, O.K. Govorova, VLA M-17562; Upper Ussuri Station, 8 Sept. 1974, E.M. Bulakh, VLA M-15838. - On the ground under the tree of *Pinus koraiensis*, Big Khekhtsir Nature Reserve, 14 Sept. 1981, E.M. Bulakh, VLA M-15340.

Scutiger oregonensis Murrill

[= *Albatrellus pes-caprae* (Fr.) Pouzar]

On the ground under the tree of *Pinus densiflora*, Nikolaevka, 21 Aug. 2002, L.N. Vassiljeva, VLA M-17594.

SPARASSIDACEAE

Sparassis crispa (Wulfen) Fr.   Plate 15: 86

On the bases of trunks of *Pinus koraiensis*, Ussuriysk Nature Reserve, 13 Aug. 1998, O.K. Govorova, VLA M-13020; Upper Ussuri Station, 19 Aug. 1974, E.M. Bulakh, VLA M-13025; Big Khekhtsir Nature Reserve, 16 Aug. 2004, Tolgor Bau, HMJAU 2955; Birobidzhan: Bastak Nature Reserve, 16 Aug. 2000, E.M. Bulakh, VLA M-15020.

TYPHULACEAE

Typhula phacorrhiza (Reichard) Fr.

On the ground under the coniferous and deciduous trees, Upper Ussuri Station, 14 Sept.

1974, E.M. Bulakh, VLA M-12487.

Typhula uncialis (Grev.) Berthier

On the culm of a grass, Ussuriysk Nature Reserve (Vasilyeva & Bezdeleva, 2006). - On dead stems of *Angelica,* Upper Ussuri Station, 14 Aug. 1974, E.M. Bulakh, VLA M-12515.

Typhula variabilis Riess

On the ground in coniferous-broad-leaved forest, Upper Ussuri Station (Azbukina & Kharkevich, 1984).

CORTINARIALES

CORTINARIACEAE

Cortinarius alboviolaceus (Pers.) Fr.

On the ground in korean pine-broad-leaved forest, Upper Ussuri Station, 13 Sept. 1975, E.M. Bulakh, VLA M-6772; in deciduous forest, Big Khekhtsir Nature Reserve, 12 Sept. 1946, L.N. Vassiljeva, VLA M-6773; Hulin, 9 Aug. 2004, Tolgor Bau, HMJAU 3341; in birch-poplar forest, Birobidzhan: Bastak Nature Reserve, 16 Aug. 2002, E.M. Bulakh, VLA M-17493.

Cortinarius alnetorum (Velen.) M.M. Moser

On the ground in korean pine-broad-leaved forest, Ussuriysk Nature Reserve, 17 Sept. 1963, M.M. Nazarova, VLA M-6793.

Cortinarius alneus M.M. Moser ex M.M. Moser

Under the tree of *Alnus* in alder forest, Upper Ussuri Station, 5 Sept. 1975, E.M. Bulakh, VLA M-6768.

Cortinarius anomalus (Fr.) Fr.

(= *Cortinarius azureus* Fr.)

On the ground in deciduous forest, Osinovka, 11 Sept. 1951, L.N. Vassiljeva, VLA M-6756; Birobidzhan: Bastak Nature Reserve, 21 Aug. 2003, E.M. Bulakh, VLA M-19162; in dark coniferous forest, Big Khekhtsir Nature Reserve, 20 Aug. 1983, E.M. Bulakh, VLA M-6755.

Cortinarius armeniacus (Schaeff.) Fr.

On the ground in coniferous forest, Arseniev (Nezdoyminogo, 1990).

Cortinarius armillatus (Alb. et Schwein.) Fr.

On the ground in deciduous forest, Ussuriysk, 3 Aug. 2003, Tolgor Bau, HMJAU 2978; Arseniev (Nezdoyminogo, 1990); Raohe, 8 Aug. 2004, Tolgor Bau, HMJAU 2673; Hutou, 8 Sept. 2003, Tolgor Bau, HMJAU 3257; Fuyuan, 7 Aug. 2004, Tolgor Bau, HMJAU 3319. - Under the tree of *Betula*, Birobidzhan: Bastak Nature Reserve, 16 Aug. 2002, E.M. Bulakh, VLA M-17490.

Cortinarius aureoturbinatus (Secr.) J.E. Lange

On the ground in korean pine-fir forest, Upper Ussuri Station, 9 Sept. 1973, E.M. Bulakh, VLA M-6759.

Cortinarius balaustinus Fr.

On the ground in dark coniferous forest, Upper Ussuri Station, 20 Aug. 1975, E.M. Bulakh, VLA M-6830.

Cortinarius betuletorum M.M. Moser ex M.M. Moser

[= *Cortinarius raphanoides* (Pers.) Fr.]

On the ground in coniferous-broad-leaved forest, Ussuriysk Nature Reserve, 19 Sept. 1961, L.N. Vassiljeva, VLA M-7145.

Cortinarius betulinus J. Favre

Under the trees of *Betula* in dark coniferous forest, Upper Ussuri Station, 16 Sept. 1975 E.M. Bulakh, VLA M-6828; Big Khekhtsir Nature Reserve, 5 Sept. 1981, E.M. Bulakh, VLA M-6826; Birobidzhan: Bastak Nature Reserve, 15 Aug. 2000, E.M. Bulakh, VLA M-16878.

Cortinarius boudieri Rob. Henry var. *pseudoarcuatum* Rob. Henry

On the ground in coniferous-broad-leaved forest, Upper Ussuri Station, 9 Sept. 1973, E.M. Bulakh, VLA M-6819.

Cortinarius brunneofulvus Fr.

On the ground in korean pine-broad-leaved forest, Upper Ussuri Station, 12 Sept. 1975, E.M. Bulakh, VLA M-6817.

Cortinarius brunneus (Pers.) Fr. var. *brunneus*

On the ground in korean pine-broad-leaved forest, Ussuriysk Nature Reserve, 26 Sept. 1946, L.N. Vassiljeva, VLA M-6806; Ussuriysk: Gorntayozhnoye, 29 Jul. 1957, L.N. Vassiljeva, VLA M-6811; Nikolaevka, 21 Sept. 1951, L.N. Vassiljeva, VLA M-6807.

Cortinarius brunneus var. *glandicolor* (Fr.) Lindstr. et Mérat

On the ground in broad-leaved forest, Ussuriysk Nature Reserve, 9 Sept. 1961, L.N. Vassiljeva, VLA M-7015. - Under the bush of *Corylus* in broad-leaved forest, Osinovka, 11 Sept. 1951, L.N. Vassiljeva, VLA M-7014.

Cortinarius bulliardii (Pers.) Fr.

On the ground in korean pine-broad-leaved forest, Ussuriysk Nature Reserve, 26 Aug. 1961, L.N. Vassiljeva, VLA M-6803; Osinovka, 11 Sept. 1951, L.N. Vassiljeva, VLA M-6802.

Cortinarius caerulescens (Schaeff.) Fr.

On the ground in oak forest, Nikolaevka, 21 Sept. 1954, L.N. Vassiljeva, VLA M-6888.

Cortinarius candelaris Fr.

On the ground in korean pine-broad-leaved forest, Ussuriysk Nature Reserve, 24 Sept. 1963, M.M. Nazarova, VLA M-6836; in dark coniferous forest, Upper Ussuri Station, 13 Sept. 1975, E.M. Bulakh, VLA M-6838.

Cortinarius caninus (Fr.) Fr.

Under the trees of *Betula* in dark coniferous forest, Upper Ussuri Station, 7 Sept. 1975, E.M. Bulakh, VLA M-6841; Big Khekhtsir Nature Reserve, 14 Aug. 1981, E.M. Bulakh, VLA M-6843; Birobidzhan: Bastak Nature Reserve, 8 Sept. 2001, E.M. Bulakh, VLA M-16798.

Cortinarius castaneus (Bull.) Fr.

On the ground in coniferous-broad-leaved forest, Ussuriysk Nature Reserve, 3 Sept. 1963, M.M. Nazarova, VLA M-6848.

Cortinarius cereifolius (M.M. Moser) M.M. Moser

On the ground in korean pine-broad-leaved forest, Ussuriysk Nature Reserve, 26 Sept. 1946, L.N. Vassiljeva, VLA M-6853.

Cortinarius cinnabarinus Fr.

Under the tree of *Betula*, Birobidzhan: Bastak Nature Reserve, 21 Aug. 2004, E.M. Bulakh, VLA M-20883.

Cortinarius cinnamomeus (L.) Fr.

On the ground in korean pine-broad-leaved forest, Ussuriysk Nature Reserve, 29 Aug. 1963, M.M. Nazarova, VLA M-6868. - Under the trees of *Abies* in dark coniferous forest, Big Khekhtsir Nature Reserve, 14 Aug. 1981, E.M. Bulakh, VLA M-6871; Birobidzhan: Bastak Nature Reserve, 17 Aug. 2000, E.M. Bulakh, VLA M-16879; in broad-leaved forest, Hulin, 9 Aug. 2004, Tolgor Bau, HMJAU 3345.

Cortinarius collinitus (Pers.) Fr.

On the ground in oak forest, Ussuriysk: Gornotayozhnoye, 6 Aug. 2003, E.M. Bulakh, VLA M-19088; in korean pine-broad-leaved forest, Upper Ussuri Station, 8 Sept. 1974, E.M. Bulakh, VLA M-6896.

Cortinarius colus Fr.

On the ground in korean pine-broad-leaved forest, Ussuriysk Nature Reserve, 12 Sept. 1963, M.M. Nazarova, VLA M-6919.

Cortinarius cotoneus Fr.

In oak forest, Birobidzhan: Bastak Nature Reserve, 8 Sept. 2001, E.M. Bulakh, VLA M-19109.

Cortinarius crassifolius (Velen.) Kühner et Romagn ex Bon

On the ground in oak forest, Mikhailovka, 23 Aug. 1955, L.N. Vassiljeva, VLA M-6926; in dark coniferous forest, Upper Ussuri Station, 17 Sept. 1974, E.M. Bulakh, VLA M-6925.

Cortinarius croceus (Schaeff.) Hølland

On the ground in coniferous forest (Nezdoyminogo, 1990).

Cortinarius crystallinus Fr.

On the ground in oak forest, Mikhailovka, L.N. Vassiljeva, VLA M- 6926.

Cortinarius cyanites Fr.

On the ground in deciduous forest, Osinovka, 14 Sept. 1954, L.N. Vassiljeva, VLA

M-6929.

Cortinarius decipiens (Pers.) Fr.

Under the trees of *Salix* in the thicket, Khanka Nature Reserve, 28 Aug. 2002, E.M. Bulakh, VLA M-19117; Bikin, 20 Sept. 1945, L.N. Vassiljeva, VLA M-6942.

Cortinarius delibutus Fr.

On the ground in dark coniferous forest, Ussuriysk Nature Reserve, 26 Sept. 1946, L.N. Vassiljeva, VLA M-6951; Upper Ussuri Station, 10 Sept. 1974, E.M. Bulakh, VLA M-6950; Big Khekhtsir Nature Reserve, 18 Sept. 1946, L.N. Vassiljeva, VLA M-6945.

Cortinarius dilutus (Pers.) Fr.

On the ground in korean pine-broad-leaved forest, Ussuriysk Nature Reserve, 24 Sept. 1946, L.N. Vassiljeva, VLA M-6954; Upper Ussuri Station, 8 Sept. 1974, E.M. Bulakh, VLA M-6957.

Cortinarius distans Peck

On the ground in korean pine-broad-leaved forest, Ussuriysk Nature Reserve (Vasilyeva & Bezdeleva, 2006).

Cortinarius elegantior (Fr.) Fr.

On the ground in korean pine-broad-leaved forest, Ussuriysk Nature Reserve, 28 Sept. 1946, L.N. Vassiljeva, VLA M-6973.

Cortinarius erythrinus (Fr.) Fr.

On the ground in broad-leaved forest, Khanka Nature Reserve (Nezdoyminogo, 1990).

Cortinarius fasciatus Fr.

On the ground in korean pine-broad-leaved forest, Ussuriysk Nature Reserve, 1 Sept. 1962, M.M. Nazarova, VLA M-6985.

Cortinarius flexipes (Pers.) Fr.

On the ground in korean pine-broad-leaved forest, Ussuriysk Nature Reserve, 10 Sept. 1961, L.N. Vassiljeva, VLA M-7004; in broad-leaved forest, Birobidzhan: Bastak Nature Reserve, 23 Aug. 2003, E.M. Bulakh, VLA M-19128.

Cortinarius fulvoochraceus Rob. Henry

On the ground in coniferous-broad-leaved forest, Big Khekhtsir Nature Reserve, 12 Sept. 1946, L.N. Vassiljeva, VLA M-6939.

Cortinarius fuscoperonatus Kühner

On the ground, Osinovka, 11 Sept. 1951, L.N. Vassiljeva, VLA M-6996.

Cortinarius gentilis (Fr.) Fr.

On the ground in korean pine-broad-leaved forest, Ussuriysk Nature Reserve, 3 Sept. 1961, L.N. Vassiljeva, VLA M-7008. - Under the bush of *Corylus* in broad-leaved forest, Big Khekhtsir Nature Reserve, 11 Sept. 1946, L.N. Vassiljeva, VLA M-7010.

Cortinarius glaucopus (Schaeff.) Fr.

On the ground under the tree of *Betula*, Tikhorechnoye, 5 Aug. 2005, E.M. Bulakh, VLA

M-20201.

Cortinarius helvolus (Bull.) Fr.

Under the the bush of *Corylus* in broad-leaved forest, Big Khekhtsir Nature Reserve, 11 Sept. 1946, L.N. Vassiljeva, VLA M-7031.

Cortinarius hemitrichus (Pers.) Fr.

On the ground in korean pine forest, Ussuriysk Nature Reserve (Nezdoyminogo, 1990); Upper Ussuri Station, 18 Sept. 1974, E.M. Bulakh, VLA M-7041; in deciduous forest, 9 Aug. 2004, Tolgor Bau, HMJAU 3201; Birobidzhan: Bastak Nature Reserve, 12 Sept. 2001, E.M. Bulakh, VLA M-16823.

Cortinarius hinnuleus Fr.

On the ground in korean pine-broad-leaved forest, Ussuriysk Nature Reserve, 25 Aug. 1962, M.M. Nazarova, VLA M-7051.

Cortinarius incisus (Pers.) Fr.

Under the trees of *Betula* and *Picea* in korean pine forest, Upper Ussuri Station, 16 Sept. 1975, E.M. Bulakh, VLA M-7085.

Cortinarius infractus Berk.

On the ground in coniferous-broad-leaved forest, Ussuriysk Nature Reserve, 12 Sept. 1962, M.M. Nazarova, VLA M-7077.

Cortinarius jubarinus Fr.

Under the trees of *Quercus* and *Betula* in broad-leaved forest, Big Khekhtsir Nature Reserve, 5 Sept. 1983, E.M. Bulakh, VLA M-7072.

Cortinarius laniger Fr.

On the ground in mixed forest, Ivanovka (Nezdoyminogo, 1990).

Cortinarius largus Fr.

Under the trees of *Betula* in oak forest, Ussuriysk: Gornotayozhnoye, 11 Sept. 1951, L.N. Vassiljeva, VlA M-7061; in birch forest, Osinovka, 11 Sept. 1951, L.N. Vassiljeva, VLA M-7062.

Cortinarius livido-ochraceus (Berk.) Berk.

(= *Cortinarius elatior* Fr.)

On the ground in deciduous forest, Osinovka, 14 Aug. 1954, L.N. Vassiljeva, VLA M-6969; in oak forest, Ussuriysk: Gornotayozhnoye, 19 Aug. 1963, M.M. Nazarova, VLA M-6970.

Cortinarius livor Fr.

On the ground under the tree of *Betula* in deciduous forest, Big Khekhtsir Nature Reserve, L.N. Vassiljeva, VLA M-7066.

Cortinarius malicorius Fr.

On the ground in coniferous-broad leaved forest, Ussuriysk Nature Reserve, 21 Aug. 1961, L.N. Vassiljeva, VLA M-7103; in oak forest, Ussuriysk: Gornotayzhnoye, 6 Aug. 2002,

E.M. Bulakh, VLA M-19078.

Cortinarius melleopallens (Fr.) J.E. Lange

On the ground in dark coniferous forest, Upper Ussuri Station, 16 Sept. 1975, E.M. Bulakh, VLA M-7109.

Cortinarius mucosus (Bull.) Cooke

On the ground in larch-oak forest, Birobidzhan: Bastak Nature Reserve, 21 Aug. 2004, E.M. Bulakh, VLA M-20887.

Cortinarius obtusus (Fr.) Fr.

On the ground in korean pine-broad-leaved forest, Ussuriysk Nature Reserve, 24 Sept. 1946, L.N. Vassiljeva, VLA M-7134.

Cortinarius orichalceus (Batsch) Fr.

On the ground in korean-broad-leaved forest, Ussuriysk Nature Reserve, 24 Sept. 1946, L.N. Vassiljeva, VLA M-7137; Upper Ussuri Station, 18 Sept. 1975, E.M. Bulakh, VLA M-7138.

Cortinarius pholideus (Fr.) Fr.

Under the tree of *Larix*, Birobidzhan: Bastak Nature Reserve, 12 Aug. 2001, E.M. Bulakh, VLA M-16829.

Cortinarius polymorphus Rob. Henry

(= *Cortinarius allutus* Fr.)

On the ground in dark coniferous forest, Upper Ussuri Station, 17 Sept. 1975, E.M. Bulakh, VLA M-6796.

Cortinarius porphyropus (Alb. et Schwein.) Fr.

On the ground under the tree of *Betula* in oak forest, Big Khekhtsir Nature Reserve (Nezdoyminogo, 1990).

Cortinarius praestans Cordier

In broad-leaved forest, Birobidzhan: Bastak Nature Reserve, 22 Aug. 2003, E.M. Bulakh, VLA M-19129.

Cortinarius praestigiosus (Fr.) M.M. Moser

On the ground in korean pine-broad-leaved forest, Upper Ussuri Station, 8 Sept. 1974, E.M. Bulakh, VLA M-7165.

Cortinarius prasinus (Schaeff.) Fr.

On the ground in korean pine-broad-leaved forest, Ussuriysk Nature Reserve, 28 Sept. 1946, L.N. Vassiljeva, VLA M-7164; Upper Ussuri Station, 10 Sept. 1975, E.M. Bulakh, VLA M-7162.

Cortinarius rapaceus Fr.

On the ground in korean pine-broad-leaved forest, Ussuriysk Nature Reserve, 24 Sept. 1946, L.N. Vassiljeva, VLA M-7177.

Cortinarius rigens (Pers.) Fr.

(= *Cortinarius duracinus* Fr.)

On the ground in korean pine-broad-leaved forest, Ussuriysk Nature Reserve, 24 Sept. 1946, L.N. Vassiljeva, VLA M-6959; in dark coniferous forest, Upper Ussuri Station, 9 Sept. 1973, E.M. Bulakh, VLA M-6958.

Cortinarius rubicundulus (Rea) Pearson

On the ground in broad-leaved forest, Tikhorechnoye, 4 Aug. 2005, E.M. Bulakh, VLA M-20285.

Cortinarius rubricosus (Fr.) Fr.

In korean pine-broad-leaved forest, Birobidzhan: Bastak Nature Reserve, 13 Aug. 2002, E.M. Bulakh, VLA M-17498.

Cortinarius salor Fr .

On the ground in korean pine-broad-leaved forest, Ussuriysk Nature Reserve, 21 Aug. 1961, L.N. Vassiljeva, VLA M-71997; Upper Ussuri Station, 9 Sept. 1974, E.M. Bulakh, VLA M-7219; in dark coniferous forest, Big Khekhtsir Nature Reserve, 7 Sept. 1983, E.M. Bulakh, VLA M-7217; in larch-birch forest, Birobidzhan: Bastak Nature Reserve, 13 Aug. 2002, E.M. Bulakh, VLA M-17533.

Cortinarius sanguineus (Wulfen) Fr.

On the ground in dark coniferous forest, Upper Ussuri Station, 9 Sept. 1973, E.M. Bulakh, VLA M-7205; Big Khekhtsir Nature Reserve, 7 Sept. 1983, E.M. Bulakh, VLA M-7208; Birobidzhan: Bastak Nature Reserve, 14 Aug. 2000, E.M. Bulakh, VLA M-15412.

Cortinarius saturninus (Fr.) Fr.

On the ground in broad-leaved forest, Big Khekhtsir Nature Reserve, 12 Sept. 1946, L.N. Vassiljeva, VLA M-7231 .

Cortinarius scutullatus (Fr.) Fr.

On the ground in korean pine forest, Upper Ussuri Station, 15 Sept. 1974, E.M. Bulakh, VLA M-7239.

Cortinarius semisanguineus (Fr.) Gillet

On the ground in korean pine-broad-leaved forest, Ussuriysk Nature Reserve, 9 Sept. 1946, L.N. Vassiljeva, VLA M-7244.

Cortinarius sphaerospermus Kauffm.

On the ground in korean pine-broad-leaved forest, Upper Ussuri Station, 21 Aug. 1975, E.M. Bulakh, VLA M-7258; Bikin, 12 Sept. 1945, L.N. Vassiljeva, VLA M-7261.

Cortinarius subferrugineus (Batsch) Fr.

On the ground in korean pine-broad-leaved forest, Ussuriysk Nature Reserve, 31 Aug. 1946, L.N. Vassiljeva, VLA M-7272; Upper Ussuri Station, 10 Sept. 1975, E.M. Bulakh, VLA M-7273.

Cortinarius sublatisporus Svrček

Under the tree of *Alnus,* Birobidzhan: Bastak Nature Reserve, 21 Aug. 2003, E.M. Bulakh, VLA M-19148.

Cortinarius trivialis J.E. Lange

On the ground in broad-leaved forest, Big Khekhtsir Nature Reserve, 3 Sept. 1983, E.M. Bulakh, VLA M-7289.

Cortinarius uliginosus Berk.

Under the tree of *Salix* in willow thicket, Khanka Nature Reserve, 28 Aug. 2002, E.M. Bulakh, VLA M-19084. - On the ground in korean pine forest, Upper Ussuri Station, 16 Sept. 1975, E.M. Bulakh, VLA M-7300. - Under the trees of *Alnus* and *Larix* in alder forest, Big Khekhtsir Nature Reserve, 31 Aug. 1983, E.M. Bulakh, VLA M-7301; Birobidzhan: Bastak Nature Reserve, 9 Sept. 2001, E.M. Bulakh, VLA M-16837.

Cortinarius umbrinolens P.D. Orton

[= *Cortinarius rigidus* (Scop.) Fr.]

In the birch-poplar forest, Birobidzhan: Bastak Nature Reserve, 8 Sept. 2001, E.M. Bulakh, VLA M-16821.

Cortinarius uraceus Fr.

On the ground in coniferous-broad-leaved forest, Ussuriysk Nature Reserve, 24 Sept. 1963, M.M. Nazarova, VLA M-7308.

Cortinarius urbicus (Fr.) Fr.

On the ground in willow thicket, Ussuriysk Nature Reserve (Nezdoyminogo, 1990).

Cortinarius venetus (Fr.) Fr.

On the ground in korean pine-broad-leaved forest, Ussuriysk Nature Reserve, 7 Sept. 1963, L.N. Vassiljeva, VLA M-7313; Birobidzhan: Bastak Nature Reserve, 13 Aug. 2002, E.M. Bulakh, VLA M-17492; in dark coniferous forest, Upper Ussuri Station, 9 Sept. 1973, E.M. Bulakh, VLA M-7310; Birobidzhan: Bastak Nature Reserve, 13 Aug. 2002, E.M. Bulakh, VLA M-17492.

Cortinarius violaceus (L.) Gray

On the ground in dark coniferous forest, Ussuriysk Nature Reserve, 26 Sept. 1946, L.N. Vassiljeva, VLA M-7321; in birch-aspen forest, Big Khekhtsir Nature Reserve, 29 Jun. 1981, E.M. Bulakh, VLA M-7406; Birobidzhan: Bastak Nature Reserve, 17 Aug. 2000, E.M. Bulakh, VLA M-20671.

Flammulaster erinaceella (Peck) Watling

On the rotten wood, Big Khekhtsir Nature Reserve, 15 Aug. 2004, Tolgor Bau, 2921.

Flammulaster ferruginea (Maire ex Kühner) Watling

On the log in broad-leaved forest, Ussuriysk: Gornotayozhnoye, 6 Aug. 2003, E.M. Bulakh, VLA M-19149.

Flammulaster limulatus (Weinm.) Watling

On the logs of deciduous trees in korean pine-broad-leaved forest, Ussuriysk Nature Reserve, 19 Jun. 2002, E.M. Bulakh, VLA M-17738; Upper Ussuri Station, 3 Sept. 1975, E.M. Bulakh , VLA M-597.

Flammulaster muricata (Fr.) Watling

On the wood in coniferous forest, Birobidzhan: Bastak Nature Reserve, 18 Aug. 2000, E.M. Bulakh, VLA M-15381.

Flammulaster siparia (Fr.) Watling

On the logs in korean pine-broad-leaved forest, Ussuriysk Nature Reserve, 18 Aug. 1975, M.M. Nazarova, VLA M-5957; in broad-leaved forest, Khanka Nature Reserve, 21 Jun. 2003, E.M. Bulakh, VLA M-19210; Upper Ussuri Station, 6 Sept. 1975, E.M. Bulakh., VLA M-5952; Big Khekhtsir Nature Reserve, 25 Jun. 1981, E.M. Bulakh, VLA M-5960.

Flammulaster wieslandrii (Fr.) M.M. Moser

On the log of *Betula* in coniferous-broad-leaved forest, Ussuriysk Nature Reserve, 25 Aug. 1970, M.M. Nazarova, VLA M-5966. - On the wood in coniferous-broad-leaved forest, Upper Ussuri Station, 11 Aug. 1990, E.M. Bulakh, VLA M-5973; in broad-leaved forest, Big Khekhtsir Nature Reserve, 31 Aug. 1983 E.M. Bulakh, VLA M-5974.

Galerina atkinsoniana A.H. Sm.

On the ground in dark coniferous forest, Big Khekhtsir Nature Reserve, 5 Aug. 1981, E.M. Bulakh, VLA M-7322; in broad-leaved forest, Birobidzhan: Bastak Nature Reserve, 20 Aug. 2003, E.M. Bulakh, VLA M-19113.

Galerina badipes (Fr.) Kühner

[= *Galerina cedretorum* (Maire) Singer]

On the wood in korean pine-broad-leaved forest, Ussuriysk Nature Reserve, 21 Sept. 1962, M.M. Nazarova, VLA M-7378.

Galerina camerina (Fr.) Kühner

On the fallen twigs in korean pine-broad-leaved forest, Ussuriysk Nature Reserve, 10 Sept. 1962, M.M. Nazarova, VLA M-7384. - On the wood of coniferous trees in coniferous-broad-leaved forest, Big Khekhtsir Nature Reserve, 27 Aug. 1983, E.M. Bulakh, VLA M-7385; Birobidzhan: Bastak Nature Reserve, 13 Aug. 2000, E.M. Bulakh, VLA M-15374.

Galerina cerina A.H. Sm. et Singer

On the wood among mosses in dark coniferous forest, Upper Ussuri Station, 26 Aug. 1973, E.M. Bulakh, VLA M-7386; Big Khekhtsir Nature Reserve, 14 Aug. 1981, E.M. Bulakh, VLA M-7389.

Galerina clavata (Velen.) Kühner

On the moist ground in willow thicket, Khanka Nature Reserve, 18 Jun. 2003, E.M. Bulakh, VLA M-19144; in dark coniferous forest, Upper Ussuri Station, 12 Aug. 1974, E.M.

Bulakh, VLA M-7396; in broad-leaved forest, Big Khekhtsir Nature Reserve, 31 Aug. 1983, E.M. Bulakh, VLA M-7397.

Galerina evelata (Singer) A.H. Sm. et Singer

On the ground among mosses in broad-leaved forest, Upper Ussuri Station, 26 Aug. 1973, E.M. Bulakh, VLA M-7405; Big Khekhtsir Nature Reserve, 16 Sept. 2005, A.B. Melnikova, VLA M-20203.

Galerina helvoliceps (Berk. et M.A. Curtis) Singer

On the ground in deciduous forest, Hulin, 9 Aug. 2004, Tolgor Bau, HMJAU 3181, 3373.

Galerina hypnorum (Schrank) Kühner

On the wood among mosses in broad-leaved forest, Ussuriysk Nature Reserve, 14 Aug. 1961, L.N. Vassiljeva, VLA M-7415; in dark coniferous forest, Upper Ussuri Station, 10 Aug. 1973, E.M. Bulakh, VLA M-7417; Big Khekhtsir Nature Reserve, 14 Aug. 1981, E.M. Bulakh, VLA M-7413; Birobidzhan: Bastak Nature Reserve, 8 Sept. 2001, E.M. Bulakh, VLA M-16799.

Galerina marginata (Batsch) Kühner

On the logs in korean pine-broad-leaved forest, Ussuriysk Nature Reserve, 10 Aug. 1961, M.M. Nazarova, VLA M-7431; Upper Ussuri Station, 9 Sept. 1975, E.M. Bulakh, VLA M-7440; in dark coniferous forest, Big Khekhtsir Nature Reserve, 14 Sept. 1981, E.M. Bulakh, VLA M-7438.

Galerina salicicola P.D. Orton

On the ground in korean pine forest, Upper Ussuri Station, 19 Sept. 1974, E.M. Bulakh, VLA M-6049.

Galerina stylifera (G.F. Atk.) A.H. Sm. et Singer

On the decayed wood in korean pine-broad-leaved forest, Ussuriysk Nature Reserve, 12 Sept. 1961, M.M. Nazarova, VLA M-7467; in dark coniferous forest, Upper Ussuri Station, 29 Aug. 1973, E.M. Bulakh, VLA M-7464; Big Khekhtsir Nature Reserve, 15 Sept. 1981, E.M. Bulakh, VLA M-7469.

Galerina triscopa (Fr.) Kühner

On the logs in korean pine-broad-leaved forest, Ussuriysk Nature Reserve, 7 Aug. 2003, E.M. Bulakh, VLA M-19176; in dark coniferous forest Big Khekhtsir Nature Reserve, 7 Sept. 1983, E.M. Bulakh, VLA M-7481; Birobidzhan: Bastak Nature Reserve, 21 Aug. 2003, E.M. Bulakh, VLA M-19114. - On the wood of *Taxus* in dark coniferous forest, Upper Ussuri Station, 15 Sept. 1974, E.M. Bulakh, VLA M-7479.

Galerina vittiformis (Fr.) Earle

On the ground among mosses in fir-broad-leaved forest, Ussuriysk Nature Reserve, 4 Sept. 1963, M.M. Nazarova, VLA M-7485; Ussuriysk, 3 Aug. 2003, Tolgor Bau, HMJAU 3190. - On the wood among mosses in broad-leaved forest, Ussuriysk: Gornotayozhnoye, 4 Aug. 2002, E.M. Bulakh, VLA M-19115; Big Khekhtsir Nature Reserve, 27 Aug. 1983, E.M.

Bulakh, VLA M-7499; in korean pine forest, Upper Ussuri Station, 13 Jun. 1975, E.M. Bulakh, VLA M-7496; Birobidzhan: Bastak Nature Reserve, 9 Sept. 2001, E.M. Bulakh, VLA M-16844.

Gymnopilus aeruginosus (Peck) Singer

On the rotten wood, Ussuriysk, 3 Aug. 2003, Tolgor Bau, HMJAU 2940.

Gymnopilus bellulus (Peck) Murrill

On the logs of coniferous trees in korean pine-broad-leaved forest, Ussuriysk Nature Reserve, 16 Aug. 1963, M.M. Nazarova, VLA M-6645; in coniferous-broad-leaved forest, Upper Ussuri Station, 17 Sept. 1974, E.M. Bulakh, VLA M-6628; Jakovlevska, 23 Aug. 1955, L.N. Vassiljeva, VLA M-6642; in broad-leaved forest, Big Khekhtsir Nature Reserve, 9 Aug. 1981, E.M. Bulakh, VLA M-6636; Birobidzhan: Bastak Nature Reserve, 12 Aug. 2002, E.M. Bulakh, VLA M-17536.

Gymnopilus hybridus (Bull.) Maire

On the stump of a coniferous tree in korean pine-broad-leaved forest, Ussuriysk Nature Reserve, 28 Aug. 1965, M.M. Nazarova, VLA M-6663.

Gymnopilus junonius (Fr.) P.D. Orton

[= *Gymnopilus spectabilis* (Fr.) Singer]

On the logs in birch forest, Ussuriysk Nature Reserve, 4 Sept. 1975, M.M. Nazarova, VLA M-6728; Ussuriysk, 3 Aug. 2003, Tolgor Bau, HMJAU 3209; in broad-leaved forest, Big Khekhtsir Nature Reserve, 19 Aug. 1983, E.M. Bulakh, VLA M-6724; Birobidzhan: Bastak Nature Reserve, 9 Sept. 2001, E.M. Bulakh, VLA M-16800; Raohe, 7 Aug. 2004, Tolgor Bau, HMJAU 3344. - On the log of *Salix* in willow thicket, Khanka Nature Reserve, 28 Aug. 2002, E.M. Bulakh, VLA M-19110.

Gymnopilus liquiritiae (Pers.) P. Karst.

On the logs in korean pine-broad-leaved forest, Ussuriysk Nature Reserve, 16 Aug. 1961, L.N. Vassiljeva, VLA M-6665; Ussuriysk, 3 Aug. 2003, Tolgor Bau, HMJAU 2833; Birobidzhan: Bastak Nature Reserve, 18 Aug. 2004, Tolgor Bau, HMJAU 3266, 6 Sept. 2001, E.M. Bulakh, VLA M-16801.

Gymnopilus luteofolius (Peck) Singer

On the wood of *Betula* in coniferous-broad-leaved forest, forest, Upper Ussuri Station, 31 Jun. 1974, E.M. Bulakh, VLA M-6668.

Gymnopilus penetrans (Fr.) Murrill

On the trunk of a coniferous tree in korean pine-broad-leaved forest, Ussuriysk Nature Reserve, 6 Sept. 1975, M.M. Nazarova, VLA M-6671. - On the wood of *Betula* in coniferous-broad-leaved forest, Upper Ussuri Station, 17 Aug. 1974, E.M. Bulakh, VLA M-6684. - On the log of a deciduous tree, Birobidzhan: Bastak Nature Reserve, 7 Sept. 2001, E.M. Bulakh, VLA M-16802.

Gymnopilus picreus (Pers.) P. Karst.

On the logs of coniferous trees in korean pine-broad-leaved forest, Ussuriysk Nature Reserve, 5 Sept. 1962, M.M. Nazarova, VLA M-6708; Upper Ussuri Station, 6 Sept. 1974, E.M. Bulakh, VLA M-6696; in dark coniferous forest, Big Khekhtsir Nature Reserve, 19 Aug. 1983, E.M. Bulakh, VLA M-6706; Birobidzhan: Bastak Nature Reserve, 14 Aug. 2000, E.M. Bulakh, VLA M-15439.

Gymnopilus pulchrifolius (Peck) Murrill

On the wood of *Betula* in coniferous-broad-leaved forest, Upper Ussuri Station (Nezdoyminogo, 1990).

Gymnopilus sapineus (Fr.) Maire

On the log of *Quercus* in korean pine-broad-leaved forest, Ussuriysk Nature Reserve, 6 Aug. 1962, M.M. Nazarova, VLA M-6723. - On the wood in coniferous-broad leaves forest, Upper Ussuri Station, 10 Sept. 1975, E.M. Bulakh, VLA M-6718.

Hebeloma album Peck

On the ground under the trees of *Salix*, Khanka Nature Reserve, 9 Aug. 2003, E.M. Bulakh, VLA M-20199; Upper Ussuri Station, 10 Sept. 1975, E.M. Bulakh, VLA M-20654; Birobidzhan: Bastak Nature Reserve, 21 Aug. 2003, E.M. Bulakh, VLA M-19127.

Hebeloma birrus (Fr.) Gillet

(= *Hebeloma danicum* Gröger)

On the ground in broad-leaved forest, Birobidzhan: Bastak Nature Reserve, 18 Aug. 2003, E.M. Bulakh, VLA M-19171.

Hebeloma crustuliniforme (Bull.) Quél.

Under the trees of *Populus* and *Salix* in poplar forest, Ussuriysk Nature Reserve (Vasilyeva & Bezdeleva, 2006); Ussuriysk, 3 Aug. 2003, Tolgor Bau, HMJAU 3212; Upper Ussuri Station (Nezdoyminogo, 1990).

Hebeloma hiemale Bres.

On the ground in birch forest, Khanka Nature Reserve, 28 Aug. 2002, E.M. Bulakh, VLA M-19112; in poplar forest, Upper Ussuri Station (Nezdoyminogo, 1990); Birobidzhan: Bastak Nature Reserve, 21 Aug. 2003, E.M. Bulakh, VLA M-19234.

Hebeloma ingratum Bruchet

On the ground in poplar forest, Upper Ussuri Station (Nezdoyminogo, 1990).

Hebeloma longicaudum (Pers.) P. Kumm.

On the ground in dark coniferous forest, Upper Ussuri Station (Nezdoyminogo, 1990).

Hebeloma mesophaeum (Pers.) Quél.

On the ground in coniferous forest, Ussuriysk Nature Reserve (Nezdoyminogo, 1990).

Hebeloma pumilum J.E. Lange

On the ground in korean pine-broad-leaved forest, Ussuriysk Nature Reserve (Vasilyeva & Bezdeleva, 2006).

Hebeloma pusillum J.E. Lange

On the ground under the tree of *Salix* in willow forest, Upper Ussuri Station, Big Khekhtsir Nature Reserve (Nezdoyminogo, 1990).

Hebeloma sacchariolens Quél.

On the ground, Ussuriysk, 3 Aug. 2003, Tolgor Bau, HMJAU 3270.

Hebeloma sinapizans (Fr.) Sacc.

On the ground in korean pine-broad-leaved forest, Ussuriysk Nature Reserve (Vasilyeva & Bezdeleva, 2006); Osinovka, 14 Sept. 1954, L.N. Vassiljeva, VLA M-6575.

Hebeloma testaceum (Batsch) Quél.

Under the trees of *Populus* in poplar forest, Ussuriysk Nature Reserve (Nezdoyminogo, 1990); in oak forest, Mikhailovka; Upper Ussuri Station; Big Khekhtsir Nature Reserve (Nezdoyminogo, 1990); in birch forest, Birobidzhan: Bastak Nature Reserve, 6 Sept. 2001, E.M. Bulakh, VLA M-16851.

Hebeloma truncatum (Scaeff.) P. Kumm.

On the ground in deciduous forest, Khanka Nature Reserve, 26 Jul. 2002, V.Yu. Barkalov, VLA M-19104; Mikhailovka (Nezdoyminogo, 1990).

Hebeloma vaccinum Romagn.

On the ground in poplar-willow forest, Upper Ussuri Station (Nezdoyminogo, 1990).

Inocybe acuta Boud.

On the ground in korean pine-broad-leaved forest, Ussuriysk Nature Reserve (Vasilyeva & Bezdeleva, 2006); Birobidzhan: Bastak Nature Reserve, 12 Aug. 2001, E.M. Bulakh, VLA M-16846.

Inocybe adaequata (Britzelm.) Sacc.

On the ground in broad-leaved forest, Ussuriysk: Gornotayozhnoye, 4 Aug. 2002, E.M. Bulakh , VLA M-198116; in korean pine forest, Upper Ussuri Station, 18 Aug. 1974, E.M. Bulakh, VLA M-6438; Birobidzhan: Bastak Nature Reserve, 21 Aug. 2004, E.M. Bulakh, VLA M-20868.

Inocybe amethistina Kuyper

On the ground in korean pine-broad-leaved forest, Ussuriysk Nature Reserve (Vasilyeva & Bezdeleva, 2006); Ussuriysk, 3 Aug. 2003, Tolgor Bau, 2891.

Inocybe appendiculata Kühner

On the ground in korean pine-broad-leaved forest, Ussuriysk Nature Reserve, 9 Sept. 1961, L.N. Vassiljeva, VLA M-6173.

Inocybe assimilata Britzelm.

On the ground in coniferous forest, Upper Ussuri Station (Nezdoyminogo, 1990).

Inocybe asterospora Quél.

On the ground in korean pine-broad-leaved forest, Ussuriysk Nature Reserve, 29 Aug. 1963, L.N. Vassiljeva, VLA M-6180; Upper Ussuri Station, 7 Sept. 1975, E.M. Bulakh, VLA

M-6175; in broad-leaved forest, Ussuriysk: Gornotayozhnoye, 30 Aug. 1963, M.M. Nazarova, VLA M-6174; in oak forest, Big Khekhtsir Nature Reserve, 11 Aug. 1981, E.M. Bulakh, VLA M-6176; in coniferous forest, Birobidzhan: Bastak Nature Reserve, 14 Aug. 2000, E.M. Bulakh, VLA M-15437. - Under the tree of *Salix* in willow thicket, Khanka Nature Reserve, 18 Jun. 2003, E.M. Bulakh, VLA M-19168. - Under the tree of *Betula* in birch forest, Raohe, 7 Aug. 2004, E.M. Bulakh, VLA M-20403.

Inocybe auricoma (Batsch) J.E. Lange

On the ground in coniferous-broad-leaved forest, Ussuriysk Nature Reserve, 24 Aug. 1963, M.M. Nazarova, VLA M-6188.

Inocybe bongardii (Weinm.) Quél.

On the ground in korean pine-broad-leaved forest, Ussuriysk Nature Reserve, 3 Sept. 1961, M.M. Nazarova, VLA M-6201.

Inocybe brunnea Quél.

On the ground in coniferous-broad-leaved forest, Ussuriysk Nature Reserve (Nezdoyminogo, 1990).

Inocybe brunneotomentosa Huijsm.

On the ground in broad-leaved forest, Mikhailovka, 14 Aug. 1954, L.N. Vassiljeva,VLA M-6210.

Inocybe calamistrata (Fr.) Gillet

On the ground in fir-broad-leaved forest, Ussuriysk Nature Reserve, 18 Aug. 1963, M.M. Nazarova , VLA M-6211; in oak forest, Raohe: Shangli State Farm, 6 Aug. 2004, E.M. Bulakh, VLA M-20267.

Inocybe calospora Quél.

On the ground in fir-broad-leaved forest, Ussuriysk Nature Reserve, 28 Aug. 1965, M.M. Nazarova, VLA M-6223; in coniferous-broad-leaved forest, Upper Ussuri Station, 16 Sept. 1975, E.M. Bulakh, VLA M-6217; in broad-leaved forest, Big Khekhtsir Nature Reserve, 21 Aug. 1983, E.M. Bulakh, VLA M-6214; Birobidzhan: Bastak Nature Reserve, 18 Aug. 2003, E.M. Bulakh, VLA M-19133.

Inocybe cervicolor (Pers.) Quél.

On the ground in coniferous forest, Upper Ussuri Station (Nezdoyminogo, 1990).

Inocybe cincinnata (Fr.) Quel.

On the ground in forest, Ussuriysk, 3 Aug. 2003, Tolgor Bau, 2891.

Inocybe cookei Bres.

On the ground in oak forest, Ussuriysk Nature Reserve (Nezdoyminogo, 1990); Ussuriysk: Gornotayozhnoye, 9 Sept. 1963 , M.M. Nazarova, VLA M-6232; Big Khekhtsir Nature Reserve, 11 Aug. 1981, E.M. Bulakh, VLA M-6231.

Inocybe corydalina Quél.

On the ground in korean pine-broad-leaved forest, Ussuriysk Nature Reserve, 6 Sept.

1961, L.N. Vassiljeva, VLA M-6235; in oak forest, Ussuriysk: Gornotayozhnoye, 30 Aug. 1963, M.M. Nazarova, VLA M-6234.

Inocybe curvipes P. Karst.

[= *Inocybe lanuginella* (J. Schröt.) Konrad et Maubl.]

On the ground in coniferous-broad-leaved forest, Ussuriysk Nature Reserve (Nezdoyminogo, 1990); Khanka Nature Reserve, 9 Aug. 2003, Tolgor Bau, HMJAU 3207. - Under the tree of *Salix*, Raohe, 7 Aug. 2004, E.M. Bulakh, VLA M-19597.

Inocybe dulcamara (Alb. et Scwein.) P. Kumm.

On the ground in birch forest, Khorol, 18 Sept. 1954, L.N. Vassiljeva, VLA M-6255; Big Khekhtsir Nature Reserve, 12 Aug. 1981, E.M. Bulakh, VLA M-6257.

Inocybe flocculosa (Berk.) Sacc.

On the ground in korean pine-broad-leaved forest Ussuriysk Nature Reserve, 29 Aug. 1963, M.M. Nazarova, VLA M-6337; in coniferous-broad-leaved forest, Upper Ussuri Station, 16 Aug. 1974, E.M. Bulakh, VLA M-6322; Birobidzhan: Bastak Nature Reserve, 17 Aug. 2000, E.M. Bulakh, VLA M-15454; in birch forest, Big Khekhtsir Nature Reserve, 5 SEpt. 1983, E.M. Bulakh, VLA M-6329.

Inocybe fraudans (Britzelm.) Sacc.

[= *Inocybe pyriodora* (Fr.) P. Kumm.]

On the ground in korean pine-broad-leaved forest, Ussuriysk Nature Reserve, 25 Aug. 1962, M.M. Nazarova, VLA M-6532; Jakovlevka, 23 Aug. 1955, L.N.Vasssiljeva, VLA M-6531; in broad-leaved forest, Big Khekhtsir Nature Reserve, 2 Sept. 1983, E.M. Bulakh, VLA M-6529.

Inocybe fuscidula Velen.

On the ground in korean pine-broad-leaved forest, Ussuriysk Nature Reserve, 3 Sept. 1962, L.N. Vassiljeva, VLA M-6356; in aspen forest, Big Khekhtsir Nature Reserve, 12 Sept. 1946, L.N. Vassiljeva, VLA M-6355; Birobidzhan: Bastak Nature Reserve, 7 Sept. 2001, E.M. Bulakh, VLA M-16842.

Inocybe fuscomarginata Kühner

On the ground in korean pine forest, Upper Ussuri Station, 16 Aug. 1974, E.M. Bulakh, VLA M-6228.

Inocybe geophylla (Pers.) P. Kumm.

On the ground in coniferous-broad-leaved forest, Ussuriysk Nature Reserve, 14 Sept. 1961, M.M. Nazarova, VLA M-6377; Ussuriysk, 3 Aug. 2003, Tolgor Bau, HMJAU 2847; in deciduous forest, Khanka Nature Reserve, 28 Aug. 2002, E.M. Bulakh, VLA M-18322; in korean pine forest, Upper Ussuri Station, 18 Sept. 1974, E.M. Bulakh, VLA M-6386; in dark coniferous forest, Big Khekhtsir Nature Reserve, 15 Aug. 1981, E.M. Bulakh, VLA M-6383; Birobidzhan: Bastak Nature Reserve, 15 Aug. 2000, E.M. Bulakh, VLA M-15438; Hulin, 9 Aug. 2004, Tolgor Bau, HMJAU 3180, 3261; Raohe: Shengli State Farm, 6 Aug. 2004, Tolgor

Bau, HMJAU 2644.

Inocybe glabripes Ricken

On the ground in coniferous-broad-leaved forest, Birobidzhan: Bastak Nature Reserve, 7 Sept. 2001, E.M. Bulakh, VLA M-16840.

Inocybe godey Gillet

On the ground in korean pine-broad-leaved forest, Ussuriysk Nature Reserve, 6 Jul. 1962, M.M. Nazarova, VLA M-6408.

Inocybe grammata Quél. et Le Bret

On the ground in korean pine-broad-leaved forest, Ussuriysk Nature Reserve (Vasilyeva & Bezdeleva, 2006); in korean pine forest, Upper Ussuri Station, 21 Aug. 1974, E.M. Bulakh, VLA M-6415; in dark coniferous forest, Big Khekhtsir Nature Reserve, 20 Aug. 1983, E.M. Bulakh, VLA M-6413.

Inocybe griseolilacina J.E. Lange

On the ground in korean pine-broad-leaved forest, Ussuriysk Nature Reserve, 15 Jul. 1962, M.M. Nazarova, VLA M-6422; Birobidzhan: Bastak Nature Reserve, 9 Sept. 2001, E.M. Bulakh, VLA M-16854.

Inocybe hirtella Bres.

On the ground in broad-leaved forest, Ussuriysk, 3 Aug. 2003, Tolgor Bau, HMJAU 3178; Raohe, 7 Aug. 2004, Tolgor Bau, HMJAU 3228; Hulin, 9 Aug. 2004, Tolgor Bau, HMJAU 3274, 3349.

Inocybe lacera (Fr.) P. Kumm.

On the ground in korean pine-broad-leaved forest, Ussuriysk Nature Reserve (Vasilyeva & Bezdeleva, 2006); in willow thicket, Khanka Nature Reserve, 21 Jun. 2002, E.M. Bulakh, VLA M-19126; in coniferous-broad-leaved forest, Upper Ussuri Station, 18 Aug. 1973, E.M. Bulakh, VLA M-6440. - Under the trees of *Betula* in birch-larch forest, Big Khekhtsir Nature Reserve, 25 Aug. 1983, E.M. Bulakh, VLA M-6449; Birobidzhan: Bastak Nature Reserve, 18 Aug. 2004, Tolgor Bau, HMJAU 3417.

Inocybe langei R. Heim

Under the tree of *Salix* in willow thicket, Khanka Nature Reserve, 18 Jul. 2002, E.M. Bulakh, VLA M-19086.

Inocybe lanuginosa (Bull.) P. Kumm.

On the forest litter in fir-broad-leaved forest, Ussuriysk Nature Reserve, 28 Aug. 1965, M.M. Nazarova, VLA M-6472; Upper Ussuri Station and Big Khekhtsir Nature Reserve (Nezdoyminogo, 1990); Birobidzhan: Bastak Nature Reserve, 8 Sept. 2001, E.M. Bulakh, VLA M-16848.

Inocybe leptophylla G.F. Atk.

On the ground in broad-leaved forest, Birobidzhan: Bastak Nature Reserve, 8 Sept. 2001, E.M. Bulakh, VLA M-16853.

Inocybe maculata Boud.

On the ground in birch forest, Ussuriysk, 3 Aug. 2003, Tolgor Bau, HMJAU 3205; Birobidzhan: Bastak Nature Reserve, 13 Aug. 2002, E.M. Bulakh, VLA M-17501; Raohe, 7 Aug. 2004, E.M. Bulakh, VLA M-20213.

Inocybe margaritispora (Berk.) Sacc.

On the ground in korean pine-broad-leaved forest, Ussuriysk Nature Reserve (Vasilyeva & Bezdeleva, 2006); in fir forest, Yakovlevka (Nezdoyminogo, 1990).

Inocybe mixtilis (Britzelm.) Sacc.

On the ground in korean pines-broad-leaved forest, Ussuriysk Nature Reserve (Vasilyeva & Bezdeleva, 2006); Big Khekhtsir Nature Reserve (Nezdoyminogo, 1990).

Inocybe muricellata Bres.

Under the trees of *Pinus koraiensis* in korean pine-broad-leaved forest, Ussuriysk Nature Reserve, 10 Sept. 1955, M.M. Nazarova, VLA M-6488; Upper Ussuri Station, 15 Sept. 1974, E.M. Bulakh, VLA M-6493.

Inocybe nitidiuscula (Britzelm.) Lapl.

(= *Inocybe friesii* R. Heim)

On the forest litter in korean pine-broad-leaved forest, Ussuriysk Nature Reserve, 21 Aug. 1961, M.M. Nazarova, VLA M-6346; Birobidzhan: Bastak Nature Reserve, 14 Aug. 2000, E.M. Bulakh, VLA M-15435. - On the ground in broad-leaved forest, Big Khekhtsir Nature Reserve, 14 Sept. 1946, L.N. Vassiljeva, VLA M-6340.

Inocybe obscurobadia (J. Favre) Grund et D.E. Stuntz

On the ground in korean pine-broad-leaved forest, Ussuriysk Nature Reserve, 6 Sept. 1962, M.M. Nazarova, VLA M-6497; Birobidzhan: Bastak Nature Reserve, 7 Sept. 2001, E.M. Bulakh, VLA M-16835; in broad-leaved forest, Ussuriysk: Gornotayozhnoye, 4 Aug. 2002, E.M. Bulakh, VLA M-19277; in oak forest, Fuyuan, 5 Aug. 2004, E.M. Bulakh, VLA M-20192.

Inocybe ochroalba Bruyl.

On the ground in aspen forest, Big Khekhtsir Nature Reserve, 12 Sept. 1946, L.N. Vassiljeva, VLA M-6504.

Inocybe perlata (Cooke) Sacc.

On the ground in broad-leaved forests, Big Khekhtsir Nature Reserve (Nezdoyminogo, 1990).

Inocybe petiginosa (Fr.) Gillet

On the ground in oak forest, Ussuriysk: Gornotayozhnoye, 6 Aug. 2002, E.M. Bulakh, VLA M-19087; Big Khekhtsir Nature Reserve (Nezdoyminogo, 1990). - On the ground under the tree of *Betula* in birch forest, Raohe, 7 Aug. 2004, E.M. Bulakh, VLA M-20402.

Inocybe posterula (Britzelm.) Sacc.

On the ground in korean pine-broad-leaved forest, Ussuriysk Nature Reserve, 20 Sept.

1962, M.M. Nazarova, VLA M-6523.

Inocybe praetervisa Quél.

On the ground in coniferous-broad-leaved forest, Ussuriysk Nature Reserve (Vasilyeva & Bezdeleva, 2006); Upper Ussuri Station (Nezdoyminogo, 1990). - Under the tree of *Salix* in willow thicket, Khanka Nature Reserve, 20 Jun. 2004, V.Yu. Barkalov, VLA M-19330.

Inocybe rimosa (Bull.) P. Kumm

[= *Inocybe fastigiata* (Fr.) Quél.]

On the ground in korean pine-broad-leaved forest, Ussuriysk Nature Reserve, 6 Sept. 1961, M.M. Nazarova, VLA M-6512; in oak forest, Ussuriysk: Gornotayozhnoye, 9 Sept. 1963, M.M. Nazarova, VLA M-6288; Khorol, 4 Aug. 1985, E.M. Bulakh, VLA M-6313; Osinovka, 14 Aug. 1954, L.N. Vassiljeva, VLA M-6314; in birch forest, Khanka Nature Reserve, 26 Jul. 2002; Raohe, 7 Aug. 2004, E.M. Bulakh, VLA M-20196, 6 Aug. 2004, Tolgor Bau, HMJAU 3237; in coniferous-broad-leaved forest, Upper Ussuri Station, 21 Aug. 1974, E.M. Bulakh, VLA M-6274; in broad-leaved forest, Big Khekhtsir Nature Reserve, 25 Aug. 1983, E.M. Bulakh, VLA M-6516, 16 Aug. 2004, Tolgor Bau, HMJAU 3268; Birobidzhan: Bastak Nature Reserve, 7 Sept. 2001, E.M. Bulakh, VLA M-16834.

Inocybe sindonia (Fr.) P. Karst.

On the ground in coniferous forest, Yakovlevka: Yelovy pereval, 23 Aug. 1955, L.N. Vassiljeva, VLA M-6506; Birobidzhan: Bastak Nature Reserve, 21 Aug. 2004, E.M. Bulakh, VLA M-20720.

Inocybe splendens R. Heim

[= *Inocybe brunnea* Quél. ss. Konrad et Maubl.]

On the ground in korean pine-broad-leaved forest, Ussuriysk Nature Reserve, 10 Sept. 1955, L.N. Vassiljeva, VLA M-6207.

Inocybe subcarpta Kühner et Boursier

On the ground in korean pine-broad-leaved forest, Ussuriysk Nature Reserve, 4 Sept. 1963, M.M. Nazarova, VLA M-6191; in oak forest, Ussuriysk: Gornotayozhnoye, 30 Aug. 1963, M.M. Nazarova, VLA M-6192.

Inocybe tenebrosa Quél.

On the ground in broad-leaved forest, Big Khekhtsir Nature Reserve, 10 Sept. 1946, L.N. Vassiljeva, VLA M-6186; Raohe: Shengli State Farm, 6 Aug. 2004, E.M. Bulakh, VLA M-19609.

Inocybe umbratica Quél.

On the ground in coniferous forest, Big Khektsir Nature Reserve (Nezdoyminogo, 1990); Birobidzhan: Bastak Nature Reserve, 17 Aug. 2000, E.M. Bulakh, VLA M-15455.

Inocybe whitei (Berk. et Broome) Sacc.

Under the tree of *Betula*, Birobidzhan: Bastak Nature Reserve, 19 Aug. 2003, E.M. Bulakh, VLA M-19172.

Leucocortinarius bulbiger (Alb. et Schwein.) Singer

On the ground in korean pine-broad-leaved forest, Ussuriysk Nature Reserve, 31 Aug. 1962, M.M. Nazarova, VLA M-7337; Upper Ussuri Station, 19 Aug. 1974, E.M. Bulakh, VLA M-7341.

Naucoria alnetorum (Maire) Kühner et Romagn

Under the tree of *Alnus*, Birobidzhan: Bastak Nature Reserve, 17 Aug. 2000, E.M. Bulakh, VLA M-15440.

Naucoria bohemica Velen.

On the ground in dark coniferous forest, Upper Ussuri Station, 17 Sept. 1974, E.M. Bulakh, VLA M-6584.

Naucoria escharoides (Fr.) P. Kumm.

On the ground in coniferous-broad-leaved forest, Upper Ussuri Station, 9 Sept. 1973, E.M. Bulakh, VLA M-6595; Birobidzhan: Bastak Nature Reserve, 8 Sept. 2001, E.M. Bulakh, VLA M-16362.

Naucoria luteofibrillosa (Kühner) Kühner et Romagn.

On the ground in alder forest, Upper Ussuri Station, 5 Sept. 1999, E.M. Bulakh, VLA M-12257; Birobidzhan: Bastak Nature Reserve, 8 Sept. 2001, E.M. Bulakh, VLA M-16376.

Naucoria spadicea D.A. Reid

On the ground in coniferous forest, Upper Ussuri Station (Nezdoyminogo, 1990). - Under the tree of *Alnus*, Birobidzhan: Bastak Nature Reserve, 20 Aug. 2003, E.M. Bulakh, VLA M-19152.

Naucoria subconspersa Kühner et P.D. Orton

On the ground in coniferous-broad-leaved forest, Upper Ussuri Station, 18 Aug. 1974, E.M. Bulakh, VLA M-6612.

Phaeocollybia christinae (Fr.) R. Heim

On the ground in dark coniferous forest, Big Khekhtsir Nature Reserve, 14 Jul. 1981, E.M. Bulakh, VLA M-7365.

Phaeocollybia jennuae (P. Karst.) Romagn.

On the ground in dark coniferous forest, Upper Ussuri Station, 23 Aug. 1975, E.M. Bulakh, VLA M-7363; Big Khekhtsir Nature Reserve, 15 Aug. 1981, E.M. Bulakh, VLA M-7361.

Phaeocollybia lugubris (Fr.) R. Heim.

On the ground in dark coniferous forest, Big Khekhtsir Nature Reserve, 14 Sept. 1981, E.M. Bulakh, VLA M-7374.

Phaeolepiota aurea (Matt.) Maire   Plate 15: 87

On the ground in broad-leaved forest near the road, Ussuriysk Nature Reserve, 18 Oct. 1986, E.M. Bulakh, VLA M-4936; Big Khekhtsir Nature Reserve, 18 Sept. 1999, A.B. Melnikova, VLA M-13611; in poplar forest, Upper Ussuri Station, 18 Sept. 1975, E.M.

Bulakh, VLA M-4941.

Phaeomarasmius erinaceus (Pers.) Schaeff. ex Romagn.

On the wood in broad-leaved forest, Ussuriysk: Gornotayozhnoye, 5 Aug. 2003, E.M. Bulakh, VLA M-19163; Ussuriysk, 3 Aug. 2003, Tolgor Bau, HMJAU 3275, 3418; Tikhorechnoye, 21 Jul. 1998, E.M. Bulakh, VLA M-12099; Big Khekhtsir Nature Reserve, 15 Aug. 2004, Tolgor Bau, HMJAU 2921.

Rozites caperatus (Pers.) P. Karst.   Plate 15: 88

On the ground in oak forest, Ussuriysk: Gornotayozhnoye, 4 Aug. 2002, E.M. Bulakh, VLA M-19091; in dark coniferous forest, Upper Ussuri Station, 23 Aug. 1973, E.M. Bulakh, VLA M-7346; Big Khekhtsir Nature Reserve, 15 Sept. 1981, E.M. Bulakh, VLA M-7348; Birobidzhan: Bastak Nature Reserve, 18 Aug. 2000, E.M. Bulakh, VLA M-15302; in forest, Raohe, 7 Aug. 2004, Tolgor Bau, HMJAU 2532.

Simocybe centunculus (Fr.) P. Karst.

On the wood in korean pine-broad-leaved forest, Ussuriysk, 3 Aug. 2003, Tolgor Bau, HMJAU 3277; Ussuriysk Nature Reserve, 11 Aug. 1961, M.M. Nazarova, VLA M-6046; in broad-leaved forest, Khanka Nature Reserve, 21 Jun. 2004, E.M. Bulakh, VLA M-19184; Big Khekhtsir Nature Reserve, 26 Jun. 1981, M-6040, E.M. Bulakh; Raohe: Shengli State Farm, 6 Aug. 2004, E.M. Bulakh, VLA M-20406; Birobidzhan: Bastak Nature Reserve, 21 Aug. 2003, E.M. Bulakh, VLA M-19056. - On the log of *Betula* in coniferous-broad-leaved forest, Upper Ussuri Station, 27 Aug. 1973, E.M. Bulakh, VLA M-6030.

Simocybe haustellaris (Fr.) Watling

On the log in ash forest, Ussuriysk Nature Reserve, 2 Sept. 1962, M.M. Nazarova, VLA M-6100.

CREPIDOTACEAE

Crepidotus applanatus (Pers.) P. Kumm.

On the logs in korean pine-broad-leaved forest, Ussuriysk Nature Reserve, 20 Jun. 2005, E.M. Bulakh, VLA M-20422; in oak forest, Ussuriysk, 3 Aug. 2003, Tolgor Bau, HMJAU 3189; Ussuriysk: Gornotayozhnoye, 23 Aug. 2002, E.M. Bulakh., VLA M-19074; in poplar forest, Upper Ussuri Station, 26 Aug. 1973, E.M. Bulakh, VLA M-6111; in aspen forest, Big Khekhtsir Nature Reserve, 26 Jun. 1981, E.M. Bulakh, VLA M-6153; Birobidzhan: Bastak Nature Reserve, 21 Aug. 2003, E.M. Bulakh, VLA M-19021.

Crepidotus betulae Murrill

On the log in coniferous-broad leaved forest, Upper Ussuri Station, 3 Aug. 1974, E.M. Bulakh, VLA M-6074.

Crepidotus calolepis (Fr.) P. Karst.

On the wood of *Populus* in poplar forest, Ussuriysk Nature Reserve, 20 Aug. 2003, E.M.

Bulakh, VLA M-16951; in deciduous forest, Big Khekhtsir Nature Reserve, 21 Jun. 1981, E.M. Bulakh, VLA M-6051; Raohe: Shengli State Farm, 6 Aug. 2004, E.M. Bulakh, VLA M-20217. - On the dead twig of *Maackia amurensis* in deciduous forest, Fuyuan, 4 Aug. 2004, E.M. Bulakh, VLA M-20274.

Crepidotus cesatii (Rabenh.) Sacc. var. *cesatii*

On the wood of *Carpinus* in coniferous-broad-leaved forest, Ussuriysk Nature Reserve, 23 Jul. 1971, M.M. Nazarova, VLA M-18198. - On the wood in deciduous forest, Big Khekhtsir Nature Reserve, 30 Jun. 1981 E.M. Bulakh, VLA M-6132; Birobidzhan: Bastak Nature Reserve, 13 Aug. 2000, E.M. Bulakh, VLA M-15351.

Crepidotus cesatii var. *subsphaerosporus* (J.E. Lange) Senn-Irlet

On the wood in deciduous forest, Hulin, 9 Aug. 2004. Tolgor Bau, HMJAU 3175.

Crepidotus cinnabarinus Peck

On the wood in broad-leaved forest, 2 Aug. 2003, Tolgor Bau, HMJAU 2989; Birobidzhan: Bastar Nature Reserve, 19 Aug. 2004, Tolgor Bau, HMJAU 2758.

Crepidotus citrinus Petch

On the fallen twigs in broad-leaved forest, Ussuriysk Nature Reserve, 7 Aug. 2003, E.M. .Bulakh, VLA M-18209; Khanka Nature Reserve, 21 Jun. 2003, E.M. Bulakh, VLA M-18318.

Crepidotus croceitinctus Peck

On the wood of *Quercus* in broad-leaved forest, Novotroitskoye, 14 Jul. 2004, E.M. Bulakh, VLA M-19497. - On the wood of *Tilia* in coniferous-broad-leaved forest, Upper Ussuri Station, 5 Aug. 1974, E.M. Bulakh, VLA M-6082.

Crepidotus crocophyllus Berk.

On the wood of *Quercus* in korean pine-broad-leaved forest, Ussuriysk Nature Reserve, 4 Aug. 1968, M.M. Nazarova, VLA M-18203. - On the wood in oak forest, Ussuriysk: Gornotayozhnoye, 6 Aug. 2003, E.M. Bulakh, VLA M-18204; in broad-leaved forest, Upper Ussuri Station, 16 Sept. 1974, E.M. Bulakh, VLA M-6084; in coniferous-broad-leaved forest, Big Khekhtsir Nature Reserve, 22 Jun. 1983, M.M. Nazarova, VLA M-6131; Birobidzhan: Bastak Nature Reserve, 20 Aug. 2003, E.M. Bulakh, VLA M-19025 .

Crepidotus epibryus (Fr.) Quél.

On the dead stems of *Carex*, Ussuriysk Nature Reserve, 18 Jul. 1962, M.M. Nazarova, VLA M-434. - On the dead stems of a fern, Ussuriysk: Gornotayozhnoye, 5 Aug. 2003, E. M. Bulakh, VLA M-18202; Upper Ussuri Station, 19 Sept. 1974, E. M. Bulakh, VLA M-443; Big Khekhtsir Nature Reserve, 14 Sept. 1981, E.M. Bulakh, VLA M-6138.

Crepidotus kauffmanii Hesler et A.H. Sm.

On the wood of *Ulmus* in korean pine-broad-leaved forest, Ussuriysk Nature Reserve, 21 Aug. 1969, M.M. Nazarova, VLA M-6134.

Crepidotus latifolius Peck

On the wood in broad-leaved forest, Ussuriysk Nature Reserve, 17 Aug. 1961, L.N.

Vassiljeva, VLA M-6097; Tikhorechnoye, 13 Jul. 2004, E.M. Bulakh, VLA M-19489; Upper Ussuri Station, 8 Aug. 1973, E.M. Bulakh, VLA M-10609.

Crepidotus lundelii Pilát

On the wood in ash forest, Ussuriysk Nature Reserve, 19 Aug. 1961, L.N. Vassiljeva, VLA M-6147; in broad-leaved forest, Ussuriysk: Gornotayozhnoye, 23 Jul. 2003, E.M. Bulakh, VLA M-19058; Khanka Nature Reserve, 21 Jun. 2003, E.M. Bulakh, VLA M-19071; Big Khekhtsir Nature Reserve, 31 Aug. 1983, E.M. Bulakh, VLA M-6050; Birobidzhan: Bastak Nature Reserve, 21 Aug. 2004, E.M. Bulakh, VLA M-19592.

Crepidotus mollis (Schaeff.) Staude

On the wood in korean pine-broad-leaved forest, Ussuriysk Nature Reserve, 7 Aug. 2003, E.M. Bulakh, VLA M-17816; Ussuriysk, 3 Aug. 2003, Tolgor Bau, HMJAU 2904; in coniferous-broad-leaved forest, Upper Ussuri Station, 19 Jun. 1974, E.M. Bulakh, VLA M-6116; in birch forest, Fuyuan, 5 Aug. 2004, E.M. Bulakh, VLA M-19561; Raohe, 7 Aug. 2004, E.M. Bulakh, VLA M-20276; in broad-leaved forest, Big Khekhtsir Nature Reserve, 21 Jun. 1981, E.M. Bulakh, VLA M-6067; Birobidzhan: Bastak Nature Reserve, 18 Aug. 2003, E.M. Bulakh, VLA M-19039.

Crepidotus subverrucisporus Pilát

On the fallen twigs in broad-leaved forest, Ussuriysk Nature Reserve, 9 Aug. 1969, M.M. Nazarova, VLA M-18197; in willow thicket, Khanka Nature Reserve, 28 Aug. 2002, E.M. Bulakh, VLA M-18205. - On the fallen twigs of *Corylus* in broad-leaved forest, Tikhorechnoye, 13 Jul. 2004, E.M. Bulakh, VLA M-19494; in birch forest, Fuyuan, 5 Aug. 2004, E.M. Bulakh, VLA M-19561.

Crepidotus variabilis (Pers.) P. Kumm.

On the wood in broad-leaved forest, Big Khekhtsir Nature Reserve, 15 Aug. 2004, Tolgor Bau, HMJAU 3392.

Pleurotellus chioneus (Pers.) Kühner

On the fallen twigs of *Betula* in broad-leaved forest, Ussuriysk Nature Reserve, 18 Jul. 1962, M.M. Nazarova, VLA M-435; in coniferous-broad-leaved forest, Upper Ussuri Station, 19 Jun. 1974, E.M. Bulakh, VLA M-6116.

DACRYMYCETALES

DACRYMYCETACEAE

Calocera coralloides Kobayasi

On the logs of deciduous trees, Ussuriysk Nature Reserve, 19 Oct. 1990, O.K. Govorova , VLA M-10797; Big Khekhtsir Nature Reserve, 26 Jun. 1981, E.M. Bulakh, VLA M-10796. - On the twigs of *Crataegus*, Khanka Nature Reserve, 26 Jul. 2002, V.Yu. Barkalov, VLA

M-18542.

Calocera cornea (Batsch) Fr.

On fallen twigs of deciduous trees, Ussuriysk Nature Reserve, 30 Jul. 1992, O.K. Govorova, VLA M-10822; Ussuriysk, Tolgor Bau, HMJAU 3197; Ussuriysk: Gornotayozhnoye, 6 Aug. 2002, O.K. Govorova, VLA M-18543; Upper Ussuri Station, 11 Aug. 1990, E.M. Bulakh, VLA M-10820; Big Khekhtsir Nature Reserve (Azbukina & Kharkevich, 1986); Birobidzhan: Bastak Nature Reserve, 18 Aug. 2002, E.M. Bulakh, VLA M-18538.

Calocera furcata (Fr.) Sacc.

On the log of a coniferous tree, Ussuriysk Nature Reserve (Vasilyeva & Bezdeleva, 2006). - On the log of *Picea*, Upper Ussuri Station, 15 Aug.1974, E.M. Bulakh, VLA M-10847.

Calocera fusca Lloyd

On the wood of coniferous trees, Ussuriysk Nature Reserve, 14 Aug. 1998, O.K. Govorova, VLA M-10851; Birobidzhan: Bastak Nature Reserve, 16 Aug. 2000, E.M. Bulakh, VLA M-15206.

Calocera glossoides (Pers.) Fr.

On the fallen twigs of *Quercus*, Ussuriysk: Gornotayozhnoye, 6 Aug. 2002, O.K. Govorova, VLA M-18510.

Calocera sinensis McNabb

On the wood, Ussuriysk Nature Reserve, 7 Aug. 1975, M.M. Nazarova, VLA M-10878. - On the log of *Picea*, Upper Ussuri Station, 10 Aug.1974, E.M. Bulakh, VLA M-10877. - On the wood of a deciduous tree, Big Khekhtsir Nature Reserve, 9 Aug.1981, E.M. Bulakh VLA M-10872.

Calocera viscosa (Pers.) Fr.

On the pine-needles in forest litter, Ussuriysk Nature Reserve, 17 Sept. 1996, O.K. Govorova, VLA M-10909; Ussuriysk, Tolgor Bau, HMJAU 3295. - On the log of a coniferous tree, Upper Ussuri Station, 5 Aug. 1973, E.M. Bulakh, VLA M-10898. - On the forest litter, Big Khekhtsir Nature Reserve, 9 Aug. 1981, E.M. Bulakh, VLA M-10895; Birobidzhan: Bastak Nature Reserve, 13 Aug. 2000, E.M. Bulakh, VLA M-15022.

Dacrymyces capitatus Schwein.

On the wood of a coniferous tree in coniferous forest, Ussuriysk Nature Reserve, 13 Aug. 1998, O.K. Govorova, VLA M-11017.

Dacrymyces chrysocomus (Bull.) Tul.

On the log of a coniferous tree, Ussuriysk Nature Reserve (Vasilyeva & Bezdeleva, 2006).

Dacrymyces chrysospermus Berk. et M.A. Curtis

On the log of a coniferous tree, Ussuriysk Nature Reserve (Vasilyeva & Bezdeleva, 2006).

Dacrymyces enatus (Berk. et M.A. Curtis) Massee

On the wood of *Quercus*, Terekhovka, 27 Aug. 1998, O.K. Govorova, VLA M-11026.

Dacrymyces estonicus Raitv.

On the wood, Ussuriysk Nature Reserve, 30 Jul. 1992, O.K. Govorova, VLA M-11030.

Dacrymyces minor Peck

On the wood of a coniferous tree, Ussuriysk Nature Reserve, 13 Aug. 1998, O.K. Govorova, VLA M-11058.

Dacrymyces palmatus (Schwein.) Burt.

On the wood, Ussuriysk Nature Reserve, 19 Oct. 1990, O.K. Govorova, VLA M-11036; Ussuriysk, 3 Aug. 2003, Tolgor Bau, HMJAU 2869; Hulin, 9 Aug. 2004, Tolgor Bau, HMJAU 2689. - On the logs of coniferous trees, Upper Ussuri Station, 27 Jul. 1974, E.M. Bulakh, VLA M-11078; Birobidzhan: Bastak Nature Reserve, 17 Aug. 2000, E.M. Bulakh, VLA M-15016.

Dacrymyces roseotinctus Lloyd

On the logs of *Quercus*, Ussuriysk Nature Reserve, 19 Oct. 1990, O.K. Govorova, VLA M-11128; Ussuriysk: Gornotayozhnoye, 23 Jul. 2002, O.K. Govorova, VLA M-18659.

Dacrymyces stillatus Nees

On the fallen twigs, Ussuriysk Nature Reserve, 30 Jul. 1992, O.K. Govorova, VLA M-11185. - On the fallen twigs of *Quercus*, Khanka Nature Reserve, 20 Jun. 2002, V.Yu. Barkalov, VLA M-18505. - On the log, Ussuriysk: Gornotayozhnoye, 23 Jul. 2002, O.K. Govorova, VLA M-18645.

Dacrymyces variisporus McNabb

On the fallen twigs of a coniferous tree, Upper Ussuri Station, 8 Aug. 1973, E.M. Bulakh, VLA M-11204.

Dacryopinax spathularia (Schwein.) G.W. Martin

On the logs, Ussuriysk Nature Reserve, 30 Jul. 1992, O.K. Govorova, VLA M-11009; Khanka Nature Reserve, 25 Jul. 2002, V.Yu. Barkalov, VLA M-18638. - On the logs of *Quercus*, Ussuriysk: Gornotayozhnoye, 23 Jul. 2002, O.K. Govorova, VLA M-18636. - On the wood of *Ulmus*, Upper Ussuri Station, 6 Aug. 1974, E.M. Bulakh, VLA M-10998.

Ditiola abieticola D.A. Reid

On the wood of a coniferous tree, Upper Ussuri Station, 10 Aug. 1974, E.M. Bulakh, VLA M-15693.

Ditiola peziziformis (Lév.) D.A. Reid

On the fallen twigs, Ussuriysk Nature Reserve, 10 Sept. 1997, O.K. Govorova, VLA M-10991; Birobidzhan: Bastak Nature Reserve, 23 Aug. 2003, E.M. Bulakh, VLA M-18662. - On the fallen twigs of a coniferous tree, Ussuriysk: Gornotayozhnoye, 18 Aug. 2001, O.K. Govorova, VLA M-18592.

Ditiola radicata (Alb. et Schwein.) Fr.

On the fallen twigs, Ussuriysk Nature Reserve, 18 Aug. 2001, O.K. Govorova, VLA,

VLA M-18592.

Guepiniopsis buccina (Pers.) L.L. Kenn.

On the log of foliage tree, Ussuriysk Nature Reserve (Vasilyeva & Bezdeleva, 2006).

GANODERMATALES

GANODERMATACEAE

Ganoderma applanatum (Pers.) Pat.   Plate 15: 89

[= *Ganoderma lipsiense* (Batsch) G.F. Atk.]

On the logs of deciduous trees, Ussuriysk Nature Reserve, 28 Aug. 2004, E.M. Bulakh, VLA M-19703; Ussuriysk, 3 Aug. 2003, Tolgor Bau, HMJAU 2979; Upper Ussuri Station, 3 Sept. 1975, E. Parmasto, VLA M-14605; Big Khakhtsir Nature Reserve, 16 Aug. 2004, Tolgor Bau, HMJAU 2762, 2768; Fuyuan, 5 Aug. 2004, Tolgor Bau, HMJAU 2636.

Ganoderma lucidum (Curtis) P. Karst.   Plate 15: 90

On the stump of *Betula*, Ussuriysk Nature Reserve, 5 Sept. 1996, E.M. Bulakh, VLA M-14632. - On the stump of *Abies nephrolepis* in dark coniferous forest, Big Khekhtsir Nature Reserve (Azbukina & Kharkevich, 1986).

GOMPHALES

GOMPHACEAE

Gomphus clavatus (Pers.) Gray   Plate 16: 91

On the ground under deciduous trees, Upper Ussuri Station, 2 Aug. 1974, E.M. Bulakh, VLA M-12290; Birobidzhan: Bastak Nature Reserve, 17 Aug. 2000, E.M. Bulakh, VLA M-15207.

Gomphus floccosus (Schwein.) Singer

On the ground under the trees of *Abies*, Ussuriysk Nature Reserve, 14 Aug. 1998, O.K. Govorova, VLA M-12296; Upper Ussuri Station, 12 Aug. 1974, E.M. Bulakh, VLA M-13260; Big Khekhtsir Nature Reserve, 19 Aug. 1983, E.M. Bulakh, VLA M-12297; Birobidzhan: Bastak Nature Reserve, 22 Aug. 2003, E.M. Bulakh, VLA M-18740.

LENTARIACEAE

Lentaria byssiseda Corner

On the fallen twigs of *Abies*, Ussuriysk Nature Reserve (Vasilyeva & Bezdeleva, 2006).

Lentaria pinicola (Burt) R.H. Petersen

On the twigs of *Abies*, Birobidzhan: Bastak Nature Reserve, 17 Aug. 2000, E.M. Bulakh,

VLA M-12891.

Lentaria soluta (P.Karst.) Pilát

On the fallen twigs of a coniferous tree, Ussuriysk Nature Reserve, 14 Aug. 1998, O.K. Govorova, VLA M-12332. - On the fallen twigs of *Picea*, Upper Ussuri Station, 29 Aug. 1973, E.M. Bulakh, VLA M-12327. - On the fallen twigs of *Pinus koraiensis*, Birobidzhan: Bastak Nature Reserve, 17 Aug. 2000, E.M. Bulakh, VLA M-13779.

RAMARIACEAE

Kavinia himantia (Schwein.) J. Erikss.

On the fallen twigs, Ussuriysk Nature Reserve, 20 Aug. 1961, L.N. Vassiljeva, VLA M-12713. - On the trunk of *Acer*, Upper Ussuri Station, 10 Aug. 1974, E.M. Bulakh, VLA M-18222. - On the fallen twig of *Populus davidiana*, Big Khekhtsir Nature Reserve (Azbukina & Kharkevich, 1986).

Ramaria abietina (Pers.) Quél.

[= *Ramaria ochraceovirens* (Junh.) Donk]

On the pine needles in forest litter in dark coniferous forest, Ussuriysk Nature Reserve (Vasilyeva & Bezdeleva, 2006); Big Khekhtsir Nature Reserve, 8 Aug. 1981, E.M. Bulakh, VLA M-13009, 18 Aug. 2004. - On the forest litter under coniferous trees, Upper Ussuri Station, 18 Aug. 1974, E.M. Bulakh, VLA M-13000; Birobidzhan: Bastak Nature Reserve, 18 Aug. 2000, E.M. Bulakh, VLA M-12821.

Ramaria americana (Corner) R.H. Petersen

On the ground in broad-leaved forest, Ussuriysk Nature Reserve, 21 Aug. 2001, O.K. Govorova, VLA M-15660428.

Ramaria apiculata (Fr.) Donk

On the wood in coniferous forest, Ussuriysk Nature Reserve, 14 Aug. 1998, O.K. Govorova, VLA M-12854; in korean pine forest, Upper Ussuri Station, 10 Aug. 1974, E.M. Bulakh, VLA M-12812; Big Khekhtsir Nature Reserve, 18 Aug. 2004, Tolgor Bau, HMJAU 3399; Birobidzhan: Bastak Nature Reserve, 18 Aug. 2004, Tolgor Bau, HMJAU 3393, 13 Aug. 2000, E.M. Bulakh, VLA M-15770.

Ramaria araiospora Marr et D.E. Stuntz

On the ground under the tree of *Quercus*, Ussuriysk: Gornotayozhnoye, 6 Aug. 2002, O.K. Govorova, VLA M-19391.

Ramaria aurea (Schaeff.) Quél.

On the ground in korean pine-broad-leaved forest, Upper Ussuri Station (Azbukina & Kharkevich, 1984).

Ramaria botrytis (Pers.) Ricken

On the ground under the trees of *Quercus*, Ussuriysk Nature Reserve (Vasilyeva &

Bezdeleva, 2006); Ussuriysk: Gornotayozhnoye, 4 Aug. 2002, E.M. Bulakh, VLA M-19402; Birobidzhan: Bastak Nature Reserve, 7 Sept. 2001, E.M. Bulakh, VLA M-15772.

Ramaria brunneicontusa R.H. Petersen

On the ground in coniferous-broad-leaved forest, Ussuriysk Nature Reserve, 4 Sept. 1975, M.M. Nazarova, VLA M-12931.

Ramaria cyaneigranosa Marr et D.E. Stuntz

On the ground in broad-leaved forest, Big Khekhtsir Nature Reserve, 2 Aug. 1983, E.M. Bulakh, VLA M-19401.

Ramaria cystidiophora (Kauffm.) Corner

On the ground under the tree of *Quercus*, Ussuriysk: Gornotayozhnoye, 6 Aug. 2002, O.K. Govorova, VLA M-19410.

Ramaria daucipes R.H. Petersen

On the ground under the tree of *Quercus,* Chuguevka, 27 Aug. 1996, E.M. Bulakh, VLA M-15099.

Ramaria decurrens (Pers.) R.H. Petersen

On the ground in broad-leaved forest, Birobidzhan: Bastak Nature Reserve, 19 Aug. 2000, E.M. Bulakh, VLA M-12831.

Ramaria distinctissima R.H. Petersen et M. Zang **var. *americana*** R.H. Petersen

On the ground in korean pine-broad-leaved forest, Upper Ussuri Station, 17 Aug. 1974, E.M. Bulakh, VLA M-13029; Birobidzhan: Bastak Nature Reserve, 22 Aug. 2003, E.M. Bulakh, VLA M-19397.

Ramaria ephemeroderma R.H. Petersen et M. Zang

On the ground in forest, Big Khekhtsir Nature Reserve, 17 Aug. 2004, Tolgor Bau, HMJAU 2953.

Ramaria eumorpha (P. Karst.) Corner

[= *Ramaria invalii* (Cotton et Wakeff.) Donk]

On the log, Ussuriysk Nature Reserve, 3 Sept. 1999, O.K. Govorova, VLA M-12757. - On the forest litter under coniferous trees, Upper Ussuri Station, 31 Jul. 1974, E.M. Bulakh, VLA M-12744; Big Khekhtsir Nature Reserve, 20 Aug. 1983, E.M. Bulakh, VLA M-12756.

Ramaria fennica (P. Karst.) Ricken

On the ground, Ussuriysk Nature Reserve, 15 Aug. 1968, M.M. Nazarova, VLA M-12908.

Ramaria flaccida (Fr.) Bourdot

On the wood, Ussuriysk Nature Reserve, 5 Sept. 1996, O.K. Govorova, VLA M-12718. - On the forest litter, Upper Ussuri Station, 15 Aug. 1974, E.M. Bulakh, VLA M-12723; Big Khekhtsir Nature Reserve, 3 Aug. 1981, E.M. Bulakh, VLA M-12730.

Ramaria flava (Schaeff.) Quél.

On the ground in forest, Big Khekhtsir Nature Reserve, 16 Aug. 2004, Tolgor Bau,

HMJAU 2774; Raohe: Shengli State Farm, 6 Aug. 2004, Tolgor Bau, HMJAU 3398.

Ramaria flavescens (Schaeff.) R.H. Petersen

On the ground, Ussuriysk Nature Reserve, 5 Sept. 2000, O.K. Govorova, VLA M-15225.

Ramaria flavicingula R.H. Petersen

On the ground under the trees of *Quercus*, Ussuriysk: Gornotayozhnoye, 13 Aug. 2002, O.K. Govorova, VLA M-19364; Nikolaevka, 21 Aug. 2002, O.K. Govorova, VLA M-19362.

Ramaria flavigelatinosa Marr et D.E. Stuntz

On the ground, Barabash-Levada: Shirokaya Canyon, 30 Aug. 2002, E.M. Bulakh, VLA M-19381; Birobidzhan: Bastak Nature Reserve, 9 Sept. 2001, E.M. Bulakh, VLA M-15788.

Ramaria flavobrunnescens (G.F. Atk.) Corner

On the ground in korean pine-broad-leaved forest, Upper Ussuri Station (Azbukina & Kharkevich, 1984); in oak forest, Big Khekhtsir Nature Reserve (Azbukina & Kharkevich, 1986).

Ramaria flavosaponaria R.H. Petersen

On the ground, Ussuriysk Nature Reserve, 5 Sept. 2000, O.K. Govorova, VLA M-15226.

Ramaria foetida R.H. Petersen

On the ground under deciduous trees, Chuguevka, 27 Aug. 1996, E.M. Bulakh, VLA M-15783.

Ramaria formosa (Pers.) Quél.

On the forest litter under the trees of *Quercus,* Ussuriysk Nature Reserve, 14 Aug. 1998, O.K. Govorova, VLA M-13026; Ussuriysk: Gornotayozhnoye, 6 Aug. 2002, O.K. Govorova, VLA M-19442; Nikolaevka, 21 Aug. 2002, O.K. Govorova, VLA M-19441; Barabash-Levada: Shirokaya Canyon, 30 Aug. 2002, E.M. Bulakh, VLA M-19444; Birobidzhan: Bastak Nature Reserve, 12 Aug. 2002, E.M. Bulakh, VLA M-19443.

Ramaria gelatinosa (Coker) Corner

On the ground under the tree of *Quercus*, Ussuriysk: Gornotayozhnoye, 6 Aug. 2002, O.K. Govorova, VLA M-19369.

Ramaria gracilis (Pers.) Quél.

On the wood, Upper Ussuri Station, 18 Aug. 1974, E.M. Bulakh, VLA M-12773; Birobidzhan: Bastak Nature Reserve, 7 Sept. 2002, E.M. Bulakh, VLA M-15776.

Ramaria holorubella (G.F. Atk.) Corner   Plate 16: 92

On the ground in korean pine-broad-leaved forest, Ussuriysk Nature Reserve (Vasilyeva & Bezdeleva, 2006).

Ramaria incognita R.H. Petersen

On the forest litter in korean pine-broad-leaved forest, Ussuriysk Nature Reserve, 14 Aug. 1998, M.M. Nazarova, VLA M-12727.

Ramaria lacteobrunnescens Schild.

On the ground under the tree of *Quercus*, Ussuriysk: Gornotayozhnoye, 6 Aug. 2002,

O.K. Govorova, VLA M-19367.

Ramaria largentii Marr et D.E. Stuntz

On the ground under the trees of *Pinus densiflora* and *Quercus*, Nikolaevka, 21 Aug. 2002, E.M. Bulakh, VLA M-12994; Birobidzhan: Bastak Nature Reserve, 17 Aug. 2000, E.M. Bulakh, VLA M-15230.

Ramaria mutabilis Schild et R.H. Petersen

On the ground in broad-leaved forest, Ussuriysk Nature Reserve, 13 Aug. 1998, M.M. Nazarova, VLA M-12716; Birobidzhan: Bastak Nature Reserve, 7 Sept. 2001, E.M. Bulakh, VLA M-15777.

Ramaria myceliosa (Peck) Corner

On the ground in broad-leaved forest, Birobidzhan: Bastak Nature Reserve, 20 Aug. 2003, E.M. Bulakh, VLA M-18713.

Ramaria pallida (Schaeff.) Ricken

On the ground in broad-leaved forest, Birobidzhan: Bastak Nature Reserve, 12 Aug. 2002, E.M. Bulakh, VLA M-19376.

Ramaria pulcherrima (Lj.N. Vassiljeva) Lj.N. Vassiljeva

On the fallen twigs, Ussuriysk Nature Reserve, 23 Aug. 1975, M.M. Nazarova, VLA M-13045.

Ramaria purpurissima R.H. Petersen et Scates

On the ground under the tree of *Quercus*, Ussuriysk: Gornotayozhnoye, 13 Aug. 2002, O.K. Govorova, VLA M-19389.

Ramaria rubella (Schaeff.) R.H. Petersen

On the coniferous wood, Ussuriysk Nature Reserve, 14 Aug. 1998, O.K. Govorova, VLA M-12762.

Ramaria rubriattenuipes R.H. Petersen et M. Zang

On the forest litter under the trees of *Pinus densiflora* and *Quercus*, Ussuriysk Nature Reserve, 4 Sept. 1975, M.M. Nazarova, VLA M-12931.

Ramaria rubrievanescens Marr et D.E. Stuntz

On the ground under the tree of *Pinus densiflora*, Nikolaevka, 20 Sept. 2000, E.M. Bulakh, VLA M-15101.

Ramaria sandaracina Marr et D.E. Stuntz

On the ground under the tree of *Pinus densiflora*, Nikolaevka, 20 Sept. 2000, E.M. Bulakh, VLA M-15224.

Ramaria strasseri (Bres.) Corner

On the forest litter under the tree of *Quercus*, Ussuriysk Nature Reserve, 23 Aug. 1975, M.M. Nazarova, VLA M-12968.

Ramaria stricta (Pers.) Quél.

On the wood, Ussuriysk Nature Reserve, 5 Sept. 1996, O.K. Govorova, VLA M-12884;

Ussuriysk, 3 Aug. 2003, Tolgor Bau, HMJAU 2824. - On the fallen twigs of *Picea*, Upper Ussuri Station, 20 Aug. 1975, E.M. Bulakh, VLA M-12888; Yakovlevka: Yelovy pereval, 23 Aug. 1955, L.N. Vassiljeva, VLA M-12837; Birobidzhan: Bastak Nature Reserve, 16 Aug. 2000, E.M. Bulakh, VLA M-15755.

Ramaria subdecurrens (Coker) Corner

On the forest litter in korean pine-broad-leaved forest, Birobidzhan: Bastak Nature Reserve, 11 Aug. 2006, E.M. Bulakh, VLA M-21342.

Ramaria suecica (Fr.) Donk

On the forest litter under coniferous trees, Ussuriysk Nature Reserve, 14 Aug. 1998, O.K. Govorova, VLA M-12787; Birobidzhan: Bastak Nature Reserve, 17 Aug. 2000, E.M. Bulakh, VLA M-12744.

Ramaria testaceo-flava (Bres.) Corner

On the ground, Ussuriysk: Gornotayozhnoye, 13 Aug. 2002, O.K. Govorova, VLA M-19380; Ussuriysk: Voshod, 29 Aug. 2002, V.Ju. Barkalow, VLA M-19379.

HERICIALES

AURISCALPIACEAE

Dentipellis fragilis (Pers.) Donk

On the wood, Ussuriysk: Voshod, 29 Aug. 2002, V.Yu. Barkalov, VLA M-17629. - On the trunk of *Quercus*, Ussuriysk: Gornotayozhnoye, 23 Jul. 2002, O.K. Govorova, VLA M-17601; Birobidzhan: Bastak Nature Reserve, 13Aug. 2002, E.M. Bulakh, VLA M-17628. - On the log of *Alnus hisuta* in alder forest, Big Khekhtsir Nature Reserve (Azbukina & Kharkevich, 1986). - On the log of *Picea* in coniferous-broad-leaved forest, Upper Ussuri Station (Azbukina & Kharkevich, 1984).

CLAVICORONACEAE

Clavicorona pyxidata (Pers.) Doty   Plate 16: 93

On the wood, Ussuriysk Nature Reserve, 5 Sept. 1996, E.M. Bulakh, VLA M-12360; Ussuriysk, 3 Aug. 2003, Tolgor Bau, HMJAU 2871, 2986; Ussuriysk: Gornotayozhnoye, 4 Sept. 2002, O.K. Govorova, VLA M-18699; Khanka Nature Reserve, 19 Jun. 2002, E.M. Bulakh, VLA M-18698; Big Khekhtsir Nature Reserve, 22 Jun. 1981, E.M. Bulakh, VLA M-12378; 15 Aug. 2004, Tolgor Bau, HMJAU 2969; Birobidzhan: Bastak Nature Reserve, 18 Aug. 2004, Tolgor Bau, HMJAU 2793; Fuyuan, 5 Aug. 2004, Tolgor Bau, HMJAU 2539. - On the wood of a coniferous tree, Upper Ussuri Station, 13 Jun. 1975, E.M. Bulakh, VLA M-12366.

Clavicorona taxophila (Thom) Doty

On the forest litter under coniferous trees, Upper Ussuri Station, 23 Aug. 1975, E.M. Bulakh, VLA M-12384.

GLOEOCYSTIDIELLACEAE

Gloeocystidiellum lactescens (Berk.) Boidin

(= *Gloeocystidiellum orientale* Parmasto)

On the logs of *Maakia amurensis,* Ussuriysk Nature Reserve (Parmasto, 1965).

Gloiodon strigosus (Sw.) P. Karst.

On the log of a deciduous tree, Ussuriysk Nature Reserve, 24 Sept. 1946, L.N. Vassiljeva, VLA M-16509.

Laxitextum bicolor (Pers.) Lentz

On the fallen twigs of a deciduous tree, Ussuriysk Nature Reserve (Vasilyeva & Bezdeleva, 2006).- On the log of *Betula*, Upper Ussuri Station (Azbukina & Kharkevich, 1984). - On the fallen twigs of *Alnus hirsuta*, *Quercus mongolica* and *Populus davidiana*, Big Khekhtsir Nature Reserve (Azbukina & Kharkevich, 1986).

HERICIACEAE

Hericium alpestre Pers.

[= *Hericium flagellatum* (Scop.) Pers.]

On the log of coniferous tree, Ussuriysk Nature Reserve, 31 Oct. 1961, L.N. Vassiljeva, VLA M-16644.

Hericium clathroides (Pall.) Pers.

On the log of a deciduous tree in broad-leaved forest, Big Khekhtsir Nature Reserve (Azbukina & Kharkevich, 1986).

Hericium coralloides (Scop.) Pers.   Plate 16: 94

[= *Hericium ramosum* (Bull.) Letell]

On the logs of deciduous trees, Ussuriysk Nature Reserve, 6 Sept. 1975, M.M. Nazarova , VlA M-15938; Ussuriysk, 3 Aug. 2003, Tolgor Bau, HMJAU 2992; Khanka Nature Reserve, 28 Jul. 2007, E.M. Bulakh, VLA M-21520; Big Khekhtsir Nature Reserve, 28 Aug. 1983, Upper Ussuri Station, 16 Sept. 1974, E.M. Bulakh, VLA M-15923; Big Khekhtsir Nature Reserve, 31 Aug. 1983, E.M. Bulakh, VLA M-15941, 17 Aug. 2004, Tolgor Bau, HMJAU 2974; Hulin, 9 Sept. 2004, Tolgor Bau, HMJAU 2660. - On the log of *Quercus*, Anuchinskyi: Ilmakovka, 12 Sept. 2005, E. Kudriavtseva, VLA M-20211; Birobidzhan: Bastak Nature Reserve, 23 Aug. 2003, E.M. Bulakh, VLA M-18590.

Hericium erinaceus (Bull.) Pers.

On the logs of *Quercus,* Ussuriysk Nature Reserve, 22 Sept. 1961, L.N. Vassiljeva, VLA M-15901; Upper Ussuri Station, 18 Sept. 1974, E.M. Bulakh, VLA M-15899; Big Khekhtsir Nature Reserve, 31 Aug. 1983, E.M. Bulakh, VLA M-15905; Raohe, 8 Sept. 2003, Tolgor Bau, HMJAU 3010; Birobidzhan: Bastak Nature Reserve, 17 Aug. 2000, E.M. Bulakh, VLA M-15906.

LENTINELLACEAE

Lentinellus brunnescens Lj.N. Vasiljeva   Plate 16: 95

On the logs of deciduous trees, Ussuriysk Nature Reserve, 6 Sept. 2003, E.M. Bulakh, VLA M-18353; Ussuriysk: Gornotayozhnoye, 4 Aug. 2002, E.M. Bulakh, VLA M-18337; Bastak Nature Reserve, 10 Aug. 2006, E.M. Bulakh, VLA M-20974. - On the log of a coniferous tree, Tikhorechnoye, 2 Jul. 1988, E.M. Bulakh, VLA M-19013.

Lentinellus cochleatus (Pers.) P. Karst.

On the logs, Ussuriysk Nature Reserve, 24 Aug. 1970, M.M. Nazarova, VLA M-390; Ussuriysk, 3 Aug. 2003, Tolgor Bau, HMJAU 2861. - On the logs of *Betula*, Upper Ussuri Station, 15 Sept. 1974, E.M. Bulakh, VLA M-389; Big Khekhtsir Nature Reserve, 28 Aug. 1983, E.M. Bulakh, VLA M-394; Bastak Nature Reserve, 13 Aug. 2002, E.M. Bulakh, VLA M-17248.

Lentinellus micheneri (Berk. et M.A. Curtis) Pegler

[= *Lentinellus omphalodes* (Fr.) P. Karst.]

On the log of *Betula*, Upper Ussuri Station, 14 Jun. 1975, E.M. Bulakh, VLA M-405.

Lentinellus ursinus (Fr.) Kühner

On the wood of deciduous trees, Ussuriysk Nature Reserve, 12 Sept. 1955, L.N. Vassiljeva, VLA M-420; Ussuriysk, 4 Aug. 2003, Tolgor Bau, 2884; Ussuriysk: Gornotayozhnoye, 23 Jul. 2002, E.M. Bulakh, VLA M-19026; Khanka Nature Reserve, 25 Jul. 2002, E.M. Bulakh, VLA M-19066; in coniferous-broad-leaved forest, Big Khekhtsir Nature Reserve, 25 Jun. 1981, E.M. Bulakh, VLA M-422, 15 Aug. 2004, Tolgor Bau, HMJAU 2994; Bastak Nature Reserve, 18 Aug. 2002, E.M. Bulakh, VLA M-17271; Longwangmiao: Mishan, 1 Sept. 2003, Tolgor Bau, 3032; Raohe, 7 Aug. 2004, Tolgor Bau, HMJAU 2508, 3182. - On the log of *Quercus,* Tikhorechnoye, 3 Jul. 1979, E.M. Bulakh, VLA M-417.

HYMENOCHAETALES

HYMENOCHAETACEAE

Coltricia cinnamomea (Jacq.) Murrill

On the ground, Ussuriysk Nature Reserve, 24 Aug. 1963, M.M. Nazarova, VLA

M-14675; Raohe: Shengli State Farm, 6 Aug. 2004, Tolgor Bau, HMJAU 2632.

Coltricia perennis (L.) Murrill

On the ground in korean pine-broad-leaved forest, Upper Ussuri Station (Azbukina & Kharkevich, 1984); Birobidzhan: Bastak Nature Reserve, 10 Aug. 2006, E.M. Bulakh, VLA M-20960.

Hymenochaete cinnamomea (Pers.) Bres.

On the fallen twigs of a deciduous tree, Ussuriysk Nature Reserve (Vasilyeva & Bezdeleva, 2006). - On the fallen twigs of *Philadelphus tenuifolius* and *Eleuterococcus senticosus*, Upper Ussuri Station (Azbukina & Kharkevich, 1984). - On the fallen twigs of *Corylus manshurica,* Big Khekhtsir Nature Reserve (Azbukina & Kharkevich, 1986).

Hymenochaete corrugata (Fr.) Lév.

On the fallen twig of *Alnus hirsuata*, Upper Ussuri Station (Azbukina & Kharkevich, 1984).

Hymenochaete fuliginosa (Pers.) Lév.

On the log of *Picea ajanensis*, Upper Ussuri Station (Azbukina & Kharkevich, 1984).

Hymenochaete intricata (Lloyd) S. Ito

On twigs of *Corylus* in broad-leaved forest, Birobidzhan: Bastak Nature Reserve, 11 Aug. 2006, E.M. Bulakh, VLA M-20965.

Hymenochaete mougeotii (Fr.) Cooke

On the fallen twigs of *Abies*, Ussuriysk Nature Reserve, 21 Sept. 1975, M.M. Nazarova,VLA M-14720; Upper Ussuri Station, 10 Sept. 1975, E.M. Bulakh, VLA M-14725; Big Khekhtsir Nature Reserve (Azbukina & Kharkevich, 1986).

Hymenochaete rheicolor (Mont.) Lév.

(= *Hymenochaete sallei* Berk.)

On the trunk of *Actinidia colomicta*, Upper Ussuri Station, 6 Sept. 1975, E.M. Bulakh, VLA M-14714.

Hymenochaete rubiginosa (Dicks.) Lév.

On the fallen twig of *Quercus*, Upper Ussuri Station (Azbukina & Kharkevich, 1984).

Hymenochaete tenuis Peck

On the fallen twigs, Ussuriysk Nature Reserve, 12 Sept. 1955, I.A Bunkina, VLA M-14716.

Inonotus andersonii (Ellis et Everh.) Černy

On the log of *Quercus*, Big Khekhtsir Nature Reserve (Azbukina & Kharkevich, 1986).

Inonotus cuticularis (Bull.) P. Karst.

[= *Onnia triquetra* (Pers.) Imazeki]

On the dead trunk of *Picea,* Upper Ussuri Station (Azbukina & Kharkevich, 1984).

Inonotus flavidus (Berk.) Ryvarden

(= *Inonotus sciurinus* Imazeki)

On the wood in deciduous forest, Raohe: Shengli State Farm, 6 Aug. 2004, Tolgor Bau, HMAU 3296.

Inonotus hispidus (Bull.) P. Karst.

On fallen twigs of deciduous trees, Ussuriysk Nature Reserve (Vasilyeva & Bezdeleva, 2006); Raohe, 9 Sept. 2003, Tolgor Bau, HMJAU 3061; Fuyuan, 4 Aug. 2004, Tolgor Bau, HMJAU 2557. - On the log of *Ulmus*, Upper Ussuri Station (Azbukina & Kharkevich, 1984).

Inonotus obliquus (Ach. ex Pers.) Pilát   Plate 16: 96

On the logs of *Betula costata*, *B. lanata and B. platyphylla*, Ussuriysk Nature Reserve, (Vasilyeva & Bezdeleva, 2006); Upper Ussuri Station, 20 Aug. 1974, E.M. Bulakh, VLA M-20086; Big Khekhtsir Nature Reserve, 2 Sept. 1981, E.M. Bulakh, VLA M-199; 16 Aug. 2004, Tolgor Bau, HMJAU 3003; Birobidzhan: Bastak Nature Reserve, 17 Aug. 2000, E.M. Bulakh, VLA M-21052.

Inonotus radiatus (Sowerby) P. Karst.

On the fallen twigs, Ussuriysk Nature Reserve, 18 Aug. 1962, M.M. Nazarova , VLA M-14776. - On the stump of *Alnus hirsuta*, Big Khekhtsir Nature Reserve (Azbukina & Kharkevich, 1986). - On the log of a deciduous tree, Upper Ussuri Station (Azbukina & Kharkevich, 1984).

Inonotus rheades (Pers.) Bondartsev et Singer

On the fallen twig of *Alnus hirsuta*, Big Khekhtsir Nature Reserve (Azbukina & Kharkevich, 1986).

Onnia tomentosa (Fr.) P. Karst.

On the wood buried in ground, Ussuriysk Nature Reserve, 28 Aug. 1965, M.M. Nazarova, VLA M-14805. - On the roots of *Picea*, Upper Ussuri Station, 20 Aug. 1975, E.M. Bulakh, VLA M-14802.

Phellinus baumii Pilát

On the trunks of *Syringa*, Ussuriysk Nature Reserve, 21 Sept. 1975, M.M. Nazarova, VLA M-14817; Ussuriysk, 3 Aug. 2003, Tolgor Bau, HMJAU 2933; Upper Ussuri Station, 28 Jul. 1974, E.M. Bulakh, VLA M-14812; Big Khekhtsir Nature Reserve (Azbukina & Kharkevich, 1986).

Phellinus betulinus (Murrill) Parmasto

On the log of *Betula*, Upper Ussuri Station (Azbukina & Kharkevich, 1984).

Phellinus chinensis Pilát

On the log of *Populus davidiana*, Big Khekhtsir Nature Reserve (Azbukina & Kharkevich, 1986).

Phellinus chrysoloma (Fr.) Donk   Plate 17: 97

On the logs of coniferous trees, Ussuriysk Nature Reserve (Vasilyeva & Bezdeleva, 2006). - On the logs of *Picea* and *Pinus koraiensis*, Upper Ussuri Station (Azbukina & Kharkevich, 1984). - On the trunks of *Picea ajanensis* and *Larix*, Big Khekhtsir Nature

Reserve (Azbukina & Kharkevich, 1986). - On trunk of *Larix*, Birobidzhan: Bastak Nature Reserve, 17 Aug. 2000, E.M. Bulakh, VLA M-21059.

Phellinus conchatus (Pers.) Quél.

On the trunk of *Salix*, Ussuriysk Nature Reserve, 6 Aug. 1961, VLA M-14823, M.M. Nazarova; Ussuriysk, 3 Aug. 2003, Tolgor Bau, 2966.

Phellinus ferruginosus (Schrad.) Pat.

On the fallen twigs, Ussuriysk Nature Reserve, 2 Jun. 1976, E. Parmasto, VLA M-14828. - On the wood of *Quercus*, Birobidzhan: Bastak Nature Reserve, 11 Aug. 2006, E.M. Bulakh, VLA M-21009. - On the log of *Tilia manshurica*, Big Khekhtsir Nature Reserve (Azbukina & Kharkevich, 1986).

Phellinus gilvus (Schwein.) Pat.

On fallen twigs of *Carpinus*, Ussuriysk Nature Reserve, 10 Aug. 1961, L.N. Vassiljeva, VLA M-14833. - On the fallen twigs of *Corylus manshurica* and *Acer tegmentosum*, Upper Ussuri Station (Azbukina & Kharkevich, 1984). - On the log of *Populus davidiana*, Big Khekhtsir Nature Reserve (Azbukina & Kharkevich, 1986).

Phellinus hartigii (Allesch. et Schnabl) Pat.

On living and drying coniferous trunks, Ussuriysk Nature Reserve (Vasilyeva & Bezdeleva, 2006). - On the trunk of *Abies,* Upper Ussuri Station, 28 Aug. 1974, E.M. Bulakh, VLA M-14814; Big Khekhtsir Nature Reserve (Azbukina & Kharkevich, 1986).

Phellinus igniarius (L.) Quél.   Plate 17: 98

[= *Phellinus nigricans* (Fr.) P. Karst.]

On the stumps and logs of *Betula costata, B. lanata and B. platyphylla, Chosenia arbutifolia*, Big Khekhtsir Nature Reserve (Azbukina & Kharkevich, 1986); in birch forest, Fuyuan, 4 Aug. 2004, E.M. Bulakh, VLA M-20271. - On the logs of *Betula* and *Alnus*, Ussuriysk Nature Reserve (Vasilyeva & Bezdeleva, 2006); Upper Ussuri Station (Azbukina & Kharkevich, 1984). - On the trunks, Ussuriysk, 3 Aug. 2003, Tolgor Bau, HMJAU 3286; Raohe: Shengli State Farm, 6 Aug. 2004, Tolgor Bau, HMJAU 2971; Birobidzhan: Bastak Nature Reserve, 16 Aug. 2004, Tolgor Bau, HMJAU 2983. - On trunk of *Abies*, Birobidzhan: Bastak Nature Reserve, 11 Aug. 2006, E.M. Bulakh, VLA M-21030.

Phellinus jezoënsis (Yamano) Parmasto

On the trunks of *Picea ajanensis*, Upper Ussuri Station (Azbukina & Kharkevich, 1984); Big Khekhtsir Nature Reserve (Azbukina & Kharkevich, 1986).

Phellinus laevigatus (Fr.) Bourdot et Galzin

On the logs, Ussuriysk Nature Reserve, 3 Jun. 1976, E. Parmasto, VLA M-14873; Upper Ussuri Station, 27 Jul. 1974, E.M. Bulakh, VLA M-14876. - On the log of *Betula*, Birobidzhan: Bastak Nature Reserve, 11 Aug. 2006, E.M. Bulakh, VLA M-21010.

Phellinus pini (Brot.) Bondartsev et Singer

On the wood, Ussuriysk, 3 Aug. 2003, Tolgor Bau, HMJAU 2976. - On the logs of

Picea and *Pinus koraiensis*, Upper Ussuri Station (Azbukina & Kharkevich, 1984). - On the trunk of *Pinus koraiensis*, Big Khekhtsir Nature Reserve (Azbukina & Kharkevich, 1986).

Phellinus pseudolaevigatus Parmasto

On the logs of *Betula costata*, *B. lanata* and *B. platyphylla*, Big Khekhtsir Nature Reserve (Azbukina & Kharkevich, 1986).

Phellinus punctatus (Fr.) Pilát

On the trunk of a deciduous tree, Ussuriysk Nature Reserve (Vasilyeva & Bezdeleva, 2006). - On the log of *Syringa amurensis*, Upper Ussuri Station (Azbukina & Kharkevich, 1984). - On the twigs of *Acer pseudosieboldianum*, *Padus asiatica*, *Salix caprae* and *Syringa amurensis*, Big Khekhtsir Nature Reserve (Azbukina & Kharkevich, 1986).

Phellinus robustus (P. Karst.) Bourdot et Galzin

On the logs of deciduous trees, Hulin, 9 Sept. 2004, Tolgor Bau, HMJAU 3289; Raohe, 7 Aug. 2004, Tolgor Bau, HMJAU 3228.

Phellinus tremulae (Bondartsev) Bondartsev et P.N. Borisov

On the trunks of *Populus davidiana*, Upper Ussuri Station (Azbukina & Kharkevich, 1984); Big Khekhtsir Nature Reserve (Azbukina & Kharkevich, 1986).

Phellinus vaninii Ljub.

On the stump of *Populus davidiana*, Big Khekhtsir Nature Reserve (Azbukina & Kharkevich, 1986).

Phellinus viticola (Schwein.) Donk

On the log, Ussuriysk Nature Reserve, 2 Jun. 1976, E. Parmasto, VLA M-14904. - On the log of *Abies nephrolepis*, Big Khekhtsir Nature Reserve (Azbukina & Kharkevich, 1986).

Phellinus xeranticus (Berk.) Pegler

On the twigs of *Quercus*, Ussuriysk Nature Reserve, 20 Sept. 1962, M.M. Nazarova, VLA M-14681.

Phellopilus nigrolimitatus (Romell) Niemelä, T. Wagner et M. Fish.

[= *Phellinus nigrolimitatus* (Romell) Bourdot et Galzin]

On the logs of *Picea* and *Pinus koraiensis*, Upper Ussuri Station (Azbukina & Kharkevich, 1984). - On the log of *Abies nephrolepis*, Big Khekhtsir Nature Reserve (Azbukina & Kharkevich, 1986).

Pseudochaete tabacina (Sowerby) T. Wagner et M. Fish.

On the fallen twigs of a deciduous tree, Ussuriysk Nature Reserve (Vasilyeva & Bezdeleva, 2006). - On the wood of *Populus davidiana*, Upper Ussuri Station, 12 Oct. 1996, Ju.I. Manko, VLA M-14738. - On the fallen twigs of *Corylus manshurica*, Big Khekhtsir Nature Reserve (Azbukina & Kharkevich, 1986).

HYMENOGASTRALES

HYMENOGASTRACEAE

Hymenogaster citrinus Vittad.

On the ground in dark coniferous forest, Upper Ussuri Station, 11Sept. 1975, E.M. Bulakh, VLA M-17922.

Tulostoma simulans Lloyd

On the ground of meadow, Khanka Nature Reserve, 18 Jul. 1947, L.N. Vassiljeva, VLA M-17819.

LACHNOCLADIALES

DICHOSTEREACEAE

Dichostereum granulosum (Pers.) Boidin et Lanq.

On the logs of coniferous trees, Ussuriysk Nature Reserve (Vasilyeva & Bezdeleva, 2006).

Scytinostroma galactinum (Fr.) Donk

On the log of a coniferous tree, Ussuriysk Nature Reserve (Vasilyeva & Bezdeleva, 2006).

Vararia vassilievae Parmasto

On the wood in larch forest, Khabarovsk: Lazo (Parmasto, 1965).

LYCOPERDALES

GEASTRACEAE

Cyathus lesueurii Tul. et C. Tul. var. *major* Tul. et C. Tul.

On the ground in forest, Ussuriysk, 19 Aug. 1945, L.N. Vassiljeva, VLA M-17834.

Cyathus stercoreus (Schwein.) De Toni

On the dung of a horse in the thicket of *Crataegus*, Khanka Nature Reserve, 22 Jun. 2002, E.M. Bulakh, VLA M-18219.

Cyathus striatus (Huds.) Willd.

On the ground, Ussuriysk, 18 Aug. 1945, L.N. Vassiljeva, VLA M-17840; in coniferous-broad-leaved forest, Upper Ussuri Station, 23 Aug. 1973, E.M. Bulakh, VLA M-17844; Birobidzhan: Bastak Nature Reserve, 24 Aug. 2003, E.M. Bulakh, VLA M-18218.

Geastrum fimbriatum Fr.

On the forest litter in korean pine-broad-leaved forest, Ussuriysk Nature Reserve, 2 Sept. 1962, M.M. Nazarova, VLA M-18004; Nikolaevka, 14 Sept. 1954 L.N. Vassiljeva, VLA

M-18005; Upper Ussuri Station, 9 Sept. 1975, E.M. Bulakh, VLA M-17999. - On the root of *Betula* in coniferous broad-leaved forest, Big Khekhtsir Nature Reserve, 9 Aug. 1981, E.M. Bulakh, VLA M-17990, 16 Aug. 2004, Tolgor Bau, HMJAU 3193.

Geastrum indicum (Klotzsch) Rauschert

On the ground in korean pine forest, Ussuriysk Nature Reserve (Vasilyeva & Bezdeleva, 2006); Upper Ussuri Station, 11 Sept. 2002, E.M. Bulakh, VLA M-17769. - Under the trees of *Salix* and *Quercus* in deciduous forest, Khanka Nature Reserve, 28 Aug. 2002, E.M. Bulakh, VLA M-18316.

Geastrum lageniforme Vittad.

On the forest litter in oak forest, Ussuriysk Nature Reserve, 23 Aug. 1945, L.N. Vassiljeva, VLA M-18136; Khanka Nature Reserve, 28 Jun. 2002, E.M. Bulakh, VLA M-18313; in broad-leaved forest, Barabash-Levada: Shirokaya Canyon, 8 Jul. 2003, E.M. Bulakh, VLA M-18350; Raohe: Shengli State Farm, 6 Aug. 2004, E.M. Bulakh, VLA M-19610; in dark coniferous forest, Big Khekhtsir Nature Reserve, 14 Aug. 1981, E.M. Bulakh, VLA M-18127.

Geastrum pectinatum Pers.

On the wood in dark coniferous forest, Upper Ussuri Station, 8 Sept. 1974, E.M. Bulakh, VLA M-18014.

Geastrum quadrifidum DC. ex Pers.

On the forest litter in the thicket of *Salix* and *Rhamnus*, Khanka Nature Reserve, 21 Jun. 2002, E.M. Bulakh, VLA M-17189.

Geastrum rufescens Pers.

On the ground in deciduous forest, Ussuriysk Nature Reserve (Vassiljeva & Sosin, 1959).

Geastrum saccatum Fr.   Plate 17: 99

On the ground in oak forest, Ussuriysk Nature Reserve, 22 Sept. 1975, M.M. Nazarova, VLA M-21208; Barabash-Levada: Shirokaya Canyon, 30 Aug. 2002, E.M. Bulakh, VLA M-18334; Big Khekhtsir Nature Reserve, 23 Aug. 1983, E.M. Bulakh, VLA M-21209; Birobidzhan: Bastak Nature Reserve, 18 Aug. 2004, Tolgor Bau, HMJAU 2772.

Geastrum schmidelii Vittad.

(= *Geastrum nanum* Pers.)

On the forest litter in coniferous-broad-leaved forest, Ussuriysk Nature Reserve (Vassiljeva & Sosin, 1959).

Geastrum triplex Jungh.

On the ground, Ussuriysk Nature Reserve, 24 Aug. 1961, L.N. Vassiljeva, VLA M-18124.

LYCOPERDACEAE

Bovista plumbea Pers.

On the ground of meadow, Nikolaevka, 20 Sept. 1954, L.N. Vassiljeva, VLA M-17853.

Bovista pusilla (Batsch) Pers.

On the ground in broad-leaved forest, Ussuriysk Nature Reserve, 13 Sept. 1963, M.M. Nazarova, VLA M-17937; in oak-pine forest, Khorol, 18 Oct. 1954 L.N. Vassiljeva, VLA M-17939; in coniferous broad-leaved forest, Upper Ussuri Station, 20 Aug. 1975, E.M. Bulakh, VLA M-17934; in oak forest, Big Khekhtsir Nature Reserve, 3 Aug. 1981, E.M. Bulakh, VLA M-17935.

Bovistella radicata (Durieu et Mont.) Pat.

On the ground in broad-leaved forest, Birobidzhan: Bastak Nature Reserve, 22 Aug. 2003, E.M. Bulakh, VLA M-17904; Hulin, Tolgor Bau, HMJAU 3313, 3315, 3321, 3322.

Calvatia craniformis (Schwein.) Fr.

On the lawn, Fuyuan, 4,5 Aug. 2004, Tolgor Bau, HMJAU 2564, 2567.

Calvatia lepidophora (Ellis et Everh.) Coker et Couch

On the ground in korean pine-broad-leaved forest, Ussuriysk Nature Reserve (Vassiljeva & Sosin, 1959).

Handkea utriformis (Bull.) Kreisel

[= *Calvatia utriformis* (Bull.) Jaap]

On the logs of *Quercus* in oak forest, Ussuriysk Nature Reserve, 19 Oct. 1954, L.N. Vassiljeva, VLA M-18152; Nikolaevka, 2 Sept. 1954, L.N. Vassiljeva, VLA M-17925; Raohe, 7 Aug. 2004, E.M. Bulakh, VLA M-20685. - On the ground in coniferous broad-leaved forest, Upper Ussuri Station, 10 Sept. 1975, E.M. Bulakh, VLA M-18158; Birobidzhan: Bastak Nature Reserve, 19 Aug. 2003, E.M. Bulakh, VLA M-18260.

Langermannia gigantea (Batsch) Rostk.

On the ground in broad-leaved forest, Ussuriysk Nature Reserve (Vassiljeva & Sosin, 1959); in coniferous broad-leaved forest, Upper Ussuri Station, 11 Sept. 1975, E.M. Bulakh, VLA M-18161; Birobidzhan: Bastak Nature Reserve, 12 Aug. 2000, E.M. Bulakh, VLA M-15336.

Lycoperdon acuminatum Bosc

On the ground in willow thicket, Khanka Nature Reserve, 25 Jul. 2002 E.M. Bulakh, VLA M-18267.

Lycoperdon areolatum Rostk.

On the forest litter in korean pine-broad-leaved forest, Ussuriysk Nature Reserve, 18 Aug. 1962, M.M.Nazarova, VLA M-21285.

Lycoperdon caudatum J. Shröt.

(= *Lycoperdon pedicellatum* Batsch)

On the forest litter in coniferous-broad-leaved forest, Ussuriysk Nature Reserve, 14 Sept. 1962, M.M.Nazarova, VLA M-21147; Upper Ussuri Station, 15 Aug. 1974, E.M. Bulakh, VLA M-21233; Hulin, 9 Aug. 2004, Tolgor Bau, HMJAU 2670. - On the rotten wood, Hulin, 19 Sept. 2004, Tolgor Bau, HMJAu 2670.

Lycoperdon decipiens Durieu et Mont.

On the ground in oak forest, Ussuriysk: Gornotayozhnoye, 6 Aug. 2003, E.M. Bulakh, VLA M-18215; Birobidzhan: Bastak Nature Reserve, 13 Aug. 2000, E.M. Bulakh, VLA M-18268.

Lycoperdon echinatum Pers.   Plate 17: 100

On the log in broad-leaved forest, Birobidzhan: Bastak Nature Reserve, 21 Aug. 2003, E.M. Bulakh, VLA M-18327.

Lycoperdon echinulatum Berk et Broome

On the log of *Abies* among mosses, Ussuriysk Nature Reserve, 23 Oct. 1944, L.N. Vassiljeva, VLA M-21282. - On the ground in deciduous forest, Big Khekhtsir Nature Reserve, 17 Aug. 2004, Tolgor Bau, HMJAU, 3177.

Lycoperdon mammiforme Pers.   Plate 17: 101

On the ground in broad-leaved forest, Tikhorechnoye, 4 Aug. 2005, E.M. Bulakh, VLA M-20306; Birobidzhan: Bastak Nature Reserve, 11 Aug. 1981, E.M. Bulakh, VLA M-21367.

Lycoperdon molle Pers.

On the ground in willow thicket, Khanka Nature Reserve, 25 Jul. 2002, E.M. Bulakh, VLA M-18275; Big Khekhtsir Nature Reserve, 17 Aug. 2004, Tolgor Bau, HMJAU, 3177; Mishan, 1 Sept. 2003, Tolgor Bau, HMJAU 3348.

Lycoperdon oblongisporum Berk. et M.A. Curtis

On the ground in oak forest, Ussuriysk Nature Reserve (Vassiljeva & Sosin, 1959); Upper Ussuri Station, 24 Aug. 1973, E.M. Bulakh, VLA M-21273.

Lycoperdon perlatum Pers.

On the ground in broad-leaved forest, Ussuriysk Nature Reserve, 6 Sept. 1963, M.M. Nazarova, VLA M-21108; Ussuriysk, 3 Aug. 2003, Tolgor Bau, HMJAU 2808; Tikhorechnoye, 21 Jul. 1998, E.M. Bulakh, VLA M-21214; Upper Ussuri Station, 17 Sept. 1975, E.M. Bulakh, VLA M-21264; Nikolaevka, 21 Oct. 1954, L.N. Vassiljeva, VLA M-21255; Big Khekhtsir Nature Reserve, 15 Aug. 2004, Tolgor Bau, HMJAU 2791, 2781; Birobidzhan: Bastak Nature Reserve, 18 Aug. 2004, Tolgor Bau, HMJAU 2798; Hulin, 20 Sept. 2003, 9 Aug. 2004, Tolgor Bau, HMJAU 2572, 2605, 2666; Fuyuan, 5 Aug. 2004, E.M. Bulakh, VLA M-20399; Raohe: Shengli State Farm, 6 Aug. 2004, Tolgor Bau, HMJAU 3356.

Lycoperdon pyriforme Schaeff.

On the wood in pine-broad-leaved forest, Ussuriysk Nature Reserve, 17 Sept. 1996, E.M. Bulakh, VLA M-18265; in dark coniferous forest, Upper Ussuri Station, 29 Aug. 1973, E.M. Bulakh, VLA M-17914; in broad-leaved forest, Big Khekhtsir Nature Reserve, 2 Jul. 1943,

L.N. Vassiljeva, VLA M-17970; in birch forest, Raohe, 7 Aug. 2004, E.M. Bulakh, VLA M-19587; Birobidzhan: Bastak Nature Reserve, 21 Aug. 2003, E.M. Bulakh, VLA M-18258; Hulin, 9 Aug. 2004, Tolgor Bau, HMJAU 2700, 2507, 2711, 3075; Fuyuan, 4 Aug. 2004, Tolgor Bau, HMJAU 2581, 2631.

Lycoperdon serotinum Bonord.

On the ground in broad-leaved forest, Ussuriysk Nature Reserve, 17 Sept. 1996, L.N. Vassiljeva, VLA M-18266; Big Khekhtsir Nature Reserve, 15 Sept. 1981, E.M. Bulakh, VLA M-17950; Birobidzhan: Bastak Nature Reserve, 21 Aug. 2003, E.M. Bulakh, VLA M-18274.

Lycoperdon spadiceum Schaeff.

On the ground in broad-leaved forest, Ussuriysk: Gornotayozhnoye, 6 Aug. 2002, E.M. Bulakh, VLA M-18352; in birch forest, Fuyuan, 4 Aug. 2004, E.M. Bulakh, VLA M-19584.

Lycoperdon umbrinum Pers.

On the ground in korean pine-broad-leaved forest, Ussuriysk Nature Reserve, 31 Aug. 1946, L.N. Vassiljeva, VLA M-17900; in broad-leaved forest, Big Khekhtsir Nature Reserve, 27 Jul. 1946, L.N. Vassiljeva, VLA M-17909; Luchegorsk: Sakhalinka River Valley, 16 Sept. 1945, L.N. Vassiljeva, VLA M-17910.

Vascellum pratense (Pers.) Kreisel

On the ground in oak forest, Nikolaevka, 2 Sept. 1954, L.N. Vassiljeva, VLA M-17925.

MYCENASTRACEAE

Mycenastrum corium (Guers.) Desv.

On the ground in a garden, Ussuriysk, 8 Jul. 1945, L.N. Vassiljeva, VLA M-17896; in broad-leaved forest, Big Khekhtsir Nature Reserve, 9 Sept. 1999, A.B. Melnikova, VLA M-13616.

MELANOGASTRALES

MELANOGASTRACEAE

Leucogaster nudus (Hazsl.) Hollós

(= *Leucogaster floccosus* R. Hesse)

On the ground in dark coniferous forest, Upper Ussuri Station, 29 May 1974, E.M. Bulakh, VLA M-17924.

PHALLALES

PHALLACEAE

Dictyophora duplicata (Bosc) E. Fisch.   Plate 17: 102

On the ground in korean pine-broad-leaved forest, Ussuriysk Nature Reserve, 14 Sept. 1975, M.M. Nazarova, VLA M-18143; in broad-leaved forest, Big Khekhtsir Nature Reserve (Azbukina & Kharkevich, 1986).

Mutinus caninus (Huds.) Fr.   Plate 18: 103

On the ground in broad-leaved forest, Ussuriysk Nature Reserve, 18 Aug. 1961, M.M. Nazarova, VLA M-18171; Ussuriysk, 3 Aug. 2003, Tolgor Bau, HMJAU 2815; in willow thicket, Khanka Nature Reserve, 28 Aug. 2002, E.M. Bulakh, VLA M-19099.

Phallus impudicus L.

On the log of *Pinus koraiensis* in korean pine-broad-leaved forest, Ussuriysk Nature Reserve (Vasilyeva & Bezdeleva, 2006). - On the ground in oak forest, Khanka Nature Reserve, 28 Jul. 2002, E.M. Bulakh, VLA M-18319; in korean pine forest, Upper Ussuri Station, 6 Aug. 1974, E.M. Bulakh, VLA M-18193. - On the decayed wood in broad-leaved forest, Big Khekhtsir Nature Reserve, 24 Jun. 1981, E.M. Bulakh, VLA M-18189.

PORALES

Anomoloma albolutescens (Romell) Niemelä et K.H. Larss.

[= *Anomoporia albolutescens* (Romell) Pouzar]

On the logs of *Abies nephrolepis,* Upper Ussuri Station (Azbukina & Kharkevich, 1984); Big Khekhtsir Nature Reserve (Azbukina & Kharkevich, 1986).

Anomoporia bombycina (Fr.) Pouzar

On the logs of *Abies* and *Picea*, Upper Ussuri Station (Azbukina & Kharkevich, 1984).

Antrodia albida (Fr.) Donk

[= *Coriolellus albidus* (Fr.) Bondartsev]

On the logs of deciduous trees, Ussuriysk Nature Reserve (Vasilyeva & Bezdeleva, 2006); Ussuriysk, 3 Aug. 2003, Tolgor Bau, HMJAU 2895; Upper Ussuri Station (Azbukina & Kharkevich, 1984). - On the log of *Quercus*, Big Khekhtsir Nature Reserve (Azbukina & Kharkevich, 1986).

Antrodia heteromorpha (Fr.) Donk

On the log of *Picea ajanensis*, Upper Ussuri Station (Azbukina & Kharkevich, 1984).

Antrodia serialis (Fr.) Donk

On the logs of *Picea ajanensis,* Upper Ussuri Station (Azbukina & Kharkevich, 1984); Big Khekhtsir Nature Reserve (Azbukina & Kharkevich, 1986).

Antrodia sinuosa (Fr.) P. Karst.

On the log of *Pinus koraiensis,* Ussuriysk Nature Reserve (Vasilyeva & Bezdeleva, 2006).

Antrodia xantha (Fr.) Ryvarden

On the dead trunks of coniferous trees, Ussuriyskyi Nature Reserve, 9 Aug. 1961, L.N. Vassiljeva., VLA M-13275; Upper Ussuri Station (Azbukina & Kharkevich, 1984). - On the log of *Abies nephrolepis*, Big Khekhtsir Nature Reserve (Azbukina & Kharkevich, 1986).

Antrodiella semisupina (Berk. et M.A. Curtis) Ryvarden

On the twigs in broad-leaved forest, Birobidzhan: Bastak Nature Reserve, 10 Aug. 2006, E.M. Bulakh, VLA M-21023.

Bjerkandera adusta (Willd.) P. Karst.

On the stump of *Carpinus*, Ussuriysk Nature Reserve, 21 Sept. 1962, M.M. Nazarova, VLA M-13286. - On the trunk, Upper Ussuri Station, 28 Aug. 1974, E.M. Bulakh, VLA M-13287. - On the trunks of *Populus davidiana*, *Quercus mongolica*, *Tilia amurensis* and *T. mandschurica*, Big Khekhtsir Nature Reserve, 16 Aug. 2004, Tolgor Bau, HMJAU 2961; Raohe, 9 Sept. 2003 and 7 Aug. 2004, Tolgor Bau, HMJAU 3059, 3078, 3365, 3400.

Bjerkandera fumosa (Pers.) P. Karst.

On the wood, Vladivostok, 2 Aug. 2003, Tolgor Bau, HMJAU 2812. - On the stump of a deciduous tree, Big Khekhtsir Nature Reserve (Azbukina & Kharkevich, 1986). - On the stumps of *Alnus* and *Populus*, Upper Ussuri Station (Azbukina & Kharkevich, 1984).

Bondarcevomyces taxi (Bondartsev) Parmasto

(= *Hapalopilus taxi* Bondartsev)

On the stump of a deciduous tree, Ussuriysk Nature Reserve (Vasilyeva & Bezdeleva, 2006).

Castanoporus castaneus (Lloyd) Ryvarden

[= *Cystidiophorus castaneus* (Lloyd) Imazeki]

On the twigs of *Pinus koraiensis*, Ussuriysk Nature Reserve, 2 Jun. 1976, E. Parmasto, VLA M-13874; Upper Ussuri Station (Azbukina & Kharkevich, 1984); Big Khekhtsir Nature Reserve (Azbukina & Kharkevich, 1986).

Ceriporia viridans (Berk et Broome) Donk

On the logs of *Ulmus* and *Acer*, Upper Ussuri Station (Azbukina & Kharkevich, 1984).

Cerrena unicolor (Bull.) Murrill   Plate 18: 104

[= *Coriolus unicolor* (Bull.) Pat.]

On the trunk of a deciduous tree, Ussuriysk Nature Reserve (Vasilyeva & Bezdeleva, 2006). - On the logs, Vladivostok, 2 Aug. 2003, Tolgor Bau, HMJAU 2844; Hulin, 5 Sept. 2003, Tolgor Bau, HMJAU 3023; Fuyuan, 5 Aug. 2004, Tolgor Bau, HMJAU 2680. - On the logs of *Acer pseudosieboldianum* and *Padus asiatica*, Upper Ussuri Station (Azbukina & Kharkevich, 1984); Big Khekhtsir Nature Reserve (Azbukina & Kharkevich, 1986).

Cinereomyces lindbladii (Berk) Jülich

[= *Antrodia lindbladii* (Berk.) Ryvarden]

On the logs of *Pinus koraiensis*, Ussuriysk Nature Reserve, 29 Aug. 1960, L.N. Vassiljeva, VLA M-13944; Upper Ussuri Station (Azbukina & Kharkevich, 1984); Big Khekhtsir Nature Reserve (Azbukina & Kharkevich, 1986).

Cryptoporus volvatus (Peck) Shear   Plate 18: 105

On the trunk of *Pinus koraiensis*, Ussuriysk Nature Reserve, 23 Jun. 1962, M.M. Nazarova, VLA M-13899.

Daedalea dickinsii Yasuda

On the trunks of deciduous trees, Ussuriysk Nature Reserve, 18 Aug. 1962, M.M. Nazarova,VLA M-13910; Big Khekhtsir Nature Reserve, 16 Aug. 2004, Tolgor Bau, HMJAU 2956, 2999.

Daedalea flavida Lév.

(= *Lenzites acuta* Berk.)

On the logs, Ussuriysk Nature Reserve, 4 Jun. 1976, E. Parmasto, VLA M-14148; Upper Ussuri Station (Azbukina & Kharkevich, 1984); Birobidzhan: Bastak Nature Reserve, 11 Aug. 2006, E.M. Bulakh, VLA M-21062.

Daedalea quercina (L.) Pers.

On the trunks of *Quercus*, Ilyinka, 22 Aug. 1955, Z.M. Azbukina, VLA M-13916; Birobidzhan: Bastak Nature Reserve, 14 Aug. 2006, E.M. Bulakh, VLA M-21006.

Daedaleopsis confragosa (Bolton) J. Schröt.   Plate 18: 106

[= *Daedaleopsis tricolor* (Bull.) Bondartsev et Singer]

On the wood in deciduous forest, Ussuriysk Nature Reserve, 3 Oct. 1963, L.N. Vassiljeva, VLA M-13919; Ussuriysk, 3 Aug. 2003, Tolgor Bau, HMJAU 2941; Fuyuan, 5 Aug. 2004, Tolgor Bau, HMJAU 2653; Hulin, 19, 20 Sept. 2004, Tolgor Bau, 2608, 2625. - On the logs of *Acer ukurunduense*, *Alnus hirsuta*, *Quercus*, Upper Ussuri Station (Azbukina & Kharkevich, 1984). - On the fallen twigs of *Padus asiatica* and *Populus davidiana*, Big Khekhtsir Nature Reserve (Azbukina & Kharkevich, 1986); Birobidzhan: Bastak Nature Reserve, 11 Aug. 2006, E.M. Bulakh, VLA M-20964.

Datronia mollis (Sommerf.) Donk

On the log of *Populus davidiana,* Big Khekhtsir Nature Reserve (Azbukina & Kharkevich, 1986). - On the fallen twig of a deciduous tree, Upper Ussuri Station (Azbukina & Kharkevich, 1984).

Datronia scutellata (Schwein.) Gilb. et Ryvarden

On the wood of a deciduous tree, Ussuriysk Nature Reserve (Vasilyeva & Bezdeleva, 2006). - On the logs of *Salix*, Upper Ussuri Station, 7 Sept. 1975, E.M. Bulakh, VLA M-13902; Hulin 9 Aug. 2004, Tolgor Bau, HMJAU 2658.

Datronia stereoides (Fr.) Ryvarden

On fallen twigs of *Sorbaria*, Ussuriysk Nature Reserve, 12 Aug. 1961, L.N. Vassiljeva, VLA M-13280. - On the fallen twigs of *Fraxinus*, Upper Ussuri Station (Azbukina & Kharkevich, 1984).

Erastia salmonicolor (Berk. et M.A. Curtis) Niemalä et Kinnunen

[= *Hapalopilus salmonicolor* (Berk. et M.A. Curtis) Pouzar]

On the log of *Picea* in coniferous-broad-leaved forest, Upper Ussuri Station (Azbukina & Kharkevich, 1984). - On the log of *Pinus koraiensis*, Big Khekhtsir Nature Reserve (Azbukina & Kharkevich, 1986).

Fomes fomentarius (L.) Fr.   Plate 18: 107

On the logs of *Betula*, Ussuriysk Nature Reserve, 25 Aug. 1959, I.A. Bunkina , VLA M-14021; Ussuriysk, 3 Aug. 2003, Tolgor Bau, HMJAU 2826; Upper Ussuri Station, 5 Aug. 1974, E.M. Bulakh, VLA M-14039; Big Khekhtsir Nature Reserve (Azbukina & Kharkevich, 1986); Birobidzhan: Bastak Nature Reserve, 17 Aug. 2000, E.M. Bulakh, VLA M-21056. - On the wood in deciduoud forest, Ussuriysk, 3 Aug. 2003, Tolgor Bau, 2826; Fuyuan, 5 Aug. 2004, Tolgor Bau, HMJAU 2682; Hulin, 20 Sept. 2004, Tolgor Bau, HMJAU 2665.

Fomitopsis cajanderi (P. Karst.) Kotl. et Pouzar

On the wood of *Abies*, Ussuriysk Nature Reserve, 28 Aug. 1967, L.N. Vassiljeva, VLA M-13903. - On the wood of a coniferous tree, Birobidzhan: Bastak Nature Reserve, 10 Aug. 2006, E.M. Bulakh, VLA M-21000. - On the log of *Picea ajanensis*, Upper Ussuri Station (Azbukina & Kharkevich, 1984); Big Khekhtsir Nature Reserve (Azbukina & Kharkevich, 1986). - On the stump, Hulin, 4 Sept. 2003, Tolgor Bau, HMJAU 3006.

Fomitopsis castanea Imazeki

[= *Melanoporia castanea* (Imazeki) T. Hatt. et Ryvarden = *Phellinus quercinus* Bondartsev et Ljub.]

On the log of *Quercus,* Ussuriysk Nature Reserve (Parmasto & Kollom, 2000).

Fomitopsis pinicola (Sw.) P. Karst.   Plate 18: 108

On the logs of coniferous trees, Ussuriysk Nature Reserve (Vasilyeva & Bezdeleva, 2006); Birobidzhan: Bastak Nature Reserve, 17 Aug. 2000, E.M. Bulakh, VLA M-21053. - On the logs of deciduous trees, Ussuriysk, 3 Aug. 2003, Tolgor Bau, 2980; Hulin, 19 Sept. 2004, Tolgor Bau, HMJAU 2651; Raohe: Shengli State Farm, 6 Aug. 2004, Tolgor Bau, HMJAU 2522. - On the log of *Picea ajanensis*, Upper Ussuri Station (Azbukina & Kharkevich, 1984). - On the logs of *Abies nephrolepis*, *Alnus hirsuta*, *Picea ajanensis*, *Pinus koraiensis* and *Populus davidiana*, Big Khekhtsir Nature Reserve (Azbukina & Kharkevich, 1986).

Fomitopsis rosea (Alb. et Schwein.) P. Karst.

On the logs of *Picea*, Upper Ussuri Station, 19 Aug. 1974, E.M. Bulakh, VLA M-14014; Big Khekhtsir Nature Reserve (Azbukina & Kharkevich, 1986). - On the log of *Pinus koraiensis*, Birobidzhan: Bastak Nature Reserve, 10 Aug. 2006, E.M. Bulakh, VLA M-20970.

Fomitopsis sensitiva (Lloyd) R. Sasaki

On the wood, Hulin, 19 Sept. 2004, Tolgor Bau, HMJAU 2712.

Funalia trogii (Berk.) Bondartsev et Singer

On the dead twigs of *Salix*, Ussuriysk Nature Reserve, 18 Aug. 1961, L.N. Vassiljeva, VLA M-14661. - On the trunk of *Quercus,* Ilyinka, Jul. 1955, Z.M.Azbukina, VLA M-13887. - On the log of *Populus*, Upper Ussuri Station (Azbukina & Kharkevich, 1984). - On the logs of *Alnus hisuta*, *Populus davidiana* and *Salix*, Big Khekhtsir Nature Reserve (Azbukina & Kharkevich, 1986).

Gloeophyllum abietinum (Fr.) P. Karst.

On the log of *Picea*, Upper Ussuri Station, 19 Aug. 1974, E.M. Bulakh, VLA M-14042.

Gloeophyllum odoratum (Wulfen) Imazeki

On the logs of *Betula*, Upper Ussuri Station, 19 Aug. 1974, E. Parmasto, VLA M-14044; Raohe, 6 Aug. 2004, Tolgor Bau, HMJAU 3317.

Gloeophyllum sepiarium (Wulfen) P. Karst.

On the logs of coniferous trees, Ussuriysk Nature Reserve (Vasilyeva & Bezdeleva, 2006); Upper Ussuri Station, 19 Aug. 1974, E. Parmasto, VLA M-14067. - On the stumps and logs of *Pinus koraiensis* and *Populus davidiana*, Big Khekhtsir Nature Reserve (Azbukina & Kharkevich, 1986); Birobidzhan: Bastak Nature Reserve, 18 Aug. 2004, Tolgor Bau, 2922.

Grifola frondosa (Dicks.) Gray   Plate 19: 109

On the ground under the tree of *Quercus*, Ussuriysk Nature Reserve, 2 Sept. 1962, M.M. Nazarova, VLA M-414.

Hapalopilus nidulans (Fr.) P. Karst.

On the log of a deciduous tree, Ussuriysk Nature Reserve (Vasilyeva & Bezdeleva, 2006). - On the log of *Betula,* Upper Ussuri Station (Azbukina & Kharkevich, 1984).

Hapalopilus rutilans (Pers.) P. Karst.

On the log of *Quercus*, Big Khekhtsir Nature Reserve (Azbukina & Kharkevich, 1986).

Heterobasidion insulare (Murrill) Ryvarden

On the log of *Abies*, Ussuriysk Nature Reserve, 2 Jul. 1976, E. Parmasto, VLA M-14121. - On the log of *Picea ajanensis*, Upper Ussuri Station (Azbukina & Kharkevich, 1984). - On the basis of living tree of *Abies nephrolepis*, Big Khekhtsir Nature Reserve (Azbukina & Kharkevich, 1986).

Hydnopolyporus fimbriatus (Fr.) D.A. Reid

On the log of a deciduous tree. Upper Ussiri Station (Azbukina & Kharkevich, 1984). - On the log of a coniferous tree in dark coniferous forest, Big Khekhtsir Nature Reserve (Azbukina & Kharkevich, 1986).

Ischnoderma benzonium (Wahlenb.) P. Karst.

On the logs of *Quercus*, Ussuriysk Nature Reserve, 23 Sept. 1995, E.M. Bulakh, VLA M-14243; Ussuriysk: Timiryasevsky, 20 Oct. 1994, P. Fisenko, VLA M-14241. - On the log of a coniferous tree, Big Khekhtsir Nature Reserve (Azbukina & Kharkevich, 1986).

Ischnoderma resinosum (Schrad.) P. Karst.

On the logs of coniferous trees, Ussuriysk Nature Reserve, 28 Aug. 1965, M.M. Nazarova, VLA M-14133; Upper Ussuri Station, 25 Aug. 1974, L.N. Vassiljeva, VLA M-14134; Hulin, 20 Sept., 2004, Tolgor Bau, HMJAU 2657, 2701. - On the logs of *Picea* and *Acer*, Upper Ussuri Station (Azbukina & Kharkevich, 1984).

Ischnoderma scaurum (Lloyd) Domański

On the log of a deciduous tree, Ussuriysk Nature Reserve, 2 Sept. 1961, M.M. Nazarova, VLA M-14135.

Laetiporus sulphureus (Bull.) Murrill   Plate 19: 110

On the logs of deciduous trees, Ussuriysk Nature Reserve, 2 Sept. 2004, E.M. Bulakh, VLA M-204; Ussuriysk, 3 Aug. 2003, Tolgor Bau, HMJAU 2934; Upper Ussuri Station (Azbukina & Kharkevich, 1984). - On the basis of trunks of *Quercus* and *Picea ajanensis*, Big Khekhtsir Nature Reserve, 16 Aug. 2004, Tolgor Bau, HMJAU 2796; Birobidzhan: Bastak Nature Reserve, 19 Aug. 2004, Tolgor Bau, HMJAU 2923; Hulin, 19 Sept. 2004, Tolgor Bau, HMJAU 2671.

Laricifomes officinalis (Vill.) Kotl. et Pouzar   Plate 19: 111

[= *Fomitopsis officinalis* Vill.) Bondartsev et Singer]

On the stump of *Larix*, Birobidzhan: Bastak Nature Reserve, 11 Aug. 2001, E.M. Bulakh, VLA M-20673.

Lenzites betulina (L.) Fr.   Plate 19: 112

On the logs of *Betula,* Ussuriysk Nature Reserve, 14 Aug. 1959, I.A. Bunkina, VLA M-14166; Ussuriysk, 3 Aug. 2003, Tolgor Bau, HMJAU 2936; Upper Ussuri Station, 10 Aug. 1974, E.M. Bulakh, VLA M-14158; Birobidzhan: Bastak Nature Reserve, 10 Aug. 2006, E.M. Bulakh, VLA M-20976. - On the logs of *Betula, Acer pseudosieboldianum, Corylus mandshurica* and *Populus davidiana*, Big Khekhtsir Nature Reserve, 12 Aug. 1981, E.M. Bulakh, VLA M-14150, 17 Aug. 2004, Tolgor Bau, HMJAU 2918; Hulin, 20 Sept. 2004, Tolgor Bau, HMJAU 2678; Fuyuan, 5 Aug. 2004, Tolgor Bau, HMJAU 2678.

Leucophellinus hobsonii (Berk ex Cooke) Ryvarden

[= *Leucophellinus mollissimus* (Pat.) Parmasto]

On the wood of *Acer*, Ussuriysk Nature Reserve. - On the trunk of *Alnus*, Khabarovsk: Mukhen (Parmasto, 1983).

Leucophellinus irpicoides (Bondartsev ex Pilát) Bondartsev et Singer

On the log, Ussuriysk Nature Reserve, 1962, M.M. Nazarova, VLA M-14169. - On the trunks of *Acer mono, Fraxinus manshurica* and *Ulmus laciniata*, Upper Ussuri Station (Azbukina & Kharkevich, 1984).

Oxyporus corticola (Fr.) Ryvarden

On the stump of *Phellodendron amurense*, Ussuriysk Nature Reserve, 1 Aug. 1961, L.N.

Vassiljeva, VLA M-14226. - On the log of *Picea*, Upper Ussuri Station (Azbukina & Kharkevich, 1984). - On the log of *Populus davidiana*, Big Khekhtsir Nature Reserve (Azbukina & Kharkevich, 1986).

Oxyporus philadelphi (Parmasto) Ryvarden

On the fallen twigs of *Philadelphus tenuifolius*, Upper Ussuri Station (Azbukina & Kharkevich, 1984).

Oxyporus populinus (Schumach.) Donk

On the trunks of *Acer mono*, Ussuriysk Nature Reserve, 14 Aug. 1961, L.N. Vassiljeva, VLA M-14220; Upper Ussuri Station, 5 Aug. 1974, E.M. Bulakh, VLA M-14216. - On the trunks of *Acer mono* and *Populus davidiana*, Big Khekhtsir Nature Reserve, 19 Aug. 1983, E.M. Bulakh, VLA M-14224; 16 Aug. 2004, Tolgor Bau, HMJAU 2794; Raohe: Shengli State Farm, 6 Aug. 2004, Tolgor Bau, HMJAU 2585; Birobidzhan: Bastak Nature Reserve, 18 Aug. 2004, Tolgor Bau, HMJAU 2928, 3303.

Oxyporus pseudo-obducens (Pilát) Bondatsev

On the log of *Abies* in dark coniferous forest, Upper Ussuri Station (Azbukina & Kharkevich, 1984).

Pachykytospora subtrametea (Pilát) Kotl. et Pouzar

On the log of *Tilia taqueti* in korean pine-broad-leaved forest, Upper Ussuri Station (Azbukina & Kharkevich, 1984).

Parmastomyces kravtzevianus (Bondartsev et Parmasto) Kotl. et Pouzar

On the log, Upper Ussuri Station (Azbukina & Kharkevich, 1984).

Perenniporia maackiae (Bondartsev et Ljub.) Parmasto

On the log and twigs of *Maackia amurensis*, Ussuriysk Nature Reserve, 9 Aug. 1961, L.N. Vassiljeva, VLA M-14230; Big Khekhtsir Nature Reserve, 22 Jun. 1981, E.M. Bulakh, VLA M-14229; Birobidzhan: Bastak Nature Reserve, 14 Aug. 2006, E.M. Bulakh, VLA M-21132.

Perenniporia ochiensis (Berk) Ryvarden

On the wood of a deciduous tree, Birobidzhan: Bastak Nature Reserve, 14 Aug. 2006, E.M. Bulakh, VLA M-21007.

Perenniporia ochroleuca (Berk.) Ryvarden

On the fallen twigs of deciduous trees, Ussuriysk Nature Reserve, 19 Jul. 1964, M.M. Nazarova, VLA M-14236; Big Khekhtsir Nature Reserve (Azbukina & Kharkevich, 1986).

Perenniporia subacida (Peck) Donk

On the logs of *Picea* and *Abies*, Upper Ussuri Station (Azbukina & Kharkevich, 1984).

Phaeolus schweinitzii (Fr.) Pat.

On roots of *Pinus koraiensis*, Ussuriysk Nature Reserve, 26 Jul. 1959, I.A. Bunkina, VLA M-14260. - On the roots of *Picea*, Upper Ussuri Station (Azbukina & Kharkevich, 1984); Big Khekhtsir Nature Reserve, 14 Aug. 1981, E.M. Bulakh, VLA M-14265.

Piptoporus betulinus (Bull.) P. Karst.

On the logs and dead trunks of *Betula,* Ussuriysk Nature Reserve (Vasilyeva & Bezdeleva, 2006), Ussuriysk, 3 Aug. 2003, Tolgor Bau, HMJAU 2937; Upper Ussuri Station (Azbukina & Kharkevich, 1984); Big Khekhtsir Nature Reserve (Azbukina & Kharkevich, 1986); Birobidzhan: Bastak Nature Reserve, 21 Aug. 2006, E.M. Bulakh, VLA M-20659; Hulin, 19 Sept. 2004, Tolgor Bau, HMJAU 2713.

Piptoporus ulmi Bondatsev et Ljub.

On the log of *Tilia,* Big Khekhtsir Nature Reserve (Azbukina & Kharkevich, 1986).

Poronidulus conchifer (Schwein.) Murrill

On the fallen twigs of deciduous trees, Ussuriysk Nature Reserve (Vasilyeva & Bezdeleva, 2006); Big Khekhtsir Nature Reserve (Azbukina & Kharkevich, 1986).

Postia balsamea (Peck) Jülich

On the logs of *Picea* and *Pinus koraiensis,* Upper Ussuri Station (Azbukina & Kharkevich, 1984).

Postia caesia (Schrad.) P. Karst.

[= *Oligoporus caesius* (Schrad.) Gilb. et Ryvarden]

On the fallen twigs, Ussuriysk Nature Reserve, 12 Sept. 1961, L.N. Vassiljeva, VLA M-14200. - On the rotten wood, Ussuriysk, 3 Aug. 2003, Tolgor Bau, HMJAU 2897.

Postia fragilis (Fr.) Jülich

On the log of *Pinus koraiensis,* Ussuriysk Nature Reserve (Vasilyeva & Bezdeleva, 2006). - On the logs of *Picea* and *Abies* in dark coniferous forest, Upper Ussuri Station (Azbukina & Kharkevich, 1984).

Postia guttulata (Peck) Jülich

On the log of *Picea* in coniferous-broad-leaved forest, Upper Ussuri Station (Azbukina & Kharkevich, 1984).

Postia hibernica (Berk. et Broome) Jülich

On the log of *Picea* in korean-pine-broad-leaved forest, Upper Ussuri Station (Azbukina & Kharkevich, 1984).

Postia mappa (Overh. et J. Lowe) M.J. Larsen et Lombard

On the log of a coniferous tree, Upper Ussuri Station, 9 Sept. 1975, E.M. Bulakh, VLA M-13338.

Postia stiptica (Pers.) Jülich

On the log in korean-pine-broad-leaved forest, Upper Ussuri Station (Azbukina & Kharkevich, 1984).

Pycnoporellus fulgens (Fr.) Donk

On the log, Ussuriysk Nature Reserve, 18 Aug. 1975, M.M. Nazarova, VLA M-14364. - On the logs of *Abies* and *Picea* in coniferous-broad-leaved forest, Upper Ussuri Station (Azbukina & Kharkevich, 1984). - On the log of *Picea ajanensis,* Big Khekhtsir Nature

Reserve (Azbukina & Kharkevich, 1986).

Pycnoporus cinnabarinus (Jacq.) Fr.

On the logs of deciduous trees, Ussuriysk Nature Reserve, 7 Aug. 1961, L.N. Vassiljeva, VLA M-14405; Upper Ussuri Station, 25 Aug. 1974, E. M. Bulakh, VLA M-14403; Big Khekhtsir Nature Reserve, 28 Aug.1981, E. M. Bulakh, M-14379; Birobidzhan: Bastak Nature Reserve, 14 Aug. 2006, E.M. Bulakh, VLA M-21011.

Skeletocutis amorpha (Fr.) Kotl. et Pouzar

On the log of *Abies* in coniferous-broad-leaved forest, Upper Ussuri Station (Azbukina & Kharkevich, 1984).

Skeletocutis lenis (P.Karst.) Niemelä

On the log of a deciduous tree, Ussuriysk Nature Reserve, 2 Jun. 1976, E. Parmasto, VLA M-13271.

Skeletocutis nivea (Jungh.) Jean Keller

On the log of a deciduous tree, Ussuriysk Nature Reserve, 3 Jun. 1976, E. Parmasto, VLA M-14374. - On the fallen twigs of *Acer barbinerve*, Upper Ussuri Station (Azbukina & Kharkevich, 1984).

Skeletocutis subincarnata (Peck) Jean Keller

On the fallen twigs *of Picea ajanensis* and *Pinus koraiensis*, Upper Ussuri Station (Azbukina & Kharkevich, 1984).

Skeletocutis tschulymica (Pilát) Jean Keller

On the logs of *Picea* and *Abies,* Upper Ussuri Station (Azbukina & Kharkevich, 1984).

Spongipellis litschaueri Lohwag

On the trunk of *Quercus*, Big Khekhtsir Nature Reserve (Azbukina & Kharkevich, 1986).

Spongipellis spumeus (Sowerby) Pat.

On the wood in forest, Big Khekhtsir Nature Reserve, 16 Aug. 2004, Tolgor Bau, HMJAU 2800; Birobidzhan: Bastak Nature Reserve, 12 Aug. 2006, E.M. Bulakh, VLA M-21014; Hulin, 20 Sept. 2003, Tolgor Bau, HMJAU 3308.

Trametes cervina (Schwein.) Bres.

On the log of a deciduous tree, Ussuriysk Nature Reserve (Vasilyeva & Bezdeleva, 2006).

Trametes gibbosa (Pers.) Fr.

On the logs of *Tilia,* Ussuriysk Nature Reserve, 17 Aug. 1961, L.N. Vassiljeva, VLA M-14476; Upper Ussuri Station, 21 Aug. 1974, E.M. Bulakh, VLA M-14478. - On the log of *Populus davidiana*, Big Khekhtsir Nature Reserve (Azbukina & Kharkevich, 1986).

Trametes hirsuta (Wulfen) Pilát

On the logs of deciduous trees, Ussuriysk Nature Reserve, 26 Sept. 1962, M.M. Nazarova, VLA M-14504; Upper Ussuri Station, 3 Aug. 1974, E.M. Bulakh, VLA M-14499; Fyuan, 5 Aug. 2004, Tolgor Bau, HMJAU 2679; Birobidzhan: Bastak Nature Reserve, 15 Aug.

2000, E.M. Bulakh, VLA M-21057. - On the fallen twigs of *Alnus hirsuta, Populus davidiana* and *Quercus*, Big Khekhtsir Nature Reserve (Azbukina & Kharkevich, 1986).

Trametes ochracea (Pers.) Gilb. et Ryvarden

On the fallen twigs, Ussuriysk Nature Reserve, 25 Jul. 1959, I.A. Bunkina, VLA M-9809; Big Khekhtsir Nature Reserve, 9 Aug. 1981, E.M. Bulakh, M-14526. - On the fallen twigs of *Corylus*, Upper Ussuri Station, 7 Sept. 1974, E.M. Bulakh, VLA M-14515.

Trametes pubescens (Schumach.) Pilát

On the fallen twigs, Ussuriysk Nature Reserve, 10 Aug. 1961, L.N. Vassiljeva, VLA M-14549. - On the wood, Upper Ussuri Station (Azbukina & Kharkevich, 1984); Big Khekhtsir Nature Reserve, 17 Aug. 2004, Tolgor Bau, HMJAU 2927; Hulin, 20 Sep. 2004, Tolgor Bau, HMJAU 2613.

Trametes suaveolens (L.) Fr.

On the trunk of *Lonicera,* Ussuriysk Nature Reserve, 9 Aug. 1961, L.N. Vassiljeva, VLA M-14553. - On the trunk of *Salix*, Upper Ussuri Station (Azbukina & Kharkevich, 1984); Fuyuan, 6 Aug. 2004, Tolgor Bau, HMJAU 3258.

Trametes versicolor (L.) Pilát   Plate 19: 113

[= *Coriolus versicolor* (L.) Quél.]

On the fallen twigs and trunks of deciduous trees, Ussuriysk Nature Reserve, 29 Jun. 1959, I.A. Bunkina, VLA M-14570; Ussuriysk, 3 Aug. 2003, Tolgor Bau, 2870; Upper Ussuri Station (Azbukina & Kharkevich, 1984); Big Khekhtsir Nature Reserve (Azbukina & Kharkevich, 1986); Birobidzhan: Bastak Nature Reserve, 12 Aug. 2000, E.M. Bulakh, VLA M-21060; Hulin, 19 Sept. 2004, Tolgor Bau, HMJAU 2707; Fuyuan, 4 Aug. 2004, Tolgor Bau, HMJAU 2652. - On the bark, Fuyuan, 5 Aug. 2004, Tolgor Bau, HMJAU 2637. - On the stump, Raohe, 8 Sept. 2003, Tolgor Bau, HMJAU 3049.

Trichaptum abietinum (Dicks.) Ryvarden

On the log of a coniferous tree, Ussuriysk Nature Reserve (Vasilyeva & Bezdeleva, 2006). - On the trunks of *Abies*, Upper Ussuri Station, 28 Aug. 1974, E.M. Bulakh, M-14417; Big Khekhtsir Nature Reserve, 23 Jun. 1981, E.M. Bulakh, M-14421; Birobidzhan: Bastak Nature Reserve, 11 Aug. 2006, E.M. Bulakh, VLA M-20979.

Trichaptum biforme (Fr.) Ryvarden

On the fallen twigs and trunks of deciduous trees, Ussuriysk Nature Reserve (Vasilyeva & Bezdeleva, 2006). - On the fallen twigs of *Quercus,* Ussuriysk: Gornotayozhnoye, 24 Jun. 1963, E.M. Bulakh, M-14446; Nikolaevka, 21 Aug. 1954, L.N. Vassiljeva, VLA M-14441; Big Khekhtsir Nature Reserve, 25 Jun. 1981, E.M. Bulakh, M-14447; Birobidzhan: Bastak Nature Reserve, 10 Aug. 2006, E.M. Bulakh, VLA M-21002. - On the fallen twigs of *Betula* in korean pine-broad-leaved forest, Upper Ussuri Station (Azbukina & Kharkevich, 1984). - On the wood, Ussuriysk, 3 Aug. 2003, Tolgor Bau, HMJAU 2859; Dongfanghong, 20 Sept. 2004, Tolgor Bau, HMJAU 2614; Fuyuan, 4, Aug. 2004, Tolgor Bau, HMJAU 2513,

2562, 2583, 2674.

Trichaptum fusco-violaceum (Ehrenb.) Ryvarden

On the log of a coniferous tree, Ussuriysk Nature Reserve (Vasilyeva & Bezdeleva, 2006). - On the log of *Abies nephrolepis* in dark coniferous forest, Upper Ussuri Station (Azbukina & Kharkevich, 1984); Big Khekhtsir Nature Reserve (Azbukina & Kharkevich, 1986).

Trichaptum laricinum (P.Karst.) Ryvarden

On the log of *Abies* in coniferous-broad-leaved forest, Upper Ussuri Station (Azbukina & Kharkevich, 1984). - On the log of *Larix*, Big Khekhtsir Nature Reserve (Azbukina & Kharkevich, 1986).

Tyromyces chioneus (Fr.) P. Karst.

On fallen twigs of *Quercus,* Ussuriysk Nature Reserve (Vasilyeva & Bezdeleva, 2006). - On the logs of *Betula* in coniferous-broad-leaved forest, Upper Ussuri Station (Azbukina & Kharkevich, 1984); Birobidzhan: Bastak Nature Reserve, 10 Aug. 2006, E.M. Bulakh, VLA M-21046.

Tyromyces duracinus (Pat.) Murrill

On the log of *Populus davidiana,* Big Khekhtsir Nature Reserve (Azbukina & Kharkevich, 1986).

Tyromyces kmetii (Bres.) Bondartsev et Singer

On the log of *Pinus koraiensis*, Ussuriysk Nature Reserve, 20 Aug. 1961, L.N. Vassiljeva, VLA M-14590.

Tyromyces lacteus (Fr.) Murrill

On the stump of *Betula lanata* in korean pine-broad-leaved forest, Upper Ussuri Station (Azbukina & Kharkevich, 1984).

LENTINACEAE

Lentinus cyathiformis (Schaeff.) Bres.

On the wood of a deciduous tree, Ussuriysk Nature Reserve (Vasilyeva & Bezdeleva, 2006). - On the wood of *Populus davidiana*, Ussuriysk, 3 Aug. 2003, Tolgor Bau, HMJAU 3278; Upper Ussuri Station, 18 Aug. 1974, E.M. Bulakh, VLA M-190; Raohe: Shengli State Farm, 6 Aug. 2004, E.M. Bulakh, VLA M-20277; Bastak Nature Reserve, 19 Aug. 2002, E.M. Bulakh, VLA M-15198. - On the log of *Betula*, Big Khekhtsir Nature Reserve, 19 08 1983, E.M. Bulakh, VLA M-191. - On the wood of *Populus*, Raohe: Shengli State Farm, 6 Aug. 2004, E.M. Bulakh, VLA M-20277.

Lentinus martianoffianus Kalchbr.

(= *Lentinus pilososquamulosus* Lj. N.Vassiljeva)

On the wood, Ussuriysk Nature Reserve, 26 Aug. 1946, L.N. Vassiljeva, VLA M-445;

Bastak Nature Reserve, 22 Aug. 2003, E.M. Bulakh, VLA M-19125. - On the wood of *Quercus*, Upper Ussuri Station (Azbukina & Kharkevich, 1984).

Lentinus strigosus (Schwein.) Fr.

On the wood of a deciduous tree, Ussuriysk Nature Reserve (Vasilyeva & Bezdeleva, 2006). - On the log of *Betula*, Upper Ussuri Station, 18 Aug. 1973, E.M. Bulakh, VLA M-154. - On the log of a deciduous tree, Big Khekhtsir Nature Reserve (Azbukina & Kharkevich, 1986).

Lentinus suavissimus Fr.

On the fallen twigs of deciduous trees, Ussuriysk: Gornotayozhnoye, 23 Jul. 2002, E.M. Bulakh, VLA M-19054; in oak forest, Khanka Nature Reserve, 27 Jul. 2007, E.M. Bulakh, VLA M-21525; Big Khekhtsir Nature Reserve, 28 Aug. 1983, Upper Ussuri Station, 6 Jul. 1973, E.M. Bulakh, VLA M-169; Bastak Nature Reserve, 6 Sept. 2001, E.M. Bulakh, VLA M-16484. - On the wood of *Acer*, Big Khekhtsir Nature Reserve, 15 08 1981, E.M. Bulakh, VLA M-163.

Neolentinus adhaerens (Alb. et Shwein.) Redhead et Ginns

[= *Lentinus adhaerens* (Alb. et Shwein.) Fr.]

On the log and near the basis of living trunk of *Abies*, Ussuriysk Nature Reserve, 20 Aug. 1969, M.M.Nazarova, VLA M-181. - On the log and roots of *Pinus koraiensis*, Upper Ussuri Station, 26 Aug. 1973, E.M. Bulakh, VLA M-179. - On the logs of deciduous trees, in broad-leaved forest, Khanka Nature Reserve, 28 Jul. 2007, E.M. Bulakh, VLA M-21522; Big Khekhtsir Nature Reserve, 28 Aug. 1983, E.M. Bulakh, VLA M-22639.

Neolentinus lepideus (Fr.) Redhead et Ginns

On the stumps of coniferous trees, Ussuriysk Nature Reserve, 6 Sept. 1975, М.М.Назарова , VLA M-187; Ussuriysk, 3 Aug. 2003, Tolgor Bau, HMJAU 2942; Upper Ussuri Station (Azbukina & Kharkevich, 1984); Big Khekhtsir Nature Reserve, 20 Sept. 1981, E.M. Bulakh, VLA M-207; Bastak Nature Reserve, 6 Sept. 2001, E.M. Bulakh, VLA M-16490. - On the rotten wood, Ussuriysk, 3 Aug. 2003, Tolgor Bau, HMJAU 2942; Hulin, 20 Sept. 2004, Tolgor Bau, HMJAU 2615.

Neolentinus sulcatus (Berk.) Singer

On the wood of a building, Tikhorechnoye, 10 Jun. 1989, E.M. Bulakh, VLA M-221. - On the log, Arkhipovka, 4 May 2004, E.M. Bulakh, VLA M-19357.

Panus ciliatus (Lév.) T.W. May et A.E. Wood

On the fallen twigs of *Betula*, Ussuriysk Nature Reserve (Vasilyeva & Bezdeleva, 2006); Big Khekhtsir Nature Reserve, 20 Aug. 1983, E.M. Bulakh, VLA M-184.

Panus conchatus (Bull.) Fr.   Plate 19: 114

[= *Lentinus torulosus* (Pers.) Lloyd]

On the log of *Betula*, Upper Ussuri Station, 19 Aug. 1973, E.M. Bulakh, VLA M-177. - On the wood, Ussuriysk, 3 Aug. 2003, Tolgor Bau, HMJAU 2966; Big Khekhtsir

Nature Reserve, 16 Aug. 2004, Tolgor Bau, HMJAU 2964; Fuyuan, 4 Aug. 2004, Tolgor Bau, HMJAU 2620.

Phyllotopsis nidulans (Pers.) Singer   Plate 20: 115

On the logs of deciduous trees in korean pine-broad-leaved forest, Ussuriysk Nature Reserve, 4 Oct. 1963, M.M. Nazarova, VLA M-452; Tikhorechnoye, 10 Sept. 1978, E.M. Bulakh, VLA M-456. - On the fallen twigs of *Acer* in dark coniferous forest, Upper Ussuri Station, 6 Sept. 1975, E.M. Bulakh, VLA M-448; Big Khekhtsir Nature Reserve, 14 Sept. 1981, E.M. Bulakh, VLA M-447. - On the rotten wood, Raohe, 9 Aug. 2004, Tolgor Bau, HMJAU 2510.

Pleurotus calyptratus (Lindblad) Sacc.

On the trunks of *Populus*, Ussuriysk Nature Reserve, 21 Jun. 1945, E.M. Bulakh, VLA M-1; Arkhipovka, 25 May 2004, E.M. Bulakh, VLA M-19351. - On the trunk of *Populus davidiana*, Big Khekhtsir Nature Reserve (Azbukina & Kharkevich, 1986).

Pleurotus citrinopileatus Singer   Plate 20: 116

On the logs of *Ulmus*, Ussuriysk Nature Reserve, 15 Jul. 1961, L.N. Vassiljeva, VLA M-15; Upper Ussuri Station, 11 Aug. 1990, E.M. Bulakh, VLA M-8; Ussuriysk, 3 Aug. 2003, Tolgor Bau, HMJAU 2993. - On the logs of *Tilia*, Big Khekhtsir Nature Reserve, 11 Aug. 1981, E.M. Bulakh, VLA M-16; Bastak Nature Reserve, 16 Aug. 2000, E.M. Bulakh, VLA M-15443. - On the wood in forest, Raohe, 7, 8 Aug. 2004, Tolgor Bau, HMJAU 2514, 2643.

Pleurotus djamor (Fr.) Boedijn

(= *Pleurotus salmoneostramineus* Lj.N. Vassiljeva)

On the trunks of *Phellodendron amurense*, Ussuriysk Nature Reserve, 16 Jul. 1969, M.M. Nazarova, VLA M-122; Ussuriysk: Gornotayozhnoye, 4 Aug. 2002, E.M. Bulakh, VLA M-17746; Ussuriysk, 3 Aug. 2003, Tolgor Bau, HMJAU 2909. - On the logs of *Maackia amurensis*, Khanka Nature Reserve, 28 Aug. 2002, E.M. Bulakh, VLA M-19062; Tikhorechnoye, 8 Aug. 1977, E.M. Bulakh, VLA M-126. - On the log of *Ulmus*, Big Khekhtsir Nature Reserve 11 Aug. 1981, E.M. Bulakh, M-129.

Pleurotus dryinus (Pers.) P. Kumm.

On the trunks of *Quercus*, Ussuriysk Nature Reserve, 25 Aug. 2002, E.M. Bulakh, VLA M-19706; Bastak Nature Reserve, 7 Sept. 2001, E.M. Bulakh, VLA M-16481. - On the log of *Fraxinus*, Big Khekhtsir Nature Reserve, 5 Sept. 1983, E.M. Bulakh, VLA M-30.

Pleurotus ostreatus (Jacq.) P. Kumm.   Plate 20: 117

On the trunk of *Ulmus*, Ussuriysk Nature Reserve, 16 Aug. 1962, M.M. Nazarova, VLA M-74. - On the trunk of *Betula*, Upper Ussuri Station, 20 Jun. 1974, E.M. Bulakh, VLA M-55. - On the wood of deciduous trees, Tikhorechnoye, 28 Jul. 1984, E.M. Bulakh, VLA M-70; Big Khekhtsir Nature Reserve (Azbukina & Kharkevich, 1986).

Pleurotus pulmonarius (Fr.) Quél.   Plate 20: 118

On the logs of deciduous trees, Ussuriysk Nature Reserve, 3 Jul. 1990, E.M. Bulakh,

VLA M-93; Khanka Nature Reserve, 21 Aug. 2002, E.M. Bulakh, M-17182; Ussuriysk, 3 Aug. 2003, Tolgor Bau, HMJAU 2505, 2756, 2804, 2830. 2938; Bastak Nature Reserve, 13 Aug. 2000, E.M. Bulakh, VLA M-15263; Raohe, 7 Aug. 2004, Tolgor Bau, HMJAU 2506, 2646, 2647; Fuyuan, 5 Aug. 2004, Tolgor Bau, HMJAU 2525, 25762687. - On the trunk of *Maackia amurensis*, Tikhorechnoye, 2 Jul. 1988, E.M. Bulakh, VLA M-105. - On the logs of *Betula*, Upper Ussuri Station, 2 Aug. 1974, E.M. Bulakh, VLA M-97; Big Khekhtsir Nature Reserve, 25 Aug. 1983, E.M. Bulakh, VLA M-108.

POLYPORACEAE

Coriolopsis aspera (Jungh.) Teng

On the wood, Raohe, Tolgor Bau, HMJAU 3429.

Dichomitus squalens (P. Karst.) D.A. Reid

On the log of *Larix,* Big Khekhtsir Nature Reserve (Azbukina & Kharkevich, 1986). - On the log of *Picea ajanensis*, Upper Ussuri Station (Azbukina & Kharkevich, 1984).

Jahnoporus hirtus (Quél.) Nuss

On the logs of coniferous trees in coniferous broad-leaved forest, Ussuriysk Nature Reserve, 21 Aug. 1963, M.M. Nazarova, VLA M-141431; Upper Ussuri Station (Azbukina & Kharkevich, 1984); Birobidzhan: Bastak Nature Reserve, 14 Aug. 2006, E.M. Bulakh, VLA M-21005.

Microporus affinis (Blume et T. Nees) Kuntze

[= *Microporus luteus* (Nees) Pat.]

On the fallen twigs of *Carpinus*, Ussuriysk Nature Reserve, 17 Aug. 1962, M.M. Nazarova, VLA M-14178.

Polyporus admirabilis Peck

(= *Piptoporus fraxineus* Bondartsev et Ljub.)

On the living trunk of *Fraxinus*, Ussuriysk Nature Reserve (Vasilyeva & Bezdeleva, 2006).

Polyporus alveolarius (DC.) Bondartsev et Singer

On the trunks of deciduous trees, Ussuriysk Nature Reserve (Vasilyeva & Bezdeleva, 2006); Khanka Nature Reserve, 29 Jul. 2007, E.M. Bulakh, VLA M-21501; Birobidzhan: Bastak Nature Reserve, 14 Aug. 2006, E.M. Bulakh, VLA M-21042. - On the logs of *Picea* and *Abies* in coniferous-broad-leaved forest, Upper Ussuri Station, deciduous forest, 31 Aug. 1974, E.M. Bulakh, VLA M-14275.

Polyporus arcularius (Batsch) Fr.

On the trunk of a deciduous tree, Ussuriysk Nature Reserve, 6 Aug. 1962, M.M. Nazarova, VLA M-14282. - On the log of *Betula,* Upper Ussuri Station (Azbukina & Kharkevich, 1984). - On the logs of *Maackia amurensis*, *Syringa amurensis* and *Vitis amurensis*, Big Khekhtsir Nature Reserve (Azbukina & Kharkevich, 1986).

Polyporus brumalis (Pers.) Fr.

On the wood of a deciduous tree, Ussuriysk Nature Reserve, 20 Sept. 1975, M.M. Nazarova, VLA M-14306. - On the fallen twigs of *Populus*, Upper Ussuri Station (Azbukina & Kharkevich, 1984).

Polyporus ciliatus Fr.

On the fallen twigs of *Quercus*, Upper Ussuri Station (Azbukina & Kharkevich, 1984).

Polyporus leprieurii Mont.

On the log in coniferous-broad-leaved forest, Upper Ussuri Station (Azbukina & Kharkevich, 1984).

Polyporus melanopus (Pers.) Fr.

On the wood of a deciduous tree, Birobidzhan: Bastak Nature Reserve, 13 Aug. 2006, E.M. Bulakh, VLA M-21043.

Polyporus mongolicus (Pilát) Y.C.Dai

On the rotten wood, Hulin, 19 Sept. 2004, Tolgor Bau, HMJAU 3415.

Polyporus squamosus (Huds.) Fr.   Plate 20: 119

On the logs of *Alnus* and *Ulmus,* Ussuriysk, 3 Aug. 2004, Tolgor Bau, HMJAU, 2987; Ussuriysk Nature Reserve (Vasilyeva & Bezdeleva, 2006); Upper Ussuri Station (Azbukina & Kharkevich, 1984). - On the wood of deciduous trees, Big Khekhtsir Nature Reserve, 22 Jun. 1981, E.M. Bulakh, VLA M-14323; Ussuriysk, 3 Aug. 2003, Tolgor Bau, 2987.

Polyporus subadmirabilis Bondartsev

On the log of a deciduous tree, Ussuriysk Nature Reserve (Bondartsev, 1962).

Polyporus umbellatus (Pers.) Fr.

On the ground under the tree of *Quercus*, Big Khekhtsir Nature Reserve, 25 Jun. 1981, E.M. Bulakh, VLA M-13771.

Polyporus varius (Pers.) Fr.

On the fallen twigs of *Carpinus*, Ussuriysk Nature Reserve, 21 Jun. 1961, L.N. Vassiljeva, VLA M-14349. - On the log of *Alnus*, Upper Ussuri Station (Azbukina & Kharkevich, 1984). - On the fallen branch of *Fraxinus mandshurica*, Big Khekhtsir Nature Reserve (Azbukina & Kharkevich, 1986). - On the wood, Hulin, 19, 20 Sept. 2004, Tolgor Bau, HMJAU 2609, 2669; Fuyuan, 4 Aug. 2004, Tolgor Bau, HMJAU 2601.

Royoporus badius (Pers.) A.B. De

[= *Polyporus badius* (Pers.) Schwein.]

On the wood of *Quercus*, Ussuriysk Nature Reserve, 7 Aug. 1961, O.K. Govorova, VLA M-14298. - On the log of *Picea* in coniferous-broad-leaved forest, Upper Ussuri Station (Azbukina & Kharkevich, 1984). - On the rotten wood, Fuyuan, 4-5 Aug. 2004, Tolgor Bau, 2555, 2638; Raohe, 8 Sep. 2003, 7 Aug. 2004 Tolgor Bau, HMJAU 3030, 2516; Ussuriysk, 3 Aug. 2003, Tolgor Bau, HMJAU 2832, 2862; Big Khekhtsir Nature

Reserve (Azbukina & Kharkevich, 1986). - On the log of *Larix*, Birobidzhan: Bastak Nature Reserve, 10 Aug. 2006, E.M. Bulakh, VLA M-21003.

RUSSULALES

RUSSULACEAE

Lactarius acerrimus Britzelm.

[= *Lactarius insulsus* (Fr.) Fr. sensu A.A. Pearson, auct. Eur.]

Under the trees of *Quercus* in oak forest, Ussuriysk Nature Reserve, 23 Aug. 1975, M.M. Nazarova, VLA M-9876; Ussuriysk: Gornotayozhnoye, 19 Aug. 1963, M.M. Nazarova, VLA M-9879; Osinovka, 11 Sept. 1951, L.N. Vassiljeva, VLA M-9874; Khorol, 4 Aug. 1985, E.M. Bulakh, VLA M-9877; Tikhorechnoye, 28 Aug. 1984, E.M. Bulakh, VLA M-9884; Birobidzhan: Bastak Nature Reserve, 14 Aug. 2006, E.M. Bulakh, VLA M-20924.

Lactarius acris (Bolton) Gray

Under the bush of *Corylus* in broad-leaved forest, Osinovka, 14 Aug. 1954, L.N. Vassiljeva, VLA M-9559.

Lactarius aspideus (Fr.) Fr.

On the ground in dark coniferous forest, Ussuriysk Nature Reserve (Vasilyeva & Bezdeleva, 2006).

Lactarius aurantiacoochraceus Lj.N. Vassiljeva

Under the trees of *Betula* in fir-broad-leaved forest, Ussuriysk Nature Reserve, 4 Sept. 1963, M.M. Nazarova, VLA M-9568; in dark coniferous forest, Big Khekhtsir Nature Reserve, 7 Sept.1983, E.M. Bulakh, VLA M-9567, 16 Aug. 2004, Tolgor Bau, HMJAU 3202; Birobidzhan: Bastak Nature Reserve, 18 Aug. 2000, E.M. Bulakh, VLA M-15344.

Lactarius aurantiacus (Pers.) Gray

[= *Lactarius mitissimus* (Fr.) Fr.]

Under the trees of *Pinus koraiensis* in korean pine-broad-leaved forest, Ussuriysk Nature Reserve, 4 Oct. 2000, E.M. Bulakh, VLA M-13572; in dark coniferous forest, Upper Ussuri Station, 15 Sept. 1974, E.M. Bulakh, VLA M-9916.

Lactarius azonites (Bull.) Fr.

Under the trees of *Betula* in korean pine-broad-leaved forest, Ussuriysk Nature Reserve, 25 Aug. 1975, M.M. Nazarova, VLA M-9616; Ussuriysk, 3 Aug. 2003, Tolgor Bau, HMJAU 2903; in broad-leaved forest, Tikhorechnoye, 10 Aug. 1977, E.M. Bulakh, VLA M-9599; Khorol, 4 Aug. 1985, E.M. Bulakh, VLA M-9585; Spassk-Dalny: Slavinka, 18 Aug. 1981, E.M. Bulakh, VLA M-9601; Big Khekhtsir Nature Reserve, 3 Aug. 1981, E.M. Bulakh, VLA M-9603; Birobidzhan: Bastak Nature Reserve, 16 Aug. 2000, E.M. Bulakh, VLA M-15327; in dark coniferous forest, Upper Ussuri Station, 20 Aug. 1975, E.M. Bulakh, VLA M-9614.

Lactarius camphoratus (Bull.) Fr.

On the log of *Betula* in korean pine-broad-leaved forest, Ussuriysk Nature Reserve, 27 Sept. 1961, L.N. Vassiljeva, VLA M-9620.

Lactarius chrysorheus Fr.

Under the trees of *Quercus* in korean pine-broad-leaved forest, Ussuriysk Nature Reserve, 27 Aug. 1963, M.M. Nazarova, VLA M-9624; in broad-leaved forest, Big Khekhtsir Nature Reserve, 8 Aug. 1981, E.M. Bulakh, VLA M-9637; Birobidzhan: Bastak Nature Reserve, 13 Aug. 2006, E.M. Bulakh, VLA M-20930.

Lactarius circellatus (Battara) Fr.

Under the trees of *Betula* and bush of *Corylus* in deciduous forest, Ussuriysk Nature Reserve, 1 Sept. 1963, L.N. Vassiljeva, VLA M-9648; Ussuriysk, 7 Aug. 2003, Tolgor Bau, HMJAU 2881. - Under the trees of *Betula* in birch forest, Khanka Nature Reserve, 28 Jul. 2002 V.Yu. Barkalov, VLA M-17478; Bikin, 3 Sept. 1945, L.N. Vassiljeva, VLA M-9650. - Under the trees of *Quercus* in oak forest, Big Khekhtsir Nature Reserve, 8 Aug. 1981, E.M. Bulakh, VLA M-9665; Birobidzhan: Bastak Nature Reserve, 19 Aug. 2000, E.M. Bulakh, VLA M-15318; Raohe: Shengli State Farm, 6 Aug. 2004, E.M. Bulakh, VLA M-20657.

Lactarius controversus (Pers.) Fr.

Under the trees of *Populus* in poplar forest, Ussuriysk Nature Reserve, 19 Aug. 1961, L.N. Vassiljeva, VLA M-9674; Osinovka, 15 Aug. 1954, L.N. Vassiljeva, VLA M-9676; Spassk Dalny: Novo-Vladimirovka, 20 Aug. 1981, E.M. Bulakh, VLA M-9672.

Lactarius deliciosus (L.) Gray   Plate 20: 120

Under the trees of *Pinus koraiensis*, *Abies* and *Picea* in dark coniferous forest, Ussuriysk Nature Reserve (Vasilyeva & Bezdeleva, 2006); Upper Ussuri Station, 17 Aug. 1974, E.M. Bulakh, VLA M-9698; Big Khekhtsir Nature Reserve, 14 Aug. 1981, E.M. Bulakh, VLA M-9700; Birobidzhan: Bastak Nature Reserve, 9 Sept. 2001, E.M. Bulakh, VLA M-16385.

Lactarius flavidulus S. Imai

Under the trees of *Abies* in coniferous-broad-leaved forest, Ussuriysk Nature Reserve, 15 Sept. 1961, L.N. Vassiljeva, VLA M-9741; in dark coniferous forest, Big Khekhtsir Nature Reserve, 14 Aug. 1981, E.M. Bulakh, VLA M-9700; Birobidzhan: Bastak Nature Reserve, 19 Aug. 2000, E.M. Bulakh, VLA M-15318.

Lactarius flexuosus (Pers.) Gray

Under the tree of *Populus davidiana* in aspen forest, Big Khekhtsir Nature Reserve, 21 Jun. 1981, E.M. Bulakh, VLA M-9754; under the tree of *Betula*, Birobidzhan: Bastak Nature Reserve, 14 Aug. 2006, E.M. Bulakh, VLA M-20922.

Lactarius fuliginosus (Fr.) Fr.

On the ground in coniferous-broad-leaved forest, Ussuriysk Nature Reserve (Vasilyeva & Bezdeleva, 2006); in oak forest, Fuyuan, 4 Aug. 2004, E.M. Bulakh, VLA M-19620.

Lactarius fulvissimus Romagn.

(= *Lactarius ichoratus* sensu auct.)

On the decayed wood under the trees of *Betula* in korean pine-broad-leaved forest, Ussuriysk Nature Reserve (Vasilyeva & Bezdeleva, 2006); in dark coniferous forest, Upper Ussuri Station, 15. Aug. 1974, E.M. Bulakh VLA M-9865; in birch forest, Upper Ussuri Station, 15 Aug. 1974, E.M. Bulakh, VLA M-9865; Birobidzhan: Bastak Nature Reserve, 19 Aug. 2003, E.M. Bulakh, VLA M-19059.

Lactarius glutinopallens F.H. Møller et J.E. Lange

On the ground in korean pine-broad-leaved forest, Ussuriysk Nature Reserve, 26 Sept. 1946, L.N. Vassiljeva, VLA M-9781; Birobidzhan: Bastak Nature Reserve, 11 Aug. 2006, E.M. Bulakh, VLA M-20928; in dark coniferous forest, Upper Ussuri Station, 17 Sept. 1974, E.M. Bulakh, VLA M-9779.

Lactarius glyciosmus (Fr.) Fr.

Under the trees of *Betula* in birch forest, Ussuriysk Nature Reserve, 4 Sept. 1963, M.M. Nazarova, VLA M-9804; Ussuriysk, 3 Aug. 2004, Tolgor Bau, HMJAU 3194; Khanka Nature Reserve, 28 Aug. 2002, E.M. Bulakh, VLA M-18097; in dark coniferous forest, Upper Ussuri Station, 17 Sept. 1974, E.M. Bulakh, VLA M-9791; Big Khekhtsir Nature Reserve, 15 Aug. 1981, E.M. Bulakh, VLA M-9806; Birobidzhan: Bastak Nature Reserve, 11 Aug. 2001, E.M. Bulakh, VLA M-16387.

Lactarius grandisporus Lj.N. Vassiljeva

On the ground in broad-leaved forest, Ussuriysk Nature Reserve, 5 Sept. 1996, E.M. Bulakh, VLA M-9813.

Lactarius griseus Peck

Under the trees of *Alnus* in alder forest, Big Khekhtsir Nature Reserve, 12 Sept. 1946, L.N. Vassiljeva, VLA M-9833; Birobidzhan: Bastak Nature Reserve, 12 Sept. 2001, E.M. Bulakh, VLA M-16076.

Lactarius hatsudake Tanaka

On the ground in broad-leaved forest, 9 Aug. 2004, Tolgor Bau, HMJAU 3347.

Lactarius hysginus (Fr.) Fr.

Under the trees of *Betula* in dark coniferous forest, Upper Ussuri Station, 16 Sept. 1975, E.M. Bulakh, VLA M-9844; in birch forest, Big Khekhtsir Nature Reserve, 29 Jun. 1981, E.M. Bulakh, VLA M-9848; Birobidzhan: Bastak Nature Reserve, 16 Aug. 2002, E.M. Bulakh, VLA M-17256.

Lactarius lacunarum Romagn. et Hora

(= *Lactarius decipiens* Quél.)

Under the trees of *Pinus koraiensis* in korean pine-broad-leaved forest, Ussuriysk Nature Reserve, 10 Sept. 1961, L.N.Vasiljeva, VLA M-9684; Upper Ussuri Station, 22 Aug. 1975, E.M. Bulakh, VLA M-9681.

Lactarius lignyotus Fr.

On the basis of the trunk of *Pinus koraiensis* in fir-broad-leaved forest, Ussuriysk Nature Reserve, 7 Aug. 1975, E.M. Bulakh, VLA M-9890. - On the ground in korean pine forest, Upper Ussuri Station, 22 Aug. 1975, E.M. Bulakh, VLA M-9901; in dark coniferous forest, Big Khekhtsir Nature Reserve, 15 Aug. 1981, E.M. Bulakh, VLA M-9907, 16 Aug. 2004, Tolgor Bau, HMJAU 3251, 3214; Birobidzhan: Bastak Nature Reserve, 10 Aug. 2006, E.M. Bulakh, VLA M-20929; Mishan, 1 Sept. 2003, Tolgor Bau, HMJAU 3351; Raohe, 6 Aug. 2004, Tolgor Bau, HMJAU 3198, 3215, 3284; Hutou, 8 Sept. 2003, Tolgor Bau, HMJAU 3305; Hulin, 9 Aug. 2004, Tolgor Bau, HMJAU 3307.

Lactarius obscuratus (Lasch) Fr.

Under the trees of *Alnus* in alder forest, Ussuriysk Nature Reserve, 28 Aug. 1962, L.N. Vassiljeva, VLA M-9962; Birobidzhan: Bastak Nature Reserve, 10 Aug. 2006, E.M. Bulakh, VLA M-20925.

Lactarius piperatus (L.) Pers.

Under the trees of *Quercus* in oak forest, Ussuriysk Nature Reserve, 23 Aug. 1975, M.M. Nazarova, VLA M-9986; Ussuriyisk: Gornotayozhnoye, 19 Aug. 1963, M.M. Nazarova, VLA M-9889; Khanka Nature Reserve, 25 Jul. 2002, V.Yu. Barkalov, VLA M-17476; Upper Ussuri Station, 7 Sept. 1975, E.M. Bulakh, VLA M-9971; Big Khekhtsir Nature Reserve, 1 Sept. 1983, E.M. Bulakh, VLA M-9981, 16 Aug. 2004, Tolgor Bau, HMJAU 3420; Birobidzhan: Bastak Nature Reserve, Tolgor Bau, HMJAU 2775, 2948; Fuyuan, 5 Aug. 2004, Tolgor Bau, HMJAU 2676.

Lactarius porninsis Rolland

Under the tree of *Larix,* Birobidzhan: Bastak Nature Reserve, 12 Sept. 2001, E.M. Bulakh, VLA M-16375.

Lactarius pterosporus Romagn.

On the ground in broad-leaved forest, 16 Aug. 2004, Tolgor Bau, HMJAU 3332.

Lactarius pubescens (Fr.) Fr.

Under the trees of *Betula* in coniferous-broad-leaved forest, Ussuriysk Nature Reserve, 15 Sept. 1961, L.N. Vassiljeva, VLA M-10014; in birch forest, Khanka Nature Reserve, 26 Jul. 2002, V.Yu. Barkalov, VLA M-17455; Upper Ussuri Station, 28 Aug. 1974, E.M. Bulakh, VLA M-10020; Big Khekhtsir Nature Reserve, 16 Aug. 1981, E.M. Bulakh, VLA M-10005, 16 Aug. 2004, Tolgor Bau, HMJAU 2920; Birobidzhan: Bastak Nature Reserve, 7 Sept. 2001, E.M. Bulakh, VLA M-16388.

Lactarius pyrogalus (Bull.) Fr.

On the ground in korean pine-broad-leaved forest, Ussuriysk Nature Reserve (Vasilyeva & Bezdeleva, 2006). - Under the bush of *Corylus* in broad-leaved forest, Osinovka, 11 Sept. 1951, L.N. Vassiljeva, VLA M-10032. - Under the trees of *Betula* in birch forest, Khorol, 4 Aug. 1985, E.M. Bulakh, VLA M-10036; Upper Ussuri Station, 17 Sept. 1974, E.M. Bulakh,

VLA M-10031; in dark coniferous forest, Big Khekhtsir Nature Reserve, 15 Sept. 1981, E.M. Bulakh, VLA M-10027.

Lactarius quietus (Fr.) Fr.

Under the trees of *Quercus* in oak forest, Ussuriysk Nature Reserve, 21 Aug. 2004, E.M. Bulakh, VLA M-20420; Ussuriysk, 3 Aug. 2003, Tolgor Bau, HMJAU 3211; Khorol, 4 Aug. 1985, E.M. Bulakh, VLA M-10039; Birobidzhan: Bastak Nature Reserve, 23 Aug. 2003, E.M. Bulakh, VLA M-19263; Hailin Mudanjiang, 9 Aug. 2004, Tolgor Bau, HMJAU 2589; Raohe, 7 Aug. 2004, Tolgor Bau, HMJAU 3389.

Lactarius repraesentaneus Britzelm.

Under the trees of *Betula* in birch-oak forest, Khorol, 14 Aug. 1954, L.N. Vassiljeva, VLA M-10068; Birobidzhan: Bastak Nature Reserve, 13 Aug. 2000, E.M. Bulakh, VLA M-15320.

Lactarius resimus (Fr.) Fr.

On the ground in korean pine-broad-leaved forest, Ussuriysk Nature Reserve (Vasilyeva & Bezdeleva, 2006); in birch-oak forest, Ussuriysk: Gornotayozhnoye, 23 Aug. 1945 L.N. Vassiljeva, VLA M-10076. - Under the trees of *Betula* in birch-oak forest, Nikolaevka, 19 Sept. 2000, E.M. Bulakh, VLA M-15127; in broad-leaved forest, Big Khekhtsir Nature Reserve, leaves, 10 Aug. 1981, E.M. Bulakh, VLA M-10074.

Lactarius rufus (Scop.) Fr.

Under the tree of *Larix,* Birobidzhan: Bastak Nature Reserve, 13 Aug. 2002, E.M. Bulakh, VLA M-17293.

Lactarius sakamotoi S. Imai

Under the trees of *Picea* and *Abies* in fir-broad-leaved forest, Ussuriysk Nature Reserve, 19 Sept. 1975, M.M. Nazarova, VLA M-10111; in dark coniferous forest, Upper Ussuri Station, 6 Sept. 1975, E.M. Bulakh, VLA M-10109; Big Khekhtsir Nature Reserve, 26 Sept. 1946, L.N. Vassiljeva, VLA M-10108.

Lactarius sanguifluus (Paulet) Fr.

Under the trees of *Pinus densiflora* in pine forest, Nikolaevka, 21 Aug. 2002 E.M. Bulakh, VLA M-17473; Barabash-Levada: Shirokaya Canyon, 30 Aug. 2002, E.M. Bulakh, VLA M-19075.

Lactarius scrobiculatus (Scop.) Fr.

On the ground in fir-broad-leaved forest, Ussuriysk Nature Reserve, 22 Sept. 1975, M.M. Nazarova, VLA M-10119. - Under the tree of *Betula* in coniferous-broad-leaved forest, Upper Ussuri Station, 8 Sept. 1974, E.M. Bulakh, VLA M-10112.

Lactarius serifluus (DC.) Fr.

Under the trees of *Quercus* in korean pine-broad-leaved forest, Ussuriysk Nature Reserve, 2 Sept. 1963, M.M. Nazarova, VLA M-10144; in dark coniferous forest, Upper Ussuri Station, 9 Sept. 1973, E.M. Bulakh, VLA M-10135. - Under the tree of *Betula* in dark coniferous forest, Big Khekhtsir Nature Reserve, 14 Aug. 1981, E.M. Bulakh, VLA M-10140.

Lactarius subdulcis (Bull.) Gray

On the ground under the trees of *Betula* in coniferous-broad-leaved forest, Ussuriysk Nature Reserve, 15 Sept. 1962, M.M. Nazarova, VLA M-10147; Upper Ussuri Station, 15 Sept. 1974, E.M. Bulakh, VLA M-10126; in broad-leaved forest, Ussuriysk: Gornotayozhnoye, 4 Aug. 2002, E.M. Bulakh, VLA M-19081.

Lactarius thejogalus (Fr.) Fr.

Under the trees of *Betula* in korean pine-broad-leaved forest, Ussuriysk Nature Reserve (Vasilyeva & Bezdeleva, 2006); in birch forest, Khanka Nature Reserve, 28 Aug. 2003, E.M. Bulakh, VLA M-19096, 4 Aug. 2003, Tolgor Bau, HMJAU 2899; Big Khekhtsir Nature Reserve, 21 Aug. 1983 E.M. Bulakh, VLA M-10172; in oak forest, Tikhorechnoye, 28 Jul. 1984, E.M. Bulakh, VLA M-10170.

Lactarius torminosus (Schaeff.) Gray   Plate 21: 121

On the ground under the trees of *Betula* in birch forest, Ussuriysk Nature Reserve, 4 Sept. 1975, M.M. Nazarova, VLA M-10190; Upper Ussuri Station, 18 Sept. 1974, E.M. Bulakh, VLA M-10182; Big Khekhtsir Nature Reserve, E.M.Bulakh, VLA M-20682; Birobidzhan: Bastak Nature Reserve, 6 Aug. 2001, E.M. Bulakh, VLA M-16809; Raohe 6-7 Aug. 2004, Tolgor Bau, HMJAU 3338, 3357; Hulin, 9 Aug. 2004, Tolgor Bau, HMJAU 3342.

Lactarius trivialis (Fr.) Fr.

On the ground in dark coniferous forest, Upper Ussuri Station, 20 Aug. 1975, E.M. Bulakh, VLA M-10213. - Under the trees of *Abies* in dark coniferous forest, Big Khekhtsir Nature Reserve, 15 Sept. 1981, E.M. Bulakh, VLA M-10209, 16 Aug. 2004, Tolgor Bau, HMJAU 3334. - Under the tree of *Larix*, Birobidzhan: Bastak Nature Reserve, 9 Sept. 2001, E.M. Bulakh, VLA M-16395.

Lactarius turpis Fr.

Under the trees of *Betula* in fir-broad-leaved forest, Ussuriysk Nature Reserve, 24 Aug. 1975, M.M. Nazarova, VLA M-9938; in birch forest, Upper Ussuri Station, 17 Sept. 1974, E.M. Bulakh, VLA M-9933; in dark coniferous forest, Big Khekhtsir Nature Reserve, 15 Sept. 1981, E.M. Bulakh, VLA M-9935; Birobidzhan: Bastak Nature Reserve, 18 Aug. 2000, E.M. Bulakh, VLA M-15337; Hutou, 8 Sept. 2003, Tolgor Bau, HMJAU 3287, 3368.

Lactarius uvidus (Fr.) Fr.   Plate 21: 122

Under the trees of *Betula* in moist birch forest, Ussuriysk Nature Reserve, 4 Sept. 1975, M.M. Nazarova, VLA M-10265; in dark coniferous forest, Upper Ussuri Station, 17 Sept. 1974, E.M. Bulakh, VLA M-10241; Bikin, 20 Aug. 1946, L.N. Vassiljeva, VLA M-10264; Big Khekhtsir Nature Reserve, 25 Aug. 1983, E.M. Bulakh, VLA M-10288; Birobidzhan: Bastak Nature Reserve, 6 Sept. 2001, E.M. Bulakh, VLA M-16392.

Lactarius vellereus (Fr.) Fr.

Under the trees of *Betula* in coniferous-broad-leaved forest, Ussuriysk Nature Reserve, 4

Sept. 1963, M.M. Nazarova, VLA M-10305; in dark coniferous forest, Upper Ussuri Station, 14 Aug. 1974, E.M. Bulakh, VLA M-1029 ; in broad-leaved forest, Big Khekhtsir Nature Reserve, 21 Aug. 1983, E.M. Bulakh, VLA M-10307, 17 Aug. 2004, Tolgor Bau, HMJAU 3001; Birobidzhan: Bastak Nature Reserve, 6 Sept. 2001, E.M. Bulakh, VLA M-16365; Raohe, 7 Aug. 2004, Tolgor Bau, HMJAU 3330.

Lactarius vietus (Fr.) Fr.

Under the trees of *Betula* in coniferous-broad-leaved forest, Ussuriysk Nature Reserve (Vasilyeva & Bezdeleva, 2006); Upper Ussuri Station, 21 Aug. 1974, E.M. Bulakh, VLA M-10326; Bikin, 20 Aug. 1945, L.N. Vassiljeva, VLA M-10328; in dark coniferous forest, Big Khekhtsir Nature Reserve, 15 Aug. 1981, E.M. Bulakh, VLA M-10320; Birobidzhan: Bastak Nature Reserve, 13 Aug. 2000, E.M. Bulakh, VLA M-15330.

Lactarius vinaceorufescens A.H. Sm.

Under the trees of *Picea* and *Abies* in dark coniferous forest, Ussuriysk Nature Reserve, 24 Sept. 1946, L.N. Vassiljeva, VLA M-10368; Upper Ussuri Station, 6 Sept. 1975, E.M. Bulakh, VLA M-10364; Big Khekhtsir Nature Reserve, 15 Aug. 1981, E.M. Bulakh, VLA M-10371; Birobidzhan: Bastak Nature Reserve, 17 Sept. 2002, E.M. Bulakh, VLA M-17252.

Lactarius violascens (J. Otto) Fr.

Under the tree of *Quercus* in korean pine-broad-leaved forest, Ussuriysk Nature Reserve, 21 Aug. 1975, M.M. Nazarova, VLA M-10395.

Lactarius volemus (Fr.) Fr.   Plate 21: 123

Under the trees of *Quercus* in korean pine-broad-leaved forest, Ussuriysk Nature Reserve, 18 Aug. 1962, M.M. Nazarova, VLA M-10418; in oak forest, Ussuriysk, 3 Aug. 2003, Tolgor Bau, HMJAU 3269; Ussuriysk: Gornotayozhnoye, 23 Aug. 1945, L.N. Vassiljeva, VLA M-10421; Nikolaevka, 20 Sept. 1954, L.N. Vassiljeva, VLA M-10406; Upper Ussuri Station, 12 Sept. 1975, E.M. Bulakh, VLA M-10404; Big Khekhtsir Nature Reserve, 25 Aug. 1983, E.M. Bulakh, VLA M-10415; Birobidzhan: Bastak Nature Reserve, 7 Sept. 2001, E.M. Bulakh, VLA M-16384; Hulin, 19 Sept. 2004, Tolgor Bau, HMJAU 2611.

Lactarius zonarius (Bull.) Fr.

Under the trees of *Quercus* in broad-leaved forest, Ussuriysk Nature Reserve, 6 Sept. 1962, M.M. Nazarova, VLA M-10450; Novotroitskoye, 22 Jul. 1998, E.M. Bulakh, VLA M-10556.

Russula adusta (Pers.) Fr.

Under the trees of *Betula* korean pine-broad-leaved forest, Ussuriysk Nature Reserve, 7 Aug. 1975, M.M. Nazarova, VLA M-8283; in birch forest, Khanka Nature Reserve, 19 Jun. 2002, V.Yu. Barkalov, VLA M-17234. - Under the trees of *Quercus* in oak forest, Ussuriysk: Gornotayozhnoye, 6 Aug. 2002, E.M. Bulakh, VLA M-19090; Spassk Dalny: Slavinka, 18 Jul. 1981, E.M. Bulakh, VLA M-8277; Birobidzhan: Bastak Nature Reserve, 14 Aug. 2006, E.M. Bulakh, VLA M-20. - Under the trees of *Abies* and *Picea* in korean pine forest, Upper Ussuri

Station, 21 Aug. 1975, E.M. Bulakh, VLA M-8254; in dark coniferous forest, Big Khekhtsir Nature Reserve, 14 Aug. 1981, E.M. Bulakh, VLA M-8257.

Russula aeruginea Fr.

On the ground in fir-broad-leaved forest, Ussuriysk Nature Reserve (Vasilyeva & Bezdeleva, 2006); in the stand of *Pinus,* Khorol, 4 Aug. 1985, E.M. Bulakh, VLA M-8295; Osinovka, 14 Sept. 1954, L.N.Vassilleva, VLA M-8308; in birch forest, Upper Ussuri Station, 26 Aug. 1973, E.M. Bulakh, VLA M-8287. - Under the trees of *Betula* in broad-leaved forest, Big Khekhtsir Nature Reserve, 5 Sept. 1983, E.M. Bulakh, VLA M-8293; Birobidzhan: Bastak Nature Reserve, 12 Sept. 2001, E.M. Bulakh, VLA M-16812; Fuyuan, 4 Aug. 2004, E.M. Bulakh, VLA M-20212; Hutou, 8 Sept. 2003, Tolgor Bau, HMJAU 3310.

Russula albonigra (Krombh.) Fr.

On the ground in korean pine-broad-leaved forest, Ussuriysk Nature Reserve, 25 Aug. 1962, M.M. Nazarova, VLA M-8338; Birobidzhan: Bastak Nature Reserve, 14 Aug. 2006, E.M. Bulakh, VLA M-20940.

Russula alnetorum Romagn.

Under the tree of *Alnus* in alder forest, Ussuriysk Nature Reserve, 2 Sept. 1993 E.M. Bulakh, VLA M-8554.

Russula alutacea (Fr.) Fr.

Under the trees of *Quercus* and *Betula* in korean pine-broad-leaved forest, Ussuriysk Nature Reserve (Vasilyeva & Bezdeleva, 2006); in oak forest, Fuyuan, 5 Aug. 2004, E.M. Bulakh, VLA M-19644; Birobidzhan: Bastak Nature Reserve, 13 Sept. 2006, E.M. Bulakh, VLA M-20931.

Russula atropurpurea (Krombh.) Britzelm.

On the ground in dark coniferous forest, Ussuriysk, 3 Aug. 2003, Tolgor Bau, HMJAU 3272; Upper Ussuri Station, 10 Sept. 1974, E.M. Bulakh, VLA M-8359.

Russula aurea Pers.

[= *Russula aurata* (With.) Fr.]

Under the trees of *Betula* in korean pine-broad-leaved forest, Ussuriysk Nature Reserve, 7 Aug. 1975, M.M. Nazarova, VLA M-8384; Ussuriysk, 3 Aug. 2003, Tolgor Bau, HMJAU 2827; Upper Ussuri Station, 12 Sept. 1974, E.M. Bulakh, VLA M-8362; in broad-leaved forest, Big Khekhtsir Nature Reserve, 2 Sept. 1983, E.M. Bulakh, VLA M-8399; Birobidzhan: Bastak Nature Reserve, 10 Sept. 2001, E.M. Bulakh, VLA M-16049.

Russula aurora (Krombh.) Bres.

(= *Russula rosea* Quél.)

Under the trees of *Betula* in birch forst, Khanka Nature Reserve, 26 Jul. 2002, E.M. Bulakh, VLA M-19107; in coniferous-broad-leaved forest, Big Khekhtsir Nature Reserve, 27 Aug. 1983, E.M. Bulakh, VLA M-9029; Birobidzhan: Bastak Nature Reserve, 19 Aug. 2003, E.M. Bulakh, VLA M-19243.

Russula brunneola Burl.

Under the trees of *Quercus* in korean pine-broad-leaved forest , Upper Ussuri Station, 22 Aug. 1975, E.M. Bulakh, VLA M-8451; in dark coniferous forest, Big Khekhtsir Nature Reserve, 15 Aug. 1981, E.M. Bulakh, VLA M-8449; Birobidzhan: Bastak Nature Reserve, 13 Aug. 2002, E.M. Bulakh, VLA M-17241.

Russula brunneoviolacea Crawshay

On the ground in dark coniferous forest, Big Khekhtsir Nature Reserve, 15 Aug. 1981, E.M. Bulakh, VLA M-8466.

Russula claroflava Grove

Under the trees of *Betula*, *Picea* and *Abies* in dark coniferous forest, Upper Ussuri Station, 15 Aug. 1974, E.M. Bulakh, VLA M-8502; Big Khekhtsir Nature Reserve, 15 Aug. 1981, E.M. Bulakh, VLA M-8503.

Russula cuprea (Krombh.) J.E. Lange

(= *Russula urens* Romell)

Under the tree of *Pinus koraiensis* in fir-broad leaves forest, Ussuriysk Nature Reserve, 28 Aug. 1965, M.M. Nazarova, VLA M-9405.

Russula cyanoxantha (Schaeff.) Fr.

Under the bush of *Corylus*, trees of *Quercus* and *Betula* in broad-leaved forest, Ussuriysk Nature Reserve, 20 Aug. 1963, M.M. Nazarova, VLA M-8521; Ussuriysk: Gornotayozhnoye, 26 Aug. 1963, L.N. Vassiljeva, VLA M-8511; Ussuriysk, 3 Aug. 2003, Tolgor Bau, HMJAU 2848; Spassk Dalny: Slavinka, 18 Jul. 1981, E.M. Bulakh, VLA M-8512; Upper Ussuri Station, 2 Aug. 1974, E.M. Bulakh, VLA M-8520; in dark coniferous forest, Big Khekhtsir Nature Reserve, 15 Aug. 1981, E.M. Bulakh, VLA M-8449, 17 Aug. 2004, Tolgor Bau, HMJAU 3002; Birobidzhan: Bastak Nature Reserve, 18 Aug. 2003, E.M. Bulakh, VLA M-20060 ; Raohe: Shengli State Farm, 6 Aug. 2004, Tolgor Bau, HMJAU 2519; Fuyuan, 6 Aug. 2004, Tolgor Bau, HMJAU 3176.

Russula decipiens (Singer) Kühner et Romagn.

Under the trees of *Quercus* in oak forest, Ussuriysk Nature Reserve, 24 Sept. 1946, L.N. Vassiljeva, VLA M-8570; Osinovka, 11 Sept. 1951, L.N. Vassiljeva, VLA M-8566; Tikhorechnoye, 4 Aug. 2005, E.M. Bulakh, VLA M-20190; Birobidzhan: Bastak Nature Reserve, 15 Aug. 2006, E.M. Bulakh, VLA M-21016; Fuyuan, 5 Aug. 2004, E.M. Bulakh, VLA M-20389.

Russula decolorans (Fr.) Fr.

Under the tree of *Larix* in larch forest, Birobidzhan: Bastak Nature Reserve, 9 Sept. 2001, E.M. Bulakh, VLA M-16804.

Russula delica Fr.

Under the trees of *Betula* and *Abies* in korean pine-broad-leaved forest, Ussuriysk Nature Reserve (Vasilyeva & Bezdeleva, 2006); Ussuriysk, 3 Aug. 2003, Tolgor Bau, HMJAU 2819;

Upper Ussuri Station, 18 Aug. 1974, E.M. Bulakh, VLA M-8624; in oak forest, Tikhorechnoye, 28 Jul. 1984, E.M. Bulakh, VLA M-8631; in broad-leaved forest, Big Khekhtsir Nature Reserve, 29 Jun. 1981, E.M. Bulakh, VLA M-8615; Birobidzhan: Bastak Nature Reserve, 11 Aug. 2006, E.M. Bulakh, VLA M-20942; Hailin Mudanjiang, 9 Aug. 2004, Tolgor Bau, HMJAU 2590.

Russula densifolia Secr. ex Gillet   Plate 21: 124

Under the trees of *Betula* in coniferous-broad-leaved forest, Ussuriysk Nature Reserve (Vasilyeva & Bezdeleva, 2006); in dark coniferous forest, Big Khekhtsir Nature Reserve, 15 Aug. 1981, E.M. Bulakh, VLA M-8648. - Under the bush of *Corylus* in broad-leaved forest, Ussuriysk: Gornotayozhnoye , 26 Aug. 1963, L.N. Vassiljeva, VLA M-8640.

Russula emetica (Schaeff.) Pers.

Under the trees of *Betula* and *Quercus* in coniferous-broad-leaved forest, Ussuriysk Nature Reserve (Vasilyeva & Bezdeleva, 2006); Ussuriysk, 3 Aug. 2003, Tolgor Bau, HMJAU 2839; Upper Ussuri Station, 26 Aug. 1973, E.M. Bulakh, VLA M-8658; in oak forest, Tikhorechnoye, 8 Aug. 1977, E.M. Bulakh, VLA M-8696; broad-leaved forest, Big Khekhtsir Nature Reserve, 5 Aug. 1981, E.M. Bulakh, VLA M-8660; Birobidzhan: Bastak Nature Reserve, 12 Sept. 2001, E.M. Bulakh, VLA M-16813.

Russula farinipes Romell

Under the trees of *Picea* and *Betula* in dark coniferous forest, Big Khekhtsir Nature Reserve, 15 Aug. 1981, E.M. Bulakh, VLA M-8707.

Russula flavida Frost.

Under the tree of *Quercus*, Raohe, 5 Aug. 2004, Tolgor Bau, HMJAU 3200.

Russula foetens (Pers.) Fr.

Under the trees of *Betula* in korean pine-broad-leaved forest, Ussuriysk Nature Reserve, 11 Aug. 1945, L.N. Vassiljeva, VLA M-8754; Ussuriysk, 3 Aug. 2003, Tolgor Bau, HMJAU 2943, 2823; in birch forest, Khanka Nature Reserve, 26 Jul. 2002, V.Yu. Barkalov, VLA M-17745; in coniferous-broad-leaved forest, Upper Ussuri Station, 6 Aug. 1974, E.M. Bulakh, VLA M-8740; Birobidzhan: Bastak Nature Reserve, 13 Aug. 2000, E.M. Bulakh, VLA M-15195. - Under the trees of *Quercus* in oak forest, Tikhorechnoye, 28 Jul. 1984, E.M. Bulakh, VLA M-8733; in broad-leaved forest, Big Khekhtsir Nature Reserve, 3 Aug. 1981, E.M. Bulakh, VLA M-8751; in forest, Raohe, 6 Aug. 2004, Tolgor Bau, HMJAU 2708, 2518, 2524; Hutou, 8 Sept. 2003, Tolgor Bau, HMJAU 3324.

Russula fragilis (Pers.) Fr.

Under the trees of *Betula* and *Populus davidiana* in coniferous-broad-leaved forest, Ussuriysk Nature Reserve, 2 Sept. 1994, E.M. Bulakh, VLA M-8758. - On the log of *Pinus koraiensis* in coniferous-broad-leaved forest, Upper Ussuri Station, 21 Aug. 1973, E.M. Bulakh, VLA M-8764; Birobidzhan: Bastak Nature Reserve, 21 Aug. 2004, E.M. Bulakh, VLA M-20838. - Under the trees of *Quercus* and *Betula* in broad-leaved forest, Big Khekhtsir

Nature Reserve, 30 Jun. 1981, E.M. Bulakh, VLA M-8767.

Russula gracillima Jul. Schäff.

Under the trees of *Betula* in dark coniferous forest, Upper Ussuri Station, 17 Sept. 1974, E.M. Bulakh, VLA M-8780; in birch forest, Big Khekhtsir Nature Reserve, 7 Sept. 1983, E.M. Bulakh, VLA M-8777; Birobidzhan: Bastak Nature Reserve, 21 Aug. 2003, E.M. Bulakh, VLA M-19214.

Russula granulata Peck

Under the trees of *Pinus koraiensis* in korean pine-broad-leaved forest, Ussuriysk Nature Reserve, 1 Aug. 1961, M.M. Nazarova, VLA M-8788; Upper Ussuri Station, 19 Sept. 1974, E.M. Bulakh, VLA M-8792; in dark coniferous forest, Big Khekhtsir Nature Reserve, 7 Sept. 1983, E.M. Bulakh, VLA M-8795; Birobidzhan: Bastak Nature Reserve, 10 Aug. 2006, E.M. Bulakh, VLA M-20938.

Russula grisea (Batsch) Fr.

Under the trees of *Tilia* in broad-leaved forest, Novo-Vladimirovka, 20 Jul. 1981, E.M. Bulakh, VLA M-8817; in oak forest, Khorol, 4 Aug. 1985, E.M. Bulakh, VLA M-8811; Tikhorechnoye, 5 Aug. 2005, E.M. Bulakh, VLA M-20300; Birobidzhan: Bastak Nature Reserve, 14 Aug. 2006, E.M. Bulakh, VLA M-21362.

Russula heterophylla (Fr.) Fr.

On the ground in korean pine-broad-leaved forest, Ussuriysk Nature Reserve, 31 Aug. 1946, L.N. Vassiljeva, VLA M-8835. - Under the trees of *Betula* and *Populus davidiana* in birch-aspen forest, Big Khekhtsir Nature Reserve, 3 Aug. 1981, E.M. Bulakh, VLA M-8836; Birobidzhan: Bastak Nature Reserve, 13 Aug. 2006, E.M. Bulakh, VLA M-20945.

Russula integra (L.) Fr.

Under the coniferous trees in dark coniferous forest, Upper Ussuri Station, 20 Aug. 1975, E.M. Bulakh, VLA M-8843.

Russula ionochlora Romagn.

Under the trees of *Betula* in birch forest, Big Khekhtsir Nature Reserve, 8 Aug. 1981, E.M. Bulakh, VLA M-8846.

Russula lactea (Pers.) Fr. var. ***lactea***

Under the trees of *Quercus* in oak forest, Ussuriysk: Gornotayozhnoye, 23 Jul. 2002, E.M. Bulakh, VLA M-19092; Ussuriysk, 3 Aug. 2003, Tolgor Bau, HMJAU 2835; Khanka Nature Reserve, 25 Jul. 2002, V.Yu. Barkalov, VLA M-17480; Birobidzhan: Bastak Nature Reserve, 13 Aug. 2006, E.M. Bulakh, VLA M-20936.

Russula grata Britzelm.

(= *Russula laurocerasi* Melzer)

Under the trees of *Quercus* in broad-leaved forest, Ussuriysk Nature Reserve, 23 Aug. 1975, M.M. Nazarova, VLA M-8889; Spassk Dalny: Novo-Vladimirovka, 20 Jul. 1981, E.M. Bulakh, VLA M-8867; Novotroitskoye, 22 Jul. 1998, E.M. Bulakh, VLA M-10482; Big

Khekhtsir Nature Reserve, 5 Aug. 1981, E.M. Bulakh, VLA M-8883, 16 Aug. 2004, Tolgor Bau, HMJAU 2788; Birobidzhan: Bastak Nature Reserve, 14 Aug. 2006, E.M. Bulakh, VLA M-20941; Fuyuan, 5 Aug.2004, E.M. Bulakh, VLA M-20187.

Russula laricina Velen.

Under the tree of *Larix*, Birobidzhan: Bastak Nature Reserve, 12 Sept. 2001, E.M. Bulakh, VLA M-16805.

Russula lilacea Quél.

Under the trees of *Quercus* and *Betula* in broad-leaved forest, Ussuriysk Nature Reserve, 21 Aug. 1961, L.N. Vassiljeva, VLA M-8901; Ussuriysk, 3 Aug. 2003, Tolgor Bau, HMJAU 2829. - Under the bush of *Corylus* and trees of *Betula* in broad-leaved forest, Osinovka, 11 Sept. 1951, L.N. Vassiljeva, VLA M-8902; Big Khekhtsir Nature Reserve, 23 Aug. 1983, E.M. Bulakh, VLA M-8916; Birobidzhan: Bastak Nature Reserve, 11 Aug. 2006, E.M. Bulakh, VLA M-20947; Raohe: Shengli State Farm, 6 Aug. 2004, E.M. Bulakh, VLA M-20391.

Russula lutea (Huds.) Gray

Under the trees of *Betula* in korean pine-broad-leaved forest, Ussuriysk Nature Reserve, 24 Sept. 1961, L.N. Vassiljeva, VLA M-8978; Ussuriysk, 3 Aug. 2003 , Tolgor Bau, HMJAU 2813; in birch forest, Khanka Nature Reserve, 26 Jul. 2002, V.Yu. Barkalov, VLA M-17479; Fuyuan, 4 Aug. 2004, E.M. Bulakh, VLA M-20392; in broad-leaved forest, Osinovka, 14 Aug. 1955, L.N. Vassiljeva, VLA M-8946; Upper Ussuri Station, 18 Aug. 1974, E.M. Bulakh, VLA M-8948; Khorol, 4 Aug. 1985, E.M. Bulakh, VLA M-8957. - Under the trees of *Quercus* in oak forest, Novotroitskoye, 13 Jul. 1998, E.M. Bulakh, VLA M-10483; Big Khekhtsir Nature Reserve, 5 Aug. 1981, E.M. Bulakh, VLA M-8961; Birobidzhan: Bastak Nature Reserve, 13 Aug. 2002, E.M. Bulakh, VLA M-17294; Raohe: Shengli State Farm, 6 Aug. 2004, Tolgor Bau, HMJAU 3236; Hutou, 8 Sept. 2003, Tolgor Bau, HMJAU 3368.

Russula luteoviridans Martin ss. Melzer et Zvara

Under the trees of *Picea* in dark coniferous forest, Upper Ussuri Station, 25 Aug. 1975, E.M. Bulakh, VLA M-8985; Big Khekhtsir Nature Reserve, 15 Aug. 1981, E.M. Bulakh, VLA M-8984.

Russula maculata Quél.

Under the trees of *Betula* in fir-broad-leaved forest, Ussuriysk Nature Reserve, 28 Aug. 1946, L.N. Vassiljeva, VLA M-8998; in broad-leaved forest, Ussuriysk: Gornotayozhnoye, 3 Aug. 2002, E.M. Bulakh, VLA M-19055; Ussuriysk, 3 Aug. 2003, Tolgor Bau, HMJAU 2977; Upper Ussuri Station, 15 Sept. 1974, E.M. Bulakh, VLA M-8992, E.M. Bulakh; Big Khekhtsir Nature Reserve, 15 Aug. 1981, E.M. Bulakh, VLA M-8997; Birobidzhan: Bastak Nature Reserve, 23 Aug. 2003, E.M. Bulakh, VLA M-19194. - Under the tree of *Quercus* in oak forest, Tikhorechnoye, 28 Jul. 1984, E.M. Bulakh, VLA M-8996.

Russula mariae Peck

On the ground under the tree of *Quercus* in broad-leaved forest, Fyuan, 4 Aug. 2004,

E.M. Bulakh, VLA M-20188.

Russula mustelina Fr.

Under the tree of *Abies* in coniferous-broad-leaved forest, Upper Ussuri Station, 12 Aug. 1974, E.M. Bulakh, VLA M-9032.

Russula nauseosa (Pers.) Fr.

Under the trees of *Quercus* and *Betula* in korean pine-broad-leaved forest, Ussuriysk Nature Reserve, 8 Sept. 1951, L.N. Vassiljeva, VLA M-9095; in oak forest, Tikhorechnoye, 28 Jul. 1984, E.M. Bulakh, VLA M-9097; in birch forest, Fuyuan, 4 Aug. 2004, E.M. Bulakh, VLA M-20393.

Russula nigricans (Bull.) Fr.   Plate 21: 125

Under the trees of *Betula* and *Quercus*, in oak forest, Khanka Nature Reserve, 20 Jul. 2007, E.M. Bulakh, VLA M-21539; Big Khekhtsir Nature Reserve, 28 Aug. 1983, - On the ground in dark coniferous forest, Upper Ussuri Station, 19 Aug. 1974, E.M. Bulakh, VLA M-9098; Big Khekhtsir Nature Reserve, 14 Aug. 1981, E.M. Bulakh, VLA M-9103, 17 Aug. 2004, Tolgor Bau, HMJAU 2984; Birobidzhan: Bastak Nature Reserve, 12 Sept. 2001, E.M. Bulakh, VLA M- 21380; Fuyuan, 4 Aug. 2004, Tolgor Bau, HMJAU 2633, 2578.

Russula nitida (Pers.) Fr.

Under the trees of *Betula* in korean pine-broad-leaved forest, Ussuriysk Nature Reserve, 15 Aug. 1962, M.M. Nazarova, VLA M-9113; Anuchino, 21 Aug. 1955, L.N. Vassiljeva, VLA M-9117; Big Khekhtsir Nature Reserve, 5 Sept. 1983, E.M. Bulakh, VLA M-9114; Raohe, 7 Aug. 2004, E.M. Bulakh, VLA M-20388.

Russula ochroleuca (Pers.) Fr.

(= *Russula citrina* Gillet)

On the ground in coniferous forest, Ussuriysk Nature Reserve (Wasser, 1990); in dark coniferous forest, Upper Ussuri Station, 10 Sept. 1974, E.M. Bulakh, VLA M-9042; Big Khekhtsir Nature Reserve, 7 Sept. 1983, E.M. Bulakh, VLA M-8494.

Russula olivina Ruots. et Vauras

On the ground in korean pine-broad-leaved forest, Upper Ussuri Station, 9 Sept. 1973, E.M. Bulakh, VLA M-9084.

Russula paludosa Britzelm.   Plate 21: 126

Under the tree of *Larix,* Birobidzhan: Bastak Nature Reserve, 14 Aug. 2006, E.M. Bulakh, VLA M-21029.

Russula pectinata (Bull.) Fr.

Under the trees of *Tilia* and *Ulmus* in broad-leaved forest, Ussuriysk Nature Reserve, 6 Sept. 1951, L.N. Vassiljeva, VLA M-9138; Ussuriysk, 3 Aug. 2003, Tolgor Bau, HMJAU 2811. - Under the trees of *Betula* in birch forest, Khanka Nature Reserve, 26 Jul. 2002, E.M. Bulakh, VLA M-19106; Big Khekhtsir Nature Reserve, 8 Aug. 1981, E.M. Bulakh, VLA M-9135; Birobidzhan: Bastak Nature Reserve, 13 Aug. 2006, E.M. Bulakh, VLA M-20935;

Fuyuan, 4 Aug. 2004, E.M. Bulakh, VLA M-20189.

Russula pectinatoides Peck

Under the trees of *Betula* in korean pine-broad-leaved forest, Ussuriysk Nature Reserve, 16 Aug. 1945, L.N. Vassiljeva, VLA M-9155; in deciduous forest, Ussuriysk: Gornotayozhnoye, 29 Aug. 1951, L.N. Vassiljeva, VLA M-9168; in willow-birch forest, Khanka Nature Reserve, 25 Jul. 2002, E.M. Bulakh, VLA M-18356, 7 Aug. 2003, Tolgor Bau, HMJAU 2825; in oak forest, Osinovka, 14 Aug. 1964, L.N. Vassiljeva, VLA M-9166; Spassk Dalny: Slavinka, 18 Jul. 1981, E.M. Bulakh, VLA M-9158; Tikhorechnoye, 21 Jul. 1998, E.M. Bulakh, VLA M-10485; in dark coniferous forest, Big Khekhtsir Nature Reserve, 15 Aug. 1981, E.M. Bulakh, VLA M-9146, 18 Aug. 2004, Tolgor Bau, HMJAU 2981; Birobidzhan: Bastak Nature Reserve, 13 Aug. 2006, E.M. Bulakh, VLA M-20944.

Russula pelargonia Niolle

Under the trees of *Populus davidiana* in aspen forest, Khanka Nature Reserve, 27 Jul. 2007, E.M. Bulakh, VLA M-21537; Big Khekhtsir Nature Reserve, 28 Aug. 1983, Big Khekhtsir Nature Reserve, 31 Jul. 1946, L.N. Vassiljeva VLA M-9197; Birobidzhan: Bastak Nature Reserve, 18 Aug. 2002, E.M. Bulakh, VLA M-17291; Raohe, 7 Aug. 2004, E.M. Bulakh, VLA M-20303.

Russula persicina Krombh.

(= *Russula rubicunda* Quel.)

Under the trees of *Quercus* and *Betula* in broad-leaved forest, Ussuriysk: Gornotayozhnoye, 29 Jul. 1959, L.N. Vassiljeva, VLA M-9320; Tikhorechnoie, 28 Jul. 1984, E.M. Bulakh, VLA M-9315; Big Khekhtsir Nature Reserve, 31 Jul. 1946, L.N. Vassiljeva VLA M-9316.

Russula pseudodelica J.E. Lange

Under the trees of *Quercus* in korean pine-broad-leaved forest, Ussuriysk Nature Reserve, 18 Aug. 1962, M.M. Nazarova, VLA M-9209; in oak forest, Upper Ussuri Station, 7 Sept. 1975, E.M. Bulakh, VLA M-9204; Big Khekhtsir Nature Reserve, 11 Aug. 1981, L.N. Vassiljeva, VLA M-9206, 18 Aug. 2004, Tolgor Bau, 2981; Birobidzhan: Bastak Nature Reserve, 17 Aug. 2000, E.M. Bulakh, VLA M-15323; Hulin, 9 Aug. 2004, E.M. Bulakh, VLA M-20195.

Russula pseudointegra Arnold et Goris

On the ground in birch forest, Big Khekhtsir Nature Reserve, 27 Aug. 1983, E.M. Bulakh, VLA M-9243, 17 Aug. 2004, Tolgor Bau, HMJAU 2771; Raohe, 7 Aug. 2004, E.M. Bulakh, VLA M-19627.

Russula puellaris Fr.

On the ground in dark coniferous forest, Big Khekhtsir Nature Reserve, 14 Sept. 1981, E.M. Bulakh, VLA M-9240; Birobidzhan: Bastak Nature Reserve, 10 Aug. 2006, E.M. Bulakh, VLA M-21361.

Russula pulchella I.G. Borshch.

(= *Russula exalbicans* Pers. sensu Melzer et Zvára)

On the ground in larch forest, Birobidzhan: Bastak Nature Reserve, 12 Sept. 2001, E.M. Bulakh, VLA M-16813.

Russula punctipes Singer Plate 22: 127

(= *Russula senecis* S. Imai)

Under the trees of *Quercus* in korean pine-broad-leaved forest, Ussuriysk Nature Reserve, 10 Sept. 1946, L.N. Vassiljeva, VLA M-9232.

Russula queletii Fr.

Under the trees of *Pinus koraiensis* in korean pine-broad-leaved forest, Ussuriysk Nature Reserve, 14 Sept. 1961, M.M. Nazarova, VLA M-9265; Upper Ussuri Station, 22 Aug. 1975, E.M. Bulakh, VLA M-9254; in dark coniferous forest, Big Khekhtsir Nature Reserve, 15 Aug. 1981, E.M. Bulakh, VLA M-9269; Birobidzhan: Bastak Nature Reserve, 12 Aug. 2001, E.M. Bulakh, VLA M-16789; Hulin, 9 Aug. 2004, E.M. Bulakh, VLA M-20301.

Russula risigalina (Batsch) Sacc.

[= *Russula chamaeleontina* (Lasch) Fr.]

Under the trees of *Quercu*s and *Betula* in broad-leaved forest, Big Khekhtsir Nature Reserve, 1 Sept. 1983, E.M. Bulakh, VLA M-8483.

Russula sanguinaria (Schumach.) Raushert

[= *Russula rosacea* (Pers.) Gray]

On the ground in coniferous-broad-leaved forest, Ussuriysk Nature Reserve (Vasilyeva & Bezdeleva, 2006); Ussuriysk, 3 Aug. 2004, Tolgor Bau, HMJAU 3260, 3280; Hulin, 9 Aug. 2004, Tolgor Bau, HMJAU 3216, 3232; Hutou, 8 Sept. 2003, Tolgor Bau, HMJAU 3312.

Russula sanguinea (Bull.) Fr.

Under the trees of *Quercus* in oak forest, Ussuriysk Nature Reserve, 18 Aug. 2005, E.M. Bulakh, VLA M-20419; Ussuriysk, 3 Aug. 2003, Tolgor Bau, HMJAU 2837; Ussuriysk: Gornotayozhnoye, 29 Jul. 1951, L.N.Vassiljeva, VLA M-9320; Khanka Nature Reserve, 28 Jul. 2002, V.Yu. Barkalov, VLA M-17483; Tikhorechnoye, 28 Jul. 1984, E.M. Bulakh, VLA M-9315; Big Khekhtsir Nature Reserve, 31 Jul. 1946, L.N. Vassiljeva, VLA M-9316; Birobidzhan: Bastak Nature Reserve, 11 Aug. 2006, E.M. Bulakh, VLA M-20943; Raohe, 7 Aug. 2004, Tolgor Bau, HMJAU 2629, 2642; Fuyuan, 4 Aug. 2004, Tolgor Bau, HMJAU 2547.

Russula subcompacta Britzelm.

Under the trees of *Pinus koraiensis* and *Abies* in korean pine-broad-leaved forest, Ussuriysk Nature Reserve, 28 Sept. 1946, L.N. Vassiljeva, VLA M-9346.

Russula turci Bres.

Under the trees of *Pinus koraiensis* in korean pine-broad-leaved forest, Ussuriysk Nature Reserve, 16 Sept. 1962, L.N. Vassiljeva, VLA M-9348; Upper Ussuri Station, 17 Aug. 1974,

E.M. Bulakh, VLA M-9377; Bikin, 10 Sept. 1945, L.N. Vassiljeva, VLA M-9380. - Under the trees of *Abies* and *Picea* in dark coniferous forest, Big Khekhtsir Nature Reserve, 14 Aug. 1981, E.M. Bulakh, VLA M-9373.

Russula velenovskyi Melzer et Zvara

On the ground under the tree of *Betula* in birch forest, Raohe, 7 Aug. 2004, E.M. Bulakh, VLA M-20302.

Russula versicolor Jul. Schäff.

[= *Russula blackfordiae* Peck sensu Lj.N. Vassileva (1973)].

Under the trees of *Betula* in oak-birch forest, Ussuriysk, 3 Aug. 2003, Tolgor Bau, HMJAU 2968; Fuyuan, 4 Aug. 2004, E.M. Bulakh, VLA M-20215. - Khanka Nature Reserve, 21 Aug. 2002, E.M. Bulakh, VLA M-17174; in broad-leaved forest, Big Khekhtsir Nature Reserve, 3 Aug. 1981, E.M. Bulakh, VLA M-8410; Birobidzhan: Bastak Nature Reserve, 13 Aug. 2000, E.M. Bulakh, VLA M-15315.

Russula vesca Fr.

Under the trees of *Quercus* and *Betula* in korean pine-broad-leaved forest, Ussuriysk Nature (Vasilyeva & Bezdeleva, 2006); Ussuriysk: Gornotayozhnoye, 23 Aug. 1945, L.N.Vasiljeva, VLA M-9425.

Russula vinosa Lindblad

Under the tree of *Larix,* Birobidzhan: Bastak Nature Reserve, 12 Aug. 2001, E.M. Bulakh, VLA M-16808.

Russula vinosobrunnea (Bres.) Romagn.

On the ground in korean pine-broad-leaved forest, Ussuriysk Nature Reserve, 15 Sept. 1961, L.N. Vassiljeva, VLA M-9446. - Under the tree of *Quercus* in oak forest, Ussuriysk: Gornotayozhnoye, 9 Sept. 1963, L.N.Vassiljeva, VLA M-9447.

Russula violacea Quél.

Under the trees of *Betula* and *Populus davidiana* in coniferous broad-leaved forest, Ussuriysk Nature Reserve, 11 Sept. 1963, M.M. Nazarova, VLA M-9450; Tikhorechnoye, 21 Jul. 1998, E.M. Bulakh, VLA M-10486; in birch forest, Big Khekhtsir Nature Reserve, 26 Aug. 1983, E.M. Bulakh, VLA M-9457.

Russula xerampelina (Schaeff.) Fr.   Plate 22: 128

Under the trees of *Betula* and *Quercus* in coniferous broad-leaved forest, Ussuriysk Nature Reserve, 17 Aug. 1962, M.M. Nazarova, VLA M-9495; Ussuriysk: Gornotayozhnoye, 19 Aug. 1963, L.N. Vassiljeva, VLA M-9518; Khanka Nature Reserve, 28 Aug. 2002, E.M. Bulakh, VLA M-18354; in oak forest, Khorol, 1 Aug. 1985, E.M. Bulakh, VLA M-9526; Tikhorechnoye, 21 Jul. 1998, E.M. Bulakh, VLA M-10487. - Under the trees of *Pinus koraiensi* in korean pine forerst, Upper Ussuri Station, 17 Sept. 1975, E.M. Bulakh, VLA M-9488; in dark coniferous forest, Big Khekhtsir Nature Reserve, 15 Aug. 1981, E.M. Bulakh, VLA M-9484; Birobidzhan: Bastak Nature Reserve, 15 Aug. 2000, E.M. Bulakh, VLA

M-15325 .

SCHIZOPHYLLALES

SCHIZOPHYLLACEAE

Plicaturopsis crispa (Fr.) D.A. Reid   Plate 22: 129

On the logs in korean pine-broad-leaved forest, Ussuriysk Nature Reserve, 7 Sept. 1962, M.M. Nazarova, VLA M-13737; Birobidzhan: Bastak Nature Reserve, 10 Aug. 2006, E.M. Bulakh, VLA M-21020. - On the fallen twigs of deciduous trees, Tikhorechnoye, 23 Jul. 1998, E.M. Bulakh, VLA M-12095; Hulin, 19 Sept. 2004, Tolgor Bau, HMJAU 2599, 2604; Raohe: Shengli State Farm, 6 Aug. 2004, Tolgor Bau, HMJAU 2542. - On the fallen twig of *Betula*, Upper Ussuri Station (Azbukina & Kharkevich, 1984). - On the log of *Acer tegmentosum* in coniferous-broad-leaved forest, Big Khekhtsir Nature Reserve (Azbukina & Kharkevich, 1986).

Schizophyllum commune Fr.   Plate 22: 130

On the fallen twigs, Ussuriysk Nature Reserve, 10 Jun. 1959, I.A. Bunkina,VLA M-14636. - On the trunk of *Prunus*, Osinovka, 14 Jul. 1959, A.A. Ablakatova, VLA M-14641. - On the wood of a well, Iljinka, 27 Aug. 1955, Z.M. Azbukina, VLA M-14657. - On the log of *Ulmus*, Upper Ussuri Station, 20 Aug. 1973, E.M. Bulakh, VLA M-14650. - On the fallen twigs, Big Khekhtsir Nature Reserve, 25 Jun. 1981, E.M. Bulakh, VLA M-14639; Raohe, 8 Sep. 2003, Tolgor Bau, HMJAU 3026; Birobidzhan: Bastak Nature Reserve, 10 Aug. 2006, E.M. Bulakh, VLA M-20651.

SCLERODERMATALES

SCLERODERMATACEAE

Scleroderma cepa Pers.

On the ground in korean pine-broad-leaved forest, Ussuriysk Nature Reserve,   14 Aug. 1945, L.N. Vassiljeva, VLA M-17865.

Scleroderma citrinum Pers.

On the ground in korean pine-broad leaves forest, Ussuriysk Nature Reserve (Vassiljeva & Sosin, 1959); in meadow, Khanka Nature Reserve, 28 Aug. 2002, E.M. Bulakh, VLA M-17778; Big Khekhtsir Nature Reserve, 19 Aug. 1983, E.M. Bulakh, VLA M-21144; Birobidzhan: Bastak Nature Reserve, 18 Aug. 2002, E.M. Bulakh, VLA M-17524.

Scleroderma poltavense Sosin

On the sandy ground in deciduous forest, Khanka Nature Reserve, 26 Jul. 2002, E.M. Bulakh, VLA M-18261.

Scleroderma sapidum (Corda) Zerova

On the forest litter in broad-leaved forest, Ussuriysk: Gornotayozhnoye, 6 Aug. 2002, E.M. Bulakh, VLA M-18262; Birobidzhan: Bastak Nature Reserve, 13 Aug. 2000, E.M. Bulakh, VLA M-15345.

Scleroderma verrucosum (Bull.) Pers.

On the ground in oak forest, Ussuriysk: Gornotayozhnoye, 23 Jul. 2002, E.M. Bulakh, VLA M-18201; Birobidzhan: Bastak Nature Reserve, 14 Aug. 2006, E.M. Bulakh, VLA M-21218. - On the wood in dark coniferous forest, Upper Ussuri Station, 15 Sept. 1974, E.M. Bulakh, VLA M-17874.

SPHAEROBOLACEAE

Sphaerobolus stellatus Tode

On the dead culm of a grass in coniferous-broad-leaved forest, Upper Ussuri Station, 5 Sept. 1974, E.M. Bulakh, VLA M-17826.

STEREALES

ALEURODISCACEAE

Aleurocystidiellum subcruentatum (Berk. et M.A.Curtis) P. A. Lemke

On the bark of *Picea ajanensis*, Big Khekhtsir Nature Reserve (Azbukina & Kharkevich, 1986).

Aleurodiscus amorphus Rabenh.

On the dry twigs of *Abies*, Ussuriysk Nature Reserve (Vasilyeva & Bezdeleva, 2006). - On the log of *Abies nephrolepis*, Upper Ussuri Station (Azbukina & Kharkevich, 1984).

Aleurodiscus diffissus (Sacc.) Burt

On the fallen twig of *Rhododendron dahuricum*, Big Khekhtsir Nature Reserve (Azbukina & Kharkevich, 1986).

Aleurodiscus disciformis (DC.) Pat.

On the fallen twigs of *Quercus* in korean pine-broad-leaved forest, Upper Ussuri Station (Azbukina & Kharkevich, 1984); on the trunks of *Quercus*, *Tilia amurensis* and *T. mandshurica*, Big Khekhtsir Nature Reserve (Azbukina & Kharkevich, 1986).

ATHELIACEAE

Piloderma bicolor (Peck) Jülich

On the log of *Picea ajanensis* in dark coniferous forest, Big Khekhtsir Nature Reserve (Azbukina & Kharkevich, 1986).

BOTRYOBASIDIACEAE

Botryobasidium bondarcevii (Parmasto) G. Langer

(= *Botryohypochnus bondarcevii* Parmasto)

On the log of *Pinus koraiensis*, Ussuriysk Nature Reserve (Parmasto, 1965).

CORTICIACEAE

Corticium roseocarneum (Schwein.) Hjorstam

[= *Laeticorticium roseocarneum* (Schwein.) Boidin]

On the log of *Acer*, Ussuriysk Nature Reserve, 2 Jun. 1976, E.Parmasto, VLA M-13694. - On the fallen twigs of *Syringa amurensis*, Big Khekhtsir Nature Reserve (Azbukina & Kharkevich, 1986). - On the log of a deciduous tree, Birobidzhan: Bastak Nature Reserve, 14 Aug. 2006, E.M. Bulakh, VLA M-20973.

Cytidia salicina (Fr.) Burt

On the twigs of *Salix,* Ussuriysk Nature Reserve, 18 Aug. 1961, L.N. Vassiljeva, VLA M-13328. - On the twigs of *Populus*, Upper Ussuri Station, 3 Sept. 1975, E.M. Bulakh, VLA M-13336.

Dentocorticium ussuricum (Parmasto) M.J. Larsen et Gilb.

On the fallen twigs of *Corylus manshurica*, *Eleutherococcus senticosus* and *Quercus*, Upper Ussuri Station (Azbukina & Kharkevich, 1984); Big Khekhtsir Nature Reserve (Azbukina & Kharkevich, 1986).

Dendrothele acerina (Pers.) P.A. Lemke

On the bark of *Acer mono*, Ussuriysk Nature Reserve (Vasilyeva & Bezdeleva, 2006); Big Khekhtsir Nature Reserve (Azbukina & Kharkevich, 1986).

Dendrothele commixta (Höhn. et Litsch.) J. Erikss. et Ryvarden

On the bark of *Quercus*, Big Khekhtsir Nature Reserve (Azbukina & Kharkevich, 1986).

Laeticorticium pilatii Parmasto

On the fallen twigs of *Tilia*, Ussuriysk Nature Reserve (Parmasto, 1965). - On the fallen twigs of *Fraxinus mandshurica*, Upper Ussuri Station (Azbukina & Kharkevich, 1984). - On the fallen twigs of *Tilia mandshurica*, Big Khekhtsir Nature Reserve (Azbukina & Kharkevich, 1986).

Laeticorticium polygonioides (P. Karst.) Donk

On the fallen twigs of *Populus davidiana*, Big Khekhtsir Nature Reserve (Azbukina & Kharkevich, 1986).

Laeticorticium roseum (Pers.) Donk

On the fallen twigs of *Syringa amurensis*, Big Khekhtsir Nature Reserve (Azbukina & Kharkevich, 1986). - On the fallen twigs of *Salix,* Upper Ussuri Station (Azbukina &

Kharkevich, 1984).

Punctularia strigoso-zonata (Schwein.) Talbot

On the log of *Populus davidiana*, Big Khekhtsir Nature Reserve (Azbukina & Kharkevich, 1986). - On the rotten wood, Hulin, 20 Sept. 2004, Tolgor Bau, HMJAU 2663.

Terana caerulea (Lam.) Kuntze

[= *Pulcherricium caeruleum* (Lam.) Parmasto]

On the twigs, Big Khekhtsir Nature Reserve, 16 Aug. 2004, Tolgor Bau, HMJAU 2766; Birobidzhan: Bastak Nature Reserve, 18 Aug. 2004, Tolgor Bau HMJAU2766.

HYPHODERMATACEAE

Atheloderma orientale Parmasto

[= *Hyphoderma orientale* (Parmasto) Jülich]

On the log of a deciduous tree, Ussuriysk Nature Reserve (Parmasto, 1968).

Basidioradulum radula (Fr.) Nobles

On the fallen twig of *Ulmus propinqua*, Big Khekhtsir Nature Reserve (Azbukina & Kharkevich, 1986). - On the twigs, Raohe: Shengli State Farm, 6 Aug. 2004, Tolgor Bau, HMJAU 2654.

Crustoderma dryinum (Berk. et M.A. Curtis) Parmasto

On the logs of *Picea ajanensis*, Upper Ussuri Station (Azbukina & Kharkevich, 1984); Big Khekhtsir Nature Reserve (Azbukina & Kharkevich, 1986).

Cylindrobasidium evolvens (Fr.) Jülich

On the wood, Ussuriysk Nature Reserve, 13 Aug. 1961, L.N. Vassiljeva, VLA M-13320.

Hyphoderma setigerum (Fr.) Donk

On the fallen twigs of *Alnus hirsuta*, Big Khekhtsir Nature Reserve (Azbukina & Kharkevich, 1986).

Poriodontia subvinosa Parmasto

On the logs of *Abies nephrolepis* in dark coniferous forest, Upper Ussuri Station (Azbukina & Kharkevich, 1984); Big Khekhtsir Nature Reserve (Parmasto, 1982).

Radulodon licentii (Pilát) Ryvarden

On the fallen twigs of *Quercus*, Upper Ussuri Station (Azbukina & Kharkevich, 1984); Big Khekhtsir Nature Reserve (Azbukina & Kharkevich, 1986).

LINDTNERIACEAE

Cristinia helvetica (Pers.) Parmasto

On the log of *Populus*, Ussuriysk Nature Reserve (Vasilyeva & Bezdeleva, 2006).

MERULIACEAE

Chondrostereum purpureum (Pers.) Pouzar

On the log of *Populus davidiana*, Upper Ussuri Station (Azbukina & Kharkevich, 1984); Big Khekhtsir Nature Reserve (Azbukina & Kharkevich, 1986).

Gloeoporus dichrous (Fr.) Bres.

On the wood, Ussuriysk Nature Reserve, 3 Jun. 1976, E. Parmasto, VLA M-14077; Birobidzhan: Bastak Nature Reserve, 13 Aug. 2006, E.M. Bulakh, VLA M-21040; Birobidzhan: Bastak Nature Reserve, 11 Aug. 2006, E.M. Bulakh, VLA M-21034; Fuyuan, 6 Aug. 2004, Tolgor Bau, HMJAU 3185. - On the log of *Betula,* Upper Ussuri Station, 16 Sept. 1973, E.M. Bulakh, VLA M-13341. - On the logs of *Acer pseudosieboldianum, Alnus hirsuta* and *Quercus mongolica*, Big Khekhtsir Nature Reserve (Azbukina & Kharkevich, 1986).

Gloeoporus pannocinctus (Romell) J. Erikss.

On the log of *Betula* and *Alnus*, Upper Ussuri Station (Azbukina & Kharkevich, 1984). - On the log of *Populus davidiana,* Big Khekhtsir Nature Reserve (Azbukina & Kharkevich, 1986).

Merulius tremellosus Schrad.   Plate 22: 131

On the wood, Ussuriysk Nature Reserve, 22 Sept. 1975, M.M. Nazarova, VLA M-13715. - On the log of *Tilia*, Upper Ussuri Station, 16 Sept. 1974, E.M. Bulakh, VLA M-13706; Hulin, 20 Sept. 2004, Tolgor Bau, HMJAU 2692; Raohe, 8 Sept. 2003, Tolgor Bau, HMJAU 3008. - On the logs of *Alnus hirsuta, Quercus mongolica, Tilia amurensis* and *Ulmus propinqua*, Big Khekhtsir Nature Reserve (Azbukina & Kharkevich, 1986).

Meruliopsis corium (Pers.) Ginns

On the fallen twigs of deciduous trees, Ussuriysk Nature Reserve (Vasilyeva & Bezdeleva, 2006); Upper Ussuri Station (Azbukina & Kharkevich, 1984); Big Khekhtsir Nature Reserve (Azbukina & Kharkevich, 1986).

Mycoacia fuscoatra (Fr.) Donk

On the log of *Acer ukurunduense*, Upper Ussuri Station (Azbukina & Kharkevich, 1984).

Phanerochaete sanguinea (Fr.) Pouzar

On the fallen twigs of *Quercus*, Upper Ussuri Station (Azbukina & Kharkevich, 1984).

Phanerochaete sordida (P. Karst.) J. Erikss. et Ryvarden

On the log of *Pyrus*, Ussuriysk Nature Reserve, 12 Oct. 1953, L.N. Vassiljeva, VLA M-13723.

Phanerochaete velutina (DC.) Parmasto

On the wood, Ussuriysk Nature Reserve, 24 Aug. 1961, E. Parmasto, VLA M-13727.

Phanerochaete viticola (Schwein.) Parmasto

On the log, Bulygo-Fadeevo (Burdsall, 1985).

Phlebia albida H. Post

On the logs of *Eleutherococcus senticosus* and *Maackia amurensis*, Big Khekhtsir Nature Reserve (Azbukina & Kharkevich, 1986).

Phlebia coccineofulva Schwein.

[= *Phlebia martiana* (Berk. et M.A.Curtis) Parmasto]

On the log of a deciduous tree, Upper Ussuri Station (Azbukina & Kharkevich, 1984);

Phlebia rufa (Pers.) M.P. Christ.

On the dead trunk of *Aralia,* Upper Ussuri Station (Azbukina & Kharkevich, 1984). - On the log of *Quercus*, Big Khekhtsir Nature Reserve (Azbukina & Kharkevich, 1986).

Phlebiopsis gigantea (Fr.) Jülich

On the log of *Pinus koraiensis*, Big Khekhtsir Nature Reserve (Azbukina & Kharkevich, 1986).

Rhizochate filamentosa (Berk. et M.A. Curtis) Gresl., Nakasone et Rajchenb.

[= *Phanerochaete filamentosa* (Berk. et M.A. Curtis) Burds.]

On the log of *Abies*, Ussuriysk Nature Reserve (Burdsall, 1985). - On the rotten wood in forest, Raohe, 8 Sept. 2003, Tolgor Bau, 3008; Hulin, 20 Sept. 2004, Tolgor Bau, 2692.

PENIOPHORACEAE

Peniophora manshurica Parmasto

On the trunks of *Acer barbinerve* and *Quercus mongolica*, Big Khekhtsir Nature Reserve (Azbukina & Kharkevich, 1986).

Peniophora quercina (Pers.) Cooke

On the fallen twigs, Ussuriysk Nature Reserve, 2 Jun. 1976, E. Parmasto, VLA M-13718.

Peniophora rufa (Pers.) Boidin

On the fallen twigs of *Populus davidiana*, Upper Ussuri Station (Azbukina & Kharkevich, 1984); Big Khekhtsir Nature Reserve (Azbukina & Kharkevich, 1986).

Veluticeps abietina (Pers.) Hjortstam et Telleria

On the log of *Abies nephrolepis*, Upper Ussuri Station (Azbukina & Kharkevich, 1984).

Veluticeps ambigua (Peck) Hjertstam et Tellerria

On the log of *Abies nephrolepis*, Upper Ussuri Station (Azbukina & Kharkevich, 1984).

PODOSCYPHACEAE

Cotylidia diaphana (Schwein.) Lentz

On the ground in broad-leaved forest, Ussuriysk Nature Reserve, 8 Aug. 2005, E.M. Bulakh, VLA M-20202.

SISTOTREMATACEAE

Sistotrema confluens Pers.

On the ground, Ussuriysk Nature Reserve, 4 Sept. 1975, M.M. Nazarova, VLA M-16630.

Trechispora mollusca (Pers.) Liberta

On the log of *Abies nephrolepis*, Upper Ussuri Station (Azbukina & Kharkevich, 1984).

Xenasmatella vaga (Fr.) Stalpers.

[= *Trechispora vaga* (Fr.) Liberta]

On the log of *Abies nephrolepis*, Upper Ussuri Station (Azbukina & Kharkevich, 1984).

STECCHERINACEAE

Irpex lacteus (Fr.) Fr.   Plate 22: 132

On the wood, Ussuriysk Nature Reserve, 24 Aug. 1975, M.M. Nazarova, VLA M-13828. - On the fallen twigs of *Corylus mandshurica* and *Acer barbinerve* in coniferous-broad-leaved forest, Upper Ussuri Station (Azbukina & Kharkevich, 1984). - On the twigs, Birobidzhan: Bastak Nature Reserve, 11 Aug. 2006, E.M. Bulakh, VLA M-21039; Raohe, 8 Sept. 2003, Tolgor Bau, HMJAU 3041.

Junghuhnia collabens (Fr.) Ryvarden

On the logs of coniferous trees, Upper Ussuri Station (Azbukina & Kharkevich, 1984); Big Khekhtsir Nature Reserve (Azbukina & Kharkevich, 1986).

Junghuhnia nitida (Pers.) Ryvarden

On the logs of *Quercus*, *Tilia* and *Alnus*, Upper Ussuri Station (Azbukina & Kharkevich, 1984). - On the logs of *Acer ukurunduense*, *Populus davidiana* and *Tilia amurensis*, Big Khekhtsir Nature Reserve (Azbukina & Kharkevich, 1986).

Mycoleptodonoides aitchisonii (Berk.) Maas Geest.

On the wood, Ussuriysk Nature Reserve, 15 Sept. 1961, L.N. Vassiljeva, VLA M-16561; Birobidzhan: Bastak Nature Reserve, 9 Sept. 2001, E.M. Bulakh, VLA M-16560. - On the log of *Betula*, Big Khekhtsir Nature Reserve, 14 Sept. 1981, E.M. Bulakh, VLA M-16563. - On the fallen twigs of *Alnus* and *Populus davidiana*, Upper Ussuri Station [(Azbukina & Kharkevich, 1984), as *M. vassiljavae* Nikol.].

Mycorrhaphium adustum (Schwein.) Maas Geest.

On the wood, Ussuriysk Nature Reserve, 12 Aug. 1962, M.M. Nazarova, VLA M-16545; Ussuriysk, 3 Aug. 2003, Tolgor Bau, HMJAU 2885, 2913. - On the ground in forest, Big Khekhtsir Nature Reserve, Tolgor Bau, HMJAU 2950; Birobidzhan: Bastak Nature Reserve, 10 Aug. 2000, E.M. Bulakh, VLA M-16541. - On the logs of *Acer* and *Tilia* in korean pine-broad-leaved forest, Upper Ussuri Station (Azbukina & Kharkevich, 1984).

Steccherinum fimbriatum (Pers.) J. Erikss.

On the fallen twigs of *Philadelphus tenuifolius* in korean pine-broad-leaved forest, Upper Ussuri Station (Azbukina & Kharkevich, 1984). - On the fallen twigs of *Padus asiatica*, Big Khekhtsir Nature Reserve (Azbukina & Kharkevich, 1986).

Steccherinum laeticolor (Berk. et M.A. Curtis) Banker

On the fallen twigs and logs of deciduous trees, Ussuriysk Nature Reserve (Vasilyeva & Bezdeleva, 2006); Upper Ussuri Station (Azbukina & Kharkevich, 1984). - On the fallen twigs of *Quercus mongolica*, Big Khekhtsir Nature Reserve (Azbukina & Kharkevich, 1986).

Steccherinum murashkinskyi (Burt) Maas Geest.

On the stump of *Tilia*, Ussuriysk Nature Reserve, 21 Jun. 1945, L.N. Vassiljeva, VLA M-13807. - On the log of *Betula costata* in coniferous-broad-leaved forest, Upper Ussuri Station (Azbukina & Kharkevich, 1984). - On the wood, Raohe, 8 Sept. 2003, Tolgor Bau, HMJAU 3314.

Steccherinum ochraceum (Pers.) Gray

On the fallen twigs of *Betula,* Ussuriysk Nature Reserve (Vasilyeva & Bezdeleva, 2006); Upper Ussuri Station (Azbukina & Kharkevich, 1984). - On the log of a deciduous tree, Ussuriysk: Gornotayozhnoye, 24 Jun. 1963, L.N. Vassiljeva, VLA M-13805. - On the wood of *Maackia*, Birobidzhan: Bastak Nature Reserve, 10 Aug. 2006, E.M. Bulakh, VLA M-21050. - On the fallen twigs of *Quercus mongolica*, Big Khekhtsir Nature Reserve (Azbukina & Kharkevich, 1986).

STEREACEAE

Amylostereum areolatum (Chaillet) Boidin

On the log of *Picea ajanensis*, Upper Ussuri Station (Azbukina & Kharkevich, 1984).

Boreostereum radiatum (Peck) Parmasto

On the logs of *Picea ajanensis* and *Salix*, Upper Ussuri Station (Azbukina & Kharkevich, 1984).

Gloeostereum incarnatum S. Ito et S. Imai

On the wood, Ussuriysk Nature Reserve, 19 Aug. 1975, M.M. Nazarova, VLA M-13347; Tikhorechnoye, 28 Aug. 1984, E.M. Bulakh, VLA M-13352; Upper Ussuri Station, 5 Sept. 1975, E.M. Bulakh, VLA M-13348; Big Khekhtsir Nature Reserve, 28 Aug.1983, E.M. Bulakh, VLA M-13354.

Lopharia cinerascens (Schwein.) G. Cunn.

[= *Lopharia mirabilis* (Berk. et Broome) Pat.]

On the trunks of *Sambucus*, Ussuriysk Nature Reserve, 16 Aug. 1961, L.N. Vassiljeva,VLA M-13793; Hulin, 9 Aug. 2004, Tolgor Bau, HMJAU, 3294.

Lopharia crassa (Lev.) Boidin

(= *Stereum umbrinum* Berk. et M.A. Curtis)

Raohe, 8 Sep. 2003, Tolgor Bau, HMJAU 3326.

Lopharia spadicea (Pers.) Boidin

On the dead trunk, Ussuriysk Nature Reserve (Vasilyeva & Bezdeleva, 2006).

Stereum gausapatum (Fr.) Fr.

On the wood, Ussuriysk Nature Reserve, 16 Aug. 1962, M.M. Nazarova, VLA M-13355; Fuyuan, 5 Aug. 2004, Tolgor Bau, HMJAU 2681; Hulin, 9 Aug. 2004, Tolgor Bau, HMJAU 3293. - On the log of *Populus*, Upper Ussuri Station (Azbukina & Kharkevich, 1984). - On the log of *Quercus mongolica*, Big Khekhtsir Nature Reserve (Azbukina & Kharkevich, 1986).

Stereum hirsutum (Willd.) Pers.

On the log of *Quercus*, Ussuriysk Nature Reserve (Vasilyeva & Bezdeleva, 2006). - On the trunks of deciduous trees, Ussuriysk, 3 Aug. 2003, Tolgor Bau, HMJAU 2864; Big Khekhtsir Nature Reserve, 3 Aug. 1981, E.M. Bulakh , VLA M-13759, 15 Aug. 2004, Tolgor Bau, HMJAU 2972; Birobidzhan: Bastak Nature Reserve, 17 Aug. 2000, E.M. Bulakh, VLA M-21061; Hulin, 5 Sep. 2003, Tolgor Bau, HMJAU 3029; Raohe, 8 Sep. 2003, Tolgor Bau, HMJAU 3011.

Stereum ostrea (Blume et T. Nees) Fr.

On the fallen twigs of deciduous trees, Ussuriysk Nature Reserve [(Vasilyeva & Bezdeleva, 2006), as *S. fasciatum* (Fr.) Fr.]; Ussuriysk, 3 Aug. 2003, Tolgor Bau, HMJAU 2872. - On the logs, Raohe, 6, 8 Sep. 2003, Tolgor Bau, HMJAU 2582, 3027; Birobidzhan: Bastak Nature Reserve, Tolgor Bau, 2998, 3419.

Stereum rugosum Pers.

On the fallen twigs of *Corylus*, Ussuriysk Nature Reserve, 2 Jun. 1976, E. Parmasto, VLA M-13768.

Stereum sanguinolentum (Alb. et Schwein.) Fr.

On the log of *Picea ajanensis*, Upper Ussuri Station (Azbukina & Kharkevich, 1984). - On the wood, Big Khekhtsir Nature Reserve, 17 Aug. 2004, Tolgor Bau, HMJAU 2924.

Stereum subtomentosus Pouzar

On the log of *Acer*, Upper Ussuri Station, coniferous broad-leaved forest, 5 Aug. 1974, E.M. Bulakh, VLA M-13767. - On the log of *Padus*, Big Khekhtsir Nature Reserve, 29 Jun. 1981, E.M. Bulakh, VLA M-13764.

Stereopsis burtiana (Peck) D.A. Reid

On the wood, Hailin, 9 Aug. 2004, Tolgor Bau, HMJAU 3413.

Xylobolus frustulatus (Pers.) Boidin

On the logs of *Quercus*, Ussuriysk Nature Reserve (Vasilyeva & Bezdeleva, 2006); Upper Ussuri Station, 5 Aug. 1974, E.M. Bulakh, VLA M-13753.

TUBULICRINACEAE

Tubulicrinis gracillimus (Ellis et Everh. ex D.P. Rogers et H.S. Jacks.) G. Cunn.

[= *Tubulicrinis glebulosus* (Fr.) Donk]

On the dead twigs of *Padus maackii*, Ussuriysk Nature Reserve, 10 Sept. 1961, L.N. Vassiljeva, VLA M-13769.

THELEPHORALES

BANKERACEAE

Phellodon confluens (Pers.) Pouzar

On the ground, Ussuriysk: Gornotayozhnoye, 4 Sept. 2002, O.K. Govorova, VLA M-17451.

Phellodon melaleucus (Sw.) P. Karst.

On the wood, Fuyuan, 5 Aug. 2004, Tolgor Bau, HMJAU 2639.

Phellodon tomentosus (L.) Banker

On the ground under the tree of *Quercus,* Ussuriysk: Gornotayozhnoye, 6 Aug. 2002, E.M. Bulakh, VLA M-17448. - Under the tree of *Pinus densiflora*, Barabash-Levada: Shirokaya Canyon, 30 Aug. 2002 E.M. Bulakh, VLA M-17446.

THELEPHORACEAE

Hydnellum aurantiacum (Batsch) P. Karst.

On the ground in broad-leaved forest, Ussuriysk Nature Reserve (Vasilyeva & Bezdeleva, 2006); Ussuriysk: Gornotayozhnoye, 15 Aug. 2002, E.M. Bulakh, VLA M-17445; Birobidzhan: Bastak Nature Reserve, 14 Aug. 2006, E.M. Bulakh, VLA M-20967. - On the ground under the trees of *Pinus densiflora*, Nikolaevka , 21 Aug. 2002, O.K. Govorova, VLA M-17426; Barabash-Levada: Shirokaya Canyon, 21 Aug. 2002, O.K. Govorova, VLA M-17442.

Hydnellum caeruleum (Hornem.) P. Karst.

(= *Hydnellum ferrugipes* Coker)

On the ground under the tree of *Quercus*, Ussuriysk: Gornotayozhnoye, 13 Aug. 2002, O.K. Govorova,VLA M-17435.

Hydnellum concrescens (Pers.) Banker

On the ground under the trees of *Quercus*, Ussuriysk Nature Reserve (Vasilyeva & Bezdeleva, 2006); Ussuriysk: Gornotayozhnoye, 5 Aug. 2002, O.K. Govorova, VLA M-17440. - On the ground under the trees of *Pinus densiflora*, Nikolaevka, 21 Aug. 2002,

O.K. Govorova, VLA M-17413; Barabash-Levada: Shirokaya Canyon, 30 Aug. 2002, E.M. Bulakh, VLA M-17423.

Hydnellum ferrugineum (Fr.) P. Karst.

On the ground under the tree of *Quercus*, Nikolaevka, 24 Aug. 2002, O.K. Govorova, VLA M-17422; under the tree of *Pinus densiflora*, Barabash-Levada: Shirokaya Canyon, 30 Aug. 2002, E.M. Bulakh , VLA M-17415.

Hydnellum scrobiculatum (Fr.) P.Karst.

On the ground, Khabarovsk, 10 Aug, 2002, M.P. Tiunov, VLA M-17414.

Hydnellum spongiosipes (Peck) Pouzar

On the ground under the tree of *Quercus*, Ussuriysk: Gornotayozhnoye, 6 Aug. 2002, O.K. Govorova, VLA M-17424.

Pseudotomentella atrofusca M.J. Larsen

On the decayed wood of a coniferous tree, Ussuriysk Nature Reserve (Kõljalg, 1996).

Pseudotomentella tristis (P. Karst.) M.J. Larsen

On the decayed wood of coniferous and deciduous trees, Ussuriysk Nature Reserve (Kõljalg, 1996).

Sarcodon fennicus (P. Karst.) P. Karst.

On the ground under the tree of *Pinus densiflora*, Nikolaevka, 25 Sept. 1999, E.M. Bulakh, VLA M-16576.

Sarcodon imbricatus (L.) P. Karst.

On the ground, Upper Ussuri Station, 14 Aug. 1975, E.M. Bulakh, VLA M-16584.

Sarcodon leucopus (Pers.) Maas Geest. et Nannf.

On the ground, Ussuriysk Nature Reserve (Vasilyeva & Bezdeleva, 2006); under the tree of *Pinus densiflora*, Nikolaevka, 20 Sept. 2000, E.M. Bulakh, VLA M-16568.

Sarcodon scabrosus (Fr.) P. Karst.

On the ground under the tree of *Pinus densiflora*, Barabash-Levada: Shirokaya Canyon, 30 Aug. 2002, E.M. Bulakh, VLA M-17419.

Thelephora anthocephala (Bull.) Fr.

On the ground under the trees of *Pinus koraiensis*, Ussuriysk Nature Reserve, 21 Aug. 2001, O.K. Govorova, VLA M-16675; Birobidzhan: Bastak Nature Reserve, 11 Sept. 2001, E.M. Bulakh, VLA M-16687.

Thelephora caryophyllea (Schaeff.) Pers.

On the ground, Ussuriysk Nature Reserve, 13 Aug. 1961, L.N. Vassiljeva, VLA M-16665.

Thelephora multipartita Schwein.

On the ground under the trees of *Quercus*, Ussuriysk Nature Reserve, 18 Aug. 2001, O.K. Govorova, VLA M-16707; Terekhovka, 27 Aug. 1998, O.K. Govorova, VLA M-16697; Big Khekhtsir Nature Reserve, 15 Aug. 2004, Tolgor Bau, HMJAU 2995; Fuyuan, 5 Aug. 2004,

Tolgor Bau, HMJAU 2618.

Thelephora palmata (Scop.) Fr.

On the ground, Ussuriysk Nature Reserve, 21 Aug. 2001, O.K. Govorova, VLA M-16732; Big Khekhtsir Nature Reserve, 11 Aug. 1981, E.M. Bulakh, VLA M-16715; Birobidzhan: Bastak Nature Reserve, 17 Aug. 2000, E.M. Bulakh, VLA M-16713; Raohe, 8 Sept. 2003, Tolgor Bau, HMJAU 3403.

Thelephora penicillata (Pers.): Fr.

On the ground, Ussuriysk Nature Reserve, 18 Aug. 2001, O.K. Govorova, VLA M-16750.

Thelephora terrestris Ehrh.

On the forest litter, Terekhovka, 27 Aug. 1998, O.K. Govorova, VLA M-16754; Ussuriysk Nature Reserve, 22 Sept. 1961, L.N. Vassiljeva, VLA M-16771; Khorol, 18 Sept. 1954, L.N, Vassiljeva, VLA M-16772; Upper Ussuri Station, 14 Aug. 1974, E.M. Bulakh, VLA M-16778; Birobidzhan: Bastak Nature Reserve, 14 Aug. 2006, E.M. Bulakh, VLA M-21048.

Tomentella bryophila (Pers.) M.J. Larsen

On the decayed wood of coniferous and deciduous trees, Ussuriysk Nature Reserve (Kõljalg, 1996).

Tomentella coerulea (Bres.) Höhn. et Litsch.

On the decayed wood of coniferous and deciduous trees, Ussuriysk Nature Reserve (Kõljalg, 1996).

Tomentella crinalis (Fr.) M. J. Larsen

On the decayed wood of deciduous trees, Ussuriysk Nature Reserve (Kõljalg, 1996); Big Khekhtsir Nature Reserve (Azbukina & Kharkevich, 1986). - On the log *of Abies nephrolepis*, Upper Ussuri Station [(Azbukina & Kharkevich, 1984), as *Caldesiella ferruginosa* (Fr.) Sacc.]

Tomentella ferruginea (Pers.) Pat.

On the decayed wood of coniferous and deciduous trees, Ussuriysk Nature Reserve (Kõljalg, 1996).

Tomentella fibrosa (Berk. et M.A. Curtis) Kõljalg

On the decayed wood of coniferous and leaved trees, Ussuriysk Nature Reserve (Kõljalg, 1996).

Tomentella lateritia Pat.

On the decayed wood of coniferous and foliage trees, Ussuriysk Nature Reserve (Kõljalg, 1996).

Tomentella lilacinogrisea Wakef.

On the decayed wood of coniferous and leaved trees, Ussuriysk Nature Reserve (Kõljalg, 1996).

Tomentella stuposa (Link) Stalpers

On the wood of coniferous and deciduous trees, Ussuriysk Nature Reserve (Kõljalg, 1996).

Tomentella terrestris (Berk. et Broome) M.J. Larsen

On the decayed wood of coniferous and deciduous trees, Ussuriysk Nature Reserve (Kõljalg, 1996). - On the basis of trunks of *Betula* and *Populus*, Upper Ussuri Station (Azbukina & Kharkevich, 1984).

TREMELLALES
APORPIACEAE

Elmerina caryae (Scwein.) D.A.Reid

[= *Aporpium caryae* (Schwein.) Teix et Rog.]

On the old fruit bodies of a polypore on the log of *Betula*, Upper Ussuri Station (Azbukina & Kharkevich, 1984).

Elmerina holophaea (Pat.) Parmasto

On the logs of deciduous trees, Ussuriysk Nature Reserve, 19 Aug. 1975, M.M. Nazarova, VLA M-12035; Big Khekhtsir Nature Reserve (Azbukina & Kharkevich, 1986). - On the wood of *Quercus*, Upper Ussuri Station, 26 Aug. 1973, E.M. Bulakh, VLA M-12032; on the branch of *Quercus*, Birobidzhan: Bastak Nature Reserve, 7 Sept. 2001, E.M. Bulakh, VLA M-15689.

EXIDIACEAE

Eichleriella alliciens (Berk. et Cooke) Burt

On the wood of a deciduous tree, Ussuriysk Nature Reserve (Vasilyeva & Bezdeleva, 2006).

Eichleriella incarnata Bres.

On the wood in deciduous forest, Hulin, 9 Aug. 2004, Tolgor Bau, HMJAU 3292.

Exidia glandulosa (Bull.) Fr.

On the fallen twigs of *Padus*, Vladivostok, 2 Aug. 2003, Tolgor Bau, HMJAU 2855; Ussuriysk Nature Reserve, 5 Jul. 1990, O.K. Govorova, VLA M-11416. - On the fallen twigs of *Crataegus*, Khanka Nature Reserve, 18 Jun. 2003, V.Yu. Barkalov, VLA M-18477. - On the wood of *Betula*, Upper Ussuri Station, 23 Jun. 1974, E.M. Bulakh, VLA M-11375; Big Khekhtsir Nature Reserve, 21 Jun. 1981, E.M. Bulakh, VLA M-11384. - On the bark, Big Khekhtsir Nature Reserve, 16 Aug. 2004, Tolgor Bau, HMJAU 2929; Raohe, 9 Sept. 2003, Tolgor Bau, HMJAU A3056; Hulin, 19 Sept. 2004, Tolgor Bau, HMJAU 2600. - On the log of a deciduous tree, Birobidzhan: Bastak Nature Reserve, 20 Aug. 2003, E.M. Bulakh, VLA M-18544.

Exidia japonica Lloyd

On the fallen twigs, Ussuriysk Nature Reserve, 21 Aug. 2001, O.K. Govorova, VLA M-15701. - On the fallen twigs of *Quercus,* Khanka Nature Reserve, 19 Jun. 2002, V. Yu. Barkalov, VLA M-18475. - On the trunk of *Maackia amurensis*, Tikhorechnoye, 11 Aug. 1977, E.M. Bulakh , VLA M-11847.

Exidia nucleata (Schwein.) Burt

On the wood of *Quercus*, Ussuriysk: Gornotayozhnoye, 23 Jul. 2002, O.K. Govorova, VLA M-18655. - On the log of *Tilia,* Khanka Nature Reserve, 20 Jun. 2002, V.Ju. Barkalov, VLA M-18642.

Exidia pallida K. Wells et Raitv.

On the log of a deciduous tree, Ussuriysk Nature Reserve (Wells & Raitviir, 1977).

Exidia recisa (Ditmar) Fr.

On the fallen twigs, Ussuriysk Nature Reserve, 23 Oct. 1956, I.A. Bunkina, VLA M-11490; Birobidzhan: Bastak Nature Reserve, 20 Aug. 2003, E.M. Bulakh, VLA M-18472. - On the fallen twigs of *Alnus*, Upper Ussuri Station, 11 Aug. 1990, E.M. Bulakh, VLA M-18469.

Exidia repanda Fr.

On the fallen twigs of *Sorbus*, Ussuriysk Nature Reserve, 18 Aug. 2001, O.K. Govorova, VLA M-15665. - On the log of *Betula*, Khanka Nature Reserve, 20 Jun. 2002, V.Yu. Barkalov, VLA M-1854.

Exidia thuretiana (Lév.) Fr.

On the fallen twigs, Ussuriysk Nature Reserve, 5 Jul. 1990, O.K. Govorova, VLA M-11555; Chernigovka, 8 Aug. 1990, O.K. Govorova, VLA M-11530. - On the log of *Quercus*, Khanka Nature Reserve, 20 Jun. 2002, V. Yu. Barkalov, VLA M-18485.

Exidia uvapassa Lloyd

On the fallen twigs, Ussuriysk Nature Reserve, 19 Oct. 1990, O.K. Govorova, VLA M-11581. - On the fallen twigs of *Quercus*, Khanka Nature Reserve, 22 Jun. 2002, V.Yu. Barkalov, VLA M-18492.

Protodaedalea hispida Imazeki

On the rotten wood, Ussuriysk, 3 Aug. 2003, Tolgor Bau, 2959; Big Khekhtsir Nature Reserve, 18 Aug. 2004, Tolgor Bau, HMJAU 2886; Raohe: Shengli State Farm, 6 Aug. 2004, Tolgor Bau, HMJAU 2541; Birobidzhan: Bastak Nature Reserve, 14 Aug. 2006, E.M. Bulakh, VLA M- 20986.

Protohydnum piceicola Kühner et Bourdot

On fallen twigs of *Picea*, Ussuriysk Nature Reserve (Vasilyeva & Bezdeleva, 2006).

Pseudohydnum gelatinosum (Scop.) P. Karst.

On the logs, Ussuriysk Nature Reserve, 24 Aug. 1975, M.M. Nazarova, VLA M-11777; Birobidzhan: Bastak Nature Reserve, 18 Aug. 2003, E.M. Bulakh, VLA M-18244. - On the wood of a coniferous tree, Upper Ussuri Station, 25 Aug.1973, E.M. Bulakh, VLA M-11778.

Sebacina calcea (Pers.) Bres.

[= *Exidiopsis calcea* (Pers.) K. Wells]

On the wood of a coniferous tree, Ussuriysk Nature Reserve (Vasilyeva & Bezdeleva, 2006). - On the twigs of *Picea ajanensis* in dark coniferous forest, Big Khekhtsir Nature Reserve (Azbukina & Kharkevich, 1986).

Sebacina epigaea (Berk. et Broome) Bourdot et Galcin

On the ground and wood, Ussuriysk Nature Reserve (Vasilyeva & Bezdeleva, 2006).

Sebacina incrustans (Pers.) Tul. et C. Tul.

On the culms of grasses, Ussuriysk Nature Reserve, 18 Aug. 2001, O.K. Govorova, VLA M-15664; Birobidzhan: Bastak Nature Reserve, 13 Aug. 2002, E.M. Bulakh, VLA M-18667. - On the ground, Ussuriysk: Gornotayozhnoye, 15 Jul. 1959, A.A. Ablakatova, VLA M-11831.

Guepinia helvelloides (DC.) Fr.

[= *Tremiscus helvelloides* (DC.) Donk]

On the wood, Ussuriysk Nature Reserve, 14 Sept. 1975, M.M. Nazarova, VLA M-11771. - On the stump, Upper Ussuri Station, 16 Sept.1975, E.M. Bulakh, VLA M-11768.

TREMELLACEAE

Tremella cinnabarina Bull.

On the wood of a coniferous tree, Ussuriysk Nature Reserve, 19 Oct. 1990, O.K. Govorova, VLA M-11723.

Tremella dysenterica Möller

On the wood of deciduous trees, Ussuriysk Nature Reserve, 23 Aug. 2002, O.K. Govorova, VLA M-18647; Ussuriysk: Gornotayozhnoye, 13 Aug. 2002, O.K. Govorova, VLA M-18626. - On the log of *Populus davidiana*, Birobidzhan: Bastak Nature Reserve, 17 Aug. 2002, E.M. Bulakh, VLA M-18630.

Tremella encephala Willd.

On the fallen branches of *Abies*, Ussuriysk Nature Reserve (Vasilyeva & Bezdeleva, 2006).

Tremella fimbriata Fr.

On the wood of *Quercus mongolica*, Ussuriysk Nature Reserve, 19 Oct. 1990, O.K. Govorova, VLA M-11605. - On the stump of *Betula,* Upper Ussuri Station, 19 Jun. 1974, E.M. Bulakh, VLA M-11603. - On the fallen twigs of *Quercus mongolica*, Big Khekhtsir Nature Reserve, 3 Aug.1981, E.M. Bulakh, VLA M-11602.

Tremella foliacea Pers.

On the log of *Quercus*, Ussuriysk Nature Reserve, 23 Oct. 1995, E.M. Bulakh, VLA M-11646; Ussuriysk: Gornotayozhnoye, 23 Jul. 2002, O.K. Govorova, VLA M-18623; Barabash-Levada: Shirokaya Canyon, 30 Aug. 2002, E.M. Bulakh, VLA M-18624; Birobidzhan: Bastak Nature Reserve, 16 Aug. 2000, E.M. Bulakh, VLA M-15008. - On the log of *Picea,* Upper Ussuri Station, 15 Aug. 1974, E.M. Bulakh , VLA M-11609. - On the log of *Betula*, Big Khekhtsir Nature Reserve, 22 Jun. 1981, E.M. Bulakh, VLA M-11620.

Tremella mesenterica Retz.

On fallen twigs of *Corylus*, Ussuriysk Nature Reserve, 18 Aug. 1963, M.M. Nazarova, VLA M-11666. - On the log of *Abies nephrolepis*, Big Khekhtsir Nature Reserve (Azbukina & Kharkevich, 1986). - On the log of *Alnus*, Birobidzhan: Bastak Nature Reserve, 17 Aug. 2000, E.M. Bulakh, VLA M-15017.

PLATYGLOEOALES

PLATYGLOEOACEAE

Eocronartium muscicola (Pers.) Fitzp.

On the mosses, Ussuriysk Nature Reserve, 6 Jul. 1962, M.M. Nazarova, VLA M-10952; Upper Ussuri Station, 7 Aug. 1973, E.M. Bulakh, VLA M-10949; Big Khekhtsir Nature Reserve, 9 Aug. 1981, E.M. Bulakh, VLA M-10965.

REFERENCES

Azbukina Z M, Kharkevich S S. The flora and vegetation of the Big Khektsir Nature Reserve (Khabarovsk Territory). Far East Sci. Center. Vladivostok, 1986, 1-228. (in Russian)

Azbukina Z M, Kharkevich S S. The flora of the Upper Ussuri Station (the south of Sikhote-Alin). Vladivostok: Far East Sci. Center, 1984, 1-130. (in Russian)

Bau T, Bulakh Y M, Zhuang J Y, Li Y. Agarics and other macrobasidiomycetes from Ussuri River Valley. Mycosystema, 2007, 26(3): 349-368.

Bau T, Li Y, Gorbunova I A, Bulakh E M, Sysuev W A. common wild edible mushrooms from Russia. Edible Fungi of China, 2008, 27(3): 9-13. (in Chinese)

Bondartsev A S. New polyporous fungi found in the Far East. Botanical materials of the Department of cryptogamic plants, 1962, 15: 103-111. (in Russian)

Bondartseva M A, Parmasto E H. Key-books of fungi in the USSR. Aphyllophorales. Part. 1. Nauka, Leningrad, 1986, 1-192. (in Russian)

Burdsall H H. A contribution to the taxonomy of the genus *Phanerochaete*. Mycologia Memoir, 1985, 10: 1-165.

Dai Y C, Bau T. Illustrations of edible and medicinal fungi in Northeast China. Beijing: Science Press, 2007. (in Chinese)

Kõljalg U. *Tomentella* (Basidiomycota) and related genera in temperate Eurasia. Synopsis Fungorum, 1996, 9: 1-213.

Kovalenko A E. Hygrophorales. 1995, 206-301. In Azbukina Z M. (ed.) Cryptogamic plants, fungi and mosses the Russian Far East. Vol. 3. Nauka. Saint-Petersburg. (in Russian)

Li Y, Bau T. Mushrooms of Changbai Mountains, China. Beijing: Science Press, 2003. (in Chinese)

Mao X L. Economic fungi of China. Beijing: Science Press, 1998, 1-762. (in Chinese)

Mao X L. The macrofungi in China. Zhengzhou: Henan Science and Technology Press, 2000, 1-719. (in Chinese)

Nezdoyminogo E L. Cortinariaceae, 1990, 207-381. In Wasser S P. (ed.) Cryptogamic plants, fungi and mosses the Soviet Far East. Vol. 1. Nauka. Leningrad. (in Russian)

Parmasto E, Kollom A. The genus *Melanoporia* (Polypores, Hymenomycetes). Folia Cryptog. Estonica, 2000, 37: 67-78.

Parmasto E. A new porioid genus of the Hyphodontieae (Aphyllophorales: Corticiaceae). Mycotaxon, 1982, 14: 103-106.

Parmasto E. Conspectus systematis Corticeacearum. Tartu., 1968, 1-261.

Parmasto E. Corticiaceae URSS. I. Descriptiones taxorum novarum. Combinationes novae. Eesti NSV Teaduste Akad. Toimet. Biol. Ser, 1965, 2: 220-233.

Parmasto E. *Leucophellinus mollissimus* (Pat.) Parm. - troopiline torikuline NSV Liidu Kaug-idas. Eesti NSV Teaduste Akad. Toimet. Biol. Ser., 1983, 32: 264-271.

Petersen R H, Nagasawa E. The genus *Xerula* in temperate east Asia. Rep. Tottori Mycol. Inst., 2005, 43: 1-49.

Tai F L. Sylloge Fungorum Sinicorum. Beijing: Science Press, 1979, 1-1527.

Teng S C. A contribution to our knowledge of the higher fungi of China. Beijing: Academia Sinica, 1939, 1-614.

Vasilyeva L N, Bezdeleva T A. (eds.) The flora, vegetation and mycobiota of the reserve "Ussuriysky". Dalnauka. Vladivostok, 2006, 1-300. (in Russian)

Vassiljeva L N, Sosin P E. A contribution to the knowledge of gastomycetous fungi of the Primorsky Territory. Reports of the Far Eastern Branch of the Siberian Department of the USSR Academy of Sciences, 1959, 11: 58-62. (in Russian)

Vassiljeva L N. Agaricoid mushrooms of the Primorsky Territory. Nauka. Leningrad., 1973, 1-331. (in Russian)

Wasser S P. Agaricaceae, 1990, 118-206. In Wasser S P. (ed.) Cryptogamic plants, fungi and mosses the Soviet Far East. Vol. 1. Nauka. Leningrad. (in Russian)

Wells K, Raitviir A. The species of *Exidiopsis* (Tremellaceae) of the USSR. Mycologia, 1977, 69: 987-1007.

Yang Z L. Further notes on genus *Oudemansiella* from Southweastern China. Mycotaxon, 2000, 74: 357-366.

Urediniomycetes: Uredinales

Zinaida M. AZBUKINA,   Jian-Yun ZHUANG

The checklist presented here is the result of our own studies based on the specimens collected by the writers during 2003 and 2004 expeditions to the Ussuri valley. We put emphasis on areas in China including Xingkaihu (Khanka) Nature Reserve, Hulin, Raohe and Fuyuan, and areas in Russia including Khanka Nature Reserve, Ussuriysk Nature Reserve and the Khabarovsk region. A total of 78 species belonging to 14 genera (including form genera) are recorded. For each species, host plants are given first, followed by field data of collections. The checklist must be regarded as preliminary. For further understanding the species diversity of rusts in the region, more collecting activities will undoubtedly be necessary.

UREDINIOMYCETES

UREDINALES

PUCCINIASTRACEAE

Melampsoridium betulinum (Fr.) Kleb.

On *Betula ermanii* Cham., Hulin: Hutou, 4 Sept. 2003, Z.M. Azbukina & J.Y. Zhuang 7307.

Pucciniastrum agrimoniae (Dietel) Tranzschel

On *Agrimonia pilosa* Ledeb., Ussuriysk: Gornotayozhnoye, 4 Aug. 2003, J.Y. Zhuang 7011, 7021; 6 Aug. 2003, J.Y. Zhuang 7056; Khanka Nature Reserve, 9 Aug. 2003, J.Y. Zhuang 7096, 7101; Hulin: 856 State Farm, 5 Sept. 2003, Z.M. Azbukina & J.Y. Zhuang 7255; Hulin: Dongfanghong, 3 Sept. 2003, Z.M. Azbukina & J.Y. Zhuang 7284; Mudanjiang: Mt. Weihushan, 9 Aug. 2004, J.Y. Zhuang 7654, 7656; vicinity of Khabarovsk, 15 Aug. 2004, J.Y. Zhuang 7764; Khabarovsk: Big Khekhtsir Nature Reverve, 16 Aug. 2004, J.Y. Zhuang 7701, 7707; Aug. 17, 2004, J.Y. Zhuang 7709, 7715, 7718; Birobidzhan: Bastak Nature Reserve, 18 Aug. 2004, J.Y. Zhuang 7728, 7735, 7742; 19 Aug. 2004, J.Y. Zhuang 7770.

Pucciniastrum epilobii G.H. Otth

On *Epilobium palustre* L., Raohe: Dadai, 7 Aug. 2004, J.Y. Zhuang 7620.

Pucciniastrum tiliae Miyabe

On *Tilia mandshurica* Rupr., Xingkaihu Nature Reserve, 1 Sept. 2003, Z.M. Azbukina & J.Y. Zhuang 7246.

Thekopsora asterum Tranzschel

On *Aster ageratoides* Turcz., Raohe: Dadai, 7 Aug. 2004, J.Y. Zhuang 7619; Khabarovsk: Big Khekhtsir Nature Reserve, 17 Aug. 2004, J.Y. Zhuang 7712, 7721. - On *Kalimeris incisa* (Fisch.) DC., Ussuriysk: Gornotayozhnoye, 6 Aug. 2003, J.Y. Zhuang 7055. - On *Kalimeris integrifolia* Turcz., Ussuriysk: Gornotayozhnoye, 5 Aug. 2003, J.Y. Zhuang 7032.

Thekopsora brachybotridis Tranzschel

On *Brachybotrys paridiformis* Maxim. ex Olivier, Mudanjiang: Mt. Weihushan, 9 Aug. 2004, J.Y. Zhuang 7659.

Thekopsora guttata (J. Schröt.) P. Syd. & Syd.

On *Galium davuricum* Turcz. ex Ledeb., Raohe: Dadai, 7 Aug. 2004, J.Y. Zhuang 7624, 7635; Khabarovsk: Big Khekhtsir Nature Reserve, 15 Aug. 2004, J.Y. Zhuang 7672, 7686; 16 Aug. 2004, J.Y. Zhuang 7702; 17 Aug. 2004, J.Y. Zhuang 7713; Birobidzhan: Bastak Nature Reserve, 18 Aug. 2004, J.Y. Zhuang 7745. - On *Galium maximoviczii* (Kom.) Pobed., Ussuriysk: Gornotayozhnoye, 4 Aug. 2003, J.Y. Zhuang 7017; Hulin: Wulindong, 4 Sept. 2003, Z.M. Azbukina & J.Y. Zhuang 7313; Fuyuan, 4 Aug. 2004, J.Y. Zhuang 7554. - On *Galium pseudoasprellum* Makino, Ussuriysk Nature Reserve, 7 Aug. 2003, J.Y. Zhuang 7067, 7074.

Thekopsora rubiae Kom.

On *Rubia cordifolia* L., Ussuriysk Nature Reserve, 7 Aug. 2003, J.Y. Zhuang 7072; Hulin: Dongfanghong, 3 Sept. 2003, Z.M. Azbukina & J.Y. Zhuang 7285; Khabarovsk: Big Khekhtsir Nature Reserve, 15 Aug. 2004, J.Y. Zhuang 7667.

Uredinopsis pteridis Dietel & Holw.

On *Pteridium aquilinum* (L.) Kuhn var. *latiusculum* (Desv.) Underw., Xingkaihu Nature Reserve, 1 Sept. 2003, Z.M. Azbukina & J.Y. Zhuang 7242, 7249.

Uredinopsis struthiopteridis F.C.M. Stoermer ex Dietel

On *Matteuccia struthiopteris* (L.) Todaro, Ussuriysk Nature Reserve, 7 Aug. 2003, J.Y. Zhuang 7081; Khabarovsk: Big Khekhtsir Nature Reserve, 15 Aug. 2004, J.Y. Zhuang 7673.

COLEOSPORIACEAE

Coleosporium cimicifugatum Thüm.

On *Actaea acuminata* Wall. ex Royle, Fuyuan, 4 Aug. 2004, J.Y. Zhuang 7524, 7531. - On *Cimicifuga dahurica* (Turcz.) Maxim., Ussuriysk: Gornotayozhnoye, 4 Aug. 2003, J.Y. Zhuang 7009, 7024; 5 Aug. 2003, J.Y. Zhuang 7037, 7040; 6 Aug. 2003, J.Y. Zhuang 7058; Hulin: Dongfanghong, 3 Sept. 2003, Z.M. Azbukina & J.Y. Zhuang 7279; Raohe: Dadai, 7

Aug. 2004, J.Y. Zhuang 7630; Birobidzhan: Bastak Nature Reserve, 18 Aug. 2004, J.Y. Zhuang 7737; 19 Aug. 2004, J.Y. Zhuang 7756. - On *Cimicifuga simplex* (Wormsk. ex DC.) Turcz., Fuyuan, 4 Aug. 2004, J.Y. Zhuang 7547; Raohe: Shengli State Farm, 6 Aug. 2004, J.Y. Zhuang 7593, 7597; Raohe: Dadai, 7 Aug. 2004, J.Y. Zhuang 7607, 7616, 7623, 7639; Mudanjiang: Mt. Weihushan, 9 Aug. 2004, J.Y. Zhuang 7645, 7653; vicinity of Khabarovsk, 15 Aug. 2004, J.Y. Zhuang 7665; Khabarovsk: Big Khekhtsir Nature Reserve, 15 Aug. 2004, J.Y. Zhuang 7670; 17 Aug. 2004, J.Y. Zhuang 7711, 7722.

Coleosporium clematidis Barclay

On *Clematis fusca* Turcz., Hulin: 856 State Farm, 2 Sept. 2003, Z.M. Azbukina & J.Y. Zhuang 7265. - On *Clematis mandshurica* Rupr., Khanka Nature Reserve, 9 Aug. 2003, J.Y. Zhuang 7103; Fuyuan, 4 Aug. 2004, J.Y. Zhuang 7537.

Coleosporium lycopi P. Syd. & Syd.

On *Adenophora pereskiifolia* (Fisch. ex Schult.) G. Don, Ussuriysk: Gornotayozhnoye, 4 Aug. 2003, J.Y. Zhuang 7013, 7026, 7028; 5 Aug. 2003, J.Y. Zhuang 7036; Hulin: 854 State Farm, 2 Sept. 2003, Z.M. Azbukina & J.Y. Zhuang 7267; Raohe: Shengli State Farm, 6 Sept. 2003, Z.M. Azbukina & J.Y. Zhuang 7320, 7327. - On *Adenophora verticillata* Fisch., Khanka Nature Reserve, 9 Aug. 2003, J.Y. Zhuang 7098; Fuyuan, 4 Aug. 2004, J.Y. Zhuang 7525, 7528, 7532, 7573; Fuyuan: Sanjiang Nature Reserve, 5 Aug. 2004, J.Y. Zhuang 7579; Khabarovsk: Big Khekhtsir Nature Reserve, 15 Aug. 2004, J.Y. Zhuang 7671, 7680; Birobidzhan: Bastak Nature Reserve, 19 Aug. 2004, J.Y. Zhuang 7743, 7768.

Coleosporium neocacaliae Saho

(= *Coleosporium senecionis* auct. non Kickx)

On *Cacalia auriculata* DC., Hulin: Dongfanghong, 3 Sept. 2003, Z.M. Azbukina & J.Y. Zhuang 7282; Raohe: Shengli State Farm, 6 Sept. 2003, Z.M. Azbukina & J.Y. Zhuang 7321; Raohe: Dadai, 7 Aug. 2004, J.Y. Zhuang 7636; Khabarovsk: Big Khekhtsir Nature Reserve, 17 Aug. 2004, J.Y. Zhuang 7710, 7720. - On *Cacalia hastata* L., Hulin: Dongfanghong, 3 Sept. 2003, Z.M. Azbukina & J.Y. Zhuang 7294; Hulin: Wulindong, 4 Sept. 2003, Z.M. Azbukina & J.Y. Zhuang 7311; Fuyuan, 4 Aug. 2004, J.Y. Zhuang 7555; Raohe: Dadai, 7 Aug. 2004, J.Y. Zhuang 7622; Mudanjiang: Mt. Weihushan, 9 Aug. 2004, J.Y. Zhuang 7657; Birobidzhan: Bastak Nature Reserve, 19 Aug. 2004, J.Y. Zhuang 7762. - On *Cacalia kamtschatica* (Maxim.) Kudo, Fuyuan, 4 Aug. 2004, J.Y. Zhuang 7530, 7545. - On *Senecio nemorensis* L., Birobidzhan: Bastak Nature Reserve, 18 Aug. 2004, J.Y. Zhuang 7751.

Coleosporium pedunculatum S. Kaneko

On *Saussurea ussuriensis* Maxim., Raohe: Dadai, 7 Aug. 2004, J.Y. Zhuang 7631.

Coleosporium phellodendri Kom.

On *Phellodendron amurense* Rupr., Hulin: 856 State Farm, 2 Sept. 2003, Z.M. Azbukina & J.Y. Zhuang 7253, 7258; Hulin: 854 State Farm, 2 Sept. 2003, Z.M. Azbukina & J.Y. Zhuang 7268, 7270; Hulin: Dongfanghong, 3 Sept. 2003, Z.M. Azbukina & J.Y. Zhuang 7276;

Fuyuan, 4 Aug. 2004, J.Y. Zhuang 7562, 7567; Raohe: Shengli State Farm, 6 Aug. 2004, J.Y. Zhuang 7603; Khabarovsk: Big Khekhtsir Nature Reserve, 15 Aug. 2004, J.Y. Zhuang 7674, 7688; 16 Aug. 2004, J.Y. Zhuang 7700, 7708; Birobidzhan: Bastak Nature Reserve, 19 Aug. 2004, J.Y. Zhuang 7769.

Coleosporium saussureae Thüm.

On *Saussurea amurensis* Turcz., Hulin: Dongfanghong, 3 Sept. 2003, Z.M. Azbukina & J.Y. Zhuang 7281. - On *Saussurea manshurica* Kom., Mudanjiang: Mt. Weihushan, 9 Aug. 2004, J.Y. Zhuang 7658; Khabarovsk: Big Khekhtsir Nature Reserve, 17 Aug. 2004, J.Y. Zhuang 7714. - On *Saussurea pectinata* Bunge, Xingkaihu Nature Reserve, 1 Sept. 2003, Z.M. Azbukina & J.Y. Zhuang 7234; Hulin: 854 State Farm, 2 Sept. 2003, Z.M. Azbukina & J.Y. Zhuang 7269; Hulin: Dongfanghong, 3 Sept. 2003, Z.M. Azbukina & J.Y. Zhuang 7291.

Coleosporium tussilaginis (Pers.) Lév.

[= *Coleosporium campanulae* (F. Strauss) Tul. = *Coleosporium ligulariae* Thüm. = *Coleosporium melampyri* (Rebent.) P. Karst.]

On *Campanula cephalotes* Nakai, Raohe: Dadai, 7 Aug. 2004, J.Y. Zhuang 7613. - On *Campanula glomerata* L., Raohe: Shengli State Farm, 6 Sept. 2003, Z.M. Azbukina & J.Y. Zhuang 7322. - On *Campanula punctata* Lam., Fuyuan, 4 Aug. 2004, J.Y. Zhuang 7533, 7543, 7556; Khabarovsk: Big Khekhtsir Nature Reserve, 15 Aug. 2004, J.Y. Zhuang 7687. - On *Ligularia fischeri* (Ledeb.) Turcz., Raohe: Shengli State Farm, 6 Sept. 2003, Z.M. Azbukina & J.Y. Zhuang 7323; Fuyuan, 4 Aug. 2004, J.Y. Zhuang 7557. - On *Ligularia intermedia* Nakai, Raohe: Shengli State Farm, 6 Sept. 2003, Z.M. Azbukina & J.Y. Zhuang 7324, 7326. - On *Ligularia sibirica* (L.) Cass., Fuyuan, 4 Aug. 2004, J.Y. Zhuang 7529, 7544, 7548, 7564. - On *Melampyrum roseum* Maxim., Ussuriysk: Gornotayozhnoye, 4 Aug. 2003, J.Y. Zhuang 7023.

CRONARTIACEAE

Cronartium flaccidum (Alb. & Schwein.) G. Winter

On *Paeonia lactiflora* Pall., Vladivostok: Botanic Garden, 3 Aug. 2003, J.Y. Zhuang 7007; Ussuriysk: Gornotayozhnoye, 4 Aug. 2003, J.Y. Zhuang 7030. - On *Paeonia obovata* Maxim., Khanka Nature Reserve, 9 Aug. 2003, J.Y. Zhuang 7104.

Cronartium orientale S. Kaneko

On *Quercus mongolica* Fisch. ex Ledeb., Ussuriysk: Gornotayozhnoye, 4 Aug. 2003, J.Y. Zhuang 7015.

Cronartium ribicola J.C. Fisch.

On *Ribes mandshuricum* (Maxim.) Kom., Khabarovsk: Big Khekhtsir Nature Reserve, 15 Aug. 2004, J.Y. Zhuang 7668.

MELAMPSORACEAE

Melampsora abietis-populi S. Imai

On *Pupulus koreana* Rehd., Hulin: Dongfanghong, 3 Sept. 2003, Z.M. Azbukina & J.Y. Zhuang 7297.

Melampsora epitea (Kunze & J.C. Schmidt) Thüm.

On *Salix abscondita* Laksch., Hulin: Dongfanghong, 3 Sept. 2003, Z.M. Azbukina & J.Y. Zhuang 7289. - On *Salix gracilistyla* Miq. var. *latifolia* Skvortzov, vicinity of Fuyuan, 4 Aug. 2004, J.Y. Zhuang 7546, 7566; Fuyuan: Sanjiang Nature Reserve, 5 Aug. 2004, J.Y. Zhuang 7580. - On *Salix integra* Thunb., Mudanjiang: Mt. Weihushan, 9 Aug. 2004, J.Y. Zhuang 7649. - On *Salix linearistipularis* (Franch.) Hao, Fuyuan: Sanjiang Nature Reserve, 5 Aug. 2004, J.Y. Zhuang 7585. - On *Toisusu cardiophylla* (Trautv. et Mey.) Kimura, Hulin: Hutou, 4 Sept. 2003, Z.M. Azbukina & J.Y. Zhuang 7304. - On *Salix rorida* Laksch., Hulin: Dongfanghong, 3 Sept. 2003, Z.M. Azbukina & J.Y. Zhuang 7287; vicinity of Fuyuan, 4 Aug. 2004, J.Y. Zhuang 7550. - On *Salix schwerinii* E. Wolf, Hulin: Hutou, 4 Sept. 2003, Z.M. Azbukina & J.Y. Zhuang 7301, 7308; vicinity of Fuyuan, 4 Aug. 2004, J.Y. Zhuang 7553; Birobidzhan: Bastak Nature Reserve, 18 Aug. 2004, J.Y. Zhuang 7740, 7748; 19 Aug. 2004, J.Y. Zhuang 7767. - On *Salix udensis* Trautv. et Mey., Raohe: Shengli State Farm, 6 Aug. 2004, J.Y. Zhuang 7591. - On *Salix taraikensis* Kimura var. *latifolia* Kimura, Raohe: Dadai, 7 Aug. 2004, J.Y. Zhuang 7638. - On *Salix triandra* L., Hulin: 856 State Farm, 2 Sept. 2003, Z.M. Azbukina & J.Y. Zhuang 7251; Khabarovsk: Big Khekhtsir Nature Reserve, 15 Aug. 2004, J.Y. Zhuang 7683. - On *Salix* sp., Ussuriysk: Gornotayozhnoye, 6 Aug. 2003, J.Y. Zhuang 7060.

Melampsora euphorbiae (C. Schub.) Castagne

On *Euphorbia discolor* Ledeb., Khanka Nature Reserve, 8 Aug. 2003, J.Y. Zhuang 7089, 7092.

Melampsora kusanoi Dietel

On *Hypericum ascyron* L., Raohe: Dadai, 7 Aug. 2004, J.Y. Zhuang 7621.

Melampsora laricis-pentandrae Kleb.

On *Salix pentandra* L., Khanka Nature Reserve, 9 Aug. 2003, J.Y. Zhuang 7099; Xingkaihu Nature Reserve, 1 Sept. 2003, Z.M. Azbukina & J.Y. Zhuang 7244. - On *Salix* sp., Khanka Nature Reserve, 9 Aug. 2003, J.Y. Zhuang 7110.

Melampsora laricis-populina Kleb.

On *Populus* x *berolinensis* Dipp., vicinity of Khabarovsk, 14 Aug. 2004, J.Y. Zhuang 7662. - On *Populus* x *canadensis* Moench., Fuyuan: Sanjiang Nature Reserve, J. Y. Zhuang 7584. - On *Populus cathayana* Rehd., Smidovich, 18 Aug. 2004, J.Y. Zhuang 7754. - On *Populus koreana* Rehd., vicinity of Fuyuan, 4 Aug. 2004, J.Y. Zhuang 7534; Birobidzhan: Bastak Nature Reserve, 18 Aug. 2004, J.Y. Zhuang 7726, 7741, 7746; 19 Aug. 2004, J.Y. Zhuang 7757. - On *Populus simonii* Carr., Fuyuan: Sanjiang Nature Reserve, 5 Aug. 2004, J.Y.

Zhuang 7576, 7577, 7583; vicinity of Khabarovsk, 14 Aug. 2004, J.Y. Zhuang 7661. - On *Populus suaveolens* Fisch., Hulin: Hutou, 4 Sept. 2003, Z.M. Azbukina & J.Y. Zhuang 7306; vicinity of Fuyuan, 4 Aug. 2004, J.Y. Zhuang 7565.

Melampsora magnusiana Wagner ex Kleb.

On *Populus* x *canadensis* Moench. cf. *"robusta"*, Khanka Nature Reserve, 9 Sept. 2003, J.Y. Zhuang 7108, 7094 ; Hulin: 856 State Farm, 2 Sept. 2003, Z.M. Azbukina & J.Y. Zhuang 7250; Hulin: 854 State Farm, 2 Sept. 2003, Z.M. Azbukina & J.Y. Zhuang 7271; Hulin: Hutou, 4 Sept. 2003, Z.M. Azbukina & J.Y. Zhuang 7305; Hulin: Wulindong, 4 Sept. 2003, Z.M. Azbukina & J.Y. Zhuang 7317; vicinity of Fuyuan, 4 Aug. 2004, J.Y. Zhuang 7542, 7560, 7575; Fuyuan: Sanjiang Nature Reserve, 5 Aug. 2004, J.Y. Zhuang 7578; Khabarovsk: Khekhtsir Nature Reserve, 15 Aug. 2004, J.Y. Zhuang 7677. - On *Populus tremula* L., Xingkaihu Nature Reserve, 1 Sept. 2003, Z.M. Azbukina & J.Y. Zhuang 7241; Raohe: Shengli State Farm, 6 Sept. 2003, Z.M. Azbukina & J.Y. Zhuang 7328; vicinity of Fuyuan, 4 Aug. 2004, J.Y. Zhuang 7526, 7527, 7571, 7572, 7574; Fuyuan: Sanjiang Nature Reserve, 5 Aug. 2004, J.Y. Zhuang 7587; Raohe: Shengli State Farm, 6 Aug. 2004, J.Y. Zhuang 7578; Raohe: Dadai, 7 Aug. 2004, J.Y. Zhuang 7612, 7615, 7627, 7633; Khabarovsk: Big Khekhtsir Nature Reserve, 15 Aug. 2004, J.Y. Zhuang 7676; 17 Aug. 2004, J.Y. Zhuang 7717; Birobidzhan: Bastak Nature Reserve, 18 Aug. 2004, J.Y. Zhuang 7727, 7739. 7749; 19 Aug. 2004, 19 Aug. 2004, j.Y. Zhuang 7761.

CHACONIACEAE

Aplopsora lonicerae Tranzschel

On *Lonicera caerulea* L., Raohe: Dadai, 7 Aug. 2004, J.Y. Zhuang 7617.

UROPYXIDACEAE

Leucotelium padi Tranzschel

On *Padus avium* Mill., Ussuriysk Nature Reserve, 7 Aug. 2003, J.Y. Zhuang 7078.

PHRAGMIDIACEAE

Phragmidium griseum Dietel

On *Rubus crataegifolius* Bunge, Ussuriysk: Gornotayozhnoye, 5 Aug. 2003, J.Y. Zhuang 7031, 7035; 6 Aug. 2003, J.Y. Zhuang 7052.

Phragmidium montivagum Arthur

On *Rosa davurica* Pall., Hulin: 854 State Farm, 2 Sept. 2003, Z.M. Azbukina & J.Y.

Zhuang 7272.

Phragmidium papillatum Dietel

On *Potentilla cryptotaeniae* Maxim., Mudanjiang: Mt. Weihushan, 9 Aug. 2004, J.Y. Zhuang 7646.

Phragmidium potentillae (Pers.) P. Karst.

On *Potentilla chinensis* Sér., Khanka Nature Reserve, 9 Aug. 2003, J.Y. Zhuang 7114. - On *Potentilla multifida* L., Khanka Nature Reserve, 9 Aug. 2003, J.Y. Zhuang 7109.

Phragmidium rubi-idaei (DC.) P. Karst.

On *Rubus sachalinensis* Lévl., Birobidzhan: Bastak Nature Reserve, 16 Aug. 2004, J.Y. Zhuang 7747; 18 Aug. 2004, J.Y. Zhuang 7752.

Xenodochus carbonarius Schltdl.

On *Sanguisorba tenuifolia* Fisch. ex Link, Fuyuan, 4 Aug. 2004, J.Y. Zhuang 7535.

RAVENELIACEAE

Triphragmium ulmariae (DC.) Link var. **anomalum** (Tranzschel) Lohsomb. & Kakish.

On *Filipendula palmata* (Pall.) Maxim., Hulin: Dongfanghong, 3 Sept. 2003, Z.M. Azbukina & J.Y. Zhuang 7273; Hulin: Wulindong, 4 Sept. 2003, Z.M. Azbukina & J.Y. Zhuang 7310, 7316; Fuyuan, 4 Aug. 2004, J.Y. Zhuang 7563; Raohe: Shengli State Farm, 6 Aug. 2004, J.Y. Zhuang 7601; Mudanjiang: Mt. Weihushan, 9 Aug. 2004, J.Y. Zhuang 7650.

PHRAGMIDIACEAE

Phragmidium griseum Dietel

On *Rubus crataegifolius* Bunge, Ussuriysk: Gornotayozhnoye, 5 Aug. 2003, J.Y. Zhuang 7031, 7035; 6 Aug. 2003, J.Y. Zhuang 7052.

Phragmidium montivagum Arthur

On *Rosa davurica* Pall., Hulin: 854 State Farm, 2 Sept. 2003, Z.M. Azbukina & J.Y. Zhuang 7272.

Phragmidium papillatum Dietel

On *Potentilla cryptotaeniae* Maxim., Mudanjiang: Mt. Weihushan, 9 Aug. 2004, J.Y. Zhuang 7646.

Phragmidium potentillae (Pers.) P. Karst.

On *Potentilla chinensis* Sér., Khanka Nature Reserve, 9 Aug. 2003, J.Y. Zhuang 7114. - On *Potentilla multifida* L., Khanka Nature Reserve, 9 Aug. 2003, J.Y. Zhuang 7109.

Phragmidium rubi-idaei (DC.) P. Karst.

On *Rubus sachalinensis* Lévl., Birobidzhan: Bastak Nature Reserve, 16 Aug. 2004, J.Y. Zhuang 7747; 18 Aug. 2004, J.Y. Zhuang 7752.

Xenodochus carbonarius Schltdl.

On *Sanguisorba tenuifolia* Fisch. ex Link, Fuyuan, 4 Aug. 2004, J.Y. Zhuang 7535.

PUCCINIACEAE

Puccinia aomoriensis Syd. & P. Syd.

On *Atractylodes ovata* (Thunb.) DC., Ussuriysk: Gornotayozhnoye, 5 Aug. 2003, J.Y. Zhuang 7045. - On *Carex* sp., vicinity of Fuyuan, 4 Aug. 2004, J.Y. Zhuang 7552.

Puccinia argentata (Schultz) G. Winter

On *Impatiens noli-tangere* L., Raohe: Dadai, 7 Aug. 2004, J.Y. Zhuang 7640.

Puccinia baicalensis Tranzschel

On *Aegopodium alpestre* Ledeb., Mudanjiang: Mt. Weihushan, 9 Aug. 2004, J.Y. Zhuang 7655.

Puccinia brachypodii G.H. Otth var. *poae-nemoralis* (G.H. Otth) Cummins & H.C. Greene

On *Poa* sp., Fuyuan, 10 Aug. 2000, J.Y. Zhuang 4490; vicinity of Khabarovsk, 15 Aug. 2004, J.Y. Zhuang 7663.

Puccinia calcitrapae DC. var. *centaureae* DC.

(= *Pucinia cirsii* Lasch)

On *Cirsium leo* Nakai & Kitag., Hulin: Dongfanghong, 3 Sept. 2003, Z.M. Azbukina & J.Y. Zhuang 7295. - On *Cirsium maackii* Maxim., Raohe: Shengli State farm, 6 Aug. 2004, J.Y. Zhuang 7588, 7604. - On *Cirsium pendulum* Fisch., Hulin: 856 State Farm, 2 Sept. 2003, Z.M. Azbukina & J.Y. Zhuang 7257. - On *Cirsium schantarense* Trautv. et Mey., Raohe: Shengli State Farm, 6 Aug. 2004, J.Y. Zhuang 7589, 7596.

Puccinia carici-adenocauli Kakish., M. Yokoi & Y. Harada

(anamorph: *Aecidium adenocauli* Syd. & P. Syd.)

On *Adenocaulon himalaicus* Edgew. Ussuriysk: Gornotayozhnoye, 4 Aug. 2003, J.Y. Zhuang 7020.

Puccinia caricina DC.

On *Carex arnellii* Christ, Hulin: Dongfanghong, 3 Sept. 2003, Z.M. Azbukina & J.Y. Zhuang 7277. - On *Carex rhynchophysa* C.A. Mey., Ussuriysk: Gornotayozhnoye,, 4 Aug. 2003, J.Y. Zhuang 7025; Ussuriysk Nature Reserve, 7 Aug. 2003, J.Y. Zhuang 7068, 7077, 7082; Xingkaihu Nature Reserve, 1 Sept. 2003, Z.M. Azbukina & J.Y. Zhuang 7247; Hulin: Dongfanghong, 3 Sept. 2003, Z.M. Azbukina & J.Y. Zhuang 7286; Hulin: Wulindong, 4 Sept. 2003, Z.M. Azbukina & J.Y. Zhuang 7309; Raohe: Shengli State Farm, 6 Aug. 2004, J.Y. Zhuang 7592, 7602; Mudanjiang: Mt. Weihushan, 9 Aug. 2004, J.Y. Zhuang 7651. - On *Carex yamatsutana* Ohwi, Raohe: Dadai, 7 Aug. 2004, J.Y. Zhuang 7614. - On *Carex* sp., Ussuriysk: Gornotayozhnoye, 4 Aug. 2003, J.Y. Zhuang 7014; 5 Aug. 2003, J.Y. Zhuang 7041; Ussuriysk Nature Reserve, 7 Aug. 2003, J.Y. Zhuang 7063; Xingkaihu Nature Reserve, 1 Sept. 2003,

Z.M. Azbukina & J.Y. Zhuang 7240; Raohe: Dadai, 7 Aug. 2004, J.Y. Zhuang 7626; Khabarovsk: Big Khekhtsir Nature Reserve, 15 Aug. 2004, J.Y. Zhuang 7682; Birobidzhan: Bastak Nature Reserve, 18 Aug. 2004, J.Y. Zhuang 7753; 19 Aug. 2004, J.Y. Zhuang 7766.

Puccinia caricicola Fuckel

On *Carex* sp., Khanka Nature Reserve, 9 Aug. 2003, J.Y. Zhuang 7111.

Puccinia caricis-siderostictae Dietel

On *Carex siderosticta* Hance, Hulin: Dongfanghong, 3 Sept. 2003, Z.M. Azbukina & J.Y. Zhuang 7278, 7283.

Puccinia chaerophylli Purton

On *Anthriscus sylvestris* (L.) Hoffm., Ussuriysk Nature Reserve, 7 Aug. 2003, J.Y. Zhuang 7070.

Puccinia circaeae-caricis Hasler

On *Circaea lutetiana* L., Ussuriysk: Gornotayozhnoye, 6 Aug. 2003, J.Y. Zhuang 7050, 7053, 7062.

Puccinia cnici-oleracei Pers. ex Desm.

On *Artemisia integrifolia* L., Ussuriysk: Gornotayozhnoye, 6 Aug. 2003, J.Y. Zhuang 7061; Raohe: Shengli State Farm, 6 Aug. 2004, J.Y. Zhuang 7590. - On *Artemisia lavandulaefolia* DC., Mudanjiang: Mt. Weihushan, 9 Aug. 2004, J.Y. Zhuang 7643. - On *Artemisia stolonifera* (Maxim.) Kom., Hulin: Dongfanghong, 1 Sept. 2003, Z.M. Azbukina & J.Y. Zhuang 7293.

Puccinia coronata Corda var. ***coronata***

On *Agrostis* sp., Fuyuan: Zhuaji, 9 Aug. 2000, J.Y. Zhuang 4487; Khabarovsk: Big Khekhtsir Nature Reserve, 17 Aug. 2004, J.Y. Zhuang 7716. - On *Calamagrostis langsdorffii* (Link) Trin., Fuyuan: Sanjiang Nature Reserve, 8 Aug. 2000, J.Y. Zhuang 4474; Fuyuan: Usu, 9 Aug. 2000, J.Y. Zhuang 4481. - On *Festuca rubra* L., Hulin: Wulindong, 4 Sept. 2003, Z.M. Azbukina & J.Y. Zhuang 7314. - On *Poa alpigena* (Blytt) Lindm., Khanka Nature Reserve, 9 Aug. 2003, J.Y. Zhuang 7093. - On *Poa* sp., Fuyuan: Usu, 9 Aug. 2000, J.Y. Zhuang 4483. - On *Puccinellia tenuiflora* (Griseb.) Scribn. et Merr., vicinity of Fuyuan, 4 Aug. 2004, J.Y. Zhuang 7570. - On *Roegneria turczaninovii* (Drob.) Nevski, Xingkaihu Nature Reserve, 1 Sept. 2003, Z.M. Azbukina & J.Y. Zhuang 7236, 7248; Hulin: 854 State Farm, 2 Sept. 2003, Z.M. Azbukina & J.Y. Zhuang 7266; Hulin: Dongfanghong, 3 Sept. 2003, Z.M. Azbukina & J.Y. Zhuang 7299; Hulin: Hutou, 4 Sept. 2003, Z.M. Azbukina & J.Y. Zhuang 7302.

Puccinia coronata Corda var. ***himalensis*** Barcl

On *Calamagrostis langsdorffii* (Link) Trin., Khabarovsk: Big Khekhtsir Nature Reserve, 15 Aug. 2004, J.Y. Zhuang 7685.

Puccinia dioscoreae Kom.

On *Dioscorea nipponica* Makino, Khanka Nature Reserve, 9 Aug. 2003, J.Y. Zhuang 7097, 7107; Khabarovsk: Big Khekhtsir Nature Reserve, 15 Aug. 2004, J.Y. Zhuang 7678.

Puccinia elymi Westend.

On *Elymus excelsus* Turcz. ex Griseb., Ussuriysk: Gornotayozhnoye, 5 Aug. 2003, J.Y. Zhuang 7042. - On *Elymus* sp., Xingkaihu Nature Reserve, 1 Sept. 2003, Z.M. Azbukina & J.Y. Zhuang 7237.

Puccinia graminis Pers.

On *Berberis amurensis* Rupr., Khanka Nature Reserve, 9 Aug. 2003, J.Y. Zhuang 7113. - On *Agrostis gigantea* Roth, Fuyuan: Riverside Park, 7 Aug. 2000, J.Y. Zhuang 4469; Fuyuan: Sanjiang Nature Reserve, 8 Aug. 2000, J.Y. Zhuang 4476. - On *Poa* sp., Fuyuan: Riverside Park, 7 Aug. 2000, J.Y. Zhuang 4468.

Puccinia hieracii (Röhl.) H. Mart.

On *Taraxacum asiaticum* Dahlst., Fuyuan, 4 Aug. 2004, J.Y. Zhuang 7558, 7568; Fuyuan: Sanjiang Nature Reserve, 5 Aug. 2004, J.Y. Zhuang 7586.- On *Taraxacum brassicaefolium* Kitag., Hulin: Dongfanghong, 3 Sept. 2003, Z.M. Azbukina & J.Y. Zhuang 7298.

Puccinia magnusiana Körn.

On *Phragmites australis* (Cav.) Trin. ex Steudel, Raohe: Shengli State Farm, 6 Aug. 2004, J.Y. Zhuang 7594; Xingkaihu Nature Reserve, 1 Sept. 2003, Z.M. Azbukina & J.Y. Zhuang 7232; Hulin: 856 State Farm, 2 Sept. 2003, Z.M. Azbukina & J.Y. Zhuang 7259.

Puccinia microsora Körn.

On *Carex rhynchophysa* C.A. Mey., Birobidzhan: Bastak Nature Reserve, 18 Aug. 2004, J.Y. Zhuang 7730. - On *Carex vesicata* Meinsh., Birobidzhan : Bastak Nature Reserve, 19 Aug. 2004, J.Y. Zhuang 7760.

Puccinia minussensis Thüm.

On *Lagedium sibiricum* (L.) Soják, Raohe: Dadai, 7 Aug. 2004, J.Y. Zhuang 7606, 7611. - On *Pterocypsela indica* (L.) Shih, Ussuriysk Nature Reserve, 7 Aug. 2003, J.Y. Zhuang 7075; Hulin: 856 State Farm, 2 Sept. 2003, Z.M. Azbukina & J.Y. Zhuang 7261; Fuyuan: Sanjiang Nature Reserve, 5 Aug. 2004, J.Y. Zhuang 7582; Khabarovsk: Big Khekhtsir Nature Reserve, 16 Aug. 2004, J.Y. Zhuang 7706; Birobidzhan: Bastak Nature Reserve, 18 Aug. 2004, J.Y. Zhuang 7738, 7750.

Puccinia opizii Bubák

On *Carex* sp., Khabarovsk: Big Khekhtsir Nature Reserve, 15 Aug. 2004, J.Y. Zhuang 7669.

Puccinia persistens Plowr.

On *Agrostis alba* L., Hulin: Dongfanghong, 3 Sept. 2003, Z.M. Azbukina & J.Y. Zhuang 7290. - On *Agrostis clavata* Trin., Hulin: Wulindong, 4 Sept. 2003, Z.M. Azbukina & J.Y. Zhuang 7315. - On *Agrostis gigantea* Roth, Birobidzhan: Bastak Nature Reserve, 18 Aug. 2004, J.Y. Zhuang 7744. - On *Calamagrostis langsdorffii* (Link) Trin., Hulin: Dongfanghong, 3 Sept. 2003, Z.M. Azbukina & J.Y. Zhuang 7288; Hulin: Wulindong, 4 Sept. 2003, Z.M. Azbukina & J.Y. Zhuang 7319. - On *Elymus dahuricus* Turcz. ex Griseb., Xingkaihu Nature

Reserve, 1 Sept. 2003, Z.M. Azbukina & J.Y. Zhuang 7233; vicinity of Fuyuan, 4 Aug. 2004, J.Y. Zhuang 7569. - On *Elytrigia repens* (L.) Nevski, Ussuriysk Nature Reserve, 7 Aug. 2003, J.Y. Zhuang 7084, 7087.

Puccinia polygoni-amphibii Pers.

On *Geranium wilfordii* Maxim., Vladivostok: Botanic Garden, 3 Aug. 2003, J.Y. Zhuang 7003; Ussuriysk Nature Reserve, 7 Aug. 2003, J.Y. Zhuang 7086. - On *Persicaria amphibia* (L.) S.F. Gray, Khanka Nature Reserve, 9 Aug. 2003, J.Y. Zhuang 7115; Xingkaihu Nature Reserve, 1 Sept. 2003, Z.M. Azbukina & J.Y. Zhuang 7245.

Puccinia polygoni-amphibii Pers. var. ***convolvuli*** Arthur

On *Fallopia convolvulus* (L.) A. Löve, Ussuriysk Nature Reserve, 7 Aug. 2003, J.Y. Zhuang 7076;

Puccinia polygoni-amphibii Pers. var. ***tovariae*** Arthur

On *Truellum thunbergii* (Siebold & Zucc.) Soják, Ussuriysk: Gornotayozhnoye, 4 Aug. 2003, J.Y. Zhuang 7022.

Puccinia polygoni-sieboldii (Hirats. & S. Kaneko) B. Li

(= *Puccinia polygoni-amphibii* Pers. var. *polygoni-sieboldii* Hirats. & S. Kaneko)

On *Truellum sieboldii* (Meissn.) Soják, Hulin: Wulindong, 4 Sept. 2003, Z.M. Azbukina & J.Y. Zhuang 7312; Raohe: Dadai, 7 Aug. 2004, J.Y. Zhuang 7607; Mudanjiang: Mt. Weihushan, 9 Aug. 2004, J.Y. Zhuang 7648.

Puccinia pseudosphaeria Mont.

[= *Miyagia pseudosphaeria* (Mont.) Jørst.]

On *Sonchus transcaspicus* Nevski, Hulin: 856 State Farm, 2 Sept. 2003, Z.M. Azbukina & J.Y. Zhuang 7262.

Pucinia punctata Link

On *Galium bungei* Steau., Hulin: Dongfanghong, 3 Sept. 2003, Azbukina & J.Y. Zhuang 7292; Raohe: Shengli State Farm, 6 Sept. 2003, Z.M. Azbukina & J.Y. Zhuang 7325. - On *Galium verum* L., Khanka Nature Reserve, 8 Aug. 2003; J.Y. Zhuang 7091; 9 Aug. 2003, J.Y. Zhuang 7112; Raohe: Shengli State Farm, 6 Sept. 2003, Z.M. Azbukina & J.Y. Zhuang 7325.

Puccinia pygmaea Erikss.

On *Calamagrostis epigeios* (L.) Roth, Hulin: Dongfanghong, 3 Sept. 2003, Z.M. Azbukina & J.Y. Zhuang 7275, 7296.

Puccinia sessilis W.G. Schneid.

On *Phalaroides arundinacea* (L.) Rausch., Ussuriysk Nature Reserve, 7 Aug. 2003, J.Y. Zhuang 7079.

Puccinia sjuzevii Tranzschel & Erem.

On *Carex arnellii* Christ, Hulin: 856 State Farm, 2 Sept. 2003, Z.M. Azbukina & J.Y. Zhuang 7254.

Puccinia tanaceti DC.

On *Artemisia sacrorum* Ledeb., Xingkaihu Nature Reserve, 1 Sept. 2003, Z.M. Azbukina & J.Y. Zhuang 7235.

Puccinia tatarinowii Kom. & Tranzschel

On *Prenanthes tatarinowii* Maxim., Ussuriysk: Gornotayozhnoye, 5 Aug. 2003, J.Y. Zhuang 7034, 7039; 6 Aug. 2003, J.Y. Zhuang 7054.

Puccinia violae (Schumach.) DC.

On *Viola collina* Bess., Khanka Nature Reserve, 9 Aug. 2003, J.Y. Zhuang 7102, 7106.

Uromyces amurensis Kom.

On *Maackia amurensis* Rupr. & Maxim., Ussuriysk: Gornotayozhnoye, 6 Aug. 2003, J.Y. Zhuang 7059; Xingkaihu Nature Reserve, 1 Sept. 2003, Z.M. Azbukina & J.Y. Zhuang 7238; Birobidzhan: Bastak Nature Reserve, 19 Aug. 2004, J.Y. Zhuang 7755; Raohe: Shengli State Farm, 6 Aug. 2004, J.Y. Zhuang 7600; Raohe: Dadai, 7 Aug. 2004, J.Y. Zhuang 7610, 7629; Birobidzhan: Bastak Nature Reserve, 19 Aug. 2004, J.Y. Zhuang 7764.

Uromyces fallens (Desm.) F. Kern

On *Trifolium pretense* L., Ussuriysk: Gornotayozhnoye, 4 Aug. 2003, J.Y. Zhuang 7016; Khabarovsk: Big Khekhtsir Nature Reserve, 16 Aug. 2004, J.Y. Zhuang 7703.

Uromyces geranii (DC.) Lév.

On *Geranium wilfordii* Maxim., Hulin: 856 State Farm, 2 Sept. 2003, Z.M. Azbukina & J.Y. Zhuang 7256. - On *Geranium sibiricum* L., Ussuriysk: Gornotayozhnoye, 4 Aug. 2003, J.Y. Zhuang 7029; 5 Aug. 2003, J.Y. Zhuang 7043, 7047; Ussuriysk Nature Reserve, 7 Aug. 2003, J.Y. Zhuang 7071; Xingkaihu Nature Reserve, 1 Sept. 2003, Z.M. Azbukina & J.Y. Zhuang 7231; Birobidzhan: Bastak Nature Reserve, 18 Aug. 2004, J.Y. Zhuang 7734.

Uromyces lespedezae-procumbentis (Schwein.) M.A. Curtis

On *Lespedeza bicolor* Turcz., Khabarovsk: Big Khekhtsir Nature Reserve, 15 Aug. 2004, J.Y. Zhuang 7681. - On *Lespedeza cyrtobotrya* Miq., Hulin: 856 State Farm, 2 Sept. 2003, Z.M. Azbukina & J.Y. Zhuang 7252, 7263.

Uromyces polygoni-avicularis (Pers.) P. Karst.

On *Polygonum aviculare* L., Ussuriysk: Gornotayozhnoye, 5 Aug. 2003, J.Y. Zhuang 7046.

Uromyces punctatus J. Schröt.

On *Oxytropis oxyphylla* (Pall.) DC., Khanka Nature Reserve, 8 Aug. 2003, J.Y. Zhuang 7090.

Uromyces trifolii-repentis Liro

On *Trifolium repens* L., Khanka Nature Reserve, 9 Aug. 2003, J.Y. Zhuang 7095, 7100; Hulin: Dongfanghong, 3 Sept. 2003, Z.M. Azbukina & J.Y. Zhuang 7280.

Uromyces veratri J. Schröt.

On *Veratrum dahuricum* (Turcz.) Loes. fil., Fuyuan, 4 Aug. 2004, J.Y. Zhuang 7541,

7559; Raohe: Dadai, 7 Aug. 2004, J.Y. Zhuang 7609, 7634. - On *Veratrum maackii* Regel, Raohe: Shengli State Farm, 6 Aug. 2004, J.Y. Zhuang 7605.

Uromyces viciae-fabae (Pers.) J. Schröt. var. ***orobi*** (Schumach.) Jørst.

On *Vicia unijuga* A. Br., Ussuriysk: Gornotayozhnoye, 5 Aug. 2003, J.Y. Zhuang 7033, 7038.

Uromyces viciae-fabae (Pers.) J. Schröt. var. ***viciae-fabae***

On *Lathyrus quinquenervius* (Miq.) Litv., Hulin: Wulindong, 4 Sept. 2003, Z.M. Azbukina & J.Y. Zhuang 7318. - On *Vicia baicalensis* (Turcz.) Fedtsch., Raohe: Dadai, 7 Aug. 2004, J.Y. Zhuang 7632. - On *Vicia pseudorobus* Fisch. et Mey., Raohe: Dadai, 7 Aug. 2004, J.Y. Zhuang 7618, 7625.

Myxomycetes

Yu LI   Pu LIU

Field investigations of myxomycetes were carried out during 2003, 2004, and 2009 between Northeast China and Russian Far East, including Heilongjiang Province (Hulin, Raohe, Fuyuan), Khanka Nature Reserve, Ussuriysk Nature Reserve, Khabarovsk region, and Vladivostok. Thus, 54 species in 15 genera were recorded. Some species were cited from references in order to furnish this list of myxomycetes in Ussuri River Valley. Those collected specimens of myxomycetes were deposited in the Herbarium of Mycology in Jilin Agricultural University, Changchun, China (HMJAU). The checklist given below was based on the identification of those specimens.

MYXOMYCETES

CERATIOMYXOMYCETIDAE

CERATIOMYXALES

CERATIOMYXACEAE

Ceratiomyxa fruticulosa (O.F. Müll.) T. Macbr.   Plate 23: 133

On rotten wood, Ussuriysk: Taiga, 4 Aug. 2003, Y. Li, HMJAU 11682, HMJAU 11727. - On rotten wood, Ussuriysk Nature Reserve, 7 Aug. 2003, Y. Li, HMJAU 11728. - On rotten wood, Khabarovsk, 17 Aug. 2004, Y. Li, HMJAU 11716, HMJAU 11717. - On rotten wood, Khabarovsk, 18 Aug. 2004, Y. Li, HMJAU 11718, HMJAU 11719. - On rotten wood, Khabarovsk, 15 Aug. 2004, Y. Li, HMJAU 11726. - On rotten wood, Vladivostok, 19 July 2009, P. Liu, HMJAU 11759.

Ceratiomyxa fruticulosa var. *descendens* Emoto

On rotten wood, Vladivostok, 22 July 2009, P. Liu, HMJAU 11774.

Ceratiomyxa fruticulosa var. *flexuosa* (Lister) G. Lister

On rotten wood, Vladivostok, 19 July 2009, P. Liu, HMJAU 11760, HMJAU 11763.

Ceratiomyxa fruticulosa var. *porioides* (Alb. & Schwein.) Lister

On rotten wood, Ussuriysk: Taiga, 3 Aug. 2003, Y. Li, HMJAU 11783. - On rotten wood,

Khabarovsk, 19 Aug. 2004, Y. Li, HMJAU 11782. - On rotten wood, Vladivostok, 19 July 2009, P. Liu, HMJAU 11767, HMJAU 11768. - On rotten wood, Vladivostok, 22 July 2009, P. Liu, HMJAU 11776.

Ceratiomyxa sphaerosperma Boedijn

On dead bark, Ussuriysk: Taiga, 6 Aug. 2003, Y. Li, HMJAU 11674.

MYXOGASTROMYCETIDAE

LICEALES

LICEACEAE

Licea pusilla Schrad.

On rotten wood, Heilongjiang, 7 Aug. 2003, Y. Li, HMJAU 10061.

Licea variabilis Schrad.

On rotten wood, Heilongjiang, 3 Sept. 2003, Y. Li, HMJAU 10093.

ENTERIDIACEAE

Dictydiaethalium plumbeum (Schumach.) Rostaf. ex Lister

On rotten wood, Heilongjiang, 31 Aug. 1991, S.L. Chen, HMJAU 10077.

Lycogala epidendrum (J.C. Buxb. ex L.) Fr.

On rotten wood, Ussuriysk Nature Reserve, 7 Aug. 2003, Y. Li, HMJAU 11677.

Lycogala exiguum Morgan   Plate 23: 134

On rotten wood, Ussuriysk Nature Reserve, 4 Aug. 2003, Y. Li, HMJAU 11676.

Tubulifera arachnoidea Jacq.

On moss and rotten wood, Vladivostok, 19 July 2009, P. Liu, HMJAU 11764.

CRIBRARIACEAE

Cribraria aurantiaca Schrad.

On rotten wood, Ussuriysk Nature Reserve, 7 Aug. 2003, Y. Li, HMJAU 11785.

Cribraria elegans Berk. & M.A. Curtis

On dead leaves, Heilongjiang, 16 Aug. 1984, Y. Li, HMJAU 10079.

Cribraria filiformis Nowotny & H. Neubert

On rotten wood, Vladivostok, 19 July 2009, P. Liu, HMJAU 11770, HMJAU 11771, 11773, HMJAU 11781.

Cribraria purpurea Schrad.

On rotten wood, Heilongjiang, 4 Aug. 2004, Y. Li, HMJAU 10082.

Cribraria tenella Schrad.   Plate 23: 135

On rotten wood, Ussuriysk Nature Reserve, 4 Aug. 2003, Y. Li, HMJAU 11754.

Dictydium cancellatum (Batsch) T. Macbr.   Plate 23: 136

On rotten wood, Ussuriysk Nature Reserve, 7 Aug. 2003, Y. Li, HMJAU 11704, HMJAU 11705, HMJAU 11706.

TRICHIALES

TRICHIACEAE

Arcyria abietina (Wigand) Nann.-Bremek.

On rotten wood, Khabarovsk, 19 Aug. 2004, Y. Li, HMJAU 11758.

Arcyria carnea (G. Lister) G. Lister

On rotten wood, Ussuriysk: Taiga, 6 Aug. 2003, Y. Li, HMJAU 11668.

Arcyria cinerea (Bull.) Pers.   Plate 23: 137

On rotten wood, Ussuriysk Nature Reserve, 7 Aug. 2003, Y. Li, HMJAU 11714, HMJAU 11715, HMJAU 11740. - On rotten wood, Khabarovsk, 17 Aug. 2004, Y. Li, HMJAU 11742. - On rotten wood, Khabarovsk, 18 Aug. 2004, Y. Li, HMJAU 11707. - On rotten wood and dead bark, Khabarovsk, 19 Aug. 2004, Y. Li, HMJAU 11708, HMJAU 11709, HMJAU 11710, HMJAU 11711, HMJAU 11712, HMJAU 11713, HMJAU 11739, HMJAU 11743, HMJAU 11744, HMJAU 11788.

Arcyria denudata (L.) Wettst.   Plate 23: 138

On rotten wood, Ussuriysk: Taiga, 3 Aug. 2003, Y. Li, HMJAU 11755. - On the fruitbody of mushroom, mossy bark, and rotten wood, Ussuriysk: Taiga, 4 Aug. 2003, Y. Li, HMJAU 11720, HMJAU 11721, HMJAU 11722. - On rotten wood, Ussuriysk: Taiga, 6 Aug. 2003, Y. Li, HMJAU 11723. - On rotten wood, Ussuriysk Nature Reserve, 7 Aug. 2003, Y. Li, HMJAU 11724, HMJAU 11725.

Arcyria incarnata (Pers.) Pers.

On rotten wood, Heilongjiang, 13 Aug. 1984, S.L. Chen, HMJAU 8780.

Arcyria insignis Kalchbr. & Cooke   Plate 24: 139

On rotten wood, Ussuriysk Nature Reserve, 7 Aug. 2003, Y. Li, HMJAU 11669.

Arcyria occidentalis (T. Macbr.) Lister

On rotten wood, Heilongjiang, 13 Aug. 1984, S.L. Chen, HMJAU 8419, HMJAU 8691.

Arcyria pomiformis (Leers) Rostaf.

On rotten wood, Heilongjiang, 7 Aug. 2004, Y. Li, HMJAU H920194.

Arcyria virescens G. Lister

On rotten wood, Khabarovsk, 18 Aug. 2004, Y. Li, HMJAU 11679. - On rotten wood, Khabarovsk, 19 Aug. 2004, Y. Li, HMJAU 11745, HMJAU 11746, HMJAU 11747, HMJAU

11748.

Hemitrichia calyculata (Speg.) M.L. Farr   Plate 24: 140

On rotten wood, Ussuriysk Nature Reserve, 6 Aug. 2003, Y. Li, HMJAU 11693, HMJAU 11694, HMJAU 11695, HMJAU 11696. - On dead bark and rotten wood, Khabarovsk, 18 Aug. 2004, Y. Li, HMJAU 11697, HMJAU 11698, HMJAU 11699, HMJAU 11700, HMJAU 11701. - On rotten wood, Khabarovsk, 19 Aug. 2004, Y. Li, HMJAU 11702, HMJAU 11703. - On rotten wood, Vladivostok, 19 July 2009, P. Liu, HMJAU 11762, HMJAU 11766. - On rotten wood, Vladivostok, 22 July 2009, P. Liu, HMJAU 11775, HMJAU 11778.

Hemitrichia clavata (Pers.) Rostaf.

On rotten wood, Heilongjiang, 11 Aug. 1984, X.D. Yang, HMJAU 8159.

Hemitrichia serpula (Scop.) Rostaf.   Plate 24: 141

On moss, Ussuriysk Nature Reserve, 3 Aug. 2003, Y. Li, HMJAU 11688. - On dead bark and rotten wood, Ussuriysk Nature Reserve, 7 Aug. 2003, Y. Li, HMJAU 11689, HMJAU 11690. - On dead bark, Ussuriysk: Taiga, 6 Aug. 2003, Y. Li, HMJAU 11757. - On dead bark and dead leaves, Khabarovsk, 18 Aug. 2004, Y. Li, HMJAU 11691, HMJAU 11692.

Metatrichia vesparium (Batsch) Nann.-Bremek.   Plate 24: 142

On mossy wood, Ussuriysk: Taiga, 3 Aug. 2003, Y. Li, HMJAU 11683. - On rotten wood, Ussuriysk Nature Reserve, 7 Aug. 2003, Y. Li, HMJAU 11786. - On mossy wood and rotten wood, Khabarovsk, 18 Aug. 2004, Y. Li, HMJAU 11684, HMJAU 11685, HMJAU 11686, HMJAU 11687. - On mossy wood, Khabarovsk: Big Khekhtsir Nature Reserve, 18 Aug. 2004, Y. Li, HMJAU 11749, HMJAU 11750, HMJAU 11751.

Trichia botrytis (J. F. Gmel.) Pers.

On rotten wood, Heilongjiang, 7 Aug. 2004, Y. Li, HMJAU H920001, HMJAU H920098, HMJAU H920099, HMJAU H920107, HMJAU H920245, HMJAU H920290.

Trichia erecta Rex

On rotten wood, Heilongjiang, 4 Aug. 2004, Y. Li, HMJAU H0016.

Trichia favoginea (Batsch) Pers.

On rotten wood, Ussuriysk Nature Reserve, 4 Aug. 2003, Y. Li, HMJAU 11678. - On moss and dead bark, Ussuriysk Nature Reserve, 4 Aug. 2003, Y. Li, HMJAU 11732. - On dead leaves, Ussuriysk: Taiga, 9 Aug. 2003, Y. Li , HMJAU 11733.

Trichia subfusca Rex

On rotten wood, Heilongjiang, 7 Aug. 2004, Y. Li, HMJAU H92-0255.

Trichia verrucosa Berk.

On rotten wood, Heilongjiang, 4 Aug. 2004, Y. Li, HMJAU H920264.

PHYSARALES

PHYSARACEAE

Craterium leucocephalum (Pers.) Ditmar

On dead leaves, Heilongjiang, 16 Aug. 1984, S.L. Chen, HMJAU 9667.

Physarum decipiens M.A. Curtis

On rotten wood, Heilongjiang, 4 Aug. 2004, Y. Li, HMJAU 10163.

Physarum globuliferum (Bull.) Pers.

On dead leaves and the fruitbody of mushroom, Ussuriysk: Taiga, 4 Aug. 2003, Y. Li, HMJAU 11734, HMJAU 11735.

Physarum nutans Pers.

On the fruitbody of mushroom, Khabarovsk: Big Khekhtsir Nature Reserve, 18 Aug. 2004, Y. Li, HMJAU 11787.

Physarum pusillum (Berk. & M.A. Curt.) G. Lister

On dead bark, Khabarovsk: Big Khekhtsir Nature Reserve, 18 Aug. 2004, Y. Li, HMJAU 11681.

Physarum viride (Bull.) Pers.   Plate 24: 143

On dead twig, Ussuriysk Nature Reserve, 4 Aug. 2003, Y. Li, HMJAU 11729. - On rotten wood and dead leaves, Ussuriysk: Taiga, 4 Aug. 2003, Y. Li, HMJAU 11730, HMJAU 11784.

DIDYMIACEAE

Didymium dubium Rostaf.

On rotten wood, Heilongjiang, 3 Sept. 2003, Y. Li, HMJAU 10159.

Didymium leoninum Berk. & Broome

On rotten wood, Heilongjiang, 4 Aug. 2004, Y. Li, HMJAU 10196.

Didymium melanospermum (Pers.) T. Macbr.

On rotten wood and twig and dead leaves, Heilongjiang, 14 Aug. 1985, Y. Li, HMJAU 9152, HMJAU 9155, HMJAU 9171, HMJAU 9229. - On dead leaves and pine needles, Heilongjiang, 15 Aug. 1985, S.L. Chen, HMJAU 9154.

Didymium squamulosum (Alb. & Schwein.) Fr.   Plate 24: 144

On dead leaves and stems of dried grass, Ussuriysk Nature Reserve, 7 Aug. 2003, Y. Li, HMJAU 11736.

STEMONITOMYCETIDAE

STEMONITALES

STEMONITACEAE

Comatricha elegans (Racib.) Lister

    On dead leaves, Ussuriysk Nature Reserve, 7 Aug. 2003, Y. Li, HMJAU 11680.

Comatricha nigra (Pers.) J. Schröt.

    On rotten wood and rotten twig, Heilongjiang, 14 Aug. 1985, Y. Li, HMJAU 9168, HMJAU 9178.

Stemonitis axifera (Bull.) T. Macbr.

    On rotten wood, Ussuriysk Nature Reserve, 4 Aug. 2003, Y. Li, HMJAU 11741. - On rotten wood, Vladivostok, 19 July 2009, P. Liu, HMJAU 11761.

Stemonitis flavogenita E. Jahn

    On rotten wood, Ussuriysk Nature Reserve, 7 Aug. 2003, Y. Li, HMJAU 11672, HMJAU 11737.

Stemonitis fusca Roth

    On rotten wood, Khabarovsk, 19 Aug. 2004, Y. Li, HMJAU 11731, HMJAU 11752, HMJAU 11753.

Stemonitis pallida Wingate

    On dead bark, Ussuriysk: Taiga, 6 Aug. 2003, Y. Li, HMJAU 11675.

Stemonitis smithii T. Macbr.

    On mossy wood, Khabarovsk, 17 Aug. 2004, Y. Li, HMJAU 11756.

Stemonitis splendens Rostaf.

    On rotten wood, Ussuriysk: Taiga, 3 Aug. 2003, Y. Li, HMJAU 11673. - On rotten wood, Ussuriysk Nature Reserve, 7 Aug. 2003, Y. Li, HMJAU 11671, 11738. - On dead barks, Khabarovsk, 18 Aug. 2004, Y. Li, HMJAU 11670. - On rotten wood, Vladivostok, 19 July 2009, P. Liu, HMJAU 11765, HMJAU 11769.

Stemonitis virginiensis Rex

    On rotten wood, Heilongjiang, 15 Aug. 1985, Y. Li, HMJAU 9228.

REFERENCES

Li Y. Flora Fungorum Sinicorum. Myxomycetes I & II. Beijing: Science Press, 2007. (in Chinese)

Yamamoto Y. The Myxomycete Biota of Japan (in Japanese). Tokyo: Tokyo Shorin Publishing Co., Ltd, 1998. (in Japanese)

Stephenson S L, Stempen H. Myxomycetes: a handbook of slime molds. New York: Timber Press, 1994.

Martin G W, Alexopoulos C J, Farr M L. The genera of myxomycetes. Iowa: University of Iowa Press, 1983.

Martin G W, Alexopoulos C J. The myxomycetes. Iowa: University of Iowa Press, 1969.

Keller H W, Braun K L. Myxomycetes of Ohio: their systematics, biology and use in teaching. Ohio Biological Survey, 1999, 13(2).

Nannenga-Bremekamp N E. A guide to temperate myxomycetes (trans: Feest A, Burggraaf Y). Biopress Limited, 1991.

Gray W D, Alexopoulos C J. Biology of myxomycetes. New York: The Ronald Press Company, 1968.

Alexopoulos C J, Mims C W, Blackwell M. Introductory mycology 4th ed. Wiley, New York, 1996.

Ashworth J M, Jennifer D. The biology of slime moulds. London: Edward Arnold Publishers, 1975.

Index of fungal genera

Index of host plant genera

Plates

From left to right: BAU, T., VASILYEVA, L. N., AZBUKINA, Z. M., LI, Y., ZHUANG, J.Y.

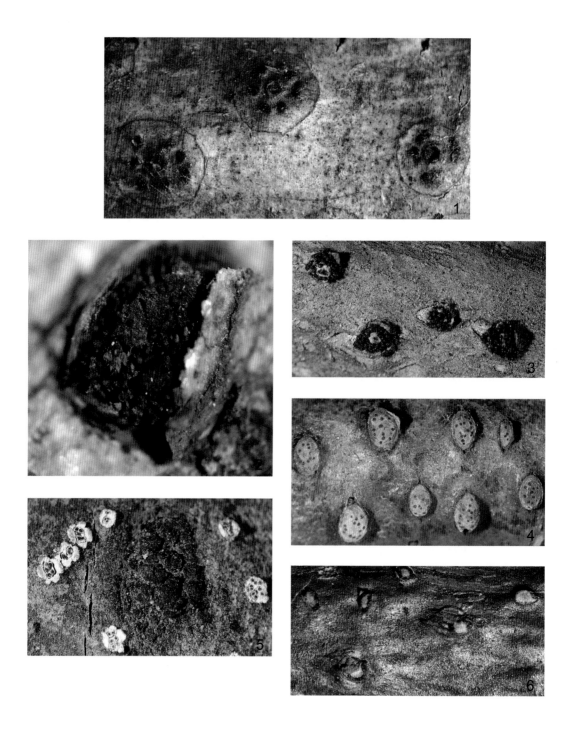

Plate 1 1. *Allantoporthe tessella* (Pers. : Fr.) Petr., 2. *Diaporthella corylina* Lar.N. Vassilyeva, 3. *Leucodiaporthe juglandis* Lar.N. Vassiljeva, 4. *Leucodiaporthe maackii* (Lar.N. Vassiljeva) M.E. Barr & Lar.N. Vassiljeva, 5. *Leucostoma pseudoniveum* Lar.N. Vassiljeva, 6. *Valsa ambiens* (Pers. : Fr.) Fr.

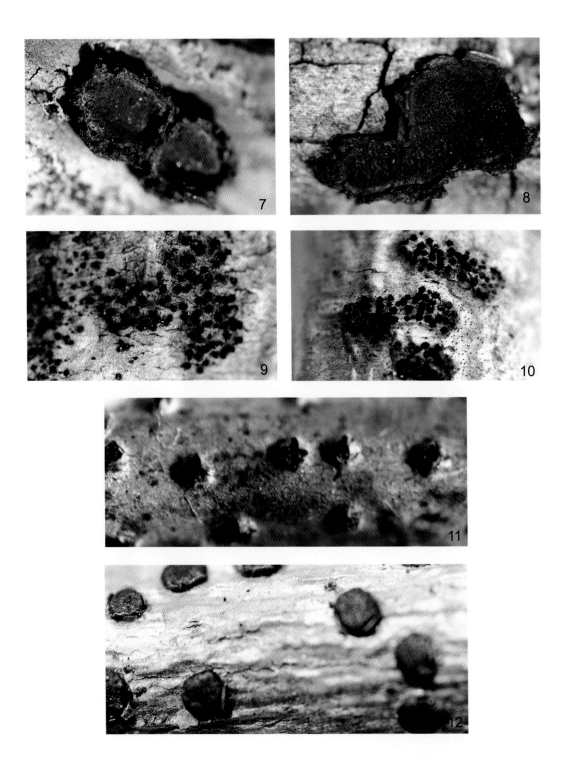

Plate 2   7. *Biscogniauxia mandshurica* Lar.N. Vassiljeva, 8. *Biscogniauxia pezizoides* (Ellis & Everh.)

Kuntze, 9. *Cryptosphaeria exornata* Lar.N. Vassiljeva, 10. *Cryptosphaeria venusta* Lar.N. Vassiljeva,

11. *Diatrype albopruinosa* (Schwein.) Cooke, 12. *Diatrype macounii* Ellis et Everh.

Plate 3   13. *Podostroma alutacea* (Pers. : Fr.) G.F. Atk., 14. *Podostroma giganteum* S. Imai, 15. *Daldinia carpinicola* Lar.N. Vassiljeva & M. Stadler, 16. *Entonaema cinnabarina* (Cooke & Massee) Lloyd, 17. *Agaricus campetris* L., 18. *Agaricus placomyces* Peck.

Plate 4   19. *Agaricus silvaticus* Schaeff., 20. *Agaricus subrufescens* Peck, 21. *Chlorophyllum rhacodes* (Vittad.) Vellinga, 22. *Leucoagaricus naucinus* (Fr.) Singer, 23. *Macrolepiota procera* (Scop.) Singer, 24. *Amanita flavipes* S. Imai.

Plate 5 25. *Amanita muscaria* (L.) Lam., 26. *Amanita phalloides* (Vaill. ex Fr.) Link, 27. *Amanita rubescens* Pers., 28. *Amanita vaginata* (Bull.) Lam., 29. *Coprinus atramentarius* (Bull.) Fr., 30. *Coprinus comatus* (O.F.Mull.) Pers.

Plate 6   31. *Coprinus flocculosus* (DC.) Fr., 32. *Coprinus micaceus* (Bull.) Fr., 33. *Entoloma aborttivum* (Berk. et M.A. Curtis) Donk, 34. *Entoloma clypeatum* (L.) P. Kumm., 35. *Volvariella bombycina* (Schaeff.) Singer, 36. *Volvariella volvacea* (Bull.) Singer.

Plate 7   37. *Kuehneromyces mutabilis* (Schaff.) Singĕr et A. H. Sm., 38. *Panaeolina foenisecii* (Pers.) Maire, 39. *Pholiota adiposa* (Batsch) P. Kumm., 40. *Pholiota aurivella* (Batsch) Fr., 41. *Pholiota flammans* (Batsch) P . Kumm., 42. *Pholiota populnea* (Pers. Kuyper et Tjall.-Beuk.)

Plate 8   43. *Psilocybe coprophila* (Bull.) P. Kumm., 44. *Stropharia rugosoannulata* Farl. ex Murrill,
45. *Armillaria mellea* (Vahl.) P. Kumm., 46. *Campanella tristis* (G. Stev.) Segedin, 47. *Clitocybe clavipes*
(Pers.) P. Kumm., 48. *Clitocybe gibba* (Pers.) P. Kumm.

Plate 9   49. *Clitocybe nebularis* (Batsch) Quel., 50. *Crinipellis zonata* (Peck) Sacc. 51. *Flammulina velutipes* (Curtis) Singer, 52. *Hypsizygus tessulatus* (Bull.) Singer, 53. *Laccaria amethystina* Cooke, 54. *Laccaria proxima* (Boud.) Pat.

Plate 10   55. *Lampteromyces japonicus* (Kawam.) Singer, 56. *Lentinula edodes* (Berk) Pegler,
57. *Lepista nuda* (Bull.) Cooke, 58. *Lepista sordida* (Fr.) Singer, 59. *Lyophyllum decastes* (Fr.) Singer,
60. *Macrocystidia cucumis* (Pers.) Joss.

Plate 11   61. *Marasmius androsaceus* (L.) Fr., 62. *Mycena lamprospora* (Corner) E. Horak, 63. *Mycena pura* (Pers.) P. Kumm., 64. *Rhodocollybia butyracea* (Bull.) Lennox, 65. *Tricholoma caligatum* (Viv.) Ricken, 66. *Xeromphalina campanella* (Batsch) Maire.

Plate 12   67. *Auricularia auricula-judae* (Bull.) Quel., 68. *Auricularia polytricha* (Mont.) Sacc.,
69. *Boletus edulis* Bull., 70. *Boletus erythropus* Fr., 71. *Boletus speciosus* Frost, 72. *Leccinum aurantiacum*
(Bull.) Gray.

Plate 13   73. *Leccinum extremiorientale* Lj. N. Vassiljeva, 74. *Leccinum variicolor* Watling,

75. *Suillus granulatus* (L.) Roussel, 76. *Suillus luteus* (L.) Roussel, 77. *Suillus plorans* (Rolland) Kuntze,

78. *Chroogomphus rutilus* (Schaeff.) O.K. Mill.

Plate 14   79. *Hygrophoropsis aurantiaca* (Wulfen) Maire, 80. *Paxillus involutus* (Batsch) Fr., 81. *Tapinella panuoides* (Batsch) E.-J. Gilbert, 82. *Chalciporus piperatus* (Bull.) Bataille, 83. *Cantharellus cibarius* Fr., 84. *Clavulina coralloides* (L.) J. Schröt.

Plate 15   85. *Craterellus cornucopioides* (L.) Pers., 86. *Sparassis crispa* (Wulfen) Fr., 87. *Phaeolepiota aurea* (Matt.) Maire, 88. *Rozites caperatus* (Pers.) P. Karst., 89. *Ganoderma applanatum* (Pers.) Pat., 90. *Ganoderma lucidum* (Curtis) P. Karst.

Plate 16 91. *Gomphus clavatus* (Pers.) Gray, 92. *Ramaria holorubella* (G.F. Atk.) Corner, 93. *Clavicorona pyxidata* (Pers.) Doty, 94. *Hericium coralloides* (Scop.) Pers., 95. *Lentinellus brunnescens* Lj.N. Vasiljeva, 96. *Inonotus obliquus* (Ach. ex Pers.) Pilát.

Plate 17   97. *Phellinus chrysoloma* (Fr.) Donk, 98. *Phellinus igniarius* (L.) Quel., 99. *Geastrum saccatum* Fr., 100. *Lycoperdon echinatum* Pers., 101. *Lycoperdon mammiforme* Pers., 102. *Dictyophora duplicata* (Bosc) E. Fisch.

Plate 18   103. *Mutinus caninus* (Huds.) Fr., 104. *Cerrena unicolor* (Bull.) Murrill, 105. *Cryptoporus volvatus* (Peck) Shear, 106. *Daedaleopsis confragosa* (Bolton) J. Schrot., 107. *Fomes fomentarius* (L.) Fr., 108. *Fomitopsis pinicola* (Sw.) P. Karst.

Plate 19   109. *Grifola frondosa* (Dicks.) Gray, 110. *Laetiporus sulphureus* (Bull.) Murrill, 111. *Laricifomes officinalis* (Vill.) Kotl. et Pouzar, 112. *Lenzites betulina* (L.) Fr., 113. *Trametes versicolor* (L.) Pilát, 114. *Panus conchatus* (Bull.) Fr.

Plate 20   115. *Phyllotopsis nidulans* (Pers.) Singer, 116. *Pleurotus citrinopileatus* Singer, 117. *Pleurotus ostreatus* (Jacq.) P . Kumm., 118. *Pleurotus pulmonarius* (Fr.) Quél., 119. *Polyporus squamosus* (Huds.) Fr., 120. *Lactarius deliciosus* (L.) Gray.

Plate 21   121. *Lactarius torminosus* (Schaeff.) Gray, 122. *Lactarius uvidus* (Fr.) Fr., 123. *Lactarius volemus* (Fr.) Fr., 124. *Russula densifolia* Secr.ex Gillet, 125. *Russula nigricans* (Bull.) Fr., 126. *Russula paludosa* Britzelm.

Plate 22   127. *Russula punctipes* Singer, 128. *Russula xerampelina* (Schaeff.) Fr., 129. *Plicaturopsis crispa*
(Fr.) D.A. Reid, 130. *Schizophyllum commune* Fr., 131. *Merulius tremellosus* Schrad., 132. *Irpex lacteus*
(Fr.) Fr.

Plate 23　133. *Ceratiomyxa fruticulosa* (O.F. Müll.) T. Macbr., 134. *Lycogala exiguum* Morgan, 135. *Cribraria tenella* Schrad., 136. *Dictydium cancellatum* (Batsch) T. Macbr., 137. *Arcyria cinerea* (Bull.) Pers., 138. *Arcyria denudata* (L.) Wettst.

Plate 24   139. *Arcyria insignis* Kalchbr. & Cooke, 140. *Hemitrichia calyculata* (Speg.) M.L. Farr, 141. *Hemitrichia serpula* (Scop.) Rostaf., 142. *Metatrichia vesparium* (Batsch) Nann.-Bremek., 143. *Physarum viride* (Bull.) Pers., 144. *Didymium squamulosum* (Alb. & Schwein.) Fr.